SEEDS OF CHAOS OMNIBUS

A GameLit Dark Adventure Series (Books 1 & 2)

Seeds of Chaos

AZALEA ELLIS

Seladore Publishing

Join the Inner Circle**

Become part of the Inner Circle.

Instantly receive a free copy of *Gods of Smoke and Stars*, a Seeds of Chaos novella.

https://www.azaleaellis.com/newsletter

I will send you new release updates, exclusive content like pre-release or deleted scenes, as well as news about giveaways or contests I'm doing (signed paperbacks, posters, etc.) and other cool stuff I think you might enjoy. Sometimes I tell weird stories about my life.

Support me on Patreon

https://www.patreon.com/azaleaellis

Read along chapter by chapter as I write the next book in my current series, with early access chapters not available elsewhere, plus exclusive short stories and bonus chapters, and even audiobooks.

Gods of Blood and Bone

To Jared. Be not afraid.

Chapter 1

You may know *of* me, but you have no idea who I *am*.
— Eve Redding

THE ELECTRICAL IMMOBILIZERS clamped on my wrists and ankles caused the skin around them to burn with a strange tingling sensation. It felt like touching my tongue to the tip of a nine-volt battery.

I tried to arch my back and kick out, and the sensation spread violently, causing my muscles to go rigid-limp against my will. I whimpered into the rubber-tasting patch covering my mouth and tried to imbue some rage into the glare I leveled at my captors. The masked woman chuckled at me. The other one, a man, placed a large metal case on the ground and unlocked it with the hissing sound of hydraulics.

"Please, you said I'd get a Seed. Can I have it now?" the boy said, desperation lacing his voice.

I turned my glare on their sniveling accomplice. How could I have been so stupid? I should have ignored his fake distress, like everyone else. I'd almost done so, but then he met my eyes, his own pitiful and full of fear. He'd mouthed, "help" at me. So I'd followed him into the alley.

And now here I was—bound and gagged by two masked people—being kidnapped. A large transport vehicle had already pulled up to hide the mouth of the alley, and thus my current predicament, from the people on the street. Not that they would have helped, anyway. Strangers would take one look at a girl being abducted by masked, vaguely military-looking people, and scurry onward, their eyes firmly pointed to the grey pavement. Got to get to work. Lucky to be among the steadily decreasing percentage with a job. No time to deal with other people's problems.

The boy looked away from me and snatched eagerly at something in the silent man's outstretched hand. "I'm sorry," he mumbled to me. "I wish I was stronger." Then he shuddered and unclenched his fist from around a little glass ball, which dropped to the ground.

"What do you think you're doing? Pick that up!" the woman hissed. "You can't leave stuff like that just lying around. There can't be any evidence we were here. None."

The boy swallowed hard and snatched it back up, then met my eyes again. "I had to. I didn't have a choice. You don't know what it's like." His voice dropped to a whisper, and his chin quivered a bit. "But you will."

"Shut up," the man said, speaking for the first time as he drew something from his metal case and stepped ominously over to me.

I tried once more to move my useless body, but my muscles had locked themselves into a painful half-relaxation. I tried to scream instead, but even though the force of it burned my throat, it came out of my nose weak and muffled.

The man bent over me and jammed a pen-sized piece of metal into my leg. It pierced the skin, and he held it there for a second before withdrawing it and handing it to the woman. She immediately plugged the other end into the side of a clunky link pad.

My breath heaved out of my lungs, and my eyes opened painfully wide, but every attempt at movement only forced me to lie more and more still.

An image popped up on the link pad screen: a picture of my face, under my name, Eve Redding, and a slew of other data.

What the hell?

It was me in a white hospital gown—the picture I'd had taken a few months before, when people had come to do a surprise, school-wide medical examination. We'd been told it was to ensure none of the students had communicable diseases. Why did they have that picture?

I swallowed. In a situation like this, there could be no good reason.

"It's her," the woman said. "Hurry. We don't have much time. We'll have to leave her here."

That didn't sound good, either. But if they were leaving me, at least I wasn't being kidnapped for human trafficking or something. I'd have made a bad slave to some rich foreigner, anyway; I was too rebellious, and not pretty enough to make up for it.

The man nodded and grabbed me by my arm, which was bound behind my back. He lifted my weight roughly, turned me onto my stomach, and brushed the hair off the nape of my neck. I felt a pressure at the base of my skull, and then a sharp pain.

I tried to jerk away, but I couldn't even move an inch. Frustration, terror, and rage boiled up in me, pushing out any forced humor, and a tear slipped down my nose onto the painfully rough concrete pressed against my cheek.

Tears—the only outlet my body had. I hated crying.

Another pain, at the base of my neck.

Another tear of rage.

He flipped me back over and the woman came forward, another glass ball in her hand, but this one was filled with creamy liquid. She knelt in front of me and pressed it to my neck. "I hope this one survives."

Wait, what?

There was one last quick, sharp pain.

She stripped off my electrical immobilizers and tapped the back of her wrist port against the patch on my mouth, causing it to disintegrate.

I drew breath to scream and tried to jerk away from her, but my muscles still wouldn't listen. The alley walls and the woman's back as she stepped into the transport vehicle all spun crazily. My eyes rolled back into my head, and I passed out.

CONSCIOUSNESS CAME LURCHING BACK to me with a wave of sickness. I rolled to my hands and knees and heaved up bitter-apple bile onto the concrete. My dark brown hair hung unrestrained around my face, and my hands got splashed with sick, but I barely noticed.

"Oh, God," I moaned, heaving once again. I retched until nothing came out, then crawled to the alley wall and used it to pull myself up. My body shuddered uncontrollably. I looked up through the smoggy air to the sky above. The sun wasn't overhead yet, but even in the shade of the towering buildings, the early summer heat made me feel like I was baking inside the city-stench all around me.

But I didn't have time to stand there contemplating my own misery.

I needed to move *right then,* or I wouldn't be able to.

I stumbled out onto the sidewalk, causing a businesswoman to rear back and sidestep to avoid colliding with me. She curled her lip in disgust and clacked away in her towering heels. Scag.

I stumbled on my way, using the walls to support myself when my legs alone couldn't. The other people on the sidewalk veered out of my way, avoiding eye-contact except to throw me the kind of derisive glance usually reserved for homeless people and half-crazed addicts.

My brain was tingling.

What the hell had they done to me? Everything spun crazily, and every time I blinked, random images and sounds flashed in my head. White walls, a frowning man in a lab coat, monitors blinking and beeping, shouting in a foreign language, a chest straining against restraints, a bright light…blindingly bright.

I opened my eyes and found myself leaning against the side of a building, hot window glass against my back, my head tilted toward the light of the rising sun. I jerked and closed my lids against the white-hot heat radiating out from the distant orb. When I opened my eyes again, I saw a man looking suspiciously my way.

Fear gave me temporary mental clarity and the boost of adrenaline needed to straighten up. "Stupid," I hissed to myself. "What the heck are you doing, on the street in broad daylight?" I took a deep breath of the dirty air and propelled myself forward, off the sidewalk and into the street. I raised my hand for a taxi pod while anxiously watching the people around me out of the corner of my eye.

My attackers had left, but what if they were coming back? What if there were others? I stood out, obvious in the stupid uniform all high school students were forced to wear. I was spaced out on the streets, looking delirious, smelling of vomit, and in serious danger. I thought of filing a report with the enforcers—the military troops that policed us civilians after the attempted air strikes seven years ago—but everyone knew they were useless when it came to actually helping the civilians, unless you had money. I didn't have money, but whoever my attackers were, they obviously did. The enforcers weren't an option.

A taxi stopped in front of me. I opened the door and threw myself inside, blurting out my address to the computer-operated vehicle. It pulled leisurely away from the sidewalk and hurled itself full-speed into the flow of traffic. My stomach lurched, and I heaved onto the plastine seat. The computerized voice said something about financial responsibility, but I wasn't paying attention.

My body started to vibrate, and when I looked down, I saw my pieces coming apart. Then I blinked, and I was normal again. "Must be hallucinating," I mumbled. When I finally looked up from the fascinating myriad lines and crags in the skin of my palms, the taxi pod was stopped outside my building.

The automated voice was loud, and I don't think I was imagining the irritation as it asked me once again, "Valued customer, we have arrived at the specified destination. The charge is three hundred twelve credits. Please swipe your identity link over the payment center and exit the vehicle promptly." I looked out the pod window to my building. Thanks to my single mother's workaholic nature, we lived in an area just far enough from the unemployment slums that it was safe to walk to school. Or should have been.

I swiped the sheath around my left forearm over the scanner in the center of the pod and climbed out. I couldn't feel my legs, and had to look down to ensure they were still attached to my torso, but somehow I made it inside, through the doors, into the elevator, and then into our house.

The dark interior was comfortably familiar. Safe.

"I hope this one survives," rang through my head again, shattering this momentary illusion of safety.

"Please," I whispered to the air. What was wrong with me? I was sick. Much too sick.

Even this simple thought was impossible to hold onto as sweat began to pour from my skin, my body growing dangerously hot. I braced one hand against the wall and waited for this to pass, but when it did, a wave of bone-creaking cold crept through me instead. My brain seemed to be tingling again, along with my spine, and when I took a step toward my room, my vision went dark and blurry. Then the cold floor smashed hard into the side of my head.

VOICES SEEPED THROUGH MY EARS, as if from very far away.

"Got a call from the school saying she was absent…Can't believe her!"

Some mumbling, and then louder, "Well, I don't work to send her to school just so she can become a delinquent and put us on the enforcers' radar! Live quietly, I say…"

The door opened. I tried to talk, to ask for help, but I couldn't muster the strength to push the air out of my lungs.

"Oh my god." Hurried steps, and someone was kneeling beside me. "Eve, are you okay?" My mother shook my shoulder.

"Something's wrong." My brother's voice. "Go get the medbot, Mom!"

Someone rolled me over onto my back, and then the medbot's cold sensors were being pushed into my armpits and mouth.

They were saying something else, but speaking in a man's deep voice, and once again it wasn't English. What? I didn't remember them being bilingual. But in any case, the sound was quite soothing, and I found I didn't care where it came from.

"Evaluation complete. Diagnosis unknown. Treatment unknown. Patient has fever of 105.4 degrees Fahrenheit. Please contact a medical professional immediately," a robotic voice announced, right next to my ear, loud enough to scramble my brains.

My mom's voice on the phone, rapid-fire and shaking, grating, loud.

Hands on my skin, picking me up and pressing so hard the pain made me black out again.

I woke up for a few seconds, in my own bed. Zed's worried face staring down at me. He just barely squeezed my hand, and it felt like my bones might disintegrate, but I couldn't move, couldn't talk.

"You're gonna be fine. The doctor's on his way."

I closed my eyes and drifted off to the sound of the other man's voice murmuring gently.

Log of Captivity 1

Mental Log of Captivity—Estimated Day: Two thousand, five hundred eighty-four.

I felt the initiation of a *blood-covenant* today. It was unlike the others, not another sordid violation. She is a Matrix, perhaps brought here in the exodus. I did not understand what was happening, at first, when I felt her. I fear that the stunted *two-leg-maggots* have captured her and are using her for experimentation, like me. But if they are the cause of my *blood-covenant* being initiated, it shows only how ignorant they are. For the first time in many cycles, I feel hope.

Chapter 2

He that dies pays all debts.
— William Shakespeare

I WAS DREAMING. In my dream, I was a thousand little sparks of light, of life, of energy. I was sinking into the flowing expanse. As I settled, I started to reach out and connect to the other pieces of myself. Vibrations traveled through us, and I felt as if I was on the cusp, about to fall over the edge into understanding. Then I woke up.

Gasping, I sat straight up in bed. My mind was reeling, dizzy, as if it had snapped back with the force of a once-taut rubber band. I found myself listening for something that wasn't there.

I let some of the tension go and looked around. I was in my room, tucked under the covers of my bed, wearing my favorite pajama set. Zed sat in a chair beside my bed, asleep. The room was still dark, just starting to grey with the approaching dawn.

I shivered and wrinkled my nose. My clothing was damp and my skin grungy from sweat. I really needed a shower. Badly. I peeled back the covers and sheets and crawled out of bed, careful not to wake my brother. It wasn't until I moved that I realized I was attached to an IV, the little needle piercing the flesh at the bend of my elbow. I've never been squeamish about needles, so I carefully pulled it back out of my skin and put pressure on the spot with my thumb for a while.

My knees almost buckled when I tried to stand. By the time I'd made it to the bathroom, just around the corner from my room, I was panting, dizzy, and completely exhausted.

I turned on the sink and leaned against the counter for support while scooping water into my desert-dry mouth. Cold water immediately entered my airway and I began to cough, spitting up a mouthful of mucus and dried blood into the sink. The sticky glob circled the drain before finally being carried down by the still-running water.

My gaze strayed to the bedraggled girl in the mirror. My dark, straight hair floated around my head in a tangled halo, my lips were dry and cracked in bloody lines, skin deathly pale, and the bags underneath my eyes looked more like bruises. My jaw was sharper, my cheekbones more defined, and I must have lost ten pounds. Just what I'd always wanted. Except…not.

I met the pale blue eyes in the mirror. "You look like crap," I croaked, which made me start coughing again.

The exertion drained me, so I sat down on the toilet. After I relieved myself—which was indeed a relief—I stayed on the toilet for a few minutes, resting. My body felt strange in a way that I'd never experienced before, even after being sick. Something was…different. And my hands and feet ached around the faint scars that still remained from having my extra fingers and toes removed as a baby. I absentmindedly rubbed at the skin where my sixth finger had been.

Memories resurfaced…strange, crazy things. Nightmares. People had grabbed me when I tried to help some random guy. They'd injected me with something.

I lifted my hand to the back of my neck and pressed around at the base of my skull, then the spot an inch below that, then ran my finger over the skin of my throat where the woman had held the marble-injector-thing. There was no pain, no nicks or cuts that I could feel. I'd miraculously made it home after they'd left me passed out in the alley.

And then what? I remembered flashes of a sterile room, strange machines, doctors, and some deep and soothing sound. I frowned and shook my head with a sigh. I wasn't remembering properly. I'd been way too out of it. Sick.

What had they done to me? Injected me with some sort of disease, maybe. We were always hearing about terrorism on the news. That was one of the main reasons for the establishment of the enforcers. Maybe I'd just been unlucky enough to meet some would-be terrorists.

But, no, that didn't make sense. They knew who I was. They'd said, "It's her." If they'd injected me with something infectious, I wouldn't be here, in my room, with Zed not even wearing a mask. I would be quarantined. So maybe it had been some sort of poison?

I groaned. I couldn't think. Maybe Zed would be able to tell me what my diagnosis was. If the doctor had come, my brother would know the result; he'd obviously been at my bedside since the day before.

Going back into my room, I sat down on my bed and gently shook Zed's shoulder.

He jerked awake, eyes wide and bleary, and looked around. "I'm up, I'm up! What's wrong?" His eyes focused on me, and then his lips parted in a relieved smile. "Oh, thank goodness. I'm so glad you finally woke up. I mean, the doctor did say we should expect you to sleep for a long time as your body fought off the virus, but when you didn't wake up for three days, I started to wonder—"

"Whoa, whoa," I said, holding out my hand to stop him. "*Three days?* I've been sleeping all this time?"

"Well, yeah. I mean, mostly. I think so." He looked uncomfortable, awkward, which was rare.

I frowned suspiciously. "What do you mean, 'mostly?'"

He grimaced. "You were having nightmares. Or hallucinations, maybe. The doctor said—"

"Mom really did pay for a doctor?"

"Well, yeah. Of course. I mean, she wanted to take you to the hospital, but you know we don't have that kind of money. What do you remember?"

I narrowed my eyes. "I got attacked on the street, and they injected me with something. People in masks. I was trying to get home, and I thought maybe they were watching, and there were doctors and machines in a small room. I was tied down…" I trailed off, frowning. "I guess I was quarantined or something? I thought you said I didn't go to the hospital."

Zed bit his lip. "Umm, okay. So the doctor said this might be a side effect. All of that stuff…it didn't happen. You were probably hallucinating, or maybe just dreaming. He said that in most cases, patients experience paranoid hallucinations during the fever, and possibly afterward, too, and that we should keep an eye on you, and he gave me some sedatives because he said sometimes they continue for a little while after the fever's over and that if you get too worked up you should take one..." he rambled.

I let myself tune out his voice as he went on. Hallucinations. Is that what everything had been? Just my stressed out, overheated brain creating imaginary terrors? "But they seemed so real," I murmured, cutting off his explanation of the sedatives. But maybe I was wrong. "What could cause something like that?"

"He said it's a new strain of virus. Usually not deadly, but there's no treatment for it yet, so he said to just give you lots of fluids and rest, and to try to make sure you stayed grounded in reality." His fingers tapped nervously on his knees, his nervous energy and the need to help overflowing.

They were testing out some sort of bioterrorism, then?

"Zed, I could have gotten you sick!"

"No. The doc said it's not very contagious and isn't normally translated through anything except blood. Do you know what may have happened?"

"I don't remember anything like that. And I promise I haven't stuck myself with any used needles lately." I smirked, then met Zed's concerned eyes and changed it to a softer smile. "Do you think you could get me something to eat? I'm feeling a bit empty."

He grinned. "Not eating in three days will do that to you, I hear. I'll go get something. Be right back."

As soon as he was gone, I picked up my ID sheath link and looked up my most recent transaction. Three hundred twelve credits, transportation and sanitation fee.

I wasn't hallucinating everything. So how could I tell what had actually happened?

THE BACK of my neck tingled, then pulsed out a little shock that felt like static electricity. *Unlike* static electricity, it caused me to go blind for a second before my vision sputtered back to life like an old car's engine.

Except now, a paper-thin, translucent screen hung in front of my face. I let out a stifled shriek and scrambled backward, kicking my covers into a pile in my haste to get as far away from it as possible. I stopped once my back was pressed firmly against the wall and I could go no further.

The screen floated unperturbed, the same distance from my face.

My eyes read the words on it without conscious thought.

WARNING: DO NOT DISCUSS THE GAME OR YOUR STATUS AS A PLAYER WITH CIVILIANS.

I reached out and tentatively hovered my hands over and around the edges of the screen, careful not to touch it. There were no wires, no strings holding it in place. I slipped my hand behind it and watched my slightly blurred fingers wiggle back at me.

"This is not good." I hesitated, then reached out and poked it with a finger. Although I didn't feel anything, it reacted to my touch, popping out of existence as if I'd burst a bubble. Another one replaced it a second later.

EVE REDDING, CONGRATULATIONS ON YOUR INITIATION TO THE GAME.

That one faded away on its own and was again replaced by another.

YOU HAVE REACHED LEVEL ONE!
YOU HAVE GAINED ONE SEED!
PLEASE EXTEND YOUR HAND PALM UP TO RECEIVE YOUR SEED.

"Oh, hell," I croaked. "This isn't real. It's not real." Even so, I couldn't help but hold my hand out, facing upward in shaky supplication. I was screaming inside, wondering what the hell was wrong with me. Resisting insanity was a much better idea, but my curiosity got the best of me. It seemed too real.

The air rippled strangely over my hand, like a heat wave rushing out from my palm, distorting my vision. It was similar to the mirage of distant water on the ground that you can see on a really hot day.

Then it was gone, replaced by a little glass ball, just like the ones used by the people in the alley.

I closed my eyes and took a deep breath, so freaked out I was afraid I might start sputtering gibberish and banging my head against the wall. My heart beat like a subwoofer inside my chest as I opened my eyes and brought the ball closer to my face for inspection.

The early morning sunlight angled through my window and glinted off the marble-like sphere. A branching, maze-like pattern was etched into the clear glass in spidery, metallic lines. Inside the glass shell some sort of shimmering liquid swirled slowly around. Across the face of the marble, a string of letters rose to the surface and flowed past my eyes. The words read "MAKE A WISH."

That was too much for me. "Zed!" I screamed.

He came rushing into the room, still holding a piece of bread in his hand and looking around frantically. "What's wrong?"

"Do you see this?" I held up the ball, my hand shuddering. "Tell me!"

"Yes, I see it. Calm down, what's wrong?" He held his hands in up a calming motion and pushed my arm down. "What's the matter?"

I pulled my hand free and shook the marble. "Look closer. What do you see?"

He frowned and peered at it. "It's a marble, Eve. Probably from a street vendor. Are you feeling all right?" He placed his hand on my forehead to test my temperature, and I brushed it away in irritation.

"What about that?" I pointed to the screen hanging in front of my face. "Do you see that?"

His eyebrows scrunched together further and his voice grew tight. "See what, Eve? What am I supposed to be seeing?"

I shook my head and pressed the palms of my hands hard to my eyes. "You'd know what I was talking about if you could see it. It's hanging in the air, damn it!"

"I'm going to get you one of those sedative pills. You stay right there, Eve. Don't move, and try to calm down. Just stay there, okay?"

Where would I go to get away from my own head? Besides, I barely had the strength to get to the bathroom. Did he think I'd run away? Jump out the window?

I took my hands away from my face and nodded, and he bolted away, the piece of bread now squished in his fist, forgotten.

The bread was so ludicrous, so removed from everything my crazy brain was trying to smash me with, that I couldn't help but laugh.

I was still giggling when another window popped up, different than the others.

—Eve, you're perilously close to breaking the rule about disclosing Game information to non-Players. You really don't want to do that.—
-Bunny-

I froze, my laughter dying in my chest.

—When he comes back, you better realize that you're feeling sick and feverish, and had another hallucination, if you care for his or your own safety.
Oh, and by the way…nice to meet you. :P—
-Bunny-

"Who are you?"

—I'm Bunny, your Game Moderator.—
-Bunny-

Chapter 3

I desire the things that will destroy me in the end.
— Sylvia Plath

ZED SAT WATCHING ME EAT, concern etched all over his face.

I ravenously stuffed the fresh sausage, eggs, biscuits, and gravy into my mouth, both to satiate my hunger and to excuse me from discussing my "hallucination" with him.

My heart was beating fast, too fast, as if I'd had too much caffeine and couldn't calm down. It was a sour feeling.

When I finished, I licked the plate and plopped backward onto my pillows with a big sigh.

Zed pushed a glass of cloudy yellow liquid toward me. "Drink this. It's vitamix and lemon water. You need to get some nutrients to help rebuild your strength."

I sighed and shot my little brother a look.

He grinned back at me and rolled his eyes. "It's good for you. Just drink it. Doctor's orders."

"Oh, really?"

"Yeah, just think of this as practice for when I join the Peace Corps. You're my dummy patient."

I snorted and complied, gulping down the mixture made only slightly better by the taste of lemon. "Okay, I feel better now. I think I just needed something in my stomach." I let out a very loud, very real yawn, not needing to fake my exhaustion. "I'm really tired now. I don't think I'll need that pill. I'm just gonna go back to sleep." I studied his worn face and bloodshot eyes. "You should probably go to sleep, too. I know you don't have anything important to do. And I'm fine, so you don't need to keep 'mother hen-ing' me."

He studied me for a moment, and I did my best to look sane, calm, and not as if I were trying to make him leave for some ulterior motive. Even though I was hallucinating invisible screens who called themselves Bunny, freaking out, and trying to shoo Zed away so I could talk to them.

"Okay. If you need anything, just shout."

"Roger."

Zed was a genuinely good person, the opposite of me in almost every way: brave, popular, handsome, and he had an unselfish nature.

That's why I sent him away without saying anything about the reason my heart was beating so frighteningly hard. Because if I *wasn't* crazy, whatever was going on wasn't good, and he didn't deserve to be involved in it. And if I was crazy, it would pass along with my lingering sickness, and no harm would come of it.

Alone, I took a deep breath and whispered, "Umm … Bunny? Are you there?"

—Yes. Now that he's gone, let me explain what's going on.—
-Bunny-

"First things first. Am I crazy? Is this a paranoid delusion?"

—No. The doctor was one of ours. He told your family that so they would ignore any strange actions or accusations you might make about being attacked, or the Game.—
-Bunny-

"That's just what a paranoid delusion would say. How do I know you're really there? Is this really happening? And why do you want to keep it a secret?"

—There will be plenty of proof, in time. The first piece being that your

brother acknowledged the "marble's" existence. It's not a marble, but it *is* obviously real.—
-Bunny-

I slid the ball from under my pillow where I'd hidden it and rolled it around my palm. "But he couldn't see these…hologram screens."

—That's because they're only in your own mind. And don't make that face. Just because the screens aren't really there doesn't mean you're imagining them. Something else *is* real. The VR chip embedded in the base of your brain.—
-Bunny-

"VR…Virtual Reality? Embedded in my brain? Is that what they were doing to the back of my neck?" I paused. "Wait, you can see me?"

—I've got access to your link camera, and our doctor put a couple different monitoring devices in your house under the guise of checking for dangerous mold spores that could exacerbate your condition, so we can keep an eye on your initiation. Sigh. If you'd just let me explain without interrupting, all of this would be a lot easier. Just be quiet for five minutes.—
-Bunny-

I raised an eyebrow but said nothing.

—You are now a Player of the Game. And as far as I know, you're not crazy. We test for that beforehand. The Game isn't the console or computer type you may be used to. It's completely interactive, completely real. The outcome is only dependent on you, and by leveling up, you can gain the ability to change everything about yourself, in real life. You level up by completing quests given to you by me, your Moderator, and by achievements in the Trials, which are game-like tests of your ability. You've been given one free Seed to use as you see fit. You may not talk about or distribute information on the Game to non-Players.
And Eve…there are no do-overs. You only have one life.—
-Bunny-

BUNNY HAD GIVEN me an introductory quest to familiarize myself with the Game's "user interface," and then left me in visual silence, writing that he had something more important to tend to.

I didn't proceed with the quest, but instead thought about what he'd said till the lingering fatigue of my sickness overpowered everything, and I slept. I woke and raided the fridge, my body ravenous for the nutrients to rebuild itself, then slept again.

The next morning, I was finally ready to deal with the situation once more.

"Bunny?" I called into the empty air of my room, hoping nothing reacted and I could write it all off as a crazy dream.

—Yes.—
-Bunny-

Tch. No such luck. "I've got some more questions."

—I have answers. Some of them, anyway.—
-Bunny-

"How are you talking to me like this?"

—We both have VR implants, and they send signals to each other. Your brain knows when you're trying to communicate with me and activates the chip.—
-Bunny-

"You can read my *thoughts*?"

—Haha, they may want us to tell you we're all-knowing, but we can't receive messages you don't want us to. Your private thoughts are your own.—
-Bunny-

"Did they do the same thing to you they did to me, or did you accept it willingly?"

—This is my job.—
-Bunny-

"Working for who?"

—Hah! Nice try.—
-Bunny-

"You warned me to keep this Game a secret. What happens if I talk about it with other people?"

—Trust me. You don't want to do that.—
-Bunny-

"But what if I did?"

—Let's just say that the information you revealed would never make it anywhere further.—
-Bunny-

I wondered exactly what that might entail, but the gist was pretty obvious. If I told someone, they'd never be able to tell anyone else. How would a powerful, secretive organization ensure someone's absolute silence? They'd kill them, that's how. "Okay. Next question. What if I refuse to play?"

—Haha. You can't refuse. You're a Player, and there's no going back. Refusing to play would really only be deciding to play *badly*. Well... perhaps you could kill yourself, but rather than 'not playing,' I tend to think of death more on the terms 'losing.'—
-Bunny-

I swallowed. "Well, what happens if I play well?"

—If you play well, you get more Seeds. And the Seeds are really the point of it all. They allow you to change everything about yourself. Well, except personality. The thirteen Attributes. They make your wishes come true, literally.—
-Bunny-

"Thirteen Attributes?"

—Part of the quest I gave you, which you obviously haven't done.—
-Bunny-

I bit the inside of my lip. "I had a lot of things to think about. This is overwhelming."

—You're going to have to become a lot more adaptable. Sigh. Let's run through it now, then.—
-Bunny-

I frowned, hesitating. "Umm, what do I…?"

—Double sigh. You're a bit useless, aren't you? Say "Display Quests."—
-Bunny-

I gritted my teeth, keeping my irritation in check. I wanted to set Bunny straight, but there was nothing I could say. There was nothing special about me at all. I wasn't a great student, I wasn't pretty, and I was especially nonathletic. I was the type of person who was mostly ignored, except for the occasional bullying. An invisible girl. But that didn't mean my jaw didn't clench and my tongue didn't burn with the desire to spit something cutting at the screen.

Instead, I said, "Display Quests."

INTRODUCTION TO USER INTERFACE–STATUS WINDOW
USE VOICE COMMAND "DISPLAY STATUS WINDOW."
COMPLETION REWARD: 5 EXP
NON-COMPLETION PENALTY: NONE

I followed the instructions, and a larger window popped up.

PLAYER NAME: EVE REDDING
TITLE: NONE
CHARACTERISTIC SKILL: NONE
LEVEL: 1 UNPLANTED SEEDS: 1
SKILLS: NONE

STRENGTH: 7
LIFE: 12
AGILITY: 4
GRACE: 4
INTELLIGENCE: 10
FOCUS: 8
BEAUTY: 4
PHYSIQUE: 5
MANUAL DEXTERITY: 7
MENTAL ACUITY: 10
RESILIENCE: 5
STAMINA: 6
PERCEPTION: 7

A SMALL, quickly fading window slid into my peripheral vision, telling me I'd gained five experience points and giving me instructions for the next part of the "chain" quest.

"These are measures of…me?"

—Yes.—
-Bunny-

I poked at the word "Strength" on the screen.

STRENGTH: ABILITY TO EXERT PHYSICAL FORCE.

"I'm level seven strength? Seven out of what?"

—Seven out of infinity. Though if you don't level up any of the balancing Attributes, you will reach a point where your body is so strong it'll destroy itself. Use the Attribute Window to display all of them at once.—
-Bunny-

"Display Attributes," I said. Another EXP gain notification popped up, along with a larger Window.

STRENGTH (7): ABILITY TO EXERT PHYSICAL FORCE.

LIFE (12): MEASURE OF HOW MUCH DAMAGE CAN BE ABSORBED BEFORE DYING.
AGILITY (4): PHYSICAL ABILITY TO INITIATE QUICK-TWITCH MUSCLE MOVEMENTS.
GRACE (4): ABILITY TO CONTROL THE FLOW AND CONSEQUENCE OF BODY MOVEMENTS.

INTELLIGENCE (10): ABILITY TO REMEMBER DATA AND EMPLOY REASONING.

FOCUS (8): ABILITY TO CONCENTRATE ATTENTION ON A SPECIFIC TOPIC.

BEAUTY (4): ATTRACTIVENESS OF THE OUTWARD APPEARANCE, SPECIFICALLY THE FACE, CONFORMING TO THE WISHES OF THE PLAYER.

PHYSIQUE (5): PHYSICAL APPEARANCE OF THE BODY'S FORM, CONFORMING TO THE WISHES OF THE PLAYER.

MANUAL DEXTERITY (7): ABILITY TO UTILIZE FINE MOTOR CONTROL.
MENTAL ACUITY (10): ABILITY TO THINK AND DRAW CONCLUSIONS QUICKLY.
RESILIENCE (5): ABILITY TO RECOVER FROM DAMAGE AND MENTAL AND PHYSICAL EXHAUSTION.
STAMINA (6): MEASURE OF HOW MUCH PHYSICAL OR MENTAL FORCE CAN BE EXERTED BEFORE BECOMING EXHAUSTED.

PERCEPTION (7): ABILITY TO SENSE BOTH THE PHYSICAL AND THE IMPLIED.
UNPLANTED SEEDS: 1
—Now pick an Attribute, hold your Seed to your wrist or your neck, and make a wish for whichever Attribute you want to increase.—
-Bunny-

I PULLED out the little marble-like ball from under my pillow and held it in my hand, studying it. The sun shone through my window and fell onto the Seed. It was beautiful, that liquid swirling around inside, glimmering in the light. Once again, the words rose to the surface, prompting me to make a wish.

"Is it addictive? Like, a drug? That guy who got me into all this, he seemed pretty desperate to get his hands on another one."

—You've already had one. Do you feel addicted?—
-Bunny-

I raised an eyebrow and snorted. "Pretty much the opposite. That thing almost killed me."

—Well, that won't happen again. Your body's already adjusted to it.—
-Bunny-

"How do you know?"

—Because you're alive.—
-Bunny-

I stilled and let out a slow breath.

—And no, there are no physically addictive properties to the Seeds.—
-Bunny-

"Physically, huh? What about mentally, or psychologically?" I wasn't stupid enough to be comforted by his not-quite-a-lie.

THERE WAS a brief pause before the next message came through.

—Some people do become obsessed. For obvious reasons. We're giving you the ability to make yourself *better*.—
-Bunny-

"Why are you doing this? All this?" I gestured vaguely to myself and the screens hanging invisibly in the air. "*Giving* us this?"

—That one, I'll leave to your imagination. Perhaps you'll discover the answer in time.—
-Bunny-

I shook my head, frustrated at the general lack of answers. A wish? What could I wish for that would make my life better, assuming it actually worked? This was the modern day, and I wasn't an athlete or a man, so things like strength would be largely useless. Intelligence would be good, but hard to measure. Would I *feel* smarter? My eyes caught on Beauty. That would be easy to compare, before and after. And people cared about appearances. Attractiveness, *beauty*, made a big difference. As someone who didn't have it, I felt its lack.

I grabbed the Seed, went to the bathroom, and locked the door, then stripped down to my underwear. I started the video recording function on both the body length wall mirror and the half-size one above the sink. "Okay. What exactly do I have to say?"

—Just say something like, "I wish I were more agile," and the Seed will inject itself into you. It's called "planting" the Seed.—
-Bunny-

I swallowed painfully and stared at myself in the mirror. Body too tall, and chubby. Slightly crooked nose. Pale, thin lips. Pimples. "There's no way this is going to work." I pressed the Seed into my wrist, above the veins. "I wish I were more beautiful."

There was a sharp pain, and the Seed injected its contents into me.

As soon as it was empty, I felt it detach from my skin, and peered at the place it had cut. The small piercing was almost gone already. As I watched, it healed itself.

I put the Seed down on the tiled counter as a horrible realization swept through me. "What have I done?" This was dangerous. Reckless.

And I just went ahead with this strange entity in my head and injected an unknown substance into myself?

I waited to feel sick or dizzy, like I had the last time. I waited to die, to feel high, anything. But nothing happened.

It seemed like an eternity, but after no more than a minute had passed, it started. My skin began to warm and tingle strangely, especially the skin of my face. It itched painfully, and when I put my hand to my cheek, I could feel the heat radiating outward.

I sat down on the toilet seat and tried to control my panicked breathing. I put my hands underneath my butt to resist the urge to claw at my skin. Just when I was about to rush out of the bathroom and do something stupid—even I wasn't sure exactly what, but *something*, anything—the tingling-burning-itching calmed down, dissipating with each passing second. As my skin cooled, I stood up and shakily walked over to the bathroom counter, leaning on it for support.

I leaned toward the mirror above the sink, looking at my face for any sign of change, good or bad. "It's my imagination."

—It's not.—
-Bunny-

I lifted a hand and ran my fingers lightly over my skin. Soft, fewer blemishes. My nose was still crooked, but perhaps not as much. My eyes, my best feature, stood out, and I brushed my fingers over the thickened eyelashes framing them, and then over my lips. Still thin and pale, but…better? I took a deep breath and closed my eyes against the view in the mirror. This could be a placebo effect—me wanting it to be true so badly I imagined an improvement.

"Calm down." I took another deep breath and said it again. "Calm down." It wasn't time to get excited yet. I stopped the mirrors' recording and downloaded the videos to my ID sheath. Then I snapped the sheath straight and replayed the two video viewpoints side by side on its clear surface. Once over my whole body, and again zoomed in to my face. Then I watched in fast forward, again, and again.

I pushed back from the counter to pace back and forth across the room. I just couldn't stay still. My hands were shaking, and I wrapped my arms around my torso as if to keep myself from exploding and flying apart. I muttered calming words to myself, trying to slow my ragged breathing.

There was a light tapping on the bathroom door. "Eve? Are you okay?" Zed's voice filtered through. "You've been in there a while."

I cleared my throat and steadied my voice. "I'll be right out. I'm fine." I slipped my clothes back on.

Zed's voice was soft, hesitant. "Are you sure?"

I flushed the toilet to give some rationale to my long stay in the bathroom, then spritzed the "fresh air scent" dispenser. I needed to pull myself together. "Yeah, I'm fine. Thanks, though."

In the mirror above the sink, I looked at myself. Pale, pale blue eyes, wide and shocked, stared back at me. The lids slid down over those eyes, and I turned on the sink to splash cold water over my face and rinse my mouth out.

I lifted the hem of my T-shirt and used it to dry my face, pushed back my shoulders, and opened the door. "Promise, I'm feeling much better."

My brother stood right outside, jaw clenched hard and a worried frown across his handsome face. When he saw me, it slipped a little. "You do look…recovered. But you were just really sick. Do you want to go lie down? I'll bring you some lemon water with a straw, if you want."

I rolled my eyes, patted him on the shoulder, and shook my head. "No, I'm really fine. Don't worry. I had to poop. Thanks for making such a huge deal of it."

Looking chagrined, he stepped aside. I slipped past him, back to my room, and closed the door behind me.

"Thinking about it abstractly is one thing. Seeing is another thing entirely," I murmured, looking at my new, slightly more beautiful face in the mirror on my wall.

I PACED the carpeted floor of my room, back and forth, back and forth. "Bunny!" I hissed into the empty air. "I need to talk to you!" It was the umpteenth time I'd called, and at this point I wasn't even expecting a response anymore.

Almost as if to prove me wrong, a Window popped up in front of my face.

—Will you stop calling me for two seconds? Every time you say my name I'm forced to divert my attention from more important things. Just be quiet, will you?—

-Bunny-

"What more important things? I'm freaking out here. I need answers! How do these things work? What just happened should be impossible." I'd searched the net for any reference to what I'd just experienced but couldn't find anything. Not surprising, as that would be a violation of the Game rules.

—I have other Players to deal with. Ones with real problems. And quite frankly, your curiosity is both tedious and pretty boring.—
-Bunny-

I paused. "Other Players? How many? Are there other Moderators, too?"

—Eve. Stop. If you'll leave me alone for now, we'll talk later. Here's something to occupy you. Don't call me again until you've finished the quest.—
-Bunny-
EXERCISE
RUN 2 MILES
COMPLETION REWARD: 15 EXP
NON-COMPLETION PENALTY: BUNNY WILL NOT ANSWER QUESTIONS.

I waved my hand across the screen as if shooing away a fly, and it disintegrated. But I didn't call for Bunny again. I was impatient, but I would wait to do as Bunny said. It—he, *she*?—was the source of all my information *and* Seeds, and its good will was valuable. Plus, fifteen more experience points would put me over the halfway mark toward my next Seed.

"Breakfast!" my mother's voice rang out from the kitchen, and I realized that I was absolutely starving.

Hurrying into the kitchen, I piled my plate high with food and flopped tiredly into a chair, then eagerly began to shovel food into my mouth.

She sat down across from Zed and me, tapping a message or report for work on her forearm sheath. I shot Zed a look, and he rolled his eyes at her bowed head with an amused smile. She always insisted that we have at least one meal per week together as a family, but still managed to be half-distracted every time. We acknowledged the irony, but that was a sort of tradition in its own right.

My mother's eyes caught on me as she looked up. Her lips tightened imperceptibly as her gaze roamed over me and then to my plate. "Eve, do you really think you should be eating…all that? If you want to be healthy, you really need to monitor yourself a bit more." Her voice paused noticeably before "healthy," and I knew what she really meant was "skinny." She herself was a beauty, but the only thing we had in common was thick, straight, almost-black hair.

"You've just lost some weight. Wouldn't you feel better if you could keep it off?" She smiled at me gently, but there was something else hiding in her voice—disappointment, and maybe some sadness, too. I was less than the beautiful, popular, perfect counterpart to Zed.

Her words stung, but I knew she didn't say them to be cruel. She was just lacking in tact. At least that's what I told myself.

"Your brother is an athlete, and a man besides that, and you're eating more than he is," she finally added.

I swallowed, the food suddenly sitting heavy in my stomach, and realized I'd lost my appetite. Besides, running two miles on a full stomach was just begging to throw it all back up. Especially considering the shape I was in.

I stood up and scraped the food on my plate down the disposal chute, then went to my room to slip on a pair of runners and a sports bra. "I'm going for a jog," I called out as I left the house, just catching the hard glance Zed threw at my mother over my shoulder.

I started out at a nice slow run. Almost instantly I was down to a jog, and not long after that I was doing some floundery, bouncing motion that had people on the street passing me at a brisk walk. I took the same path I normally walked on my way to school, which took me by the alley where it had happened.

It was empty. Innocent-looking.

I stopped jogging and walked toward it, my chest heaving, air and smog burning in and out of my lungs.

They'd known where I was going to be that morning. They'd known who I was. And Bunny could see me, I knew, though they hadn't affirmed my suspicion. Which meant…

I looked around suspiciously. Was I being monitored, watched? That guy across the street had just shot me a look. Was he following me? I looked behind myself, and a woman briefly met my eyes and then looked away.

"Just being paranoid," I gasped to myself. But even so, I started pushing my body harder. I took an abrupt turn at the next alley, and then ran through it, turning once again when it opened up on the parallel street. I kept going till a Window slid up, telling me I'd completed my quest. I found myself in an old dilapidated parking lot, gasping for breath and unable to keep moving.

—Good job. Though…you look kind of like a seal giving birth, all sweaty and gasping like that.—
-Bunny-

"You were…watching me?"

—Hmm. More or less. I didn't have anything more pressing to do at the moment, since I dealt with my other situation.—
-Bunny-

I hobbled over to a light pole and leaned against it. That was why I didn't like to exercise; I hated being reminded of the things I was terrible at. "Do you have people…following me?" I sucked in a few deep breaths of filthy city air. "Keeping tabs on me?"

—Why would we waste resources like that? Your location is tracked electronically, and at any second, I can find a camera to monitor you.—
-Bunny-

"You've got GPS on me?"

—Yes. Duh. You're an asset. Do you think we'd just let you run around without knowing where you are and being able to find out what you're doing?—
-Bunny-

If they had both GPS and the ability to see and hear me, the people behind all this must have had access to the government's internal surveillance network. And probably satellites, too.

Around the time they'd created the enforcers, the government planted listening devices and cameras throughout every city to monitor and search for potential threats to the nation's safety, which meant they could find me almost anywhere in public.

"Plus you put cameras in my house?"

—Yes. But don't bother trying to find them. You won't.—
-Bunny-

"Do other people watch me, or is it just you? Is Bunny even your name? What kind of name is that? You could be a hundred different people for all I know, all pretending to be 'Bunny.'"

—Rude much? I don't insult *your* name. >:(
My superiors have access to the files of individual Players, but they never use them. It's just me watching you, almost exclusively, and I'm not a hundred guys. Just one guy. It's my job to keep tabs on you and write reports that no one ever reads about your progress and achievements.—
-Bunny-

I closed my eyes. These people were powerful, had extensive resources, could access my high school medical tests, and had forcefully implanted a wish-fulfilling substance into me. "Who *are* you?"

—That's a secret.—
-Bunny-

Chapter 4

Everyone is a moon and has a dark side which he never shows to anybody.
— Mark Twain

I RAN-WALKED AS QUIETLY and inconspicuously as I could through my school's halls. I'd left the last class of the day early, saying I had a stomachache. Honestly, I had very little idea what I was doing. While I was ignoring the on-screen lectures in class, a quest Window had popped up almost directly in front of my face, as if Bunny were trying especially hard to attract my attention.

OPEN LOCKER 113 IN C HALL AND REMOVE THE KNIFE WITHIN, WITHOUT GETTING CAUGHT.
LOCKER COMBINATION: 13-49-01
COMPLETION REWARD: 3 SEEDS
NON-COMPLETION PENALTY: POSSIBLE PUNISHMENT FROM SCHOOL FACULTY AND/OR ENFORCERS.

Along with it, another, smaller screen popped up, displaying only a two-minute countdown. No matter how I looked at that, it screamed "dangerous!" and I didn't know if I'd be able to pull it off within the time limit. C Hall wasn't close. Then I thought of getting three Seeds, and started running as fast as I could in the opposite direction of the infirmary. As if I could refuse! My legs screamed in pain with every step, sore from the previous day's run, but I ignored them.

I skidded to a stop in front of locker one-thirteen and used a voice command to pull up the quest information again. "Thirteen…forty-nine…one," I whispered, twisting the combination into the lock. It popped open, and I quickly rifled through the locker, finding the butterfly knife easily. It belonged to a guy named Adam Coyle according to the label on the back of his school link. I stuffed it into my pocket and was about to close the locker door and leave with plenty of time to spare when a strange, niggling thought popped into my mind. I hurried to tear out a piece of paper from the back of one of the notebooks inside and scribbled, "I saved your scalp. You owe me one." Rolling the note up small, I slipped it inside the cap lying on top of the locker's jumbled contents.

An enforcer turned the corner just as I closed the locker door. Our eyes met for a split second before I turned and started walking away as nonchalantly as I could. I felt like a puppet on strings, walking stiffly and comically, until I turned the corner at the end of the corridor.

At that moment, the bell rang and students poured into the hallway, rushing out of their classrooms and creating a wonderful, sprawling sea of chaos. I slipped between the rushing, inconsiderate bodies, and felt a gleeful smile tug at my lips when the quest completion screen slid up in my peripheral vision.

"SO, Bunny, what was that all about?" I asked, walking safely home.

—What?—
-Bunny-

I dodged a mother with two screaming toddlers taking up most of the sidewalk. "That quest. Why did you need me to do that? Who does that locker belong to?"

There was no immediate response, and I wondered if Bunny was trying to figure out what to say. "Just tell me. That locker belonged to another Player, right?" I couldn't help the excited grin growing on my face. "And you were trying to protect them from that locker search?"

—Yeah, something like that. But more importantly, what are you going to do with your three Seeds?—
-Bunny-

I raised an eyebrow and smirked. Was he trying to divert my attention? Way too obvious. "That's another thing. Three Seeds? Quite a reward. You were pretty desperate to make sure they didn't get caught. Why?"

—Because that person was on their last chance. If they got caught, they'd have been sent to a juvenile detention center. And if he were under surveillance, it'd be kind of hard for him to do the Trials. And Players have to do the Trials.—
-Bunny-

"What happens if they can't?"

—Unless they're dead, a Player will do the Trials.—
-Bunny-

"And this made you panic because…?" I trailed off, thinking out loud. "If they have to do the Trials, but you don't want people to know about what you're doing…" I stopped walking and looked up at the sky, visible only in patches between the towering buildings. "If he got caught, you were going to kill him. Maybe not you, specifically, but one of your people, like the ones that grabbed me."

There was a pause before the response came back, and that told me the answer as clear as anything.

—I'm sure we could have found another way. We have a lot of influence, resources. But it's not something to worry about, because thanks to you, he didn't get caught.—
-Bunny-

I didn't know what to say to that, so I kept my silence for a while, until another thought popped into my mind. "What happens in the Trials that you don't want people to see?"

—I'm not an Examiner. I don't really deal with the Trials. All I will say is that you should prepare, Eve.—
-Bunny-

I entered my building and rode the elevator to our empty house, then went inside to my room. "Let me get those Seeds, Bunny."

—Hold out your hand.—
-Bunny-

I did so, and three creamy spheres appeared after the mini wave distortion. I went into the bathroom again after stashing the knife in my closet and recorded as I put another of the Seeds into Beauty. Now that I knew what to expect, I was much better able to handle the side effects. This time I watched in the mirror as my slightly crooked nose, which I'd focused on specifically while planting the Seed, straightened slowly, almost imperceptibly.

Once the crazy burning and itching wore off, I looked at my nose in the mirror and thought that perhaps one more Seed would make it straight. But I hesitated to plant the other two into Beauty, because of what I sensed was behind Bunny's unwritten words. I needed to prepare for something. And if it didn't matter which Attribute I planted the Seeds into, why would he have brought it up? Perhaps it was meant as more than a distraction. A subtle hint that I shouldn't just choose Beauty over and over again, maybe.

I pulled up the Attribute screen and looked them over. Intelligence or Mental Acuity seemed like a smart choice, but perhaps I would be better off putting a Seed into one of my weaker areas. I sighed. Without knowing what I might need to do in the Trials, it was hard to choose.

In the end, I chose Resilience and Stamina. They seemed like areas that could be useful in many different situations, and dealt with the mind *and* the body.

I injected the Seed for Stamina and waited tensely for painful side effects like those of Beauty. But instead, my whole body tingled with pleasant warmth, even my brain. It felt good, like a very mild, slow-burning coffee had been injected directly into my veins. If I were a pod, I would have said my gas mileage just got better.

Resilience didn't hurt, either. Warmth and tingling spread through me, but after it was over, I didn't feel much of anything different. In fact, it was a tad bit disappointing.

But I'd gained three valuable things that day: one, I now held a debt over another Player; two, the knowledge that Bunny did, reluctantly, care for the wellbeing of his Players, which meant that with the right stimulation, he could be coerced, manipulated; and three, the foreboding reminder that behind all this seeming magic, there was bound to be a catch.

I wish I'd listened to that bad feeling. But even if I had, there's no way I would have been prepared for what came next.

Chapter 5

If death has no cost, life has no worth.
— Ilium Troia

BUNNY WOULDN'T GIVE me any more information on the Game, but instead gave me exercise quest upon exercise quest. Each one came with a Seed, so of course I did them all. I put a few Seeds into different areas, but mostly Beauty. My nose was now straight, my skin clear, and my body was sore from head to toe. My mother and brother had both commented on how lovely I was looking lately, but of course didn't realize the reason. It was strange and wonderful to look in the mirror and think I was pretty. I worked out hard at Bunny's urging, pushing myself to meet the requirements of his quest. If I didn't, I would fail it, and there would be no experience points. Already, it was getting harder and harder to reach the next level, as each one required even more points.

Zed had offered his company in my new workouts, and he did a great job at being a secondary motivator. He was extremely fit, always a member of the school's sports team, and the baffling type that actually liked to work out even if he didn't strictly have to. I think he thought I was working out to lose weight so I could be prettier and live up to our mother's expectations, and he'd taken to giving her silently accusing looks whenever he thought I wasn't paying attention. He'd never liked the way she seemed to be perpetually disappointed in me while conversely praising him. I guess he thought I'd finally broken under the pressure, and it was like he couldn't decide whether to be happy I was finally taking care of myself or angry at her for being so unfair. He settled on doing both at once.

I'd continued to search the net for clues to my situation, but found nothing. I felt a strange mixture of trepidation and glee at the amazing things I was doing and the cost I knew deep in my bones had to come along with the ability.

After a night run, I stood with Zed in my building's backyard, a small park area with a few tall trees and some benches, and looked up at the night sky.

"You're getting better quickly," he said, breathing hard but not nearly panting. "Just be careful not to push yourself too hard. Your joints and tendons might not strengthen as quickly as your muscles, and you don't want to injure yourself while you're still just getting started."

I grinned and gave him a light shove, catching him off guard and making him stumble. "Hah! Just watch, Mr. I'm-going-to-be-a-doctor. In a few months, I'm going to be the one telling you to 'take it easy and make sure you don't hurt yourself, okay kiddo?' And then you'll look back on this moment and realize this is where it all started going downhill for you."

He gaped at me in mock shock for a moment, then drew himself up to his full height, which wasn't actually taller than my own Amazonian frame. "Just because I'm your little brother doesn't mean you can push me around. Someday I'll be bigger than you, and you'll regret it!" He lunged for me, wrapping an arm around my neck and pulling my torso down, then proceeded to rub his knuckles over my head, completely mussing up my ponytail.

"Miscalculation!" I shouted, wrapping one of my own arms around his waist to keep him from escaping and using the other to tickle him. "You played right into my evil plan."

He shrieked in a way that was quite unmanly and immediately let go of my neck, trying to escape my fingers. He finally struggled free and ran a few steps away from me, then turned to see if I would give chase. This time it was him gasping for breath as he recovered from his laughter.

I waved an arm limply at him, faking a disappointed whine. "Oh, no… He's run away and I can't catch up. Drat."

We both burst out laughing at ourselves, and he left to go into the house and finish up some homework. I chose to stay outside, relishing the way my body ached in a way that meant I was growing stronger—and was one step closer to getting another Seed out of Bunny.

I let the warm evening breeze blow over my skin and through my hair. I was a bit euphoric, and a bit exhausted. My Agility and Stamina Attributes had each spontaneously leveled up from the workouts, no Seed input needed. As I watched, more and more stars appeared, and seeing them spread out infinitely before me, I felt a tingle in my chest at my own tininess, and how very *not* tiny the universe was.

I smiled into the darkness, listening to faint strains of music. As I listened, they grew louder. It was a bit creepy—a child's voice singing softly in what could have been English, but…wasn't, wind chimes and reed instruments adding a level of strangeness. A shiver ran up my spine despite the warmth of the evening, and I wrapped my arms around myself.

It grew louder and louder, seeming to be coming from the air around me, from every direction at once. The child's voice sang nonsense words, and they echoed off the inside of my skull as if it was suddenly empty, like the noise had squeezed out my brain to make room for itself.

I couldn't move, couldn't think. The song was in my chest, in my bones, and then, in a wave that rolled out from the center of me, it was gone.

I was on my hands and knees, eyes clenched tight. My head spun dizzily, and I choked down bile, suddenly nauseated.

Deep, slow breaths helped to settle my vertigo.

But then I opened my eyes.

The manicured grass was gone. My hands rested on dead leaves, twigs, and damp soil. My eyes traveled upward, and my first inane thought was that the trees had grown, or maybe I had shrunk. But realization set in quickly. These definitely weren't the trees from my communal backyard. They towered above me, reaching so high into the sky that I wasn't sure where they ended and the night sky began. Moonlight filtered through the branches as if through mud, just bright enough to see by.

I stood and turned in a slow circle. My body felt like it had weights attached to it, like I'd just crawled out of a pool with soaking wet clothes on. My building, the park, the constant urban noise…it was all gone.

In the city where I lived, there was a constant hum of life and energy. Distant noise and the undercurrent of electricity ran through everything, vibrating inaudibly beneath the surface. Here, the lack of that hum was like a dark blanket that, instead of muting my senses, brought them to life. It was terrifying.

A twig snapped beneath my foot, the sound so sharp and cutting I jumped and barely held back a scream. Somehow the thought of adding noise to the darkness seemed horrible.

The wind blew across my body, suddenly chilly, and I realized it smelled of cut grass and peaches. My legs shook, and I wrapped my arms around my torso, trying to hold myself together.

A Window popped up in front of my face, causing me to jump and almost let out another scream of surprise. I half-choked on keeping it inside, but didn't make a sound.

The Window was a two-dimensional mini-map with an arrow labeled "Eve" and a blinking "X" positioned almost all the way across the map.

Attached to it were a quest Window and a timer, counting down the time from fifteen minutes.

GATHER
USE THE MINI-MAP TO MAKE YOUR WAY TO THE PLAYING FIELD.
COMPLETION REWARD: ENTER THE TRIAL
NON-COMPLETION PENALTY: DEATH

"Bunny? What the hell is going on?" I asked, putting as much force into my quiet voice as possible. There was no response, so I called again. "Bunny, answer me!"

Then I realized. Bunny had said he didn't deal with the Trials, which were some mysterious tests that I should prepare for. And the "Gather" quest's reward was to enter the Trial. "Hello? Is there a Moderator listening? Or—what was it again—an Examiner?"

There was no response, and the time limit was still ticking away. I was down to fourteen minutes. I raised my left arm to try and make a call from my ID link, but it was missing. I had left it in my room for its weekly charge. "Stupid, stupid, stupid."

There was no choice but to start walking. The X on the mini-map was a long way away from the little Eve-arrow, and I didn't know how long it would take me to get there. "Hopefully not more than fourteen minutes," I muttered. As I continued, my eyes grew more accustomed to the inky darkness, and allowing me to move faster. Every rustle of the forest made my heartbeat quicken. The hair on the back of my neck stood up straight. Something was wrong.

Something moved to my right and I froze, listening, watching, my eyes open wide to let in as much light as possible. Whatever it was moved again, low to the ground, a shadow amongst shadows.

Then a terrified scream pierced through the air, high-pitched and drawn out.

I bolted, sprinting as fast as I could, jumping over fallen trees at the last second, whacking into low-hanging branches with my bare face and arms. Something was chasing me, and catching up fast.

My instinct was to turn and look, but I kept my head straight and continued running like my life depended on it—which, for all I knew, it might. I wouldn't be one of those stupid girls in the horror films who looks back to see her pursuer gaining on her, and then trips and falls. My breathing was loud, but even so I heard another *something* keeping pace to my right. They were pinning me in.

Then something slammed into my right side. I tumbled to a stop with it on top of me, and small hand clamped over my mouth to prevent me from screaming. "Be quiet!" a young girl's voice hissed in my ear. "Do you want to lure more of them? We've only got a few seconds till it comes back. We've got to fight."

I nodded, and the girl dragged me to my feet.

"Do you have a weapon?"

"No, I don't. I'm sorry, I don't know what the hell is going on. What was that thing chasing me?"

"There's no time for that." There was a loud cracking sound, and then something hard pressed against my chest. "Here, take this."

I closed my fingers around it and realized she'd broken off an old branch to form a sort of staff.

"Is this your first Trial? Never mind. Of course it is. Damn," she muttered. "It's here!"

There was a shuffling sound. She stumbled against me and grunted with effort. At the same time a meaty *thunk* came from in front of me. Something snarled, and the shadows shifted again as the two struggled. Then a wet *snuk,* a low whine, and one of the shadows slunk off into the darkness, whimpering.

We waited a few moments in silence, and then she grabbed my hand. "Come on. We've got to get to the starting point. I'm Chanelle, by the way."

"Eve," I replied.

We moved quickly, but she pointed out things that might cause me to stumble, seemingly able to see in the darkness.

"I'm—what—" I stopped and gathered my thoughts. "What was that thing? Where are we?"

"That was a monster. They don't have a name, or if they do, I don't know it. And where we are is the big mystery. One of them, anyway." She paused. "I think it's not Earth. Or maybe it's all in our heads. Super-vivid, shared hallucinations caused by whatever they put in us."

"The Virtual Reality chips? So all this is just a game?" Air eased out of my lungs along with the tension.

"It's not a game!" she snapped. "Believe me, this is as real as anything you'll ever experience. You get hurt here, you're hurt in real life. You die here…"

I didn't need her to finish that sentence. "What happens in the Trials?"

"The Trials are always different. They test different things, play to different strengths. Most of them have some physical aspect, though." She paused to jump over the eight-foot-high trunk of a fallen tree. "If you're breathing that heavy already, you're in trouble."

I felt a bit self-conscious, but there was nothing I could do to disguise my panting. "Exercise. Got it. How do you know what the Trial will be testing?"

"You know when you're told how to get through it—what the objective is. Or if there's no Examiner, then it's usually a mental-type, and you have to work out how to survive all on your own."

Another scream carried through the strangely scented night air, morphing from piercing and clear to gurgling, and then finally strangling out into silence.

"Monster?" I said.

"Yes. Let's be quiet now. Sound draws them."

A few minutes later, the gargantuan trees opened into a small clearing, where the unobscured moonlight was bright enough to read by. Other people were standing about, obviously waiting.

"Other Players," I murmured. There must have been fifteen of them. "So many!"

"This is only a few of us. There are other Trials going on simultaneously right now."

I looked down and saw the source of my helper's voice was a small blonde girl. She scanned the group of Players with a frown and bit her lip.

"What's wrong?"

She shook her head. "My sister's not here."

Even as we entered the clearing, others were appearing from under the trees and hurriedly joining together in the middle. I walked slowly forward, watching. "Maybe she just hasn't arrived yet."

"Maybe." But the girl didn't sound reassured.

Some of the Players seemed confused, disoriented, and frightened like me. Others' moods varied from watchful preparation to absolute terror. I couldn't help but wonder what they knew that I didn't. One extraordinarily gorgeous latte-colored girl seemed to be warming up. She must have spent a lot of Seeds on Beauty, because I'd never seen a more alluring face.

In the center of the clearing, a black cube hung in mid-air. A message was written across its surface, the same on every side.

HERE YOU WILL BE TRIED, YOUR MEASURE TAKEN. THE WORTHY WILL BE GRANTED THE POWER OF THE GODS.

"What does it mean?" I asked Chanelle.

She shook her head, looking distracted. "I don't know. It's part of the Game. You get Seeds after the Trial's over if you 'perform' well."

"How—" I started to ask, but a screaming voice cut me off.

"People, it's a trap! It's a lie!" A boy stood at the edge of the forest, waving urgently at us. "If you stay there and enter the Trial, you're all going to die. Please, believe me. I've done this before. It's a death trap—" His voice cracked, either from the stress of screaming or the force of his memories.

People inside the clearing murmured to each other, some unsure, some shaking their heads at him.

Chanelle gripped my arm. "Don't even think about it. Remember the penalty for not completing the quest? At least we have a chance of living if we can win the Trial. If we leave, we're dead for sure."

The beautiful girl heard Chanelle's words and cracked her neck back and forth. "He's obviously a newbie." She had an accent. Spanish? "Watch what happens to him."

"Please, believe me. At least out here we have chance. We can help each other survive," he called.

Across the clearing, a girl let out a whimper and raced toward him.

He took her hand and squeezed it, then yelled to the rest of us again. "Run away before it's too late. We can—"

His voice cut off again as the fifteen-minute timer reached zero and winked out of existence in front of all our eyes.

I drew a deep breath to calm myself. The fear and uncertainty were fraying my nerves.

Clutching each other's hands, the girl and boy took a step backward toward the blackness of the forest. The tree above them moved, its whole form writhing, and something like fallen leaves sprinkled down onto the two of them. My stomach turned as they started frantically brushing at their bare skin. Their movements grew more and more frenzied, and then the girl started to scream. She flailed wildly as she began running back toward us. The boy stumbled along behind her, his voice scratching roughly out of his throat as he chanted, "No, no, no, please, no."

As they got closer, I saw that whatever the tree had dropped onto them was sticking. I frowned and pushed forward through to the edge of the group of Players.

The boy stumbled first, and then the girl. "I take it back. I'll do the Trial! Please, *forgive* me!" she wailed, clawing her way forward.

"Oh, damn," I said aloud as I saw what was happening to them.

The things that had fallen onto exposed areas were burying themselves within the skin, growing, pulling at the flesh. As I watched, a tendril sprouted from the boy's cheek, and a leaf grew from it, so rapidly it was like watching one of those time-lapse videos of the life of a plant over weeks. From seed to thriving adult, they only took a few minutes.

These "seeds" were using the boy and girl as fuel. As the plants grew from them, unfolding beautifully, they sucked up the flesh beneath through their roots. The pair screamed, and kept screaming, wordless in their pain and terror.

The girl looked like a corpse, skin thin enough that her bones were almost visible through it. Her voice trickled away into silence. An eyeball burst as a tendril forced its way outward, then shriveled as it was sucked up. But she didn't move, and her expression of terror didn't change, because she was dead.

I took an involuntary step backward but couldn't look away as the two of them were consumed. The plants grew thicker and higher. The only sounds now were that of branches creaking and snapping, their leaves rustling as they reached for the sky, and the Players' flesh and bones squelching and crumbling.

Finally, two trees stood in the place where the Players had fallen. The bases of the trunks held the vague memory of the shapes of their tortured bodies, like surrealist sculptures. The trees were miniature versions of all the others in the forest, and still growing upward.

I choked on nothing, my throat spasming involuntarily. I thought I might throw up. "They failed the quest," I murmured under my breath, but the sound was loud enough to carry in the absolute silence of the clearing.

"Oh, we've got a smart one here!" a mocking voice rang out from behind me. A man in a three-piece suit walked out of the trees. He was dressed immaculately, from his white, starched collar to his shiny black dress shoes. Incongruous with his otherwise fashionable clothes, a huge costume wolf head completely covered his own head.

The cube hanging in mid-air rose higher and grew bright, causing those standing next to it to jump. It lit up most of the clearing, a spotlight shining down and forming a distinct circle of brightness. The newly grown additions to the forest stood just outside the light.

The costumed man stopped and took out a gold pocket watch from his vest. "Seems like time's up." He looked us over. "And a few are missing?" The huge wolf's head shook back and forth. "Tch. Too bad. So sad."

I moved back to Chanelle, who'd been my savior. She shook her head at me before I had a chance to open my mouth. "It's over. The Trial's started now. Focus on that," she said.

I had a sudden realization. "Your sister…?" I clenched my trembling hands and tried hard not to think about what I'd just witnessed.

"China's not here. Maybe she entered a different Trial," she said, looking grim.

I knew we were both thinking of those anonymous screams we'd heard from the forest. The image of a new tree growing in the darkness flashed in my mind, and I shuddered from deep in the pit of my stomach.

The suited man moved farther into the circle of light. He bounced on his toes, and I could swear the wolf's head smiled just a bit, its felt tongue lolling from the side of its mouth. "There are consequences. You were all warned. This isn't just some child's game…" He trailed off, giggling to himself. "Well, except it is, tonight."

He clasped his hands formally behind his back, stood up even straighter, and announced, "This Trial will be a game of 'What's the Time,

Mr. Wolf?' Has anyone played it before?" It seemed almost as if the costume head moved a bit, the tongue adjusting itself to lie properly inside the mouth instead of hanging lasciviously over the side.

No one said anything.

"Well, that's fine. You'll all get the hang of it quickly, I'm sure. I am Mr. Wolf, obviously." He gestured to his head and paused as if for laughter.

There was none.

He let out a heavy, disappointed sigh. "I stand in the center of the playing field with my eyes closed. You all start around the edges, wherever you want. You will all ask me 'What's the time, Mr. Wolf?'" He called out the last part in a high-pitched, singsong voice. "And I will respond with, say…'Three o'clock.' You must all take three steps at that point, and then you ask me again. You may not take any more or any less than the amount given. Repeat ad nauseam, until it's 'Dinner Time.'"

The lips of his wolf head stretched back from the teeth in a strange parody of a smile.

I swallowed. Rather than being ludicrous, it was terrifying. The teeth looked sharper and harder than stuffing-filled cloth possibly could, the eyes brighter, and the gums pinker.

He snapped his fingers in the air.

From the forest, dark shadows moved forward, slinking up to Mr. Wolf's heels. They looked like feral dogs, except that their eyes and ears were bigger than any dog I'd ever seen, and they had teeth that curved out of their mouths like saber-tooth tigers.

"What the hell are those?" I whispered, afraid to draw attention to myself with noise.

"The same monsters that attacked us in the forest," Chanelle whispered back.

"When 'Dinner Time' is called, my wolves will eat you"—he waved a pointed finger, encompassing our group—"who are dinner. *If* they can catch you before you get back past the safe line again, that is. If you can make it out of the light, you'll be safe. So run fast, little bunnies."

The gorgeous girl with the Spanish accent cracked her knuckles. "How do we win this game?"

He focused on her intently for a few incredibly long seconds.

She didn't seem fazed by the psychological pressure at all, as I knew I would have been. Instead, she took the time to crack her neck again and roll her shoulders backward in a circular motion.

"The game is won either by surviving for twenty rounds, or if one of the prey is able to touch me before I call 'Dinner Time.' Everyone who makes it to the end will be rewarded with Seeds according to their performance, as always."

"Got it." She nodded. "But…I'm not the prey here. I'm the predator." She licked her chops exaggeratedly and grinned.

Mr. Wolf threw back his head and laughed. His eyes shone wetly when he looked at us again. "Let the Trial begin."

Chanelle gripped my hand and pulled me out of the circle.

I stumbled, my legs feeling weak. My eyes twitched instinctively toward the newly grown trees.

She let out a sigh, gripped my face, and pulled, forcing me to bend over and look her straight in the eye. "Things are about to get dangerous, okay? You need to pull it together. Focus. From now on, concentrate on staying alive. Don't think about what happened to those other people. There's no room for that."

I stared into her big blue eyes and tried to stop trembling.

She gripped my face tighter. "Do you want to live, newbie?"

I swallowed past the swollen lump in my throat. "Yes."

"Then stop thinking about those two. Forget them. The Trial and surviving it are the most important things in the world to you right now. Got it?"

"Why are you being so nice to me?"

She let go of my face and stepped back, turning toward the light. "Does there need to be a reason? That's not important."

Mr. Wolf placed himself in the center of the circle, his hands covering his eyes. "Let the Trial begin. Loudly, now, and all of you together."

"What's the time, Mr. Wolf?" we said in chorus.

"Twelve o'clock, little bunnies!"

We stepped forward twelve times, moving from the outside of the circle inward. This repeated with different "times" until a few Players drew dangerously close to Mr. Wolf and his saber-tooth dogs.

It would be the next round, I knew. And it was.

"Dinner Time!" he sang, uncovering his eyes and turning around to look at all the Players who'd chosen to walk toward him from behind, which was the majority of us.

His stuffed animal head was no longer stuffed. It had become a grotesque, disproportionate wolf's head, alive atop his human body. His too-large eyes moved, taking in our positions relative to him, and the dogs sprang forward. His nostrils flared, and saliva swung from his hanging tongue, falling toward the tip of his polished shoe.

Seeing it hit snapped me out of my trance, and I turned around to sprint back to the safe line. Someone screamed. I didn't turn my head to look back, didn't wonder about the safety of my fellow Players, and didn't think about my own already aching legs. I just ran.

Ahead of me, a guy stuck out his foot to trip another, and the second guy went down hard. I jumped over him and kept running.

I passed the line by quite a bit before turning around to make sure I was safe. Others stampeded toward and past me, obscuring my view of Mr. Wolf for a moment. When the small field had cleared of terrified people, I saw him standing still in the middle of it.

Two of the dog-things had caught someone, and one was the boy who'd been tripped. The monster's jaw was clenched around his upper arm, long curving teeth piercing into the flesh. Blood mixed with saliva ran down into the fabric of the boy's blue T-shirt, soaking it. His face was white and contorted with pain and fear.

Someone laughed beside me—the same boy who tripped him. Our eyes met, and he gave me a small shrug and a smile. "Less survivors means more Seeds for the rest of us."

The fallen boy reached out a pleading hand to all of us watching safely from behind the line, and then his eyes rolled back in his head and he started to convulse. He looked like he was having a seizure, except foam was dripping down his chin. The other downed Player started to flail, too. The dog-monsters retreated back to Mr. Wolf's side, and soon the bodies lay still.

Not saber-tooth tiger teeth, then. More like cobra fangs. Venomous.

People screamed and cried all around the edge of the light.

But then the boy in the blue T-shirt twitched. Silence crashed over the stunned Players as every eye fixed on him.

He moved bit by bit, jerky, like a battery-powered doll running on the last of its juice. He stood up, but his stance was strange, alien. Limp arms hung down past slightly bent knees, and his head lolled to the side. His eyes were vacant, and he turned his back on us to join Mr. Wolf in the center of the light.

Mr. Wolf giggled. "Oh. Bitten Players become wolves. I may have forgotten to mention that."

Chapter 6

What reinforcement we may gain from Hope. If not, what resolution from despair.

—John Milton

AS THE NEXT ROUND STARTED, the ring of Players inched forward with each number, our feet moving just enough to be called steps and no more. When "Dinner Time" was called, the two bitten Players turned and chased after us, just like the monsters. The boy's mouth was stretched in a wide grin, and slobber ran down his chin and neck.

Once I'd reached the safety of the shadows, I turned and watched a thin guy run desperately from the strangely loping former Player. He...*it* reached out a hand and grazed the back of the guy's shirt. Terrified, he took a dangerous chance and tried to feint away. He stopped abruptly and turned to run at a different angle, but he wasn't counting on a dog-monster being right where he needed to go. The creature vaulted at him, catching his neck between its massive, wide-open jaws, his head disappearing inside the mouth.

Blood gushed out between the teeth.

My knees were shaking. I took deep breaths and looked away from the gruesome scene. I wanted to deny that this was real, just pretend it was all a horrible dream that I would wake from soon. But I couldn't do that, because I knew the fear was the only thing keeping me going. Without the slight edge that it gave me, boosting my slow, ungainly movements with adrenaline, I would die here tonight.

I knew that, and so I didn't pretend it wasn't real. I looked away, swallowed, and tried to steady my shaking legs.

Chanelle caught my eye and gave me a silent nod of approval.

We started forward again. The speed was glacial, each of us doing our best to move forward less than the others.

Even though I was panting for breath and my muscles were burning and trembling, I felt extremely grateful to Bunny for enticing me to exercise. He knew, I realized. He knew about this, and he understood that I lacked the strength to survive here.

Chanelle crept beside me on one side, the beautiful Spanish girl on the other.

I felt incrementally safer between them, and found myself focusing in on Chanelle's white runners dragging through a puddle of dark blood where the last Player had fallen. Her pretty white shoes were ruined.

I realized my mind was playing tricks on me to disconnect from the horror. I grabbed the pad of my left hand between my forefinger and thumb and pinched as hard as I could. Pain brought some clarity to my mind, and I focused on it, trying to get a grip.

"Dinner Time" was called again, and we all turned to run. Out of the corner of my eye, I saw the Spanish girl slip in that same puddle of blood covering the ground. But I didn't stop. How could I?

When I reached the safe line and looked back, she was pinned to the ground by the "wolf" in the blue T-shirt. He snarled down at her, drool dripping onto her cheek.

The fingers of her left hand were wrapped around his neck, holding him off. She formed the other into a fist and slammed it into his ear. Once, twice, three times.

He fell sideways off her, eyes unfocused for a second. He shook his head and rallied, but she'd already scrambled to her feet.

She pulled back her right fist and slammed it down into the back of his head, propelling it with the force of her entire body.

His face smashed flat into the ground. He twitched, and she pulled back and punched once more. He didn't move that time, but she kicked him in the side before racing back to the safe line, weaving to avoid the remaining monsters and bitten Players.

I watched her in awe. What kind of strength was that?

By the start of the next round, we were down to almost half of our original number while Mr. Wolf's had grown again.

The tension neared its breaking point as we got closer and closer to Mr. Wolf. A girl tried to bolt back to the safety line early, but vines burst from the earth, tripped her, and held her down. She screamed and struggled, but she was trapped. When Mr. Wolf sang out "Dinner Time!" all the attackers ignored her, leaving the easy pickings for last.

Only a few seconds from the safety line, a turned Player lunged for a boy running close to Chanelle. The boy swerved and spun to avoid it, smashing his elbow hard into her temple.

She went down.

I stumbled the last few meters across the line and looked back, gasping.

She knelt on her hands and knees, blood dripping down the side of her head. Beside her, the boy who'd elbowed her howled as the turned Player gnawed at the exposed skin of his forearm.

"Run!" I screamed at her.

She crept forward a few inches and tried to stand, but couldn't get her feet solidly under her. After only a few stumbling steps, she fell forward again.

The turned Player released its catch and turned to her.

I took a step into the light.

"Get back!" she snarled, her voice slurred and groggy.

It grabbed her head between two hands and bit into the curve where her neck met her shoulder. It ripped its head back viciously, and a bite-sized chunk of flesh went with it.

She flopped awkwardly in its grip, like a fish stranded on the shore, and let out a choked scream.

"No!" I shouted.

"My sister…China. Find her. Thirteen hundred Brine Street. Tell her…to live!" She squeezed the words out, rapid-fire.

It bit into her neck again, this time digging its teeth in and shaking its head like a dog with a toy.

She ignored it, keeping her eyes locked on mine.

Hands over my mouth, my throat so tight I couldn't have spoken even if I knew what to say, I just nodded.

Chanelle's eyes rolled back into her head, and she started to thrash around in the blood-soaked mud.

I pinched the inside of my thumb pad, hard. The pain helped me to focus, but it wasn't enough. Thinking of the Players-turned-wolves, I bit my bottom lip until the iron taste of blood blossomed on the tip of my tongue and spread throughout my mouth.

MR. WOLF, drool running down the collar of his once immaculate suit, looked at the number of new "wolves" and laughed.

Our numbers were severely depleted, and the danger of each round grew exponentially greater.

I looked at his grotesque, laughing head, and I hated him. I hated him, and I was absolutely terrified. I shuffled forward as the next round started and thought of the Seeds I'd wasted. What good was Beauty to me now, when my life was on the line?

Each round seemed to be taking longer and longer, as if Mr. Wolf was trying to get us as close to him as possible before calling "Dinner Time." And because we were moving so slowly, it was a tedious affair of constant, mind-eroding tension. But Mr. Wolf never called for any time greater than ten o'clock.

When he finally turned and called "Dinner Time!" I pivoted toward the starting line as quickly as I could. As my head swung around, I met Chanelle's eyes for a second, as if in slow motion. The connection broke as I sprinted away.

Behind me, I heard light footsteps and bubbling gasps, a noise like someone breathing through water.

My heart beat so fast it felt like it might literally burst out of my chest. I'd never understood those words before, but now I could feel it, expanding large and squeezing hard with each hummingbird-fast pump. My legs felt like fat, heavy logs that wouldn't move like I wanted. They were slow, too slow—much too slow compared to the light footsteps gaining on me from behind.

As I approached the safe line, I started to let out great, gasping sobs. I was almost there when something hit the back of my knees. I went down hard, smashing into the ground and sliding in the muck.

I flipped over onto my back, scrambling to protect myself.

The thing that had once been Chanelle was on its knees, grabbing desperately onto my legs. Her jaw hung halfway open, and so much saliva bubbled up in her mouth that her breathing rattled with the fluid she was inhaling. There was no compassion, no recognition in her wide blue eyes, only hunger.

I pulled back a knee without even thinking and slammed my foot into her face, hard enough that her small hands lost their grip on my legs, then scrambled backward like a crab, clumsily, but my arms slipped and I collapsed. She came for me again, and I kicked her again, keeping her off for just a few more feet.

From the other side of the division between light and darkness, her eyes met mine again.

She seemed to strain forward, but was held back by some invisible force. I searched for some semblance of humanity in her, but there was nothing. Then even the hunger faded and her interest in her escaped prey seemed to slip away. She limply rose to her feet and returned to Mr. Wolf.

On the field, two more people were convulsing in their own blood.

My arms collapsed from the weight of my upper body, and I rolled into a ball with my eyes facing the ground and my torso bent over my knees.

It was too much. I couldn't do this again. I didn't even want to stand up.

And yet I was on my feet when the next round started.

Mr. Wolf called out "twelve o'clock" for the first time since the beginning of his sick game. I took my twelve shuffling steps forward. How many rounds had it been? Not close enough to twenty. I didn't think I could make it till the end. But I would keep trying until I couldn't take another step or got turned into a "wolf."

There was a quick movement to my right, making me look up. The tough Spanish girl jumped forward with a huge, half-leaping, half-running step. What was she doing? My weary brain struggled to compute.

But then I saw the shrinking distance between her and Mr. Wolf.

I gasped, and in an instant, I was urging her on with every fiber of my being.

She grinned viciously, and I remembered what she'd said in the beginning about being a predator. Her jumps weren't like anything I'd ever seen before. Something was slightly off about them, as if, despite the heaviness of this place, she was bending the rules of gravity, moving too high from the pull of the Earth, and traveling too far.

Jump, jump, jump, she went, drawing dangerously near Mr. Wolf.

How many steps did she have left? I hoped it was enough.

She jumped and landed one last time, stopping obviously too far away to reach Mr. Wolf without moving her legs. "Damn it!" she growled. The sound carried easily in the taut silence.

I felt the pit in my stomach yawn open and suck the air out of me.

Mr. Wolf chuckled.

But before we asked the time again, she straightened her body, stood up on the tips of her toes, and extended her hands toward the sky. Even her fingers were straining to move higher.

It looked like she was trying to fly away.

Then, with her body extended and stiffly clenched, she started to tilt forward. She tilted until she was falling, and didn't flinch even a bit as she slammed face-first into the ground.

A few moments of frozen silence passed. Her feet were still planted on the ground where she'd stopped, at exactly twelve steps.

But Mr. Wolf's ankle was caught in her outstretched hand.

"She's touching him," I whispered. Then I repeated it, shouting desperately, as if making sure everyone heard it would make it irrefutably true.

The Spanish girl stood up stiffly. She'd probably knocked the air out of her lungs when she hit the ground. She rested her hands on her knees for a moment, taking a few deep breaths. Then she let out a low chuckle, spit, and straightened, wiping her mouth with the back of her hand. "Screw you," she said succinctly.

Mr. Wolf stood frozen for a long moment before turning around. His head was once again an innocent stuffed costume head, but I could still see the saliva drenching the lower half of it. "It would've been a waste to eat you, anyway," he told her. Then he lifted his arms wide, palms facing toward the sky. "The game is won, and the Trial completed. Congratulations, Players!" His voice was jovial, pleased.

The sound made me shudder. I knew his true nature.

He took a step toward us, and I flinched, but he didn't move to bite the Spanish girl or chase after any of us. He walked through our pitiful group and away, into the darkness of the trees from where he'd come. On his whistle, the ones who'd been bitten followed him, shuffling off into oblivion.

Was it over now that she'd won the Trial? No, not yet. Don't trust, don't relax, I ordered myself.

In the middle of the field, where we'd first gathered, the floating cube sank down to head-level once again.

I waited to make sure that nothing happened to the Players who moved close to it, and then followed.

CONGRATULATIONS ON SURVIVING THE TRIAL. THERE ARE NO BESTOWALS.

The beautiful girl scowled, pacing back and forth in front of the cube.

I watched her without realizing what I was doing. Every step made my wire-taut nerves stretch even more precariously, her agitation feeding my own. Every sense was alert for danger, and the hair on my sweat-slick skin stood up. I couldn't take any more.

Then the cube's message changed.

DO YOU WISH TO RETURN FROM THE TRIAL?
YES / NO

The girl's face lit with relief, and she lunged forward to press "Yes" without hesitating. A mirage-like wave, like those that formed when I received new Seeds, rolled out of her body, and then she disappeared.

Nothing remained where she had been standing. She was just gone.

After her, others began to press "Yes" one after another, and the same thing happened to them.

I swallowed, reached out, and touched the cube before I could worry about it any longer. I thought I heard a snippet of the eerie children's song again, loud in my bones, and then it exploded out of me.

I was dizzy and nauseated, but my knees didn't buckle this time.

The breeze was warm on my skin, and the grass under my feet was the normal grass of my backyard, not the too-green, too-sharp stuff of the Trial.

The tree was a normal oak, large but not towering, and the smell of the air was fresh with a smog-like tang. The darkness wasn't true-black pierced only by distant light from the expanse of sky, but the grey-tinged, half-sick haze of an insomniac city.

I threw up from relief, all over my shoes.

Chapter 7

Death is not the greatest loss in life.

The greatest loss is what dies inside us while we live.

— Norman Cousins

WHEN MY STOMACH WAS EMPTY, I noticed the Window hanging in front of my face.

YOUR ACTIONS IN THE TRIAL HAVE AWARDED YOU TWO LEVELS.
YOU HAVE GAINED TWO SEEDS.

I wiped the back of my hand across my mouth and stared at the words for a long time.

It was easy to slip into the house without my family noticing me. I went into the bathroom, stripped off my dirty, torn clothing, and stepped slowly into the tub, pressing my hand against the wall to support myself. Every muscle in my legs was shivering violently, so I turned on the faucet and sat down in the tub before I collapsed.

A bath was better, anyway, because I wouldn't have to close my eyes under the stream of water.

My skin had been scraped and sliced everywhere it'd made direct contact with the ground and grass of that place, but I hadn't even noticed. Now that the overwhelming tension was gone, though, the raw skin started to hurt.

I ran the water hot, as hot as I could stand it, and soaked in it till it turned tepid. Then I got out and went to my room. I shoved my clothes to the bottom of my trashcan so my mom wouldn't see them. My shoes went into a plastic bag in the closet until I could find time to wash them in secret.

I dressed in a long-sleeved shirt, pants, and socks, wanting to have as much of my skin covered as possible. I twisted my hair into a single braid and tied it off with a hair band, out of the way. Then, with my light on full brightness, I checked in every corner and possible hiding spot of my room, just in case. There was no one, nothing new.

As prepared as I was going to get, I turned off my light so that no one would think I was still awake and come checking in on me during the middle of the night. I couldn't handle that right now. I crawled into bed and tucked myself into the corner so I could see both the door and window, and any movement, without turning.

"Bunny?"

—I'm here.—
-Bunny-

"What was that?"

—I think you know.—
-Bunny-

"No, I mean, it was a Trial. But what *was* it? What happened—it was… It's not freaking possible! It's not possible."

—Don't be obtuse. It happened, didn't it? Therefore it *is* possible. You just don't understand it.—
-Bunny-

"But…how?" I whispered.

—I can't tell you that.—
-Bunny-

"Why not?"

—I just can't. I'm not involved with the Trials, Eve. I'm just your normal Game Moderator.—
-Bunny-

He didn't *know*, I realized. He *couldn't* tell me. "Please, can't you let me go? I don't want to be a Player. I'll give back all the Seeds. You can change back the things I leveled up. Just, *please* let me go. I don't want to do this anymore."

—There's no way out but through. Once you're a Player, there's no going back.—
-Bunny-

"How do you get through?"

—I don't know.—
-Bunny-

"Has anyone ever done it before?"

There was a delay in the answer.

—Not yet. Not that I know of.—
-Bunny-

I didn't say anything, just lay curled in the corner, my sheets balled into my fists like a toddler holding onto her favorite blankie.

Bunny didn't prompt me for more words, and left me alone in the dark, almost-silence of my room.

Perhaps it was then that I began to change.

If any evidence of the true nature of humanity was needed, I only had to look at myself. I wasn't thinking about those Players' families or the tragedy of their deaths. I wasn't sad, or guilty about not being brave enough to stop and help them.

I was only scared for myself. My mind was focused not on regret, but rather on exactly how I could ensure I didn't lose to the Game, like them. I wanted to live.

I tucked my knees to my chest, wrapped my arms around my legs, and stared into the darkness. There was no way I would be able to sleep, despite my physical and mental exhaustion. Even if I could, I didn't want to. I was afraid I'd dream of the Trial, but never wake up.

I stayed curled up on the far corner of my bed till morning, watching my room, my door, and my window. The sunrise was like a relieving balm to my strained mind. After all, humans always feel safer in the light. Instinct and genetic memory would never let us truly forget the time when there were far more dangerous creatures than humans living in the dark.

I CRAWLED STIFFLY OUT of bed shortly after the first hint of sunrise and dressed in silence. Then I peeked in on my sleeping mother and brother to make sure they were okay. They had to be kept separate from all of this. Safe. So far, at least.

I went outside to examine the ground where I'd been the night before, when *it* happened. There was only grass, manicured and sedate, and completely unhelpful. I stood up and sighed. "Fine."

I angled my left arm across my body and used my right hand to type an address into my forearm sheath link. "China, right?" I muttered to myself as I started walking toward the street.

Two public transport pods and a short walk later, I was in front of the house at the address Chanelle had given me.

It was nice. Not mansion-rich, but it wasn't stacked next to or on top of any other houses, and there was a large, fenced backyard exclusive to their family. Even the pollution was lighter, so far from the jobless slums.

I stood awkwardly, shifting from foot to foot. "What now, dumbass?" It didn't seem right to just knock on the front door. What would I say? 'Hi, I think one of your daughters is gone forever, possibly dead, because she got bit by a crazy, salivating Player in a secret Game your daughters and I are being forced to play. But no worries, because I'm here looking for the other daughter?' Probably not a good idea.

I slipped around the side and hauled myself painfully over the tall wooden fence enclosing their backyard. My fatigued muscles gave out and dropped me on the other side with a painful *thud*.

Holding in a groan, I pushed myself up into a crouch and started to move gingerly through the huge bushes, flower plants, and trees of the backyard garden. Sneaking around and peeking in the windows probably wasn't the best way to earn someone's trust, but I didn't want to interact with anyone but China if I could help it. No non-Players.

I paused next to one of the tall, leafy trees, watching the windows for any movement, my thoughts on Chanelle and China, unsure what I even wanted to say. It was in that moment of distraction that something dropped out of the tree onto my back, flattening me to the ground and knocking the air from my lungs.

Panic flooded me as I struggled wildly to turn around, sucking desperately for air that just wouldn't come. I was ready to kick, bite, and claw—whatever was necessary…until I saw my attacker.

A small girl with blonde hair and big blue eyes scowled down at me. "Who are you? Why are you here?" she whispered.

"Chanelle?" I croaked. "What are you doing here? I thought—"

She pressed her hand over my mouth and leaned over to hiss in my ear. "Where is she? What did you do to my sister?" Her hand pressed harder, and I could only let out a muffled, "mmph."

"Be quiet. If you alert the others, I'll kill you." She took her hand away. "Now tell me. What did you do with Chanelle? Where is she?"

China, I realized belatedly. She looked exactly like her sister.

I shook my head. "I didn't do anything to her, I swear. After the Trial, she went with the Examiner. She told me to come find you." I paused as a horrible thought filled my head. "You *are* China, right?"

She nodded, scowling.

"And you're a…Player?"

Hesitation, then another nod.

I hadn't broken the silence rule then. "I know this looks suspicious, me sneaking around and all, but I promise I'm not here to do anything bad. I was just trying to find you."

"What do you mean, Chanelle went with the Examiner? Is she all right? And what are those people doing in her room?"

When I didn't answer immediately, she leaned down, eyes narrowed dangerously, and said, "Talk! Just because you're a Player doesn't mean anything. For all I know, this could be a quest, and you're here to trick me. If I don't start getting answers right away, you're going to start hurting."

I nodded. "China, I'll tell you everything I know. I promise I'm only here because of Chanelle." I tried to imbue my voice with calm trustworthiness and confidence. "You can trust me. But you just said someone's in her room. What are they doing?" I said the last slowly, emphasizing the importance.

She pulled back and frowned. "I don't know. Going through her stuff. I snuck out here to hide, but then you came. I wouldn't even have noticed them if I hadn't been waiting up all night for her." Her eyes were wide, half wild, and unstable from fear.

I nodded again, swallowing. If I was going to gain her as an ally, now was the time to act, to be confident. "Let me up, China. We should find out what they're doing. It could be important—about what happened to Chanelle."

She stared down at me for a few seconds before the tension in her face loosened. She scrambled up and offered me her hand.

I took it, and the two of us hurried to the back of a huge, leafy bush. China pushed aside one of its branches, and I saw there was enough space in the center for the two of us to crouch uncomfortably. I crawled in, and she came after me.

From within, we could see out through the leaves, but anyone who looked in our direction would see nothing but a bush.

"My sister and I used to play in here all the time when we were kids," China said quietly, her voice catching on the word "sister." "It was our secret place. And it's got a perfect view through her bedroom window." She pointed.

Through the window, I saw three masked people moving around inside the bedroom. One was on Chanelle's computer, one was rifling through her drawers, and the other was waving a scanning wand of some kind over every inch of her room. Visible through the breathing holes in the masks, their mouths moved silently behind the window glass. I scooted forward in a futile attempt to hear. "We're too far away."

China shook her head and closed her eyes. "I think I can hear them. I've got a lot of Seeds in Perception. Give me a second to focus."

She took a few deep breaths, then went utterly still and silent, concentrating so hard I found myself holding my own breath for fear of disturbing her. After a few seconds, she started to speak. "Hurry up! The sun's almost all the way up. We need to be out of here soon."

"I'm going as fast as I can. It's not our fault that Davis girl had a party going on at her house. Took us forever to get in and out without being seen."

The other laughed. "Yeah, but with a girl like that, no one would have any trouble believing she ran away."

I let out a slow, silent breath. She was relaying their conversation to me, somehow hearing their voices clearly through a window and ten meters of air. Amazing.

"Wonder what NIX is going to do with all of them," she continued.

"Research, idiot. They're going to study them three ways from Tuesday. I bet we'll be doing the Mendell drop with samples from them within days."

"Would you two *shut up*? There are other people in this house, you know. What if they hear you and decide to come check up on the little sleeping girly? Keep it quiet."

China waited for a while longer and then opened her eyes again. "Seems like they listened to him. I can't hear anything."

I nodded. The masked figures inside weren't moving their mouths anymore. They took some of Chanelle's things and put them in a bag. A couple minutes later, they climbed deftly out of the window and climbed over the fence on the other side, much the same way I had, only more graceful. The gentle rumble of an engine cut the silence, and a plain multi-member pod slipped off down the brightening street.

I relaxed in their absence. "That was amazing, China. Good job."

She looked away, plucking a leaf off the bush and crumbling it in her fingers. "Not amazing enough. All we got was some cryptic conversation. I should have been listening from the beginning, but I was too focused on hiding."

I smiled. "It was more than just some cryptic conversation, China. We got plenty."

China closed her eyes and took a deep, deep breath, then released it along with some of her tension. "Yeah. Chanelle's still alive." She opened her eyes, and they locked on mine. "At least for now. Tell me everything that happened last night."

I did, starting from the time Chanelle tackled and protected me to the point where she followed Mr. Wolf into the darkness, conveniently glossing over my weaker moments and general uselessness.

"So…NIX has her. Who, or what, is NIX?"

"They're probably the ones who created this Game. Not a person. An organization. They're too powerful for anything else," I said.

"And as long as they've got tests or whatever to run on her, they'll keep her alive, right? What's the Mendell drop?"

I shook my head. "I don't know. Maybe it's some sort of testing facility. They said they'd be taking samples. And when I was made a Player, they matched my blood to confirm my identity." I bit my much-abused bottom lip and held a finger to my lips. "Bunny might be listening," I mouthed silently.

She nodded, understanding, and took off her link, tossing it away. She motioned for me to do the same. "There aren't any mics out here," she said. "Chanelle and I searched."

"How?"

"If you concentrate really hard, and your Perception is really high, you can hear them."

That was definitely a useful skill. Making sure to consciously keep my thoughts shielded from any intention to communicate with Bunny, I said, "Did you have a medical test at your school a few months ago?"

Her pale eyebrows drew down. "Yes. Blood and tissue tests, physical exam, and they took our pictures…" She trailed off. "You think that was them? NIX?"

"Maybe. They had access to that test, even if it wasn't them implementing it. It makes sense though, doesn't it? I've got a theory. They're using us like test subjects. Human rats. That's what the examination was for. To make sure we were healthy, because they didn't want to waste their money on a faulty product." I leaned forward, talking faster. "I mean, can you imagine how expensive we must be? The technology they're displaying, I can't imagine what kind of funding they must have…"

"Why are they doing this to us?" She looked like a small, wounded animal, a look practically designed to inspire protective feelings.

But I was reminded of my goal instead. "I don't know. But remember the message Chanelle gave me for you?"

"She said for me to live?" China frowned. "What does that mean?"

I shrugged. "I think it means exactly that. She wanted you to be safe, to stay alive. And she sent me to you so we could help each other. As long as we're alive, there's hope that we can escape. For us, and for Chanelle. I want to help you, if you'll do the same for me. I want us both to live."

The truth was that *I* wanted to live, and I thought she might be able to help me with that. "In the Trial, I saw people trip each other so they could get more Seeds. Killing people who are stuck in the same hell right next to them, just to get ahead a step or two. That's not right." It wasn't *smart*. "Let's have each other's backs. I'll look out for you if you do the same for me." I held out my hand to her. "Allies?"

She stared searchingly into my eyes, then nodded and gripped my hand with her smaller one. "Allies."

We talked for a bit longer, exchanging contact information and speculation, and then I left for my home, and she for her room. If Bunny were to check in on me, I didn't want my GPS to reveal my knowledge of the cleanup crew. I looked back at the house, standing deceptively sturdy against the backdrop of the sunrise-stained sky. "I'm sorry, China," I whispered, so low I could barely hear my own voice, safe from even her superhuman hearing. "But I need your strength. I'm not going to die yet."

Chapter 8

We stopped checking for monsters under our beds when we realized they were inside us.

— The Joker

TWO DAYS LATER, the song played again, and I entered my second Trial.

I'd been walking down a crowded street, thinking about the things my most recent net searches had uncovered. With more information, I knew better what clues to search for, and found a few different online conspiracy groups who questioned the increased number of child runaways and mysterious disappearances. It had started five years ago. The theories ranged from serial-killer cover ups to human trafficking to government experiments. The enforcers of course found nothing, and these were dismissed as the crazy ravings of distraught parents. And then there were the parenting groups, where they worried about their children being victims of a bullying ring or part of some sort of secret fight club. Of course, their children *were* fighting —for their lives in the Trials—but the Players had to keep it a secret from their families, so other explanations for the wounds were created.

When the first faint strains of music entered my head, I panicked a little. I scrambled for the nearest side street, and the nearest alley from there, all the while muttering urgently under my breath, "Bunny? Bunny, I need to talk to you. Now!"

—What is it?—
-Bunny-

"I'm hearing the song again, that one that filled me up, and then I was in the other place, in the Trial, and it's too soon. I'm not ready, I haven't prepared yet, and I thought I'd have more time—" I took a deep breath and swallowed hard to cut off my babbling.

—It's probably a special Trial, separate from the normal ones. I think this is your Characteristic Trial. It's going to test your reactions, and then you'll get a Skill based on your performance.—
-Bunny-

"It's too soon, Bunny! I'm not even recovered from the last time yet! I thought we were supposed to have ten days! That's what China said, and I'm—" Once again, I cut myself off. I was scared. But I didn't want to say it aloud, because if I didn't, I could pretend the fear wasn't real. And then maybe it wouldn't be.

—Suck it up. You don't have time to whine. The Boneshaker doesn't last for long, and you're almost out of time. Pull it together, kick some ass, and we'll talk about it when you get back.—
-Bunny-

I wanted to throw a few choice cuss words back at Bunny, but the song was in my bones. I closed my eyes to keep them from rattling out of my head, and it stopped.

I was prepared for the nausea and dizziness, so I stood up and observed my surroundings despite the sickness, knowing it would pass.

I was standing in the middle of a field with tall green grass up to my chest. The sun shone down so brightly I had to squint until my eyes didn't burn from the light. The colors were somehow *deeper* than any I'd seen before. The sky was a clear, piercing blue, a bit too dark a color. The grass was a green that made me think of strength, life, and the insatiable desire to *grow*. The air smelled…*off*, fruity and earthy and green. I breathed it in and shuddered. Normally it would be a pleasant smell, but I couldn't help but associate it with blood and death.

I saw that other Players were there too, poking out of the gently waving green sea. Furrows were cut through the grass in straight lines, paths leading to a few scattered buildings a couple hundred meters away. The buildings weren't like any I'd seen before. They seemed to have been built for beauty rather than economy of space, and twisted and lounged in strange, sometimes organic and sometimes geometric shapes.

On the other side, the field stopped abruptly at the edge of a line of thick trees. These weren't the giant trees of my last Trial, but thick and so closely spaced they blocked out the light beneath their leaves.

Players were moving to where the paths in the field all converged. Another black cube hung in there air there. I started toward it as well, slowly, aware of my own heaviness, which made me clumsy. I stumbled from the grass onto a narrow road. It was lined with thin strips of metal running along the stone path in straight lines.

I leaned down to touch them, and my eyes widened at the sight of my trembling arm. "My ID link!" It was basically a computer, mobile phone, and official identification all rolled into one. I tried to call my mother, but the screen was blank, and the link lay unresponsive on my forearm. Was I out of range? But the only places out of range were caves and lead boxes. "Don't screw with me! I can see the sky, so I should have service." I smacked the forearm sheath in sudden desperation, but it continued to ignore me.

A young boy giggled at me and shook his head. "They don't work here. I tried last time. You shouldn't bring electric things with you. They get scrambled and broke by the Boneshaker."

Bunny had used that word before, too. The Boneshaker must be the creepy song that brought me to the Trials. "But the VR chip in my neck still works, even though it goes through the Boneshaker."

The kid shrugged. "It's inside your body."

"Oh." I looked more closely at the kid. He was…young. Really young. "How many times have you been here?"

"Once before," he said, and a different emotion wiped the smile off his face.

I knew that feeling all too well after my last Trial. "Me too."

A guy my age laughed softly. "Oh, that's too bad. Usually you've got time to strengthen a bit more before the Characteristic Trial."

I focused on his handsome face. "You know about this, about what's going on?"

He smirked, looking me up and down. "I do. This is our chance to gain the weapons to become gods."

"What does that mean?" I took a step forward, wanting to drag an explanation for all this out of him.

"That's the point of all this, you know. They're seeing who can become a god." He gestured to the floating cube. "What did you think it meant?"

Unsure what me meant at first, I stared at the cube until the words scrawled across each side coalesced into meaning.

HERE YOU WILL BE TRIED, YOUR MEASURE TAKEN. THE LIVING WILL BE GRANTED A POWER TO MATCH.

I wanted to scream, but restrained myself to a flurry of questions. "What does that mean? Who's 'seeing?' What is this place, this game? What weapons do you mean? Illegal things, like guns or knives?"

He smiled again and looked up at the sky. A flapping sound filled the air, and I followed his gaze. Hundreds of crows flew towards us from every direction.

I threw myself backward into the grass and crouched down.

The guy gave me a surprised look and laughed. "It's only the Examiner. Relax."

The small boy smiled at me, an innocent expression that made me wonder just how old he was. Definitely too young to be playing in this Game. Just what kind of monster would do that to a child?

The crows settled around the group of Players in the small stone clearing like a shimmering black shroud over the earth. When nothing happened, I crept back out again.

One crow, larger than the others, landed on top of the cube and looked down at all of us with a cocked head and beady little bird eye. It opened its mouth, and a half-mechanic, half-cute voice came from it. "Hello, Players. I am this Trial's Examiner." Its beak stayed constantly open while the words came out, as if a speaker in the back of its throat did all the "talking."

"These are my eyes and ears." It gestured to the other crows with its beak.

Their little eyes glittered, a sea of sparkles. It was unnatural, revolting, and the hair of my arms and the back of my neck prickled stiff.

The crow's voice came out again. "This Trial is a special type of test. All the choices and actions you make, your every move, is measured. If you survive until the end, you will be given a Skill that matches your assessment. Please reach into the cube and retrieve your token."

The handsome guy sunk his hand eagerly into the wall of the cube, which melted over his disappearing skin, and then drew something out.

Nothing happened to him, so I thrust my own hand forward. I clenched my teeth when the cube didn't stop me, instead seeming to suck and pull at my flesh. I felt something small and hard, clenched my fist around it, and yanked backward. In my hand was a little black ball.

I examined it for markings while the other Players took their own tokens, but it was perfectly smooth, and surprisingly heavy. I tucked it into my shirt pocket.

The crow started to speak again. "There are only two rules to win. Do not give up possession of your token. You will not be able to return without it. And do not die. You may take each other's tokens through battle or trickery, but greater potential rewards create a harder challenge. If you are not prepared for an increase in difficulty level, do not take additional tokens." It cocked its head as if listening to something in the distance. "Let the Trial begin." With that, all the crows flapped into chaos, rising into the sky like a cloud of darkness.

I COVERED my face with my hands to protect it from the crows' beating wings and claws. It was only when I pulled them away that I saw everyone else had burst into motion. Some were running through the field for the trees in the distance, while others had already started fighting over each other's tokens, and a few ran for the strange buildings. The small boy and the guy who'd known what was happening were both gone already.

I hesitated for a moment, and then ran down the lined stone path toward the buildings. Protective walls around me and a small place to hide sounded perfect.

The path split in three directions, and I turned to the right. The path split again, and I took the right again, which led to an oval building that looked like a gargantuan, half-sunken egg. Vines sprung from the ground and curled up its surface as if anchoring it to the earth.

A shriek, like that from a bird of prey, cut through the air behind me like a high-pitched razor. Someone shouted, and then the shouting changed to a desperate, terrified shriek.

I shuddered and didn't look back as I entered a small doorway cut through the side of the vine-covered building. Which was stupid, because the floor dropped away beneath my feet as soon as I touched it, and I fell, screaming.

My scream cut off abruptly as my landing knocked the air out of my lungs. I rolled to my hands and knees and sucked desperately for the dust-filled air. Something *snicked* above me, and every last ray of light cut out. When I could once again breathe, I patted at the ground, sweeping my arms around to get my bearings. Heavy dust and…sticks. I followed the sticks to other, attached sticks, and came to a horrible realization. "Not sticks…" I snatched my hands back, coughing and gagging.

I fumbled with my link, but its display wouldn't come on. Instead, I closed my eyes and waited. When I opened them again, they had adjusted to the low light in the small compartment. A large skeleton lay beside me. I scuttled back only to rattle another stack of old bones. Turning in a circle, I realized that I was in a seamless square box, about three meters in every direction. Three large skeletons and one normal-sized one kept me company.

There was a small black ball amongst the half-inch layer of dust made of their decayed bodies. I picked it up to brush off the dust, realized it was a token, and dropped it immediately. The crow had said having more than one made the Trial even harder, and I didn't want the walls to suddenly start pouring water down on me and filling up the room, or some other equally deadly twist. I only needed my own token to get out alive.

I stood up and put my hand on one of the walls, hoping to feel some seam or crack I could get at, but it slid away at the touch of my hand, meshing into the adjacent wall. A corridor stretched out in front of me, lit with warm light. Beautiful pale blue flowers with large, droopy petals stretched out over the floor and walls.

I stared into the hall, and then back to the four skeletons lying inside the room. "Unless they were moved here after dying, there's a reason they didn't escape," I muttered.

I turned back to the bones and noticed something on the normal-sized skeleton's arm. I slid it off and held it up. "Damn." It was an old ID link, completely out of power.

My heart was beating faster and faster, the fine hairs on the back of my neck standing up in warning.

I turned in a circle, searching for danger, but nothing had changed. I tried to fold the link to tuck it into my waistband and take it home, but it was as brittle as if it had been lying there for decades, and crumbled in my hands. I clenched my jaw and went to examine the three larger skeletons.

All wore armor of some sort. Among the bones was a large hammer and a short, wide sword. I couldn't lift either weapon. But there were two strange bands crossing the empty chest cavity of one skeleton, and I dragged them off, shifting the heavy chest, arm, and skull until I had pulled them free.

The bands seemed to be made from hundreds of pieces of metal stuck together into straps. I examined them quickly as the feeling of danger grew and the sweet scent of the flowers from the hall floated toward me. I looked around again, as I slipped the bands over my head and positioned them across my chest in an X, like the corpse had. I couldn't wait any longer.

I stepped cautiously into the corridor, droopy petals crushing beneath my feet and releasing their perfume. Adrenaline burned as it flowed into my veins. Danger. Death was coming.

I started to run, breathing heavily. The faster and farther I went, the more the sweet scent filled my lungs, and the more I shuddered with irrational fear. I bit the inside of my cheek. The blossom of pain and taste of blood distracted me from the danger for a moment, and I realized something was wrong. The panic was raging out of control for no apparent reason. The farther I went, the worse it got. There was something bad was ahead. I could feel myself getting closer to it as the instinctual sense of danger increased.

I stumbled over a branching vine and fell to my hands and knees. The blue flowers puffed their cloying scent right into my face, and my heart squeezed so hard I became lightheaded from the fear.

The flowers. I took another breath, thinking back to the safety of that small room with the skeletons. I knew I should go back. I'd be safe there.

"Damn."

I stood up and ripped off my shirt's sleeve, then wrapped it twice around my head, covering my mouth and nose like a mask.

The flowers were messing with my head. Something in their scent made my brain think of death and torment. And as I went farther, they grew thicker and thicker, and the fear grew worse.

I started running again, gasping for air through the thick filter. It helped somewhat, and I was able to continue until the corridor grew so thick with flowers that I had trouble moving. Finally, the hallway ended abruptly, and I stumbled into a large room with steps leading down from the outside to the center, like a coliseum or a small version of a football stadium.

I looked around and shuddered. The room was filled with new monsters, and they were all looking in my direction. For a few awkward seconds, we all just stared.

The corpses of strange animals littered the floor, some newer, some old enough that the bones had been picked clean. There were a few human skeletons, too.

The monsters were short, close to the ground. The bigger ones had six stubby legs, three on either side of their grub-like bodies. Their heads resembled a retarded pug dog's. Their eyes bulged out on either side of their skull, and their mouths dripped thick green slime.

They had been slurping up the liquefied flesh of the bodies. Smaller monsters with no legs, the babies, wormed around like maggots, blindly sucking up the fleshy slush beneath them. Even corpses of their own species were left to rot in the soup before being cannibalized.

One of them sniffled loudly, lifting its head as if to scent the air. Then it ran toward me, moving surprisingly fast on its six stubby little legs. The other adults followed, mouths hanging open like happy dogs. Most of them were on the lower levels of the room, and they struggled to move up the large steps.

I turned and ran, heading sideways around the outside of the stadium, close to the wall on the highest level. One of the grub-pub things was snuffling right behind me, and I ran faster, barely keeping ahead of it. Looking frantically around for an escape, I spotted a door at the other end of the room.

Fetid breath warmed the back of my calf, and I snapped from fear, just a bit. I took a huge leap out over the abnormally large steps leading down to the middle. Things seemed to slow down for a moment as I hung in the air, falling forward toward the steps far below. Then I was plummeting downward at full speed.

I landed on my feet, but my legs couldn't handle the pressure or the forward momentum, and I tumbled over. I came down on my back and flung out my arms to keep from rolling any more. Despite knowing I must have hurt myself quite a bit with that little stunt, there was so much adrenaline pumping through my veins that I didn't feel it.

I'd put some distance between myself and the grub-pug on the top level, but conversely put myself closer to the ones still struggling to climb up from the bottom. I stood and ran forward, careful to maintain my footing on the vines and small plants that grew everywhere at this lower level.

When I reached the far end of the room near the second doorway, I started up the stairs again, my thighs burning from the exertion of moving my weight upward at such a fast pace, especially under the effects of the increased gravity. When I reached the top, I couldn't help but chuckle, even though I barely had enough air in my lungs to do so.

The grub-pug on top had followed me down and across the room, but was now struggling along with the others to move up the steps below me. Its short legs scrabbled desperately before finally heaving it over the edge of a step.

I pointed at it and spit. "Screw you! I'm not that easy to kill."

Of course, fate took that moment to show me the consequence of my hubris. A sniffling sound came from the doorway behind me, and I jumped out of the way just in time to avoid the huge grub-pug lunging for me. It sniffed again, then came for me at full speed.

I spun and ran all the way back to the blue-flower doorway, then down and back up again, avoiding the decaying bodies along the way.

Some of the grub-pugs were thrown off, but more flooded through the doorway, and others caught on to my trick, ignoring my descent and waiting for me at the top level. Soon I found myself trapped on three sides with my back to the outside wall. I was caught, too far away from either of the doors to escape into them. Helpless rage took hold of me at the unfairness of my situation. I hadn't asked for any of this, had done nothing to deserve it. My whole life I'd gone about silently, invisibly, never standing out or voicing the anger, irritation, and derision that filled my head.

I screamed at the monsters, a wordless shriek of challenge. Let them try and fight me, eat me, if they could. I wouldn't hold back my rage at Death's attempt to take me any longer.

So I put my back to the curve of the wall and braced myself for the first one to come close. I was ready when it did. I kicked it in its drooling face as hard as I could.

Its pug-nose squished in a little bit, and it fell back, dazed. Another came, and I did the same to it. But they were big creatures, and my kicks weren't having much effect other than to keep them off.

So I kicked harder. I slid my back farther down the wall, so that my legs could push outward rather than just down.

The drooling, maggot-like monsters gathered around me, watching warily, looking for a chance to rush me. Thick, slimy fluid from their mouths coated the stone floor, making it slippery.

When I kicked them from my lowered position, they slid away, tumbling over the side of the step. But for each one I kicked away, another one crawled up from the lower levels, a constant incoming tide of monsters.

I let out a choked sob. There were too many of them, and I wasn't strong enough.

Then, one of them made a horrible snorting sound, like it was gathering up a stubborn loogie from the back of its throat. It spit at me, a wad of green slime flying forward and hitting me in the middle of my left shin.

I shook my leg, and most of the spit glob dripped reluctantly to the floor. But my pants were wet where it had hit, and they clung to my leg.

Then another snorted, and another.

I didn't know what the heck the green stuff was, but the fact that they were standing at a distance and spitting it on me meant it couldn't be good. I only had to look around to see it had to be a poison or acid of some sort. I highly doubted they were just going for the gross-out factor.

They aimed for my legs, and I use my left shin to shield my still loogie-free right leg.

The heavy fluid soaked through my pant leg and pooled in my shoe.

I was prepared for the pain of acid eating through my skin or something equally horrible, but nothing happened. In fact, my lower left leg and foot didn't hurt at all. I'd had blisters all over my foot and my calf had been absolutely screaming in suppressed pain, just like my right leg. I tried to wiggle my left toes but couldn't feel them to tell if they'd moved or not.

Blood rushed in my ears as I comprehended my situation. They would keep me pinned, spitting on me from afar until I was paralyzed, and then they would eat me, feeding their young on my dissolving, putrid body.

"Screw that." I spit back at the monster that'd spit on me first. Then I screamed and pushed forward from the wall. I balanced on my good leg and used the numb one to kick out viciously, knocking two grub-pugs down a few steps as they slid in their own green slime, and then limped after the ones still on the top level. I kicked one in the head hard enough that it wobbled drunkenly, and I used the opportunity to shove it over the edge.

The last one on the top level made the snorting, gathering sound again, but I kicked it before it could spit. Its head snapped sharply to the side, sending a trail of slime splattering down on the others. It opened its mouth wide and rushed me, but I threw myself at it, stomping with all my weight down on its head. My foot was so numb I couldn't even feel the impact, but I saw it sink down in the blubbery creature's head.

I did it again and again, as hard as I could. My breath shuddered in and out of my lungs, and I sobbed desperately, a sound of fear and mindless rage.

It had stopped moving, its skull thoroughly smashed in, its eyes bulging out of the sockets. I stepped back from it and placed my back against the wall again.

"I killed it," I said to myself. And then again, "I killed it! It's dead!" It was a giddy feeling. And when the monsters I'd kicked down a few steps reached the top, I killed them, too. I screamed my defiance at them, a grin stretching my mouth painfully wide.

More came from below, and still more from the far door, but their skulls weren't designed for stability against hard impacts. I stayed in my circle of slippery, smashed carcasses and killed my attackers with vicious kicks when they came close.

I didn't know how much time passed, but eventually they stopped coming, and I realized that all the adults were dead, too stupid to realize my superiority and run away.

I stood panting in the circle of squished-headed monsters for a bit, then limped away and sat down with my back against the wall. I leaned my head toward the low-hanging ceiling and laughed, a hollow sound that quickly soured as I started to cry. "I'm alive," I whispered. I hadn't thought I would be.

Lethargy started to crawl over me, and I struggled to my feet. If I didn't keep moving, I might fall into the sleep of exhaustion and never wake again.

Chapter 9

I knew nothing but shadows and I thought them to be real.
— Oscar Wilde

I LIMPED through the far doorway and dragged myself up the huge steps of a dark stairwell. The remnants of light evaporated as I climbed, until I moved in absolute darkness. It frightened me at first, but as I went on, I lost even the strength for fear, and thought longingly of rest. My dragging left leg felt like a heavy log.

By the end I was panting, my legs so worn that even the good one felt numb, and I couldn't tell if my dizziness was imagined or a result of overexertion. The stairwell ended abruptly, and my face smashed into something solid. The pain made me jerk away and brought me tingling back to a level of awareness I didn't remember losing.

I felt along the wall I'd run into. It was actually more like the ceiling. It slanted toward me, and warmth radiated from the stone in waves that felt soothing despite the heat of my body. I pushed, and the stone slid away. Hot air wafted down on me, and I peeked my head up through the floor and looked around.

The room was a compact cylinder with a low ceiling and images of different kinds of strange animals carved into the walls at regular intervals.

No monsters appeared. I spat as far as I could into the room and ducked down, waiting for a reaction. When nothing happened, I climbed up the rest of the way into the room. As soon as I was in, the opening *snicked* closed behind me, as seamless as if it had never been there.

The air around me let out a pulsing *boom*. It hit me from every side at once, and suddenly I was burning. Heat tightened my skin, and my dust-dry eyes stung with tears that evaporated before they even wet my eyeballs.

I screamed but couldn't hear myself, and ran mindlessly, trying to get *away*. I slammed into a section of the wall with a gazelle-like creature on it. The stone once again slid open, this time onto a room full of deer-like monsters, separated from me by what looked like a seamless sheet of water.

A thin, muscular monster turned to look at me. It reminded me of a cross between a Chihuahua and a deer. Rather than hooves, two claws tipped each of its four legs. Its snout was long and pointed, and its teeth sharp. Two triangular ears swiveled around warily, and it ran towards me before stopping at what it seemed to judge a safe distance.

I pushed my fingers through the layer of water. They cooled immediately, and I had to resist the urge to plunge my body through, too.

The creature let out a high-pitched chattering sound. "Tikitiktiktik!" Its eyes were locked on my own, and something about it, small bony frame and all, conjured back the fear I had been momentarily too tired to feel. Even though it was kind of cute, I knew immediately that it wanted to kill me. Drawn by its call, others slipped into my line of sight, one after another, until a crowd waited on the other side of the barrier.

The taut skin of my lips cracked from the heat, and a drop of blood fell to the bands across my chest, then dried up and flaked away like dust.

I could fight the monsters. I couldn't fight the heat.

The curtain of water ran over my burning, aching skin as I stepped forward. The absence of the burning felt so pleasurable I wanted to weep in relief—but I didn't have time.

I knew from their body language they were going to rush me all at once, so I made the first move. I stepped forward and crushed one of them under my left foot with one giant stomp.

Its legs snapped out from underneath its body at a bad angle, and it died with a pitiful, high-pitched scream.

I almost felt bad for it, until its friends jumped at me from all sides. Their little legs propelled them through the air as if they were made to run and jump. But unlike the delicate creatures they resembled, they were the hunters, not the hunted. Their legs clawed at my clothes, my face, and my arms, and their teeth ripped at my skin.

They came at me from so many different directions I could only flail around and try to protect my head. But there were too many of them, and I was already weakening. I bled from a myriad of tiny slashes, and each time they sank their teeth into me, they tore loose small chunks of flesh.

It was instinct to react defensively to something I couldn't fight head on, but I realized with a sickening lurch that it was going to get me killed. Clenching my jaw, I uncurled, exposing my head but freeing up my hands.

A tik-tik was on my leg, biting into my thigh with its Chihuahua-sized jaw. I grabbed it by the nape of its neck and twisted with both my hands as if wringing out a washcloth. Its bones crunched and broke, and I used the body to bat away another that jumped at me. It slammed into the ground, hard, and didn't get up again. Some were attached to my back, so I stumbled against the nearest wall and crushed my body against the stone once, then again, and again.

Blood ran from me, and some splashed against the metal bands I'd taken, right in the middle where they crossed each other. Metallic scales rippled out from the center point in waves, rising like the back hair of a frightened cat. Then it tightened over me, and the bands started to spread, the little scales filling in the gaps between the bands. In less than a second, my torso up to the neck and down to my waist was covered. I gave it a sharp rap of my knuckles, and it silently spread the force of the impact with a ripple of scales. "Freaking body armor," I croaked. "Hell, yeah."

The creatures sank back for a second, wary, and a few of them let out the high-pitched "Tik!" sound again.

I knew I needed to finish them quickly, before they overwhelmed me again. I was already exhausted and losing blood to boot. So I lunged forward aggressively, picking them off one by one.

They wouldn't run away, and instead encircled me, trying to keep me contained. I had the feeling they were stalling for time until reinforcements were drawn by their cute calls.

I used the bodies of their dead against them. If a little deer got knocked over, I was on it, and it was dead before it had the chance to stand back up. I killed them, and kept killing them. They were so weak compared to the grub-pugs. But more came, and more. They were determined, smart, and vicious. One would dart in and make a feint at me while two more attacked when my attention was diverted. My torso was protected, but they ripped at my legs, arms, and head. Rather than latching on like in the beginning, they'd dart in to give small wounds, and then dart right back out to rejoin the encircling swarm. They were like a pack of relentless arctic wolves, hell-bent on bringing down their prey.

But fear of death is a powerful motivator, and I refused to fall. I killed more and more of them, their broken little bodies piling up like crisp autumn leaves until finally one let out a sharp "Tik!" and they all backed up a few steps and repeated the sound.

I made a feinting lunge toward them as if to attack, screaming with all the intimidation I could muster. My dry throat cracked, and my voice broke under the pressure, turning my scream into a growling shriek of bloodlust.

They jumped in surprise and dashed away almost quicker than I would have thought possible, going "Tik! Tik!" in alarm.

After that, I took a long minute to just lean against the wall and rest. I knew I needed to keep moving. I knew that. But at that moment, I couldn't. That scream had been a desperate attempt to scare them. And luckily it had worked, because no matter how much I wanted it to, my body couldn't keep going without a break.

As I sat among the small carcasses, I felt a kind of vindictive elation cutting through my fatigue. I'd won, with my own strength. I'd fought and won.

I SAT near the entrance barrier and looked around the room. I'd been too busy with the more immediate danger to examine it before.

It was a section of the top of the building, cut somewhat like a piece of Bundt cake, the center being the heat-room I'd come from. Each slice was undoubtedly filled with other types of monsters. There were three doorways in the far wall, each leading into darkness. But the small criss-crossing grooves lining the walls and the holes in the ceiling that let in beams of sunlight were of more interest to me.

I looked to the three doors, and then to the skylights, and then to the grooved walls. "Damn. I wish I'd exercised more." With one last deep breath, I swallowed to moisten my still-dry throat, crawled to my feet, and hobbled toward the doors.

When I reached the outward facing wall, I carefully avoided the doorways and the danger I knew would lurk somewhere on the other side.

Instead, I wedged my fingers and toes into the slanted grooves in the wall and started to shuffle diagonally upward. When I'd gone to the far wall, I carefully moved to a higher set of grooves and started in the other direction, inching my way toward the ceiling.

As I neared one of the glassless windows, I realized it was eerily silent outside, and the faint smell of something else mixed with the light perfume of the air. When I'd entered the building, the Trial grounds had already echoed with a chorus of horrible screams, but they were absent now. When I reached the window and hauled my upper body through the opening, I discovered why.

"Oh. God," I murmured.

It was a scene of carnage. Countless bodies were strewn across the ground in every direction, lying on the stone paths and amongst the trampled grass of the fields. Many of them were monsters, but I saw a human head with brown hair lying below my vantage point, face down.

It was just the head, the body nowhere to be seen.

I reared back from the opening, gasping for air as my stomach heaved. But even so, the taste of the air, filled with the scent of blood and feces and the meaty, food-smell of raw meat and internal organs…the smell filled my mouth, and I could taste it on my tongue and the back of my throat.

My stomach convulsed, and I spewed down onto the floor below. I wiped my mouth with the back of my hand and looked out again.

Under a nearby tree, whose trunk had broken like a snapped toothpick, a pack of the tik-tiks piled on top of something on the ground, ripping and biting. A small arm flailed out, helpless, and I gasped. It was the boy, the small boy from earlier. They were killing him.

I shouted and waved my hands, but none of the monsters so much as twitched. Crawling out of the opening, I angled my feet and pushed off down the outside of the curved building. The descent was even faster than I'd anticipated, and I shot off the side almost straight down.

Sharp pain shot up through my un-numbed ankle, my knees, and my hips as I hit the ground and rolled. The scaly vest I wore absorbed some of the impact and protected my spine. A dry groan escaped me as I stumbled to my feet and began hobbling toward the monsters, shouting in rage.

They saw me coming and lifted red-stained muzzles, teeth bared in warning.

When I reached them, I snapped one's neck with my hands while I cracked the spine and brittle legs of another under my foot, screaming all the while. The rest ran off, chattering at me resentfully.

I knelt in front of the small Player. It looked like maybe he had been hiding in the branches of the tree, which had been knocked over by some huge force. He was bleeding badly—way, way too much blood.

My hands shook as they hovered above him, trying to figure out the best spot to apply pressure. "Oh, god. Please. Are you okay?" I knew the answer. There were too many wounds, he was too small, and he'd already bled so much. It was everywhere, the blood.

He gasped up at me, chest heaving for breath, eyes wide and terrified.

I smiled at him, hoping it looked honest. "You're going to be fine, okay? They're gone, and I'm here now. I'll keep you safe, and as soon as this is over, we're going to get you out of here—to a hospital—so don't you worry." I looked around for someplace to hide. "Everything's okay," I chattered, not sure if I was trying to soothe the boy or myself with my words.

The sleeve I'd wound around my face earlier had fallen down around my neck. I took it off, tore it down the middle, and used it to tie off both his arms as close to his body as possible. Then I tore off my other sleeve and did the same to his upper thighs. "Need to keep the blood near your core," I explained.

His torso was still leaking blood everywhere, but I didn't have anything to bind it with.

I heard a shriek, and a huge shadow passed overhead, blocking out the heat and glaring harshness of the sun for a fraction of a second. Glancing up, I just caught the tail end of a huge flying bird creature streaking through the sky. "Crap. We need to move."

I looked around for somewhere small, somewhere defensible. Definitely not another mysterious, *surprise-it's-a-trap*! building. Somewhere I could keep the boy safe. A crow sat in a nearby tree, watching us with its beady little eyes. Beyond it, overturned on one of the grooved stone paths, was a bullet-shaped glass container big enough to fit a couple humans inside.

I slid my arms under the boy's light body and lifted him, trying not to jostle him despite my limpy leg, and carried him to the human-sized bullet. It had metal tracks on one side, and as I stared at the aerodynamic shape, I suddenly understood. "It's a pod! A transport pod."

I set the boy down on the ground and wedged my shoulder against the side of the pod, giving it a hard shove. It lifted slightly but settled back down again. I shoved harder, and kept shoving, and it lifted, then rolled over and settled with its tracks along the grooves in the stone path. I pulled at the handle I'd uncovered and opened the glass door, then lifted the boy and slid him inside.

He groaned and tossed his head back and forth, pale with pain and blood loss.

My body dragged against the side of the pod as I moved around behind it and pushed, trying to get it moving. It did move, but ground roughly against the stone, and I had to stop almost immediately. I just didn't have the strength or energy.

I peeked my head inside the door to check on the boy, but instead noticed a cartridge in the front of the pod, attached to the end of the metal tracks. On the floor of the pod lay another, covered in rust.

I picked it up and buffed it thoughtfully against my pants, blew hard into its end, and took the other cartridge out of the slot. They were the same. I slipped the old one into my waistband, and then put the one from the floor into the slot. It took a good hard shove to push it into place, but when I finally got it, the pod hummed to life.

After only a few seconds, the glass tinted over to protect the interior from the sun. I laughed aloud. "Hell yeah!"

The boy giggled despite his injuries. "This is awesome."

"How do you drive this thing?" I wondered aloud, eyeing the pod's interior.

Something moved on the other side of the pod.

I stilled in fear as a large creature stalked around the corner of a nearby building, straight toward us. It looked like a humongous wildcat, except for the third eye in its head. I had half a moment to hope that it had already eaten someone or something else and wasn't hungry anymore. Then its nose twitched, and it shot forward, slamming into the side of the pod and almost rocking it off the path again, clawing at the glass as if trying to get inside.

The boy screamed shrilly.

The three-eyed wildcat growled and scored lines into the tinted glass with its claws.

I took an involuntary step back, and it pushed away from the pod, padding purposefully around to my side. I stepped backward, and then remembered something I'd heard once about dealing with wildcats. I spread my arms and legs wide to try and look large and resisted the urge to turn my back and run.

It merely threw me a warning snarl and turned to the boy, exposed by the open door of the pod.

"Damn it," I groaned. I lunged forward and slammed the pod door closed, leaving the boy protected inside.

The creature seemed to assess me anew—almost as if it were surprised —and bared its teeth in warning. It's low, rumbling growl was the sound of far-away thunder rolling across the earth.

"I can't let you. He's just a little kid," I said aloud, though I knew it wouldn't make a difference to the creature.

It lunged for me, and I pushed sideways just quick enough to avoid its long claws. I fell onto my numb leg, now unfeeling all the way up to the hip, and scrambled backward. My hand landed on a rock, which I immediately threw at the cat, but it struck nothing more than a glancing blow.

All three of its eyes focused on me unwaveringly, a hunter's glare.

I continued to scuttle away as it stalked forward, until I came up against the trunk of the split tree from earlier.

The cat let out a series of raspy coughs, almost as if it was laughing.

I used the trunk to haul myself to my feet and snatched one of the snapped branches, pointing the sharp end toward the cat and shouting in wordless, empty threat.

It swiped one large paw and ripped the awkward weapon from my grasp. Another step and another swipe, and it knocked me into a tumbling roll across the ground.

I crawled to my hands and knees, holding the bleeding scratch marks on my arm and wondering if the bone might be broken. My ID link definitely was, cracked and split like the ground of a desert land.

The cat pounced on me again, batting at me like a toy and sending me flying.

I dragged my limp left leg toward the pod and used its smooth side to haul myself to my feet. My eyes met the boy's through the tinted glass, and I saw my own fear mirrored within them. I also saw the reflection of the cat behind me, and I knew that it would play with me until it killed me, and then it would eat me, and the boy would still die.

There was no escape.

So I turned around, balled my hands into tight, bloodless fists, and screamed defiance at the monster. "Come on!"

It smashed me against the side of the pod and pinned me with its front paws, towering over me on its hind legs.

I punched and flailed and even tried to bite at it, but it held still, looking at me with those three beautiful golden eyes. It opened its mouth to bite off my head.

I refused to close my eyes against death. But when it lowered its head, instead of teeth biting at me, a sandpaper tongue rasped against my forehead. I blinked twice as my mind stuttered in confusion. A lick?

The creature pushed back and landed on all fours, looked at my astonished face once more, and let out another coughing laugh. Then it ambled away, disappearing around a bend of the stone path between the tall grasses.

I shakily opened the door of the slim pod and sat down inside. "Are you okay?"

The boy nodded faintly. "I'm glad…you're okay," he whispered, taking rapid, shallow breaths.

I let out a sharp, disbelieving breath almost like a laugh. "Me too." There was a small lever in the center of the pod. I pushed it forward, and, with a rusty groan, the pod started to slide forward.

The boy was shivering, and when I placed my hand on his forehead, it was cold and clammy. I pushed the lever down harder, and the pod shuddered with the effort to add more speed.

With some difficulty and a lot of worrying, we finally made it back to the starting point and the cube, the pod dying as the clearing came into view.

I got out, lifted the boy into my arms, and hobbled toward the still black cube. I laid the boy at the edge of the clearing and went to poke and prod at the cube, but got no reaction. I smashed my palm against it in frustration before returning to the boy. "It'll be over soon, and then we'll be able to go back. I'll get you help."

He smiled sweetly at me and whispered, "No, you won't. But that's okay. Take it." He gestured to the front pocket of his jeans.

"What?"

"Take it."

He fumbled with the stiff fabric, so I reached into the small denim pouch to help him and drew out his black token.

"No." I shook my head, moving to put it back.

He smiled again, and blood ran out of the corner of his mouth as he whispered, "It's okay. Thank you." And then…he was gone. I didn't want to believe it, but there's a horrible sense humans have for the souls of others. His was gone.

I blinked and let out a hitching, sobbing breath, though my eyes stayed dry.

Then the crow flapped down from the deep blue sky, landing atop the cube once more.

A screen flashed in front of my face.

THE TRIAL IS OVER. PLEASE RETURN TO THE STARTING POINT.

I waited numbly until others started to drag themselves back to the cube, weary and half-beaten. Then I stood up, clenching the second token in my fist. Words appeared on the cube.

YOU HAVE PROVEN YOURSELVES WORTHY.

I watched as the survivors filtered back. A man and woman came back okay, or so I thought. He dragged her, her arm thrown around his shoulder. Her eyes were wide and staring, and her throat had been slashed open, deep.

He was chanting mindlessly to the dead woman, as I had done to the boy. "It's okay, Honey. I'm here with you, and everything's going to be okay. It'll all be back to normal once we get back to the real world. It's okay, Honey…" This time, I knew for sure that the words were to comfort him, not her.

The cocky guy I'd spoken to at the beginning of the Trial popped out of the tall grass and stumbled over the body of the boy. He grimaced in distaste, and then knelt down to pat the boy over and search his pockets.

"He doesn't have a token," I said without thinking.

He looked up and smiled at me. "You made it, huh? Though a bit worse for the wear, I see," he said, looking at my bleeding, bedraggled, and bruised body. "How do you know he doesn't have one?"

I stared at him emotionlessly, and his lips twisted into a knowing smile. "You took it, that's how. Well, well. I must say I'm impressed. Going for the weaker targets doesn't pay in strong Skills, but you decrease risk that way, too. Personally, I prefer the ones with fight in them. That way you know you'll get something good." He nodded at me approvingly. "And you got some armor. You've got more guts than I thought. You might do well in this Game."

I turned my head away without responding, watching the others.

There had been many at the start, but we were fewer now. "More than fifty percent casualty rate," I muttered.

"How else to cull the weak from the strong?" he said.

The crow Examiner opened its mouth. "Everyone has arrived. Congratulations on surviving. Now, for the special awards! Please take out your tokens."

I slipped my finger between my strange vest and my shirt and pulled out my original token from the pocket where I'd stashed it. As the cube hummed, both tokens started to vibrate sympathetically, and then melted and reformed into strange shapes that reminded me vaguely of old Chinese characters, or maybe Egyptian hieroglyphs.

Words rolled out across the screen from left to right.

WISHER'S PENNY: JENNY SHEEN
GREEN WHISPERER: JACK URBAN
SECOND WIND: VAUGHN RIDLEY
AURA OF LIGHT: VAUGHN RIDLEY
FLICKER: VAUGHN RIDLEY
MADRIGAL'S SHELL: VAUGHN RIDLEY

I watched the guy next to me. As Vaughn Ridley's name rolled out, over and over, his smile grew wider and wider. He held a handful of transformed tokens in his hand, watching the screen.

I grew cold inside but was soon distracted as my own name rolled across the screen.

TUMBLING FEATHER: EVE REDDING
SPIRIT OF THE HUNTRESS: EVE REDDING

"Wow," Vaughn said. "You got a spirit-type Skill? Impressive."

I frowned at him. "What does that mean? What are 'Skills?'"

He shook his head at my ignorance. "They're just like the 'skills' in a video game. They let you do special things once you plant them, things you couldn't do normally. They're quite useful."

I stared at the two tokens, sitting so innocently in my palm. "They'll help me survive?" For a second, I was elated at my good fortune. I could hardly wait to plant them.

"They help you do more than survive. They allow you to become god," he announced, looking at me with narrowed eyes. "I am the strongest Player to ever enter the Game, and I'm aiming for the ultimate power. I'm looking for allies to help me on my way. Strong people who will do whatever it takes, and don't mind getting their hands dirty. How about it?"

It took a minute for my overwhelmed brain to understand what he was asking. "You want me to join you?"

"Yes. You're the only one here with more than one token, besides me. Even if you did only kill a little kid to get it, at least you're ruthless. And I know you're a bit strong, because you've got a spirit-type Skill. I'm going to dominate this Game and all the other useless Players. I could take you with me to the top."

I almost said yes. But then I saw the happy, charming smile on his face, and over his shoulder, the empty little body lying on the ground. Putrid disgust for myself washed over me. I hated myself, truly, at that moment.

"No. I'm not the one you want." I turned and dragged my left leg slowly toward the cube, which now displayed the "Do you want to leave?" message, and pushed "Yes."

Chapter 10

I carry death in my left pocket.
— Charles Bukowski

THE FEEL of my suddenly lighter body and the sight of concrete walls rising up into smoggy air to either side allowed me to let out a sigh of relief. A Window popped up, telling me I'd earned a few levels and Seeds. As the tension left my body, the pain and exhaustion washed over me like the waves of a rising tide. My head spun, and I fell against the wall and started to shiver. Blobs of light and dark swam across my vision, and a distant voice shocked me to alertness again.

With a gasp, I looked around. I didn't know how long I'd been sitting on the ground, but numbness had overtaken my whole left leg and butt and was spreading through my torso. I was shivering and clammy from blood loss, and my heart was beating too fast trying to keep my body oxygenated. "Damn it. No, no." I shook my head helplessly. Soon, the numbness and paralysis would spread to my lungs.

I jabbed at my ID sheath, but the shattered surface didn't respond. No phone call possible. I called out weakly toward the sidewalk, but the alley took a sharp turn, so no one could see me, and I was too weak to shout.

One last resort. "Bunny?"

He responded immediately.

—You're back.
Shit. You look like crap.—
-Bunny-

I swallowed. "I need help. If I don't get to the hospital, I'm going to die."

—What's wrong? What exactly happened?—
-Bunny-

My tongue felt furry and thick. "Got spit on by some monsters and my whole body's getting paralyzed. Bit up pretty bad, blood loss…" I struggled for another breath. "Maybe a couple broken bones. Please, call an ambulance."

—I can't do that. What are you going to say happened to you? There'll be questions.—
-Bunny-

"If you don't help me, I'm going to die right here on the ground!" I said, rage and desperation fueling me, even if only for an instant. "You will remember my death forever. How I begged you for help, and how you murdered me."

No response, and then,

—I can't call an ambulance. But maybe I can get help…—
-Bunny-

The rage slipped away, and with it went my strength. My eyes closed. When I opened them again, I was somehow lying on the ground.

A bright orange screen pulsed inches from my face.

—Stay awake! Help is on the way.
Talk to me.—
-Bunny-

I heard a deep voice speaking, panting and hoarse, but I couldn't make out the words. I roused a bit, tried to tell it I couldn't understand, but all that came out was a ragged wheeze. I thought my eyes were open, but black crept in from the edges of my vision, wiping out the alley.

Running feet appeared in my last pinprick of sight, and then I knew only black nothingness.

I WOKE with a gasp to a blonde boy giving me CPR.

He drew back with a relieved sigh and slumped against the opposite wall of the alley as I sucked for air, every cell in my body screaming for oxygen.

When I was re-oxygenated, I sat up and stretched carefully. My legs both moved, and though the left one was considerably stiff and still numb, I could now feel the ankle swelling painfully.

What had he done to save me? My eyes narrowed as I looked him over. Sandy blond hair, blue eyes, white teeth, and clothes that were worth more than everything in my closet put together. He was shivering with exhaustion and had a strange look in his eyes.

"Did Bunny send you?" My voice scratched against my throat and sent me into a fit of coughing.

He slipped off a light backpack and tossed me a half-empty water bottle from within.

I downed the contents in a few gulps, water overflowing and running over my cheeks and down my throat. "Thanks." I handed the empty bottle back. "So? Did he?"

The boy took a deep breath, nodding.

"Did you heal me?"

He nodded again.

"How?"

He raised the corners of his mouth in an unhappy smile. "It's my Skill."

"Your Skill? You mean from the Characteristic Trial?" I didn't wait for his response. "Show me."

He frowned at me, not moving, so I smiled back as innocently as possible. "I'm Eve. What's your name?"

"Sam. Samuel, but I go by Sam." He smiled back at me, wide and open, and I decided that I liked him.

"How long have you been a Player, Sam?"

"A few months."

"Wow. I'm a new Player. I don't have any Skills yet, and I'd love to see yours in action. Would you show me?" I tried again, this time with a smile.

He'd stopped shivering and gave me a half-shrug. "I guess something small couldn't hurt." He moved toward me and took my hand, which had long scratches along the palm, outlined in blood.

He held out his other hand. His skin separated and started to bleed, the same pattern as the cuts on my hand. Then it closed up again, gone as if it had never been.

He wiped the blood off on his jeans and showed me the unmarred skin. Then he rubbed at my cuts with his thumb, and the dried blood flaked off, showing skin just as smooth as if I'd never been cut.

My mouth hung open and I flexed my hand. It didn't hurt. "It's gone. You took the injury from me?"

He nodded. "That's my Skill. I take the injury on myself and heal it." He looked down for a moment. In the blue depths of his eyes, I saw a shadow move, but when he looked back up, it had passed.

"That's completely amazing!"

He gave me a small smile. "Not really. I can't heal everything as easily as that cut. For instance, your poison. I only took a bit of that. I can't do anything about your previous blood loss, and I'll have to do a few more passes before you can be safely left alone. But I took care of the lung paralysis, so we've got time."

I shook my head. "No. It really is amazing. And you've been a Player for months. That in itself is amazing, too. Do you have others to help you?"

He shook his head. "No. I play alone."

Good. That meant I might be able to use him without the hindrance of other Players.

"And you'll want to burn or bury these pants. Don't wash them. The saliva might be reactivated if you do, and you don't want that spreading through the city's water system." He placed his hand on my hip, and some of the numbness from that area receded. He took a few minutes of rest while his body fought off the effects of the poison, and then did it again, and again, moving down my left leg toward the original point of contact.

Next, he placed his hand on my ribs and some of the pain of each breath flowed away. My armored vest had returned to its original state of two black bands crossing my chest sometime while I'd been too out of it to notice.

"You've got a few fractures there. I'm not healing them completely, but I've given you a jumpstart on the process."

"Why did you come?"

He shrugged. "I came because I heard you needed me. What else could I do?"

"You could have ignored me," I said matter-of-factly. "Or you could have used my weakness against me."

"Well, I guess I could have. But for what?"

"I can think of a few things. Like Seeds. But you wouldn't do that, would you? Because you're a genuinely good person."

His eyes rose to mine in surprise. "I'm not, really. I use good behavior to mask the truth."

"The truth?" I parroted.

"I'm not an angel. I'm the harbinger of death," he murmured, pushing himself up the wall so he was standing over me. By the way he struggled even to pull his backpack on, it was obvious that he was exhausted from his efforts. "I've got to get home. My parents might be wondering where I'm at."

I nodded and rose carefully to my feet. If he didn't want to discuss his secret with me, that was fine. I could understand that. But it didn't change the judgment I'd made of him. "Thank you, Sam. Really. You saved my life." I met his eyes, trying to project that judgment of him clearly.

He looked at me for a moment, then smiled happily, gave me a nod of acknowledgment, and started to walk away.

"Wait!"

He turned.

"Give me your contact information."

He hesitated, so I stepped forward, limping from the pain of my sprained ankle. "Please. I just want to be able to contact you in case something happens. You can trust me."

He held out the ID link on his wrist, but my own link was too broken to accept the flashed information.

"Just tell me. I'll remember your number," I said.

I stood in silence for a while after he'd gone before speaking into the empty air.

"Bunny. Thank you."

—You're welcome, Eve.—

-Bunny-

I ENTERED my house carefully in case my mother and brother were there. My clothes were once again ruined, and despite what Sam had done for me, injuries riddled my body. How would I explain that? 'I got mugged by a meat processor?' I placed my hand on the doorknob to my bedroom and turned the handle slowly so as not to make too much noise.

"Where were y— What happened?" Zed's urgent voice came from his bedroom doorway, which had just opened.

My mouth bobbed open and closed like a suffocating fish as I tried and failed to give my brother some excuse.

He looked me up and down, then rushed toward me and grabbed my shoulders as if I might collapse at any moment. "Oh my god. Are you okay? What the hell happened?"

I shook my head sharply. "Shh! Be quiet."

He frowned down at me as if I was crazy. "What do you mean, be quiet? You're hurt bad, Eve! I'm going to call Mom."

I clapped my hand over his mouth and shook my head vehemently, then dragged him into my room. When the door was closed and locked behind us, I turned back to him. "You can't tell anyone about this. Please."

"Tell anyone about *what*? Were you bullied? Did someone hurt you? Just tell me who it was, Eve. I'll make sure they never touch you again."

I smiled and shook my head, looking at his clenched fists. He wanted to be the savior, but there was nothing he could do about this. He couldn't know. I didn't want him to be the subject of one of NIX's cleanup operations. Would they make it look like another runaway? Or maybe an accidental death? "Trust me, Zed. You don't understand. I'm doing this for your own good. Please, just listen to me. Trust me. Have I ever led you wrong before?"

He sputtered and shook his head. "I can't just *ignore* this. I—"

I cut him off. "I'm not asking you to ignore it. I'm asking you to keep it a secret. I'm asking you to not ask questions. Please. I need you to do this for me." I looked into his eyes and imbued my voice with as much sincerity as possible.

He clenched his jaw and frowned at me as if in pain. After a long, tense moment, he said, "Can't you let me help you?"

I smiled widely, knowing I'd won. "I can. Help me put on some ointment and wrap up all these little cuts," I said, though I knew that wasn't what he meant. I went into the bathroom and pulled out the small energy cartridge digging into my stomach. It was strange to see it in my ordinary bathroom, something from *that place* infiltrating my mundane life. I wrapped it and the armored vest bands in my ruined clothes to hide it and took a quick shower.

When I returned to my room, now more comfortable in baggy pajamas, Zed was waiting with the medbot. I tossed the bundle of clothes into my closet.

He helped me to rub the disinfectant cream over most of my cuts. "What did this to you? Never mind." He snorted. "I suppose you won't tell me."

I smiled. "That's right. Thank you."

The sound of the front door opening filtered through the house, and we looked at each other in panic.

Zed quickly shooed me into my bed and pulled the cover over me, then slipped the first aid kit and medbot next to my feet as my mother called out to us.

"Go," I said.

"I'll keep her away." He opened my door and called, "Welcome home," then turned and threw me a glance over his shoulder. A look that said I owed him one.

I raised an eyebrow and smiled. I did owe him one. But I couldn't repay him with the answers I knew he craved.

When he was gone, I slipped quietly out of bed and locked the door again, then immediately fell tiredly back into it. I extended my palm, and Seeds appeared in a ripple of air and dropped into my hand. I chose two and held them to my neck, planting them into Resilience.

By the morning, I had healed more than I thought possible. "Note to self. Resilience is useful."

Log of Captivity 2

Mental Log of Captivity—Estimated Day: Two thousand, five hundred ninety-seven.

My link to my master has been growing stronger, but only today did I realize how weak she is. She must be still young, still new. I am needed as a protector, and yet I am confined by these *two-leg-maggots* while she is in danger. I could do nothing but send my words to her again, but I received nothing back. I suspect this is because the *blood-covenant* is still incomplete, only one-sided. I despise my own uselessness. If my *mother-lord* saw me, she would spit at my feet.

Chapter 11

The caged bird sings of freedom.
— Maya Angelou

I OPENED my window to let warm summer air flow through my room and placed the two black tokens on the windowsill. My own token, sharp and bold, with hidden edges that just might cut if touched the wrong way. The boy's, looping and delicate. It matched him, too fragile to protect himself.

An exploding heat inside of me forced its way out. Hatred, helplessness, and self-loathing raged in me, and I swallowed them down, slumping boneless to the floor. Small sounds like those of a wounded animal came from my throat as I cried—great, heaving sobs.

I'd thought I deserved better than the horror NIX put me through, thought I was just another victim, thought I was good. But it turned out I was just a hypocrite.

Zed would have made a better Player than me. He wouldn't have used his first Seeds so selfishly, so stupidly, and he would never have seen a small child gather for a Trial, only to leave to protect himself without a second thought for the boy.

I cried until snot and tears soaked into the rough carpet under my face. When I finally stopped, I felt slightly less horrible. Zed would have handled the situation better, definitely, but thank god the universe didn't see fit to punish him that way and make him a Player. However, I *was* a Player, and that wasn't going to change.

"Who I am isn't going to change, either." I wiped my wet face against my sleeve. I couldn't change, and I didn't want to. I cared about my own survival. I wanted to live, and I would do anything to make that happen. But if I could do it all again, I'd protect the kid from the beginning. Now it was too late for him, but there would be other chances. Other chances to make sure I didn't regret my actions.

I went to the bathroom, washed my face with cold water, and looked at myself hard in the mirror. Blotches covered my face, and my eyes were puffy and red from crying, but my gaze didn't waver.

I wouldn't feel guilty again, I vowed. I returned to my Skill tokens and picked them up. I would need power to back that promise.

"DO PLAYERS EVER COMMIT SUICIDE?" I asked Bunny, a question I'd been wondering about for a while.

He took his time answering.

—Yes. You're not thinking of…—
-Bunny-

"No, no, I'm not. I'm more the type to cling to life with my fingernails. I don't have the constitution to kill myself. I was just curious."

—Well, I've only heard rumors from other Moderators. It hasn't happened to me.—
-Bunny-

"What happens to them—the Players that kill themselves?"

—Well, they'd be dead. But other than that, we send out the cleaners for the body, make sure there's no suicide note with incriminating evidence, etc. No one will find out what happened to them.—
-Bunny-

"What do the cleaners do with the bodies?"

—I don't know. That's not part of my job, and I'm not privy to that information.—
-Bunny-

"Well, I've never seen someone start out as a dead body at the beginning of the Trial. That happens later," I joked bitterly. "So at least they escaped that."

—Dead Players are taken off the lists of active Players. What would be the point to send a dead person to the Trial?—
-Bunny-

"Yeah," I said, and dropped the issue. But I filed that tidbit away in the back of my mind. All information was important when it came to NIX and the Game. I never knew what might someday save my life.

That didn't end up being the information that saved my life, though. In fact, it very nearly got me killed.

I HELD THE DELICATE, twisting token to my neck and spoke aloud, experimenting. "I wish I had the Skill 'Tumbling Feather.'"

I felt a familiar pain as it pricked my skin and injected its hidden contents into me.

A Window popped up.

YOU HAVE GAINED A NEW SKILL: TUMBLING FEATHER

I waited for side effects, something strange or burning or a sense of strength or well-being, but nothing happened. I repeated the process with my own token. "I wish I had the Skill 'Spirit of the Huntress.' "

Again, no response in my body.

I looked out over the communal park stretching out beneath my fourth-floor window. My backyard. A tree obscured some of the view, its branches almost close enough to touch. I leaned forward absentmindedly to brush my fingers over the wide green leaves.

A small bird fluttered toward me, chirping angrily, and then disappeared into the thick foliage.

My breathing slowed as I watched for it to appear again. A flutter, a flap of wings, and a flash of movement between the leaves. I crawled onto my windowsill and reached forward, then pulled myself onto the closest branch. It dipped under my weight.

I crept forward and found the bird again. It darted away, chittering in outrage as I intruded on its territory. My head snapped around to follow its path, and I pressed myself closer to the branch. I wanted to chase it, to see if I could catch it.

Then, like someone threw a bucket of ice water in my face, I realized what I was doing. The trance-like state snapped away.

I gasped, freezing. My vision went blurry, my head started to spin, and my whole body began to burn and tingle. I wrapped my arms around the tree branch and hung on, terrified to find myself in that in-between place where I couldn't be sure if I was about to fall off or not. My stomach rolled and I heaved a little, bile biting at the back of my teeth. My fingers felt like burning hot knives were piercing through the tips of them, and suddenly something was cutting my skin where my hands overlapped the opposite forearm. It hurt, but I was too disoriented and terrified to loosen my grip. Was I dying? Was NIX finally killing me?

"No," I groaned, heaving again, spewing sourness as my body started into mini convulsions. I bit my lip until the iron taste of blood spilled onto my tongue. I realized I was probably having an adverse reaction to the Skills I'd just gained. If so, I only had to wait a few minutes and it would subside.

All I could do was hold on even tighter as both stars and waves of darkness burst across my eyes, my arms bled, and my body burned and shook.

But the symptoms didn't subside; they grew worse. My grip on the trunk slipped, and my body twisted around it, and I fell.

The wind brushed my skin like a caress as I plummeted, and I slammed into the branch below and bounced off. Then the next branch, and the next. I felt like a little metal ball in one of those old pinball machines. But somewhere on the way down, I started to understand the twisting of my body, the pushes and pulls that moved it. I caught a branch with my arms and almost ripped them out of the sockets trying to slow myself. The next branch I hit with both feet, but still slipped.

Then I slammed into the ground. Instinctively, I threw myself into a sideways roll, spreading the force of the impact over the surface of my body. A few bruising tumbles later and I came to a stop, four stories below where I'd started out, and still alive.

I crawled to my hands and knees, making a mental examination of my body. The wounds from the day before, though somewhat better, were all still there, but the pain, shaking, and sensory disorientation were gone. A few cuts, definitely some bruises. But nothing serious compared to what I'd been through lately. Except that below my face, pressed into the weak grass, short, bloody claws tipped my fingers.

I rose to my feet and held my hands in front of me, curling and uncurling my fingers. Everything was strangely clear and light, as if the sun had gotten brighter. I looked around to make sure I hadn't been transferred to a Trial without realizing it, but I was still in the building's communal backyard, unexceptional except for me, the girl who'd just fallen four stories out a window and landed on her feet.

My forearms bled from puncture wounds, no doubt caused by the claws when I was clinging onto the branch for dear life. I spit red and tried to wipe the blood from my ravaged lip. I was shaking, tired, and feeling half-drunk. I took a few deep breaths to steady myself and shut out the outside world. "Display Characteristic Skills," I choked out.

CHARACTERISTIC SKILLS
TUMBLING FEATHER (KINETIC CLASS): INCREASES GRACE AND AGILITY. IMPROVES SENSE OF BALANCE AND MOTION. SKILL EFFECTS WILL EXPAND AND STRENGTHEN WITH PLAYER GROWTH.

SPIRIT OF THE HUNTRESS (SPIRIT CLASS): INCREASES GRACE, AGILITY, PERCEPTION, FOCUS, PHYSIQUE, AND STAMINA. NAILS EXTEND AND SHARPEN ON COMMAND. INCREASES CHANCE TO LAND ON FEET AFTER A FALL. AGGRESSIVE TENDENCIES INCREASE. SKILL EFFECTS WILL EXPAND AND STRENGTHEN WITH PLAYER GROWTH.

I SWALLOWED. "OH. MY. GOD." This type of thing was something I hadn't even imagined. The bonuses were amazing. "Bunny! What just happened? This Skill, it's—I've—" I searched for words, hitching.

—Hey. Looks like you've got a couple Characteristic Skills. And one is

quite good. The percentage of Spirit Class Skills is very low, from what I understand.—
-Bunny-

A few moments passed while I took it all in, and then a slow smile spread across my face. "Lucky me."

I slunk back into my house and hid out in my room, stashing the empty Characteristic token shells in a side pocket of my pack. Somewhere along the way my nails returned to normal, which I was grateful for. I decided to skip school and stayed in my room trying to make the claws come out again.

Zed helped to cover for me again with my mom, though not without some frustration when he saw the new cuts on my forearms. I felt guilty for causing him so much worry, but I couldn't tell him the truth. Even if I did, it would do nothing but cause him more stress.

I fell asleep at some point, with the sun shining on me through my open window, but woke when a shadow passed in front of the light, darkening my closed eyelids. Something poked my shoulder.

I jumped and shot straight up, attacking.

By the time I registered that little China was the one standing in front of me, I had both of her thin arms squeezed in my hands, extended claws pressing into her soft skin, my lips pulled back from my teeth in silent menace.

Her eyes and mouth gaped open, surprised and speechless.

I relaxed my grip on her and sat back onto the bed. "Sorry, China. You surprised me."

"Yeah, apparently." She rubbed her arms where I'd grabbed them. "You weren't at school today, what happened?" Her eyes caught on the cuts and bruises that covered my exposed skin. "Are you okay?"

I frowned and nodded. "Yeah. But why are you here?" I pushed my hair back from my face as if scraping the cobwebs from my mind. "How did you know I wasn't at school?"

"I go to Jefferson High, Eve. Didn't you know?"

I looked her up and down. She didn't look old enough to be a high school student.

She must have seen the doubt on my face, because she said, "I do!" and punctuated her words with an emphatic stomp of her small foot. "Why does everybody think I look like a little kid?" She crossed her arms.

I chuckled. "Well, maybe you would be more convincing as a high school student if you didn't stomp your foot like a little girl."

She opened her mouth, closed it, looked down at the offending foot, and uncrossed her arms. "Well, I'm a freshman."

I resisted the urge to continue teasing her, instead saying, "I didn't know you went to Jefferson."

"Well, I do. But that's not the point. What happened to you? You look like you just had a Trial, or got hit by a train, but there shouldn't be any Trials for another six days or so, except for people with a Characteristic…" She trailed off. "Did you just have your Characteristic Trial?"

I paused, then nodded. "Yeah."

"Oh. I thought those normally happened somewhere in the first few weeks. I assumed you'd already had yours."

That's because I wanted her to think I was more experienced, so she'd trust me more and accept my usefulness. But not too experienced, so she wouldn't think it was weird when I pumped her for information. I shrugged and grinned. "Well, I'm relatively new. But I got some good Skills, apparently. Just haven't quite figured out how to use them yet."

She sat down in my chair, grinning. "What did you get? I might be able to help."

"Something called Tumbling Feather, and Spirit of the Huntress. Spirit of the Huntress is the one I'm more focused on. It gives me these claws." I held up my hands to show her, but my fingertips had already gone back to normal. "Well, I don't know how to make them come out. Seems to just happen involuntarily."

"Like when you're scared or angry?"

"Yeah. How'd you know?"

"Because they came out when I startled you just now. Good thing you just grabbed me and didn't slice. Why don't you try and step back into that same emotion again?"

I took a deep breath and searched for the feeling again. Something like anger, but more confident. My fingertips itched, and I looked down to see the short claws poking out once again. I flexed my fingers and felt the longing to assert my superiority over something, someone.

China stared at me in awe, and I felt a heady sense of pleasure at her open acknowledgment of my power.

I willed my fast-pumping heart to calm down, and the exhilarating feeling slipped away, along with the claws. "Damn. That was crazy." I let out a shuddering breath. "Aggression is one of the side effects. Maybe not the best idea for me to do that with you around right now."

After a moment of incomprehension, her eyes widened and she leaned backward. "Oh. Yeah. Good thinking. Umm…so how was the Trial?"

I stared down at my now normal hands. "I'd rather not talk about it."

She frowned and shook her head at her lap. "Of course. That was stupid. Sorry."

I shrugged. "No big deal. But what about you? Your Skill, I mean? Will you show me?"

She hesitated for a second before moving to my still-open window. "I can speak to animals."

I almost snorted, thinking she was joking, until I saw the bird from earlier fly to the edge of the sill and hop onto her finger, cheeping curiously.

"He says you jumped out of the tree earlier." She lifted wide eyes to me.

I coughed behind a fist and looked away. "Uh…well, that's impressive, I'll admit. But you said there'd be another Trial in six days?" I asked, changing the subject.

"Yeah." The bird flew away. "The normal ones happen every ten days or so. I heard that it used to be longer, before, but then it just suddenly changed. Who knows? It might change again someday, but for now you can pretty much count on ten days in between."

"So if we know we've got six days, we should start to prepare. There are some things I think would be useful for the Trials. I'd also like to spend some time with you practicing our Skills and working out strategies for different scenarios."

"If we're lucky enough to get the same Trial," she muttered.

"What?"

She looked up, startled. "Oh. It's just that the Trial you enter is somewhat randomized. Unless you form a recognized team, from what I understand it's just luck if you get put with the same people. Being close together when the Boneshaker starts helps, but it's no guarantee."

"Well, how do you form a recognized team? Bunny?"

When he acknowledged me with a pop-up screen, I repeated my question.

—You have to have more than two people.—
-Bunny-

"How many?"

—Four or more. One leader, three or more followers for a team, which is the first level of command.—
-Bunny-

My mind was racing. "And once I've got them, what then? Just tell you we're a team?"

—Yes, basically. At that point you'll be grouped together for Trials. Teamwork is a recognized, important part of the Game, and being part of a group gives certain extra rewards.—
-Bunny-

"Four." I grinned. "That's not so hard."

Chapter 12

I must not fear. Fear is the mind-killer. Fear is the little-death that brings total obliteration. I will face my fear. I will permit it to pass over me and through me. And when it has gone past I will turn the inner eye to see its path. Where the fear has gone there will be nothing. Only I will remain.
— Frank Herbert

I SPENT the next six days planning and preparing for a Trial. My link was broken, and my mom refused to get me a new one, so I met in person with China to discuss her previous Trial experience. From her, I gained knowledge of the different types of Trials, and some insight into Skills and the effects of the various Attributes.

I continued to train my body, level up, and put Seeds into Intelligence and Mental Acuity. Being able to think quickly in a tight spot might allow me to avoid situations where I *needed* brute strength or speed. Plus, the brain was much harder for me to spontaneously level up with training than my physical Attributes were.

I also practiced my new Skill, sheathing and unsheathing my claws until they obeyed more reliably.

Zed continued to keep my secret. Although he reluctantly stopped asking me to confide in him, he still watched me suspiciously.

On the day of the Trial, I was woken from a dead sleep by the Boneshaker, letting out a choking gasp like I'd been drowning and just broken the surface of the water. I clenched my thin summer blanket so hard I felt the bones in my hands creak like the hinges of a rusty door.

After a few seconds of panic, I scrambled out of bed, already dressed in cargo pants, a long sleeve shirt, and a jacket—the closest I could come to military-type gear. Underneath it all I had the two-banded, transforming vest armor that I'd taken off the skeleton during my Characteristic Trial.

Quickly starting a recording with a small mirror I'd brought to my room, I grabbed the small backpack I'd prepared and slung it on. I stood there in the dark, trembling as I waited to be taken into the Trial by that dizzying wave.

The song filled me and burst outward.

I was in a city. The buildings were taller, twisting and flowing and more beautiful than any I'd seen before, and overgrown with tenacious greenery. Only the occasionally boring rectangle disrupted the organic shapes, unlike the city where I'd come from.

The little map popped up, and I followed its directions to a big, squat building. Light peeked out through its windows, making it stand out. The only other light was that of the stars and the...*two* moons? I stared up at the sky for a few seconds, trying to figure out what the heck I was seeing.

I rubbed my eyes to make sure I wasn't seeing double, even though the two orbs were different sizes and had different markings on their surfaces. My brain simply didn't want to accept what it was seeing, unable to believe the two moons could be real.

Then the side of the building opened as a piece of the wall slid upward. I jumped in surprise, but then saw other Players and the floating cube waiting inside. Steeling myself, I joined them.

Players milled about, but I didn't have much time to observe them, because one of the pieces of wall slid upwards, and a large mouse walked into the room. It was four feet tall even walking with all paws on the ground, and probably seven or eight standing on its hind legs. A spiked ball that looked like it could do serious damage tipped the end of its tail. The creature wore a military hat and jacket with colorful stripes and medals decorating the collar and chest.

The mouse—or maybe it was a rat, I wasn't sure—walked silently across the room, sniffing the air and inspecting us Players, all of whom had gone silent. Someone whimpered.

It sat up on its haunches to address us. "Time is up. Those who are not here will be summarily executed." The lights seemed harsh and bright under the weight of its presence. It twitched its whiskers, and another door slid up in the side of the wall, releasing an orderly row of long-limbed creatures dressed in soldier-like uniforms. Their arms and legs seemed abnormally elongated, but still corded with wiry muscle. Black goggles hid their eyes, and their noses were long and wide-nostriled. Something about their pale skin and twitching noses reminded me of rodents.

"I am the General." The rat's voice was loud, rebounding jarringly off the bare walls. "For every two of you, there is one soldier. Once you leave this building, you are effectively fugitives, and they will be hunting you. You will escape to one of the extraction points."

A mini-map popped up in front of me, and everyone else, too, I assumed. It showed a 3-D model of the organically designed city, with blinking yellow dots marking the extraction points. An arrow showed where I was, right at the center of the map. I played with the model, using hand movements to turn the view and zoom in and out as the giant mouse continued to speak.

"If you are able to escape from enemy territory to the extraction point without being captured, you survive, and you win. If you are caught, you lose. Along the way, there are a few 'concerned citizens' of this wonderful city." It grimaced. "They will give away your location to your pursuers if they notice you, so beware. You will be given a small window of opportunity to leave the starting point. Exactly three minutes will pass before my soldiers are deployed." It gestured with his tail to the creatures standing tall and silent behind it. "Are there any questions?"

I bit the inside of my cheek until blood flowed, then wetted a finger with the blood and rubbed it onto the center spot of the armor bands hidden beneath my shirt. Right over my sternum, they fit together with a small opening for their fuel. After accepting the blood, the armor unfolded quietly beneath my clothes, secretly protecting me. I was as ready as I could get.

"What happens if the soldiers catch us…but we kill them?" a familiar voice called out lazily.

My head snapped around. It was the girl from my first Trial, the gorgeous one who'd caught Mr. Wolf and ended the game of terror.

The General's tail swished dangerously as it eyed the girl. "My soldiers are authorized to use deadly force to ensure fugitives do not escape. You are free to do the same to ensure the opposite." He seemed impatient.

"There will be no more questions. When the doors go up, you all have thirty seconds to leave this safe point. Then the countdown will start." And at that, pieces of the walls all around us opened to the darkness.

I watched as the crowd hurriedly disbursed through the various exits. The Spanish girl passed me on her way out but didn't spare me a glance. I would have called out or followed her, but I needed to stay and make sure no kids had been put into the Trial again. I saw a few confused and scared people, but they weren't children, and I knew I didn't have the power to expend protecting them. And since China didn't seem to be in the Trial either, I left the safe point alone.

Outside, most of the Players dispersed through the unlit streets, sprinting frantically to gain distance from their pursuers, while a few huddled in groups, discussing plans in quiet murmurs.

Behind me, the wall slid shut and a three-minute timer popped up. The seconds ticked away at a seemingly impossible speed, pushing a sense of urgency on me.

I looked at the city map again, trying to figure out the smartest move. My brain spun but could only come up with best guesses. I didn't have enough to go on. The seconds flashed away. I took a deep breath and ignored the timer. If I didn't have enough information, that meant I needed to gather more.

Instead of running away, I went to a nearby building with windows that overlooked the starting point. It didn't have any doors, and I supposed whatever pieces of the wall would have slid open for me were powered off, but one of the windows was broken.

I leaned my back against the wall and jabbed my elbow at the remaining chunks of glass, then crawled through the cleared opening.

My eyes adjusted to the lack of moonlight quickly, and I saw something had caused part of the ceiling to collapse. I peeked up into the hole, which went through every floor of the tall building, all the way through to the roof and into the night sky. A huge chain with links I could fit my arm through hung down from somewhere above. I resisted the urge to tug on it. The ground below the opening was cracked and crushed in a circular crater. Whatever caused that, I wanted to stay far away from.

I climbed up the staircase and crouched in front of an intact window. The remaining Players below ran off as the last few seconds ticked away, and the doors of the starting building slid up, spilling light and rat-men soldiers out into the street.

Their silhouettes moved into the darkness silently. Inhuman heads tilted and noses twitched, scenting the air. A few bent to the ground and sniffed, then pointed in the same direction many of the Players had run. With a few whistling sounds among themselves, they scattered, following scent trails.

I kept my eyes on the streets below and pulled up my map again, mentally marking the directions the rat-men had taken. I breathed shallowly, huddling in the dark and hoping they wouldn't smell me.

A different silhouette against one of the silver moons drew my attention. Someone stood atop the building adjacent to mine. I squinted and focused, able to distinguish the features of the Spanish girl. I didn't know her name yet, but I wanted her for my team.

She crouched and sprang off the edge of the roof toward my building. As she moved through the air, a sick feeling built in my chest. I pushed, much too slowly, away from the wall toward the hole piercing the building.

Sure enough, a muffled shout of surprise resounded down the hole, and then a few frantic scrabbles, like she had tried to grab onto something. She was falling, and I couldn't move fast enough to catch her.

My hand was outstretched, too far away from the tunnel hollowing the building's core. Not that I would have been strong enough to catch her anyway. She plummeted through the air in front of me, her hand outstretched as well, like she was reaching for me.

Our eyes met for a second, the image of her splattered on the broken stone of the ground floor already in my head. It would happen because I was too weak to save her.

Then she grabbed the huge metal chain with her outstretched hand.

I reached the edge of the hole just in time to see her body slam hard into the crater below. But, as she'd slowed her descent with the chain, the impact wasn't hard enough to kill her.

Above, I heard a cracking sound, and a few pebbles fell past my head. I looked upward just in time to see the huge ball at the end of that chain roll through the hole in the roof, a perfect fit. It started to hurtle down through the opening that it had obviously created in the first place, blocking out the light from the sky. As it fell, the chain below piled up on top of itself like a messy soft-serve ice cream cone.

"Move!" I screamed.

She was just starting to look up at her impending doom, too late to save herself, when something smashed into her from the side.

I jerked my head out of the tunnel less than a second before the huge ball smashed down, loud and hard enough it shook the whole building. "Crap. Someone definitely heard that," I said.

I listened for movement below, wondering whether I should go down or not. Whatever had knocked the girl out of the way might be dangerous. And the rat-men would be coming back soon, too. Then I realized what I was doing and clenched my fists. Not again.

I rushed back down the stairs, finding the girl and someone else lying in a tangle of limbs a few feet away from the metal ball. I dropped hard to my knees on the dusty stone beside them. "Are you okay?"

The other one, a boy, was panting hard.

She was still, and I smelled blood.

I patted her cheek. "Are you okay?"

She groaned and her long, thick eyelashes fluttered open. Dark eyes stared at me blankly, and she stiffened. She looked at the boy next to her and jerked back, flailing frantically in an effort to disentangle their limbs and get away.

He groaned in pain as she pushed at his body, and I had to wrap my arms around her shoulders and drag her back to protect him from her panicked blows.

She clung to me in a vice-like grip, burying her face in my stomach.

I hesitated for a moment, and then patted her head. "It's okay. You're fine."

She started to shake and let out strange noises, and I realized with discomfort that she might be crying. She'd seemed a much stronger type than that. But when she drew her head back, I realized she was laughing. It wasn't a beautiful laugh to match her looks, but it made me smile and want to laugh with her.

"*Mierda*, I thought I was gonna die," she said.

"But you didn't," I said. I looked to the boy lying on the ground and clutching his arm, dark curly hair that was slightly too long hanging into his face. "But we need to move. The rat-men are probably already on their way. Both of you, come on."

She grew serious and stood up, but weaved dizzily on her feet, and I had to grab her arm to keep her from falling. She pursed her lips apologetically. "Hit my head. Ground keeps tilting under me."

"My arm's broken," the guy said through clenched teeth, "and my leg's not feeling great either. I'm bleeding pretty bad. You guys better move soon, cause they're going to smell the blood."

The scent was everywhere, and I knew if I smelled it, the rat-men would, too. “Crap. Okay, we can’t travel, but at the least we need to move a bit. Somewhere less visible.” I scanned the room and pointed to a corner blocked off by a half-wall only a few feet high. “There.”

I threw the girl’s arm over my shoulder and walked her to the corner.

As soon as she sat down, she struggled to rise again. “I don’t hide. I’ll fight ‘em if they come.”

“Okay.” I didn’t want to waste time arguing. Plus, even with a possible concussion, she would likely prove herself more useful than me in a fight. “For now, just wait. They’re not here yet.”

I went back for the boy and knelt beside him. “Can you move? I’ll help. If we can just get you to the corner…” I trailed off, not wanting to give him empty assurances that ‘things would be fine.’

His left arm was badly broken. The bone punctured jaggedly through the skin of his forearm, and the wound had already pumped a puddle of blood onto the floor. He was squeezing just below the elbow with his other hand to strangle off the blood flow but not doing a great job.

“Shit.” The breath left my lungs in a whoosh.

He was gritting his teeth and panting in pain, but still found the will to roll his eyes at me, as if to say, “No shit, Sherlock. I’m screwed.” What he said aloud was, “Just leave.”

“No thanks, I’d rather stay.” I reached into one of the pockets of my pants and pulled out a roll of medical gauze and unwound a long strip. I looped it around his bicep as tight as I could and rolled it into a tube that clung even tighter, helping to cut off the blood flow. Then I leaned over him and wrapped my arms around his torso. Being careful to avoid his arm, I helped him to his feet, and we hobbled to the corner together.

I went to the nearest window and peeked out. Two rat-men were already slinking up to the building, their noses twitching as they whistled softly at each other.

I felt warmth at my back, and the girl whispered in my ear. “They coming?”

I nodded. “If they come in, I’ll take the first, and you get the partner before it can call for help.” My whisper sounded barely louder than the rush of blood in my veins, but I knew she heard me.

A rat-man’s ears shifted slightly, and I prayed that it hadn’t heard me, too. But perhaps it hadn’t, because the two moved to the window I’d crawled through, their noses twitching furiously, and then one crawled through, headfirst and weasel-like.

Or maybe they were just confident in their ability to take us in a fight.

My claws slid out and my vision sharpened, and I held in a sigh of relief that my Skill hadn't failed me.

The girl's eyes met mine for a moment as the rat-man stood up and its partner moved to follow it. We attacked at the same moment.

I punched at the first soldier's neck, hoping to stop it from calling out. My fist caught, but not firmly enough to cause real damage, and it jerked back and automatically swung a fist at me. There was a dark grin on its face that suggested perhaps they *had* known where we were.

I moved back, but not fast enough, and it struck me on the shoulder. The pain made anger flow through me, instead of the fear I'd been expecting, and I moved back in aggressively. I jumped and kicked at its knees, and we went down.

It was a better fighter, and stronger than me, too. But it didn't have a Skill that gave it claws and made it want to rip me open for daring to oppose it.

I did.

I clawed at its face and throat, and when it moved to protect its head, I went for the belly and groin. When it let down its guard to go on the offensive, I grabbed the front of its throat. The claws let my fingers get a better grip, sinking into the flesh. I braced my other hand on its face for leverage and ripped away. Its throat opened, and blood guzzled out onto the stone below as it jerked spasmodically.

When the last bit of life was gone from the body, I stood up and looked for the girl.

She was leaning against the wall, grinning at me. Her opponent lay motionless with its hind end hanging out the window and blood dripping from its forehead where she'd smashed its face into the windowsill. "Took you long enough."

I was panting, the rush of triumph making my head tingle, which made it hard to concentrate. My claws slipped away. I looked back down to the body in front of me and stumbled back. "Oh, god." Unlike the monsters before, it was distinctly humanoid, long arms and legs splayed awkwardly in the puddle of dark, metallic-smelling blood.

She shook her head and pushed off the wall. "So you're one of the crazies, yeah? Pretty gruesome."

I shook my head, but what could I say to negate the thing I'd just done? The evidence was the mutilated carcass at my feet. "Not crazy. I just need practice controlling myself," I muttered.

She opened her mouth to reply, but I saw movement out of the corner of my eye and cut her off with a sharp hand motion.

Down the street, another rat-man stood still, looking suspiciously in our direction. The girl's opponent still lay with his hind end hanging out the window. If it noticed… It was much too far away for us to keep it from sounding an alarm and calling more of them down on us.

Someone screamed, far away and in the opposite direction. It turned its body toward the sound, and, with one last backward glance toward us, it slunk off, long limbs sliding around the darkness of the street corner.

We both let out silent sighs of relief, I jerked my head toward the boy, and we went back to him.

She held out a fingerless-gloved hand to me over his body. "I'm Jacqueline Santiago. Call me Jacky."

I gripped it firmly. "Eve Redding." The blood still on my hand clung to her as I pulled away. I looked down at the guy. "And you?"

"Me what?"

"Your name," I urged.

He scowled at me. "Adam."

I stared back at him, undeterred. "What were you doing? Why were you here, I mean?"

"I was watching them. NIX. Gathering information."

"What kind of information?"

"Any information," he said, staring at me mulishly, obviously unwilling to continue talking.

I understood his lack of trust. I also understood the import of his information gathering. "Knowledge is power," I agreed. And I was in the process of accumulating power. Plus, I'd seen him tackle Jacky out of the way. Humans couldn't move that fast, not without what I calculated must be a large number of Seeds. Meaning he had experience surviving the Game.

I dug around in my pack and pulled out the makeshift emergency kit I'd brought. I ripped the top off a foil kit and sprinkled blood-clotting powder over his wound. Next, I took my can of numbing spray and applied it generously over his entire forearm. "I'm not sure how well this will work on an injury this bad, but any relief is probably good in your situation."

He relaxed by a few degrees, so I knew it must have been helping.

I took an old skirt from the pack and ripped a strip from it. My claws came out with a second of concentration, and I used them to slice holes in the larger piece of fabric to wind the strip through. I held up the product of my efforts. "A sling. Hope it works okay." I'd packed the skirt for just such a need, along with many other things I wished I'd had in my last Trial.

He reached for it, but I brushed his hand out of the way. "I've got two hands free. I'll do it." As I leaned over and carefully slid the cloth around his broken arm, I noticed a stylistic, Celtic knot-like design snaking up and down his arms. I sat back on my heels and studied it. It was intricate and beautiful, delicate even. It ran from above his wrist to his bicep, the knot losing intricacy and finally disappearing as it rose. The inked skin was torn and scraped off around his wound.

"Your tattoo. Sorry, but I think it's ruined."

"I'll just redo it when everything's healed. It'll be good as new."

I stopped studying it and looked up at him. "You do that yourself?"

He was frowning at me. "Yes," he snapped. "Why are you doing this?"

I didn't pretend to misunderstand him. "Because I want to. You saved Jacky. Thank you for that."

"You know her?" He winced as he used his good arm to adjust the sling and stood up on one leg.

I shook my head. "No, not really. But I will. And I'll know you, too."

He raised a derisive eyebrow.

"I will. Don't think I'm doing this just to be nice. You'll owe me." I stared hard into his eyes, refusing to be the first to look away. He needed to know I was serious, that I meant what I said.

He looked down at his body. "Why did I do something so stupid? Basically guaranteed I'd lose the Trial," he grumbled before looking back to me. "I'll accept my debt to you, but only after you get me out alive. If you can."

"I will." I held out my hand.

After a pause, he shook it with his uninjured one.

"Do you have a weapon? Something to defend yourself with?"

He pulled something small from his pocket, and a familiar butterfly knife glinted in the darkness, bright to my sensitive eyes. "I've got a few skills besides fighting, too. If the situation demands, I'll show you something impressive."

I couldn't help the wolf-like grin that stretched across my face.

Chapter 13

I am your worst nightmare. And your wildest dream.
— Sonya Chloe

"SHARE MAP DISPLAY," I said. The three-dimensional model of our Trial arena popped up in front of me, and Adam's and Jacky's eyes focused on it as well. Sharing my displays was a little trick China had taught me.

"Okay, this is us." I pointed to the blue arrow in the center, in the middle of a rectangular building. "We'll be going here." I pointed to a blinking yellow dot on the top of a building only a few streets removed from our location.

"Why?" Adam frowned. "That's not the closest one, and it's all the way on the roof."

"We need to stay downwind of the rat-men as much as possible. Most of them went this way." I pointed in the direction I thought was east. "We want to keep them between us and the wind. As for the ones that went the other way, we'll just have to deal with them."

Jacky licked her finger and raised it to the air to catch the direction of the breeze that filtered through the broken windows of the building. "Why don't we just roof-jump? It'll be faster than goin' through the streets."

I mentally mapped the route we'd take for both options. "Yes. That's a good idea. We'd leave no scent trail on the ground, so finding us might be a bit more difficult. And the faster we can get out of here, the better our chance of survival." I looked to Adam. "Could you make a jump like that with your arm?"

He took a beanie from his pocket and shoved it onto his head with his good hand, flattening his hair in the process. "I'll have to, won't I?"

I hoped he could keep to that statement when the time came. "Okay. Let's go."

We moved up the stairs, Jacky taking the lead, seemingly to avoid Adam, while I stayed beside him to make sure he could keep up despite his injuries. Halfway up the third-floor staircase, she raised her hand, and we froze. I snuck up to her and saw what had caused her to stop.

A small plant-like creature with slowly wriggling limbs spread out across the steps above our head. One long stalk rose from its base, on top of which sat an eyeball like a snail's. "Concerned citizen?" I whispered.

She stepped forward like flowing water in the darkness. Her feet made no sound on the ground, and her movement seemed to stir no air. I thought it was a Skill.

The creature didn't have time to let out more than a gasping squeak once it noticed her presence.

Her hands shot out and wrapped around its neck, squeezing and twisting while she ground her boot into its body. The eyestalk snapped off, and the stump squirted some sort of fluid that smelled sweetly of antifreeze. The limbs at the base stopped wriggling, and the whole body seemed to deflate onto the ground like a popped balloon.

She looked at me, and I nodded.

We continued upward, Jacky taking the place of our scout again, until we reached the fifth floor.

Adam panted and leaned on the wall for every step, the pain of his injured leg wearing on him. I couldn't help but think that if he hadn't saved Jacky, he'd probably be well enough to survive all on his own. But I was glad for his recklessness, because otherwise she would have died, and I would never be able to gain her alliance.

In the middle of the fifth floor, the staircase abruptly disappeared, having collapsed for about six steps. Big steps, as always.

My heart sank in my chest. Going back down wasn't an option. But then I remembered the way Jacky had ended the first Trial.

I judged the distance of the gap. "Jacky. Could you jump that?"

She pursed her lips. "Yeah...probably. Maybe."

I nodded. "Okay. Give me a second." I rummaged in my bag and pulled out a coil of plastine rope.

They watched me as I tied the rope into a noose-like harness on both ends, pulling on my knots to test them. Thank god for the Internet, and my foresight in studying some survival channels during the last week. "Jacky, you're strong. I've seen your power. Could you lift one of us?"

She looked from me to the two-sided harness and nodded. "Yeah, I'm strong. And I can be lightweight, too. I dunno if I can make it, but I'll try."

"Brace yourself around the corner at the top of the stairs so our weight doesn't pull you off the edge," Adam said. "It doesn't matter how strong you are if you can't keep your body from sliding because you're too light."

She grinned and wrapped one slipknot around her stomach, throwing the other over her arm. She stepped back down the stairs, and, with a mutter that sounded like "fingers crossed," she lunged up the steps and sprang off the edge. She slammed into the side of the upper step, knocking her air out with an audible *oomph*, but she was able to scrabble the rest of the way up, gasping for breath but otherwise making it look easy. Hopping to her feet, she adjusted the rope around her waist, then flashed the victory sign, two fingers spread into a "V."

Adam stepped to the edge and reached out his good hand. "Lower down the other end." He wrapped it gingerly around his waist and she stepped backward to brace herself on the edge of the stairwell.

A piercing screech split through the air, like a siren made of knives.

We all flinched, and Jacky turned around and ripped off the eyestalk of the "concerned citizen" that had sounded the alarm. "Sorry. I didn't see it," she said.

Adam shook his head. "Just hurry and pull us up." He swung off the edge gently. Jacky slid for only a few inches before getting a good grip and pulling him up.

He sat panting afterward, his eyes closed against the pain while she took the tightened harness from around him like he was made of maggots.

I went next, my weight causing the harness to tighten around my torso with bruising strength. I moved upward and rolled over the edge coughing as Jacky pulled unstoppably on the rope. Her body didn't look strong or heavy enough to stand firm and lift one man-sized person, let alone *two*, but it was impossible to deny the facts. I crawled to my feet, pulled my slipknot over my head and handed it back to her. "Impressive.

Let's go. I'm sure they're on their way. Hopefully that little gap slows them down a bit." Unfortunately, I had a feeling it wouldn't.

We were all gasping for breath when we burst through the door to the rooftop. I shot a glance to my map to get our bearings and pointed to the roof of a nearby building. While we had been climbing, storm clouds had oozed across the sky. The wind whipped at me, threatening to push me off my feet.

I took a few breaths of the electrically charged air to regain some strength, stepped back, and ran to the edge of the roof. I leapt out into the empty space between buildings, feeling the extra weight of that place pulling me down.

I landed barely inches away from the deadly drop and rolled over before coming to my hands and knees. My claws were out, digging into the cold material of the building's roof. I stood and moved to the edge. The shadowy forms of rat-men rushed past a window halfway up the building we'd just ascended.

"They're coming!" I warned, hoping that fear would lighten our steps and bolster our recklessness.

Jacky came next, landing smoothly, and then tossed the harness back to Adam. He wrapped it around himself, took a few limping lunges, and jumped off. He didn't quite make it, but Jacky was already moving forward, taking up the slack in the line.

He smashed into the side of the building with a *thump*, letting out a muffled scream.

I crawled to the edge and grabbed the back of his hoodie and his good arm and helped to pull him up.

He rolled to his back, half across my lap, and lay there shuddering visibly. He'd bitten through his lip, and blood trickled down the side of his face. "Can I get some more numbing spray?"

I nodded and pulled off my backpack, fumbling around in it until I felt the can. I sprayed inside the makeshift sling, close to the skin. "Do you want some for your leg too?"

"No. Wouldn't do any good." He stood up, wavered on his feet for a second, and then started toward the far side of the roof. "This way next, right?"

This time the jump was easier, and he made it on his own.

But the next roof was slightly higher than our own, and I worried that even Jacky might not be able to clear the gap.

I had her wait to jump until I'd positioned myself with bent knees and cupped hands at the edge of the roof.

She moved to the far edge and came running at a full sprint, stepping right into my cupped hands and jumping as I pushed upward to give her a bit more lift.

She sprang away like she was flying, landed lightly atop the roof above, and then tossed the harness back to me.

I jumped, slammed into the wall on the end of the rope, and was dragged up the building's rough side to the top.

When I turned back to throw the harness to Adam, lightning shattered the sky in a burst of blinding light, highlighting the rat-men as they sprinted out onto the roof. Thunder rumbled, passing through the air like a physical force, and the wind was screaming, whistling in my ears so I had to shout to make myself heard.

"They're on the roof! Hurry!"

Jacky was already moving forward as Adam swung through the air, but the impact still jostled his whole body. His eyes rolled back in his head as his broken arm hit the wall, and he hung limp and still for a second before consciousness returned to him.

"Brace yourself with your feet and just walk up," I shouted.

He did, moving upward as Jacky moved forward.

I grabbed his good hand and gave him a boost over the edge.

The rat-men were standing on the edge of the roof of the first building, and as I looked, the first of them jumped across to the second building, landing easily. It turned to urge its fellows on. They would be on us soon.

I turned around and looked to the far side of our rooftop, where a long, oval-shaped pod stood on its end. I pulled up my mini-map and zoomed in as we hurried over to it. Sure enough, it was the extraction point. The front had an indentation like a shrunken handle, so I grabbed it and pulled. It popped open with the sound of hissing hydraulics.

I waited for a moment, but nothing happened.

"We have to get in," Adam said. "This type of teleportation pod will take us one by one. I've seen them before."

Jacky looked to the rat-men and then to Adam. "You go first."

He frowned, but she pursed her lips. "You're useless in a fight, *chico*. I don't wanna have to protect you *and* me, so you better get safe. Plus, I owe you one."

He stepped in with a single frustrated nod and sealed the door, stood there for a few moments, and then looked around in confusion and opened it again. "It's not working. It's not powering up."

"What?" Jacky ground out.

"It's broken," he snapped. "Like I said."

I turned to the rat-men. They would arrive in less than a minute at the rate they were going. "Shit." I pulled up my map to search for another extraction pod. There was one a few streets away, but on the ground, and the roof we stood on had no door, no way to move down through the building. Except for the one we'd just come from, all the buildings around were either too high to jump to or in a weird shape that we'd just slide right off of. There was no way we were going to jump all the way to the ground, and climbing down wasn't possible either. "Shit," I said again.

We had only one option. "Okay. We're going to fight. There are more of them, but being on the high ground gives us an advantage. We'll kill them all, and then go find a working extraction point."

Despite my words, I doubted we'd be leaving the Trial alive.

When I turned back to the others, Adam was kneeling awkwardly at the back of the pod. He peeked around it. "One of the power sources has corroded. The other one's a bit rusted, but I think it still works. I might be able to fix the pod, if I could get a charge in it."

I looked to the rat-men. Less than thirty seconds. I slung off my pack and tossed it to Adam. "There's another power cartridge in the side pocket. I don't know if it'll work, but I got it from a transport pod the last time I was in-Trial. I don't think it has any power."

He grabbed the pack, looking at me with surprise and a kind of consideration that bordered on respect. "I'll show you what I can do besides fighting, if you can keep them off me." He grinned with a sort of cockiness that made me smile back.

"It better be impressive," I said before turning to the rat-men.

I watched the pack run across the roof below and felt a strange exultation melt through me. I would not die here today. I would destroy them. My claws tingled out and my senses sharpened and focused on them. I could hear their panting breaths and almost smell their eagerness.

Meeting Jacky's eyes, I bared my teeth in an expression that was half smile, half animalistic snarl. "Are you ready?"

She cracked her knuckles with more pops than should have been possible with ten fingers and smirked. "Are you?"

I didn't answer, instead readying myself for the oncoming enemies.

The first rat-man reached the edge of the roof and sprang at me. I lifted one knee to my chest and kicked outward and down, catching it at the base of the throat and sending it plummeting into the chasm of darkness between the buildings. Its hands reached toward the heavens as it fell to its death.

I raised my head and sucked in a breath of energy-charged air as the next three came. I spun and clawed across the face of one as it reached me, and Jacky pummeled two with flurries of heavy blows and kicks that obviously stemmed from extensive training.

I aimed a kick to the knee of my opponent. He dodged and I thought for a minute that I would fall, off balance, but something instinctual kicked in, and I slid to my hands and knees and swung a leg to take him off his feet. Then I thrust my hand at his throat, fingers straight, and cut into it, still crouching. I curled my fingers before ripping them out, and then drug him by his ears and dropped him off the edge.

More of them had already jumped across the gap, and I turned to fight without thinking.

As I fought, I caught a glimpse of Jacky, far outnumbered and overwhelmed. Two grabbed her from behind while another three attacked her from the front. She snapped her head back and aimed a kick at their knees, but they were undeterred. They moved to the edge and swung her much smaller body out over the deep chasm between buildings.

I moved before I realized what I was doing, springing like an animal onto the back of the rat-man leading their effort to pitch Jacky off the roof. I clawed into the front of its throat and sliced my hands backward, opening its jugular veins to the world. "She's mine," I said. Jacky had the type of fighting power that would significantly increase my chances at living through both this Trial and those that followed. "I won't let you take her."

It dropped to its knees and loosened its grip on Jacky, dropping her over the edge.

I pulled myself atop its shoulders and lunged for her. My hand barely caught her wrist, and my claws dug into her. But I'd caught her. I drug her up as the rat-men punched and kicked at my unprotected, kneeling body while the rat-man under me jerked and bled out like a slaughtered animal.

My armored vest spread some of the impact of their blows but could only do so much. A blow to the back of my skull rattled my balance and made the darkness seep in around the edges of my vision.

But Jacky had already regained her footing. With a scream, she attacked with a new savageness born from the fear of her near-death. She held them off while I regained my feet, both of us now in the disadvantageous position of being surrounded on the edge of the roof and cut off from Adam.

Light exploded on the other side of the roof, knocking us all off our feet. My ears rang as I crawled to my hands and knees, my blinded eyes streaming tears from the sudden brightness.

I heard faint shouting, and then Adam's voice filtered through the ringing. "Working! Hurry…not much…"

I stood on shaking legs and blinked till I could see the pod, lit up and powered on, Adam leaning on it with a charred rat-man at his feet. He waved to me urgently, still shouting, then bent over at the waist and hung onto the pod as if to keep himself from collapsing.

Jacky was still lying on her back with her eyes closed. I fumbled over to her, stepping on the still-disoriented bodies of our enemies.

She didn't move when I smacked her face and yelled at her to get up, and then I saw the blood seeping from the side of her head. She must have smashed it into the ground for the second time that evening when the blast hit.

"Crap," I muttered, unable to hear myself over the ringing still echoing through my skull. I grabbed her by the collar of her shirt and stepped forward, pulling until her smaller body started to slide. I dragged her slowly across the roof, right over the rat-men when necessary, until we reached the pod. The ringing and disorientation had already decreased, and I could hear the rat-men rising to their feet behind me.

I shoved Jacky's unconscious body into the pod and shut the door on her. The pod started to vibrate and hum, and then it let out a familiar shockwave, and she was gone.

I turned back to the group of rat-men, already stumbling toward us. "Hurry and get in, Adam."

He was as tense as a tightly strung guitar wire as he watched them, but he shook his head. "I have to be here to charge it again. Get in. I'll be right behind you."

I hesitated, and he turned on me. "Go! You're wasting our time."

I stepped in and closed the door.

He reached upward with his good hand, the other resting on the power cartridges, and another explosion of light connected the ground and sky as he called down the lightning.

I had a last glimpse of him before the wave of energy filled my bones and took me away. A half-blind image of his back, his silhouette standing against the low-hanging moons while the rat-men encircled him menacingly.

I FOUND myself back at the starting building, the familiar dizziness and nausea making the room spin, along with the effects of being less than five feet away from a lightning strike only moments before. My claws had slipped away sometime without me realizing it, but my hands were still covered in layers of dried and drying blood, sticky and uncomfortable. I lay on the ground for a few moments, and then crawled over to Jacky's body to check her head wound. She lay motionless except for the slight rise and fall of her chest as she breathed.

"At least she's alive," I sighed. A quick glance around showed me that only a few others had made it back so far. The General was also there, his small eyes staring around at the Players, whiskers twitching, expression entirely unreadable.

I waited for Adam, my heart sinking with every passing moment. It had been too long. If he were going to return, he would have done so already. The rat-men must have gotten to him. With his arm like that, there was no way he could have fought them all off.

But in the space between one moment and the next, Adam appeared in a shockwave. His beanie was gone, and his hair floated around his head with static electricity. Little sparks jumped around him, and I could literally smell the charge suffusing his skin.

Our eyes caught, and he smirked again. "Told you I'd do something impressive." Despite his words, his muscles were rebelling in mini spasmodic tremors, and he smelled burnt.

I nodded, nothing clever coming to my weary brain. "Glad you made it." I looked him over. "You left my pack?"

He opened his mouth and then closed it again. "Uh, yeah. Sorry. I hope there wasn't anything important in there."

"It's fine." I'd gladly pay the contents of my pack in exchange for his life.

He slipped the energy cartridge into his pocket with a weary nod, then we sat next to Jacky's prone form and waited.

No other Players returned, and after a few minutes the General boomed out, "Eleven survivors. That is everyone. Quite a surprising number this time."

"Surprisingly high or surprisingly low?" I murmured.

The floating cube buzzed, rolling out the same words I'd seen before.

CONGRATULATIONS ON SURVIVING THE TRIAL. THERE ARE NO BESTOWALS.

"No bestowals? That's…" Jacky said weakly, then cursed in Spanish. She sat up, grinning at my surprise. "I'm pretty damn tough. A little knock on the head isn't gonna put me down."

DO YOU WISH TO RETURN FROM THE TRIAL?
YES / NO

She turned to Adam. "Consider my debt to you paid. You saved me, and I helped get you through."

He snorted. "We saved you again after you passed out. How do you think you got back?"

She scowled. "You're the one who knocked me out in the first place, no? Twice, I believe. I don't owe you nothing."

"Knocked you out? If I hadn't been there—"

I put my hand up to stop their bickering. "Guys. Each of us saved the others out there. None of us would have survived if we hadn't all been there. We made a great team." I smiled at them both in what I hoped was a winning kind of way.

Jacky grinned back. "We kicked their asses, crazy Eve."

But Adam obviously noticed the deeper intention beneath my words. His eyes narrowed, and he stayed silent.

"Will you two meet me in the real world? Tomorrow?" I asked.

"Why?" he asked.

"I've got something I want to talk about, a proposition I think you'll want to hear. Just come and listen. I'm not going to force you to do anything, but if we're talking about who owes who…maybe you'll remember a little note in your locker?" I knew it was him from the combination of name and the twin to his butterfly knife, which I had hidden in my closet.

His eyes widened. "That was *you*? You thief! You stole my—"

"I *saved* your ass," I snapped. "They were about to do a locker check on you."

That gave him pause. "Well, do you still have it?"

I nodded. "I do. If you come tomorrow, I'll bring it for you."

"How do I know I can trust you?"

"Well, it's obvious, isn't it? You *don't* know that. But come anyway. You won't regret it."

He thought for a while, and then said, "Where?"

"I'll message you the information. Give me your contact info."

He did, reluctantly, and then I turned to Jacky. She grinned like the Cheshire cat and said, "Give me *your* contact info. I'll call you in the morning, and you can tell me the meeting place then."

I laughed, letting some of my tension out. It was unavoidable, and when Jacky's infectious snorting joined me, even Adam couldn't hold back. I stood up and walked to the cube. "I'll see you guys tomorrow."

My bones vibrated as the cube returned me to my room, back in the dark, and alone.

MY LEGS TREMBLED as my body realized that the danger was gone. A window popped up, telling me I'd gained three levels. The Seeds appeared from the ether, and I tucked them into the back of my bedside drawer. I'd decide what to do with them later.

"More importantly…" I murmured, picking up the small mirror I'd set to recording. I hit 'stop,' and then 'replay' in fast forward to see what had gone on in my room for the hour or two I'd been absent.

I saw my nervous self from before the Trial disappear like the product of special effects, and then a few minutes of empty, silent room, and then I was back again, stumbling, dirty, torn, and tired, and full of relief. "What? That can't be right," I muttered.

I rewound it to the beginning and played through again. Only fourteen minutes had passed in the recording, but I knew the Trial had lasted for at least an hour. "Maybe it's broken."

I checked the time on my clock. Less than one hour had passed since I left for the Trial, and I'd already been back for half of that time.

I showered and laid down to try and sleep, my mind spinning with the possible implications of my discovery.

Chapter 14

Our torments also may in length of time
Become our Elements.
— John Milton

"YOU WANT US TO DO WHAT?" Adam snorted incredulously.

"Join me," I said again, looking at the four others I'd called together to China's backyard after school. Adam, Jacky, Sam, and of course China herself. Her parents had gone to her grandparents' house, so no one would be able to observe us.

"I want to create a team that works together to survive the Trials and the Game. People that we enter every Trial with, who can have each other's backs in the Trial, and in the real world with the ones behind it. We'll be organized. Prepared. It would increase our chances of survival," I said.

"How do we know we can trust any of these people?" Adam looked at the others. "I don't know them. Why should I trust them to have my back, with my life? How do I know I can trust you? This could be a trap."

I resisted the urge to grind my teeth. I'd known he'd be difficult, but I'd still asked him to meet, and more than ever I wanted him for my team.

Before I could say anything, China spoke up. "We're not tricking you.

What would we gain from that anyway? We want to team up, not make enemies."

"Even if that's true, what would I gain from allying with you? I've been playing for months, and I've gotten by just fine on my own. It just creates more risk for me if I've got to look after someone else along with keeping myself alive."

I settled back in my seat at one of the benches in China's backyard garden. "That may have been true in the past, Adam. But you're vulnerable right now." I looked pointedly at his arm. "You wouldn't have made it out of that last Trial if not for Jacky and me."

He opened his mouth to respond bitingly, but I held up a hand and continued. "And we wouldn't have made it without you, either. That's exactly my point. We all gain if everyone in the group looks out for the best interest of everyone else. You can trust us because you know that by looking out for you, we're really just looking out for ourselves. A symbiotic relationship." I stared into his eyes, knowing that my honesty would be more compelling to him than any reassurance of my good nature and morality.

Any such reassurance would be a lie anyway. My own survival was my top priority. I didn't feel guilty for that; it was just biology. I smiled after I judged our silence had gone on long enough. "Plus, I know you understand the importance of gathering more information about our…situation. I have some things I'd like to share with you, that I think you'll find valuable."

He stayed silent, scrutinizing me with narrowed eyes.

I turned to the others to allow him time to decide. I didn't know how to persuade him further. "China, I know you're in. What about you, Jacky?"

She leaned back on her perch atop the back of a bench and shrugged. "That all sounds good to me. I know already you make a good teammate. I'll go with you, for now. But"—she leaned forward, suddenly serious—"I won't be confined. I will not be trapped in this. I will leave when I want. I will follow what orders I want. I will not be forced."

I nodded. "That is as it should be. If you will listen to my reasoning and consider it, that is all I ask. The Game is more than enough enslavement for all of us, I think."

She grinned and spat on the ground. "Screw the Game."

China repeated it, the vehemence extra shocking coming from her child-like frame and angelic face.

Adam laughed, the barrier he'd been holding around himself seeming to fall away. "Screw the Game," he said with relish. "I guess I'm in."

I turned to Sam, who'd stayed noticeably silent until then. "Sam, what about you?"

He smiled but shook his head. "I don't think being part of a team is for me, sorry. I'll be going." He turned to leave.

"Wait, Sam," I called out. "Why don't you want to work with a team?"

He looked at the ground for a second, and then back to me, but I caught the white-knuckled fist he made and then quickly released. It wasn't anger. He had the type of skin tone that blushed at a moment's notice, and he would have flushed with anger. Instead, he was pale beneath his tan. "I don't work well with others. Honestly. I'm better off alone."

What secret was he hiding? "I don't expect you to be best friends with any of us. Just to work together so that we can all live."

He frowned. "That's the problem. I'm not the one you want to have at your back in a life and death situation."

What was holding him back? Fear? I could understand that. "Sam, I know what you can do." My expression and tone softened. "I don't want you fighting at my back during a life and death situation. I want you safe right beside me so that when I need you, you'll be ready and able to help. We've got fighters. I didn't ask you here to be one of them."

He shuffled his feet. "But still, I don't think—"

"I have no doubt that you'll save all our lives at least once. If you walk away now, you'll be leaving us to die without you if something happens. We need you, Sam. Please join us."

"You're kinda manipulative," he said wonderingly.

I smiled widely. "I am. But I'm also being honest. I want you on my team. I want each of you, specifically. That's why I called you here."

He still hesitated, and I rolled my eyes. "You know you want to, Sam. Just say yes."

He took a deep breath. "Okay, yes. I just hope you don't regret it."

I settled back in my seat again, legs and arms spread wide to show my confidence. "I won't. I made a promise to myself to never regret anything again."

"Bunny, you heard all that, right? I've got a consenting team. Register us."

—Already? You move fast.—
-Bunny-

"I'm single-minded." Singly focused on my own survival, to be exact. But I didn't say that last bit aloud.

A Window misted into existence like a mirage in front of my face.

YOU HAVE BECOME THE LEADER OF A TEAM.
SPECIAL CONDITION ACTIVATED.
YOU HAVE GAINED THE SKILL "COMMAND."

A new Skill? My eyes widened and I sat forward. "Display Skill Window," I murmured under my breath.

COMMAND (MUNDANE CLASS): ALLOWS LEADER ACCESS TO THE TEAM MANAGEMENT WINDOW. LEADER CAN COMMUNICATE WITH TEAM MEMBERS THROUGH GAME WINDOWS, SEE LOCATION OF TEAM MEMBERS ON TEAM MANAGEMENT MAP, AND IS ABLE TO ACCESS BASIC GAME INFORMATION OF TEAM MEMBERS.

My tongue twitched with the desire to display the team management Window, but I held myself back. "Did you guys get a Skill?"

China tilted her head to the side. "It says we can communicate with our leader via Game Windows."

Adam frowned at the invisible screen in front of his face, and then at me. "And I suppose that would be you," he said resignedly.

"Yes. It is me." I hadn't known the leader would be appointed like that, but I wouldn't apologize that it was me. The situation and my seeming power play made me a bit uncomfortable, but I kept it hidden and tried to begin as I meant to go on, with outward confidence and control.

Sam shuffled his feet and looked between Adam and me nervously.

Jacky chuckled. "Did you expect different? It's not like anything changed. There's just a pretty label on it now."

We stared each other down for a moment, and then Adam relented. "So I'm your subordinate now. What information do you have that you thought I'd be interested in?"

"You're my ally," I corrected. I very deliberately took off my link and handed it to China, who put it in her bag.

Adam's eyes widened, and he did the same.

When everyone in our group had removed their links with varying levels of understanding why we were doing so, China carried her backpack away, out of the links' audio receptors' range.

"Everyone, be careful to shield your thoughts from Bunny. Just consciously acknowledge that you don't want him to overhear this." When China returned, I looked to her. "What I have is a name, I believe."

She knew immediately what I was referring to. "Mendell."

"Mendell? One name? Is that first or last? What context is the name in? How, exactly, is something like that going to be useful?" He was rolling a coin over and between his knuckles with angry energy, tiny sparks of static electricity jumping off it.

China replied before I could. "My sister was taken by them, by NIX. We think that's the name of the people who run the Game." Her voice wavered in the beginning but strengthened as she continued. "Eve was there when it happened. And then people in masks came to my house to make it look like my sister ran away. They were talking about what they would do with the ones they'd taken, and we listened. They said they'd be taking samples from them to Mendell. That's the context."

The irritated look slipped off his face, replaced with intense focus. "A research lab, maybe? A place, or maybe a person…" He'd already begun tapping on the ID arm sheath link clamped onto the cast around his arm, entering in information.

"That's what I want you to find out," I said.

He took a deep breath and held his hand up in the air, and as he let the breath out, his hand started to spark visibly, and his curls floated upward from the electricity coursing through his body.

Sam and China watched him with avid curiosity, while Jacky stepped back in alarm, probably remembering her last incident with his abilities.

Adam laid his hand onto his arm sheath, and though his body was still, his eyes twitched back and forth with bug-like, skittering speed, focused on nothing in the real world.

I pulled up the team control Window under my breath while the others were all focused on him.

PLAYER NAME: ADAM COYLE
TITLE: NONE

CHARACTERISTIC SKILL: ELECTRIC SOVEREIGN
LEVEL: 58
SKILLS: HYPER FOCUS

STRENGTH: 13
LIFE: 11
AGILITY: 28
GRACE: 13
INTELLIGENCE: 19
FOCUS: 22
BEAUTY: 8
PHYSIQUE: 13
MANUAL DEXTERITY: 15
MENTAL ACUITY: 29
RESILIENCE: 14
STAMINA: 10
PERCEPTION: 8

HE OBVIOUSLY FOCUSED his points in the mental Attributes and Agility, and Electric Sovereign would be the Skill that allowed him to manipulate electricity. Hyper Focus was also self-explanatory. It was a little irritating that the average level of his Attributes was far above mine. He must have started out with high scores, because even fifty-eight level-ups didn't explain those numbers. If he hadn't broken his arm, he would never have needed protection from Jacky and me. He was definitely the highest leveled Player in the group.

Adam fairly vibrated with the intensity of his concentration for a while. When he finally took his hand away from the ID sheath and its connection to the Internet, he let out a shuddering breath. "I've found something," he said, rubbing his now bloodshot eyes.

We all leaned forward in anticipation, holding our breath after the display he'd just given us.

"A person," he continued. "An engineer, slash physicist, slash biologist, former genius that's been out of the scientific community and public eye for a while now. It's not much, but he's suspicious. I hacked into the city property databases and found a place under the name of his deceased sister that's paying extraordinarily high electricity bills. Which doesn't mean much, but when I tried to figure out where the money was coming from to pay those bills, I couldn't."

I nodded, understanding the direction his thoughts had gone.

Jacky pursed her lips. "So? That doesn't tell us nothing."

Adam smirked. "I'm able to understand the electrical impulses that run through a computer and manipulate them. There should be no hiding the money trail from me, but it was in the form of a large credit deposit from a company I'd never heard of, and beyond that I couldn't track its path." He paused for emphasis. "It was purposefully hidden. Now, who would want their mysterious payments to a genius hermit researcher to be untraceable?"

China bounced on her toes and grabbed my arm in excitement as if to stop herself from flying away. "Oh my god. Yes! He's connected to NIX. He has to know something about Chanelle, and maybe she's even there right now, being held in some sort of research lab…" She tugged on my arm. "Eve, we have to go get her, before it's too late."

I refused to bring the team that very instant to look for China's sister. She would have rushed to Mendell's secret lair alone, but I was able to dissuade China with a compromise that we would go after the team had some time to prepare and gather more information.

"But I'm not going to keep waiting indefinitely, Eve. If my sister's in there, I'm going to save her." She frowned at me with that face identical to Chanelle's.

I nodded and laid a hand on her shoulder. "I know. But if she is there, it's better that we wait until we're actually able to save her, rather than making an attempt and failing, and her being trapped forever."

Adam snorted. "I'll go there with the team, but no way am I risking my life for some random girl I don't even know."

I smirked but said nothing. What was it exactly that got him that broken arm? Saving some random girl he didn't even know, if I remembered correctly. If the situation arose, I'd bet credits that Adam would save Chanelle and a hundred others, grumbling about it all the while.

But Sam, who knew him even less well than I did, frowned. "If there are people there that need our help, we have to help them. We have the responsibility to do what we can."

"Right. While you're being a martyr, I'll be keeping myself alive," Adam said.

I raised a hand. "Guys. We don't even know what we're going to find there yet. We'll deal with that when we come to it. Right now, let's get to know each other better, so I know exactly what we're working with and how best to allocate our limited manpower."

Jacky tilted her head back and forth to crack her neck. "So basically you want us to tell about our Skills, right?"

"More or less. Skills, Attribute point delegation, any other special skill or ability you might have…basically anything that might be useful for me to know."

Jacky gave a mischievous smirk and grabbed a short branch from a nearby decorative tree, ripping it off.

I pulled up her statistics in the leadership Window to compare her real stats with what she told us. Her Characteristic Skill was "Gravitational Autonomy." When I touched the Skill, the words "Kinetic Class" appeared, but that was it.

She squeezed hard enough that her arm trembled with the effort, and her fingers sank into the wood, sap leaking from between her fingers and dripping onto the ground in milky spatters. With another smirk, she opened her hand and showed the pulverized wood pulp within. "I'm strong. Really strong, and sturdy enough to support my own strength—so I don't rip my own muscles and bones apart. My points are almost all in the physical Attributes. My Skill lets me change the force of gravity on my own body, just a little bit. I can't fly or nothing, but it's good for fighting." She wiped her sap-covered hand on the ground, and then moved to me and placed her hands on my shoulders. First, she bounced up and hovered just an instant longer than she should have, and the weight of her on my shoulders was surprisingly light. Then she pressed down on me, and I had to strain to keep my posture straight under the pressure her significantly smaller frame exerted on mine.

I could imagine the surprising strength behind a punch aided by the force of gravity.

"I've never put even one point into Beauty." She looked at each of us like she was challenging us to argue. "I didn't need to, since I was born beautiful, yeah?"

I couldn't help but laugh at her aggressive confidence, though inside my emotions were tinged with more than a hint of jealousy. To be born that beautiful…it was like a blessing from a fairy godmother, or a cheat code for the game of life. That beauty must have made things easier. No doubt it had much to do with her almost arrogant confidence. "I've seen you fight, too," I prompted.

"Yes, I'm also a fighter. Even before the Game. Since I was a child."

"Do you think you could train us to fight more effectively?" I asked.

"I've never taught, but I remember what my teachers did. Maybe I can teach. I'll try, but I'll need to watch you all fight, yes?" Jacky returned to her perch atop the bench.

China stood next. "My Skill…I can understand some animals, more or less."

Sam's eyebrows rose. "Like a Disney princess?"

She scowled at him, but her peach and cream complexion, big blue eyes, and thick blond hair showed a definite resemblance to a small Disney princess from the films. Except if this were a film, it would be a horror film, not all fun, acapella songs, and happily-ever-afters.

Jacky started laughing, hard. Not a beautiful laugh to match her appearance, but a snorting, rough sound that shook her whole body and irresistibly drew a laugh from me, as well. She laughed so hard she fell off her perch, and then we were all laughing.

China continued, after the mirth subsided. "I can't understand animals completely, but I get better at it as my Perception increases. And I can kinda talk back to the easiest ones, though they don't always understand me. It's a Skill of limited use. I'm not good at close combat, but I use throwing knives and that kind of thing."

Adam stood next, once again rolling a quarter between his fingers, perhaps unconsciously. "You've already seen both of my Skills. I can manipulate electrical currents and increase my brain's processing speed for short periods of time. High Intelligence, Mental Acuity, and Focus. Indirectly, I use all of those things to allow myself direct access to a computer's processes, and through that, even to the Internet."

"And you can call down lightning," Jacky added.

"Yeah." He smirked. "I focus mainly on Agility when fighting. In and out, critical hits with the least possibility of damage to myself."

I nodded, pleased that he'd been honest.

Sam shook his head wonderingly. "Wow. This group's powers are strange enough, even I feel relatively normal."

"What do you do?" Jacky asked.

I had already pulled up his Window and was looking at his Characteristic Skill in confusion.

He hesitated for a moment, and something about the strained look on his face made me step in to save him. "Sam's a healer. He saved my life after my Characteristic Trial. It was pretty amazing."

He looked at me with an indecipherable expression that might have contained relief or gratitude, but with something else locked away beneath the surface. "Yeah. I can heal wounds, and poisoning and stuff like that, as long as it's not too serious. I can't bring anyone back from the dead or anything, but"—he pointed to Adam's arm—"I could probably do something about your bone."

While Sam used Adam's broken forearm to do a demonstration, I examined his status window.

PLAYER NAME: SAMUEL HAWES
TITLE: NONE
CHARACTERISTIC SKILL: HARBINGER OF DEATH
LEVEL: 33
SKILLS: NONE

STRENGTH: 11
LIFE: 19
AGILITY: 12
GRACE: 12
INTELLIGENCE: 13
FOCUS: 9
BEAUTY: 13
PHYSIQUE: 12
MANUAL DEXTERITY: 10
MENTAL ACUITY: 9
RESILIENCE: 30
STAMINA: 18
PERCEPTION: 7

I TRIED to bring up more information on the Harbinger of Death Skill, but I could only see basic Player information with the Command Skill. Even so, the words "Ruination Class" popped up. What did that mean? The first time we met, he'd said his good exterior hid something else beneath, and he'd been reluctant to join us. Because he wasn't the type I wanted at my back…

I watched him kneeling next to Adam, controlling a grimace as the broken bone he'd taken from the other boy started to heal, and then grinning hugely at Adam's look of amazement at his own half-healed hand

and wrist.

No. I wasn't wrong to call on Sam, whatever he thought of himself. The types of people I didn't want on my team were those like Vaughn, who may have gained power and Skills through his actions in the Characteristic Trial, but who was rotten on the inside. That type of person would corrupt my soul, only feeding my own desire for control and cowardly power. I'd take Sam any day.

I stood up. "My turn then. I don't have any exceptionally high Attributes. More or less an all-rounder for now. I'm a close-combat fighter. I'm the leader of this team, so I've got a Command Skill that lets me know where you guys are in relation to me, send you Windows like Bunny does, and I can also see your basic statistics."

Sam's gaze snapped to mine, but I didn't let my face acknowledge anything out of the ordinary, and continued on. "I have two Characteristic Skills. One is a spirit-type." I willed my body to perform its now-practiced transformation. My claws slid out and my senses sharpened with a rush of excitement that made me want to run and jump. "The other Skill basically just makes me more graceful—acrobatics and stuff."

I held each of their gazes in turn. "To be explicit, since I know we're not being listened to at the moment, my goal is really to survive the Game, but I don't want to do that just by getting better at the Trials. The real threat to us are the ones who control the Game, and the disparity of power and knowledge between us. I want to level the playing field.

"So, why don't we go check out this Mendell person's house?" I grinned at them.

Chapter 15

I am terrified by this dark thing that sleeps in me.
— Sylvia Plath

A COUPLE NIGHTS LATER, I put pillows and an extra blanket under my sheets to fake a sleeping body, like I'd seen in teen movies, and hoped no one would notice my absence. Then I grabbed my backpack and climbed out my window, tentatively reaching for the tree limb just outside.

—Eve, do you really think this is a good idea?—
-Bunny-

When the monitoring devices in my room had picked up my suspicious actions, Bunny had happened to notice and asked me what I was doing. I took a risk and decided to tell him. I wanted his aid someday, and despite the danger, I had a feeling he'd stay silent for us.

My heart pounded crazily and I had to force myself to move toward the trunk, but my body reacted to the danger, my claws slipping out to grip the wood better, and my balanced sharpening noticeably. "Yes. I do."

Since learning our plan, Bunny had spent the rest of the evening trying to change my mind. But he was appalled by the fact we even knew

NIX's name, and the more he tried to stop me, the more I thought we were doing exactly the right thing. Otherwise he wouldn't have cared so much.

—You don't know what you're getting into. As soon as you break in, you've committed a crime. And what if it really is one of NIX's research labs? Do you think they'll just let you take the Players and leave?—
-Bunny-

I moved from the base of the limb to the one below, and then the one below that, again and again until I reached the wonderfully stable ground. It had been much easier than I expected, and I reveled a bit in my body's new power as I headed on foot to the meeting point. "We've done our research. We've watched the place and accessed the recorded satellite feeds. If NIX had a base with a lot of people, there'd be more traffic in and out of the property. Even if this Mendell person does have guards or assistants, it can't be very many."

—You've done your research? Please. It's only been a couple days. We have no idea what you're going to find inside. Do you even know how you're going to get in? This isn't safe, Eve. You're endangering yourself and your team.—
-Bunny-

He was worried. And he'd used "we" instead of "you," a slip that gave me confidence in my earlier assessment of him. He felt sorry for us, though he tried to hide it, and, if I could cultivate the compassion in him, I could use that weakness against him.

I knew he was right about the danger, though. Even the GPS chip in our necks might give us away when we got too close. But from the observation we'd been able to do, we hadn't noticed a lot of people at the house. In fact, the only people in and out seemed to be fast food and delivery pods. I didn't know what to do except take a risk and hope it paid off. And, for whatever it was worth, it wasn't technically against Game rules to search for info on NIX, as long as we didn't talk about it to civilians.

I let out a panting laugh as I ran. "*This* isn't safe? Come on, Bunny. Think about that. I'm a Player. Every day I have to wonder whether or not I'm going to survive my next Trial. We all do. If we can learn something here that will help us survive, the danger is an acceptable risk. And the sooner, the better." I softened my voice. "You know we have to do this. We want to live, so please don't try to stop us. And don't get us caught."

There was a long pause before his next Window appeared.

—Don't get yourself killed.—
-Bunny-

"I'll do my best," I said sarcastically, noting his silent acquiescence for what it was.

I ran quickly and quietly, reaching the meeting point to find Sam already waiting for me. The others would all arrive separately, in case we needed to leave in a hurry. I slipped into the passenger seat of his pod. No doubt an expensive gift from his parents when he'd reached driving age.

"You know…that my Skill isn't just healing, don't you?" Sam said into the silence.

"Well, you don't waste any time, do you?" I laughed. "I wasn't sure, but you've just confirmed it."

He opened his mouth, but stalled out, apparently unsure what to say. "Oh. Umm…" He clenched and unclenched his fingers around the steering wheel.

"It's okay, Sam. We don't have to talk about this now. I don't need to know all your secrets. I just need to know that you're loyal to the team." I would find out his secrets eventually, anyway.

"Okay." He let out a big breath.

We drove to a deserted side road far from the edge of town and parked the pod between a couple trees.

"Psst! Over here." A hand waved to us from the darkness, and we headed for it.

China, Jacky, and Adam were crouched in a semicircle on the ground, and I sank down beside them, trying to quiet my breathing. "Any new developments?"

China rubbed her arms, apparently cold even though the temperature was perfect. That's what came of being so thin and waif-like. "Nothing, really." She'd been observing for most of the last twenty-four hours, watching for movement and determining what security measures were in effect.

Jacky chuckled and pulled a twig she was chewing out of her perfectly shaped mouth. "Except this guy's loaded. I mean…really, really, *rich*."

Adam nodded. "Which is going to make breaking in much more difficult. From my best guess, there's an automatic alarm system set up all around the property. No dogs, but there are cameras and motion detectors."

Jacky smiled cruelly, her teeth white in the darkness. "Good thing he's a long way away from the nearest police station. We'll have plenty of time to get away if things go bad."

Sam bit his lip. "But what if the alarm doesn't go to the police station? What if…?"

"It's connected to NIX?" I finished for him. "Well, there's a simple solution. Let's just not get caught."

Jacky sighed and shook her head. "No way we're gonna break in under an alarm. Not all of us, anyway. If it's cops, they'll be here in twenty, and we'll have time to get in and out. If it's not the cops…we'll be screwed."

I shook my head. "There has to be a way."

Jacky shrugged. "I say we just move in fast and get out fast. They'll never tell who we are from the cameras since we brought the masks like you said."

Just then, the sound of another vehicle driving up the winding road behind us filtered through the trees. "China," I hissed, "go see what it is."

She gave me a sharp nod and murmured, "Got it," then sprinted off into the darkness.

We all waited in apprehension for almost a minute before she came back, breathing hard. "It's a pizza delivery pod. Must be going up to the house."

I grinned and took off my backpack. "Great." I pulled out a mask and a pair of gloves, and slipped them on.

Jacky watched me with an excited grin on her face. "We gonna do what I think we're gonna do?"

"Yep." I turned to the others. "We're hijacking that pod. Pizza delivery pods get free access onto the property, all the way to the front door. No one suspects them."

By the time the old pod came rumbling up, we were prepared. China stood in the middle of the road with her hoodie pulled up to hide her features. The delivery boy would see just her small, fragile-looking form standing in the middle in the road.

He stopped the pod and rolled down the window. "You okay?" he called to her, his head sticking out the window.

China shook, sobbing loudly.

He opened the door, but only had one foot on the road before Jacky rushed out from the trees and gave him a quick chop to the back of the neck.

He crumpled to the ground, and she dragged him off the side of the road.

"Neat trick," I said.

"Dangerous if you dunno what you're doing." She nodded sagely. "Lucky it worked, since I dunno what I'm doing." She grinned at Sam's shocked expression.

China pulled a small knife with a blue sticker from a sheath wrapped around her waist and pricked the boy's arm. "Coated with sleeping poison. Chanelle had the idea to collect it in one of our Trials. He won't wake up for a while."

"He'll be fine to stay here until we're finished," I said, nudging his still form with my foot. "If something happens, he'll be safer here anyway." I turned to the car. "Sam, you're going to be our pizza delivery guy. Strip him and take his clothes."

He looked back and forth from the unconscious boy to me. "Really?"

"You're the most trustworthy-looking out of all of us. Except China. But she looks like she's twelve. No one would believe she's old enough to drive."

I laughed under my breath at her protestations against my teasing jibe, and in a few minutes we were pulling up to the mansion's gate. The rest of us crouched down, out of sight of any cameras that might cause suspicion over a pizza delivery car full of people, while Sam drove.

"Pizza delivery?" Sam said.

A man's voice crackled back through the speaker. "Please wait. I will be down shortly."

SAM STOOD at the front door wearing the stolen outfit and a nervous smile on his face. He had a pizza in his hands, but a hat pulled low over his head for the benefit of the cameras. There was a beeping sound as someone on the other side entered a code, and then the door opened. Without giving the man time to react, Sam dropped the pizza, stepped forward, and pushed him backward, clamping his gloved hand over the man's mouth.

We rushed in behind Sam and helped him hold down, tie up, and gag the man.

Jacky brought in the pizza box and closed the front door behind us while Adam made sure the alarm system was disabled and turned off the home security system, along with NIX's possible view of the break-in. China helped him, checking for hidden cameras like the ones in Players' houses.

I looked around curiously. "Wow." The inside was a modern, open-air design, everything spacious and bright. The air smelled clean—evidence of a carbon filter air purifying system. A small fountain burbled in the middle of the lounge area beneath the stairs to the upper floors, and everything seemed to be made of marble and genuine wood. The place was beautiful, and must have cost a fortune. It was also messy, with empty takeout containers and trash strewn around.

Jacky, Adam, and China did a quick recon of the mansion to make sure no one else was there while Sam and I stayed with the man. I grabbed his ID link and pulled up his information.

Dr. Blaine Mendell.

He was in his early thirties, wore thick glasses, and had floppy brown hair and a smile that made him look like he sponsored a child in Africa, volunteered at the nearest orphanage, and saved sick puppies in his spare time. If I hadn't been almost positive he worked for the most evil people in the world, I would have thought he looked like a nice person.

I maneuvered him into a chair and took the gag out of his mouth. "Don't scream. If you do, I'll take you over to that fountain and hold your head underwater until you learn to conserve your air for breathing."

He nodded.

"Doctor Blaine Mendell, tell me, who do you work for?"

His eyes darted back and forth between me, dressed in a black mask, gloves, and sturdy clothing, and Sam, still in the pizza delivery outfit, which was somehow more disturbing.

I sighed, steeled myself, and backhanded the doctor across the face, making Sam jump in surprise. "Focus! I'm speaking to you," I said. I wasn't as strong as Jacky, but he'd have a bruise. "Let's try again. Who do you work for?"

He swallowed. "I—I do not work for anyone. I am unemployed; I just live off my savings and investments. I—I am truly unsure what is going on here. Who are you people, and what do you want with me?"

Jacky came back into the room, having found no one in her section of the mansion. She opened the pizza box and took a slice, and then came to stand beside us, looking down at him with malice as she took a huge bite.

Though clearly confused, Blaine was looking at the three of us with too much curiosity and not nearly enough naked terror.

His eyes met mine again, and I smiled calmly. "There are other ways to make you talk, if asking nicely doesn't work." I wasn't bluffing. I would do anything necessary to get the information from him, but I hoped that he saw my resolve and would spare me from having to do anything messy.

"I think you should see this!" Adam called from the doorway.

China stood behind him, eyes wide and breath shallow, her body almost vibrating.

"What is it?"

"I'm not sure yet. It's best if you see for yourself, I think. It's downstairs," Adam said, jerking his head toward the stairs.

Blaine's eyes widened, and I saw the first hint of true fear come into his eyes.

"Well, Blaine, let's see what you've got down there, shall we?" I said.

He looked between Adam and me. "Who are you? Why are you doing this?"

I nodded to Jacky. "Bring him, please."

She dragged him by his bound legs, bouncing him painfully behind us down the stairs to the cement and metal basement door, where Adam proceeded to override the electronic locking system.

China was as tense as a coiled spring, ready to shoot toward whatever was on the other side.

The door opened into a large lab. It had stone chemist tables and drains in the floor, research equipment and electronics everywhere, half-built gadgets scattered all over, a wall lined with computers, and vials of strange liquids all laid out haphazardly. There were several other closed cement doors leading through to other basement rooms.

Jacky bumped Dr. Mendell down the last few stairs, ignoring his loud protests. "You've been quite naughty, have you not, Doctor?" she said, her Spanish accent growing strong.

Sam grabbed him by the arms and helped him to sit on one of the stools. "Why don't you tell us all what you've been doing here? We're not here to hurt you, if you'd just talk to us…"

He swallowed, but croaked, "I am doing medical research. Attempting to find a cure for cancer."

My heart beat faster as adrenaline surged through my veins. He was lying. I knew, because on the table in front of me lay something that definitely didn't look like cancer research. Pinched between two slides under one of the microscope lenses was a fluid that sparkled like a Seed.

I looked through the lens and saw wiggling, teeny-tiny, microscopic organisms—little bug-like creatures—so thickly packed I could barely tell where one ended and the next began. I pulled my face away from the microscope's eye piece and unclipped the slide, gently removing it and holding it up to the harsh light above.

It shimmered and swirled over and under itself, moving constantly.

My breath came hard, and my hands shook. I cradled the slide in my hand and walked back to Blaine, showing it to him.

His loud protests, declarations of innocence, and wriggling ceased.

I touched him under the chin with the forefinger of my free hand and forced him to look at me, barely keeping my sharp nails from sliding out. "Do you know what this is?"

He didn't shake his head this time. He didn't say anything. He just swallowed and looked into my eyes, desperation growing in his own.

"*I* know what it is," I said. "And I know you do, too. I also know who you work for. You absolutely *are* going to tell us what you know. Because we're patient, you haven't been trained to withstand torture, and no one is coming to save you."

I turned to Jacky. "Please pulverize the pinky finger of his left hand from the last knuckle to the tip." I turned to him. "And do it slowly, please."

Sam's voice came out, almost silent. "Is this really necessary?"

"If he's going to talk without it, then no." I raised an eyebrow. "Well, are you? Tell us everything you know, and we won't hurt you. How about it?"

Blaine had stilled, but he said nothing.

"So be it. This is my question. What are you working on, down here in your secret lab?"

Jacky had grabbed his left hand already, a vicious, white grin stretching behind her mask. She pressed on the tip of his pinky, pinching it harder and harder until his face grew white with shock.

He turned red, and then white again, and started to pant and buck against his restraints.

Sam stepped forward. "This isn't right. Torturing him makes it like we're the bad guys."

Jacky looked to me, still pressing, obviously reluctant to quit.

I nodded to her and motioned with my hand, and she released him with a disappointed sigh.

Sam sighed as well, giving me an appreciative look.

"Move on to the next finger," I said.

Sam's eyes widened, and he hurried to stand in front of Blaine. "Come on, guys. Just stop!"

I stepped forward, placed a hand on his arm, and murmured so that the scientist couldn't hear. "I know this is difficult. But you have to understand we're not the ones in the wrong. He knows about what NIX does. He helps them. Think about the people whose lives he's had a hand in destroying, how many people he's helped them kill. He's one of the people that did this to you, to *us*. He doesn't deserve your protection." I pulled gently, and, as if the strength to oppose me had left him, Sam stepped away. "If it's too much for you to watch, why don't you go explore the other rooms with those two?" I pointed to Adam and China, who were trying to open one of the concrete doors.

He swallowed. "No, I'll stay."

Blaine held his trembling hands in front of his face. His left pinky was flattened unnaturally, a white color that was quickly turning purplish red as it filled with blood. Jacky had pulverized it, similar to what she'd demonstrated with the tree limb in China's backyard.

She shook her head ruefully. "That's gonna be hard to use from now on. You shoulda cooperated from the beginning. There's no mercy to be found here."

Sam swallowed again, staring at the crushed finger intently. He looked away after a second and took a deep breath, but his own hands were clenched at his sides, and he didn't try to stop us.

"She's right," I said. "Now, once again. What exactly are you working on?"

Blaine sputtered and panted. "I am working on a cure for cancer," he repeated.

Before Jacky could start to press again, China stomped past her, grabbed Blaine by the hair on the back of his head, and held a knife to his throat. She was panting and red-faced. "Where is she?" she demanded, her voice cracking.

I looked over my shoulder to Adam, who shook his head. All the doors were open, but apparently none of the rooms contained human subjects.

When the scientist didn't respond, her voice morphed into a scream.

"Where is she? Where? Tell me right now!" She pressed the knife forward, and a generous line of blood started to run down his neck.

He held himself still to avoid cutting his own neck. "What? I don't know who you are talking about."

She screamed again, spit flying into his face. "Don't. *Lie!* I *know* you took her. NIX took her to do research on. I know you have her. My sister! Where is she?"

His shoulders slumped, whatever had been keeping him strong slipping away. "They took your sister?"

"Why the hell do you think I'm here? They were supposed to bring her here. You're doing research on her! I'm going to save her, and if you don't tell me where she is, I'll slit your throat, right now."

He closed his eyes for a second, pain radiating from him. "I am sorry. She is not here. I don't have her." He looked at me over China's shoulder. "I'm sorry. I was told if I revealed information about them, they would…" He swallowed against the blade. "They took my niece and nephew, too. As hostages."

"WHAT? You have to have her. If she isn't here…" China stared at him for a few moments, and then slipped away like she'd been de-boned. "Where is she?" She looked to me, her face pale and wan, suddenly looking much too old and haggard.

I shook my head. "I don't know. But it's not the end yet. There's still hope."

She leaned forward until her head rested against my torso, then wrapped her arms loosely around my waist. "Promise me we'll find her, Eve. I can't stand it, imagining what she's going through. If they haven't killed her…" Her small body shuddered, and she squeezed tighter.

Despite myself, my heart clenched in response. I petted her blonde head and said, "She's strong. She's a fighter. You know that better than anyone. We'll find her. I promise." The last part felt like it might be a lie, but even I couldn't tell for sure. I looked up at the doctor. "You'd better start talking, right now."

He nodded quickly as Jacky reached for his bound hands again. "I was a researcher. Before all this. A physicist, an engineer, and I loved it, the work, the respect, the money," he blurted. "Then, my sister got diagnosed with cancer, and when she died, I quit all that because I promised I would take care of her kids. NIX contacted me, requested I work for them, but I refused. So they took my remaining family to use as blackmail against me. I had no choice but to work for them. They furnished this place with equipment and deposit money into my bank account every month. In return, whenever I am able to produce something valuable—research, or an invention—for them, they give me proof of life."

Adam's eyes narrowed. "How do you turn over your results to them?"

"I send them a message"—he jerked his head toward the computers lined up against the wall—"and they respond with a time to meet and GPS coordinates."

"How far away and how far in advance is the average meeting they give you?"

"It's usually quite immediate. A couple hours of warning, and most of the time is used up driving to wherever they want to meet." He looked at China, who had calmed down but was still letting herself be petted, and then to me. "I am sorry. I had no options. I didn't know what to do. I had to keep my sister's kids safe, and it is not like I could go to the police. Even now, if they learn that you were here, I don't know what they will do. But if they are doing this to other people, too… You are the same as me. I don't know what, but if there is anything I can do to help, I will do it."

"I'll take you up on that offer," I said immediately.

Adam's head snapped toward me with a deep frown, but I ignored him and continued talking. "But you must be willing to accept the risk involved."

Blaine smiled for the first time, despite the fact he was still tied up by four masked people who'd tortured him, and his crushed finger must have been screaming with pain. "I have been in danger since they decided they wanted my help in the first place. I don't want things to continue on as they have been, so something must change. It is insanity to keep doing the same fruitless thing in the hope that it will suddenly become profitable. They are never going to give my niece and nephew back on their own."

China pulled back from me and gave him a weak smile. "Sorry for threatening to kill you."

"I would have done the same," he murmured, "if I thought the kiddos were being held here."

I untied Blaine's bonds and nodded to Sam, who I knew had been itching with the desire to heal him. "Go ahead."

Blaine's eyes grew wide as he watched Sam's Skill go to work. When it was done, he gently touched the healed finger, his mouth hanging open. "Spontaneous regeneration. That is amazing. This is decades ahead of the research in the field right now. What did you use to do that? Could I see it? I would like to examine how it works." His eyes searched Sam's empty hands for the cause of his healing, and then went back to his finger.

"Do you know what NIX does?" I asked.

He dragged his eyes to mine for a second. "From the things I have been asked to research, I have gathered that they are an arms manufacturer. Advanced weapons technology, biological warfare, that sort of thing. Maybe selling on the black market to the highest bidding country, or maybe they are a military operation."

"Do you know what this is?" I held up the slide of shimmering Seed material.

His face brightened. "It is the most amazing thing—completely autonomous organisms that seem to share a common consciousness. I have never seen anything like them before. I received that sample just a few days ago. Honestly, I think…I really do think they might be a cure to cancer." He blinked. "Isn't that ironic? But of course that's not what they want me to do with them. Even so, my research could be beneficial, if I could release it to the world."

—Do it and you'll die, dumbass. NIX would never allow that to happen.
—
-Bunny-

"Have you heard of the Game, Blaine?" I ignored Bunny's warning to Blaine, who'd couldn't receive our Moderator's message anyway.

—Don't *you* do something stupid, Eve. Don't you remember the first rule?
You can't divulge information to non-Players.—
-Bunny-

"Are you going to kill him if I do? He's already unable to tell anyone else. And he's already involved in all of this. Hell, he's studying the Seeds! Just because he doesn't use them like we do doesn't mean he's not the same as us. He's trapped, too, already dealing with everything. He just doesn't know what that is. I'm not going to *reveal* it to him, just *explain* it."

Bunny didn't respond, and I knew it was because he couldn't technically argue with my logic.

Blaine was staring at me strangely. "Umm, who are you talking to? Are you wearing an earpiece?"

I laughed. "No. It's the voice in my head." I ignored his look of bewilderment as I explained the Game and Trials, our status as Players, and the little we knew about NIX. While Blaine's head still seemed to be spinning from that, I had him show us around his laboratory and explain what he was working on.

Projects in various states of completion were strewn all about the room. "I prefer to work on defensive capability things, rather than weapons, though I do both types of projects. I've got a few going on right now, as you can see." He gestured all around us. "But most recently I have been examining the samples they sent to me…the Seeds, you called them, and something else, which I now assume are samples from…the ones they took, like your sister. I am trying to figure out how exactly they work, and from there how I can make them do other things. Other than that, I am working on a lightweight synthetic armor—better than Kevlar—a serum that temporarily stops the pain receptors in your brain from working, and a substance that can stay strong while being thin enough to slice apart molecules. I just finished an electrically powered framework for soldiers to wear—a mecha suit, in layman's terms—but the energy requirements make it unfeasible for extended use in combat. Of course, I am particularly excited about the Seed material, and the things you've just described to me. I'd gotten some things from NIX to research before, things that made me wonder why they even needed my help if they had technology like that. I even considered that they might have excavated some ancient alien city." He laughed.

That gave me pause, and I didn't know how to respond, but Adam spoke up. "Why *does* NIX need you? I find it hard to believe an organization like theirs is lacking in scientists of their own. And even so, why do they allow you to do your research here? Why not just keep you wherever their actual base is and have you work there?" he challenged.

Blaine shrugged. "They need me because I am very, very good at what I do. And I have always preferred to work in solitude, no assistants, no distractions. I'm kind of known for not wanting a research team; idiots only hinder me. Maybe they want to preserve my working environment. Or maybe they don't want me anywhere near my niece and nephew, or they don't want me within their base for some other reason. Honestly, I don't know."

I walked around to investigate the connecting basement rooms. One was a quarantine room with a large, air-sealed glass box within, making me wonder just what he worked on that might require such precautions. Another was a storage room for supplies and equipment, another a small closet with a cot in it, but the last was pay dirt.

"Hell yes," I said aloud. Windows cut into the concrete walls near the high ceiling right at ground level would have let light into the large room, if there were any outside. But it didn't matter, because my eyes automatically compensated.

It was dusty and cobwebby enough to be on the set of a horror movie. Random, rusty bits of metal, tools, and various boxes lay all around and stacked against the walls. Two staircases on either side of the room led up to a second-story loft that ran a third of the width and the whole length of the room. I stepped forward. "This place is awesome."

I waved away a spider web and stepped onto the bottom step of the nearest staircase. A probing push with my foot proved it to be stable. "Except for the dirt." I turned to Blaine. "You said you wanted to help, right?"

He nodded, tilting his head to the side in an unspoken question.

"Guys"—I spread my arms wide—"behold our new base."

Chapter 16

For evil to triumph it is enough only that good men do nothing.
— Edmund Burke

I CREPT BACK into my house late that night and curled up in bed. Adam had of course protested my decision, not trusting Blaine Mendell or his house-slash-secret-laboratory. We'd compromised by locking Blaine in the quarantine room and changing all the passwords to his security system. The scientist hadn't enjoyed that, but I'd told him to suck it up, because as punishments go, the things he'd participated in deserved much worse. That shut him up, and I told him I'd be back for him soon. I'd even left him the rest of the pizza and some water.

I'd told Adam to work on making our base safe from NIX, including cutting off their access to the security cameras and microphones without them realizing. China's job was to thoroughly comb the house and make sure there weren't any other monitoring devices. My house was next on the list, but I figured the base took priority.

A weariness like the weight of an ink ocean crushed me, suffocating me in dark silence. I'd crossed one more line tonight, created another barrier against my naivety, my normalcy, and my original invisible self. I felt like all the soft parts were being squished out of me, both mentally and physically. When the Game was done with me, all that would be left was a hard, jagged knife of a girl, able to cut through anything and everything. It would shave everything that wasn't survival away. If I didn't shatter in the process, that is.

I hugged my legs and rested my head on my knees, speaking into the darkness. "Don't you ever get tired of it, Bunny?"

—Of what?—
-Bunny-

I'd known he would be there. "Of what you do. Kidnapping, human experimentation, murder…knowing how your Players live in fear?" When I paused, silence reigned. "How do you do it? Do you just not care? I know that's not true. So how do you do it?" Maybe if he explained it, I could do it, too.

More silence, and then a bright Window appeared against the darkness of my room.

—I do this because it's my job. And they wouldn't do it if there weren't a good reason. I know it must seem like NIX is evil, but this is all necessary. They're working toward something.—
-Bunny-

"What could possibly be important enough to make this okay?"

—I don't know. That's above my security level until I pass muster as a Moderator. But I'm just here to monitor and guide you. I may not like what happens, but I do what I can to help. Haven't I done that for you?—
-Bunny-

"You don't know why this is supposedly necessary, and you just blindly believe? You're saying you're not *directly* involved, just a bystander, so that makes it easy? That's how you deal, how you cope? That makes it okay in your head?" I laughed. I took it back; I couldn't take any lessons from him. If I was dirty, I at least wanted to see the truth of it clearly in the mirror.

"Listen to yourself, Bunny. 'They' and 'you' are the same. You work with them! Those people kidnap children, inject them with microchips, force them into a game of death and abomination while experimenting on their bodies and having them monitored by cameras and microphones and...*you*!" I ran out of breath. "Do you realize what they did to China's sister? They turned her into a literal flesh-eating monster, and then took her and others like her somewhere to experiment on them. But it did double duty, since they let us watch, to give the survivors extra incentive to use the Seeds and play their Game even better, because we're afraid to end up like the losers. Chanelle wasn't even human anymore..." My scrambling voice petered off.

—It's horrible, yes. Do you think I don't realize that? But we have to pay the price for urgent advancement. What do you want me to do?—
-Bunny-

I took a shuddering breath and let it out, the weight of everything too tiring for me to continue. It was late, and I was tired. "I just want you to face the fact that maybe you *should* be doing something about it, even if you don't know what it is yet." The anger had gone out of me, leaving behind only crushing loneliness. "You've been decent to me, Bunny. But you can't keep hiding behind your intentions. Inaction is an action, too."

I LET myself into Blaine's house the next morning, breathing hard and dripping sweat after running from the closest bus stop. I had asked everyone to come early to get a full day of cleaning and training in while the weekend was still in full swing. Soon, class would be out for seniors, and I'd be graduating. It's funny how the relative importance of graduating from high school had plummeted so abruptly.

The others were already, busying themselves cleaning our new base while Blaine fidgeted in the quarantine box.

I grabbed a rag and bucket of already cloudy water and began to wipe things down. None of us had noticed anything unusual or worrying from NIX, which reassured me that Bunny had kept our actions to himself. Or if he'd written a report, no one had read it, like he grumbled about.

Sam, up above clearing the spider webs from the loft area, leaned down to call a greeting. "Did you run here?"

"Yeah. Part of the way, anyway. I don't have a car." I shrugged. "Good exercise, and god knows I need every extra bit I can get."

Adam frowned. "It's best to have a vehicle. What if there's an emergency and you need to get somewhere fast, or get *away* fast? Except for

China, who's too young, you're the only one of us who doesn't have a ride."

"Both you and Jacky own motorcycles, right?" Sam called down.

"I have one," Adam said. "Not sure what you'd call what Jacky does."

Sam cocked his head to the side. "What do you mean?"

Jacky pursed her lips. "I may have…*borrowed* that bike."

I considered for a second if that bothered me, but only found myself wondering what skills that might entail and if they could be useful. The law was another thing that mattered so little now.

Sam smiled, innocent. "Oh. That's nice of your friend, to lend their motorcycle to you."

China, who'd been silently working beside him in the loft, stopped and stared at him incredulously along with the rest of us.

"What?" He looked back and forth at our faces.

"When she says borrowed, she doesn't mean *borrowed*," Adam said.

"Borrowed?" Sam's mental dialogue played clearly across his face, changing from "I'm totally lost," to "Oh!" to "Oh-my-god-I-can't-believe-it," to "I'm worried," over the course of a few seconds. "But what if you get caught? Won't you get in trouble with the law? And your parents?" he said aloud.

"I'm an orphan, *chico*," Jacky said with a smirk. "And I've already been in trouble with the law enough it doesn't really matter. I'm living in a detention center already. What more are they gonna do to me? I'm a minor."

Sam froze, horror and then shame washing over him along with a dark blush. "I—I'm sorry. I didn't—I… God, that was so rude of me."

Jacky stared up at him expressionlessly for a few seconds, and then busted out laughing. She laughed loud and hard, a sound that reminded me of the braying of a donkey. After pounding at her knee and gasping for air, she finally calmed down enough to say, "Oh, Sam. You were just…" She slipped into mirth again. "I say that, and you just stand there looking at me so horrified. Like you just said…like you just told me my baby was ugly. And then you look like you don't know how to apologize because I'm not even the mother. It's not my baby, I'm just fat!" She broke down again, wobbling over to the wall and leaning on it for balance.

Sam looked like he wasn't quite sure what she was saying but was relieved all the same by the fact she wasn't angry. He cracked a smile, and a laugh of his own slipped out.

I thought about what Jacky had revealed. An orphan, and living in a detention center. "Jacky, how is it you're able to meet up with us at all hours of the night if you're in a detention center? Don't they have curfews and restrictions and things like that?"

She straightened, the residual mirth slipping from her. "The warden has a soft spot for me. He lets me go out for some 'extracurricular classes', and beyond that, I just don't get caught." She grinned her cocky grin again.

But the look that had twisted her features for half a second when she spoke of the warden's soft spot was revulsion, maybe even hatred. It made me remember how she'd panicked when Adam had landed on top of her after saving her. I gave her a searching look that she resolutely ignored, then returned to my cleaning. We weren't close enough for me to probe further, and maybe I was just reading things between nonexistent lines.

After I judged the water in my pail dirty enough, I took it back to one of the sinks in Blaine's lab. Instead of returning to the others, I opened the door of the smaller quarantine room.

"Oh, god, thank goodness. I've been dying to get out of here," Blaine said.

"If you do anything stupid, I'll slice you up a bit, then I'll knock you out and lock you right back in here," I replied, sitting down at one of his lab tables. "Or I might kill you, if whatever you do is extra stupid."

He swallowed. "I want to help. But if I ally myself with you, and NIX discovers my duplicity, I may be putting the kiddos in danger."

"This is your chance to get them *out* of danger, for good, not just until the next time you can come up with something valuable to give to NIX. How long do you think your current situation can last? What if they decided that killing one of your 'kiddos' would be even better incentive for you to try and keep the other alive?"

He paled.

"And it's too late for you to go back now, you know. You're already our accomplice." I let my voice go gentle around the threat, but my gaze stayed hard and locked on his. "The only option is to get your family hidden, somewhere far away and safe."

"I am not going to do anything nefarious. Believe me, I fully understand the situation I am in. And like I said, I want to help. But"—he looked me up and down—"you may be tall, but you are still a girl, and I don't see any weapons. You said you'd kill me… How? Are you crazy strong, like that—"

I knew what he was asking, and since that's what I wanted to talk about anyway, I decided to just show him. I held my hands up and let the claws slide out. They'd grown sharper and more menacing since the first time they'd appeared, and I saw his eyes dilate as he sucked in a choked breath.

Instead of scrambling back like I half expected, he stepped forward and grabbed my hand to examine my fingers, pushing and prodding at the tips and around the base of the claws. "A weaponized biological mutation, under active control…" he muttered.

"Have you seen something like this before?"

"No, not in person. I mean, there is speculation, DNA splicing and all that, but no one has been able to figure out how to feasibly implement it." He drew a deep breath. "Would you mind if I…I'd like to study this. Study you." He waved his hand to encompass the whole team.

I grinned. "Glad you're on board. I want to know exactly what the Seeds are doing to us, and how NIX is causing all this to happen."

We sat down at one of his tables and chatted while he took samples of my blood, spit, hair, and skin, and shavings of both my claws and my normal nails, then prepared the samples for examination.

"You said they knew who you were? When they attacked and made you a Player?" he asked.

"Yeah. From what I've gathered it's more or less the same with everyone. They take you, inject you with a VR chip, tracking device, and a Seed. You get sick, and then you wake up a Player. Or you don't wake up. The ones who turned me said some things that make me think not everyone survives the process." I recounted the five minutes of helplessness that had concluded with me becoming a Player.

When I was finished, he frowned. "So the question that stands out to me is, 'Why you?' Other than the fact you are all young, I don't see an obvious pattern. I speculate there might be some genetic marker they are looking for. Something that increases your chances of adapting to the Seeds."

"Exactly. Then the next question is, 'What do they hope to accomplish?' It's got to be something big…" I thought about everything Bunny had told me and what Vaughn had said. "Every Trial, we're trying to gain the power of the gods, the incentive being fear of death…" I mused. "Which means that's what NIX wants, too. They use fear to push us toward gaining it."

Adam walked through the open door and pulled out a stool to sit on.

"Heard you talking and thought I'd join in. Next question, what would you do with the power of god if you were NIX?"

I frowned. "Before that, what exactly *is* the power of gods?"

Adam rubbed a hand through his floppy hair, making sparks jump between his fingers. "Miracles, right? Things we shouldn't be able to do, but we can because we gained something extra special as a Trial reward. Like this." He snapped his fingers and a spark jumped at me, stinging lightly where it landed. He grinned with childish smugness at my scowl.

"Which leads back around to two questions," Blaine held up a finger. "One, why do they want that power? What are they hoping to accomplish through their actions? And two, *how* are they doing this?" He bent over a microscope, peering at a slide of my blood. "Your blood has the Seed organisms floating around in it, but…something is off. Oh." He looked up at me, then back down to the slide. "Fascinating, never seen something like this before."

"What?" My voice sounded strained. "What do you see?"

He looked reluctantly away from the eyepiece. "The Seed organisms seem to have modified some of your blood cells. The majority are still normal, but a few seem to have been…enhanced. What I wouldn't give to know how they made those Seeds."

Know thine enemy. "Blaine, I have a present for you," I said. "Adam, do you still have that energy cartridge?"

"Of course."

"Lend it to the good doc." I turned back to Blaine. "I heard you had some issues with high energy requirements on one of your inventions. We've got something from the Trial world with enough capacity to power a single person's teleportation. It might help your research. Though it likely won't work, after coming back to Earth. The Boneshaker seems to have a deadly effect on electronics."

"Are you serious? An artifact from within the Game? Wait. So where exactly are they transporting you? What is the Game world?"

Adam and I exchanged a glance.

"That's a great question," I said. "Wherever it is, it's a real place. I mean, I'd considered it being a hallucination, or some sort of Virtual Reality simulation, but bringing back both injuries and objects…it wouldn't make sense."

Adam nodded, looking down. "I'm thinking…maybe an alternate dimension? Or maybe we're being beamed away to an alien planet. Or they're sending us way into the past or future. Some of the things we've seen would make sense, if the Trials are the future of Earth in a few thousand years. If NIX could gain advancements from the future—the technological and genetic advancements—they'd have a monopoly on… everything. They could take over the world."

"But what about the double moons?" The question popped out of my mouth as I thought it. "Earth has one moon."

"I don't know, maybe we got crazy and decided we'd build another one up there as a resort destination or something." He snorted. "But I was thinking, maybe something happens in the future. Some extinction-level event. That might explain an extra moon, and why there's no sentient life, despite evidence of humans."

"*Giant* humans?"

"Yeah. Which also makes me think it's thousands of years in the past. We have a few fossils of extremely oversized humans. Maybe before the dinosaurs, when the Earth could support life that large. Or maybe it's Atlantis." He snorted again.

I frowned, trying to understand the implication of any of his theories.

"Wait," Blaine said. "If it's the ancient past, that means bipedal, humanoid life evolved on Earth…twice. The ramifications of that…"

Adam shrugged. "Maybe. Or maybe it's an alternate dimension. Or it's *not* Earth at all. It kinda feels like hell to me." He grimaced at his own quip. "This really isn't my area of expertise. I'm just speculating."

Blaine's eyes had grown even brighter with fascination. "So where is this energy cartridge? Perhaps I can gain some clues through examination!"

Adam rolled his eyes. "Not here. I'll bring it for you tomorrow."

I decided to interrupt Blaine's impatient eagerness. "I don't want you to give NIX complete projects anymore. Withhold as much as you can from your best effort, keeping it at the point where they won't notice. And keep the real product for us. Can you do that?"

"Maybe…I don't think they would know the difference, either way. If they were intelligent enough to figure that out, they would not need me. But why?"

I ignored the question, knowing both men at the table were more than smart enough to work it out. "How soon do you think you can have something ready to hand over to NIX?"

"If it doesn't have to be perfect? Maybe…two weeks?"

"Okay. Make it happen." Two weeks. I hoped it was enough time for the team to prepare, and for me to turn a plan into reality.

It would have to be.

ADAM AND CHINA came to my house the next day, when I was alone, to stop all the monitoring equipment from giving NIX accurate information. They hopefully wouldn't know the difference, but I would be able to speak and act a little more freely. The two of them left before my brother or mom came home, leaving me alone with my thoughts. My mind was still consumed by our lack of information. Later, Adam called and sent me a link to video from the Net to the new ID sheath my mom had reluctantly bought me, pulling me out of my spiraling thoughts. "Take a look at this. I think he might be one of us," he said.

I sat on the chair next to my bed and flicked up the video.

A young man stood in the midst of a kneeling group, brushing his fingers against their outstretched hands. His body was surrounded by a faint glow, and when his skin touched theirs, a ring of light pulsed from the joining, and for a second, they also glowed. He walked through them toward a large stone chair sitting on a pedestal and sat looking out at his supplicants with a grim smile. His eyes flicked to the camera. "I am your god. Let those who recognize my power join me." The video clip cut out.

"What do you think? That thing about being god, and the light…it might just be fancy tricks, but maybe not," Adam said.

I shook my head. "No, it's not a trick. I know him. Vaughn Ridley. See what you can find on him and let me know. ASAP."

"Got it. Give me a couple minutes."

I dressed to go out and opened my door to find my brother standing outside it.

We both jumped, and he smiled ruefully. "Hey, sorry. I was just going to ask, do you want some food? I made enough for both of us…"

"Um, I'm going out. But I am starving. I'll grab some to go, thanks."

"Where are you going?"

"To see a…friend." Vaughn was the farthest thing from a friend, but I couldn't say 'Oh, I'm going to see someone who I hate, even after only knowing him for ten minutes total, because I need information he might have about how to stay alive. After all, he may be a sociopath, but I'm dealing with a whole organization of sociopaths, and the enemy of my enemy is my friend…'

"You've got a lot of new friends lately," Zed said.

I frowned. "Yeah. I do." His suspicion was understandable, but it was just one more burden, one more thing to deal with, and I didn't have the strength to carry it.

"I'd like to meet them, if that's okay with you," he said, relenting in the face of my stare.

"Yeah, maybe sometime." I slipped past him, grabbed some food to sate my now constantly ravenous appetite, and left the house.

Adam sent me the location where the video had been taken, and I headed straight there at a loping run I never could have sustained when I was normal. Before the Game.

I arrived a half-hour later at an out-of-the-way, rundown building. It was in the jobless slum section, and, despite knowing I could handle myself better than any normal girl, I couldn't help the wariness that prickled as I felt hungry, despairing eyes follow my running form. Before the attempted terrorist air strikes seven years ago, the area had been normal, if slightly lower-income. Now even the air was bitter and faintly slimy. My breathing was heavy, and I was covered in sweat, so I stopped to compose myself before going further, and got bowled over by a large golden blur.

My first instinct was panic, followed instantaneously by the urge to attack, but the feel of a wet tongue on my face and the stink of an unbrushed mouth calmed me. It was only a dog.

But the dog was followed close on its heels by a laughing Vaughn. When he saw me, his eyes widened in surprise. He hesitated a second, then reached out one hand to pull the dog back, and the other to help me up. "Well, if it isn't Little Miss Spirit-Type. Come to join me? If it's for you, I've got space in my ranks anytime."

I ignored his hand and rose unaided to my feet. "Vaughn. You know my name. Please use it."

He chuckled. "Eve. What brings you here? And how did you find me?"

"I found you through that video you posted online. Are you trying to get yourself killed?"

"Hardly. I'm not revealing anything that I shouldn't. I'm simply… drawing attention. I'm surprised to have a response so quickly, though I somehow doubt you're here to answer my summons. That video only went up hours ago. How did you find me?"

"I've got resources. Not unlike yourself, I think?" I tilted my head to the side and forced a smile. "Though why you would want to draw attention to yourself, I still don't understand."

"Ooh. Charm and flattery will get you…" He trailed off suggestively.

"Your attention?" I supplied.

"But you already have that. Why are you here, Eve?"

I nibbled on the inside of my lip. "When we first met, you told me that you were aiming to become a god. That the Trial was weeding out the weak from the strong. What did you mean by that?"

"Ah, you're here because you want information. I meant exactly what I said." He winked at me. "You'll have to ask more specific questions if you want more specific answers, Eve."

The subtle smirk twisting one corner of his mouth made me want to claw his face. He hadn't really done anything to cause my current ire, but perhaps it was the fact I saw myself in his eyes and didn't like the reflection. "Tell me about NIX. And how do the Seeds work?"

"You go right for the jugular. You've toughened up a bit since that Trial, burned off some softness. I like it." He looked me up and down, obviously giving his statement double meaning.

"Please, just answer the question."

"Now why would I do that? You obviously understand that information is valuable. What would I get in return, of sufficient value to match the knowledge I'd be sharing with you?"

Damn it. "What do you want?" What could I offer him that he didn't already have? And more important, what was I willing to give?

"Information would be good, but if you're coming to me, I assume you don't have anything I don't already know." He quirked an eyebrow, silently asking if he was right.

I wasn't so sure he *was* right, but I didn't want to test that by comparing notes. Any information I had that he didn't was likely specific to my team and would only make us vulnerable to him. So I kept my voice silent and my face impassive.

"If you agreed to join me, I'd tell you everything I know, but I don't think that's going to happen," he continued. "So, I think I'll have to settle for one favor, the specifics of which are to be determined at a later date."

"One *small* favor."

"Those questions you asked weren't small. One large favor."

"You're only giving me words, which I have to take at face value. It's not big enough to qualify for a large favor. I'll do small-to-medium, and that's it. And whatever you tell me better be good and thorough."

He laughed. "Okay, I'll take it. NIX, though I don't know how you found out that name, is an organization searching for strength, for excellence. A type of power you can't find on Earth. The Seeds allow them to search it out. A catalyst, you know? Those things separate you from all the other mere humans on the planet. They're like limit disablers. When you wish on them, they change your current self irreversibly from what you were before, but they also augment the bounds of what you can become. Eventually, if we prove ourselves worthy, we'll pass certain limits. The ones that separate humans from gods. The way—"

He stopped talking abruptly and looked over my shoulder. "You brought backup, I see."

I tensed, turning around slowly and following the direction of his gaze. I took three steps forward and looked around the corner of the building.

My brother stood there, eyes wide and mouth open, but no sound escaping.

"What the hell are you doing here, Zed?" I said, my voice low and grating.

He looked back and forth between Vaughn and me, still wordless.

"How long have you been standing there?" I demanded.

Vaughn stepped forward and touched the back of my elbow. "Please tell me he's a Player."

My heart seized for a minute as I took in the meaning of his words, and then crashed against my chest in a painful thump. My eyes snapped to his in wordless fear.

Reading my expression, Vaughn's face twisted in a way that almost ruined his handsomeness. "You set me up. Trying to get NIX to take me out for revealing information? Screw you."

I shook my head. "What? No. No, they can't know. I've got to get him out of here." I strode forward, grabbed Zed's arm, and yanked him away. "This never happened, Vaughn," I called desperately over my shoulder.

"What—what was going on back there, Eve?" Zed said. "What did he mean, 'take him out'? Are you in trouble? I mean, is something going on?"

I yanked harder on his arm, looking around in paranoia. Had they been monitoring our conversation? Did they know what Zed had heard? How soon could NIX's cleaners track him down? "How long were you there?" I snapped.

He looked around in confusion, following my darting eyes. "I'm sorry

I followed you. I was just worried. You've been different lately, Eve. You don't talk to me anymore, and every time you think no one's looking, you've got this look on your face like…I can't even explain it." He pried my fingers off his arm and tugged to slow me down. "Scared, angry, exhausted, I don't know. But you're not happy, Eve. Please talk to me."

I grabbed him by the arm again and kept dragging. "Zed, what the hell?! What did you think you were doing? Following me, sneaking around, spying on me?" My voice got louder as I went, and I had to take a deep breath to calm myself.

I dragged him the rest of the way home, ignoring his worried pestering at me to talk to him. When we arrived, I slammed the door behind us, did a frantic search through the house to make sure no one had broken in, and then turned on him. "You've got to mind your own business. It's not cool to…do what you did!" I sighed, stepped forward, and placed my hands on his shoulders, level with my own. "Please. I'm absolutely fine. You don't need to worry about me. I'm doing great. I've been working out as part of a group, sort of an exclusive club of friends. You just snooped on a private meeting."

He looked at me as if he didn't recognize me and shook his head. "Just talk to me. Let me help you."

"I don't need your help, Zed. Because nothing's *wrong*! Well, *one* thing's wrong, and it's you, acting like this. Why can't you just accept that for once I might have some friends? For once, I'm not the invisible girl. Just. Back. Off. Okay?" I wished I was still the invisible girl, the one nothing extraordinary ever happened to. I'd been bitter, not even knowing how wonderfully good I'd had it.

He stared at me a while longer, and then stepped forward and wrapped his arms around me. "I'm sorry. I didn't even realize that's what I was doing. Of course you should have friends. I'm just not used to not being a part of every aspect of your life. I'll give you some space." His voice was contrite and sincere, but I couldn't see his face and didn't catch the look in his eyes.

"Wait, Zed," I called out. I sighed deeply, letting some of the tension and anger go. "Sorry I got so upset," I mumbled reluctantly. I hated apologizing. "Do you want to…help me make pudding?"

He paused for a second, and then nodded.

In the kitchen, we got the ingredients for homemade pudding out quickly, working in easy harmony.

"Do you remember the first time we made pudding?" he asked. I did, but I let him keep talking. "It was my first day of school, and I saw those kids teasing you in the hallway because you were so tall. I got mad and started yelling at them, but you just grabbed my hand and told me they were stupid and *short!* Then you laughed and we made up all those short-people jokes. 'You shouldn't listen to short people 'cause their body is too worried trying to make them grow to work on their brain. The air is different all the way down there where short people breath, so if they say stupid stuff just take a good breath and feel sorry for them. A blonde and a short person walk into a bar, and then a chair, and a table. Short people never clean the tops of their refrigerators, filthy animals!" He laughed. "We were so silly, but you distracted me from being upset. I remember when we got home Mom was still at work, and I was hungry, so you said you knew how to make pudding. You totally didn't!"

I elbowed him lightly. "But at least I was smart enough to look up a recipe!"

"Which I promptly screwed up. Hey, I didn't know how to read yet! How was I supposed to know the difference between flour and starch? And you're the one who added the yum-powder."

"It's supposed to make everything taste better! That's what the commercial says!"

He affected a high-pitched little girl's voice. "Oh, it's okay you added the flour, we'll just put the pudding in the oven and make pudding-cake! It'll be delicious! I'm sure the huge warning on the yum-powder not to cook it isn't important!"

I flicked some starch into his face, making him sputter and shutting up his mimicry. "I did not sound like that."

His eyes narrowed, and his own hand darted out for a fistful of starch. "That's the part you're going to focus on?" He eyed me up threateningly. "Not the fact that you almost blew up the stove and turned the kitchen purple?"

I backed up slowly, eyeing him warily. "*Me*? I seem to remember—" I was cut off by a fistful of starch flying at my face in a cloudy explosion, and then our argument descended into a food fight.

I was kneeling on Zed's back and rubbing an egg into his hair with one hand as I incapacitated him with tickling from the other when our mother walked into the room, just home from work. I froze, and Zed choked on his laughter.

My mother's eyes tracked over the food-strewn kitchen and back to the two of us on the floor. "Pudding is cursed in this house," she said succinctly, and then walked away.

Zed started guffawing first and I followed, laughing so hard I rolled off him and couldn't pick myself up off the floor for a long while.

Pudding had always been the thing for us to make together, especially when we were feeling down about something. It never failed to lift our moods, no matter how many years passed. That hadn't changed, and, for a while, I forgot everything else that wanted my attention and just had fun with the only person in the world who I could count on to have my back. Which was also the reason he was the only person in the world I wanted to protect from myself.

Later, I went back to find Vaughn again, but he was gone, with no trace that he or any of his fanatic followers had ever been there.

Chapter 17

Corruption, do not take it gently. You must rip it out and burn it. Then spit on the ashes.

— Kaiser Fell

I JERKED from sleep to the sound of my alarm before the sun had risen all the way over the horizon. Seniors didn't have school that week as we'd already taken our exit tests, and I needed every spare second to prepare. I stood and dressed, thinking wistfully of my soft, comfortable bed. Then I thought of the Trial in a few days and suddenly rest seemed much less alluring. "I can rest when I'm dead," I croaked in a sleep-roughened voice. "And if I live, sleep is something I'm willing to give up indefinitely in return."

After the incident with Vaughn, I'd been extra wary of NIX. I supposed Vaughn might have just changed locations, but I thought it more likely NIX's cleaners had something to do with it. But they hadn't come for me or Zed, and I could only hope that meant they weren't going to. I'd questioned Bunny as subtly as possible, but he didn't seem aware of any danger to either myself or my family. I would have liked to keep watch over Zed constantly, but he would have grown even more suspicious, and I had other obligations.

Still, it made me think hard about how I would keep my family safe, because my team and I weren't the only ones in danger from NIX.

I ran to Blaine's house again, arriving drenched in sweat but feeling surprisingly good. I'd leveled up my Stamina twice.

A gratifying scene greeted me when I walked into the basement room I'd commandeered. Jacky and Sam were already there, moving furniture in. The windows high above were clean, and the extra light shining through them brightened the room.

Training mats covered a large portion of the cement floor. Weights and bands sat in one corner, and in another stood a swiveling upright cylinder of wood with rods sticking out of it all around, the kind I'd seen people training with in kung-fu movies. Large punching bags hung by huge chains from two big hooks in the ceiling. Smaller bags hung under the loft, and large mirrors had been attached to the long wall so we could keep an eye on our form while training.

Blaine stepped up beside me. "Jacky said you would need these things, so I bought them and had them delivered last night. They have been unpacking the whole morning."

"You paid for this?" I asked.

"Yes. But it is no big deal. I have money, and you needed things that money buys. Easy solution."

"Nice." The type of wealth my new ally had might come in extremely useful. Money created opportunities where none had existed before. I stepped in to help move the rest of the furniture to the upstairs loft and set up the training equipment. While we were working, Adam and China joined us, and Blaine ordered Chinese takeout for everyone, joking that he wouldn't be getting pizza delivered again for a long time.

I stuffed my stomach in silence, like the others, while Blaine watched in amazement. Something about being a Player seemed to ramp up our metabolisms, so we were always hungry. When the hunger had subsided somewhat, I said, "We need to set up training regimens for everyone. Get stronger before the Trial."

With her mouth stuffed full of chicken, Jacky said, "I'm the best fighter here, so I'll be in charge of training and exercise."

I nodded. "Anyone else have something?"

China looked around before raising her hand. "I can teach everyone how to throw knives. And I don't know if it's important enough, but I do yoga and meditation, and it helps to increase Grace and Perception. If you want, I'd be happy to help with that."

I wasn't sure how useful that would be, but any increase in Attributes was a bonus, and I knew I for one could do with some relaxation. "That sounds great."

I looked to Adam, who snorted. "Sam of the Second Coming may have helped, but my arm's still fractured. Fight training's out for me. And I can't teach you guys to be smarter." Jacky scowled, but Adam ignored her. "I can draw and do magic tricks. Not exactly something you guys need. But," he conceded, "I might be able to show you and the doc how my computer monitoring programs work. That way, if I die you'll still be able to get updates."

Sam said, "I can't really teach how to heal people, but I could give some basic first aid and trauma stabilization training. In case something happened and I…wasn't there," he finished, obviously uncomfortable with the thought of his own death.

Blaine cleared his throat. "Umm…it would take years to teach you guys to do what I do, but I have got some ideas for things I could make to help you in the Trials."

"Okay, wonderful," I said, beaming around at the others. "I don't have any skills to share that you don't already have, but I have ideas, and a plan for getting out of all this. I'm working with Blaine to figure out exactly what the things they put into us are. I'm still working on getting more information and figuring out fine details, but I'll share my plan with you all when I've got something more complete. If we survive till then, that is."

Jacky raised her eyebrows and pursed her lips. "On that note, I need to see everyone spar so I can figure out a good training plan for each of you. Don't use no special Skills, just your natural abilities. I don't wanna get someone killed." She glanced at China.

Adam and China both tried to question me about my plan, but I fended them off. I was still trying to figure it out myself, and my ideas and the snippets of things I'd learned hadn't formed into anything solid I could share. Giving them hope was enough for now. If I explained what little "plan" I actually had, it might take that hope away.

After explaining what she wanted, Jacky paired me up against Adam, and Sam against China. The latter two went first, China dancing around Sam and throwing playing cards at him in place of her knives, along with darting in and "stabbing" him with them. He refused to attack her, but nevertheless failed to properly defend himself.

Adam and I were next. Despite the handicap of his healing arm, he seemed more than confident enough in his ability to fight me. "You're going down, Eve Redding."

I raised an eyebrow and grinned at him. "Go ahead and try." I was fully aware that I didn't know how to fight. And without my claws, I would be just a slightly uncoordinated girl flailing against a guy who'd been in his first street fight long before becoming a Player. Steeling myself for pain and humiliation, I tried to imitate his loose, ready stance.

Jacky grunted to herself, but I didn't take my eyes off Adam and the way he held his legs, arms, feet, and back.

He shot forward, I felt a tap on my chest, and then the world was tilting off its axis. I slammed hard into the floor, half knocking my breath out. I groaned and rolled over, ignoring a tap on my side as he mimed a kick while I was still down.

I got to my feet and readied myself. My subconscious had responded to my instinctual fear, and though I held my claws in, focus sharpened all my senses. I could smell the new plastic of the pads under my feet, my own sweat, and the scent of my opponent.

He lunged forward again without warning, tapped me on the side of the head and the side of my left knee, and then kicked my legs out from under me.

I didn't lose my breath when I landed on my back that time.

He stretched out a hand to help me up, and a mischievous thought popped into my head. I didn't pause to think long enough to seem suspicious as I reached out my hand to him. As soon as I had a good grip on him, I braced myself against the floor with my other arm and swung my leg around low to the mat and fast.

His eyes widened as my leg made contact with his calf, and I felt a flicker of satisfaction as he started to fall.

But then my grip on his hand was broken, and he half-jumped, half-twisted over my head and behind me, wrapped an arm around my throat, and squeezed. While not painful, it was definitely uncomfortable.

I tapped his arm twice and he released me. I grinned, turning to look up at him. "Sorry. I just couldn't resist."

Jacky started laughing. "You did well, Eve. Next time isn't gonna be so easy, I think."

Adam pushed his hair off his forehead. "No, it won't."

I stood without his help and prepared for his attack once again. A giddy feeling rose within me, a mix of fierce competitiveness and laughter. I breathed deeply and focused on him.

He lunged, and I followed each subtle movement he made, how far his steps took him, and where he slipped his leg behind my own.

The world tilted in a way that was becoming familiar as my feet were ripped from under me. He thrust his good hand at my face to smash my head toward the ground. It would have been a devastating move if there weren't thick padding below us.

I grabbed his wrist in both hands and pulled my legs toward my chest as I fell, tucking my head forward so it didn't land first. When my back hit the mat, I slammed my legs forward into Adam's chest and pushed upward, using my grip on his arm to swing him over my head and smash him full length onto the mat behind me. As he hit, I released his arm and used my backwards momentum to flip onto my hands and knees. I crouched by his head and snapped my hand to his unprotected neck.

Everything was still except for his heartbeat thumping against my fingers. After a moment, I realized I was panting as if I'd just run a race. Somehow my claws were out, pressed against the skin of his throat. I stood, forced my claws back, and held out a hand to help him up. "Sorry about the claws. I got a little carried away."

He stared up at me, then slowly grabbed my hand and allowed himself to be helped up.

"Holy…crap," Sam said from the sidelines.

Jacky walked over and smacked me hard on the back with a grin. "Seems you're a bit of a natural. Quick to acclimate."

Adam started to laugh. "That was amazing. Let's go again."

After that, Adam wasn't so careless and didn't try to throw me again. Instead, he danced around and jabbed at me, light taps on various exposed areas that I knew would have quickly left me dead if he had one of his butterfly knives in his hand.

I tried to learn from his movements, and by the end of our sparring match we were both dripping sweat onto the mat, but at least I'd gotten a few taps of my own in.

"HEY, SAM," I called. "Do you think you could help me out? I think I tweaked my neck a bit." I rubbed the completely uninjured muscles.

"Sure," he said, giving me and innocent nod and following me to a corner of the room. He put a hand on my neck, then shifted it around, frowning. "I don't sense anything. Where does it hurt?"

"It doesn't," I murmured to him in a low voice. Only China would have the hearing to make out our conversation, and a glance confirmed she was busy getting instruction from Jacky at the moment. "I just wanted to chat with you."

"What's wrong?" he whispered gravely.

"Nothing!" I chuckled. "I just wanted to talk about your Skill."

"Oh." That didn't seem to reassure him.

"I know there's something you held back when you were explaining. I respect your right to privacy, but as the team leader I can see some Game information on you, remember?" I smiled in what I hoped was a reassuring way. "Will you explain the Skill to me?"

His lips were white, but he nodded. "My Skill isn't strictly for healing. It's like a sick joke. Whatever I heal, my body assimilates and understands—to recycle as a morphed attack. And the more horrifying and twisted the injury, the better I learn it."

I stared at him for a few minutes. "So...that paralyzing saliva?"

He nodded.

"Show me," I commanded.

He hesitated, then placed his hands on the bare skin of my neck again. Almost immediately, my skin started to go numb. It wasn't the same as the feeling of the grub-pug's saliva. Sam's version made me want to scratch and claw at the numb patch till it ripped away.

"Okay!" I urged, and he touched my neck again, returning sensation to my skin and stopping the torture.

"Wow," I said.

"That was mild. It gets worse. Way worse. This Skill is a punishment. I hate it." He glared at his hands. "I don't want to use it, Eve." He looked up to meet my gaze.

"Not even against monsters? You'd fight them anyway, right? That's a really great Skill, Sam, and if—"

"No!" he snapped, then, a bit more subdued, "No, I don't want to use it. Just like with any Skill, it gets stronger the more you use it. I'll use the healing side, but, as much as possible, I want to avoid making it even easier for me to kill someone. I won't use it."

I searched his eyes for a second. "Okay."

"And...don't tell the others?" he added hesitantly.

"You're our *healer*, Sam." When he didn't pick up my meaning, I added, "And that's it."

He let out a sigh of relief, and we returned to the others.

Jacky set me up on one of the lighter punching bags and showed me a few simple combinations of punches and kicks she wanted me to practice until I could do them in my sleep. "Your fancy move back there might'a worked, but being efficient and effective is better than being flashy. When you've got these moves down by instinct, it reduces the chance of failure."

She watched me till I started to get the hang of it, and then showed me how to hit with my elbow. "The elbow can do a lotta damage at close range. At the point you're closest to the bag, start to add that into the combo." Once again, she watched me attack the bag. "You need practice with combat. But even so, I would trust you to fight at my back."

I hid my surprised grin behind my shirt as I used it to wipe away the sweat dripping down my face. "You know, aren't you supposed to start off training me with basic blocks and evasion? Defense first?"

She laughed and cracked her knuckles. "The best defense is an overwhelmingly powerful offense, I always say."

With that, she left me to my practice. I alternated between starting the combo with my left and right hand, and repeated until my knuckles were raw and bleeding, my wrists wobbly and weak, and my shoulders felt like they were being ripped out of their sockets every time I moved my arms.

Sam placed a hand on the bag in front of my face to get my attention and jerked his head to China standing on the mat. "Time for a cool-down."

China told us to follow her lead, then ran us through some seemingly easy movements that were, in fact, anything but. Something like yoga mixed with a martial dance, each movement slow and controlled. She watched us all in the mirrored wall across from the mat, correcting our form when needed.

I was shaking like I had a car battery attached to my central nervous system, and so was incredibly relieved when China finally had us sit down. We folded our legs, laid our hands on our laps, and closed our eyes. As I breathed deeply, I became aware of the blood rushing in my veins and the air entering and leaving my lungs. The sweat on my skin was cool, and I could feel the currents of the air moving around me. Heat radiated off my flushed skin in waves. I focused harder and realized I could hear the others breathing. I could smell their sweat mixed with the piney scent of the cleaning liquid we'd doused the place with. Outside, the wind blew gently. I knew because it made a low, smooth noise as it parted and cut around the corner of the house above. I reached farther all at once, and something different happened.

My eyes were closed, but whiteness fogged the backs of my eyelids. As I concentrated harder, it solidified. My body hurt with cold and fatigue. I felt something come alert, and then a sense of amazement. My wrists and ankles started to hurt, and I realized that my body was yanking against something, though I wasn't consciously moving it. The room around me shone with painfully bright light, and, as my view changed, chunks of hair fell across my face and blocked some of it out. Dirty blonde hair, not my own almost black strands.

A deep, croaking voice spoke in a language I didn't know but seemed familiar all the same. Adrenaline built until I couldn't keep my concentration, and I felt my mind ripping away from that place despite something trying desperately to grab and keep me there.

My eyes opened and I jerked violently backward, an awkward half-shout bursting out of me. I looked around at the familiar base again and held my hands up in front of my face, moving them deliberately. I was there. I was me.

The others stared at me.

"Are you okay?" Sam asked, his brows furrowed in concern.

"Cramp?" Jacky gave me a sympathetic look as she stretched her own forearms. "Stretch it out."

I shook my head. "No, I, um…" I swallowed and lost track of what I was saying when a Window popped up, telling me I'd leveled up Perception and Focus. "I had a mini hallucination, or maybe…a dream? I couldn't have fallen asleep in that amount of time, right? I saw a white room, and I couldn't move my arms and legs…"

"You're probably exhausted," Sam said. "You should go home and get some rest. We all should, actually. There's only so much our bodies can take in one day."

My head ached so badly that it felt like something was literally pounding on the inside of my skull. "Yeah, you're right." I needed to be strong, not seem panicked and crazy. But I remembered where I'd heard that language before. It had sounded in my head when I was first made a Player. "I'm going to go get some juice. I think I might be a bit dehydrated." This was probably true, considering the amount I'd sweated out.

Instead of getting a drink, though, I plunked myself down in front of Blaine, who was scribbling formulas onto the screen of a glass pad in tiny, scrawling handwriting. "I need you to figure out what they put in my head, and what it's doing to me. I just had a hallucination," I said.

He kept scribbling for a moment as if he hadn't heard me, and just when I was about to repeat myself, he stopped writing, put the pen down, and said, "Great! I have been wanting to do more tests, but the others all seem a bit wary of me, and I haven't been able to get a willing subject."

I rubbed the back of my neck, remembering the two sharp pains I'd felt as they inserted something under my skin. "They put something at the base of my skull, and something else a little lower down. From what Bunny's told me, one's a virtual reality chip, and the other is probably a GPS tracker. Can you get them out?"

Blaine pushed his glasses up and walked away to grab some weird device from his supply closet. He mounted its two halves on my shoulders, on either side of my neck, and fiddled around behind me.

I felt a warmth, and then he put something sticky on either side of my neck, picked up a smartglass tablet from the table, and pulled up what looked kind of like an X-ray on its screen, except I could see shooting pulses of energy moving along my spine and into my brain.

"Like you stated, there is one at the base of your skull, and one a little lower down." He pointed to two different spots of discoloration, then pinched and flicked at the screen, and the picture zoomed in to the base of my skull.

A little spider-like thing nested there, except it had too many legs to be a spider, they were too long, and each of them was digging upward into the base of my brain.

I swallowed.

"I am assuming this would be the Virtual Reality chip. Of course, it is not fully integrated, but those tendrils likely extend into your visual cortex, which is what allows you to see the Game Windows," he said.

"Can you get it out?"

"Not without risking serious damage to your brain and spine. It has embedded itself like a tick. Honestly, I doubt you will ever be free of it."

"Well, could you just kill it, then?"

"It is attached to your brain and has a power source strong enough to control your visual cortex. If I were to risk doing anything to it, I could damage your brain beyond repair. I am not a neurosurgeon, Eve. The most I could offer you would be a signal blocker between NIX and your brain, but I would need some time to make it work."

I lifted my hands and sent a blank message Window to Adam using my new Command Skill. The nestled spider let out a flurry of small bright pulses.

Adam sent me a message back, and it pulsed again.

—Is everything okay?—
-Adam-

"Did you just use the Game interface?"

I nodded.

"Well, that proves my theory." Blaine went off again, returning quickly with another gadget, a bright smile on his face that kind of annoyed me, seeing as the situation was decidedly not cheerful.

Adam popped his head into the room. "What's going on?"

Blaine waved him over. "Oh, come look at this. We are scanning the implants NIX put into Eve. It is quite fascinating. Do it again, Eve," he said, stepping back and pointing a small, curved satellite-like dish at me.

I sent Adam another message.

"Ooh. Interesting. The lower implant, which is definitely a GPS, is sending out timed pulses to nowhere, but I can also see the data transfer between you and Adam. Each of the chips must have some kind of local-area wireless technology built in. I wonder if we might be able to do some tracking of this data between you and Bunny." Blaine lifted his head over the device and grinned at me.

That, I could see the cheer in.

We spent the next hour doing little tests on Adam and me, and Blaine came to the tentative conclusion that he might be able to create something to block Game interaction from NIX while keeping the localized access between me and my team. As for the GPS, it was also embedded into my spine, but not my brain, and though he didn't want to try and remove either of the implants, he thought he might be able to create a localized shock that would render the GPS useless without much damage to the rest of me.

But he had no idea what might have caused the hallucination, especially as the VR chip wasn't connected to my auditory cortex, and I knew I'd *heard* things. He hypothesized my problem was too much stress and extended physical and emotional trauma, and seconded Sam's advice to get some rest.

After a while, our resident scientist sat down and began to draw diagrams and make notes to himself while glancing at the videos he'd taken through the gadgets on my neck.

"Do you need a ride home? You ran here again, right? I can take you on my bike," Adam offered. "I have a feeling you'd get a few feet past the door and collapse, in the state you're in."

My eyes widened at the offer. I must have looked even worse than I felt. But riding home while someone else drove sounded wonderful. No thinking, no moving. "Yes, thank you. That would be great."

"Okay. Wait here while I get my stuff."

When we were alone, I turned to Blaine. "What plans do you have in place to keep yourself safe if you were ever able to save your niece and nephew from NIX?"

He stared at me from behind his glasses, but then his surprise faded away and he started to talk. We laid plans for a few minutes until Adam poked his head back through the doorway and told me he was ready to leave.

I stood up and made my trembling way to the door. I needed to rest, and then try for a repeat of the hallucination, if that was what it was. I could feel it was significant, and I needed to find out exactly *why* I believed that.

Log of Captivity 3

Mental Log of Captivity—Estimated Day: Two thousand, six hundred eleven.

I do not know how, but my master reached out to me today, as I have been doing to her, though the *blood-covenant* is still incomplete. She touched my mind, fairly *skin-jacked* me! It was only for a moment, and then she withdrew, but I am filled to bursting with these strange feelings I barely remember. Pride and happiness suffuse me, because I know she is in this way acknowledging our *blood-covenant.* A Matrix has accepted me, and I can only be selfishly grateful that she must be still too young to know the worth of her bond.

Chapter 18

I wanted to find one law to cover all of living. I found fear.
— Michael Ondaatje

I SPENT the next few days worrying fruitlessly about Zed, sparring, endlessly smashing different parts of my body against the unfeeling sandbag till I felt like I would fall apart, and learning how to throw knives and darts from China. I also spent a fair amount of time trying to reach that hyper-aware state again. Although I gained points in Focus from trying so hard, I had no luck. In addition to Focus, I levelled up and gained several other Attribute points through the sheer amount of work I was putting in, so my efforts weren't exactly fruitless.

On the tenth day, we gathered in the base and waited for the Trial to start. I'd told Blaine about the video I'd taken of my teleportation and asked him to monitor and study our disappearance. We were attached to wireless biometric monitors and surrounded by high frame rate cameras. Tension filled every corner of the room as we anticipated what was to come, checked and rechecked our equipment, and tried in vain to relax.

Finally, after hours of my understandably fruitless attempts to meditate, the Boneshaker played. The five of us gathered together, and we left together.

My knees tried to buckle under the sudden added weight after the transfer, but I was prepared. My stomach roiled, and I took a deep breath of the strangely flavored air.

We were all standing together, as we had been. I turned in a circle, looking around. Under my feet lay black, granite-looking stone, reaching far and unbroken in every direction until it met with what looked to be a waterfall reaching into the sky. It was almost as if someone had placed us upside down on a huge black penny, turned on the sink, and placed us under a running faucet.

It wasn't what I was expecting. There was no greenery, no buildings, no rioting mass of strong colors and strange shapes. Ahead was the familiar black cube that always welcomed us to a Trial, but with a little extra this time.

HERE YOU WILL BE TRIED, YOUR MEASURE TAKEN. THE WORTHY WILL BE GRANTED THE POWER OF THE GODS. TAKE YOUR PLACES ON THE BOARD.

Almost immediately, a timer appeared in front of my face with a three-minute deadline. The other Players milled around the cube, speaking with despair-tinged voices.

"What's going on?" I asked.

Adam's voice was grim. "It's going to be an Intelligence-type Trial." Something about his tone put a heavy stone pit in the bottom of my stomach.

Jacky nodded. "Every once in a while we get the mental Trials." She cracked her knuckles. "They're…hard." Her voice cracked along with her joints and her face was pale.

Sam was studying his own hands intently, his breathing suddenly heavy and desperate.

I'd heard of mental Trials from the others before. There was often no Moderator, and the Players had to use clues and deductive reasoning to figure out how to survive and win. And there was usually a cruel twist of some sort. They were almost always a bloodbath, with higher fatality rates than any other type of Trial.

This was bad. Very bad.

I looked around for a clue to the cube's message and noticed an aberration in the smooth stone ground. Circles about a meter in diameter were etched into the stone. I focused on one, which was bordered in complex, almost Celtic looking knots, and, on the inward-facing side, small, ornate letters spelled out the name, "Adam Coyle."

"Adam!" I called. "This one's got your name on it." I pointed to my feet, then walked to the one directly next to it and saw my own name. "And this one's mine, I guess." Good, that was good. Adam had the highest Intelligence in our group, and I the second highest, after recent increases.

I turned to my team. "We'll make it through this, working together." I reached out and grabbed both China and Jacky by the hand.

Jacky squeezed back. "This isn't my specialty. Gimme a monster to fight any day, not puzzles and silence."

China took a deep breath and stood as tall as possible with her small body. "I won't die here. I've still got to find Chanelle."

"None of us are alone." I squeezed their hands and met the eyes of both Adam and Sam, trying to instill confidence in my words. "Everyone!" I called out loudly. "Find the circle with your name on it and get inside. Before the time runs out."

Slowly, the whole group of Players in that Trial obeyed. As soon as the last person stepped into their circle, the timer abruptly disappeared, and clear bars shot up around each of us.

I reached out and touched one. It was warm and buzzing, but unmovable. There wasn't enough room between the bars to squeeze through. We were trapped.

Angry calls rang out at me from around the ring, as if I was responsible for this.

Adam tried to shake and rattle his bars in the cage next to mind, but to no avail. He caught me watching and took a deep breath, pushing his hair out of his face. "I don't know what's going on. But this worries me."

I smiled. "That's okay. Neither do I. But we'll figure it out."

He cracked a small smile, and then another timer popped up in front of our faces, this time for thirty minutes.

The ground of my circle moved strangely, causing me to stumble. An opening had appeared just in front of me, out of which a small black cube rose up and settled at my feet. I bent to touch it tentatively, and when nothing happened, picked it up.

It was shiny and smooth, except for an infinity symbol on one side and hairline cracks dividing the surface with curves and lines. I tilted the box back and forth and ran my finger over the surface, trying to see the cracks more clearly. They seemed to be geometrically shaped, not the random lightning branches of true cracks.

"It's a puzzle box, Adam," I said as soon as the thought formed in my mind.

I tried to take a step to turn and face him, but the floor had softened beneath my feet. I sucked in a shuttering breath; pretty, ink-black hands had curled around the bottom of my boots. The floor was grabbing me, and, as I watched, the fingers wriggled, as if pushing out of the restricting stone, moving a bit further up my shoe.

"Adam!" I choked out.

He looked at me, and then followed my eyes down. "Oh, no." Though I couldn't tell exactly what was coming out of the ground underneath him, he swallowed. "A puzzle box," he repeated, focusing on my previous words. "Which means, logically, we have to solve it before the time runs out. I used to love these things as a kid," he said bitterly. "I had a Rubik's cube that I would solve over and over again."

"Will the skill translate?"

He laughed. "Damn. I hope so."

"The infinity symbol on the front, I'm thinking that might be the shape of the finished puzzle."

"Sounds good to me," he answered, his voice tight with nervous energy.

After a few minutes of intense thought that drove me crazy waiting, he wriggled one of the corners. It spun away from the rest of the box, swiveling along with his fingers. Then, he started to twist in earnest.

I watched his intense concentration for a few moments before twisting the same corner of my own box, hurrying to catch up with his movements. Staring at his hands, I mimicked him frenetically, always a few moves behind, until a few minutes later he stopped.

"I've got it," he said. In his hands was a twisting infinity sign, kind of like a double helix.

Just as I was about to make the last twist on my own puzzle, screaming erupted on the other side of the ring.

The boy opposite from Adam threw himself forward. The bars around his circle were gone, but that didn't matter… The stone of his cage had fully risen up, and huge stone spiders and snakes rushed over him, holding him down and biting again and again.

The guy's screams gurgled and finally fell silent. The stone forms seemed to sense his death, melting back into the ground, the empty circle now looking perversely innocent. Discarded at his side, his uncompleted puzzle had turned from black to red.

The silence permeated everything as we all stared at his silent form.

When I tore my eyes away to look back to Adam, I saw his bars were gone, too. But the floor of his circle had stopped attacking and solidified, whatever had been coming out of it suppressed.

He stared down at the looping double helix, expressionless.

"Adam," I said, my voice low.

His wide eyes met mine. "I just killed him." He blinked. "I escaped the cage, and he was devoured by it."

I shook my head. "That wasn't your fault. That was a coincidence. And…even if it wasn't, you couldn't have known."

He ran his hand through his hair roughly, and then seemed to gather himself together. "Yeah. I didn't know. But everyone else does now."

I bit my lip. "This is going to get bad." I was now doubly grateful that our whole team was on the same side of the circle. But maybe that wasn't coincidental. "We're a team, after all. Wouldn't do to have us killing each other," I murmured without thinking.

Adam nodded. "Yeah," he said, but was obviously distracted, looking across the circle.

I followed his gaze to the girl directly across from me. The boy's body lay still on the ground in front of her. She frantically twisted her box's pieces around, glancing up at me every now and then.

Adam took an experimental step out of his circle. When nothing happened, he walked over to the bars surrounding me and wrapped his hands around them. "She's going to kill you if you don't fix that puzzle before she does." His eyes were intent on mine, the dark brown irises looking harder than I had ever seen them. "You have to solve it, Eve. And you need to hurry."

I clenched the misshapen shape in my hand. "But…I'll kill her," I protested.

He reached through the bars, grabbing me by the wrist. "She's trying to kill you, right now, as we speak."

I looked at her.

She desperately twisted and turned the pieces. Around her feet, the stone had risen to form a low-hanging, bubbly cloud of blackness.

"She's afraid, Adam."

He closed his eyes as if in pain, then clasped my hand between both of his. "We're all afraid."

The ground under my feet shifted again, and I would have lost my balance except for his steadying grip on my hand. Beneath me, faces were pressing out of the stone along with the hands crawling up my legs. They looked familiar, too familiar, and then I realized they wore my own features, staring up at me with eyes of stone.

I started to tremble, and squeezed one of Adam's hands desperately hard with my own. The sight of myself in that black abyss moved something sick in the pit of my stomach and raised the hair on the back of my neck. "It's like a nightmare," I whispered, my voice too shaky to speak properly. The light dimmed further with every passing moment, and the thought of being in the dark as the stone swallowed me made me want to slam myself against the bars until either they broke or I did.

"It's our personal nightmare," he whispered back to me. "Each of these is different. Spiders and snakes for that guy, something else for me, and something else for you. Eve, if you don't win here, you're going to lose either way. She doesn't have to solve the puzzle for you to die. What do you think happens when the timer runs out?"

He looked down at the floor of my cage pointedly. "Do you want to be killed by them?"

I shuddered visibly, unable to stop myself.

The bodies pulled themselves out of the ground, inch by inch. Each face was my own, the arms and hands my own, but the *eyes*…

I slipped my hand out of his and squeezed the puzzle. My fingers shook, but I kept a good grip because I was too afraid to drop it.

Adam let out a deep, relieved breath. "Thank you. We need you to live, as much as I hate to admit it. With you gone, the team would dissolve."

I chuckled without humor. "I'm doing this for selfish reasons, believe me. And what's this? You, protecting the team? I'm surprised. I thought you'd resent being coerced into joining it."

"I see the value in what you're trying to create. And besides, don't you know by now that I don't do anything I don't want to do? I could have said no, when you asked."

I paused before the last twist, staring at the almost completed puzzle.

Then someone else solved theirs. Not the girl across from me. A guy. Across from him, a woman, one of the very few adult Players I'd seen, tried to run, ripping out of the animated stone holding her. She got a few feet before the completely freed stone form knocked her down.

It was a giant, muscular man with a curly beard and hands like clubs.

He straddled her and began hitting her. Again and again, until blood splattered outward with every blow. Until her face was unrecognizable, caved in.

I couldn't look away, couldn't move, throughout the whole thing. I wanted to, oh, I wanted to, but my body wouldn't listen, and so I watched.

The meaty thunking…*squelching* went on and on, and the scent of blood and raw meat filled my nostrils.

She must have finally died, because the stone man melted away and flowed back into the circle. The only evidence he'd ever existed was the corpse lying in a puddle of blood in the middle of the ring of Players.

My own stone tormentors were grabbing at my hips by then, and I could swear they moved faster as they freed themselves further from the floor. My hands were slippery with sweat, despite how very, very cold I was.

I breathed in through my nose and out through my mouth, ignoring the smell of her. I forced myself to calm down and focus, to ignore the terror and unyielding hands on my body. I closed my eyes and focused on the breath in my lungs, the sound of blood rushing through my ears with every heartbeat, and the shape in my hands.

I opened my eyes and twisted the last piece into place, staring at the girl. The *snick* of that piece sliding together with the others sounded like thunder in my ears. The last move, perfect and horrible. The puzzle was without any edges or discernible cracks, smooth and unending.

In her hands, I saw a shape almost exactly like my own. But the timer had disappeared. The clear, warm bars were gone from in front of me, and the faces of my destruction melted and formed back into the floor, staring at me as they sank. The stone beneath my feet was once again solid, harmless.

The girl's screams were loud, sobbing. She pleaded with no one, with everything, to save her, to spare her. The black cloud rose around her body, a swirling, amorphous mass. As each particle of stone touched her, it sizzled into her skin, and kept sizzling till it had eaten its way through.

Her cheeks shrunk in, and then her face collapsed as the bones melted away, her eyeballs sinking down and inwards without the support of her cheekbones. Her legs crumpled under her, and she sank to the ground like a deflated balloon.

Please, please, let it be over, I thought. Let it be done already.

But she didn't die. She just kept screaming, and screaming, and screaming.

And then she finally stopped, her body little more than a pile of burn-riddled skin wrapped around an oozing sludge. Her hand still held the misshapen, now red puzzle. Silence reigned.

My stomach revolted, bile rising up in my mouth. I retched onto the ground. "Oh, god..." I could not keep thinking about it. Could. Not. What was important right now was...the team.

Adam and I were okay, but what about China, Jacky, and Sam?

I stood and spit, then wiped my mouth against my sleeve. No time to be squeamish now.

Adam already stood by China's cage, resting his hands on her shoulders as he guided her through each twist and turn.

Two others solved their puzzles. One of their opponents screamed and cursed, spewing vitriol across the circle as some large creature I didn't look at long enough to identify devoured him.

But what interested me was the other girl who'd solved her puzzle. She immediately threw away the twisting infinity symbol in horror. It flew through the air and landed with a harsh clatter, and then its color seeped from black to red, as if wounded.

The girl shrieked as the floor of her cage reanimated like the rush of a tidal wave. Huge twisting vines—no, snakes—shot out and caught her, slithering around and around, and then squeezing until bones crunched and blood seeped out from between their coils. Her opponent had died, too, not spared by the death of the winner.

Damn. Note to self. Do not throw your completed puzzle away.

Standing beside Jacky's cage, I reached for her. "Okay, what have you got?"

She ground her teeth together audibly, then forced out, "Nothing." She took a deep breath. "I've been trying and trying, but I'm just making random moves. I dunno how to do *this*." Her voice broke, and I could literally hear the creak of her knuckles as she clenched her free hand around nothing.

Stone men had formed from the ground, their reaching hands pressing lewdly into the flesh of her thighs and hips.

I grabbed her fisted hand between both of mine, passing warmth into her clammy digits. "You're going to be okay. We'll figure it out." Once again, I was reminded of the empty reassurance I'd given the boy. I would not let these words be empty. "Look at me, Jacky," I said. I had to repeat it before her terrified brown eyes met my own. I spoke clearly and slowly, putting weight into my words. "I won't let anything happen to you. I'm here now, and you're going to be okay. Believe in me."

She looked into my eyes for several long moments, and then nodded. Her body sagged as she released some of the iron tension she'd been clenching in her muscles. "You know how to solve the puzzle?"

"No, not quite yet." I could probably solve the puzzle from scratch again, but Jacky had changed the positioning of its pieces who knows how many times, so I couldn't go on memory alone. I needed to fully understand the puzzle. I was halfway to the answer from walking through the solution with Adam as guide, but not close enough to save Jacky. "But I'll figure it out."

I slung off the pack I'd prepared for this Trial, the contents of which were mostly useless since we hadn't ended up fighting as I'd predicted. But I'd also stashed something extremely valuable in it, on the chance that I might need it. And I needed it now. I brought out a small pouch and poured three unused Seeds into my palm.

Though I'd never tried it, I believed I'd be able to use them even with a Trial in progress. If not, we were screwed. Adam was helping China, and after that would move on to Sam, who had seemingly frozen in fear and not made a single move with his puzzle box. By that time, the constantly ticking timer would have reached zero. Saving Jacky was up to me.

I held the first Seed up to my neck. "I wish I was more intelligent," I said, and it injected itself into me in that all-too-familiar way. I held the second Seed up to my neck, but paused before repeating myself, as something Vaughn had said played through my head again. The Seeds were wish-fulfillers. I debated with myself for a moment. Was it really the time to be experimenting? But if my hunch was right, it could mean the difference between Jacky's life or death. "I wish I could better visualize three-dimensional movement." It injected itself into me, recognizing my words for a wish, even if it wasn't for one of the thirteen Attributes. And for the third Seed, "I wish I had better pattern recognition and could make better projections based on said patterns." Splitting the last Seed between two wishes was an even riskier move, but I was all in on the high-stakes bet.

I stared at the puzzle in Jacky's hands and focused everything I had on it, waiting for the tingle in my brain to come and pass. I breathed slow and deep, imagining the possible moves and their countless different outcomes. The pieces seemed to click together in my brain, and I thought I understood.

I placed my hands over hers and started to guide her soundlessly in rapid-fire movements of the puzzle. I made a few mistakes but realized in time to correct them without much time lost. I knew, finally, that the next turn would be the last. I paused for a moment, and then pushed against her fingers for the last time.

The bars surrounding her disappeared and I fell forward, wrapping my arms around her. I turned her so her back was toward the center and hugged her to my chest with my hands over her ears. She wouldn't see the price of her continued life, and maybe the screams would be muffled, too.

I watched for her as Jacky's former opponent bucked in what was either defiance or maddening pain as stone chains attached to his arms and legs literally ripped him apart. Drawn and quartered.

When it was done, I released Jacky and gripped her shoulders.

Her eyes let out a steady stream of tears, though she made no sound.

"You did well. It's over now," I said. I led her to stand together with China, who was also free, and turned to Sam.

Adam threw up his hands and turned away from Sam's cage, stomping back to us with a face twisted in anger and disgust. Our eyes met as he passed, and he shook his head once, a silent explanation of his anger.

I moved to kneel beside Sam, pressing against the buzzing bars.

Tiny hands were dragging him down into the soft stone, but instead of becoming frantic to solve his puzzle, he was holding his head in his hands as if trying to block out the world, hyperventilating.

"Sam. What's wrong?"

He raised his head, looking bleak and distant, as if he'd already lost. "I'm afraid. I'm so afraid. But if I give in, that person is going to die. I can't. But, it's too late for me now, already." He nodded as if consoling himself, but his face pinched together at the words, and he panted faster. "There's not enough time left. It's too late. I already made it. But I'm scared."

I reached through the bars and took his hand, as Adam had done me and I'd done Jacky. I knew the comfort touch brought, and with that comfort, the increased willingness to listen to whatever the comforter said. To let them guide you. "Sam, I'm here."

He looked at me uncomprehendingly.

I squeezed his hand and rubbed it chafingly, trying to bring some heat back into it. "I'm here. We're all here with you. I'm going to help you, if you let me. We need you, Sam. You're part of our team." It seemed he had given up any hope for himself. But maybe I could push him to have hope for the good of someone beside himself.

"I can't. And it's too late anyway," he repeated, as if those were the only words in his head.

"That person? The one who you're protecting? He's trying to kill you. Right now, Sam, he is trying to kill you. And the only reason is so he can live. You know that's wrong. It's why you're refusing to try and win against him. Because you know it's wrong to sacrifice someone else so that you can live."

He relaxed. "Yes. You understand. I can't do that again."

"You can."

He stiffened again, drawing back from me.

"You can, because we need you to. You can't do it to save yourself, but you can do it for me. For us." I squeezed his hand.

He took a sobbing, heaving breath. "Why are you doing this to me?" he pleaded. "Why are you making it okay for me to do what I know I shouldn't? I can't kill that guy. It's cowardly and wrong." His voice was firmer, but he hadn't taken his hand away from mine.

I continued rubbing. "It's wrong to kill someone else in cold blood. But this isn't your fault. You didn't ask to be a Player. The Game is forcing you to act in self-defense, just like it's forced the rest of us."

He shook his head, denying me, and closed his eyes.

"It's also wrong for you to stand back and do nothing when someone needs you, Sam," I said more firmly, deciding on a change of tactic.

His eyes opened, bloodshot and blue, and locked on my own. "What?"

"This isn't just about you anymore. You're not playing this Game by yourself. You are part of my team. A team of four others who are depending on you, and you…you're trying to take the easy way out."

"The easy way out?" his voice rose in indignation. "I'm trying to do the right thing!"

"No. The right thing to do is to live, to listen to me now. I'm right, Sam, and you know it. The team needs you, which means I need you to listen to me, and do what I say. The team is my responsibility, but as a member of my team, it's your job to follow me." Not my most subtle work, but I didn't have much time to convince him.

Luckily, he was terrified, and just selfish enough to hand over his responsibility, along with the power to command him. He focused on me as if I were his last lifeline. As if I were a piece of driftwood in a turbulent sea storm.

I nodded, giving him silent permission. "He is not pleading to be saved. He is not begging for mercy." I pointed to the boy across from Sam and spoke low and calm, trying to give my voice import. "He is trying to kill you, and it is not wrong for you to defend yourself. You will stop him from hurting the team."

He hesitated, and then nodded. "But it's impossible, Eve. There's no way. It really is too late." His face crumpled in the despair that came from having hope for a split second, only to have it ripped away. "There's only thirty seconds left."

All around us, people in their cages were panicking, dropping their unsolved boxes, fighting with the liquid stone crawling up their bodies, and clawing desperately at the bars. But the boy across from Sam was still controlled, almost finished with his puzzle. He would make it in time. Shame he wouldn't live to see the benefits of his efforts.

I dropped Sam's hand and put my own on his shoulder. "There's hope, if you'll do as I say. Listen."

He nodded, and I gave him my orders, spewing them out quickly as the last seconds counted down.

His opponent completed his puzzle.

As soon as the bars disappeared, Sam ripped away from the tiny stone hands and threw himself forward into the middle of the circle, sprinting toward the other boy, who was also free of his bars. Childlike stone bodies followed Sam with unnatural speed, pumping their little legs in a blur.

I followed at a slower pace, ready to lend a hand if needed.

The timer reached zero, and as the arena erupted into a death circus around us, Sam smashed into the other boy. He wrapped his hands around the guy's throat and squeezed.

I expected the boy to fight back, but instead he jerked in surprise, and then threw himself backward and tripped.

Sam stalked forward calmly. When the downed guy tried to kick out, Sam grabbed his leg.

The boy started to convulse, shaking the leg free from Sam's grip.

Sam moved forward again and straddled the boy. He pressed his palms down hard and flat on the guy's stomach, where the shirt had ridden up and the pale skin lay exposed.

The stone children reached Sam and crawled onto his body, weighing him down and dragging at him, but he ignored them as if they didn't exist.

Sam's opponent shook and screamed, convulsing, trying to wiggle free. His skin turned dark and started to split open in a million tiny spots as bloody crystals grew from beneath it, bursting outward like a time-lapse video of ice crystals forming on the surface of a lake.

Sam kept pressing and pressing, shaking with effort. A drop of sweat fell off his nose and dripped onto the boy, mixing with the bloody crystals beneath his hands.

Finally, the guy was still.

Sam grabbed the completed black puzzle from the dead hand and hugged it to his own chest. The granite boys pulling at him paused for a moment, seeming confused, and then melted away.

I let out a sigh of relief that my guess of the winning conditions had been correct: We needed to be in possession of a winning—black—puzzle. Solving it wasn't enough if we didn't keep it. Otherwise, the girl who'd thrown hers away wouldn't have died. And the only reason to release the cages of both the winner and the loser was to give the loser a chance to turn the tables.

Sam sat atop the body, staring down at his handiwork.

I moved to him and placed a hand on his shoulder. "Sam."

He looked up at me, startled. His bloodshot eyes were blank and wide in the growing darkness, but, as they focused on me, his face twisted in sick anger. "You."

I frowned. What was wrong with him? "It's over now. Are you okay?"

"Don't touch me." He yanked his arm back and stood up, tripping on the hardened corpse as he turned toward the rest of the group.

I watched in bewilderment as he walked away, then knelt to the body of the boy. His eyes were still open. I closed them with my fingertips. He was warm, still, and I realized I'd expected him to be frozen. His stomach had two patches of normal skin in the outline of hands, like a child had traced Sam's hand on the boy's skin. Around the outlines, blood crystals sprung up and outward, like magnetized metal shavings drawn towards a lodestone.

I touched them with the tip of my finger, finding them rigidly sharp and still radiating the warmth from inside the dead body. I remembered what Sam had told me. He was the harbinger of death.

Sam, the healer.

Chapter 19

And what constitutes evil, real evil, is the taking of a single human life. Whether a man would die tomorrow or the day after or eventually…it doesn't matter. Because if God does not exist, then life…every second of it…Is all we have.

— Anne Rice

I THOUGHT the Trial would end there, but we waited for several minutes and nothing happened. The cube stayed still and displayed no message. No instructions came to us, no timers appeared, and we began to grow worried in a whole new way. What if we hadn't completed the Trial properly and weren't allowed to return to our lives?

Then I felt vibrations through the soles of my shoes. The black stone turned white in the center of the Trial board, then rippled outward, changing color as it went.

"Get ready, everyone!" I called out, not taking my eyes off the ground as I tucked my completed puzzle safely into a large pocket in my pants. When the ground beneath us had turned all white, threads burst upward from the rippling stone, thick and so fast I had no time to react.

They surrounded me in sheets so dense I couldn't see anyone else. I screamed for my teammates, but no one called back in response.

Within moments, thick walls of glowing strings enclosed me, twisting and winding together to create a large room shaped like a smooshed ball. Helixes, columns, and bridges made of the strands filled the inside haphazardly, stretching from wall to wall and formation to formation.

I took a step around a random column, and the floor vibrated outward in a ripple of light and sound. I froze, not because of the unexpected reaction of the strings, but because of the huge woman crawling out of the floor.

She rose and detached herself from the string, standing almost twice my height, maybe twelve feet tall. Her body was made of black stone and full of holes and strange facets. Tears flowed constantly along lines carved down the middle of each of her cheeks, as if eroded by hundreds of years of crying. She wore a crown upon her head, and had a beautiful, regal face.

She looked around, and then seemed to see and focus on me. "You. You are the supposed descendant?"

"Are you the Moderator?"

She barked a laugh. "I am no such thing, tiny one. In your language, you would call me the Oracle."

"My language? What language do you normally speak? What does an oracle do in the Game?"

She slashed her hand through the air to cut me off, and the sound it made was sharp and commanding. "I will answer no more questions. It is not the time for it. I am here to test you."

She moved to the side and plunged her hands into what looked like a birdbath standing on a musical string pedestal. Another stood across from it a few yards away. If there had been birds, I would have no doubt of their function. But there were no birds, and somehow I knew the pedestal's purpose was not so innocent. Her tears dripped down into the water like little diamonds. She moved her fingers within, and some of the strings connected to the birdbath spontaneously lit up and rang out with sound, causing a ripple effect that ran outwards, transferring to connected strings until it reached me and stopped, falling dim and silent.

A half-formed image of the Oracle split away from her. The shadow's movements caught the air, and its body created a beautiful haunting melody, a thousand different wind instruments harmonizing with each other. The sound of its movements mimicked the sound she'd played through the water. Though it was as large as her, and deliberately ponderous, a few gargantuan steps brought it in front of me. It slammed the back of its forearm into my chest, sending me flying backward.

I crashed into the threaded ground and slid, throwing out light and discordant sound with the friction. The shadow disappeared, but the Oracle was already playing a new tune and creating a string-path with the birdbath.

My lungs shrieked in silent pain, begging for the breath that had been crushed from me. I cradled my torso with an arm, so, *so* grateful I was wearing the banded armor vest beneath my clothes. It had absorbed some of the impact, which perhaps was the difference between me rising again and being incapacitated by that single blow.

The new shadow was already on me, though, and I didn't have time to lie around. I slipped by it, running back toward her original body. I couldn't breathe, and every movement of my arms shot pain through my chest.

Something caught me in the back, and I smashed into the floor and slid once again, this time skinning my jaw and ripping my clothes.

The Oracle let out her barking laugh, somehow still beautiful even in its sharpness, and I knew she had anticipated my movement. There was no other way the huge, somewhat lumbering shadow would have hit me.

This time, I stood up faster, and ran toward her before she could sic her after-image on me.

The room was already filled with music, but I was quick enough, and lead with a low kick to her ankle, and then a hard swipe to the side of her knee.

Her leg buckled, but she didn't go down, and with a flick of her fingers, an ephemeral copy shot from her and blew me backward with a lunge, two palms smashing into my chest.

My body caught on a twisting double helix and bounced to the floor, facedown. This time I didn't get back up right away. I couldn't. I hadn't gotten a good breath since the first hit, and stars sprinkled around in the darkness were creeping through my vision.

But I had to move, I had to, or the next one would kill me. I crawled to my hands and knees and scuttled behind the helix, gripping it to hold myself off the ground.

She was unfazed by my little attack. Tears still streamed down her face into the water and music poured out of the strings in ripples, moving my way. They were more complex that time, and two different paths played intertwining melodies, coming from either side of me.

I regained some space in my lungs, but two copies split from her, moving toward me in a pincer formation. Knowing that I needed to stop her from making more of them, to get her away from the pedestal, I shot forward between the two copies, but they had shifted course, already moving to intercept me. My feet skidded over the strings as I furiously tried to backpedal, but one had only been feinting my interception and had slipped around behind me faster than I could change my direction.

I was falling backward towards its waiting fists. My claws slipped out —I wondered very briefly why I hadn't conjured them sooner—and in the space between one heartbeat and the next, I plunged a hand into the strings of the floor while pushing myself sideways with a foot.

My claws gave me the purchase I needed to twist my backward fall so that I ended up crouching on my hands and knees. I tried to throw myself sideways between the two shadows, but a third one already waited for me to move toward it.

It grabbed me by the arm as I tried in vain to backpedal once again. With a twist, it threw me across the room like a stuffed doll.

My shoulder popped and crunched as the arm twisted, and I couldn't help my scream of agony, even though in truth my scream came more from the horror of realizing I'd just been broken like a twig. The pain hadn't hit yet. No, it didn't hit till I smashed into the curve of the ceiling, bounced from it to a branching column, and smacked into the floor like a tenderized steak. The pain hit then, bursting outward from no specific point and flaring bright.

My eyes rolled back in my head, and I lost track of myself for a moment. When I found myself again, I allowed pure terror to take over. It overwhelmed the pain and stood me up, looked for the Oracle and her shadows through the blood in my eyes, and hobbled away from her to give me distance from my attacker—and maybe time to regroup.

The shadows had once again disappeared, but she was still playing more intertwining melodies, the music growing consistently more complex.

I had no time, and no power to win against her. I took a quick inventory of my body: a dislocated shoulder, possibly broken and screaming in pain from the weight of my pack's strap over it; twisted knee; fractured ribs, I was pretty sure; cut on the head bleeding a lot, maybe a concussion; and lots of other small hurts, too many to count. All in all, the worst shape I'd been in yet.

I realized I might die there. The thought slipped into my mind to feed my terror. No, no, no. I wouldn't die. Would not. Would. Not. I just needed to figure out how to beat her. She seemed to literally anticipate my every move, but that didn't mean I couldn't win. There had to be a way.

"Ah," I puffed. The Oracle anticipated my movements? "Stupid, stupid," I mouthed venomously at myself. By name alone, I should have realized the clue she gave me toward her power. I'd been treating this like the other Trials, but this one was based on my mental faculties, not my ability to kill monsters. Why had I forgotten that?

Even understanding that, however, I had no idea how to beat her if she could predict the future. Already the strings around me played in complex interweaving patterns, and soon the shadows would echo through the music. I wouldn't make it through the round.

An arch close to me lit up with a final smash of light and sound, and instinctively I thrust my good arm toward it. I touched my blood-covered fingers to the strands before the sound faded away, and in front of my eyes I saw an ephemeral image of my body dodging one of the Oracle's shadows, only to be hit by a hammer-fist from another. The ragged-looking girl's neck broke downward with a grinding crunch, and her skull caved inward from the impact.

The sound faded away, and with it, the glimpse into my future. "Hell, no." I wouldn't let that happen.

The shadows came at me, five strong. I dodged them as best I could with my body not working at full capacity. Each movement had my blood flowing faster and my focus deepening. No more panic, only a goal I would achieve, or literally die trying.

I felt deja-vu in my next twisting dodge and knew my death swung down from above. But then I slipped, tilting backward as my legs shot out from underneath me.

My back smashed hard into the ground, but I received no broken neck or collapsed skull. I bucked and arched, bringing my feet right back under me, and slipped through the already-fading shadow's legs. I headed straight for the other birdbath, ignoring the Oracle and her bell-tone laugh of surprise.

I reached it before her shadows could stop me and plunged both my good hand and the one hanging limply from my ruined shoulder into the water. Blood mixed with the crystal-clear liquid in silky tendrils, and my mind exploded like a crackling firework.

I understood how the cocoon-room worked, what each string signified, and exactly how to play them to get the melodies I needed. Even so, my brain wasn't equipped to hold all the information, and pieces of the puzzle slipped into and out of focus as it strained to hold everything.

I breathed deep and focused on the blood in my veins, and then outward to the blood swirling in the water, and then the water itself. The focus helped, and I twitched my fingers, sending out an experimental thread of sound and tumbling light to meet one of the melodies she'd sent my way.

I knew what would happen even before the shadow actually followed my instructions, so I focused my energy on stopping the Oracle's other shadows from coming to remove me from my place of power and kill me.

In the water, I saw all the moves she could have made, and all the ways I could respond and counterattack. At first, I played out only the strands of my future that would stop her from killing me. My waves met hers in just the right way to cancel out both sides, silence resounding where they met. But as I focused harder, my brain bent with more dexterity to the task, and I began to send out preemptive strikes of my own.

We matched each other through a myriad of possible futures for a long time, long enough that I began to lose concentration. Each time I slipped up, I stopped her from killing me later and later. Soon I would be too late, and I would die.

I started to tremble with the effort of sustaining so many different fights, even if I was only thinking through them while standing still. I knew I couldn't go on for much longer, but she showed no signs of wearying. I needed a way to stop her from attacking.

The next strand she sent toward me was a simple, lilting thing.

I split a larger portion of energy than I could truly spare away from my other futures and played one strand of my own in an exact match. The sounds and lights playing on that thread synced to each other so exactly that they meshed, and as she tried to finish it, I pushed in another direction, continuing the music in an unexpected tumble, then let it fall into a soft silence.

She let out another laugh. "That's it, tiny one. Show me your worth."

I'd let the other futures slip too far from my control and had to push extra hard against them for a moment to buy myself some time. She pushed back, but not overwhelmingly, and strand by strand, piece by piece, I matched her melodies, taking them over and changing their course.

Finally, I wrested them from her control even as she began to play them, laying each violent attempt to rest. From there, it wasn't so difficult to play her as she was at that very moment, drawing her hands from the water in gentle contentment. I played docility into her, straining to my breaking point. The last notes were little more than a squeak.

Finally, I slumped over the water, shuddering and gasping. If there was more, I could not fight it. I had pushed for life with everything I owned, and nothing remained. Even as I had the thought, I defied my own exhaustion, already gathering strength to match her next attack.

But it never came. Her strange, stone mouth stretched in a soft smile, and the lines down her cheeks no longer flowed with tears. She walked to the middle of the room and knelt on one knee, bowing her crowned head to me. When she raised her head, her chest opened strangely, folding in on itself, creating a twisting slot. She was still, then, her eyes focused unwaveringly on me.

I had won. Why hadn't I gone straight for the second birdbath in the beginning? But I knew it wouldn't have worked, because there had been no blood to mix with the water. It was something I understood in the way you remember understanding a complicated concept in a dream, an understanding that slipped from me as I withdrew my hands from the small pool and broke the connection with its reservoir of borrowed knowledge.

I shuffled to the Oracle, keeping a wary eye out for any sudden movements. "What now?" I wondered aloud.

She flicked her eyes downward, leading my own to the hole in her chest.

I pulled the puzzle from my pocket, placed it at the opening in her chest, and pushed. It slid in, but met resistance, so I twisted slightly, and it slid further, continuing until the last bit lay flush with the surface of her body.

With a small click, her chest folded inward once again, opening up to a large cavity about a foot wide. Inside were three piles of what looked to be silver loops. Small, medium, and large.

She whispered to me with a voice made from the splashing of spring water and wind across the tops of glass bottles. "You are worthy. These are my three gifts to you, that they may guide your path. May you walk through the midst of tribulation, and not waver from the way."

I frowned, said, "Umm, thank you... I guess," and reached into the space within her chest. I pulled out the smallest set of loops first. Each was bent strangely, connecting to the others in a chain. I placed the small and medium pile in my pockets, and the large loop in my pack of crushed and broken supplies, as it was too big to fit anywhere else.

The Boneshaker began to hammer into me without warning, and I stared into her sad stone eyes as it carried me away.

Chapter 20

People often believed they were safer in the light, thinking monsters only came out at night.

— C.J. Roberts

I CRUMPLED to the floor of the base, surrounded by my team, and ignored the level up window that appeared.

"You're alive!" China screamed, smashing into me and wrapping her arms around me. "Oh, we thought maybe you were dead, but you're alive."

She squeezed, and I let out a gurgling scream as my shoulder moved under the pressure.

Jacky grabbed China by the forearms and yanked her arms open and away from me. "She's hurt," she snapped. "Sam, come now. Fix her." Her finger pointed at me imperiously.

Sam sat beside me, stony-faced, and placed his hands on my shoulder.

"I'm so sorry, Eve. I shouldn't have hugged you. I was just so excited," China whispered.

Blaine saw me and went pale. "Oh, my god. What happened?"

I let out a humorless laugh. "Got in a bit of a tussle. No big deal. Tell me what happened to you guys."

Jacky crouched in front of me and grabbed the hand of my uninjured arm. "The spider egg thing swallowed you up, and you were inside for a long time. We tried to cut through it and get to you, but nothing worked. Then the cube said congratulations on surviving, but you were still inside. We all pressed the button to return from the Trial, but nothing happened. Honestly, we were starting to panic a little, but then all of a sudden the song started and we were back here, and you were with us."

"Right before that, the cube popped up with one last message," Adam said. "No one else was paying attention."

"What—" I broke off and bit my tongue to stifle a scream as Sam did something with my shoulder that caused it to pop and grind. I went light-headed for a moment and had to take several deep breaths before I could think again. "Ouch. What—what did it say?"

"Eve Redding has been found worthy, and granted the blessing of the Oracle," Adam said. "It seems similar to the message when someone gets a new Skill but worded differently."

"Interesting."

"What happened in there, Eve?" he said.

"I met…something. A huge, huge woman made of stone crawled out of the ground. She called herself the Oracle, and said she was there to test me. She could see everything I was going to do, and I couldn't win. But then I figured out how to play the same game as her, and beat her. She said I'd proven myself worthy and gave me these little silver chains. Then the Boneshaker started playing, and I was back here." What an extremely simplified version of events… It felt like everything in my life was spinning around in a tornado of pain and fear and the illusion of strength I'd tried to wrap around myself. I needed to grab hold of things before I could talk about what had just happened in more depth.

I squeezed Jacky's hand. "But I'm fine. How about you guys. Are *you* okay?" I let my voice soften on the last sentence, speaking directly to her.

"Yeah, because you saved me. Thank you. Words don't even cut it." She squeezed my hand painfully, swallowed, and shook her head, blinking suddenly shiny eyes.

"Good." My gaze shifted to the other member of the team I had been most worried about. "And you, Sam? Are you all right?"

His face was pale from the injuries and pain he'd been absorbing from me, but his cheeks flushed at that. "I killed someone today. I took a life, with my bare hands, while you—*because* of you. Do you *think* I'm okay?"

Adam stepped forward and yanked on his arm, pulling Sam away from me. "She saved you, you idiot. She kept you alive when you were too stupid to stand up and save yourself. If not for her, you'd be dead."

Sam stood and yanked his arm away, still staring at me. "You didn't save me. You made me betray myself. You're a murderer. *I'm* a murderer." His voice broke on the last bit, and he choked off any more words.

I stood up to match him, feeling the sharp pain of my heart breaking for him. "No. I helped you choose to live. NIX made murderers of us all tonight. There was no other choice for us. Kill or be killed. If I'd let any of you die when I knew I could stop it, would I be any less a murderer, then? This is…horrible beyond words. I know it. But we can't blame ourselves. You can't blame yourself. If not for this Game, tonight would never have happened. We are monsters of circumstance, not of choice."

I knew the words weren't enough. Nothing external could absolve someone from guilt if they couldn't forgive themselves. And in truth, I called myself a murderer, too, just not out loud. "There's nothing we can do about this except get out of this Game. What happens if the next time, it asks us to turn on one another?" I looked at my team. "It won't ever stop, not as long as we're forced into the Trials, unless we die or find a way to escape. So we've got to find a way, because I won't let any of you die."

I turned to Blaine, who'd watched the exchange with wide eyes from behind his glasses. "Please tell me you got something useful from monitoring the transfer."

"W-well, I will have to examine the data more closely, but I think so…"

Sam clenched his fists and left the room in red-faced silence.

China smiled bravely. "We'll find a way."

I gave her a small smile of gratitude and started to hobble toward the bathroom. Sam had left before getting to my twisted knee, but hell if I was going to call him back and ask for his services now.

Jacky immediately slipped my arm around her neck and half-carried me, despite her smaller size. "What crawled up his butt and died?" She snorted. "And what the hell was that thing he did? Damn, he turned that kid into one of those pretty rock crystal things. What are they called?" She looked to the others for help.

"A geode?" Adam supplied.

"It was a Skill," I cut in. "One he wishes he didn't have, for obvious reasons. Let's leave it to him to talk about, when and if he feels like it."

Jacky pursed her lips. "Just seems like he's been holding back on us. If I had a cool Skill like that—"

I shot her a look, and she clamped her mouth shut, pursing her lips. "Let me know if you need me," she said as she deposited me at the bathroom entrance.

"Thank you." I opened the door and limped inside. The mirror over the sink showed a face covered almost completely in blood from a cut at the edge of my hairline. My clothes were torn and bloody, and my skin was covered in scrapes and string-burn.

I struggled to take off my jacket, but paused in surprise when the door swung open.

Adam stepped through with a chair in one hand and a first aid kit in the other. "Sit down," he said as he set the chair behind me.

I did, gratefully, and reached for the first aid kit.

He pulled it back from my reach. "Nope. You're in no shape to fix yourself up right now. Let me help you, since the self-righteous jackass didn't finish his job. Besides, I brought numbing cream." He held up the tube of numbing antibiotic ointment with a teasing grin.

"Hurry up, then," I said, grimacing in return. I was exhausted and in pain, and I'd take any break I could get.

He unwrapped some steri-pads first and wiped my bloody face down with them till they came away clean. He did the same to the rest of my cuts and scrapes, squeezed a small bit of salve onto his slender forefinger and carefully applied it to the cuts, then bandaged them with a layer of camouflaging, second-skin patches. They would help me heal without scars, and also disguise the events of my evening from my family.

His fingers were gentle, and I relaxed into the chair and closed my eyes, letting some of the pain flow away. Salve, bandage, repeat, until my little surface cuts were all clean, numb, and hidden.

When he finished, I tried to stand up, but he held me back down. "I'm not done yet." He pulled out a can of numbing spray, pushed up my pant leg, and misted the bruise already forming on my shin from when I'd tried to kick the Oracle. "Feel better?"

"Yes," I sighed.

"You did the right thing today. With Sam, I mean."

"Did I?"

"Yes. We become what we need to, to survive. He doesn't understand that. Someday he will, or he'll die or cause someone else's death because he can't make the hard choice. But you can make those choices. That's what leaders do."

I thought I should put some strength in my spine, thank him, and leave. "Leader? Is that what I am? Because I don't feel like it. I'm flailing just as much as the rest of them," I said instead.

"But you don't show it."

"What am I doing right now, if not showing it?"

"I can handle it. Besides, I know that when the time comes, you'll do what you always do when it counts."

"And what is that?"

"You'll get your way."

We both laughed.

He sprayed the side of my face, noticeably avoiding eye contact. "I'll be the first to tell you when I think you're making the wrong decision. But as a leader, you did the right thing today. I understand that. I understand what you're dealing with. And I know you're not made of stone."

Was this Adam offering support?

He clamped his mouth shut and finished spraying. "Okay, all done. You ready to go?"

"Yeah. Uh, do you think I could get a ride? Home, I mean? I'd rather not go on foot, and paying a transport pod leaves records."

"Of course. Let me bring my bike around. I'll come get you when it's ready."

I nodded silently, and when he was gone, slumped into the chair. I took my link sheath out of my bag and slipped it onto my arm. "What a crappy day," I said into the silence.

—You don't look so good.—
-Bunny-

"I've heard that one before. When do I ever look good after a Trial?" I worried for a second Bunny must have cameras in the base to be able to see me, but then I realized he was using the ID sheath. He must have been waiting for it to be taken from its protective spot in my pack.

—Are you okay?—
-Bunny-

I took a breath, and then another while my answer built in me. "No, I'm not freaking okay. Tonight, I killed three people! I—" I stopped myself as I heard the resemblance to Sam's earlier reaction. "Do you know what the Trials are like, Bunny?"

—Basically, yes.—
-Bunny-

"No, not basically. Do you *know*?"

—I'm not an Examiner. I don't follow my Players to the Trials.—
-Bunny-

"Let me tell you about them, then. I'll try to help you truly understand. NIX takes kids, children, sometimes ones even younger than China. They put them into the Trials, places where nothing but monsters live, with no explanation and no help. Everything within the Trial is designed to either terrify or harm you in some way. Did you know, in my Characteristic Trial, a little boy died in my arms? He must have been younger than twelve. Did you know that, Bunny? Did you?"

—No…I didn't know that.—
-Bunny-

"He was innocent. He did nothing to deserve this. Why would NIX do that to him? What kind of people could hold down a little kid and make him a Player, even knowing what it meant? That he could die in the acclimatization process? That dying before becoming a Player might actually be the *kinder* option?"

Bunny didn't respond.

"What about what happened tonight, then? We were trapped in cages where the floor rose up in the shape of our nightmares. We had to kill the person across from us to be released, so that we could live. If neither of us was able to kill the other, then both of us would die. What could possibly be a good reason to do that to a group of kids? To *anyone*? Do you seriously believe there's some good purpose behind all of this? That they're doing it because they need to? That's what you told me, but I think you were lying. Bunny, let me tell you what the Trials do. They make us so desperate to survive that we'll do anything for more Seeds. We'll do anything to become less and less human, and further the course of this sick little experiment. We're like little ants in a terrarium to them. You watch us, monitor us, give us drugs to enhance our performance, do tests to examine our behavior…"

My claws dug into the arms of the chair. "Have you ever killed someone, Bunny?"

I waited a long while for him to respond.

—No, I've never killed anyone. But you're trying to say I *have* killed, through being a part of all this.—
-Bunny-

"You said it. You said it because you know the answer in your heart. You've judged yourself, Bunny. And I think—I think you've been found lacking."

—What am I supposed to do, Eve? I can't just stop being a Moderator. It doesn't work like that. I don't have anything to do with the Trials. I can't stop them, and I can't help you through them. The most I can do is give you quests in between so you can get more Seeds and protect yourself.—
-Bunny-

"You're lying again, Bunny." My voice was soft, but the words were hard, and as forceful as I could make them. "I and my team are going to escape NIX and its Game. You can lie to me, but not to yourself. And that's why you're not going to try and stop us. If you won't help, the least you can do is keep silent and not get us caught or killed. Because then you *will* have killed someone, no escaping or denying it. And trust me, you don't want to know what it feels like."

I stood and moved stiffly out of the bathroom and to our resident scientist. "So what did you get?"

Blaine looked up from the screen in front of him. "How they are doing it is a bit of a mystery. Well, that is obvious. They are teleporting you like some science fiction film! They must know *exactly* where you are. The sensors picked up the anomaly instantaneously. But the algorithms that know how to keep you clothed, now those must be interesting…"

I'd lifted my hand to my neck. "They must use the GPS to teleport us. When we short them out, they'll lose connection, right?"

"I would imagine so. Unless they have some other way of tracking your exact location, I do not see how they could possibly continue to do…whatever it is they are doing."

Chapter 21

This horror will grow mild, this darkness light.
— John Milton

I JERKED from a nightmare into the afternoon sun knifing my bleary eyes. The light through my window cleansed my memory of the dream I'd been having like bleach. Except the dark stains of the nightmare remained, in the way I felt sick to my stomach, and my sheets, damp from sweat. A shiver swept through me, and every inch of my body ached. Every injury seemed to have bloomed into maturity during the night. I grabbed loose clothes that would cover as much skin as possible and snuck into the bathroom without being noticed.

After a long, hot shower, I looked at myself in the mirror. "God. That's going to be hard to hide." I could have easily passed for someone who'd just been in a pod accident. "Or fallen out of a plane with no parachute," I muttered to myself. Sam had healed the serious injury—my shoulder—and no more than that. I debated for a moment whether or not to put one of the Seeds I'd earned into Resilience. I had gained a record six Seeds from the Trial.

Instead, I snuck into my mother's room while she messed around in the kitchen making breakfast, and took her makeup. I didn't know what I was doing, but we had similar pale coloring, and thirty minutes later I'd managed to cover up most of the bruising on my face. More liquid skin camo bandages over the cuts and scrapes, some powder to make them blend in, and I was ready. My face wouldn't stand up to scrutiny, but if I hung my now-dry hair over it and didn't interact with Zed or my mother too much, I might be able to slip by.

I passed by my brother on the way around the table, trying not to walk too stiffly.

My mom bustled around the kitchen, cooking with the commanding concentration of a conductor at a symphony.

"Whoa, Eve," Zed said.

I gritted my teeth, wondering what had given me away.

"Did you get taller than me again?" He tilted his head and looked me up and down with a frown.

As children, we'd traded places for the title of "tallest" for years. It had been a bit of friendly sibling rivalry when we were younger, and in recent years, a title I gladly conceded to him. I had a model's height, if not one's thinness, but any taller and it would start to stand out as strange. My mother said our father had been huge, head and shoulders above other men. That was all well and good for Zed, but as a girl, I didn't *want* to be head and shoulders above other men.

But better that question than the one I'd been expecting. "No, I'm the same size. It's just that you're sitting down."

He considered for a moment, and then shook his head. "No, I don't think so. Here, let's go check." He stood and grabbed my arm to pull me to the wall where my mom had hung the piece of wood she'd always measured us against. We'd moved house to house often in my younger years, so instead of a wall, she'd measured us against a flat panel of wood that moved along with us. At least one childhood memory wasn't left behind.

Though I managed not to jerk away from his painful grip on my left arm, which had suffered more than its share of abuse from the Oracle, I couldn't stop my wince of pain in time to avoid notice.

"What's wrong?" he said.

I looked slightly down at him and shook my head. "Oh, it's just a bruise." I smiled convincingly—I hoped. "No big deal. But I guess you were right. I've grown. Again." I nodded toward my old height mark, now at my eye level.

He frowned. "I've got some salve for bruises, if it's bad." Before I could react, he'd leaned over and lifted the end of the baggy sleeve of my shirt, exposing the bruise.

He paused, and then raised the sleeve higher, and higher still when the discoloration didn't end. He stood silent, staring at my completely exposed arm and shoulder.

I knew what he was seeing. It was a mottled mess of blue and purple from the top of my shoulder down, fading out to a strange yellow-green around my elbow.

It looked like I'd been attacked by a semi.

When he spoke, his voice was low and forcefully controlled. "Just a bruise?" His brown eyes met my own silver-blue ones with scorn. "How did this happen?" His grew louder, and my mother looked over, gasping when she saw my arm.

She walked around the table and brushed her fingers lightly over the colorful area.

I was careful not to react to the pain even her gentle touch caused me. "What happened, Sweetie? I should call the doctor." She paused for a second with her hair shielding her lowered face. "Did someone hurt you?" she asked, her voice low, almost a threat.

Zed latched onto that idea, his eyes narrowing. "Did someone hit you?"

I drew back from them both, pushing my sleeve down over my arm again and frowning. "God, no! What's with you two, jumping to crazy conclusions, going all over-protective on me?" I shook my head and gave a half smile. "I was riding my friend Adam's bike. He let me borrow it. He told me to be careful, but this bunny ran across the road, and I swerved and fell off. I'm completely fine, it just bruised really bad. That's all. It doesn't even hurt very much."

My mother backed off a bit, but her frown was still skeptical. "Are you sure?"

I rolled my eyes. "Of course I'm sure. It happened to me, didn't it? How would I not know for sure?"

She turned back to the kitchen at that. "Well, serves you right, you silly girl. There's a reason they require a license to drive a bike. One for a pod is *not* the same thing."

"I know, Mom. I was being stupid. No more joyrides for me, okay?"

She nodded and sat a plate on the table. "Damn straight."

Biting back the deep, relieved exhalation I yearned to let out, I took my seat at the table and started to load my plate with food. I was so hungry it felt like my stomach might turn inside out with the sucking need for sustenance. I ate till my stomach was so full I couldn't keep another bite down without throwing up, despite the censoring looks of my mother.

When I left the table to go back to sleep, Zed was still staring at me in silent, pointed anger. He didn't believe my story about the bike, and he was making it obvious.

I ignored him, too tired to deal with it. I couldn't tell him the truth, so the only way to alleviate his suspicions was to continue steadfast in my secrecy and lies. At least if he thought I was being bullied or abused by my "friends," he wouldn't be on to the real secret.

To my surprise, he came to my room a few minutes later with a small jar in hand. "For the bruise," he said simply.

"Uh, thanks," I mumbled, reaching for the jar.

He shook his head. "Roll up your sleeve. I'll do it."

"That's okay, really. I can do—"

He sighed exasperatedly. "You know I'm better at stuff like this than you. Just let me help."

I grumbled, but did as he asked, rolling up my sleeve all the way to my neck.

He sat on the edge of my bed and stared silently at my arm and shoulder again, his lips pressed together in a white line. But he didn't say anything, just dipped his forefinger in the jar and applied the salve gently to my skin, rubbing it in slowly with butterfly-light touches.

Almost immediately, I felt a decrease in pain of the areas he'd covered. I let out a sigh of relief. "You've got those magic hands. I'm sure all your future patients will love you." I still remembered my faint jealousy as a child toward Zed, who apparently was born with normal hands and feet, which my mother cooed over to no end. I'd, somewhat snidely, started calling his hands "magic," and it seemed to be true. Everything Zed touched flourished. My father had six fingers and toes, like me, but his parents hadn't chosen to have the extras amputated as a baby like mine were. I'd questioned my mom about my father a lot when I was younger, but she didn't like to be forced to remember him, and I learned to stop asking.

"I'm sure I developed this magic patching you up every time you got into trouble as a kid. Remember how many times you skinned your knees?"

I laughed. "I was so gangly and awkward! And you, my little brother, getting out the med kit every time and taking care of me."

"Someone had to." He grinned. "Or all those sidewalks and gym floors would have beaten you up mercilessly. It was like your knees were magnetically drawn to anything that could hurt them. I see things haven't changed too much." He raised an eyebrow at my shoulder. As kids, we would joke that whatever inanimate object I'd gotten my latest injury from had purposefully hurt me and scheme ways to get back at it. Zed had deliberately tracked dirt onto the gym floor for months after I'd ripped the skin off the bottom of my feet running too fast on it.

"Don't worry, I'm much tougher now. If you think this is bad, you should see the tree I got into an 'altercation' with." I winked.

"A tree?" He shook his head and sighed. "Oh, Sis, you do stupid stuff sometimes."

"Tell me about it," I grunted, wincing as he rubbed a particularly sensitive part of my arm.

He stayed and rubbed salve into my arm and shoulder till his jar ran out, and we chatted and laughed like we hadn't in a while. Not since before the Game. I didn't realize how much I missed it.

I WOKE AGAIN to a light flashing in my face. I shuddered at the abrupt detachment from another nightmare. I never slept without them now. What I'd thought was a light was actually a Window, sent from Jacky using the Skill gained by joining my team. There was only one word, but it made me throw myself out of bed and grab my shoes.

—Help—
-Jacky-

I sent a response, asking what was wrong and where she was.

—I'm in his office.—
-Jacky-

That wasn't useful, but she ignored my request for clarification, so I pulled up her location on the map using my Command Skill, snuck into my sleeping mother's room, and took the keys to her pod. I drove faster than I'd ever driven in my life, uncaring if an enforcer might see. Jacky may have been in danger from NIX. I sent another Window, asking what was wrong.

—I think he's dead. Definitely dead.—
—Please come.—
-Jacky-

After that, I couldn't get any more out of her, and I gunned the pod till I reached the home for "troubled" girls. It was a large, fenced-in detention center. She'd mentioned it before, but it was still strange to realize Jacky lived in a place like that.

I parked the pod in a tree's shadow and took a running jump at the barbed wire-topped fence. I held down the spiraling row of metal thorns with one hand and crawled over. The nearest door into the building was locked.

"Damn it!" I growled. I was wasting time.

Checking my map again, I pinpointed Jacky's location to a room on the fourth floor. Its glowing window was visible from down below. "Okay, let's try this," I mumbled. I took off my shoes and unsheathed my claws, then walked a few yards away from the building. I sprinted toward the wall as fast as I could and took a running leap at the last second, smashing into the concrete with my claws out.

I scrabbled and dug in desperately, but my claws finally found purchase. I hung for a second as my still-healing body screamed out in pain, and then found a seam in the concrete for my toes to grip. Then I began to scale the wall, digging in my claws and gripping with my toes as I dragged myself upward till I made it to the window on the fourth floor.

Inside, Jacky paced back and forth, biting a clenched fist. An old, overweight man lay on the hardwood floor across from her. His skull was caved in, blood puddled around it like a red halo.

I ripped the windowsill away, squinting as glass burst outward into my face, then twisted the frame to the side and scrambled through.

Jacky gasped and took an automatic step toward me, her features sagging in relief. But just as quickly, her eyes darted back toward the corpse, and she stopped herself. "I—I killed him. It was an accident. I just…panicked." She bit down on her knuckles again, her head shaking wordlessly.

The old man wore a button-up shirt and socks. No pants, no underwear. His lifeless hand clenched a fistful of shiny brown hair. Jacky's hair, ripped from her head.

Her shirt was torn, hanging half open and exposing her bra and stomach.

"What happened?" I asked.

"They're gonna send me to jail," she said in a low voice, letting her hands fall to her sides. "It'll be just like before, but worse because I'm older and I've got a record, and he's the *warden*, and he's *dead*."

"Just like before?"

"My first foster family. Distant relatives of my dad, back here in this country. I was already beautiful, even as a kid. They had a son, older than me. They wouldn't believe me when I told them what he was doing, and he tried to… I hurt him, and I ran away. When the cops finally picked me up on the streets, my relatives said I was violent, that I attacked their son cause I was an animal.

"The second home, it was the husband. The wife was nice. I told her, hoped she would help, yeah? But she was jealous, not surprised. She hit me with the rollin' pin she used to make biscuits. When they were asleep, I burned down the house."

"And then you came here?" I swallowed against the lump in my throat.

She shook her head before continuing in a soft voice. "After that, it was the streets again. I found another martial arts gym, like the one my father used to take me to. I cleaned the place at night to pay for lessons. And I used the lessons to fight. For money. That's where the enforcers found me again. I was still too young, and nobody died, so they brought me here. And it all started over again." By the end, she was drooping with cynical fatigue. "I just murdered the warden. I'm so screwed, Eve. I dunno why I even called you."

I strode forward and grabbed her by the shoulders, pushing backward and forcing her to stand straight. "You called me because you knew I would help you. This time is different from before. You're not the only one standing up for yourself anymore. You're part of my team now."

"But I killed him. I murdered him."

"He tried to hurt you?"

"He tried."

"And he hurt others?" I guessed.

She nodded.

"He deserved it. You did the right thing, Jacky. And I'm not going to let you be punished for that."

She stared at me for a moment. "What are you going to do?"

"I'm getting you out of here. And you're never coming back."

"How? They're gonna investigate, and they're gonna figure out what I did. Even if I run, they'll find me eventually."

"The first step is to destroy the evidence you were even here." They'd have Jacky's prints, and maybe even her DNA on file. "Give me a hand. He looks heavy."

We maneuvered his torso and head into position beneath his huge, antique liquor cabinet. I carefully removed Jacky's hair from his fist and handed it to her. Then we toppled his liquor cabinet onto his already damaged skull, crushing it even further with a satisfying crunchy squelch that was almost overwhelmed by the shatter of glass.

"One last thing," I said. "If he's got a liquor cabinet, he's got to have cigars." Already, the alcohol fumes burned my sensitive nostrils.

Jacky rummaged in his desk and came back with a cigar and an old-timey zippo.

"Perfect." I lit the cigar with some effort, stepped back, and paused as a thought came to me. "Jacky, is there anything you need in this place? We're not coming back."

"There's nothing. Nothing of my own anymore."

I flicked the cigar at the warden's head, and the room roared into flames. "Let's go. The fire will draw attention." I jerked my head to the window. I jumped first, landing in a roll, but the impact still knocked the breath out of my lungs, and I felt the pain of it all the way up through my body.

Jacky came next, slamming to the ground and sinking down into a graceful three-point crouch with enough force to make dust rise from the ground around her. Normally she would have grinned and bragged about being a badass, but she followed me wordlessly to my mother's pod.

"Where are you taking me?" Jacky asked.

"To our base. You're getting a room in the main house," I replied. I set the pod to semi-autopilot, since I was no longer in a hurry, and pulled up my Command Window to send a quick wake-up message to Adam.

—I'm awake.—
-Adam-

. . .

—Good. I need you to do something for me.—
-Eve-

—What is it?—
-Adam-

—Hack into the security cameras and the release records of the New Life Home for Troubled Girls. They should state Jacky has been released from custody of the state, as of yesterday, and any incriminating evidence on the security cameras from 12:00AM to 2:00AM never happened. Can you do that?—
-Eve-

—Give me 30 mins.—
-Adam-

I LET OUT a sigh of relief. "In half an hour, your records will reflect that you are no longer a ward of the state," I said to Jacky. "And the evidence you had anything to do with what happened to the warden will be either erased or burned away." The claw marks I'd made in the wall would be the only evidence remaining. Good luck interpreting that, I thought with a silent smirk.

"How?" she asked simply.

"You're not the only useful one on the team, Jacky," I teased.

She stuck out her tongue at me, but whispered, "Thank you." There was a kind of force behind those words, as if she were binding herself to me with chains of gratitude.

I set Jacky up in one of the many spare bedrooms in Blaine's house. He was enraged when I gave him a vague explanation of why Jacky would no longer be staying in the detention center, and was more than willing to house her.

Adam successfully completed his assignment, less than thirty minutes after my request, and sent me a message saying only,

—The bastard's better off in Hell. But no one else will ever know exactly how he got there.—
-Adam-

I stayed with Jacky till the morning, then left to replace my mom's pod before the sun had fully risen.

Chapter 22

Nobody really cares about your existence, but they will pretend.
— Raja Molanthe

THAT AFTERNOON, Blaine presented me with his latest invention, through which we would find NIX.

I called the team together to explain the plan and the preparation necessary to carry it out. "Blaine's got something ready for NIX. He's going to set up a drop to exchange his research for proof of life on his niece and nephew, and when it's done, we're going to follow the people who come."

Adam grinned, tossed a coin high above his head, and caught it behind his back without looking. "I knew it. That's the next logical step, after the doc told us about the drops. But it's quicker than I thought we'd be able to prepare."

"Well, we'll be giving them an inferior product, of course," I said with a smirk. "Why don't you tell them, Blaine? It's your accomplishment, after all."

Blaine stepped forward, "I have two things I've been working on at Eve's request." He held up a small silver disk. "This is the most efficient battery this world has ever seen. Well, except for the one you brought me." He nodded to Adam and me. "I created it based on the model from the Game. It is inferior, because I had to use the most similar known elements I could find. The original uses some previously undiscovered elements. Actually, it is quite amazing…" He visibly restrained himself from going off on an intellectual tangent. "But that is beside the point. We will give this to NIX. The perfected product will be for us."

"What's the second thing?" Adam asked, doodling on the back of his hand.

I gave China a wide grin. "You're going to like this."

Blaine held up a sealed vial of amber liquid in his other hand. "It's an antidote to meningolycanosis. That's what I dubbed the parasitic samples from NIX." He looked to China. "The ones that infected your sister. I used samples of Eve's blood to do a series of tests, and found that the Seed organisms would fight off other infectious diseases with varying degrees of efficiency. But meningolycanosis, they completely ignored. The Seeds can't see them, and thus don't recognize them as a threat. So, I thought, *why not*? Long story short, it's because the meningolycanosis camouflages itself."

China leaned forward and gripped my forearm, not taking her eyes off Blaine. "But you figured out how to make it visible, right?"

He cleared his throat. "Well, yes. Unfortunately, stripping the coating off them creates a sort of acidic reaction. The Seeds can kill them, but they have a harder time dealing with and disposing of the acid. I am working on a second step to the serum that will neutralize the acid after stripping off the coating, but I haven't finished it yet. It is proving more difficult than I thought. However, when I have the completed serum, we'll keep it for ourselves."

I placed my hand over China's. "And we can use it on your sister."

Her eyes filled with tears as she looked at me, and Jacky smiled at us with approval. Even Sam, who hated my guts at the moment, gave me a grudging nod.

I felt the burden of their trust and expectations weigh heavy on my shoulders. Both girls looked at me as if I was some great person, a trustworthy leader, a loyal friend.

I was not a hero. I was the leader of this team by necessity. My own necessity. My need to stay alive. Sure, I tried to take care of them, but it had nothing to do with being a good person. An intact, well-oiled, loyal team meant better chances for my own survival. Couldn't they see that?

But of course they couldn't. And so I accepted the burden of their ever-deepening trust, and hoped that I wouldn't have to betray it someday.

"I want to give us a couple days to prepare for this, but it's happening soon, and we need to be ready. Blaine will be working on the serum two-point-oh and with Adam and me on our preparations. Sam, I'd like you to help Blaine with the second step of the serum, since your abilities might give him some clue how to augment it."

He nodded immediately. "Sounds good."

At least Sam didn't have a problem taking orders from me, despite his resentment. "Adam, you're in charge of a tracking device. It's top priority. Also, let's see if we can't trace their response to Blaine's request for a drop."

"I'm on it," he said.

"China, if he's got the technical side down, you'll have the physical. With your Perception and Grace, you're the most likely to be able to follow someone organically without being detected. In case something goes wrong."

She bounced on her toes. "I can't believe this is happening! I'm so excited. We're going to save Chanelle, and we'll find a way to get out of this Game and the Trials, and everything's going to go back to normal. I can't believe it. I can't wait!"

I couldn't help but laugh. China's excitement was contagious. "Well, we need to find NIX, first. But at least it's a start. Jacky, you're our fighter, and you'll keep teaching us as you have been. Sound good?"

"Hell yeah." She cracked her knuckles and her neck, all evidence of last night's ordeal gone, though I knew at least part of it was an act.

"Okay, then. Time to brainstorm," I said.

TWO DAYS LATER, I crouched in the corner of a field, behind the rusted shell of an old pod, watching as a large black transport vehicle pulled up to Blaine's sportier pod. Two men jumped out and scanned the field of tall grass and the tree line on the far side. I could only be grateful they didn't have access to our GPS data, or we'd be given away. Blaine was still working on shorting it out safely, along with all the other projects he'd been spreading his energy among. In the meantime, he'd created lead collars we could wear around our necks that mostly stopped the signal from transmitting.

"Whatcha got for us this time, doc?" the larger man said. He wore a dark blue shirt, and the other man a black one. Except for that, they wore exactly the same outfit.

I could have heard them faintly with my increased hearing, but the henchman's tinny voice came instead out of an ear bud tucked into my ear. It was connected to a small mic on the inner corner of Blaine's glasses, and the whole team had ear buds, just in case.

Blaine held up the energy disk cushioned within a Styrofoam bed and a folder of papers explaining his research. The file was clipped on top with a simple metal clamp. Inside the clamp was a tiny tracking device, which Adam was monitoring with his computer.

"Just this," Blaine said. He sounded nervous, but I thought that was acceptable given the circumstances. He was probably nervous every time he did this, even when he didn't have a group of Players hiding all around the field where he had set up a meeting with a secret organization.

They brought out a lock box, and the blue-shirt henchman opened the door while the black-shirt took the energy disk and file from Blaine and placed it inside.

There was a faint beep when he did so, and Blue and Black shared a look before turning on Blaine. "It says something's sending a signal."

"Shit," I hissed, quickly sending a message to Adam.

—Turn it off!—
-Eve-

Blaine was stammering, trying to convince them that was impossible.

They took the vial and file out, and the box beeped again.

He grew more flustered.

—I said turn it off!—
-Eve-

—I'm trying!—
-Adam-

BLAINE HELD up a hand as the two henchmen's expressions changed to promise violence. "Wait! I know what it is. I know what it is."

Blue took a threatening step forward. "Well, what is it?"

Blaine pulled a pen out of his pocket and held it up. "This! It's a magnet pen. It's not sending a signal; it's just a magnetic field. The clip on the file is metal, and it's catching the magnetic field, sending out a disturbance to the box's sensors. Look, I'll show you." He walked to the back of his pod with the pen and stuck it to the metal side. It hung there while he walked back to the men, buying us time.

"Try it again," he said.

Black nodded at Blue, and Blue placed the file inside again. No beep.

I melted with physical relief. Blaine let out a tiny puff of his own through the bud in my ear.

Blue henchman pulled off the clip and turned it around in curiosity. "All the same, we'll leave this," he said, tossing it into the dirt beside Blaine's pod.

—We're screwed.—
-Sam-

—I hope China's ready to do some tracking.—
-Adam-

THE TEAM SENT me a flurry of messages. Adam had been unable to track the electronic source of NIX's response to Blaine without being detected, so we were forced to rely on physical means.

The disappointment was just starting to seep into me when I saw a movement in the tall grass beside the pods. Suddenly, a group of birds erupted on the other side of the field in a cacophony of squawks and flapping of wings.

The attention of both henchmen was drawn in that direction, and they put their hands under their jackets, reaching for their guns.

While they were distracted, China crawled from the grass, scrambled around Blaine's pod low to the ground, and grabbed the clip.

—What the hell is she doing?—
-Adam-

—China's going for it!—
-Jacky-

I ITCHED to send her a message telling her to get the hell away, but I didn't want to distract her and get her, and thereby all of us, caught.

She slipped around behind all three men without them noticing and put the clip in the side pocket of a messenger bag sitting inside the open door of the transport pod.

Black turned away from the spot where the birds had erupted and scanned the rest of the field while Blue went to investigate what had scared them.

China had nowhere to escape. Just as the man turned toward her, she slipped underneath the black pod in one fluid motion.

She must have made some noise, because the man looked to the spot where she'd been standing, and then crouched to look under both pods.

I held my breath, sure he'd find her, but a moment later he stood with a shrug, apparently seeing nothing. I let out the breath. China must have tucked her small body into the underside of the pod, holding herself aloft in some indentation in the mechanics of the underbelly.

The man shook his head. "Probably a snake or something."

They gave Blaine a smartglass tablet, and I vaguely saw the faces of two dark-haired children pop up. Proof of life for his niece and nephew. He had a quick conversation with them that I tuned out in my worry over China's situation.

Then the men took away the pad, got into their pod, and drove away with China still hanging underneath.

Just before they turned a sharp corner on the small path, she dropped off and rolled into the grass.

Blaine got into his small pod and drove away, oblivious to the whole adventure of China's involvement, muttering, "Sorry guys. Looks like it failed. It is up to you now."

—Wait a few minutes, guys.—
-Eve-

I sent the message to the whole team. After I was fairly certain we weren't being secretly observed, and the men had put distance between themselves and us, I gave the okay to move.

China stood up and ran back to us without bothering to brush off the dirt and grass all over her. She was trembling visibly, but had the biggest grin on her face. "I did it. I did it."

Adam scowled. "What you *did* is almost get yourself caught. And all of us along with you."

Her grin slipped a bit, but she didn't back down. "I don't think we could have tracked them all the way there without the beacon. Following them in a car would have been dangerous, too. They're probably trained to look for a tail. Besides, I couldn't just let this chance go. Who knows when we'd get another? And every day we waste, Chanelle's still in there. Who knows how much time she has?"

Adam pressed his lips together, but pushed the hair back from his face with a sigh and ruffled her hair. "Well, you didn't get caught. You're okay, and that's the most important thing. But don't do something so stupid again, okay?"

She grinned and nodded, but there was an obvious lack of remorse on her face.

I couldn't help but laugh, and it felt good. It had been a long time since I last laughed for real, and the relief of our small victory made me feel lighter inside than I had since before I was a Player.

THAT NIGHT, we sat around the tables in Blaine's lab.

"Don't be such a lily, Sam." Jacky shook her head. "What did you think we were tracking NIX for? Like we weren't gonna actually *find* them?" Jacky snorted, more on edge than usual. The fire and the warden's death had been on the news. All the residents of the juvenile center had escaped unscathed, thankfully, and it was reported as a strange drunken accident. Whether the enforcers were investigating despite that, I didn't know. Time would settle both Jacky's mood and any suspicions, I hoped. If my claw marks in the side of the building had been noticed, I could only laugh at the enforcers' inevitable confusion.

"My sister is in there," China said simply, steel in her voice.

Adam rubbed his fingers together, sparks jumping over his knuckles. "I want to go. But Sam's not wrong. It's dangerous to jump into this. You guys do remember that we all have a GPS chip embedded in our necks, right? They could have alarms set to go off if Players get too close."

"They might not," I speculated aloud. "They keep some Players who failed Trials there for research. And if anyone but Bunny were actually monitoring us, they'd notice that we're in the house of one of their contractors-slash-blackmail-victims."

"Unless they know and don't care. Or they're keeping an eye on us secretly." Adam shot one of his sparks into China's side, making her jump, then grinned mischievously when she smacked the top of his head.

I rolled my eyes at them. "We need more information. That always seems to be the problem..." I rubbed the back of my neck and sat up straight. "But we do have a resource on the inside, which we've forgotten about."

"You want to ask B—*him*?" Adam asked.

"Not overtly, of course. But if we could tease some information out of him, think how useful that would be."

Sam's eyes widened. "What if he realizes what we're doing?"

I leaned forward, my mind racing. "That's why we'll have to be careful. We'll slip the information-gathering into conversation secretly, and each of us will try for different pieces of the puzzle so he doesn't even realize everything he's told us."

CHINA WAS the one to end up getting most of the information we gathered out of Bunny. She learned more about NIX's physical and organizational structure, as well as some hints about security, all the while bonding with Bunny and subtly planting seeds of empathy toward our little team. She was amazing. When I told her so, she just shook her head sadly. "I just want us all to be safe."

From what we gathered, NIX wouldn't know if we snuck up on them unless someone checked in on us specifically and noticed our location. This was least likely to happen late at night, because, while Bunny had constant access to all the Players he moderated, he did need to sleep. And he did it on a fairly regular schedule.

So, late at night a few days later, after driving to a spot Adam had deemed suitably removed from NIX, our actual target, the team got out of the pod and spent hours in the government-property forest, circling in toward the tracking beacon. We moved cautiously, scanning for any electronic security devices hidden among the trees. When we found them, we marked a way around in their blind spots and continued on.

Finally, we got close enough to see what we'd been hunting for. It was a huge compound cut from the inside of the mountain cliff. The front side had windows and air vents cut into the stone face, little bright points of light or deeper dark in the night.

The back side was a bowl depression into the mountain, with a huge metal ball on a concrete tower shooting out of the middle surrounded by mostly open courtyard and some smaller individual buildings. The walls were made of glass in places on the inside, and we could see people moving along the curved hallways. We had no way of knowing how far the underground construction went, but I had no doubt it was extensive. The inside had stairs running up the wall for convenience, while the other side plunged to rock, river, and trees far below. Because of the way the compound had been built, it almost seemed as if the ball tower was surrounded by huge stone walls made of mountain, like a king's castle or city of olden days.

Guards walked around atop the outside of the walls, on constant patrol. They carried large guns strapped to their bodies, as well as hand-held radios and binoculars. The whole place was well secured and easily defensible on all sides.

My team crouched at the top of a hill, hidden among the trees and underbrush at the base of a nearby mountain.

"This place isn't on any official map," Adam murmured. "We've definitely found NIX." He pointed to the river. "That runs through the bottom of the mountain they've built into. They must be using it as an energy source to keep this place running."

"What's that?" I jerked my head toward the huge ball elevated above the courtyard. Bands of different colored metals spun around it in all directions, as if in moving orbit.

"No idea." He shrugged.

"I didn't expect NIX to be quite so…big," China said in a small voice. "How are we supposed to…?" She trailed off.

"Yeah. I hate to say it, Eve, but how does this help?" Sam asked. "Now we know more about them, but that only makes us more of a threat to them, and gives them a reason to kill us."

"They already try to kill us every ten days in the Trials, so not much has changed then, huh?" Adam said.

"Sam, do you know what the casualty rate is for Players?" I asked.

They were all silent for a few moments as the weight of my words settled on them.

"High. Over fifty percent. But once you've survived a few times, the survival rate goes up," he whispered.

"Does it? What about our last Trial? Even if every one of those Players had been able to solve the puzzle, *half* would still have died. Because that's what NIX wanted. They don't want us all to survive." I carefully emphasized every word. "Otherwise they wouldn't put us into the Trials. How long till one of us slips up and dies, or we're sent to a Trial where we're forced to work against each other? We can't keep this up forever."

He was silent, so I continued. "It's like I've said from the beginning, we need to escape. As soon as possible. And I've got an idea. I had an interesting conversation with you-know-who." I lifted my eyes skyward to indicate Bunny without saying his name and drawing attention to our current situation. "He told me that when Players commit suicide, NIX takes them off the list of active Players—the ones that enter Trials."

Adam twisted onto his side to face me, the weaving tattoos on his arms making him blend into the darkness like camouflage. "I know you're not going to have us kill ourselves, so what's the plan?"

I grinned. "That's where you come in." I could feel the weight of everyone's anticipation for my next words. "It's only logical that they keep records of all their past Players, right?"

"Right."

"And as you-know-who's the only one that watches us enough to know who we are, if suddenly we disappeared, no one would notice as long as nothing drew their attention to our absence?"

"Probably not…but—"

"So, if suddenly Adam Coyle's status changed to 'dead for the last six months,' and somehow also happened to be the exact same information as Joe Schmoe, some random guy that actually did die, and already had the cleaners erase suspicion on him…"

"Whoa. That might actually work. Of course, they probably have tracking and audit programs in place to find discrepancies, at least they do if they're smart. And I'm sure they've got backups, too. But they'll likely be digital for security purposes, and even if not, I'd bet there's a self-destruct protocol for invasion or takeover scenarios. If I could write a program designed to spread like the zombie apocalypse and wipe out our real information and any traces that it had been changed…plus set off the backup self-destruct…" He trailed off, the rapidly turning gears in his head practically visible behind his eyes. "I'm going to need to level up some more to be able to create something that robust. And I'll need a direct linkup. But I can do it. If I can get in there"—he jerked his head toward the compound—"for long enough for the program to work undetected."

"I've got some ideas for that," I said.

Chapter 23

We are what we pretend to be, so we must be careful what we pretend to be.

— Kurt Vonnegut

MY MOM CALLED us into the kitchen and sat us down for a particularly fancy breakfast. She rubbed her manicured hands together with a mixture of excitement and nerves. "I've got something to tell you."

I bit back my smile.

"I've received a job offer from the marketing department of one of our sister companies. They're expanding into some products with high profit potential, and they want me to lead the team. They're willing to compensate for our relocation, and the pay is high enough—"

"Relocation?" Zed interrupted. "What are you saying?"

"The decision is already made, children." She met both our eyes challengingly. "It would mean a higher standard of living, less hours of work for me after the initial push, it's got a significantly better enforcer presence, and the school is top notch."

Zed looked to me for help.

Sorry, brother, I won't be giving a hand with this one, I thought with a shrug. "I'm out of school anyway, so it doesn't matter to me."

My mother smiled, relaxing subtly. "There are some wonderful opportunities for secondary education, Eve, as well as job opportunities if you can't pass the entrance exams..."

Zed glared between the two of us and stalked out of the room, leaving the elaborate meal untouched.

My mother sighed.

"He'll come around," I said to her, piling my plate with his abandoned food. I couldn't just let it all to waste, now. I snickered to myself.

"At least I have one reasonable child," she sighed.

I smiled at her around a mouthful of melon. If only she knew. If all went well, the others in my team with families to protect would all be having similar discussions. It turned out Blaine's wealth could create connections and opportunities seemingly out of thin air.

THREE DAYS LATER, the power went off as I was lying on the floor in the living room with Zed. I sat up in vague curiosity, letting the indirect sunlight through the window wash over my body in the now-darkened room.

"Power's off," Zed stated the obvious, putting down his school pad.

"I'm sure it'll be back on soon." I frowned down at the small chain I'd been fiddling with while quizzing him for his year-end test. I couldn't see well enough without the light, and obviously couldn't activate my Huntress Skill to improve my night vision while in a civilian's presence. "Probably just a rolling blackout."

But then I heard faint musical tones, and my insides started to vibrate in harmony. "Oh, shit. Shit, shit, shit," I muttered, launching myself off the floor and sprinting to my room.

"What's wrong, Eve?"

"Uh, nothing!" I called back distractedly. "I just forgot I was going to go to a friend's house tonight. I'm late!" I grabbed the pack that I always kept prepared and nearby from my closet. I lifted the edge of my mattress and fumbled for the Seeds hidden within, tossing them into my pack. I barely remembered to strip off my link and toss it on the bed so it didn't get scrambled. "This shouldn't be happening. It's only been nine days, not ten. It's not time yet!" I hissed. Were the others going to Trial, too? Or was NIX singling me out, sending me off-schedule to see if I would die by myself? Before I had time to even put on shoes, my bones shivered me into my fifth Trial. I was understandably distracted, and so didn't feel the eyes watching me in secret through the crack in my doorway. If I had, maybe things would have been different. But…I didn't.

I found myself transported into mid-air and falling fast, and any thoughts beyond the moment quickly blew their way out of my head. I landed hard on a knobby brown tree limb, bruising my knees, scraping my hands, and half knocking the air out of my lungs.

I was sucking at the shockingly warm air, disoriented by the huge, huge distance between myself on the limb and the tawny ground far below, when a warning shout from above caused me to rear back, just fast enough to have my face smashed into the branch as something large landed on me from above.

My nose flattened, my bottom lip got caught between my teeth, and the little air I'd managed to retain after the first impact was forced from me.

"Oh crap. I'm so sorry," Sam's voice said from above. "I just got transported right into the sky and fell on you. Are you okay? I'm going to move. God damn it, this is high."

I twitched my fingers and nodded slightly, unwilling to respond further past the pain of my face and the sick feeling of fear you get when your lungs temporarily stop working.

Sam inched awkwardly off me and helped me to sit up. He put a hand between my shoulder blades and started to cough, and I was suddenly able to draw in a small breath. I used that to fight for more, and finally said, "God. How many times am I going to get the air knocked out of me?" I gathered up the bloody saliva in my mouth and spit. Some of the pink liquid landed on one of the tree's knobs and was absorbed immediately.

The knob unfolded, spreading large, pale petals wide as if seeking more moisture. The petals were almost translucent, and I could see my spit running through their veins, being sucked into the branch. As my bloody saliva traveled, the branches around me stirred in hungry anticipation.

I raised my head slowly and took in my surroundings. I was straddling a tree branch, probably a thousand feet above the desert ground. In the distance, reddish, rocky buttes jutted from the sand, throwing a shadow towards us from the harsh light of the setting sun. Except for the stone cliffs reaching toward the sky and the patch of trees we'd been dropped into, everything lay barren. The sand stretched out for miles around us, rolling in hills and rippling waves like a dry ocean in the midst of a storm.

The heat was enormous even all the way up in the sky, and the air below shimmered unceasingly, like a second layer of ephemeral water above the sand ocean.

Someone screamed as they were dropped from the air a few yards above us. They didn't catch on our level, and with each foot they fell, their chances of grabbing one of the lower, thinner branches decreased. They screamed all the way to the ground, though their voice grew thin and distant after a while. Finally, their body became just a bug-speck of red splatter, half buried by the sand.

The body lay there for only a few moments before something dark and tapered shot out from the sand, arced through the air, and swallowed the entire red-stained area before disappearing back beneath the surface.

Sam shuddered. "Sand sharks. I've heard of them." His face was pale despite the beads of sweat already plastering his hair to his forehead.

The trees around were thin and slender, their limbs reaching horizontally out of the trunks at similar intervals. The pale branches wove together, making an interlocking copse with levels at each interval. The branches grew more plentiful up higher, eventually becoming so thickly woven together that I couldn't see through the branches more than a few levels above my own. "You'd be able to walk around up there," I mused aloud.

Blood from my just-smashed nose dripped into my mouth when I spoke, and I instinctively spat again. The petals all along the limb beneath us unfurled, faintly pink with the blood.

I heard a sound overhead and jerked my gaze upward.

The higher limbs shifted to create a tunnel of visibility to higher levels. I didn't get a good look before they shifted back into place, but I caught the glint of reflective eyes far above—and I definitely heard the scratchy roar that followed.

"Crap. Something's up there, Sam," I said. "Watching us."

"But it hasn't even started yet! Where's the Examiner? Is this another mental Trial? Where's the cube?" He looked at me accusingly, as if it was somehow my fault.

I let my claws out and scanned the surrounding trees with my improved vision. I could see better through the branches than Sam, and caught sight the cube floating on the level above us. "Cube's right up there." I didn't know about the Examiner, but I hoped to god this wasn't going to be a repeat of the last Trial. "Let's go."

Climbing up turned out to be relatively easy. My skills were well-suited to scrambling through the trees without climbing gear—or even shoes. I helped Sam a few times, and we quickly reached the next level of branches. It still wasn't quite stable, but the chance of falling was less. I kept an eye toward the higher levels, but our growling watcher didn't reappear.

Other Players arrived below, popping into mid-air one by one, the rest of my team among them. We called them upward, and I pointed out the best path as Sam waited impatiently, his eyes jumping to the cube every few seconds.

Despite Sam's nervousness, we reached the cube well before most of the others. As we waited, I overheard a couple Players talking about the early start of the Trial. "Nine days? This is getting really short. It's like they're trying to see how far they can push us before we break."

"I remember when it used to be twelve," the other said.

I turned to Jacky, who had been a Player the longest of our group. "Do they do this often? Change the length of time between Trials?"

"Every four to six months it happens, from what I've heard and the shifts I've seen. But it hasn't been ten days for long. We should've had more time before it changed again."

Adam pulled out his butterfly knives and started to twirl them around in both hands with a distant frown on his face. "I wonder why they're doing that? Interesting."

"It is," I agreed.

After even more waiting, our Examiner, a baby elephant with gigantic ears that it flapped like wings, flew in and crash-landed clumsily, shaking the whole platform a little with its weight. It blinked cutely as it climbed back to its feet, reminding me uncomfortably of a certain elephant from a children's cartoon. Even its voice was cute, high-pitched and childlike. But there was nothing innocent or cute about its words as it explained the Trial.

There was to be a battle between monsters, and we were to choose sides and fight in the battle. If we could stop our own side from being annihilated, or if we completely defeated the opposing monsters and Players, we won. If we didn't die, of course.

"Yep, I think that's it. Good luck!" the creature said, letting out a comical toot through its trunk.

Out of the buttes in the distance, dark dots started to appear, jumping off the cliffs and flying in our direction. Even from so far away, I could hear their distant roars. "Damn. It's started," I said aloud.

The branch under my feet jerked, as the tree it was connected to shuddered. Far below, the sand sharks were attacking the base of the trees, smashing into them and gnawing away at the wood.

Adam sighed. "And that's the requisite time limit. No matter what happens with the battle, as soon as they topple this structure, we're dead."

"So we just have to win before that, right?" Jacky said, and they all looked to me.

"Yeah. One group of monsters is a few levels above. I say we go up and see what we're dealing with." I spoke loud enough that the other Players could hear. None of them seemed to be low-leveled newbies, which I found interesting. That could be bad, if NIX thought only stronger Players would be fit for this Trial. The upside was none of them looked helpless enough to trigger my guilty need to protect them.

We started climbing, and some of the Players followed.

Each level grew increasingly thicker, until it was hard to squeeze through the dense weave of branches. A few levels up, a large, slanted tunnel led from our level to the next.

China and I both listened and smelled for anything or anyone on the other side of the tunnel, or traps within it. Sensing no obvious threats, we walked through.

Same thing on the next level, though there were huge piles of feathers, obviously used as beds or nests by something huge. On the level above that, we heard snuffling, soft growls, and the pad of feet walking around over our heads.

The others looked to me expectantly, and, with an internal groan at the danger, I waved them back and walked into the tunnel.

Light from the setting sun streamed into the opening, blinding me as I reached the end. I stopped before exiting and squinted out.

Something smashed into my back, and I stumbled forward. I immediately fell into a fighting stance, knees slightly bent, lips drawn back in a snarl, and claws ready to rip and tear.

This level was open to the sky, at the top of the little patch of trees. All around me, huge, winged cats sat or stood or crouched as if ready to tear my guts from between my ribs. Each was as big as a medium-sized horse, and some were bigger.

One large, dark brown, heavily muscled creature lunged forward in a feint and roared straight into my face, its hair and feathers all standing on end. The force of the sound blew my hair back from my face like a wind tunnel, almost knocking me back.

Instead, I dug my toes into the woven floor and leaned into it.

When it was over, I wiped away the spittle that had landed on my face and tried to ignore the dizzying ring in my ears. "You sound like a kitten," I said. "Maybe if you took up smoking you could deepen that voice a bit." I knew it couldn't understand me, but if it had wanted to kill me, it would have attacked immediately. It wanted to scare me, so I couldn't show any self-doubt. I hoped it couldn't smell fear, though, because there was nothing I could do to stop the emotion from running through my veins and prickling along my skin.

Other cats around us leaned forward, eyes trained on me. A low, rumbling growl started from one and was picked up by the others, like the chant of an audience. They harmonized together until I felt like I was standing in a massage chair made of air and sound.

Behind me in the tunnel, Adam and Jacky were calling my name, and I heard thuds like they were pounding on the wood, for some reason unable to get through.

I was just about to attack, so that at least I could go down fighting, when a shadow blocked the sun, and something plummeted out of the sky to the floor in front of me.

It was another of the creatures, bigger than the others, and with the more slender build that I associated with females. Its wings were spread wide and protective in front of me, reaching several yards in each direction. It roared back at the dark brown male and stared down the others until they stopped growling and backed away.

She made growling sounds at them, mixed with coughs and the occasional yowl.

The male responded in kind, but then lowered his head and exposed his neck to her.

With that, she turned to me and licked my face. Her huge tongue rasped away the blood from my nose, along with the top layer of skin.

She stared into my eyes for a moment, and I found the hair on the back of my neck raising as I realized the large orbs didn't have slanted pupils like a cat. They looked…human. Deep and clear and intelligent. Expressive.

The creature swallowed, and her eyes widened. She leaned back and roared joyfully into the sky.

The others looked at her all at once as if shocked. After a few moments of still silence, they leaned back and roared, too, screaming with all the power in their lungs.

I put my hands over my throbbing ears and cringed. "Ever heard of an inside voice?" I muttered.

The huge female returned to all fours and licked my face again, which was more painful the second time, then pressed her nose to my forehead as she stared into my eyes.

My brain felt like it was being punched through my skull, but I couldn't pull back, and then I started to see things—pictures and clips of movement and sound and emotion.

I saw the group of winged cats as they lived, as if I was one of them, isolated from all others here in the desert, hunting the other creatures of this wasteland to survive, and trying to keep their race alive. They were close-knit, all related to each other in some distant way or another. They knew joy in each other and the hunt and the occasional child, and sorrow in their dwindling numbers, and hunger, and the sick-deaths of their hatchlings.

I saw images of the other creatures flying towards us now. Huge, scaled, with lumpy bodies and sagging skin. Carrion eaters and nest robbers. I knew of feuding with them over the passing of countless seasons, at first beating them easily, and then, as the numbers of my family dwindled, with more difficulty. Less than a season ago, there had been a night attack, such as the one about to begin, and they had lost almost all their eggs along with the warriors set to protect the nests.

The group was weakened; they would lose this time. All the eggs would be destroyed, their children killed and eaten before ever knowing a world bigger than the inside of their shell. They would fail in their only purpose. I felt a sense of despair that made tears well in my eyes and roll down my face.

But then hope bloomed from her to me.

I saw my own face from high above, glaring at the snarling male. Flashing images of the one-eyed wildcat from my Characteristic Trial, humans dressed in strange clothes speaking a strange language, landscapes of beauty stretching out before me as I flew, an image of mold and putrid spores devouring and subsuming a patch of purity, and the vicious exhilaration of flying into battle with my brethren, ripping and killing and obliterating my enemies.

Then she pulled back. My eyes rolled back in my head, and I dropped to my knees. My vision tumbled and my stomach heaved, but I stopped myself from throwing up or falling over by taking deep breaths of the thin air and digging my claws into the wood.

Behind me, wood cracked, and cracked again. "We're coming, Eve!" Adam called.

"Stay alive!" Jacky ordered.

I took a few more deep breaths, then croaked out, "I'm okay," then again, louder, "I'm okay. They're friendly." I didn't know if that was exactly true, but they hadn't attacked me, which was the best I could say of any monster I'd ever met in the Trials.

The door broke, and throwing knives *thwacked* into the floor on either side of me, warding off potential attackers.

Adam rushed forward and wrapped his arms around me, dragging me backward to the mouth of the tunnel.

"Where are you hurt?" Sam asked, moving alongside Adam.

China and Jacky maneuvered to stand in front of me, a wall between me and my perceived attackers. China had multiple throwing knives ready in each hand, and Jacky's fists were clenched.

The cats stood still, watching us small, "threatening" humans in curious amusement.

"I'm never letting you go first again," Adam said. "Stupid. You're just gonna get yourself killed."

I rolled my eyes. "I'm fine. I'm fine, guys!" I called, louder. My pounding headache had seceded, and I struggled out of Adam's grip. "They didn't hurt me. Well, not intentionally, anyway. The big one"—I pointed—"was just talking to me."

They looked at me in worried disbelief, and Jacky said, "They did something to her head. Fix her, Sam. I'll hold them off."

Sam stepped forward and laid clammy hands on my forehead.

I swatted him away. "Stop it! Okay, so she didn't speak English. But they've got some sort of psychic power. She showed me things. They're not going to hurt us, as long as you don't attack. They're just trying to survive, but they're about to be wiped out by those other twisted monsters." I flung my arm wide to encompass the mass of forms in the sky growing ever closer.

The floor shuddered beneath our feet, probably from something the sand sharks were doing.

"Guys, they're intelligent. And I want to communicate more with them. I can't do that if they're dead. We're going to fight on their side, against the attackers."

Jacky lowered her fists immediately and turned to face the group moving through the sky. "Damn. That's definitely the harder option."

The others looked between the two groups of monsters, and the winged cats preened and stretched their wings under the attention, showing off.

"Are you serious, Eve?" Sam said. "You're going to decide for all of us, just like that? What if I don't want to die? Because we're definitely going to lose if we do what you just said. They've got three times the numbers!" He pointed to the misshapen flying monsters. "And there's a whole other group down below trying to topple this nest of gigantic, supposedly psychic cats! Why the hell would I follow you? You're focused on nothing but what you can gain, no matter how dangerous it is. Think about something besides yourself for once. I know you don't care about what it *means* for someone to die," he said pointedly, "but my *life* is more important than your *curiosity*," he finished, out of breath and flushed from the force of his tirade.

I'd waited silently for him to finish, wondering how to handle the situation. Sam had an invaluable Skill, which had already saved my life, and I needed him around in case we needed it. But I could do without the open resentment, which had been hovering at various distances from his emotional surface since our last Trial.

I wanted to walk over to Sam and beat him into submission, the urge heightened by the irritating ringing in my ears, but I ignored the instinct. It was sure to backfire.

While I was thinking, China surprised me by stepping forward. "You're a coward, Sam," she said calmly. "And you're mean."

He gaped down at her, as did the rest of us.

"Eve saved your life, because you were too afraid to give yourself permission to save your own. You made the choice to listen to her, and you were the one that killed that guy. No one blames you for it. You had to do it, and if you hadn't you wouldn't be here to help us today. But don't *you* blame *Eve*, because it's not her fault. You feel guilty, because you listened to her, and you think it was wrong. But she's never been anything but good to you, to all of us. She's helping me save my sister."

"She helped me when I needed her," Jacky added.

"Eve's always there to help us," Adam said after a reluctant pause.

"She's given you a place to belong and people who have your back," China said. "We all have your back, and you should have ours, too." With that, she spun away from him and climbed up the side of a tree-branch hill, where she began to methodically dip the points of the knives criss-crossing her chest into a small jar of poisonous goo.

Sam was red-faced, silent.

I cleared my throat. "I'm not a perfect person, Sam. Sometimes I can be quite the opposite. But I know you're good, in your heart. You want to do the right thing. And if you listened to what their leader has to say, if you could see what she showed me, I think you'd want to protect them all on your own." I stepped forward and put my hand tentatively on the female's nose. "Could you show him what you showed me? Why you need help?" I didn't know if she could understand my words, but she watched intelligently as I brought my hand to my forehead where she'd touched me, and then pointed to Sam.

She gave a nod and turned to him.

He swallowed heavily, but stood still as she approached and touched her wet nose to his skin.

I turned away. "Okay, guys," I called loudly, knowing there were other Players on the level below, too cautious to come up after the series of threatening roars they'd no doubt been half deafened by. "The attackers are almost here. My team and I are siding with the ones who live in these trees. The cats. They're friendly to humans as long as you don't attack them, but the ones that are coming aren't. Even if you're fighting on their side, they won't recognize that, and they'll attack indiscriminately. Your best bet is to side with the rest of us." I had no idea if what I'd just said was true, but we needed all the help we could get. Lying didn't cause me a second of guilt.

The female drew back from Sam, and, after a few moments of pale dizziness, he said, "I'll fight with you."

And that was it. We waited less than a minute for the others to arrive, the trees underneath us shuddering and swaying subtly back and forth constantly.

The enemy monsters looked like a cross between a Shar Pei dog with extra saggy skin and a flying lizard. Their necks hung down in pink wattles, like a vulture's, and the wind carried a stench of rot from them.

The cats roared their defiance, and many leapt up to meet the attackers in the air while others moved to protect the "cave" China stood atop. "Their eggs must be in there," I murmured.

The first of the wrinkled lizards to make it past the front line crashed hard enough onto the platform to cause everything to sway. China threw a knife at it, and almost immediately it seemed to have trouble finding its feet. It collapsed in a twitching heap, and Adam sprang forward to cut open its throat.

Thick, dark blood oozed out, which the trees ignored, and Adam stepped back with a grimace of distaste, then wiped his knives clean on its hide.

There was a beat of silent waiting after that, and then everything exploded into chaos. More wrinkle-lizards broke through, and the Players and cats on the ground began to fight.

My claws were useful weapons, but I soon found myself dripping with the sluggish, thick lizard blood. The smell of it was indescribably horrible, like I'd been dunked in a slurry of rotten flesh.

The treetops were filled with screams and the roaring growls of monsters, and the pink bloom of the trees sucking up the non-gunky blood of both cats and humans. I found myself forced to the edge of the platform together with Sam and was just finishing off a monster that he'd brought down with his crowbar when a small dark blur whizzed past my cheek.

I looked behind me and saw a wrinkle-lizard drop to the ground with a knife in its eye. It had been about to bite down on my head.

China nodded acknowledgment to me, and then turned to continue throwing at other targets.

"Whoa, that was close," I said to Sam. But almost immediately, I heard a roaring shriek right behind our backs. I started to duck and twist, but something large and sharp caught me on the shoulder, lifting me and ripping my flesh. I flipped into the air violently, spinning around like a tossed toy soldier. My Skill kicked in, allowing me to turn in midair so I was facing the huge creature that attacked me. I could feel the heat of the putrid breath coming out of its open maw.

A cat barreled into the monster from the side, huge teeth ripping into its neck and taking it instantly out of play.

I relaxed for half a heartbeat. Then I realized I had been tossed out too far. There was nothing beneath me to land on. In just a few seconds, I would be another dark smudge on the canvas of beige a thousand feet below. I stretched out my hand, but I was too far away to reach any of the branches.

My wide, terrified eyes locked on Sam's, and I felt the insane urge to apologize for everything that had happened between us.

But he was not horrified, for once, not hesitant. His teeth were bared in effort as he lunged toward my outstretched hand. Moments before it would have been too late, his hand closed around my clawed fingers, crushing them with the force of his grip.

The sudden stop wrenched my hand and wrist and elbow and shoulder. It was the same side I'd been attacked on, and I felt a strange tearing in the already injured skin of my shoulder. Warm blood pooled in the curve of my neck and ran down between my breasts and over my back.

Sam grunted against the force of gravity on my large body, and I saw that he only had a grip on the platform with his other hand.

"Eve!" Adam's hoarse shout filtered through my ears past the rushing of the blood in my veins and the wind pushing on us.

I ignored him. This wasn't the time to be reassuring Adam that I was okay. It was the time to be focusing on making sure I *stayed* okay, stayed alive.

Sam's fingers were slipping.

I tried to breathe deeply and stay still. "Sam, you need to swing me back and forth. I'm too heavy for you to pull me up. If you can get my trajectory far enough inward and let me go, I'll be able to catch myself on the level below."

He shook his head minutely, desperately, straining too hard to talk.

I clenched my teeth. "You can do it. There's no other way for us. You can't hold on much longer, and when you slip, we're both gonna die." I grabbed onto his wrist with my other hand, and began to wriggle myself back and forth, like I was on a swing. If I'd been a better person, I might have told him to drop me. I knew his grip wouldn't last much longer, and my movements were making it harder for him to hang on. If he fell when I swung inward, I likely wouldn't be able to save him like he'd done for me. But I wasn't a better person, so I didn't even consider sacrificing myself to save him. Like he'd said, I was selfish. He was the only one who came close to realizing just how selfish.

I looked down to try and time my release, but could only gasp in helpless fear when he grunted out, "Sorry," and we began to fall.

Chapter 24

Time held me green and dying
    Though I sang in my chains like the sea.
    — Dylan Thomas

I LOOKED DOWN, down, and down. There was nothing below us for so far. I vaguely heard my name shouted again, but both Sam and I were screaming too hard for me to listen. My stomach was trying to rise through my chest when my fall stopped abruptly and unexpectedly, for the second time in the last half hour, this time on something warm and scratchy.

Sam landed half on top of me again, twisting my ankle strangely underneath his weight.

Our unsuspecting mount—a wrinkle-lizard that had flown just below us—bucked sharply at the unexpected weight on its back. It was barely big enough for its two unwelcome passengers, and I dug my fingers into the skin of its back, holding on for dear life.

Sam grabbed onto my leg with one arm and clenched a handful of lizard hide with the other.

I met his terrified eyes and couldn't help but laugh. "This wasn't quite what I had in mind when I said drop me onto the level below, but I guess it'll do. Good job."

He shook his head, lips pressed together in a white line, and looked as if he might throw up.

The creature beneath us shrieked angrily, flapping hard as it struggled between staying afloat under the extra weight and throwing us off.

I started to inch forward, drawing myself toward its shoulders with handful after handful of skin. My right shoulder screamed out in pain, begging me to stop, and I left a shiny trail of blood on the brown and green skin of its back, but I kept going until I reached the base of its leathery wings.

Cautiously, I sat up and wrapped my legs over its huge back, squeezing to keep myself steady as I looked around breathlessly and took our bearings. We were swinging back around to the trees again, luckily not too far from where we needed to be.

I felt its wings strain to lift us higher and saw where the creature's eyes were focused. "Hold on tight!" I blurted out, ducking down between the flapping wings.

Seconds later, the creature smashed into the bottom of the top tree level, crushing and scraping its back along the myriad branches. It dropped away, shaking its head, half-stunned by its own maneuver.

I sat up and looked back.

Sam was still there, hanging off the side and looking both surprised and terrified.

"Just hold on!" I screamed above the rush of the wind. I turned back and grabbed onto the strange lumpy growths on the sides of its neck, squeezing hard and pulling.

The creature stiffened and jerked, causing Sam to cry out in alarm.

But it angled its flight toward the side where I applied the most pressure. Just as I'd hoped, the lumps were sensitive, and the wrinkle-lizard was trying to relieve the pain by turning into it.

I didn't know how long it would work, so I pulled harder and faster, and the creature followed the direction of the circular protrusion on its neck. I guided it upward, swung back around to the trees, and crashed us hard into the middle of the platform, almost hard enough to flip me forward and off the creature's back. But I dug my claws into its rough folds and held on as if my life depended on it, somehow staying mounted.

It struggled to its feet, tossing its head back and forth and flapping its wings experimentally. I could feel that it was about to take off again. "We can't have that, now," I said, pressing my face into the side of its head, where an ear might be. "But I also can't just get off and let you attack me.

So…" I hugged its neck, similar to something I'd seen Jacky demonstrate, and twisted with all my strength.

The neck snapped around, and something broke with a loud crunch. One of the bulges on the side of its neck popped, and a small red organ spilled out, pulsing like a heart and hanging by a few fleshy cords. The creature slumped gently to the ground and collapsed, never to move again.

"I have to kill you," I concluded, though it couldn't hear me anymore. As I climbed off, I saw three wrinkle-lizards attacking a single cat guard in front of the eggs' hatchery.

Sam was already fighting with another lizard, but seemed to be holding his own.

I leapt forward to aid the outnumbered cat, feeling somewhat numb, and attacked one of the lizards. Claws to the neck seemed to be the fastest way for me to stop them, but they were quick and vicious, and it took me a few moments to bring my opponent down.

By the time I'd done so, more lizards had joined the other two. The guardian fell beneath them.

He let out one last gurgling roar before he died, calling for backup, but the lizards were already into the hatchery.

Large eggs sat nestled into beds of fur and feathers, and the blooming flowers of the tree were clipped above them so that blood spilled down onto their shells. The surfaces of the eggs were pockmarked, and they drank up the dark red liquid as it touched them.

The first lizard inside grabbed the nearest egg and bit down on it. The hard shell punctured its gums, but that didn't stop it from biting down again on the newly exposed, half-formed kitten within.

The kitten's limbs flailed uselessly, and then it was swallowed with a bobbing jerk of the lizard's head.

The rest of the lizards flew into a frenzy, stomping and biting the eggs, some even swallowing them whole.

I threw myself at the nearest lizard, righteous rage nearly blinding me. I fought quickly and viciously, but there were too many, and I was too weak.

Then the cats' leader was there.

She smashed into the mouth of the hatchery, so big she scraped against the walls of the entrance. Teeth, wings, and legs lashed out in every direction, ripping the lizards apart. For a second, I felt relief.

But more enemies came, and the floor beneath our feet was now pitching back and forth like the deck of a ship during a storm. Between my constant flurry of attacks on the lizards, I saw glimpses of the outside. Corpses lay everywhere, and almost the whole platform had bloomed, the bloodsucking flowers now a dark, rich red. But despite the number of dead lizards, they kept coming, and there were no reinforcements arriving on our side.

The cat leader and I were pushed toward the back of the hatchery despite our best efforts, with more and more of the unhatched kittens being slaughtered each second. My stomach filled with despair and heartbreak at the futility of it.

They might have been cats, and monsters of a type, but the female had shown me they were people, too, with feelings and lives to be lived. And the eggs were babies, being killed before they even had a chance to experience those lives.

Even I would do anything to stop tragedy like that when it was happening right in front of me.

The female used her wing to knock me behind her, then took a huge breath and let out a roar like nothing I'd ever heard before. It literally knocked back the lizards filling the front of the hatchery, stunning them with its force.

She spun then, using her claw to cut through a piece of the wall. A flap swung open, and she pushed me through before wriggling in and securing it again with a thick branch across the back of the newly revealed swinging door. She pushed past me toward the back of the hidden room, where an egg lay on a bed of feathers the same color as her wings. Blood dripped down onto it from one of the tree's clipped blooms, like the others. She nudged it gently, then scooped it up in her wing and held it toward me.

I lifted my hands, and she dropped it into them.

Behind me, the lizards were attacking the door, and I knew they would be through soon.

"Is this…your egg?" I asked.

She stepped forward and pressed her nose to my forehead again. A burst of pain followed, and I started receiving her message. It was like a dream this time, me thinking and moving, but at the same time watching myself and knowing it wasn't real. I had the understanding that I must take her egg, the thing most important to her in the world, but also important in a different type of way that I couldn't understand. Maybe it was next in line for the cat-leader throne? I watched myself wrap it in protective arms and fly far away, though I knew I didn't have wings; it was meant as a plea to leave this place behind and protect her child.

She stepped back quickly so that I wasn't incapacitated by the aftereffects of our communication.

I wrapped my arms around her egg and nodded. "Got it."

She nodded back to me, then ripped open the wall of the hatchery. I stepped out, and she followed for a few steps, making sure I wasn't attacked.

I sent a Window to the other members of my group telling them to retreat to the lower levels as quickly as possible and headed that way myself, screaming loudly for any other Players to follow—if any were still alive. I was pretty badly injured, and my ankle kept trying to collapse under my weight, but I could barely feel the pain.

China arrived the quickest, holding two branches in lieu of her knives, which had apparently run out. Her cheek was bleeding, and she had an already swelling black eye, but other than that she seemed fine. She sagged in relief when she saw me, and I realized she must have thought I died when I fell off the edge.

Sam and Jacky arrived next, both of their eyes widening when they saw me, and then Adam. Adam was bleeding from a deep cut along the palm of his hand, and had blood finger-painted across his face like Native American warpaint. They were all injured with varying degrees of severity, but at least they'd all made it. Most hadn't.

"Eve, you're hurt," Sam said, reaching out to me.

I shrugged it off. "Everyone's hurt. We don't have time for that. Come on, we've got to get out of here."

I led the way, running as fast as I could with the surprisingly heavy egg, my pack, and my unreliable ankle. We descended faster than we'd risen, and when I turned around to check, I saw that a few other Players had made it in addition to my team. That was good.

When we reached the cube, I saw the count of each team's forces. Two columns separated "TAILOS" from "RETCHIN," and showed the number of monsters still alive. The tailos had a much longer list of Players than the retchin, but the number of tailos was dwindling quickly, decreasing even as I watched.

I reached out and placed a hand on the cube, which pulsed but didn't respond further. "I've got an egg. One will live, though the rest may never see another day. One will live. The tailos will not be annihilated." I hoped to god it would let me through, accepting the unorthodox winning conditions I was providing.

The cube pulsed, and the words across the screen changed.

CONGRATULATIONS ON SURVIVING THE TRIAL!
EVE REDDING HAS GAINED THE UNHATCHED EGG

With a series of cracks and shudders from down below, the tree started to pitch sideways.

"No time, hurry up!" I snapped.

The cube complied, skipping ahead to the return message.

DO YOU WISH TO RETURN FROM THE TRIAL?
YES / NO

I slammed my hand onto "Yes" and wrapped my arms tight around the egg.

Sam leaned forward and put his hand on my back. "What's your address, Eve?" he shouted.

I frowned at him but rattled it off. "Why?"

"I'm coming for you, okay? Just stay alive. I'll be there soon."

Then I returned, riding on the vibrating melody of the Boneshaker.

I COLLAPSED onto the beige carpet of my room, and the tailos egg rolled out of my arms. I was suddenly freezing, and there were stars floating in front of my eyes and blackness creeping in from the edges of my vision. I let out a shuddering breath as the pain I hadn't felt before hit me like a tsunami. I looked down over myself and saw the blood staining my clothes dark and felt the frantic beating of my heart as it tried to pump what little was left inside me around fast enough to keep me alive.

"Damn," I whispered.

I fumbled at the pack on my back, pulling the half-shredded strap out of the wound the retchin lizard had given me. "I'll need a new one," I mumbled inanely, speaking to myself as a way to keep my eyes open. I dug clumsily for the pouch I'd stuffed inside it before the Trial.

When I shook, three Seeds rolled out, two landing in my hand, and the other bouncing off and rolling away to the far corner of the room, under my bed. I ignored it and held both Seeds to my neck at once. "I wish for more Life," I said. They shot into my veins, and within a few seconds I felt some strength return, and the edging black behind my eyes was pushed back. Only then did the Game notification telling me I'd earned seven Seeds pop up. Waiting to see if I'd live, I thought caustically.

As I fumbled the large, sturdy tailos egg into my pack, I sent a Window to Sam, telling him I'd be at the base of the tree in the community park behind my building. He couldn't come to my house, into my room. Not without sparking my family's curiosity, and thus alerting them to my situation. No, I needed to meet him somewhere else.

I pushed at the window latch till it broke, too exhausted to use fine motor control. After waiting a few seconds to make sure no one came running in to check on me, I tossed my pack over my good shoulder, crawled out onto the tree, and looked down onto the manicured grass below. Suddenly the world twisted like a marbled ice cream cone, and the green changed to the grey-blue of a smoggy summer sky. My pack floated strangely around to my front. I could see the sparkling stars, even though it was daytime.

I was still pondering this enigma when everything went black.

I woke up on the ground with a gasping, white-faced Sam bent over me, his eyes closed, his hands pressed into my sternum between my breasts.

My head was resting on something warm and supple, and I felt the familiar sting of a Seed injecting into the skin beneath my jaw.

"Are you groping me right now, Sam?" I whispered, the effort of which made me cough violently.

He gasped again and opened his eyes.

A barrage of muddled and overlapping exclamations assaulted my ears, and suddenly my vision was filled with the faces of my team leaning in around me.

China took the Seed from my neck and handed the empty shell to Adam. He added it to a handful of other empty Seeds and put them in his pocket.

"Did you guys…use your Seeds on me?"

He scowled down at me, also pale-faced. "Well, we had to, you idiot. What the hell, Eve?"

"What?" I asked, taken aback.

"How could you let this happen to yourself?" He clenched his hands at his sides, for once not twiddling his fingers.

I gaped at him, at a loss for words as a couple seconds of silence passed. "Um, it wasn't on purpose, trust me." I quirked my mouth in as much of a smile as I could muster.

His pale face reddened in anger. "Yeah, we saw that."

"I'll pay back the Seeds to whoever gave them up," I muttered, moving my hand a tiny bit as I prepared to sit up.

"Nobody's worried about the Seeds!" Adam snapped, grabbing my forearm and holding it, and me, down. He turned to Sam. "I know what you did. That wound was meant for you! If you hadn't stepped out of the way, or if you'd at least moved her with you…" Adam's long, dexterous finger trembled as he pointed accusingly. "You may be angry at her, but what you did is inexcusable."

Sam flinched visibly and swallowed, looking down at me with a sick expression. "It wasn't intentional. I mean, I just—I just dodged. I saw the retchin coming and I moved. I didn't know it'd end up hitting you instead. I swear, it was an accident. I would never, never do something like that on purpose."

Jacky scowled at him. "You shoulda taken that hit. You woulda healed from it just fine."

He opened his mouth but was cut off by Adam. "Bullshit, you didn't do it on purpose. How *convenient.*"

What was going on here? "Adam. Stop it. All of you." It was news to me that the creature had been aiming for Sam, but it made no difference to the situation.

Adam turned to me and opened his mouth angrily once more, but I cut him off before he could continue. "Sam wasn't at fault. We may not always agree, but he's never done anything to make you distrust him. If he didn't want to be here, be part of this team, or wanted harm to come to me, it wouldn't be too hard for him. Look at him. He looks like he was drowned. If he wanted to hurt me, he wouldn't have jumped off the side of the tree tower to save me, risking his own life in the process. He wouldn't be *here, now*, and I wouldn't be alive."

Adam knelt beside me but didn't touch me. "If not for him, you wouldn't have *needed* saving, or be hurt this bad in the first place."

My breath hitched as I struggled for air, and Sam turned his attention back to my chest.

"What if he hadn't been there to dodge," I asked once I had the air to speak, "and the monster had been aiming for me in the first place? I just got the accidental swipe. And, except for an apparent fall out of my own backyard tree, I'm barely hurt at all."

Adam sputtered, his eyebrows raised. "Barely hurt? Have you seen yourself? You look like a zombie!" He was shouting again.

I chuckled. "Well, thanks. Tell me I look like shit. What a great way to make me feel better."

He gaped at me as if I was crazy.

I felt fine, if a little weak. I moved to sit up and prove it, and screaming pain erupted from every inch of my body with the force of a sonic boom.

I blacked out again.

Chapter 25

She's mad but she's magic. There's no lie in her fire.
— Charles Bukowski

I WOKE up in Blaine's house, on the little bed in the closet attached to his lab. An IV bag dripped into a tube attached to my arm.

China leaned forward and smiled at me brightly. "You're awake!"

I frowned. "Guess I passed out again."

"Yeah. Sam healed you up as best he could, then we brought you here. We sent your mom and brother a message from your sheath saying you were staying the night at a friend's house. Hope that was okay?"

I raised an eyebrow, considering my mother's no doubt pleased excitement that I actually had friends to spend the night with. "Yeah. They're already a bit freaked out at my suddenly booming social life, but it'll be fine. It's not like they'd ever suspect the truth."

China giggled, a surprisingly young sound, and I was reminded again of how difficult it was to live life like this. And how much it had to have aged her, that I only heard sounds like that from her on the rarest occasion.

"What time is it?"

"It's late afternoon, Sunday."

"Whoa. I slept over eighteen hours?" I lifted my arms to push the covers back, wincing as the movement woke the angry wounds all over my body, especially my back.

She shot over and pressed my forearms back down into the bed. "No moving! Blaine gave you something to let you sleep. You shouldn't even be awake right now, but your body keeps adjusting to the dose and metabolizing the sedative faster and faster. I'll go get him, and we'll up the dose again."

"No, no. I don't want to sleep any more. There's a lot to be done."

"You are not to move from this bed," she commanded imperiously, drawing her small frame up so that she towered over me with her hands on her hips. "Is that clear?"

I stared at her for a moment before leaning my head back into the pillow. "Okay, but could you at least get me my pack? I won't move from the bed, but my mind can still work, even if my body doesn't, right? I have a puzzle I need to solve."

She hesitated, but when I gave her a puppy dog look that was as pitiful as possible, she relented and brought me my ripped and blood-soaked pack.

After checking to make sure the dark red-brown egg was okay, I dug out the silver chains I'd gotten from the Oracle and started to fiddle with the smallest one, the one with the fewest rings. We'd been so busy since the last Trial that I'd barely had time to think about the Oracle's strange gifts, much less actually work on solving them. It was almost relaxing to just lie back and focus on nothing else.

There were eleven bent links in the chain, and I had the idea they were a puzzle that would hold together if I could just figure out exactly how they fit. I knew they must be important, but the way to bring out whatever hidden potential they had was a mystery to me. It was quite frustrating, but I didn't plan on letting a little thing like that stop me.

I slept again for a few hours that afternoon. It was night when I finally woke.

Sam sat beside me this time, looking thoroughly exhausted. "Hey, how are you doing?" he said, smiling weakly.

"Peachy keen," I responded with a sarcastic smile.

"Well, that's a lie," he chuckled. "But you're going to be okay. In fact, you got quite a few extra Seeds, so once you're mended and the ones you lost along with all that blood have replenished themselves, you'll be better than ever."

"Thanks."

He leaned forward as if he wanted to grab my hand, but settled for smoothing down the edge of my blanket instead. "I hope you know, I didn't—I didn't let this happen to you on purpose. I would never do that. I mean, I was angry at you, and to be honest I still am. But it's really just anger at myself, because I let you convince me to kill that guy so I could save myself. I wouldn't ever try to take revenge or anything—anything like that." By the end, he was whispering.

I slipped my hand out from beneath the cover and patted his own lightly. "I know, Sam. I didn't think you would. I know you better than you think. We're not so different, in some ways."

He raised his eyebrows at that, but didn't respond, and after a few more awkward moments, started to leave for some work in the lab with Blaine; everyone was busy preparing to carry out my plan for NIX.

He stopped at the door. "I'm not brave, Eve. I told you before, I'm not the person you want at your back in a fight." Then he left.

With no one there to stop me, I made my way out of bed by increments, slipped out of the small room, and moved to a seat at one of the chemistry tables. I'd been fiddling with the Oracle's puzzle for a few minutes before Blaine, Sam, and Adam, all working in intense silence, noticed my presence.

Adam tried to tell me to lie down again, but I waved him off. "I'm fine. I'm sitting down, and I'm not straining myself. There's no need to coddle me."

"You said something similar the last time we spoke, if I remember correctly. And then you tried to move and passed out," he said, deadpan.

I raised a challenging eyebrow at him. "Yes. That happened. But I'm staying right here, in this seat, and you're not going to stop me."

He returned my challenge with a glower, but bit back the words he obviously wanted to say and returned to typing away furiously.

I took a measured breath, so as not to stretch my back with the movement, and returned to messing with the puzzle chain.

Blaine noticed and moved over to peer at it. "What is that?"

"I don't know. I got it in the Intelligence Trial. The Oracle said it would guide my path. I think it's a puzzle, but I've got no freakin' idea how to make it work. I need to figure it out, though. All this not knowing is dangerous. I hate it."

He held out a hand. "May I?"

"Sure." I dropped it into his palm, and he took it to a microscope.

After a few minutes of silent inspection, during which he turned the links around and examined them from every angle, he sat back and returned the chain to me. "It's a puzzle ring. The bands join together around your finger, designed to come apart when you take it off. This one has minuscule grooves and protrusions, so unless you match all the bands to each other exactly, they won't join. It is quite complicated. Impressively so. You said you got that in a Trial?"

I only nodded, left speechless by his quick understanding of something I'd spent several futile hours on already. I bent my head to study the bands, trying to see the imperfections in their surface.

"Interesting. I have some ideas about the place you go to when you're transported away…"

I jerked my head up, suddenly remembering, and interrupted him. "I've got something else you might want to take a look at. It's in my pack. Will you get it from the closet?"

He brought the pack to me, laid it gently on the table, and opened it.

The egg lay inside, clearly visible, and as big as a cantaloupe.

"Good thing it didn't break in the fall." I shuddered at the thought.

Blaine removed it reverently, holding it cupped between both hands. "What is it?"

"It's a tailos egg. The tailos are…big cats with wings. And I think they're telepathic. Its mother gave me the egg to protect. It's probably the last of its kind."

He blinked, staring through thick glasses at the heavy, porous, blood-crusted orb. "You brought back an unhatched…Trial monster?"

"Umm, yeah?" Suddenly the idea seemed questionably dangerous.

"If I'd known you could bring them back, I'd have had you bring me more. I could be dissecting them right now!" He flicked it with a finger, leaning close to listen.

"Well, usually the monsters are quite…large. We can only bring back small things, things we can kind of wrap ourselves around. And besides, I don't even know if they could survive in this world."

He sat the egg down on the table and scurried away. When he came back, he was holding a tube of gel, a stethoscope-like device, and a series of small metal hammers.

"Whoa, you're not going to try and crack it open," I said, wrapping an arm around the egg to shield it. "I promised the mother I'd protect it. If it's still alive, being born prematurely could kill it."

"Relax, I'm only going to do a sonogram."

He spread the gel over a patch, and then placed the pad at the end of the stethoscope into the gel.

Some gel ran down into one of the pores, and a tiny but forceful puff of air from inside sprayed it away and onto the table.

My eyes met Blaine's, and Sam and Adam joined us at the table as the air filled with a charge of excitement.

Blaine chose the smallest mallet and tapped gently on the shell. His eyes widened, and I had to resist the urge to rip the stethoscope-thing's tips from his ears when he said, "It moved. Something's alive in there."

"Let me," I said. I put the tips in my own ears and tapped gently on the shell. A sloshing wriggle came from inside, along with what might have been an irritated squeak.

My face stretched in a huge grin, and I reluctantly gave up the stethoscope to Adam and Sam.

Blaine was frowning into the pores. He scratched at the dried blood on the surface. "I wonder if it's cold. Should we incubate it? What temperature, though, and for how long?"

Thinking back to the tailos hatchery, I slid off my chair and made my way to Blaine's supply closet while the others were too focused to notice. I grabbed a handful of scalpels and made my way back. Then I took the stethoscope back from Blaine, put the tips in my ears, and ripped open the packaging of one of the scalpels.

"Hey, be careful there. I thought you didn't want to hurt it," he said. "Cutting it open isn't any better than cracking it. And either way, a scalpel isn't the tool for the job."

I ignored him as I lifted my left wrist above the egg and cut into the side, away from my veins but deep enough so the blood flowed well.

Adam gasped and slapped the scalpel out of my hand while the others were still gaping at me.

He clamped a large hand around my bleeding wrist and pulled it up to elevate the cut. "Get some blood-clotter and some bandages. Wait. Sam, just heal her."

Sam moved to obey, but I pulled weakly at Adam's restraints, scowling. "Stop it, you two. The tailos eggs drink blood. I was just giving it some. Look."

The blood that had made it down into the pores was being sucked up, and, when it was gone, I heard more wriggling from inside, and a muffled squeaky sound.

I carefully pulled my arm away from Adam and let more blood drip onto the egg.

It continued to suck up the liquid until Sam put his hand on my wrist and stopped the bleeding.

"You just lost a crazy amount of blood. Now is not the time to be slicing open a vein to feed some cat egg," Adam said.

I laughed, but realized that I did feel a little lightheaded. "Yeah. You're right." I nodded to Sam. "Thanks."

Sam nodded back, and the slice healed to a raw pink patch of skin before my eyes.

Blaine had watched the whole exchange in avid silence. "It drinks blood. And you said the adults are telepathic?"

"Yeah," Sam responded. "They don't use words, but it's like they push sensory input and feeling right into your brain."

"And they're good. I mean, they're pretty vicious, but they don't attack any and all humans indiscriminately, and they have families and…a culture," I added.

Blaine blinked owlishly. "You realize what this means, right? There is a sentient, communicating race in these Trials. One that's never been seen on Earth."

"Well, at least not for a long time, right? What if…have you guys ever heard of a gryphon?" I asked. "They're not the same, but…what if there's some sort of connection? And some of the places we've gone, it's like an ancient city of ruins. I mean, what about that energy cartridge, Adam? There's something…more, going on here. There's something missing, something we don't understand."

Blaine sighed wistfully. "I wish I had access to the Trial world. I would love to get my hands on everything you guys keep telling me about. The technology of a futuristic society…it's incredibly exciting."

"No," I countered. "You don't wish that. If any of these speculations are true, then it's pretty damn amazing. But that doesn't negate the fact that the lifespan of a Player bears some resemblance to the lifespan of a fruit fly. It's short. I'd give up all the 'excitement' in a second, to live an ordinary, miserable life here on present-day Earth till I was old and pollution-wrinkled."

There was a silence, and then Blaine handed me a bundle of unopened syringes. "At least don't cut yourself open. Use these instead."

Adam snatched the syringes away, glaring at him, and I left the boys to bicker and went back to sleep.

—We'll be ready.—
-Adam-

I NODDED to Adam's reassurance, though I knew he couldn't see me, and packed another box into the back of the huge transport pod my mother had rented. My back twinged with the movement, but I was careful to keep any hint of pain off my face.

Zed stared at me not-quite-secretly from the corner of his eye as we passed each other, something he'd been doing for the last few days.

"What?" I snapped. I was hungry, tired, sweaty, and stressed out about both getting my family to safety and the team's plan for NIX that evening. "You're irritating the hell out of me."

"*I'm* irritating *you*?" His eyebrows rose, then lowered into a scowl. "I'm worried about you, Eve."

"Well, stop. I'm fine! Better than fine."

"What happened to you the other night? You disappeared without even saying anything."

"Didn't Mom tell you? I messaged her. I stayed the night at my friend's house. And what does it matter? I don't have to report my every move to you."

His fingers squeezed dents into the box in his arms, and he glared at me silently for a few moments. "Why are you so freaking obstinate?"

"I'm not the obstinate one. You don't have to be involved in every aspect of my life, Zed. Stop thinking something has to be wrong just because my life is changing for the better. I'm getting tired of having this same conversation over and over."

"Eve, I *know*—"

My mom stepped around the pod and dusted off her manicured hands, which had somehow managed to stay perfect through the packing and loading of almost our entire house.

Zed cut off whatever he was about to say.

"All done now, children. I'm going to make a last pass through the house. Say bye to your sister and get in the pod, Zed. You're driving this one." She tossed him the keys.

She and Zed were moving to the new location ahead of me. I'd be following them soon, I hoped, and we could resume our mostly normal lives. Free from the Game and NIX, though I knew I'd feel the need to look over my shoulder for the rest of my life.

I sighed, and my expression softened. "You don't need to worry about me. I've got everything handled, I promise." I stared into his eyes, trying to make him believe.

He said nothing, but after a few long moments, his own stubborn expression morphed to something I couldn't quite read, and he gave me a hug.

My mother came back down, satisfied the only things left were mine, and they left for the safety of the new home and life I'd created for them with Blaine's help. A life away from NIX and its influence.

Chapter 26

Who overcomes
    By force, hath overcome but half his foe.
    — John Milton

I CROUCHED JUST outside the line of NIX's security, my team behind me. I was tense and sick with fear. I wished we could wait, but NIX implemented a shift rotation every couple weeks, and that was the best time to slip in unnoticed. If I could have delayed till the next rotation, I would have. An operation like this should be the work of weeks or even months, not a couple weeks. But in another four days, we'd be going back to the Trials, and I wasn't sure we'd all *live* till the next shift rotation. Plus, we'd been working day and night on almost no sleep to get everything ready. No matter what happened, we'd all be leaving the city in less than twenty-four hours.

Even if I hadn't given the go-ahead, China would never have waited. Her whole focus was on saving her sister, and she would be there that night whether I wanted her to or not. I'd tried to at least convince her to stay behind to carry out our plan B, but she'd found a way around that, too. I was glad to have her, though, even if her presence was one more thing to worry about. Her sonar-like senses would be invaluable to us on the inside—so long as she focused on the mission at hand and not just her sister.

I motioned with my hand, and we crept around to the side of a large military transport pod, properly keeping to the path of disabled motion sensors and cameras that Jacky had created with Adam's guidance. Once behind the pod, we stood up and strode forward with Adam at the front, as if we knew perfectly where we were going and had every right to be there.

My hands felt cold with sweat, and I hoped the uniforms we'd mimicked held up to casual inspection. We had no guns, because they were too strictly regulated in our country, and, though Blaine had the money to get pretty much anything off the black market, there wasn't time to prepare them. In addition to that, China was too small to be a guard, so we'd put her in a different type of uniform, like those worn by the Players NIX kept for experimentation. I only hoped that she wouldn't arouse suspicion as long as she was with us, and had instructed Sam to keep a firm grip on her at all times, as if she was a prisoner under our guard. If things got complicated, she would be our backup access key to the captives.

Bunny hadn't contacted any of us in a few days, probably because of the last accusing conversation I'd had with him, but that worked well for what we were planning.

We moved to one of the doors, and Adam held up a little device to the security pad there. After only a few seconds, it beeped, the pad flashed green, and a click announced that the door had unlocked itself. Adam opened the door and threw a grin over his shoulder. "Got that little trick from an online acquaintance. Pretty useful."

We stepped through the door into a well-lit hallway that had small cameras positioned at regular intervals. We wore military caps, like many of the other guards, but the real protection was a little powder Blaine had given us in a moment of gleeful excitement, like a kid unbearably eager to have their gift opened. The powder gave off only the slightest sheen to the naked eye, and could be disguised as the shimmer of a woman's foundation or a light misting of sweat. But to a camera, our faces looked like a thousand beaming facets of light, and were completely unrecognizable.

Blaine hadn't been idle for a moment, working like a crazy man to meet all my demands.

As we walked, I started using the Game interface. "Bunny," I said. "Stay still and listen to me. Don't make any indication that we're talking.

Check your map for my location." Before he had the time to send a response, I continued. "You're going to keep silent and let me do what I need to do. If we get caught, I'm going to know whose fault it is. And I'm going to come for you. I know where you are. I'm watching you, just like you've been watching us." That last part was a bluff. Blaine's tracking of our chip data only showed direction and distance from the person we were messaging; I didn't have access to any cameras.

"When they go crazy trying to figure out what happened, you're going to keep all of this a secret, because you're part of it. If you say anything, they will wonder why you didn't report us earlier, when we were planning all of this. And if you try to say you didn't know what we were doing, they might wonder what use they have of someone so incompetent. By now, I hope you've developed a better understanding of exactly how much mercy NIX has."

—What R U doing, Eve?—
-Bunny-

"I'm escaping. If you interfere with that, your employers won't be your only problem. So you'd better sit tight and pretend you're clueless."

Jacky knocked out the first lone guard we saw with a chop to the back of the neck, took his ID sheath, and locked him in a supply closet that Adam located with the map he took from said ID sheath.

Then we were on our way properly. Largely due to the obsessive reconnaissance China had been doing, we had a good idea where everything was already, but the detailed map of the inside was necessary to move within the maze-like compound. We passed other guards, but none paid much attention to us or our ward, China.

A few minutes later, Adam held up a hand at an extra-securely locked doorway. It stood no chance against Adam's little gadget, and after a few tense moments when China notified us of footsteps coming our way, we slipped in to the unlit room.

It was full of glass-circuit servers, stacked one atop the other on shelves that reached from the ceiling to the floor and stretched the span of the room.

Adam set up his computer and connected it to a random port. "We're in!"

Jacky had just given a triumphant chuckle when the room lit up, light shining from all the glass into every shadow.

I jumped about a foot, I'm not ashamed to admit.

And I wasn't the only one.

Adam looked up quickly, but then back down to the keyboard his fingers were literally blurring over. "It's just an acknowledgment of access. And...uploading."

The glass-circuits and screens on the walls started to give off a beautiful light show that almost looked like splashes and beams of light fighting against each other.

Adam grunted almost as if he was in pain, and moved his hands from the keyboard to the sides of his computer, where he'd modified it to have holes to the inside just the size of his fingers. He closed his eyes and let the sparks start to jump from his skin, communicating directly with the computer.

China was biting her nails, looking between Adam and the hallway outside through the window cut into the door.

"I don't mean to interrupt, but is everything going okay?" Sam asked, frayed nerves giving an edge to his tone.

Adam snarled at the computer. "It's freakin' fighting me. It's adaptable. Every time I get past it, it tries to push me out again. If I get kicked out even once, it'll be too late. So please let me concentrate."

He took a deep breath, and I knew he was activating his Hyper-Focus Skill. His sparks jumped even faster, and the sound turned into the buzzing of a live wire, each zap indistinguishable from the others. His curly hair rose around the sides of his cap eerily, static making it twist and turn as if it was alive.

"The lights are visible," China said.

My heart gave one sick thump in my chest, and I whipped around to the door, which had a window to the outside running right through the top half of it, just as the handle turned.

It swung open as if in slow motion, and Jacky, who'd been next to the door, stepped quickly behind it, putting the metal as a barrier between herself and the guard.

The guard. He took in all of us. In the mainframe computer room. One frantically buzzing with electricity.

I TRIED TO RELAX, leaning against the shelves behind me. "Hi. Doing some testing in here. Hope we didn't alarm you."

He frowned. "No one's authorized to be in here."

I nodded. "Yeah. That's what we're testing. The security system's resistance to intrusion during a non-authorized time frame. You weren't notified of this?"

He shook his head.

I sighed and lifted my face to the ceiling. "How many times do I have to send out notification to get anything official done around here? This is ridiculous. Your C.O. probably has the memo somewhere in his computer, unopened. What happened to compliance training? God."

He frowned, hesitant but still not convinced.

Maybe I just wasn't that good of an actor.

"I've never seen you before. Where are you from?" he asked. But instead of staying locked on mine, his eyes began to travel over each of us thoughtfully. "I've never seen any of you before."

"Of course not." I raised an eyebrow. "We're not stationed here. It's just a routine audit."

His eyes stopped for a moment on China, who was staring at him intensely. He looked first at her face, then at her uniform, the only one different from ours. "Why do you have a Player in here?"

He didn't allow me to answer the question, instead pulling back and waving to what I assumed must be his buddy while lifting his radio wristband to his mouth to say something to someone on the other end.

We never found out who that someone was or what he was going to say to them, because Jacky punched her hand through the door window and grabbed the wristband, snapping it off and crushing it. She swung around the door and punched him in the face, then pulled his instantly limp form into the room.

"Don't kill him," I snapped as she reared back. Just in case.

She grimaced, so maybe that had been a good idea on my part. Instead, she struck the back of his neck, and his eyes rolled up and back.

That move was just as cool, every time.

Unfortunately, she couldn't undo the guard having alerted his buddy, who kicked the door open wide, gun at the ready. She dropped like a rock, kicking both feet out in front of her and taking the second guard's legs out from under him while I knocked up the barrel of his gun and ripped it out of his hand so that he couldn't shoot us.

I grimaced at the distinct crunching sound of the guard's trigger finger breaking. Not pleasant, but also not something I would let myself feel bad about. Anyone who was a part of NIX deserved that and more.

The guard flipped over and gained his feet again right away, much more of a challenge than his partner. I doubted a normal soldier could have stood against us for even as long as he did, and suspected Seeds had increased his fighting skills. But he was still no match for both Jacky and me.

After he went down, the radio at his wrist crackled again. "Reinforcements on the way. Report your status, Decker." When no response came, it crackled again, "Status report, Decker!"

I turned to Adam. "You've got to hurry. We don't have much time."

"We can't hurry," he snapped, breathing hard. "Data only transfers so fast, and if the program doesn't have time to finish properly, we might as well not have come here in the first place."

I took a deep breath, trying to calm the piece of bubbling lava inside me that reacted to my fear and tension, and pushed my claws back into my fingers. "Jacky, China. Time to implement Plan B."

Jacky ripped a storage port with built-in Wi-Fi from her back pocket and shoved it into the slot on the fallen guard's ID sheath she hadn't crushed. It would forcefully override the locks and open all the doors in this section of the compound, thereby setting off a slew of other alarms. In a few minutes, the anti-fire system would engage, drenching everything non-essential in water and sucking the oxygen out of non-water-friendly rooms. Plan B was to create widespread chaos so we could slip around and away undetected in the midst of it.

"I need to know when the reinforcements get close, China, and how long we have till they get to this room."

She nodded silently, pale-skinned and round-eyed. Her fingers were curled into white-knuckled fists, but she uncurled them deliberately and cupped them behind her ears to increase the amount of sound she could capture from the specific direction she wanted, like the ears of a dog or cat. After a few moments, she said, "Now. I hear them."

"How long?" I asked, pulling on the steel-fingered gloves I'd brought to hide my possibly identity-revealing claws.

"A minute?"

I turned to Adam. "You've got thirty seconds to get out of the system. Everyone get the charge sticks ready."

He growled but gave no other response. Twenty-eight seconds later he said, "Now!"

We all pressed the charge sticks into our necks, a couple inches below the VR chips, and gave a heady jolt to the tracking devices embedded under our skins.

The lights stopped abruptly as he disconnected his computer.

"Did you do it?"

"Of course." He tried to smirk but looked too afraid and strung out to pull it off. "You know who I am, right? I always perform. Ouroboros is in motion. She'll eat every bit of the surveillance from the last few days, along with everything for the next fifteen minutes, till she's devoured her own existence. Along with any trace we ever existed."

"Good job. Let's go." We left the room and ran down the hall, just slowly enough for China to be able to run at the forefront and still listen at the same time.

The holding area was in a different section of the compound, but China thought Chanelle and Blaine's remaining family would be there, judging from snippets of information she'd gotten from listening to the guards' conversations. If we could get there and take Chanelle, Blaine's niece and nephew, and some other random decoy prisoners and test subjects without being noticed, we had set up getaway motorcycles and rent-a-pods all throughout the nearby forest. Untraceable back to us, of course.

Honestly, I would have left at that point without Chanelle and Blaine's niece and nephew. If we could just get out, we'd be off free. But I knew China wouldn't come, and I couldn't exactly leave her to be caught and tortured by NIX, likely leading them back to the rest of us.

Adam guided us toward the lightly trafficked connecting hallway that would lead us directly to the holding area. We turned the corner into a lounge-type area. It had a large wall-to-wall window looking out over the edge of the mountain we were dug into, onto the river and forest beneath.

Just in front of us stood a tall, thin man, cutting off our route of escape. He smiled thinly. "Well, well. What have we here?" He breathed deep. "I can smell the fear on you. Real fear, felt so often and so recently it's become part of your blood. I haven't smelt a guard like that here. Let alone four of them, together with a Player."

"Oh, no," China said, her voice calm, which only made her fear more plain.

Chapter 27

You monsters are people.
— Jacqueline Santiago

CHINA GRABBED me by the sleeve and tried to force me back, away from the man.

"What's wrong?"

She shook her head, never taking her eyes off him. They were wide and filled with a kind of blank terror. "We need to run, now. He'll crush us."

Jacky didn't seem to hear her, confident in her own abilities. She rushed him. As soon as she got close, she was blown away. Literally. She smashed into the window, and spiderweb cracks spread from where her body had hit, branching outward as she seemed to fall in slow motion to the ground.

China whimpered. "They're coming from behind. And up ahead. We need to run. He's a snake…I can feel it, Eve. I can tell."

Jacky got to her feet again with stiff movements, and my mind struggled to comprehend this stringy man's strength and speed.

I could hear the pounding of feet behind us, too, even through the blaring of alarms. "What can you tell?"

A tear slipped down her face. "We're going to die."

I straightened. "We're not going to die. We just need to get past him. There's still time to move forward before we're boxed in."

Adam rushed forward as Jacky came from the thin man's side. He zigzagged back and forth, trying to use his speed as a distraction, but was stopped by a bony punch to the gut. Adam retched bile onto the floor as he hung suspended, bent over the snake's fist.

Behind us, footsteps skidded to a stop, and I turned my head to see a gasping, rumpled man take the situation in. "Oh my god," he said, meeting my eyes. "Seriously?" he asked, as if he knew me.

What? I opened my mouth to question him, but the group of guards turning the corner behind him diverted my attention. They pulled him back behind the first line of bodies as if to protect him. Their guns immediately lifted, but then they saw the snake-like man and lowered them. The ones in the front line edged backward, like they were trying to increase their distance from him, jostling the ones behind them.

Well, that wasn't good. Just who was this snake?

Sam spun in a circle, looking trapped. "What do we do?"

"We move forward." I gripped him by the arm to steady him. "We do whatever we can, whatever we *have* to."

He stared at me, and then shook his head. "No. I know what you mean by that. I'll help us get past him, but I'm not going to hurt another human being. And I'm not using my Skill. Not again. Besides, aren't we supposed to be incognito? My Skill's pretty distinctive."

I grimaced, but there was no time to discuss it. The snake man shoved Adam, sending him skidding across the floor to slam into my legs.

The snake man smiled. "I think I'll play with you for a while, until it's…*safe* for the guards to take over."

Adam groaned. Behind the man, Jacky was holding a now injured left arm close to her body.

My claws had slipped out without conscious thought in response to the threat, luckily hidden by my gloves. As Adam rose from the ground, we all prepared to fight.

—Keep any of those distinctive Skills hidden, just in case.—
-Eve-

Adam took out a collapsing baton from one of his many pockets and, with a flick, sent electricity crackling through it. It wasn't a stun baton, just normal metal he was using to disguise the origin of the electricity.

I jumped forward this time, with Jacky coming in from the back, Adam beside me, and Sam moving around to the side. China held back, but the few throwing knives she'd managed to hide on her person were out and ready to back us up. The guards made no move to stop us, instead watching the scene with unnatural silence.

I thrust one gloved hand forward, aiming for his eyes. My other hand was ready to smash my claws into his gut when he instinctively protected his face, but he didn't even blink.

Instead, he unflinchingly grabbed my outstretched hand and whipped me around like a rag doll. I felt the gashes in my back rip open again as I swung around and flew into the window. More cracks spread outward, crisscrossing those Jacky's body had created. The urge to scream in pain might have been overwhelming…if my lungs had any air with which to do so.

I stood again despite that, and when the black dots cleared from my eyes, saw that the others had fared no better than me.

Jacky was crouched on the floor, blood dripping from her head. She kept trying to get up, but, as if drunk, couldn't find the balance to stand and kept falling back to her one good hand and knees. Our best fighter, down. I couldn't help but remember when the same thing had happened to Chanelle.

Adam was trying to help Jacky up, and Sam was standing back and clutching a broken wrist.

China threw her knives at our opponent with just enough delay to keep him focused on her, drawing out the time for the rest of us to recoup.

He dodged every one, weaving and bending his body like some supernatural martial artist.

And things kept getting worse. Not only were we failing to make any headway against this one enemy, but another group of guards had come up the hallway leading away from the windowed room. We were boxed in.

—Sam, I know you've got qualms about hurting others, but we could really use your help here. Maybe you could paralyze him? Kinda like the grub-pug poison you healed me from?
Or something else you can't see from the outside. His heart, or lungs…—
-Eve-

. . .

—What!?—
-Sam-

—He's got to be a Player. We'll kill his GPS, take the body.—
-Eve-

SAM GLARED at me and snapped, "*No.*"

I ground my teeth and snapped back, "Then at least make yourself useful!"

"I am!" He held up his already healing wrist and laid his other hand on Jacky's neck.

I'd never wanted a gun quite so badly before. As I had this thought, I eyeballed the groups of guards plugging both exits. A forced breath and a few sprinting steps later, and I was in front of them. I ripped a gun out of one of the guard's unsuspecting fingers and turned to shoot at the snake. I got a few rounds out before the anti-theft system recognized that I wasn't the proper owner and locked the gun.

The snake man flexed his fingers open wide with enough strength that they almost bent backward, and the bullets veered around him, smashing into the wall behind him and barely missing Adam's head.

Adam's eyes widened and he looked back to the hole in the wall, and then met mine for a moment that seemed to last forever.

I felt like we both had an *"oh crap"* moment of understanding, and then time started moving again at a frantic pace. It was time to escape while we still lived.

But there was nowhere to run.

My eyes caught on the hairline fractures running through the window, and then focused past them to the dark line of the river rushing far below. I dashed toward the window and slammed the butt of my stolen gun against it as hard as I could. The force of the impact made my hands go numb and my bones hurt, but the cracks spread, and I turned to Jacky. "Help me."

She nodded, for once without her cocky grin, and grabbed a sturdy looking coffee table on her way to me.

The snake waggled a finger. "Oh, no, kids. Don't be getting any ideas now."

Adam picked up two chairs and threw them at him one after the other. The snake was distracted for a moment, long enough for Jacky to smash through the first layer of glass, and then the second. The wind whipped along the cliffside and slipped into the room, ruffling my clothes with the force of its passing.

The program we'd plugged into the system kicked into the next stage, and the ceiling sprayed water down on us in a distractingly heavy torrent.

She looked at me. I nodded, sending a Window to the team with barely muttered voice commands. "Down him, then get out. There's a river below." I focused on widening the break enough for a human to pass through as the others turned all their energy to distracting our opponent. I could hear them fighting, but I didn't look back, and tried not to imagine the loss of my fighters.

When the opening was large enough, I turned back to the room. Sam was standing beside Jacky and clutching his arm, but hers had been healed enough that she could lift it at least.

The snake had a huge grin across his face. It twisted his features grotesquely, as if his cheeks were made of putty. He still hadn't moved from his place.

China crouched beside me, picking up sharp pieces of glass.

"I'm sorry, China. It doesn't look like we're going to be getting Chanelle today," I said in a low voice, knowing her Perception was high enough to pick up my words.

"She's strong. She'll survive until we find a way to come back for her and Blaine's family," she said firmly, as if to deny the possibility of any other outcome. And then she looked at me and nodded, like I was the one who'd suggested such an unlikely happy ending.

I turned my attention to the others, unable to face her optimism and the reflection of that idealized version of me in her eyes.

Jacky faced off with the snake warily, making no move to attack. Her gaze flicked to mine, and I jerked my head to the broken window.

China threw the shards of glass at him, two at a time. Three quick volleys, quicker than even my eyes could see.

The snake's mouth twisted in surprise, but he smashed them out of the air, disintegrating them into fragments that exploded away from him. The little crystal dust pieces mixed with the wind and pouring water and whipped around.

Not a piece reached him. But they did distract him as China, Jacky, and Adam shot in all at once from three different directions, moving low to the ground and aiming for his legs while Sam threw a decorative plant at his head. They took him down, and his forehead smashed against the edge of a splintered coffee table.

"Hurry!" China screamed, pointing out the window.

They didn't hesitate or try to finish him while he was down, instead running or limping toward me as quickly as they could.

Sam made it first, jumping even before my nod and quickly disappearing into the darkness below.

Jacky was next. She waited a few seconds to hear Sam splash in the water below, and then jumped far out into the empty air to ensure she didn't have an unfortunate meeting with the cliff or rocks at the edge of the water below.

China waited to jump next.

Adam was limping badly, and I moved to go help him.

I'd wrapped his arm around my neck and almost made it to the window.

China was about to jump, leaving only Adam and me in the room, but she froze, and then turned around to look behind us.

I followed her gaze to see what had made her stop.

The thin man had risen and was walking toward us. His face seemed to almost glow from within. Not with actual light, but a terrible power.

Behind him, the soldiers had their guns out and pointing at us, but for some reason weren't firing. Instead, there was again a general scrambling as they all tried to back up into the ones behind them.

He raised his fingers to his forehead and took them away bloody, then looked at me.

I flinched.

Adam grabbed my arm and pulled me closer to the edge. "Jump, China!" he snapped.

The snake raised a hand, and the hair on the back of my neck rose in a burning instant, screaming at me to run.

Adam's other hand snapped out to grab China, but she'd stepped forward out of his reach, screaming, "NO!" at the top of her lungs.

Then Adam's arms were wrapped around me, and he was pushing me backward, jumping out of the window and taking me with him, his body a shield between me and the thin snake of a man.

But China.

China's body crumbled and twisted and fell apart, wringing her head around to me as Adam and I launched outward. Even the air and water around her contorted, an instant twister mixed with squirts of blood.

Her eyes met mine and held for a long, long time. And then her broken, mangled body was falling, taking her face with it.

The man grimaced in distaste at the mess of her corpse, and I heard his murmured, "What a waste," through the rushing wind and now distant-seeming sirens.

I vaguely noticed a commotion from one of the groups of guards as the rumpled man who'd from earlier strained forward and they held him back.

But we were falling, too. I was surprised that my stomach could still protest at the plunge, trying to rise through my mouth in vertigo, even with what I'd just seen. Or maybe it was trying to leave *because* of it. I didn't know.

I stared up at the stars as we fell—our sky with only one moon floating through the heavens—and tried to figure out if she'd still been alive when her eyes had met mine, or if he'd already killed her, and she was just still on her feet for that last second.

Then I smashed into something hard and cold, and Adam's body above mine pushed me down into the blackness.

Chapter 28

God kills, and so shall we; indiscriminately ... for no creatures under God are as we are, none so like Him as ourselves.
— Anne Rice

ADAM DRAGGED my half-senseless body out of the water downstream, then bent me upside down over a boulder like a kid about to get whipped over their father's knee, except he pushed hard on my back instead.

Water spewed out of me, and he did it again.

Once the water was mostly gone, I gasped for air and spewed more on my own, throwing up a bit in the process. I shuddered and coughed, crawling off the rock and retching into the pebbly sand until he helped me to my feet. We started to run toward the nearest escape point.

Behind us, spotlights were shining from the compound and scanning the river and the bank, encouraging us to hurry. If we were to be caught...I shuddered.

We made it to a motorcycle stashed in the woods, and he helped me on behind him. We navigated away through the darkness, clear-headed enough to remember not to turn the vehicle's lights on.

Jacky had warned us of that, along with suggesting the muffling pads around the engine.

I held on tight, my mind too dazed to thank Adam for saving me not once, but twice.

In my head, the gruesome scene replayed itself over and over. "No, no, no," I whispered, pressing my head into Adam's back and closing my eyes. But my mind wouldn't listen to me, and I was unable to stop seeing it—her eyes, her body, and the man's little grimace of distaste. Her body crumpling limply to the ground, no longer in the right shape to support itself. Her eyes.

Adam drove for a long time, till we were out of the woods and into town, and then took a long, circuitous route that we'd laid out beforehand to make sure we weren't followed.

We were the last to arrive at the base. When we entered Blaine's lab, everyone's eyes swiveled to look at us.

Blaine looked drawn out and weary, so I knew he'd already been told of our failure to save his family.

Jacky let out a relieved breath and stood up. "You took so long, we were worried." She leaned to the side to try and look around us. "Where's China? Didn't she come with you?"

I choked.

After a few moments of silence, she asked again. "Where is China?" But this time, her voice had lost the higher pitch of excitement and relief.

"She's dead," I managed, stripping my claw-concealing gloves off. "That man…" My throat convulsed, and I couldn't force any more words out. My knees threatened to buckle beneath me, and I struggled them to straighten and hold. I couldn't let the team see me so weak. They needed someone strong, especially now.

Blaine flattened his palms on the table and stood. "What is she saying?"

Adam stepped forward. "China…was killed. He was able to do things, inhuman things. Skill-type things." He pulled up his shirt and fake uniform jacket, showing us the skin of his back. It was swollen and dark purplish-red in artistically strewn swaths where the membranes of skin and blood vessel had been pulverized. The edges of that twisting force had just licked at his back. "I was lucky," he said, his voice rough. He cleared his throat and clenched his jaw, blinking back tears.

The snake had been a Player, a powerful one. I'd known NIX had Players, but I'd thought they were more like captives or test subjects. He'd been on their side.

Sam shook his head, staring at the marks. "No, no, that doesn't make any sense. Why would he kill her? China was just…a kid. Completely innocent."

The full force of my emotions turned on him and started to spew out of my mouth. "But he did! He was too strong for all of us, and he killed her. While she was trying to protect us, protect me. He reached out his hand, and she turned into an ice cream swirl. He. Killed. Her!" I was screaming by the end, my voice hoarse, a half growled warning shriek like one of the Trial monsters.

They all leaned back, their eyes widening in surprise and maybe even fear, and I realized that my teeth were bared and my claws out in an explicit threat. I closed my mouth and willed the swirling burn inside me back down.

Jacky opened and closed her mouth, then started to cry. Her tears lasted only a few moments, and then she turned on Sam, snarling. "You shoulda stopped him. You're the only one who maybe coulda, and the only one who refused to try. You coulda done what you did in that puzzle Trial, turned him into a crystal-thing. China coulda escaped with us if you took him out."

He paled and stepped back as if she'd hit him, but didn't rebut her words.

"Did the mission work? Do they know it was you?" Blaine asked. What he meant was, 'Are they coming after you? Is my family in danger?'

"Adam did his job," I said. "There's no record of us or anything relating to us, and we shorted the GPS chips. But they've got her body. They still have her body," I repeated. "And they've still got Chanelle, and your niece and nephew."

"What does that mean?" Jacky asked.

"It means we are all in danger," Blaine said. "Eventually, they'll figure out who China was. And they've got people imprisoned, but with the wrong information. They are going to notice, and they are going to realize what we did. Somehow, they are going to connect this to us. Maybe through Bunny. Just because they no longer have any records of you in their system doesn't mean you're safe. We are not safe."

"How long do we have until they figure it out?" Sam asked.

"My program had an ouroboros clean up code. There aren't traces of tampering in the system, other than the empirical evidence of those three with all the wrong information. The computers won't give us away. Our downfall will be some person, someone who remembers their real information, and knows who Blaine is," Adam said.

"Then we just have to go back and get them, right? If we can finish the plan, take away any evidence that connects to us, we'll be safe, right?" Sam perked up a bit, a desperate plea in his eyes.

Jacky snorted. "China won't be safe. It's too late for her. And how the hell do you think we're gonna get back in after what just happened?"

"We might make it in, but we'd never leave again. Especially not with Chanelle and the other two," Adam said.

Sam deflated and returned to staring at his hands.

"Their names are Kris and Gregor," Blaine said, low.

Adam paused, then nodded. "Sorry. Kris and Gregor. But it's only a matter of time before they connect all this to us. It's not like they're just going to let it go and write it off as bad luck. If there's something to find, they'll find it. And us."

"So what do we do?" Jacky looked to me.

"We run," I said. "And we hide. If they don't know where we are, they can't use teleportation to take us to the Trials. So at least there's that." It was a small victory, considering. Why didn't I feel better about it?

I smelled our defeat in the air, saw it in the curve of our spines, bowing under the weight of fear and loss.

Sam clenched his fists. "We were so close."

"Blaine already had a more fugitive-style escape plan, since we wouldn't have been able to make NIX forget about him just because his information disappeared. None of us were planning to stay in this city anyway," I said. "We were already going to run. We'll just have to do it a little more…seriously." Desperately. My voice felt dead, but I steeled myself to get through the next few hours of planning. I was shivering. I didn't feel cold, but maybe I was, because I was still damp from the river, and I couldn't feel my fingers.

"I am not running," Blaine said. "I can't just leave the kids to NIX's mercy, especially if they were to decide the reason for keeping them alive as hostages just ran away."

Adam sighed. "You don't know what they'll do to you."

"But I have to take responsibility for my actions. I helped you because I wanted to save the kids and hurt NIX any way I could. Well, we failed. I can't just run away from that burden."

"That's your choice to make, Blaine," I said. "And I think you're a good man for making it. But the rest of us aren't in your situation. I'd rather not face NIX ever again, and I'm definitely not going to wait for them to come find me."

He smiled. "I wouldn't expect you to. And I will still help you to get away. I just won't be coming with you."

I sat down at one of the tables and called for a blanket, some coffee, and Sam's Skill to help my re-wounded shoulder. We were settling in for a long night. I couldn't be weak, couldn't let my body or my mind fail me and the team again.

A FEW HOURS of planning and discussion later, and I'd grown even more frustrated and irritable, half expecting agents from NIX to break down the door to Blaine's lab and take us all any second. Either that or call us up to tell us they'd taken our families, too, and were holding them hostage. I could only be grateful I'd had the foresight to move them to safety, away from any memories those at NIX might have of them. I hoped desperately it had worked. But now I had put them into more danger.

I wondered if I should go ahead and tell them everything so they could be on their guard if I wasn't around to watch their backs. But what if that made things worse? They could both be stubborn and reckless, especially Zed.

My pack in the corner started to vibrate and lit up, distracting me from my thoughts. I'd put my ID sheath inside and left it at the base, so, in case something went wrong, NIX wouldn't be able to use it to identify me. I retrieved my pack and the ID sheath from within it. It was an unknown caller. The call went to message when I didn't respond, but, after only a few seconds, the person on the other end redialed.

I answered, sending a warning look to the others to stay quiet. "Hello?"

"Eve?"

"Who is this?"

"It's Bunny. Listen, everything's going crazy—"

"How do you have this number?" I demanded, my heart racing. If he knew, NIX new, and we were screwed.

"I…I just happened to remember it. Listen, this is a secure line. They don't know I'm calling, and I don't have much time. They don't even know I know who you are."

"Why are you calling me?"

"Just listen! Everything's in chaos here. The whole place is on lockdown because some unknown people with Seed augmentation broke in, but they don't know who you are. They know you had Seed augmentation, so they know you're probably Players, and they're going to find you using the next Boneshaker if they don't get any other leads before that."

"But we killed the GPS," I said, taken aback. "How would they find us? They can't use the Boneshaker without knowing where we are."

"That's what I'm trying to tell you. I figured out what you did. Tried to cut yourself off from NIX's access to you, escape the Game? I mean, it was smart, but I heard them talking. They said as long as you're alive and have any Seed material from our facility in your body, the Trial will take you along with the others. They're going to run scans on the Shortcut, the huge metal ball-thing above the courtyard. At the moment of transfer, it's going to show them where all the transfers are coming from. They'll track all the ones they know, and the ones they don't must be you guys." Bunny took a deep breath, then added, "They're worried you might be Players from an unknown entity, in which case they won't be able to track you. But you are one of ours. So, they'll find you."

Disappointment sucked the strength from me. "What? I—I thought…"

"I thought so, too. When I realized what you'd done, honestly, I was so glad for you, but then…"

Suspicion flared. "Why are you telling me this?" I stared blankly out at the others sitting around the table. They were each staring at me with almost identical expressions of horror.

"I couldn't go along with it anymore. What you said to me before…I realized it was true. And when I saw you guys fighting in that room, and then what happened to China, I—I just couldn't, not anymore."

"You were that guy?" I remembered thinking the guy who ran up before being shielded by the soldiers looked at me with familiarity. Now I knew why. He'd had access to every waking and sleeping moment of my life for the last few months, except for the Trials.

"If they find out, I'm screwed," he said with a whine. "But I had to do something to stand up to them."

"How can I trust you?"

"Well, there's no way to…*prove* it, but does it matter? If I was trying to betray you, you'd know soon, because they'd be tracking this communication signal right now, and you'd have an army crashing down around your ears in a few minutes. But you won't."

"That doesn't mean I can trust you. This could be a trap."

"So don't trust me. But I'm here to help, if there's anything I can do. Look, I've got to go. If you need to contact me, call me and hang up. I'll get back with you as soon as I'm able."

The line went dead.

I dropped my ID sheath back into my pack and practically fell back into my seat. "You guys heard all that, right?"

Adam dropped his head into his hands. "It was all…for nothing. The Trial is coming again in four days, and when it does, we're going to be caught by NIX. We've only made things *worse*."

I felt hollow. All of it was my fault. I'd gone to China and told her about her sister so she would agree to help me. I'd gathered the rest of the team and convinced them to help me escape from the Trials. I hadn't forced China to stay behind, even though I should have kept her safe. I hadn't forced her and the team to wait till NIX's next shift change so we had more time to prepare and grow stronger.

The only thing I'd accomplished was to get China killed and put the rest of us on NIX's hit list. So much for my promise not to regret my actions ever again.

"We have to get as far away from here as possible," I said. "So far that they won't be able to retrieve us, even if they do know where we are. And we have to keep moving so they can't pinpoint our location from Trial to Trial. If you've got family we sent away, you might want to talk to them. It could be a while before we get the chance again. Don't alarm them. We don't want our faces on the news when we disappear. That would just be a chance for someone at NIX to notice them and happen to remember we used to be Players. If we can, we want to keep our families safe."

"We'll have to come up with some other story, then," Adam said.

EARLY THE NEXT MORNING, after a long night without sleep, I called my brother to give him a reason why I'd be disappearing, and to say good-bye. Instead, everything fell apart.

"What?" I growled across the connection.

"I'll go join Mom later, when you do. I used your bed last night, since you weren't here and mine's gone. Hope you don't mind."

"Weren't you supposed to drive the moving pod?"

"Err, yeah. Mom was livid." He snorted. "But she makes enough to afford a driver now."

I stood up, my chair scraping on the ground as I pushed it away from the table. "You should have gone with her. You need to leave, Zed."

"Why?"

I ground my teeth together. "Cause that's the plan. There's stuff waiting for you there. Are you just going to leave Mom to deal with everything? What about the summer programs you were going to enroll in? You should go, Zed."

"I don't think so. We need to talk."

I strained to keep my claws sheathed. "I'm going to be home soon. Stay there." I disconnected the call and quickly explained the situation to the others.

"It's dangerous to be seen going home," Adam warned.

"I don't have a choice," I snapped.

"At least change your clothes first. You've got blood on you."

I nodded. "I'll be back in an hour. Get everything ready to go." I dressed as inconspicuously as I could, covering my face like a paranoid film star. As I made my way back to my house, which I'd scheduled to be sterilized of any trace of living inhabitants later that day, rage bloomed in my chest like a flower whose infinite petals just kept spreading open. How could Zed be so willful? Didn't he know how much danger he was putting himself in? Undoing all my hard work to protect him.

As I opened the front door of my house, even my anger couldn't keep me strong. Of course he didn't know. I stepped through the entrance in silence. My strength had been grated away, hour after hour, and I felt like a creature of trembling tendons and hollow bones. My thoughts had the fuzzy distance that came from extreme fatigue.

I moved to the doorway of my room, bracing for an additional weight to land atop the wobbling burden already crushing me.

Zed sat on the side of my bed, hands clenched in front of him. He looked up at me with bloodshot eyes, obviously not having slept. "Hey." He smiled at me gently. "You don't look so good. Wanna sit down?" He patted the edge of the bed beside him.

I didn't know what to say. I just stood there in the doorway to my bedroom, staring at him. Anger, I could deal with. Accusations would strengthen my backbone long enough to get me bluffing through the conversation. Even threats would have been preferable. At that moment, compassion slipped through my defenses like a burrowing weasel.

Some hint of this must have shown on my face because he said only, "Oh," then stood and wrapped me in a hug.

It was so surprising that it startled a tear right out of me. One, and then another. Then I was sobbing, being nasty and slobbery and unwashed all over him, but he didn't seem to mind.

Finally, I calmed down and pulled away from him. I wiped my face on the bottom of my shirt, beyond caring about propriety at that point.

He led me into the room and sat me down on the bed, one fist still clenched tight. "You're in trouble," he stated, voice calm.

"No, no, I'm really not, Zed. You don't have to worry about me." After crying so hard—after everything that had happened since the last time I slept—I barely had the strength to keep sitting up. But I couldn't leave him fretting about me when I disappeared for what might be the rest of his life. "You're way overprotective." I rolled my eyes. "I haven't slept in a while, my body's tired from working out, and I…I'm probably not going to see you for a while."

"What do you mean?"

"I got an offer from the foreign relations branch of enforcers. If I join their training program as a recruit right out of high school, I'll get the chance to travel the world, have adventures, get more schooling…all while getting paid. It's a wonderful opportunity." I tilted my head to the side and smiled as cheerfully as I could. "I think I'm going to accept. I just realized I'm going to miss you and your stupid overprotectiveness. That's why I started blubbering like a sea cow." I elbowed him playfully.

He stood and started to pace back and forth. "Don't lie to me, Eve. I *know* you." He reached the far wall and turned to stare at me.

Maybe at one point that was true, I thought. But who I was had changed over the last couple months. He didn't know me, not anymore. I didn't say any of that, but I saw the recognition of it in his eyes and realized how sad this must all be for him. We'd been so close before the Game. We looked out for each other. But all of a sudden, with no explanation, I'd started distancing myself from him, cutting him out of my life. And he could never know why.

"You look so tired you might as well be wearing panda makeup, you've got dried blood behind your ear"—he nodded when my hand flew to my ear, giving me away—"and you're so freaking scared all the time now."

I opened my mouth to protest, but he held up a hand and talked over me. "I've listened to you pretend everything's okay, that you have everything under control, over and over now. But whatever's going on, it's obvious you're *not* 'handling' it." He took a deep breath, clenched his fist, and said, "So I have to force my help on you." His fist opened to reveal a Seed.

As my mind stuttered for a response, any sensible excuse, he did the one thing that could make everything that had come before seem like a trivial test of my ability to hold myself together.

As the words, "I wish I was," began to form on his lips, I lunged across the room toward him, reaching for his hand and the Seed it held. Our eyes met, and I wanted to scream for him to stop, that he didn't know what he was doing, but I choked on the fear, and was too slow to stop him from finishing.

"—like Eve."

I clamped one hand down around his wrist hard enough to force his fingers loose and used the other to slap the Seed out of his grip with stunning force.

It flew across the room like a bullet and left a dent in the wall.

"Ahh!" my brother screamed, yanking back and cradling the hand I'd slapped. "What the hell!"

I ignored him and pulled his hand forward, inspecting it for a small incision that might soon be gone. Sure enough, even as I watched, the small puncture wound disappeared, knitting itself back up so quickly and so flawlessly I might have believed it a figment of my imagination if I hadn't experienced it so many times before in my own flesh.

Chapter 29

Part of my soul I seek thee, and claim thee my other half.
— John Milton

"NOW, whatever you're caught up in, I'm part of, too," he said.

"What the hell did you do!" I screamed.

"I saw you, Eve. The other day when the power went off and you disappeared. And then you reappeared, hurt. Bad hurt. You left your link here, though. I…I used it to access all your files stored in the cloud over the last few months, since you started acting strange. You tried to hide those videos, I could tell. Even a password. But I've known your favorite password for years…" He trailed off and took a deep breath, frowning.

Rage overwhelmed me, and I nearly punched him. I'd been trying so, so hard, and he'd just ruined it all. Instead, I forced him to the bed and made him sit down. "How did you get the Seed?"

"That marble thing? You dropped it when you reappeared." He plopped a hand on my shoulder, eyes drooping. "You don't realize it, but you can't fix everything alone. Now you don't have a choice. Whatever that was I just did, you'll have to let me in… Whoa." He blinked in disorientation and swayed on the bed.

"You're okay," I muttered, scrabbling with inept fingers at my link.

"I'm not feeling too grlll..." he slurred, and then his eyes rolled back in his head.

"No, no. Stay awake. Don't pass out, Zed!" I slapped his cheek, but it had no effect, so I turned my attention back to my ID link and finally managed to dial the number Bunny had called me from. My hands were trembling, and, when I heard the first ring, I forced myself to hang up and wait for him to call back. I shook Zed, slapped his cheeks, and yelled at him, but he was unresponsive. "They'll take you to the Trials, too. No, don't do this to him," I pleaded.

My ID sheath rang only once before I picked up Bunny's call. "Bunny! Please help me. Don't let this happen to him. I'll do anything, just help me!" I said, basically sobbing by the end.

"Calm down. Speak clearly. What's going on?"

"It's Zed, my brother. He took a Seed. He saw me use one right after the last Trial and found one of mine and he just made a wish and took it and now he's passed out and I'm so afraid." I took a deep breath. "He can't be a Player. I'll do anything, just please, tell me how to stop this. He doesn't deserve this." I breathed hard, waiting for Bunny's response.

"Eve...once the wish is made, there's nothing to be done. If he's been injected, it's already spread through his system. The acclimatization process is already starting. There is nothing I can do. There's nothing anyone can do. But..."

"What?" I snapped. "But what?"

"He would have been tested, too. If he's not a Player already, I can only guess that means he doesn't have the compatibility gene. Which means he's in serious danger."

"Explain."

"NIX chooses candidates that have the highest chance of surviving the acclimatization process the body has to go through to adapt to its first Seed. You were chosen. He wasn't."

"Are you saying he's going to die? No. No, he's not."

"I'm sorry," he replied, his voice subdued.

It barely reached my ears; I was too busy throwing Zed's limp body over my shoulder. I thanked the Seeds wordlessly for making me strong enough to carry him, at the same time cursing them for putting us both in this situation.

I made it back down to the pod I'd arrived in unnoticed and stuffed him onto the empty back seats. Then I took the driver's seat, sent a

Window to Sam, and floored the acceleration pedal on my way back to the base.

Sam and Blaine met me at the door to help carry Zed, and we laid him in Blaine's lab.

"Keep him alive," I said. "He took one of my Seeds and it's killing him. You two need to keep him alive."

Blaine hurried around the room, grabbing monitoring equipment and bags of IV fluid from their storage places while Sam bent over Zed with one hand on his head and the other on his chest.

"I won't let him die," Sam said quietly, his eyes closed.

I wondered for a moment if that was a promise he could keep, then shook the thought from my head. Sam could work miracles, literally. He would save my brother, because if he didn't, I would kill him.

"I can't stop the process that's been started," he added, "but if I can heal him fast enough and for long enough, I think I can keep him strong enough to survive it."

"You *think*?"

"I—I will. And Eve, I just want to say, I was wrong. Wrong about everything since the Intelligence Trial. I feel so responsible." His voice broke on the last bit, but his eyes didn't waver from mine.

I gave him a half smile. It was all I could afford without cracking into a quivering mess. "I can't judge. I've screwed *everything* up."

THE WHOLE TEAM had gathered in Blaine's lab, watching Blaine and Sam work as I paced back and forth anxiously, asking how Zed was doing every five minutes. We'd postponed our departure a few hours to let the two work on him.

Finally, Sam took one last frustrated breath and snapped at me to leave. "The Seed is attacking his body on a cellular level. Keeping him stable is very difficult. It takes a lot of power and concentration, and you're making it harder."

I clenched my jaw, but Blaine laid a hand on my shoulder. "He will be fine even if you don't stay here and watch over him. We know what we're doing. Especially Sam. Go, get some rest."

I nodded and left the room after one last look at Zed. Instead of going to lay down, however, I went outside in my bare feet.

Early afternoon sun shone down with determined strength. The lack of smog in the air around Blaine's remote property was noticeable in the subsequent absence of a near-constant burning sensation in my nostrils. I dug my toes into the pleasantly cool grass and breathed deeply. Just as I had begun to force some tension out of my muscles, my ID sheath rang with Bunny's secret number. I picked up immediately.

"They've got your face," he said.

"What?"

"Your face, they've made drawings from the witness accounts. I've been sticking my nose in as much as possible without getting noticed, and I heard they're calling in some guy that monitors Players with potential. Apparently you were on the watch list because of some Bestowals, which are special accomplishments in the Trials. If anyone can remember any of your information from looking at the drawing, you're screwed, Eve."

"I thought you were the only one who watched us?"

"I thought so, too. But you stood out, did well, and apparently it drew attention."

"Crap."

"Yeah. If they figure out who you are, and they will, I think, then they're going to know I've been keeping your identity a secret. I'll be screwed, and I'm not going to be able to keep you safe."

"God. They're going to question you." I crouched down and buried my head between my knees.

"I won't tell them anything, I promise."

"You can't promise that. What if they torture you?" It wasn't really a question, and he knew it, too.

"I'm sorry, Eve," he said after a long pause. "I never wanted it to turn out like this."

"Yeah." I couldn't keep talking to him. I needed to be alone. "I've got to go, Bunny." I hung up before he could respond, stood, and walked into the forest surrounding Blaine's mansion.

The news wasn't so crushing. They would have found us all sooner or later, I knew. But it added a pressure just a little too heavy to bear on top of all the rest.

I walked under the weight for a long while, forcing my legs to bear the grueling burden that had built up over my never-ending day. Finally, I stopped and let it all out in a scream that ripped through the woods around me like a ravenous beast.

Birds exploded out of their nests in terror, and small things chittered and squeaked as they raced away through the underbrush.

I screamed and kept screaming, pushing everything within me out into the air till my mind was a ringing, empty place. Then I crumpled to the ground and flailed at the dirt and decaying leaves with my claws, ripping at it so I didn't cut into my own flesh.

I opened my mouth in a straining, silent scream, flexing my muscles as I lost control of everything I'd been holding back for so long. Barriers inside creaked and cracked and broke, and everything slipped away from me.

Then something within the aching emptiness reached out to me. It enfolded me, wrapping around and holding me together with warmth and darkness.

I shuddered and sank into the comfort.

It spoke to me, but I couldn't understand.

I shook my head and my concentration slipped from the sound.

Hesitantly, warmth pulsed acknowledgment of my hurt, a feeling rather than words.

I shook my head again. I wasn't hurt, not really. I was just broken, defeated. Like a small beaten animal.

It questioned. Who hurt me?

I remembered Zed's eyes as he passed out from the Seed, the snake-man and China, the Trials, and the masked duo at the beginning who'd started it all. NIX had done this to me. NIX had broken and destroyed me.

Anger seeped into me then, and along with it, strength. It showed me what it was like to crush my enemy with power, enough to lay a blanket of dread and reverence over all who would oppose me.

The feeling was wonderful. But I was weak. I couldn't even save one person from NIX.

It gave me the solution. Become strong.

It was simple. So simple. All along I'd been going about it wrong. The only way to defeat a huge power was with an even more overwhelming power. Fear was the most effective tool against my enemies. Along with that understanding, more strength flowed into me, and the warmth bound me tighter and tighter till I opened my eyes and saw the forest around me.

I lay in a fetal ball at the base of a tree, and I was alone. I sat up slowly, feeling as if I might fall apart if I moved too quickly. But inside, a burning mass fed strength to me.

Hours must have passed, because the light was different, fading and yellow as it slanted through the leaves above. I stood and looked around. At my feet, the ground was scored and gouged, and there was dirt under my nails, but no sign of anyone else.

I took a cavernous breath and let it swirl in that ball of heat within me, then blew it out. "Time to plan," I said aloud, and typed Bunny's number into my ID sheath. When he called me back, I said, "I need to restore Chanelle, Kris, and Gregor's info into NIX's database without NIX knowing. And you're going to help me."

Log of Captivity 4

Mental Log of Captivity—Estimated Day: Two thousand, six hundred twenty-nine.

The lacerations I tore into myself trying to escape throb. I felt her come close to where they keep me captive, and I struggled to join her as I know she wished, but I failed. I failed to go to her side, and she was hurt. Later, she reached out to me in pain, but I, useless as I am, was only able to give her my anger as fuel. It is the one thing I have in abundance. She grabbed it like a true *warrior-queen* and rose again. She grows quickly, even without my help. Thank the gods, for if she were weaker, I would be the first *blood-covenant-champion* to let their master die before even meeting her.

Chapter 30

Do not go gentle into that good night.
— Dylan Thomas

I SPOKE with Bunny for a long while, brainstorming and asking questions while still keeping my newfound goal hidden from him. He may have been willing to help when I and my team were innocent, helpless victims, but I didn't know if he'd ally himself with a wolf baring teeth in his direction. When I was ready, I sent a message to the group asking them to gather for a meeting. Then I headed back through the darkening forest, planning my persuasion.

They were all waiting for me nervously when I arrived back dirty-footed and somewhat disheveled.

Before talking to them, I went to Zed's beside and bent over him.

He was breathing shallowly, and sweat beaded up on his skin. An IV needle pierced through his arm and fed fluid into him.

Sam cleared his throat. "He's stable," he said. "I'm checking on him every ten minutes, but the Seed seems to have moved past the first stage. I'm just waiting for the second to start."

"And you can handle it when it does?"

"I will keep him alive through this, Eve. I promise." He drew himself up straight and looked me in the eye with more steel in his bearing than I'd ever seen.

I nodded. "Okay." I turned to address the whole group. "I've got a new plan."

Adam leaned forward. "Oh? A better way to hide from NIX?"

"No."

He tilted his head to the side. The rest of them just gave me blank looks.

"The old plan isn't going to work," I continued. "It's only postponing the inevitable. Soon they'll be tracking us through the Trials. Even if we somehow manage to keep surviving, how long before we're too badly injured to escape afterward? NIX may not have our information, but they have my face, and maybe some of yours, too. And soon—"

"What?" Sam interrupted, his face going pale.

"Bunny contacted me earlier and told me they had sketches from the witness statements of my face. Someone outside of the Moderators was keeping track of me specifically, and they're going to recognize me."

Adam shrugged. "Well, that sounds bad, but…" He paused and frowned. "Oh. They'll be tracking us through the cameras. If they know our faces, they might not even need to wait for a Trial to try and get us. They'll just have to find us in any monitored area. Which means we'd have to stay away from civilization in general…" He took a deep breath. "Which means we're going to be hard-pressed to lose them after the Trials, because satellite imaging will be on us, and we'll have to be creative to escape its eyes. It's not impossible, but…" He trailed off again, lapsing into glowering silence.

Blaine adjusted his glasses. "But is not the point of all this to buy yourselves time? It's not like you can just give up. Either run or sit there waiting for them to come for you. Even if there are some unforeseen difficulties, it does not change the situation."

"Buy ourselves time? Time to what? Keep running? Always be looking over our shoulders, living in fear?" I ground my teeth, holding back the anger that was both fueling me and threatening to overflow onto my allies. "You have Kris and Gregor to consider, which I understand, but nothing is going to change if we don't force it to. The situation can only get worse with the playing board the way it is now. We're screwed, either way. But…there is a third option."

They stared at me in confusion, as I'd been saying the opposite only hours before.

I took a deep breath before continuing. "We take pre-emptive action. Rather than letting NIX control this, we change up the rules."

"What do you mean?" Adam said.

"I mean, I want to do more than figure out how to escape being Players in the Game. I want to completely stop NIX from coming after us."

"And…how do you propose we do that?" he asked.

"We attack. We crush them." I turned to Jacky. "Didn't you tell me once that the best defense is an overwhelmingly powerful offense?"

She leaned forward and clenched her hands together, fingers entwined so hard they turned white. "Hell, yes. That sounds wonderful. I'll go wherever you decide, but if it's to fight, hell yes. Payback."

While Adam was looking at her incredulously, Sam spoke up. "I'm with you, too, if you can think of a way to make it work." He rubbed at his worn and tired face. "I've been afraid to really fight for a long time, because I don't want to be…a murderer. And it's way, way too easy for me because of my Skill. But from now on, I'm going to fight properly, whether it's a suicide mission or not. Some people—those people at NIX…they deserve to die. If I'd realized that sooner, maybe someone who was innocent would still be alive." He looked around self-consciously, and we all knew who he meant.

Adam gaped at him next. "Are you freaking serious?" he spat. "Have you forgotten what happened the last time we fought with someone from NIX? I haven't. I've still got internal bruising! We were totally outclassed."

Blaine nodded. "He is, I must say, correct. You barely escaped last time, and China was killed less than a day ago. You are not thinking clearly, Eve. Understandable, with the tragedy you've just been through. Maybe you should sleep for a while. NIX will be on the alert for any attacks. The one reason you made it as far as you did is the element of surprise."

"An element which is now *lost*," Adam said. "And not only are we too weak to go against them, we no longer have a way to get stronger now that the Game interface and our location are blocked from NIX. No more magically appearing Seeds, remember? There's no way in hell I'm ever going back there. In fact, I plan to stay as far away and as hidden as possible."

Sam had paled as Adam spoke, but he didn't take back his statement. Jacky only rolled her eyes in derision.

I smiled. I hadn't expected it to be so easy. I'd expected Jacky to be with me. She was the type to jump into any fight with glee, and lately she'd been hero-worshipping me. But Sam? A surprise, there. "Any other concerns?" I asked, looking at each of them. Once they laid each objection out, I could find a way to shoot them down all at once.

"I caution you against this path of action, Eve. It is illogical and reckless. And I fear that it would endanger those still held by NIX," Blaine said.

"Other than the fact that you're being *stupid* and reckless, no. I think those two things should be reason enough," Adam added.

"Okay, good," I said. "Blaine, I want to fix Kris, Gregor, and Chanelle's information in NIX like it was never erased. That will give them some protection, and it might keep you safe too."

Adam cut in. "How are you going to do that?"

"Well, you're going to help me." I smiled. "Bunny's on the inside, and he's willing to access the computer system for us. It wouldn't have to be too fancy. Just something so any erasing we did won't be noticed at first glance."

Blaine beamed at the possibility of protecting the kids. "Oh, wonderful! If Adam can get the program ready, I can send the data through to the Moderator's link device."

"Good. That'll keep those three safe. And yes, Adam, we're not strong enough right now. In fact, we were blown away in terms of power. And we won't be getting any more Seeds. But you know that new Seeds aren't the only way to get stronger. They replicate organically if your body displays a need for them. Like muscles. That's where our spontaneous Attribute level-ups come from."

"That takes *time.* Which we are decidedly lacking right now," Adam ground out. "Didn't you just say running wouldn't work? Your 'plan' doesn't avoid that. The amount of training we'd have to do to face that superhuman strength… We'd be running forever, trying to survive the Trials while organically leveling up."

"Exactly." My smile was a sharp thing full of menace I didn't bother to try and hide. "Which is why we need to create more time."

Jacky pursed her lips. "I know you've got a plan, Eve. But I dunno what this one is. Explain, please."

"If you've noticed, when we're in the Trials, much more time passes there than what the clock says when we return. In fact, it seems to be about five times as much. Plenty of time to train ourselves uninterrupted."

"You want to stay there, after the Trial is over," Jacky inferred. Her voice was low, scratchy.

Sam stood up and laid his hands on Zed's chest, took a deep breath, and shuddered as he began to heal again. "What if we get trapped?"

"What if we get *killed*?" Adam snapped, scowling at me.

"Being trapped shouldn't be a problem. I've talked to Bunny about it. Getting killed is a real possibility. But in our current situation, it's not so different than if we stayed in the normal world."

Sam sat back down. "I'll go."

Jacky nodded. "Me too. I'm not a yellow-bellied coward."

Adam stood up, sparks jumping along the dusting of hair on the back of his arms up to his head. "This is idiotic, Eve. You're leading them into danger, just like with NIX. I've supported you in the past, but I'm not going to agree to this. I won't die just because you hate NIX so much you want to find a way to get back at them, and I won't go with you and watch you do it, either. I'm going with the original plan, the one with the least risk to my life." He started to stride away but stopped and turned back. "And I hope you all come to your senses and stay with me. You're the leader, Eve. The team needs you to *lead* them, beyond your desire for revenge and panic for your brother." Then he left, disappearing through the doorway, though his angry footsteps could still be heard.

I sighed. I'd have to keep working on him.

Blaine took off his glasses and rubbed them briskly. "This is not my decision to make. I am not a Player, so I couldn't go even if I wished. But I do have a lot to lose if you screw up."

"You also have a lot to gain. Freedom from NIX, for both you and the kids."

"I trust that you are not leading all of us to our deaths or a life of being test subjects—or enslaved scientists, in my case," Blaine said. "You must have a plan, knowing you. What is it?"

"I want to hit them where it hurts. *Everywhere* it hurts. A multi-pronged attack that will make them recognize us as anathema to their operation, a caustic poison they don't want to touch with a ten-foot pole. And if I can't escape the Game, I want to destroy it."

Chapter 31

Whenever a thing is done for the first time, it releases a little demon.
— Emily Dickinson

A COUPLE DAYS LATER, Zed finally woke up.

We were in a small village off the coast of some city whose name I couldn't pronounce, hidden from NIX's watchful eyes as well as possible. Sam and I had been watching Zed every moment, day and night, but at some point, we'd drifted into a fitful sleep next to his bed. The sudden, unexpected movement made me jump and startled Sam so badly he sent his chair crashing backwards in his rush to leave it.

Zed looked around blearily and croaked like a chain-smoking frog.

Stumbling past his overturned seat, Sam rushed to get him some water while I helped him to sit up.

"He's awake!" I said loudly, letting the others know.

Zed gulped down the liquid and handed the cup back to Sam. "What's going on?"

"You were sick, really sick," I said, my grin so wide I felt like my lips might split. "But you made it."

He frowned. "What was I sick with? I feel like crap."

"You..." I trailed off, unsure exactly how I was supposed to explain.

Jacky moved to stand beside me and gave Zed a grin even wider than my own. "You've just been initiated into a super exclusive club."

"You injected yourself with something, remember?" I asked.

He nodded. "Yeah. One of those glass balls you use."

"Those are called Seeds," Sam said.

"Do you remember a few months ago, when I was so sick?" I asked

"Yeah. Is that what this was?"

I nodded. "The Seed is…something that changes your body on a cellular level. Little microscopic organisms go in and change things according to the wishes you make when you use the Seeds. And using the Seed makes you a Player." I paused to swallow past the lump in my throat.

Adam picked up the explanation for me. "We're all Players. We've all taken the Seed and survived. Well, except him." He pointed to Blaine. "He's just got beef with the people behind all this. And rightfully so. They took his family and blackmailed him into helping them. The rest of us just hate them because of the Game."

"Wait, slow down, I'm lost. What does it mean when you say you're a Player?" Zed asked.

Jacky butted in again. "It means you're a kinda superhuman badass now."

Adam rolled his eyes. "Sorry, but the other side of that is you're teleported away and forced to play in a death game every handful of days."

Sam shook his head at the both of them. "Guys, you're kind of horrible at explanations. You're being confusing and frightening by turns." He turned to Zed and said, "Hi, I'm Sam. I'm a member of your sister's team. This must all be very confusing."

Zed nodded at him in relief. "Yes, it is." He looked to me. "Please, someone just start making sense."

"When I got sick that time, I wasn't actually sick. Not in the conventional sense. There's a secret organization called NIX that forces people to play something they just call the Game. They do that by injecting us with a Seed, a tracking device, and a virtual reality chip. Since you did it to yourself, you only have the Seed. But you'll still have to go to the Trials. When you saw me disappear, that's what happened. It's basically teleportation, as far as we can tell. Or maybe time travel. Every few days, that happens to us, and we appear at something called a Trial. Basically, it's a test of our ability to survive using the Skills and Attributes we gain from the Seeds." I continued trying to explain for a few more minutes, with the others interjecting periodically.

At the end, Zed just stared at me. "I feel like I'm dreaming."

A laugh bubbled up from my stomach. "You're not dreaming. But I remember when I thought it was all a crazy hallucination, too. That changed quickly enough. Here, let me show you." I looked to the others. "Quick demonstration?"

Jacky picked up the ceramic mug Zed had been drinking from. She squeezed, and the handle crumbled away in her hand. She held out the dust for Zed's inspection, and then blew it into the air, creating a little cloud of floating particles.

Which Adam then poured little sparks of electricity through until it looked like a cutely menacing storm cloud.

I allowed the now-familiar feeling of power to roll through my veins, turning my fingernails into thick, slightly curved claws. Looking down, I saw that my toes had changed a bit, too. The joints and bones of my foot seemed to have thickened and spread out, and the nails had grown pointed. "That's new," I said, using my superior balance to raise my leg straight up from the ground to show the others.

"Fascinating," Blaine said, leaning in. "You say this has not happened before? I would love to spend a little more time examining your transformation…"

I rolled my eyes and gave him an exasperated smile, then turned to Zed, whose eyes were wide enough to show the whites. I picked up his hand and ran my index fingernail across the palm.

He yanked the hand away and stared up at me in horror as blood started to bead along the scratch. "What the hell?"

"It hurts, right? I don't know if it's true, but they say you can't feel pain in a dream. Plus, I needed to set something up for Sam to show you what he's capable of."

Sam took Zed's hand gently. Within a few seconds, the scratch had transferred to Sam, and in a few seconds more, it was gone.

Blaine wiped the blood off Zed's hand with a cotton swab and moved away to examine it at the nearest microscope.

"This is insane," Zed said. "You guys are all…mutants?"

After a few seconds of surprised silence, we all started to laugh. I chuckled at first, and then noticed Zed's obvious confusion and started to laugh even harder.

Jacky's immense strength deserted her under the effects of her mirth, and she sank to the ground, snorting like a pig on every inward breath.

Finally, I was able to open my mouth without laughing. I wiped my eyes and said, "Yeah, kinda like that."

ZED HAD GONE BACK to sleep as his body fought to regain strength, and I lay on a pallet in the large room we'd rented, working on the smallest puzzle ring the Oracle had given to me. Technically, I should have been sleeping like the others, but I felt a constant pressure to do something to give us all a better chance at survival.

My weary eyes grew a sort of tunnel vision, allowing me to see the irregularities in each band's surface. I'd slipped it over my left forefinger, because without something to hold onto and wrap around, the bands kept slipping apart.

I'd found that my claws were better suited for the finesse required to fit the bands together. I could use their tips like tweezers, instead of the clumsy flesh of my fingertips.

After a long, intense period of fiddling, twisting and turning, and matching protrusions to grooves, the last piece of band matched up with its companions, and the shiny ring became one solid piece.

I made a fist and pumped it in the air. Finally, I'd finished it!

Then the ring seemed to come alive, grabbing at my skin, sliding down, and shrinking around my finger till it fit snugly. It pierced inward and injected into me, just like the Seeds.

YOUR NON-SENSORY PERCEPTION HAS INCREASED!

The window hung in front of my face, prompted by the sensors of the now local-access-only VR chip still embedded in my skull.

I stared at my hand in a mixture of curiosity and horror.

Then the seizure started, and all curiosity slipped away. Pain ruptured my consciousness, and my eyes rolled back in my head as my body flailed on the couch.

There was only pain and flashing lights behind my eyelids for a while, but then I started to see things in the lights. Most of them passed too fast or were too strange for me to understand: blood, yellowing teeth, mold growing over a sick child's cheek, and then a dizzying rush of sensations and images that I didn't catch but which filled me with fear and the sick feeling of decay and ruination.

Then I saw a huge mountain towering above a beautiful land filled with dark-rippling fire. I stood on the mountainside and knew that at the top sat power unimaginable. The ground trembled beneath my feet and my perception changed, like a child that looks up at the sky and realizes they are about to fall off the bottom of the world. I understood the power dwelt not at the top, but beneath me, that I stood on a gargantuan body only pretending to be a mountain.

When I woke—or thought I had—my physical eyes would not open.

Instead, I lingered in a body not my own. A man's body, his thoughts, his world. A vague part of me realized that I was dreaming of being someone else, but the other part of me was too caught up in the sensation of the moment to care.

I looked up at the moons showing through the still brightening morning sky. I stood at the top of a small grassy knoll looking out over a lake. This place, at least, still lay untainted. I smiled and lifted something over my shoulder with a strength I'd never experienced in my real body. I wanted to protect this land, my land, and my people. I turned then, and saw a face peeking out at me from behind a tree. A beautiful girl grinned at me, and my heart filled with happiness.

I woke gasping, able to see nothing but the peeling-plaster ceiling of our rented room. I rolled off the couch onto my hands and knees, gulping back choking sobs. Tears dropped rapidly onto the wooden boards between my hands. I felt a deep-seated sense of loss, heartbreak almost, as if something precious had been ripped away from me.

A cool hand gently touched my back. I jerked away from it, looking up to see Adam.

He knelt beside me on the floor and just rubbed my back silently.

After a while, the sobs calmed down, and I wiped my face. "J—just a dream," I hiccupped. I doubted the truth of that. The ring puzzle had given me a vision, but the second part had been different. It had a kind of mental scent to it, which I'd felt before. First, when expanding my senses under China's tutelage and had felt like I was somewhere else, and again when I'd been in the woods at our base, breaking under the pressure.

"The crazy thing is, it was k-kind of a nice dream."

"Sometimes those are the hardest. When you wish they were real, and then have to wake up to reality," he said quietly, the soothing hand still on my back.

That wasn't quite it, but I didn't have the desire or the energy right then to try and explain what had happened, so I just nodded. "Sorry I woke you," I sniffled.

He shook his head. "I was already awake. It's one of the side effects of the Seeds augmenting my body. I just can't sleep as much as I used to."

"Oh."

"You should go back to sleep, though. Come on." He waved me back up onto the pallet and pulled a light blanket over me. "I'll stay with you until you fall asleep."

"Adam…" I said hesitantly.

He smirked. "I'm not going to tell anyone you were crying like a little girl, Eve. Just turn over and go to sleep."

I wrinkled my nose and turned my back to him.

He rubbed my back soothingly, over and over till I fell asleep, but all I could think of was that feeling in my dream, that happiness.

ON THE NINTH day since the last Trial, Blaine drove us all into what remained of the real countryside. We thought the Trials would be nine days apart from the last one on, but the exact time the Boneshaker would start was uncertain.

I sat next to Zed, berating myself that he was seated in this van, facing this fear along with us because of me. "I should have never let this happen to you," I murmured.

He turned to me in surprise. "Let this happen to me? You didn't have anything to do with it. Well, except…"

"That you did this for me. Right? You did this for me, and if I'd been more careful, hadn't left that Seed, hadn't let you know anything was wrong…"

"You mean if you'd lied and kept secrets from me better." He clenched his jaw.

"Yes. Exactly! No matter what, I should have kept you safe and separate from all this."

"And then I'd go about my life blissfully unaware and happy? Is that what you think?" he said, disbelief dripping from the words. "That's not how it works. If I didn't figure it out now, it would have happened eventually. Or maybe I'd never understand, and just go about my life wondering what happened to you and why you disappeared. That's not what I want. You didn't cause this. I chose this."

"You didn't know what you were choosing!" I hissed. "Not knowing is better. It's better than knowing because you're forced to live it!"

"If you'd told me, I'd have known! And I would still—" He cut off as the Boneshaker started to play, reverberating through us. "What is that?"

"The Boneshaker," Jacky said grimly. "It will get loud."

Adam grunted. "At least it's better than listening to you two bicker," he said.

"Better step on it," I said to Blaine.

He nodded and started to accelerate past the point where the pod beeped an incessant speed limit warning and started to shudder lightly.

Sam gripped the seat beneath him and took a deep breath. "Are you sure this is safe?"

Blaine frowned. "It should be safe?"

"*Should* be?" Sam's grip tightened more, and he looked out the window at the blurring scenery as the pod shot down a straightaway.

"Yes. Whatever teleportation device is being used to take you to the Trials, it seems to take into account the movement of your body and neutralizes excess kinetic energy. So, you should be fine."

"But you don't know."

"Well..." Blaine cleared his throat. "I do not have access to the technology, so it is technically just speculation. But I am rarely wrong, and the speed should help to mask your signal from NIX when you go. They will still find you, but it might take a minute or so longer."

"That's not much time, guys," I said. "We need to finish this quickly so Adam and Zed can return and get away before NIX comes for them. We've got the upper hand this time, because they don't know we know how they're going to track us."

As the song grew louder, I swung the large pack on my lap around to my back and wrapped my arms around Zed.

Across from me, Adam did the same.

Because Zed wasn't officially a Player, Bunny couldn't add him to my team, and thus we needed to forcefully take him with us to the Trial so I could make sure he was safe.

A few seconds later, the pulse slammed through the pod.

Zed's eyes were closed. I stepped back from him in case he threw up, keeping a hand on his arm to stabilize him against the dizziness. He opened his eyes warily, but they grew wide as he took in the world around us.

We were on a white-sand beach under a tree with drooping leaves that looked like cocoons. We'd been deposited about a mile from the base of a colossal mountain that seemed like a lot of flat-topped buttes and mesas gathered together and stacked into a tiered tower. Huge waterfalls came from openings in the rock faces and spilled down from the top, which was obscured from view by the thick clouds of mist that rose like a veil of waves all around the mountain before coalescing into an opaque layer higher up.

Multiple vast lakes cut through by what seemed to be randomly shifting sandbars reached out from the base of the mountain in all directions and spilled into rivers that cut through the lush land we stood on. The sun shone bright even through the clouds, and the colors were deep and richer than any I'd seen except in the Trials. For the first time, I thought this place had something which I, living on Earth, might be envious of.

But that thought was quickly replaced by a mix of tension and watchfulness because I remembered this view. In fact, I'd seen it the night before, in the painful dream I'd received after the Oracle's first gift had been solved and it had injected itself into me.

"It's beautiful," Zed said, taking a deep breath of the invigorating air. "And it smells like it comes out of a scent bottle. An expensive one. I've never seen water so vibrant."

I grimaced. "Yeah. Wait till the water turns out to be acid. Or better yet, a paralytic, so you drown peacefully if you try to take a swim in it." I wiggled my bare toes in the sand, suddenly rethinking my decision to forgo shoes on my mutated feet. They would be in the way when my claws slipped out, but my boots offered great protection.

He took a step back from the water's edge. "Really?"

Jacky walked over and poked a finger in. When nothing happened, she took the finger out, sniffed it, and then put the tip in her mouth. "Just water," she said, just before she started to convulse.

Sam lunged forward, grabbing onto her face with his hands, ready to heal.

Zed sucked in a breath, eyes wide, and both Adam and I tensed in horror.

Jacky stopped twitching and pulled back with a grin on her face.

Sam frowned in confusion. "I can't feel anything, I don't—" He cut off, and his eyes widened, then narrowed at her mischievous look. "You were faking."

She snorted a loud laugh. "Sorry. The idea popped in my mind, and I couldn't resist."

I let out a loud breath, along with the rest of the team. "God, Jacky! Get away from the water. You scared me half to death."

She pursed her lips and walked back to us, then turned to look up at Zed, her mirth sliding away. "That was a joke, but it was in bad taste, no? Because here, it would more likely be real. And maybe I did just eat poison, and it's only waiting, like a cat in the bushes, to strike me."

Adam spun in a circle, his eyes taking everything in as he scanned for danger. "It's beautiful here. And it's just as dangerous as it is amazing. Don't do anything without testing it out first, or watching someone else do it without dying."

We'd been deposited close to the cube this time, so we waved the other Players over as they arrived. As always, I checked for children. When one appeared, I stiffened for a moment, but a group of older Players gathered around her, obviously protective. I nodded to them in acknowledgment and allowed myself to feel relief. Zed would be enough to protect today.

Jacky gathered up her spit and loudly shot it into the sand.

The ground started to tremble underneath our feet, causing gentle ripples in the otherwise glassy water.

We all took a collective step back into the cover of the trees.

"What did you do, Jacky?" Sam said, looking a tiny bit sick.

Her eyes widened, and she shook her head mutely.

Zed imitated Adam's scan of his surroundings as the shuddering grew more pronounced.

"Guys, you remember that Intelligence Trial? The one with the puzzles?" I said.

Sam stepped closer to the rest of the group, starting to scan the surroundings as well. "Who could forget? Do you think this is another one?"

"I don't know. But that's not the point. Do you remember when I got caught in that string-room-thing with the Oracle?"

"Yeah? We never saw this Oracle, but I remember the cube said you got some sort of reward for that."

"Puzzles. Last night, I solved one of them." I held up my left hand to show the ring. "It turned out to be some sort of Seed. It increased my Perception and made me pass out. I had a…dream. Maybe you'd call it a vision. I saw this place. Except I saw fire falling from the sky. I mean, it looked kind of like fire. But also like water. And it was dark. And the mountain was alive."

Adam stared at me, nonplussed. "Why didn't you say something?"

I bit the inside of my lip. "What would I have said? I had a weird, freaky dream and saw all this stuff I can't explain, most of which I can barely remember?"

He nodded slowly. "Yeah. If you said, 'Hey guys, I was just injected by this strange Seed I got from an intelligent Trial monster, and then I passed out and had a weird dream-slash-vision. Just thought you should know,' that might have been nice."

I scowled. "Well, if I'd known this was going to happen, I would have."

"Umm, guys," Sam said, "is this really the time?"

We fell silent, waiting for something to happen and throw us into action.

Shortly after that, one of the tree's cocoon leaves started to wiggle.

I grabbed Zed's arm and dragged him away from it.

The team moved with me, each of us scanning our surroundings in a different direction so nothing snuck up on us while we were distracted.

The cocoon unfolded, and an ancient looking old man emerged from within, hanging from his head, which sprouted brightly colored feathers in lieu of hair.

He dropped to the sand with a *pop*, steadying himself with a cane. His back bent like the curve of a fruit-laden tree branch, and he gave us a kindly smiled, which only wrinkled his raisin-like face even more.

"Hello, children," he said, his voice like cat's tongue in my ear. "I see that you are all here and appear to be ready."

At least it wasn't an Intelligence type Trial. From all our combined experiences, the Intelligence types never had Moderators.

When there was no response, he continued. "Very well then. That volcano," he pointed with his cane, "is about to erupt. To win the Trial, you need to capture some of the fire and bring it back to me. Inside the Cube are containers for that purpose. Everyone please take one. And be quick about it. We don't have much time."

He continued to speak as the Cube doled out clear glass bulbs. "Point the end toward some of the flame and snap the seal. It will suck inward and hold the fire."

"Is that all?" someone asked.

His eyebrows drooped over his eyes, along with the feathers on his head. "You must survive, too. That is enough."

The ground gave a rolling heave, and a booming wave of sound followed, forceful enough to almost knock me off my feet. The clouds around the mountain were writhing, but I still couldn't see above them to the tip of the volcano.

The feather-headed old man reached upward with his cane and prodded the tip of the leaf-cocoon.

It reached down and wrapped around his body, then drew upward along with the other branches, all of which were then pulled in close to the trunk. It shivered, then settled, its color changing to a dark grey that spread out from the trunk to the tips of the cocoons.

One of the Players rapped their knuckles on the tree. "Stone," they announced.

All around us, the trees started to pull their limbs in close and do the same.

Adam ran to one of the cocoons and patted on it, trying to get it to open, but it pulled away, stiffening as its color leached away. He turned to me and shook his head in futility.

Something started to fall through the clouds. Something that flickered dark and light, and was headed our way.

"Uh oh," Jacky croaked.

"Fire," I said. In my dream, the land for miles and miles had been covered, cleansed by the flame. "There's no outrunning it."

I looked to Zed, whose eyes reflected the light of the flickering sky. I willed the panic down and started doing mental calculations. In less than two minutes, the fire would reach the ground. Since there was no way to escape the mountain's spewing wrath, we needed a way to weather through it.

The trees around us curled up and turned to stone in ever-widening ripples. "Find us a place to take shelter," I snapped to the group, already racing toward the still-green trees. If the Moderator was hiding in one, I knew they could keep us safe.

I launched myself at the side of the tree, using my momentum to take a few more steps vertically up the trunk, and grabbed one of the folded green leaves. With a firm grip, I pressed my feet against the trunk and used both leverage and gravity to rip the leaf off. It tore away from the stem with a milky white spray and started to calcify even as I fell to the ground. Once it had completely hardened, though, I couldn't unfold it, and I tossed the useless thing to the ground in frustration.

I repeated the process, but this time snapped the leaf as if I was airing out a dirty rug before the grey spread through it. It straightened and hardened in that position, a makeshift leaf umbrella against the coming firestorm. I dropped the stone leaf at my feet and moved on to the next green tree. When I'd used up as much time as I could, I turned and sprinted back to the others, snatching up the huge leaves I'd harvested as I ran.

I pulled up a map Window through my Command Skill and followed the moving dots on it to the rest of the team. Adam was leading the others over the lake, across the sparse sandbars rippling a path through its depths and toward a large rock jutting diagonally out of the water. I followed them out into the deeper water, each lunging step sending up a big splash of the crystal-clear liquid.

Zed looked back to see me, relief softening his expression.

A dark shadow moved across the water in the corner of my eye. "There's…something in the water," I screamed in alarm, gasping for air.

They immediately started to move faster, but the resistance of the water impeded their progress, while the shadow raced toward them. They weren't going to make it.

My heart crashed around in my chest, and the sick feeling of fear and helplessness made me want to scream. I pushed myself harder, but even though I started to catch up with the group, the creature slicing toward them like a bullet would reach them first.

I threw the leaves like Frisbees towards the rocky overhang, slipped off my pack and hurled that, too, and then turned to intercept the creature. I inserted myself between the team and the approaching monster with only seconds to spare, jumping as hard as I could. My body twisted in the air, and I brought my clawed left hand down first, thrusting into the water as the monster passed beneath me.

I caught a glimpse of the legged, spiky-spined shark in the second before I thrust my hand into the lake and hooked my claws into it. They tore through its thick, rubbery skin, just behind the head, and continued to tear as its momentum forced my hand along the body. I realized it was going to rip itself free in a frenzy of pain and anger, so I curled my clawed fingers inside even harder and wrenched, swinging my other arm around. That hand slammed into it right above the tail, and then we were both under the water, and it was thrashing around with a strength I had no hope to match.

My claws ripped free, and I saw only huge, curved teeth in the opening of its tube-like throat before it was on me. I sliced my pointed fingers through the water as quickly as I could, slamming my right hand into its jaw right behind the mouth to throw off its toothy aim. With the other hand, I raked across its murky black eyes, slicing them open.

It tried to get away, but I dug the fingers of my right hand in even farther, far enough to clench them together on the inside of its throat cavity. If it left, it was taking me with it.

With my left hand, I continued to thrust, holding my hand and fingers straight and compact like I was going to karate chop it, but using my claws like daggers. They allowed me to pierce easily, and I did so, again and again, stabbing indiscriminately.

The volcanic fire started to hit the top of the water, its fall not dampened by the liquid. A piece hit the creature's torso and evaporated some of its flesh into a flashing, dark mist. I prayed none fell on me, because I was too busy fighting the monster to focus on anything else.

My lungs burned and my arms weakened from lack of oxygen, but the creature finally slowed, having lost too much blood to continue. I ignored my exhaustion and searched desperately for the surface of the water, disorientated after the shark's mad, blind flight. Luckily, we were close. If not, I'm not sure I would have made it.

I burst through the surface with a gasp, and only after a few breaths of air cleared the blackness from my eyes did I realize I was still holding the huge creature in a death grip with my right hand.

Blood dyed the water, splashing into my face and rolling over my head as the fire rained down all around me. If these creatures were anything like the sharks of Earth, others would come soon, and I knew I didn't have the strength to fight them. If I didn't get incinerated first, that is. But as I tried to remove my forearm from the monster's throat, I realized I was stuck. Somehow, the corpse had tightened around me, and something hard pressed together around my wrist. I couldn't release my fist to make my hand small enough to slip through the entrance wound, and so the huge bleeding beacon was stuck to me.

With a single sob of exhaustion, I started trying to swim back to the rock overhang with one arm, dragging the shark-like monster. Water kept finding its way into my mouth and nose as I struggled to stay afloat. I could hear indistinguishable shouting on the shore, but despite trying to focus, I couldn't make sense of it.

Adam's voice cut through the noise and exhaustion. I looked blearily upward to Jacky, who was holding a huge length of rope in her arm. I was too winded to shout acknowledgment, but she threw it anyway, spinning her body and releasing the rope so that it flew in a wide arc through the air, unwinding as it went.

It landed in the water not far from me, and I grabbed on with just enough time to wrap the loop around my shoulders before they started hauling me forward. I sliced through the water, the rope never losing tautness, and was soon being grabbed by the hands of my team.

I coughed, spitting up some water, and then collapsed onto the warm sand beneath me. Someone dragged me, shark and all, under the protection of the jutting rock and hardened leaves.

Behind me, I heard the wet sounds of slashing and stabbing, the evidence of my team fighting the monsters that had followed.

After a while, the fighting died down and I regained some of my energy.

Adam leaned over me and pried at the flesh gripping my right hand. He let out a shuddering laugh. "I thought you'd lost the arm, because you weren't using it to swim. I thought…"

"No worries," I said, giving him a weak smile. "My arms don't come off that easily."

Jacky knelt beside me and gave me a quick visual inspection, letting out a sigh of relief only when she didn't find any wounds. "You are *loca.* We thought for sure…" She stopped herself. "You were under for a long time."

"I'm just glad you guys kept an eye out for me. If you'd given me up for shark bait, I don't know if I'd have made it back."

She scowled. "You'd definitely be dead, stupid. If not for me and my crazy good tug-o'-war skills, no?" She sniffed and pursed her lips.

"Thank you. Now stop bragging," I said, giving her a light smack on the arm.

Zed finished helping Sam use the rock leaves to create a barrier around the opening of the scoop-cave we were all huddled in. He knelt beside me, his dark eyebrows pulled down in a horrible scowl. But when he saw me lying there, his eyes started to fill with liquid.

I frowned and shook my head. "Zed, everything's fine. It's okay. This is no big deal, I promise. I've dealt with much worse."

He shook his head and bit his lip hard as he worked to push down the tears. "Is this…what you've been doing? Stuff like this, is what you've been going through?"

Adam cut away the shark that was gripping my hand and gently slid the appendage out of the carcass.

I flexed my stiff fingers and muttered, "Thanks," then turned to Zed. "This is why I didn't want you involved. This Game runs on fear and death. But if one of the team needs help, we help. Like I helped stop the monster, and everybody helped me just now."

He pressed his lips together and clenched his jaw.

"Are you hurt?" Sam asked. "Do you need my help?"

"I'm fine, just a little winded," I said.

When I stood up, Jacky gave a whooping cheer and flipped the bird outward, to everything that was making our little makeshift hiding place quiver and shake.

We stayed huddled up under the rock as the world rumbled around us for what seemed like hours. Finally, things seemed to settle down, and I tentatively shifted one of the leaves covering the opening and looked out.

Fire no longer fell from the sky, so I removed the leaf and crawled out, climbing up the rock for a higher vantage point. Except for the large landmarks like the mountain and the water down below, the landscape was completely different.

The lakes had spread and changed shape, and the greenery on the shore sprung from the sand, a riot of brightly colored blooms sprinkled among the transformed vegetation. Only the stone cocoon trees remained the same. Mist from the mountaintop was quickly spreading to create dark clouds, but for the moment the sand sparkled clear and bright, reflecting light from the water and the sun. Here and there, patches of dark flame shone, giving off rippling shadows as they burned a new land into existence.

Chapter 32

Into this wild Abyss/ The womb of Nature, and perhaps her grave—/ Of neither sea, nor shore, nor air, nor fire,/ But all these in their pregnant causes mixed/ Confusedly, and which thus must ever fight,/ Unless the Almighty Maker them ordain/ His dark materials to create more worlds, —/ Into this wild Abyss the wary Fiend/ Stood on the brink of Hell and looked a while,/ Pondering his voyage; for no narrow frith/ He had to cross.

— John Milton

WE HURRIED to grab samples of the last of the flames before they burned themselves out, and then went immediately to the feather-headed Moderator, who had survived, protected by the stone trees.

He detached from the tree, then took the bulbs from us and secured them in a padded briefcase. "It gladdens my heart to see you alive," he said. "May your strength lead you on." His gaze grew distant, an obvious dismissal as he waited for any remaining survivors. Besides us, there would not be many.

The Cube popped up with its usual message.

DO YOU WISH TO RETURN FROM THE TRIAL?
YES / NO

I stepped forward, a shaking finger hovering over the cube surface. I pressed, "No," and let out a breath.

IF YOU DO NOT RETURN NOW, YOU WILL NOT BE ABLE TO UNTIL THE NEXT ALIGNMENT. ARE YOU SURE?
YES / NO

I picked "Yes."

Jacky went next, and Sam after her, both repeating my actions.

I turned to Zed and Adam, who would both be staying on Earth. "I guess we'll see you guys in about nine days, your time. Good luck." I bit the inside of my lip, wishing things could be different, and I didn't have to worry about the two.

Adam ran a hand through his hair, pushing it back from his face. "Ah, damn it. With things like this, you leave me no choice, Eve." He stepped forward and quickly chose the option to stay in the Trial world rather than return to Earth. "If I leave you alone with these two"—he flicked his fingers to Jacky and Sam—"how can I trust you'll survive? I have to be here to watch your back, especially when you keep putting yourself in dangerous situations."

"Hey!" Jacky said. "I… Well, I'd be offended, but I'm just glad you decided to stay. We're a team, and we should stick together, no?"

Zed stepped forward and pressed "No," too, but I grabbed his hand in a crushing grip before he could confirm his selection.

"What the hell do you think you're doing?" I hissed.

"I'm going to stay, too. I can help you, Eve. I want to be here." He wriggled his hand in my grasp, trying to force the issue. "Just let me stay and help."

I thrust him back hard enough that he stumbled. "You're not staying," I growled, my claws fully extended.

He steadied himself and stepped forward again. "This isn't your choice to make. The whole reason all this happened is because I wanted to keep you safe. There's no way I'm going to just watch you go into danger and not do anything to help."

My heart clenched, because I knew I'd be saying the same thing to him in this situation. But I also knew what would hit hard enough to make him stay away despite all that. "I don't want you here, Zed," I said clearly.

"You want me to be safe, I know. But it's no safer if I go back, now.

Adam was supposed to be with me, help protect us, but now it will be just me and Blaine."

"NIX doesn't know you exist. I want to keep it that way, and I'll need you on the other side as a point to return the team to next time. And it's not just that I want to protect you by keeping you out of this Trial. You're weak," I said, stepping forward and poking him in the chest with my claw. "If you stay, you're going to put me and my team in danger. We'll have to look out for you every step of the way. If I needed your help, I would ask for it." I took another step, pushing him backward, glaring at him with every ounce of malice I possessed. "I don't need your help, and I don't want it. So do as I say and quit making trouble for me."

He stared at me for a moment, searching for something in my eyes that I made sure he didn't find. "O-okay. Are you sure?"

"I'm damn sure. Now please, hurry up and go back so we can get on with it." I pointed toward the Cube.

He moved forward, and, with one last glance back to me, he selected the option to return to the normal world and popped out of existence.

There was a moment of silence, and then Jacky let out a low whistle. "Damn, that was vicious." She laughed ruefully and clapped me on the back.

Sam pinched his lips together. "She was doing what she had to, what was needed to get the job done. It was the right thing to do."

"Sam, my boy, you're coming 'round." Jacky clapped him on the back with a laugh, hard enough that he stumbled forward.

I took a deep breath and turned toward the mountain. It stood towering over the land like a giant. "In my dream, there's something important up there. Who's up for some rock climbing?"

As if the world itself had a sense of humor, the sky chose that moment to open up, and we were immediately soaked to our bones in a torrential downpour.

WE DOVE FOR COVER, but it seemed to be ordinary rain, aside from how much of it there was. It dried up quickly, but not before putting out the last of the fires.

We made our way to the base of the mountain, wary of shark monsters, but either they had all died or they were in hiding, because none showed up to attack us.

When we reached the base, my gaze tracked along the side of the tiered mountain, up and up and up. "This is gonna be great training, guys," I said, wiggling my still bare toes in the sand and adjusting the straps of my heavy pack on my shoulders. I extended my claws and tested them against the rock; they made satisfying scores in the surface. "Jacky, we're going to need your rope again. I want us all tied together, but leave some slack in the line so we're not all tugging on each other. I'll go first and cut hand and footholds with my claws so you all have something to hold onto. We're going to go diagonally across the rock surface, moving in zigzags. We'll stop once we reach the top of this first section and reassess. Don't slip, it's still wet from the rain. Got it?"

Jacky was grinning and clenching her muscles, Sam was looking up at the mountain in apprehension, and Adam seemed to be absorbed in his own thoughts, his eyes constantly scanning, but they all nodded to show they understood.

Thus, we started a climb of many days.

A plateau topped each butte. Each one was its own little ecosystem, with water either falling down from above or springing up out of the rocks, and all containing a plethora of monsters trying to kill us. In just the first few days we encountered more than enough danger and hardship to last a few Trials, and we grew stronger at every turn. When we weren't fighting against our environment, Adam spent his time quizzing us and teaching strange theories and complicated math we'd never need in real life. But these lessons stretched my mind in new ways, and I found, to my surprise, that we could level up the mental Attributes spontaneously. In another surprise, my Beauty also leveled up spontaneously. I could only guess it was because I was so much more fit than I'd been before the Game. My Physique was a high level, and the two things obviously went together. I had no mirror, but I could feel cheekbones instead of vague pudge on my cheeks.

A sucking-mud swamp gave Jacky a chance to practice her Skill when we chose that plateau to rest on for the night. It was safe enough as long as we didn't walk into the mud, which sucked down anything that touched it as if some huge monster was slurping at it through a straw. Although it looked to me like she was just playing in the mud, she nonetheless was able to hone control of her body's adherence to the law of gravity to the point that she could float through it. She also liked to use her Skill to reduce her gravity while we scaled the mountainside, grinning cockily at the rest of us who grew tired from climbing with huge packs on our backs.

Another plateau held what seemed to be a fruit orchard, a notion that was quickly disproved when Jacky ate some small, bright cherries, and Sam had to heal her when she started to asphyxiate. She smiled euphorically while choking to death, after which Sam had an idea, and ate a few himself. When I snapped at him, he reminded me of his Skill. Every time he healed something, his body grew a natural resistance to it. But at the same time, it also grew the ability to replicate that damage, slightly augmented. He was hoping to add the berries' effects to others of the same type he already had and create a harmless, painless paralytic ability that he could use to fight.

On another plateau, swarming bugs camouflaged themselves expertly until we had settled in for a meal. They came after us in sheets and waves, biting and clawing and wriggling at us until Adam sent a jolt of electricity through the damp air. Their crunchy carcasses smelled like roasted almonds covering the ground.

My biggest concern wasn't monsters or the terrain, but our food supply. If my calculations of the time in-Trial versus the time in the real world were correct, we would be there for about forty-five days. We were pushing our bodies hard, and, like I'd wished, we were leveling up many of our different Attributes through old-fashioned hard work. But that also meant we were eating like ravenous hyenas and would run out of food within days, despite having filled our packs to the brim with little else.

Ten days into our climb, I was sitting the early morning watch against danger and contemplating our situation. I groaned and rolled my shoulders, then pushed up from my rocky perch to stretch my sore and stiff muscles. I felt like I'd gotten only a few hours of rest. Sleep was difficult with the luxurious damp stone mattress, the insects, my grumbling stomach, and the constant worrying at the back of my mind that I would need to get up and fight at a moment's notice.

Water was a non-issue, seeing as the stuff was everywhere—like in the group's shoes, in our blankets, and hanging heavy in the air. But delicious and energizing as it was, it had no calories. We would run out of food in a day or two, and I'd already noticed the others self-rationing to try and make it last. Doing that would only make it harder for us to get stronger.

"We're going to have to acquire a taste for monster," I muttered to myself. "Hope it's edible."

I sat down on the edge of the large rocky outcropping we had made camp on and looked out into the darkness of the trees and heavy jungle-like foliage that covered a large portion of this plateau. I let the familiar feeling of power roll through me, allowing my eyes to pull in light through the fog cover from the bright, milky stars and single moon, hanging low in the sky at that time of night.

Adam walked over, holding a glowing bulb on a stem—a makeshift light bulb created from a carnivorous plant he'd ripped the leaves and teeth from. With a tired sigh, he plopped down beside me. He wasn't wearing a shirt, since the night was warm and the bugs had mostly dispersed this late. The intricate design of his tattoo had spread significantly since the last time I'd seen it, having crawled up his arms and started to reach across his upper back.

I wondered how he'd done that to himself. A mirror? "Have you been up all night?" I asked in a low, hoarse voice, and then coughed and cleared my sleep-scratchy throat.

"I've been doing some work on augmenting my program to help get past NIX's security again. It'll be more powerful, more robust. They won't know what hit them. I just wish it wasn't so humid here. If I'd known, I would have brought some cooling gel."

"That's funny, because when we went into the Trial, you were still saying you wouldn't be coming with us. What would you have needed cooling gel for?" I raised my eyebrow, suppressing a smile.

He looked away with an embarrassed half-grin. "I may have been having second thoughts."

"That's great, but you should be sleeping. Your watch was over hours ago."

"I need less sleep now, remember? Unfortunately, the less sleep I get, the less I seem to need. It's gotten to the point where I can barely sleep five hours straight. So I figured I'd be productive. And I don't just mean with the program." He smiled in excitement, a rare expression on him.

"So, what have you been doing?" I raised a curious eyebrow.

"I"—he paused for effect—"have been practicing with a new, absolutely awesome Skill. This is going to blow your mind."

I grinned, unable to help being infected by his enthusiasm. "Show me."

He nodded and pulled out a large berry from his pocket. We'd found them in the poisonous fruit orchard and dubbed them inkberries, both because of the instant-staining, abundant black juice they provided, and their bitter taste. Adam had gathered tons of them. He crushed the berry into the palm of his other hand, letting the dark fluid pool in his palm.

"Wait." I held up a hand. "You're about to show me a new Skill, right?"

He nodded.

"So…I seem to recall you jumping on me when I revealed I'd solved the Oracle's puzzle and had a strange dream that turned out to be prophetic."

He bit his lip, obviously understanding what I was getting at.

"But you got a new Skill," I said. "Something obviously of interest to the rest of the group, and you kept it a secret? When did you get this awesome Skill?" I teased.

"The desert Trial. And before you continue, I didn't tell everyone partially because of all the other important things going on, and partially because I didn't know how to use it properly. It's taken a lot of practice to get to this point. And it's kind of…personal. I haven't shown anyone yet. "

I elbowed his bare arm. "I'm just messing with you. And I'm honored that I get to see it first. So hurry up and show me!"

His fingers tilted toward the stone between us, letting a drop of ink slide down onto it. He frowned fiercely, his eyes locked onto the dark liquid.

It moved, seemingly of its own accord, spreading out into thin lines and blobs on the stone.

My breath caught in surprise as the ink moved eerily, forming the easily recognizable image of a giraffe.

Adam let out the deep breath he'd been holding. "I'm not used to drawing in front of other people."

"Whoa," I whispered, staring down at the cute creature. "You just drew that with your mind. Awesome! Can you do it with your eyes closed? How far away can you be from the drawing for it to work? I'm assuming you could do words, too, and not just images. Adam, that could be *extremely* useful," I rattled, my mind already spinning with possibilities.

Then, he took another deep breath and whispered, "Animus."

The ink climbed out of the rock, the giraffe poking its head and neck out, then lifting itself with a hoof on the stone and pulling the rest of its body upward.

My eyes went as wide as they could go, and I forgot to breathe. I'd seen a lot of fantastical things, but this was new.

The giraffe was a thing of ink and air, black and clear, and three-dimensional. It sniffed curiously, and then started to move around.

Adam blew on it. It flattened its ears under the relatively strong onslaught of wind, and seemed to glare at him fearlessly before running around to hide from the artificial gusts behind my knee.

It peeked its head out from behind my protection, almost tauntingly. After a few more seconds, it disappeared, disintegrating into clearness and falling away on the air. Where it had been, there was no trace of ink, no flat drawing on the ground, no anything.

"Adam, that was amazing!"

He grinned, self-satisfied and smug.

"Can you do other animals? How big can they go? Is that the time limit on them?"

He chuckled at my rapid-fire questions. "I can do anything I can draw, and they have the personality traits I'm imagining when I create them. A real giraffe would probably be scared of me if I leaned over and blew on it. I can go bigger to a certain degree, but it takes a lot of concentration, and the Skill isn't very strong yet. I haven't tried to animate any words, and I can't animate something far away from me. I haven't tried to do it with my eyes closed. And right now, the time limit is twenty-one seconds.

"You know," he continued in a low voice, "I think one of the tailos made it happen. We fought together, and I'd used some of the monster's blood like warpaint in the heat of the moment. I was just angry." He shrugged, looking away in embarrassment. "The tailos seemed interested in it and my tattoos, and when he died, I wiped some on him, too. A useless gesture, you know? I just wanted…to let him know I thought he was a great warrior, and that he wasn't alone. And now I've got this ability to make my drawings come to life for a few seconds." He smiled again, less cocky and more melancholy.

I was about to ask for another demonstration when I heard a snuffling sound from the direction of the jungle. I grew absolutely silent, pushing my slightly enhanced eyes to their limit as I peered into the shadows. The fog was heavy, as it always seemed to be, and it obscured things in the darkness even more.

Adam slipped out his knives, which had gotten a great workout from all the battles we'd been through lately. He, too, scanned the dense foliage.

I saw movement and the tip of a snout and shouted, "Attack!

Incoming from the trees," over my shoulder, not taking my eyes off the tree line.

Behind me, my sleeping teammates jumped awake at the same time monsters poured out of the deeper darkness into the edge of the sky-lit clearing.

By the time we had eradicated them all, the sun had risen, and everything from our camp to the tree line was covered in blood and dead monsters.

I had Sam cook up a haunch of one of the monsters and sample it. If his body gained any Resistance or anti-poisoning Skill upgrade from it, it wasn't safe for us to eat.

His eyes widened in surprise, and he took a bigger bite, juice dripping down his chin.

We all stared at him avidly, our stomachs grumbling jealously and our mouths watering at the smell of cooking meat.

"Well," Jacky snapped, "can we eat?"

He nodded. "It's safe. And it tastes freaking amazing."

A WEEK LATER, we had nearly reached the top of the mountain. We stopped on a small plateau to rest, eat, and prepare before we faced whatever power was waiting for us—a power that was making the hair on the back of my neck stand up just from being close to it.

By my estimate, we'd only been gone from the real world a little over three days. But to us, it felt like we'd been climbing for seventeen days. The air was thinner near the top, and the water ran fresh like nothing I'd ever tasted. The bottled water companies in the real world had been ripping us off. Fresh mountain spring-water, my ass. Everything from the monster meat to the misty-yet-scantily oxygenated air here seemed designed to make us stronger, pushing us to our limits.

We pulled out food from our packs, all stuff that we'd hunted and gathered on the way up, and sat down in a circle. In the center, we laid out the bugs, fruit, and smaller animals to share, and Adam gave everyone's meat a quick zap to warm it up.

Difficult though the ordeals of the climb had been, the team had changed for the better, growing not only in power, but in the sort of deeper confidence and camaraderie that came from making it through hell together.

Sam let out a deep sigh and rolled his shoulders. "I've been wondering, what happened to Bunny? We didn't make plans to save him."

"I did make plans," I said. "By now, Bunny's told NIX some of the things he knew about us, with some key differences between his story and the truth. Keeping Zed a secret, and that we died here, or committed suicide by Trial, to name a few. Most of what he knows doesn't matter for our safety anymore, but they'll think he's on their side, so he'll be safe, and we'll have a man on the inside when we go back."

Sam nodded with a thoughtful frown. "So, what's the plan? For right now, when we reach the top, I mean," he asked me.

Jacky took off her gloves and dug into a comically large drumstick. In her hands, it looked like a barbarian meat club. "We go up there and destroy the enemy, no?"

He rolled his eyes and passed her his flask of water. "That may be your plan, she-hulk, but the rest of us would like to act in a way that's going to get us through the fight alive."

She jostled him with her shoulder and took a swig of the water, no longer so averse to the touch of the boys, when once she could only stand to touch them if she was inflicting violence. "She-hulk? What're you spewing out of your ass? For some reason, it doesn't smell good…" She cracked her knuckles, play-threatening him.

He leaned back so far, pretending to cower in fear, that he fell off the rock he was sitting on.

While Jacky was busy pointing and laughing at him, Adam took a handful of inkberries from his pocket and crushed them in his fist, which was perpetually black-stained lately because of all the practicing he'd been doing.

Well, maybe not so much *practicing* as entertaining the group. Jacky begged for a show almost every time we stopped to rest, never-endingly delighted to see his creations come to life.

The drops of ink running from his fist burst into action almost before they even hit the ground, spreading into a cute, flowery meadow that looked like it came from a children's book. Small animals played among the flowers and peeked out from behind rocks.

Jacky's laughter sobered, and we all focused on it, what we'd been doing forgotten.

The fairytale meadow sprang upward, and then a small form pulled itself over an invisible edge, climbing into the frame. It was a comically muscular creature, broad-footed and club-fisted. Veins popped from its arms, and it had a small hunchback and no visible neck. Atop the body sat Jacky's pretty face, twisted in anger.

"It's a she-hulk," I gasped, struggling to hold back a laugh.

Mini Jacky-hulk roared, shaking every blade of grass and petal in the meadow and causing the animals to freeze. She beat on her chest like a monkey and stomped around. The animals leapt away, keeping a safe distance from her and her crushing hands and feet.

Real Jacky's eyes were wide as she watched her counterpart go uselessly berserk, lumbering around the meadow in circles as the more nimble creatures teased her.

By the time Adam's Animus Skill wore off, his shoulders were shaking, and the rest of us were gasping on the ground, unable to breathe past our hilarity.

"That…is not…me!" Jacky finally got out, suppressing a smile of her own.

I wiped the tears of laughter from my eyes. "Of course not," I said. "Those rabbits *never* would have escaped you!" I fell back into laughter as she scowled at me.

Once we had all calmed down a bit, we finished our quick meal, continuing to joke amongst ourselves. I'd grown closer to the team than ever. Though I wished I could say I wasn't so weak, I feared for what might become of them if my plan didn't work.

Whatever awaited us on the mountaintop was powerful. Likely the most powerful thing we'd ever encountered.

When I was ready, I took a few deep breaths, focusing on my heartbeat, and slipped into the hyper-aware state that had once been so difficult to achieve. I'd been practicing, sometimes even as we climbed the mountainside. It was getting easier and easier, as though perhaps solving the ring had given my ability a boost, but I still hadn't been able to reach out to that other presence again. It worried me a bit, though I wasn't quite sure why. Maybe because I didn't like the unknown, especially when it could be important to my survival.

When I threw my senses out, I was almost blinded by an aura that assaulted every sensory channel. After completing the ring puzzle, the smallest gift from the Oracle, I'd gained a vague perception of something new, an energy that couldn't be seen with the naked eye but that flowed through all of my team, brightening when we used our Skills. But here, that was overwhelmed by power seeping from the rocks beneath, thrumming in the air we breathed, and sliding through the water around us. But overpowering all of that was a large mass above us.

It was unmoving, planted in the center of the caldera we'd have to descend into once we reached the lip at the top. It had roots longer and thicker than I could see, and all around it were smaller points of strength.

I gathered my seeking senses back into my body and opened my eyes.

The others were all watching me intently, the layer of mirth wiped away as they waited for news of the coming danger.

"Well, that vision was right. Whatever's at the top, it's powerful. Very, very powerful."

"Powerful enough to defeat NIX?" Jacky asked.

"If it could be used as a weapon, I don't see how it could fail to defeat them."

"But that's just it," Adam said. "What *is* it? How do we know if it's going to be useful for us? Or even something we can take back?"

"I'm…not sure," I said. "It's so strong, it sort of overwhelmed my senses. I could only get a vague idea of where it is, I couldn't tell what it is."

"How do you know this is safe, Eve? I mean, some Trial creature gives you something that makes you have visions of the future, but not before trying to *kill* you. What if this is just its way of finishing the job?" Adam asked, ever the pessimist.

Sam looked between Adam and me, taking deep, slow breaths to keep himself calm despite Adam's words.

"Adam, something's going on that we don't understand here. That Trial monster you're talking about was…intelligent. It talked to me. Yeah, it tried to kill me, but it was just a test. When I proved myself to it, it gave me its blessing and wished me well. And what about the tailos? They were telepathic, sentient beings!" I patted the side pouch of my pack, where the tailos egg was nestled. I had brought syringes in my pack and fed it frequently. "You said yourself you think one gave you the Animus Skill. Consider the possibility that not everything here wants to kill us indiscriminately."

He let out a sigh. "Fine. We're already here, anyway. If you think it might be the answer, I'll follow you," he said, but then he muttered something under his breath that sounded suspiciously like, "not *everything* may want to kill us, but ninety-nine percent of everything sure as hell does."

Chapter 33

Yet from those flames
No light, but rather darkness visible.
— John Milton

I CROUCHED DOWN on the edge and looked over into the steep, huge bowl cut out of the top of the mountain. Clear blue water bubbled and steamed like a witch's cauldron. It spewed up from nowhere and spilled out through cracks in the rocks, no doubt creating the numerous beautiful waterfalls that tumbled down the precipitous cliffsides before feeding into the lake below. Submerged beneath the water, orange and red spots glowed hot and caused the water to bubble more furiously around them. Large, flat stones broke up the surface of the whole caldera. We'd have to cross on those to get to the middle.

I still couldn't figure out what was in the center, though I was squinting right at it. Steam rose from the water there, with huge wafting clouds making a shrouding column so thick I couldn't see through it. "That's where we need to go," I pointed. "But I felt other points of power, too. There might be monsters lying in wait. Or traps of another kind." I fed my armored vest a few extra drops of blood to make sure it was ready, though I kept it unfurled all the time at that point.

After a few minutes to psyche ourselves up, stretch muscles, and sharpen knives, we left our packs at the top and started the descent, jumping from ledge to ledge along the inside wall. Before coming to that Trial, I may not have been able to make those jumps, but I'd grown stronger.

When we reached the bottom, gathering on one of the flat stones, the water around us started to splash as if it noticed our presence.

"That's disturbing," Sam said, stepping away from the edge of our platform.

We jumped forward, moving from stone to stone toward the tower of steam in the center of the caldera. With each step, the water leaped and popped more frantically, and the heat grew so oppressive that even the stones beneath my bare feet burned.

Suddenly, one of the red-orange spots below us shot up from the depths. It burst out, steaming with the sound a drop of water makes in a too-hot pan.

The first thing that came to my mind was that it was a rock and lava golem. It was humanoid, with a featureless lump for a head, and limbs of rock held together by flowing lava. The second thing that came to my mind was that it was damn scary.

Jacky was closest to where it appeared, and it caught her pant leg with a swipe of its rocky hand. She kicked it in the head hard enough to make the stone crumble, and it fell away from her into the water, leaving a smoking hole in the fabric of her pants.

Almost immediately, it recovered and shot to the surface again, this time climbing onto the rocky platform.

She carefully avoided the lava-flowing parts of it as she aimed crushing blows at its rocky limbs and head. One solid roundhouse kick to the abdomen cracked through its chest, and the thing collapsed into a steaming pile of rock and quickly cooling lava.

"Go for the chest!" she shouted.

The water started to boil and jump even stronger all around us, and more lava golems shot upward. I bit my lip nervously at the number, but noticed that there were no more red lights shining up from the bottom of the water, so at least there wouldn't be more than one wave of the creatures.

We started to attack, making surprisingly short work of them. We'd gotten stronger. A lot stronger. I was grinning cockily when the crushing sound of a lot of water crashing down blew past us, and a huge wave rolled out of the bottom of the column of steam, rushing out in all directions. "Damn," I said, my grin erasing itself instantly.

There was nowhere to run, nothing to hold on to except the rocks beneath our feet.

"Jump when it reaches you!" I called out as I followed my own advice. I came back down into shallower rushing water, but the depth and strength of the tail end was still enough to knock me off my feet, and it was scalding hot.

I grabbed onto the edge of the platform and managed to pull myself back up after a few moments of spluttering. As I tried to look around to check on the others, something grabbed my foot. I had less than a second for the alarm to sound in my mind before the clear, watery fist yanked me off the edge and down into the water.

I kicked and struggled to swim away, but my efforts had no effect. When I looked down, I saw nothing, but I could still feel the fist around my ankle.

It pulled harder, dragging me down fast and far enough that the pressure of the boiling water began to feel uncomfortably strong. Finally, it stopped pulling and released my ankle, but before I could swim away, something wrapped around my torso and pressed against my face, pinning my arms to my sides and pushing against my nose and mouth, trying to force the burning water into my lungs.

I bucked and wriggled, but the liquid creature only swirled around me more strongly, completely dominant against my clumsy underwater maneuverings. Bug-eyed, I felt the air being squeezed out of me and knew the burning panic of a person who's about to drown.

Then Jacky shot by like a rocket, ripping my assailant away and setting me free.

I swam toward the surface and sucked in a breath of air along with a little water. I choked and started to cough, but my head cleared and I was able to swim to another of the platforms. I spent a few seconds clearing my lungs and letting the dizzying heat of my skin cool, careful to keep away from the edge of the platform.

When I stood and peered into the water's depths, I saw Jacky shooting around like a superhero, decimating vague watery outlines left and right. She would burst out for a breath of air every minute or so, then dive back in.

Above, Adam was still dealing with the remaining rock and lava golems. Sam fought by his side with his crowbar.

A roaring crackle sounded from the direction of the column of steam, and out of its center burst a ring of that strange light-and-dark fire. The fire separated, and pieces of it formed into bird-like shapes and flew outward in all directions. They eyed us for a few moments, circling overhead, and then one made a dive for me.

If not for Sam's screamed, "Don't touch it!" I would have counterattacked with a rake of my claws or a kick as it went by. I skipped out of the way instead, teetering on the edge of my platform for a second.

The water below me bubbled and burst upward in a vague humanoid shape, arms reaching for me.

Jacky shot out of the water, spearing through its chest with a single punch before crushing a fistful of harder clear liquid within her fist. "Gravity Skill comes in handy," she gasped. "I can go side to side, if I just pretend that way is down. I got the water. You can handle these, no?"

I nodded. "Thanks for the save. We've got this."

She took another deep breath of air and shot downward, feet first.

I moved to Sam and Adam, jumping along the stone platforms and avoiding the swooping fire birds. "What's wrong, Sam?"

"Anything they touch gets…unmade." He held up his crowbar, which was missing one end.

"How the hell are we supposed to stop them, then?" I moved my eyes to the sky, scanning for signs of an attack, which would be especially dangerous since all three of us were together.

Adam lifted his hand and shot a bolt of electricity at one flying dangerously close to us.

It jerked at the hit, then seemed to burn out of control and devour its own body. A few chunks of flame hit the water and sank, still burning.

"I guess that's how," Adam said. "I hope I've got enough power for this." He slipped a cylindrical energy cartridge from his pocket. "I've been saving this for an emergency. I think this qualifies."

He lifted his free hand. Another bolt shot from his fingertips, crackling outward through the damp air and hitting two targets at once.

"You handle them," I said to Adam. "Sam, you and I are going to go take care of the source of our problem." I pointed toward the billowing column.

He stifled a groan and adjusted his grip on his shortened crowbar. "Lead the way."

My chest had a strange tightness in it, because something big was moving within the mist and steam of the column, and I could feel it in the air. As we moved closer, the humidity made it hard to breathe, and I started to cough. If we stayed too long, I worried we might be steam-cooked, like my mom used to do with vegetables and chicken.

But then a huge arm made of stone and water appeared, clearing a swath of steam. Another gargantuan arm swung, wider this time, and almost hit me as it passed. More of the obscuring mist cleared, revealing the colossal torso of a woman literally rooted to the mountain. She had distinct features cut into the stone of her face, and more graceful arms and torso than the smaller golems.

Bright, clear water ran over her body to connect her limbs and fill the large cavity in the center of her chest. It seemed to completely defy gravity —and maybe a few other rules of physics, too. Right where her heart might be if she were human floated a small object, suspended in the glimmering water. Fire burned in lines around her base, and the stone near it ran a bright liquid orange.

She saw us then, and sound came out of her with the slow booming of an avalanche. "Bugs, you dare to come before me? I am not so weakened as to fall," she said. Then she brought down her palm in a flat arc to smash us as if we were insects.

I PUSHED Sam into the lake and jumped onto a platform just far enough away to avoid her hand. The force of her slap caused the water all around to jump higher than my head. It reminded me of a child playing in the bath, slapping the water's surface and making it splash. "Except you're not that cute," I grunted.

Sam rose pink-skinned from the water, and I grabbed the end of his crowbar and helped him back onto the platform.

"Really? Push me into the water?" he gasped, dripping.

"I made sure you didn't get hit."

"Well, couldn't you have just yelled, 'Run,' or 'Jump,' instead?"

"What if you hadn't reacted in time?" I slapped him on the back with a wet squishing sound. "This way I was sure. The chest seems to be the weak spot. I'm going to make a run for it."

A few running leaps brought me to a platform close to her base, which looked like hips growing into the mountain's core. Another leap brought me to her waist, where I used the claws on my hands and feet to scurry up the rock of her body like a spider.

I'd just reached the chest and was extending a clawed hand towards the water-filled chamber that held her "heart" when she brushed me off with a bone crushing slap. I went flying, my whole right side feeling as if I'd slammed hard into a stone wall, which I guess technically I had.

I flew like a skipping stone toward one of the platforms. Thankfully, my Skills let me twist around to land on all fours, and I dug all my claws into the stone, gouging strips out of it. I still had enough momentum to slide off the edge into the scalding water, and had to scramble back out of it, gasping in shock at the temperature. No wonder Sam had been perturbed. A few minutes in there and he'd have been cooked like a lobster.

Sam ran around her base in a circle, whacking the stone with his crowbar. It barely even chipped her, so he tossed it away, then positioned himself behind her and put a hand on her in an attempt to use his Skill.

The mountain-slash-woman scowled in frustration as she unhinged her water-jointed arms and twisted them backward, over her head.

Sam stepped away from her. A chunk of her base, crystallized and sparkly, crumbled away with him. He ducked her swing and made it a safe distance away from her on the other side. To some punch-drunk, tired part of my brain, it looked like we were playing a doomed-to-fail game of monkey in the middle.

But then she roared, and out of her burst another wave and ring of fire. Almost immediately, the water golems popped out of the water, sliding around half submerged on snake-like tails of water, and the fire creatures looked bigger and fiercer.

"We have to stop her," I called across the caldera to Sam.

The veil of mist had cleared, and I saw that the other two were still busy fighting their respective golems. It was just us, and we didn't have much time before she multiplied again and the number of golems became insurmountable.

"I won't lose here," I whispered to myself, and then I flexed my claws and sprang forward to attack the thing again. From the other direction, Sam did the same. This time, I crawled up to her shoulder to hack and gouge at the joint, trying to break off her arm and reduce her offensive capabilities.

Any piece of her rock I broke loose was immediately replaced with the glass-clear water, and I didn't know if my actions made a difference.

Once again, I saw her other hand racing toward me, but this time I jumped out of the way, landing on her collarbone at the base of her neck. I thought I was safe, and so was caught by surprise when the shock of her hand's impact with her shoulder shook her whole body like a large earthquake, sending me falling down her chest. I tried to claw my way to a stop, but her other arm came around and smashed into me again.

She was moving faster than she had before, almost as if she were waking up, or maybe warming up, judging by the heat radiating from those huge stone fingers when they smashed into my ribs and arm.

This time, I landed in the water, shooting a good few meters into it before slowing and starting to pull my way back to the surface.

When I reached it, barely escaping a water golem, I climbed onto a steaming platform and began to cough and shudder as my head swam from the heat and lack of oxygen combined.

I looked up just in time to see a huge stone hand throw Sam spinning end over end across the caldera like a skipping stone. He looked like a rag doll when he hit the water bouncing. He was stopped by a firm bodily meeting with the far wall, where his unmoving form sank into the water. I flinched at the sight, hoping against hope that Sam was all right. I wasn't sure how he could be, though. Not after being thrown like that. He was our healer, and without him, the aftermath of this fight didn't look so good.

I sent a Window to Jacky to help Sam, but in my state of distraction, I didn't notice the huge hand rushing down toward me, the air swirling noisily with the force of its movement, until it was far too late. I tried to roll away, back into the water, but knew that I wasn't going to make it. The shadow from above was already darkening the stone. There was no way.

But then Adam's voice was shouting, "Animus!" above me, and there was a huge gust of wind as something collided with enough force to create a shockwave.

I looked up and saw that the beautiful tattoos from his arms and shoulders, which he'd so painstakingly and lovingly grown, were holding both her arms in place. They had sprung from his flesh, huge and thick, and were rooting him to the ground, and her to him, in unmovable knots.

She brought her full weight to bear, trying to crush him into the platform along with me, even as he held her still. The sound of stone grinding on stone filled the air.

He looked over his shoulder to me, wet dripping hair hanging over his face. "Move!" he screamed, his voice raw and shaking.

I sprang to my feet and started running as fast as I could, digging my toe claws into the stone for more grip.

Adam's Animus Skill must have gotten stronger, but I knew I didn't have much time until that tattoo disintegrated into the air, and she flattened him, crushing his bones and internal organs beyond repair.

This was the perfect chance, maybe the only chance, and I needed to stop her immediately, before it was too late and he died.

I sprang up, clawing frantically at her chest.

She felt me moving, I know, and tried to pull back to brush me off or crush me again, but Adam held her in place even as I felt her stones tremble under me in the effort to pull back. His control of her must have been difficult, because I heard another hoarse scream from him.

But she didn't move, and I reached her chest cavity and plunged myself into it with all the force I could muster. I shot through the water, grabbed the black, blob-like heart floating in it, and held it to my chest with all my might. I burst out the other side and was falling, falling, and then crashing hard into a platform.

I looked up and saw that she had started to tip backward, the direction she must have been pulling when Adam's tattoo disappeared.

That was wonderful, because she wouldn't crush him out of sheer momentum now. It was also horrible, because she would crush me instead if I couldn't get out of the way.

So I ran, leaping from stone to stone like a football player hurdling opponents, her heart tucked tightly to my chest. When the shadow from her back started to grow dark around me, I jumped into the water, slicing downward like an arrow.

The force of her impact still shook me hard enough I thought I might lose the air I held in my lungs, but I was safe and able to swim under her and out to the surface.

—I made it. Make sure Adam and Sam are okay.—
-Eve-

I knew what it must have looked like when the creature fell onto the spot where I'd been, and I didn't want any of the team to worry about me. The others were the main priority.

I spent a little while just breathing and cooling down, and then held up the heart I'd taken from her chest cavity.

It was a black, shimmering mass, sort of like what the Seeds looked

like except for the color, and about the size of a basketball. It flowed around my hand, moving like the water of the creature's body, and seemed to notice my inspection because it started to ripple.

"Oh, wow," I whispered. "Treasure. I guess the Oracle was looking out for me after all."

I STOOD up and started to limp across the basin of that huge bowl cut into the top of the mountain, skirting the fallen creature. The water had succumbed to the force of gravity and flowed away from the body, so it was only a few ginormous rocks lying still on the ground, but they were still somewhat terrifying

The substance around my hand, the woman's heart, was so dark that my eyes seemed to fall into it, and yet it shimmered light back toward me. As it flowed and rippled around my hand, having attached itself to my fist, I couldn't help but think it both the most beautiful and terrifying thing I'd ever seen. Something about it gave off the feeling of a writhing sea of darkness, despite the points of light and energy that swarmed through it.

Jacky had helped Adam to a seat on the ground next to Sam's motionless body. My two conscious teammates drew back from the substance on my fist as soon as they noticed it, and then leaned in to look more closely at it for a few seconds. This didn't seem to alleviate their hesitation toward it at all.

Jacky was pale, wet, and shivering despite the heat radiating from her surroundings.

"Is he…okay?" I asked, looking at Sam.

She pursed her lips. "He's alive. For now. I dunno what to do for him. I really hope he can heal himself."

"Yeah. That's probably why he's sleeping. He needs to focus all his strength on healing himself." I laid my free hand on her shoulder. "You sit down. The fight's over. You did good."

She stared at me with an expression I couldn't decipher for a second, but eventually gave me a half-smile. "Thank you."

Adam waved at me from his seat on the ground, looking pale. "I'm fine, too. Just a little worn out from saving you from a huge crazy rock monster. Who also happened to birth little elemental minions every other minute. No biggie. Thanks for asking." His eyes were red and bloodshot, having strained so hard the tiny vessels broke under the pressure, and his voice was hoarse from screaming.

I smiled. "What, you mean that was hard for you? I think you should be asking me if *I'm* okay. I just defeated the monster that gave you so much trouble."

He chuckled, and then started to cough. "So glad you made it in time, though. Otherwise I'd be a pancake."

"But…what about your tattoos? I know how long you must have spent on them, how much effort. They're gone."

He held up his newly bare arms and looked them up and down. "It was pretty bad-ass that I did that, huh?" He pulled his knees to his chest and coughed again. "I'll draw another one. Even cooler this time."

I bit the inside of my lip and nodded, then went to grab the packs from the rim of the caldera. I awkwardly fumbled the bedrolls and blankets from within the packs with the hand not covered in goo, and then helped get camp set up in a smaller niche in the rock side, being careful not to jostle Sam when we moved him. I forced everyone to eat something, including doing my best to feed Sam some broth made from meat and bone juices. It was kind of hard with only one hand free of the black substance, but the others were in no condition to help me. They'd really given their all in the fight. I thought I might have a couple broken ribs, and I'd definitely have full-body bruising from being swatted and tossed around, but I could still function.

When everything was as settled as I could get it, I looked over Sam's sleeping body for obvious injuries. They were everywhere, and told me nothing. So I sat down next to him and closed my eyes, laying my hands lightly on his body like he did whenever he was going to heal someone.

"No shit," Jacky said. "Can you do that? Heal him like he does us?"

I opened one eye. How awesome did this girl think I was? "I'm not a healer. But I might be able to tell if there's anything wrong inside."

"Oh." She drew back and nodded, wrapping her blanket tightly around her shoulders.

I slipped into the hyper-aware state with a bit of a struggle. I was so tired, and my body hurt. It was hard. My mind struggled to focus so much Perception energy in one small place, but I was able to get a vague idea of his injuries. "He's healing himself," I said, opening my eyes and drawing my hands back. "It looks pretty bad in there, but I think—I *hope*—he can handle it. I don't know what to do to help him."

Jacky rested her forehead on her knees. "He better make it. He…is such a trier. He tries harder than anyone I've ever met. Cares so much."

"He doesn't deserve to die," Adam said.

I sighed, and then gave myself a mental slap on the cheeks. Sighing didn't fix anything. I looked at the mass of strange goop still attached to my right hand. It took power to fix things, to change them. *Real* power. And I had an idea. "Guys, I want you all to stay tucked away in here, hidden. I'm going to do something potentially very stupid, and I'd like you all at a safe distance when I do."

Despite looking altogether like crap, half flushed and half pale, with his wet hair plastered to his head and face in a way that made him look like a twice-drowned dog, Adam forced himself to his feet. "You need backup if you're doing something stupid."

"You're in no shape to be my backup," I said gently, putting a hand on his shoulder to push him back down.

"True! Better yet, how about you just don't do anything stupid? That would be awesome." He read my expression and muttered, "Guess that would be too much to ask for."

I turned away, looking back toward the still form lying in the caldera's center, and all around at the water that had ceased to flow. "I'm either crazy, or I'm a freaking lionhearted genius," I said to myself. I moved towards the she-mountain corpse. "Why not both?"

Chapter 34

...a dark
Illimitable ocean, without bound,
Without dimension; where length, breadth, and height,
And time, and place are lost.
— John Milton

I APPROACHED the stone chest of the fallen boulders and stopped at the now empty cavity within it. With my free left hand, I reached for the substance on my right. It reached out part of itself as if to meet my hand, which gave me pause. I made a pinching motion in the air, and the smaller glob formed into a separate mass, connected to the whole of itself with only a thin string. When I pulled on this smaller portion, it separated easily, and then started to flow around my left hand.

I hesitated, then put some of the baseball-sized globe on my left hand back into the bigger mass surrounding my right. I then dropped my left hand into the empty air of the chest cavity and shook a bit, making it clear that I wanted the substance to detach and thinking hard about it doing so.

It slipped off the end of my fingers and hung in the air. The shallow water beneath the cavity began to flow upward to it, surrounding the small ball with an ever-thickening layer of clear water.

"I'm giving you back some of your heart," I said. "Be good and don't attack me when you wake up."

Once the chest cavity was filled, the she-mountain stirred, seeming to take a deep breath, though I doubted whether a rock could even need to breathe.

I chose that time to retreat to a suitably safe distance, where I sat down to wait for enough water to gather in and around the creature that it could move once again, hoping desperately that I hadn't just done the stupidest thing since my birth.

Besides stopping to help that traitorous guy who allowed NIX to give me the Seed in the first place, of course.

The rock-and-water woman sat up and looked around in bewilderment, then down at me, sitting cross-legged on the stone below her with the majority of her heart flowing happily around my right hand. "You…" Her voice was weaker than before, but still a crashing rumble.

"Hi," I said.

"You have restored my physical form?"

I swallowed down the lump in my throat and tried to sound confident. "I've got a few questions. I hope you can be friendly, otherwise I'll have to take it back."

She threw her head back and her chest shook up and down with a roaring, breaking, booming sound.

It made me tense up for a moment before I realized it was a laugh. Then I had to wonder if her being amused at my threat was really a good thing.

She lowered her gaze to me. "Confident, for such a puny little thing. All right. I have decided not to kill you. You have gained my interest. Who are you?"

"My name is Eve. Who are you?" I decided I didn't need to remind her again that we'd just beaten her. I didn't know that we could do it again, so I didn't want to start another fight.

"I am the Goddess. The one that came before and was formed."

"I don't understand. What does that mean?"

"I am the formless mass, the void." She tilted her head, as if I should get what she meant.

I shook my head. "Also, you're a volcano." Time for another line of questioning.

"I have taken many forms, and I carry many now," she boomed. "This form is one of my branches, constrained to a physical presence. It pleases me, for now, though the order of it changes my power, as it must channel through those constraints. Still, it allows me to easily cleanse some of the land."

"Cleanse it from what?"

"The sickness that is not my child. The abhorrent."

Yeah. Still not understanding. "What is this place?" I gestured around me. "I mean, obviously this is a mountain. But the whole thing? What is this planet?"

"The small ones call it Estreyer. Or they did, the last time I was among them."

"So it's not Earth, then." I'd suspected. Two moons in the sky *was* kind of a dead giveaway.

"There is earth." She nodded. "Also sky and water and wood and much else."

"Right…" Was this the language barrier? I thought I could understand her words, the way you know what someone's saying in a dream by instinct even when they're making an unintelligible jumble of it, but something seemed to be getting lost in translation. "Okay, then. Are there other living beings, ones like me?"

"Yes, though they disappear along with the rest."

Perhaps she meant they disappeared when they teleported back to the real world. "Have you heard of NIX?"

"The night was born of me." She made a fist at my confused look. "You do not understand, even though you are the one asking me. And your deficient communication method confuses me, as well. What use have I for speech? Be done with your questions, tiny one, for I grow impatient with this."

"Do you know what the Trials are?" I tried.

"Your kind supplicates before us in hopes of gaining power. Most fail. Many die. You are the first to gain my interest in a long time. To come after me when I am weakened, you are bold."

"This power you speak of, it's the Seeds, right? I've never seen this black type before, but I've got something similar." I pulled out a Seed I'd reserved for an emergency and showed her.

She drew backward and sniffed in pointed offense, hard enough to make my hair flutter around my face. "My power is nothing like that flesh-power. Do you know nothing? Why is one so ignorant even here!?" Heat started to radiate from her, and the water swirled faster along her body.

"I meant no offense. I just don't understand the ways of this world, or what's happening to me."

She settled as fast as she'd grown angry, giving me a wry smile. "Well, I cannot expect a head as small as yours to understand all that I do. The thing you hold, it is from a mixture of lower powers, focused on the physical. It is not a higher power, like me."

"A higher power…like this?" I held up my hand, where the dark substance swirled excitedly.

"You hold a part of my strength, condensed. Holding it here within me"—she pointed to her chest"—is what allows me to maintain the physical form you see before you. It is not a power of the flesh."

"What would happen if I…consumed it?"

"You seek to gain my patronage and ascend?"

"I don't know what that means," I admitted. "There are some people I need to fight back against, and I have to be strong. I don't know if you know who the Oracle is, but she gave me a gift, and the gift gave me a vision of this place. I think it might have been leading me to you."

"The Oracle? Hmm…perhaps…" she trailed off. "If you take that, it will likely kill you. At best it will change you. You have given power to your body. My power will do that, too, but it will also change the void of you, your center…ah, I have not the words for it. But you will probably die instead."

"And if I don't die?" I stared at the huge Seed, something in my abdomen tightening up.

"You will surely die. My heart is too much for a puny bug like you, amusing though you may be."

"What if I only took a little?"

She laughed again. "So greedy! I like it. Perhaps your body could contain a small amount. But, as with all power, it likes to grow, and mine especially. Perhaps someday it would rip you apart."

I continued to stare at its shimmering blackness, reflecting the yellowing light of the setting sun. "How soon would it be?"

"Eventually," she answered unhelpfully. "You would trade time for power?"

"Without power, I have no time, and neither do those who I care for. How much Seed can I take?"

"Not much. You are small."

I nodded and sent a Window to the others.

—I'm going to take a bit of a risk, now. If I die, please head back on your own. If you ask her nicely, the mountain might be willing to give you a hand getting out of here.—
-Eve-

I ignored the Windows and shouts that came back at me. A couple motions and the thought of what I wanted made the black goop form a normal Seed-sized ball, which I popped off. I held it in my hand as it flattened itself to me and started swirling in little tendrils between my fingers.

Then I opened my mouth and let it run inside and down my throat. It tasted like…something beyond the sensory range of my tongue.

When it hit my stomach, it started to spread outward from that pit inside me.

There was pain, and more pain, and then the expanse.

I KNEW FORMLESSNESS AND CHANGE, as the shore knows the endless ocean. I slipped in and out of fevered dreams my brain couldn't comprehend when it knew what I was, but fell into wholeheartedly when the burning chaos gained the upper hand. My body's fight was an ebb and flow of power as it struggled to maintain itself against the Seed, which tried to make me one with the sea.

I was not myself for a while, and then I started to draw back, folding and squishing in on my body in an agony of pain. The endless ocean that I'd been part of slipped away from me, but I was left with a portion of it folded in the back of my mind.

When I woke, it was full night, and I did not know where I was, or who I was. This did not bother me until my mind started to gather together, and I realized that it should. Then I was frightened, and scrambled to regain my memories and control of my body.

Then I saw the stars shining bright and as thick as if a child had dumped out a bucket of glitter on the canvas of the sky, and it snapped together.

"So, you are awake."

The sound blew through me, shaking me even from the inside. It hurt, as if I was one big bruise.

"Yes." My voice felt strange, but I couldn't remember why.

"I am glad. Though it is curious that I should be worried for one so small and fleeting."

The rest of the black Seed was gone from my right hand, once again floating within her chest. I probably should have been at least slightly worried by that, but the notion never crossed my mind. "I feel strange."

"Of course. You are different than you were before."

That made perfect sense to me, vague as it was. "I lived. Am I powerful now?"

"What is your name?"

"Eve. Eve Redding. Don't tell me you forgot so easily."

She leaned forward and touched my chest with the tip of her huge stone finger. "You are my progeny. I welcome you to the existence of power, child god Eve-Redding. May you go without chief or ruler, free and wild."

I could hear in the way she said it that she'd missed the concept of a first and last name, but that was fine. "May the waters without light flow unfettered," I replied, the words coming unbidden from that space in the back of my mind. It seemed like a good idea to respond in turn to her formal blessing.

She smiled and let out a deep humming sound, which was slightly more pleasant and easy on the ears than her usual repertoire of avalanches, exploding bombs, and earthquakes. "I go by many names, and my real name cannot be spoken with a tongue or heard with ears. But in this form, you may call me Behelaino. Now go to your subjects. They have been mewling for you, and step on my patience. In the morning, you will begin your training."

"Training?" My ears perked up.

"Yes. You must train your puny body to contain and channel the drop of Khaos, if you are to live. Now, go." She pronounced the "K" and "H" separately, but I was pretty sure I understood what she meant.

Chaos? Is that what I'd swallowed? When she put it like that, it didn't sound so good. Right dangerous, in fact.

I TURNED AWAY from Behelaino to go check on the others and was surprised by a Window popping up. Blaine and Adam had done some complicated things with "double encryption and spiked firewalls" that I didn't understand, but which allowed the VR chips to keep working, and the team to use them amongst each other, but blocked NIX from any access. Not that they would have been able to reach us here in the Trial world. Estreyer, I reminded myself.

YOU HAVE GAINED THE SKILL "—NAME UNKNOWN—"
WOULD YOU LIKE TO NAME THIS SKILL?
YES / NO

I chose "Yes," and named the Skill "Chaos."

SKILL "CHAOS" HAS UNKNOWN CLASS.
WOULD YOU LIKE TO ASSIGN A CLASS?

On a whim, I dubbed it "Godling" Class. Then I pulled up my Attribute Window, out of curiosity. I knew I'd been getting a lot of spontaneous level ups lately, but I hadn't checked my stats.

PLAYER NAME: EVE REDDING
TITLE: TEAM LEADER(3)
CHARACTERISTIC SKILL: SPIRIT OF THE HUNTRESS,
TUMBLING FEATHER
LEVEL: 38 UNPLANTED SEEDS: 2
SKILLS: COMMAND, CHAOS

STRENGTH: 13
LIFE: 20
AGILITY: 19
GRACE: 17
INTELLIGENCE: 16
FOCUS: 15
BEAUTY: 10
PHYSIQUE: 11
MANUAL DEXTERITY: 9
MENTAL ACUITY: 18
RESILIENCE: 12
STAMINA: 18
PERCEPTION: 17

MY ATTRIBUTE LEVELS were much higher than the level I held might suggest due to all the hard work my team and I had been putting in. But it still wasn't enough. Hopefully the new Skill would be helpful. "Display Skill Window," I murmured.

CHARACTERISTIC SKILLS
TUMBLING FEATHER (KINETIC CLASS): INCREASES GRACE AND AGILITY. IMPROVED SENSE OF BALANCE AND MOTION. SKILL EFFECTS WILL EXPAND AND STRENGTHEN WITH PLAYER IMPROVEMENT.

SPIRIT OF THE HUNTRESS (SPIRIT CLASS): INCREASED GRACE, AGILITY, PERCEPTION, FOCUS, PHYSIQUE, AND STAMINA. NAILS EXTEND AND SHARPEN ON COMMAND. GREATER CHANCE TO LAND ON FEET AFTER A FALL. AGGRESSIVE TENDENCIES INCREASE. SKILL EFFECTS WILL EXPAND AND STRENGTHEN WITH PLAYER IMPROVEMENT.
SKILLS
COMMAND (MUNDANE CLASS): ALLOWS LEADER ACCESS TO THE TEAM MANAGEMENT WINDOW. LEADER CAN COMMUNICATE WITH TEAM MEMBERS THROUGH GAME WINDOWS, SEE LOCATION OF TEAM MEMBERS ON TEAM MANAGEMENT MAP, AND IS ABLE TO ACCESS BASIC GAME INFORMATION OF TEAM MEMBERS. MAY ADD ADDITIONAL TEAM MEMBERS AT HIGHER LEVELS OF COMMAND.

CHAOS (GODLING CLASS): UNKNOWN—PLAYER USE DATA WILL BE GATHERED TO SUPPLEMENT LACK OF INFORMATION.

"OH, *THAT'S* USEFUL." I shook my head and continued on, slowly. My team was already out and waiting beside the small niche where I'd left them. There'd be no sleeping with Behelaino's voice assaulting their eardrums.

Sam stood on his own two feet, though a bit the worse for wear.

Adam was the first to hug me, wrapping his arms around me so tightly I literally felt my painful ribs creak, despite my body's Seed-enhanced fortitude. He smelled like sweat. Hell, we all probably did at this point. "I'm really glad you're okay." But his relief quickly turned to outrage. "How could you do something so stupid!"

I drew back. "It wasn't stupid. It worked. Which means it was genius! I took a new type of Seed from her, the thing that was powering her physical body. I'm probably going to be strong enough now to take on NIX. We got what we came here for, essentially." I turned to the others. "It worked."

"Probably? Is that worth endangering your life, and ours too, for that matter? What if it hadn't worked?"

"It did work. And yes, it is worth it. We don't have a lot of options, Adam." I forced my surprisingly instantaneous anger back. "That's why we're here in the first place. We grow strong or we die. When you think about it like that, I made a pretty simple decision."

He took a deep breath and let it out again. "You're right. I was just… tense." He stepped back and moved to the little niche in the rock wall, setting out food.

Jacky's grin was huge as she moved to hug me next.

I held up a hand. "Don't crush me, okay? I'm feeling a little tender."

She laughed and crushed me anyway. "You're awake. I didn't know when you'd get up, and that crazy creature wouldn't let us go to you! I was getting ready to go over there and kick its ass again. But now you're here, so you spared me the trouble." Despite her bravado, the slight tremble in her voice let me know how worried she'd been.

I refused to feel bad, though. I'd done what needed to be done, and if feelings would be the sacrifice for power, so be it.

Sam threw his arm around me and walked with me toward the small camp area. "They told me what happened when I woke up. I can't believe you did something so crazy. Eve," he murmured, "you can't go dying on us. We need you. The last three days…it hasn't been fun."

"Three days?" I gasped. "Wow. No wonder you guys were so worried. But I was just sleeping it off. I'm fine, and believe me, I'm not going to give up my hold on life voluntarily."

Only when we sat down to eat from a smorgasbord of strange foods, which apparently Behelaino had supplied them with while they waited, did I realize how absolutely starving I was.

I gorged myself until my stomach was literally distended, and then had just a little bit more.

Adam brought out the tailos egg. "Figured you might want to see to this thing." He placed it tenderly in my lap. "It's been making sounds for the last couple days. I think it might be close to hatching."

I laid my ear on the dark, pocked surface. "Or maybe it's just hungry. Unless one of you fed it, it hasn't eaten in a couple days." I fumbled in my pack for one of the syringes Blaine had given me and quickly drew some blood from my arm.

The egg sucked up the blood I was squirting into the pockmarks, but then it started squeaking even louder. After a few minutes, the baby tailos moved inside its egg with enough force to rock back and forth in my lap.

The other three gathered around, watching with avid curiosity.

When the first crack appeared in the surface, Adam gave a hiss and bit down on a knuckle, maybe the most excited I'd ever seen him. "It's hatching. I told you, it's hatching!" He nudged Sam and Jacky, as if to make sure they knew even though they were watching just as wide-eyed as him.

The first piece of shell broke off, clattering to the ground. After that, the rest was short work.

A creature small enough to be cradled in my hands struggled out into my lap, pieces of shell sticking to its back. It let out a croak, coughed, and then let out louder, scratchy mewl.

"A baby tailos," I whispered in awe.

It had the body of a baby wildcat, but with fragile little wings covered in matted fuzz attached to its back.

It mewled again, and Adam reached out to clean the pieces of shell off its sticky body.

It snapped at his fingers with sharp teeth and made a hilariously pitiful attempt at a growl.

Adam gripped his bleeding finger, which Sam reached over to heal without conscious thought. "Wow. Vicious little creature." Adam scowled at it as he licked the blood off his already healed digit.

Jacky laughed delightedly and clapped her hands.

The tailos cub looked up and met my gaze. Its eyes still had the blue sheen of a baby, but I thought they might be green when it grew up. It licked its chops and mewled at me, louder.

"Aww, he's just hungry," I said. "Do we have anything tender for him to eat?"

While Sam moved to get food, Adam raised an eyebrow. "That thing doesn't need something tender. Have you seen its teeth? I thought babies weren't supposed to have teeth right away. And how do you know it's a boy?"

"He's a warrior cub. Of course he'd have teeth," I said approvingly, scratching at the cub's head. "And he just kinda seems like a boy. That's the impression I got from his mother when she gave him to me."

Sam handed me some chunks of meat, careful to keep his finger out of reach of the tailos cub, which sniffed pointedly at his food-filled hands.

I took it and fed the cub bite after bite, which it didn't bother to chew at all.

A glimpse of its mouth showed primarily canines, so that made sense.

When it had finished one handful, it licked at my empty hand with a rough tongue and mewled at me pointedly.

"Hungry. That's good, means he's strong." Jacky nodded her approval.

"What should I call you?" I said to the creature. "Hmm? Do you have a name? Can you do that telepathic thing like your mother?" I touched a finger to the tip of its nose, and it jerked back in surprise, and then let out a large burp, which seemed to surprise it even more.

We all laughed at its comically wide-eyed, slightly alarmed expression.

The cub looked around at us for a moment, and then mewled in affront.

"Okay, okay," I chuckled. "Birch it is. We'll just say we named you after the mighty tree."

"I wish China were here to see this," Sam said suddenly.

We all fell silent, the sadness pushing out the happy atmosphere.

"Me too," Adam whispered.

Jacky angrily knuckled away tears. "I'm gonna make them pay. I swear it."

I swallowed the lump in my own throat. I felt like I should say something, but I didn't know what, so I just said, "Me too."

I fed Birch until his stomach was even rounder than my own food-stuffed belly, and then fell asleep with him tucked in the crook of my arm, my organs and bones aching and burning as the Seed continued to fight against me.

Chapter 35

I am the creator and the destroyer, I am he that defines all worlds. I bring life to the lifeless, I rain death on all that lives. My judgement is supreme. I encompass all things, I am the progenitor of good and evil. I created sin, I cause its every pain. Hell is one of my works. I am the source of all gods. I create gods on a whim, I destroy gods with a thought. I am man.

— Craig Smith

WHEN I WOKE UP AGAIN, with a hungry Birch pawing and licking persistently at my face, another whole day had passed. I fed my new little companion and stuffed myself, too, but this time resisted the urge to fall back asleep.

The sounds of shouting and grunts of effort drew me out of our small camp, and the first thing I saw was my companions locked in combat against a small army of golems. My muscles tensed, and I berated myself for trusting Behelaino, but I just as quickly realized what was really happening.

Behelaino had transformed a large section of the lake into a smooth stone floor, and the team was using it to spar against creatures summoned by the goddess.

"Whose idea was this?" I asked, jogging out onto the combat platform.

Jacky gave me her now characteristic grin. "I asked the big lady to help us train. It's a welcome distraction from the boredom of watching you sleep, *chica*."

I only rolled my eyes and waved for them all to carry on, then turned to Behelaino, whose attention I wanted for myself, eager to begin learning about my new Skill. She waited for me to approach, and I sat cross-legged at her base.

Birch followed me, curling up in my lap to sleep off the huge meal. After only a day he was walking, though it was more like a stumbling wobble than anything.

"Disorder naturally runs free and resists control," she rumbled at me. "While this is as it should be, if you allow it, you will die. You must learn to enforce order. That is the way of life."

"Okay, so how do I do that?"

She drew back and tilted her head. "You mold my power. Guide it, rather than allowing it to run freely through you."

"Okay…but how?"

She frowned, head still tilted. "How?" she repeated. "Can you not feel it?"

"Feel it? I don't have some instinctual knowledge of how to channel power, if that's what you mean. Can you explain from a human point of view?"

She huffed, blowing the hair back from my face. "I am not the God of Knowledge, how would I know the training of a mortal to a godling?"

"I thought you'd done this before?"

"Yes, many years ago, but that one was different than you. Smarter. I did not need to teach them what to do with something so natural."

The heat of anger burned up in me, but Birch woke up and gave a scratchy little growl in Behelaino's direction. The cute threat startled both her and me, and my anger slipped away. "I'll try to figure it out. In the meantime, maybe you'd like to continue your sparring with the others," I said.

Her growing irritation seemed to have dissipated as well, and she smiled, but said, "If I must. I'd be embarrassed for my godling to be seen with such followers. They must grow stronger before you leave."

I let the insult pass, taking a few deep breaths and forcing my mind into the hyper-aware state. I focused on my own body, ignoring all outside distractions.

I slipped deeper and deeper into my own body, looking closer and closer, till I could see my cells struggling and dying against the onslaught of the Seed. I healed at an accelerated rate, but even the best healing power wouldn't be enough without being able to stop the constant attack. I tried to focus my will and calm down the erosion, but while I could control a few of the strange Seed organisms, the countless others went on unchecked, and if I took concentration away for a moment, the stilled Seed pieces would surge back to life and immediately begin attacking my body again.

I opened my eyes when Birch stirred on my lap and began to pester me for food.

"You did not succeed," Behelaino said before I had a chance to say anything. "I could feel it. I cannot teach you how to control it, but once you learn, I will train you to do it better, faster, and in different ways."

"If I can figure it out," I mumbled back, feeling defeated and so very, very tired.

I carried Birch back to our little camp spot and fed us both again, giving only lethargic responses to my teammates' conversation attempts before going back to sleep.

The cycle of eating ravenously to power my body's healing, trying futilely to control the Seed, and sleeping as if I was a newborn babe continued for days. I grew increasingly frustrated and irritable at my failure and the constant pain, enough that the others started to avoid talking to me or getting in my way. The only one who didn't feel the lash of my tongue was Birch, but he was just as snappish as I toward anyone who wasn't me.

Enough time passed that I felt insidious doubt that I would ever be able to control the Seed, and a growing certainty that I would die from my reckless consumption of it. I walked along the rim of the caldera's lip, taking in the spectacular view, which was like nothing I had ever seen back on earth. At least, the glimpses I got when the ocean of clouds surrounding the mountain's peak would clear momentarily. The land stretched away beneath me, so far that I could see the curve of the planet.

Birch followed behind me, tentatively letting his wings catch the wind. They were still more fuzzy than feathered, but he'd grown significantly in the time since he'd hatched and was the size of an adult cat, with all the playfulness and body shape of a kitten.

My claws slipped out involuntarily as I paced back and forth, and I resisted the urge to yank at my own hair in frustrated rage. Tears prickled behind my eyes, and I choked on my own fear. I focused my mind inward, pushing past the emotion with some effort, and begged wordlessly with the Seed to listen to me, to stop attacking me.

It didn't listen, and so I screamed. I opened my eyes and screamed again, all the rioting emotions within clawing out through my throat. As I did, a strange power burst from me along with a dark-tendrilled smoke, and the slippery rock at my feet turned to sand.

I stared down in amazement, unblinking, as the little grains slid off the edge. The wispy black smoke had dissipated almost immediately, and left me feeling empty. Then the rock crumbled and started to fall away beneath my feet, taking me with it.

My stomach lurched at the sudden change in velocity, but already the tumult of conflicting emotion in my mind was back, and stronger than before. My body convulsed with pain, and I blacked out as the wind of my fall brushed against my cheek.

WHEN I WOKE, Adam sat beside me, redrawing his tattoo with inkberries, wincing as he embedded the dark liquid into his skin. This design was even more intricate than the last one, twisting up his arm in fractal knots. It reminded me of bindings, holding any broken pieces of Adam secure beneath his skin.

Perhaps I should get some, I thought. I was falling apart, too, and could use something to help me hold it together. I giggled at the thought, causing him to break concentration.

He smiled. "You're awake." The smile slipped away almost immediately, morphing into a stern look I'd seen before.

"Yes. And let me guess, you're upset because I was reckless and hurt myself."

He sighed. "Birch gave this crazy yowl when you fell—he's awesome—and Jacky caught you. It's just lucky you fell toward the inside, rather than down the mountainside. Otherwise you'd be dead right now." He stared at me somberly, his eyes searching my face. "What happened? Sam said you didn't hit your head, but you passed out, and there's this crater and cracks in the rocks above where you fell."

I cleared my scratchy throat, and he handed me a flask of water without looking away. I drank, and said, "I got the new power to work for the first time. Or rather, I kind of lost it up there, and suddenly I'd destroyed part of the rock where I was standing. Then it was like all the different emotions went full volume, all together, and I just…passed out. It's the Seed. It's…chaos, Adam. Behelaino…she told me she's formlessness and the void, and I have that inside me. I don't know how to control it. Even now—" I broke off, swallowing the sudden and furiously strong urge to cry. "I feel like I'm vibrating apart into a million pieces."

He stared at me for a second, then said, "When I was a kid, I had some trouble…coping." He looked down to his hands, idly rubbing his fingers together.

I clenched my teeth, holding in an unexpected surge of anger. He was going to tell me he knew how I felt, try to sympathize with me? How dare he? He knew nothing, had never experienced something like this. What advice could he give me?

"My dad drank…*drinks*," he corrected. "But back then my mom was still alive. He'd get angry and do these little clever, hurtful things. Sometimes, those can be harder to take than the physical pain."

My anger slipped away, replaced by a burning shame at its existence only seconds before.

"I'd get angry and sad, and it would all get to be so much I just couldn't handle it. I'd hole up in my room, screaming into a pillow and punching the headboard of my bed." He rubbed his scarred knuckles absentmindedly, and was silent for a while.

"Adam," I whispered, unsure what to say, but he began talking again as if he hadn't heard me.

"My mom found me one day, like that, just kind of…unreachable. She pulled me onto her lap and rocked me for a long time, until I calmed down. Then she taught me a way to help control all the negative emotions when things got overwhelming. She told me to make a house in my mind, and in that house, to make a room. In that room, to make a box, and in that box, to put the things that were making me crazy. If I felt ashamed, she told me to think of the thing that had made me that way, acknowledge it, and then put it in the box. Then to cover the box and fill the room with things that made me feel confident and proud and safe, so that the shame wouldn't be as loud. If you put the bad feeling in a room made of bad things, it'll stay hidden, but it starts to fester and poison you secretly. That's why you hold it with its opposite."

He took a deep breath and met my eyes again. "Maybe you can do that with this new Seed. Take it and lock it up so it can't keep making you crazy." He gave me a pointed look and a small quirk of a smile.

"Maybe," I said. "At this point, I'm willing to try just about anything."

With Adam's serene voice guiding me, I made a house with many rooms waiting to be filled. I chose one of the rooms and put the sea of chaos within my body and mind into a small wooden box made of silence. I locked it and put the box in a chest made of stillness. I left them in the middle of my room made of serenity and closed the door. Then I built a towering wall of protective stone all the way around the house, because it made me feel safe.

I opened my eyes, and then closed them again almost immediately, moving my concentration inward in a different sort of way, checking on the Seed within me. It was still there, spread throughout, but it no longer pushed so strongly against the natural order of my body, and other than relief, I had no overpowering emotion coursing through me.

I was exhausted by the intense mental effort. In moments, I fell asleep again, with a muttered, "Thank you," to Adam.

The next day, I told Behelaino of my conquest, and she began to instruct me in the use of my newly contained power. She was a harsh taskmaster, constantly impatient and fickle, and my body was still weak from its extended battle. Learning even a modicum of control was grueling. According to Behelaino, I was also singularly untalented.

"You must leave soon," she said to me a few days later.

"Yes. The Trials will be starting soon, and then I will go back to my world. There's not much time left," I said, sparring lightly with a man-sized tornado of jagged pebbles and steam she'd conjured.

"I have not much control left. My strength replenishes by the day, and I struggle to hold it in check so that you and your subjects do not die. I cannot continue to do so for much longer," she rumbled.

I frowned and released a short burst of my new power, scattering and disintegrating the twister with a poof of fleeting dark tendrils. I quickly clamped back down on the Chaos, locking it up again before it could attack me in a frenzy of sudden release. The effort exhausted me. It would be a while before I could use the Skill again, though I was getting better… at least compared to fainting the first time. "You're regaining the strength lost from when you…erupted?" She'd hinted as much a few times before.

"Yes. If you do not take some distance from this place, your lives in mortal form will be gone, your energy mixed with my own. Prepare your subjects to travel. If this Trial does not take you when you have said it will, you will need to run. I have grown…*fond* of you, and would like you to live on."

But it did take us, shortly afterward. When the Boneshaker started to play, a cube formed in front of us, and we were given the option to go to the Trial or not. Behelaino could somehow tell. "You do not bear my power in vain, Eve-Redding. May you go free."

I met the swirling orbs of water that represented her eyes, and then my team and I were snapped away to a Trial. For the first time since my first Trial, I felt no overwhelming fear.

Chapter 36

A child weaned on poison considers harm a comfort.
— Gillian Flynn

AS I'D GUESSED–OR rather *hoped*—Zed was there, so we could protect him. When he saw me, his face lit up, as happy as I'd ever seen him. But instead of rushing forward to hug me and make sure I was alright, he hesitated, and his eyes searched mine.

I was puzzled for a moment, and then realized what was going on in his mind. I remembered the last time I'd seen him, the things I'd said. Instead of waiting for him, I stepped forward and wrapped him in a crushing hug. He wheezed from the force my strength could now create, but when I pulled back, he was beaming. "I'm glad you're okay," I said. "And…you know, those things I said—"

"You wanted to keep me safe," he interrupted. "I know. Sometimes we do things we shouldn't, trying to keep each other safe. Must run in the family," he said pointedly.

My eyes widened in surprise, and I finally let go of the last bit of anger I'd been holding against him for taking my Seed. "Yeah. I guess we do."

He nodded, but I knew that even if all was forgiven between us, it would be a while till the wounds healed and things were back to normal. Maybe they would never be normal. And that was okay, too.

After the Trial, which seemed designed to test our speed, dexterity, and endurance, the team returned with Zed to the normal world, wrapping our arms around him in a kind of bulky group hug in the hopes that he'd take us with him to the point where Blaine was waiting with an escape route.

It worked, and we all piled into Blaine's dark-tinted pod, ignoring the queasiness that came with teleportation. He peeled away through a network of mostly empty underground tunnels, which he navigated with ease.

My eyes had adjusted to the dark, so when the pod burst out into the brightness of day and merged with flowing traffic, I flinched and lifted an arm to block my face.

Zed, who was sitting beside me, did the same. When we'd had time to adjust to the brightness, he turned to me. "You seem different."

Jacky grinned and poked her head forward from the backseat. "Yah. That's because we're bad-ass strong now."

Sam, on my other side, sighed and leaned his head back against the seat. "Training in Hell will do that to you." He paused for a moment, then added, "I never realized before how bad Earth stinks. I'd gotten used to the freshness."

"No," Zed shook his head, "that's part of it. But there's something else, too."

Adam flicked me a look from the front passenger seat, which I pointedly ignored.

Zed looked from Adam to me. "What is it?"

I shook my head. "We just have a lot more experience with danger than we did before. We've become veteran Gamers, kind of in the space of nine days. It's been a lot longer than that for us. That disconnect is probably what you're sensing."

"How long were you over there for?"

"About six weeks."

He nodded and let the questioning go, but the frown on his face said he wasn't quite satisfied. He was more sensitive to lies and evasion after everything that had happened. "Well, you're crazy, crazy powerful now."

I couldn't blame him for being suspicious, but I didn't know what to say about the Seed I'd taken, or how to explain it, and I didn't want him to worry. But…I felt a guilty twinge at the idea of lying to him again, and decided to elaborate anyway. "I also have a new…Skill-type-thingy." I made vague hand motions meant to play down its importance rather than explain.

He perked up with interest, but I gave vague answers and kept the true danger and side effects to myself.

The others knew the truth, more or less, but they wouldn't go against my word.

Blaine took us to a hotel suite that he'd paid for using a fake ID link. He had some lab equipment set up, though not even close to the realm of the laboratory in his basement.

When I let Birch out of my backpack, where I'd firmly ordered him to stay hidden, still, and quiet before the Trial, Blaine went into a state of frenzied, ecstatic curiosity, and lamented that he didn't have better equipment to examine the animal. Birch bit him when Blaine tried to touch his wings, but the scientist seemed even more excited by that, asking a series of questions about him and the Trial world that I was too tired to answer properly.

Luckily, Adam was more than happy to rave about my new monster companion. He adored the little tailos, a fact Birch seemed to have picked up on quite quickly considering the way he mercilessly bullied Adam. Every time Adam got close, Birch swatted or made coughing sounds at him. And when Adam tried to feed him scraps of meat, Birch always deliberately nipped his fingers, too. It was obvious the tailos found it all great fun, and for some reason Adam only liked him even more.

After a few hours to rest and recuperate, I sat down with Blaine and Birch to satisfy his curiosity and my own. While I kept up a constant stream of petting, praise, and reassurance toward the sleepy cub, Blaine took samples of his various bodily fluids, fur, and feathers.

"Give me an update on the real world," I said. "What's been happening while we've been gone? Have you been able to safely avoid NIX?"

Blaine spoke without looking at me, intent on his samples of an alien life form. "Yes. We have been a step ahead of them the whole time. However, if not for my…especially wide skill set, that would not be the case. Everything we buy is on untraceable credit, and I've put some additional measures in place to avoid recognition by the satellites or cameras. It is not perfect, though. I may be a genius, but I am only one person, and they have resources most people can barely imagine."

"That can work against them, too. They may be big and powerful, but they're also secretive. They haven't let the world find out about them. It'll end up being just one more incentive for them to decide we're more trouble than we're worth, no matter how much power they have. Have you made any progress on verifying their method of teleportation?" I asked.

"From the feedback on the monitoring system, it seems your hunch was right. The sphere device in the courtyard of NIX's compound is in control of the Boneshaker. I still do not understand how it works, unfortunately. I cannot block it."

"That's okay. I know another way."

He was silent for long enough that I thought maybe he wasn't going to continue the conversation, but then he said, "What do you think the chances are? That you will be able to pull this off, I mean? This commitment you have made to all of us, it is quite…large. Save my sister's kids, free the rest of the team from the Game, strike a blow to NIX and force them to leave us alone afterward… Can you do it?"

"Blaine, there's only one answer I can give you. I won't allow a future in which I fail. I'm going to keep everyone safe."

He pulled out a syringe and pierced my arm, drawing blood. "What if you cannot? What if NIX is too strong for us, even now?"

I suppressed a small surge of anger at his doubt, recognizing it for the emotional volatility born of my new power. I hadn't been to my mental room of peace for a while, and I needed to visit it and tend the box within. "I won't fail. You may see something new in that blood when you examine it, Blaine. I asked about what's happened here, but I haven't told you about our little trip yet."

We talked for a couple hours after that, exchanging information and more plans. Though I wasn't willing to accept aloud the possibility of a second defeat at NIX's hands, I still made plans to keep Zed far away and safe in the event that I was wrong. I was cocky, yes, but never let it be said that I didn't learn from my mistakes.

Log of Captivity 5

Mental Log of Captivity—Estimated Day: Two thousand, six hundred forty-two.

She is back again, though she was gone long enough I worried myself to distraction. I have tried to reach her, and though I can feel our *blood-covenant-bond*, I cannot touch her. She has adapted some sort of *warrior's-technique* to protect her mind. I am grateful that she grows strong, but I feel her coming close to this place of *two-leg-maggots*, and I worry that she will attempt to find me again. It is shameful that my child-master must save her *blood-covenant-champion*. But my *mother-lord* would approve of her.

Chapter 37

They shall have stars at elbow and foot;
Though they go mad they shall be sane,
Though they sink through the sea they shall rise again;
Though lovers be lost love shall not;
And death shall have no dominion.
— Dylan Thomas

I SAT on the mountainside behind the bowl of NIX, which I'd just realized was similar to Behelaino's peak, only less defensible and harsh. A map of NIX floated in front of my face, and I'd shared it with Jacky and Adam, who sat on either side of me. We were going over the plan for our attack and reviewing the myriad variations we'd come up with, in case of surprises.

The sun had just risen, and its cleansing light was almost harsh despite the early hour. We would come at dawn instead of in darkness this time. I let the wind whipping along the mountainside rush over me as I contemplated what was to come, willing my victory into existence.

—We're ready.—
-Sam-

I'd sent Sam around to the other side of NIX with Blaine. Sam would be able to heal the hostages if needed, guaranteeing that everyone would be in condition to escape without being a burden. When they were finished, Blaine would take off with the kids and Chanelle, and Sam would come back around as backup for my group.

Bunny, now officially our man on the inside, had unlocked a door for them. Blaine would be going for the prototype of the electronically powered armor suit he'd given to NIX first, which would augment his fighting ability and hopefully allow him to hold his own while they broke Chanelle and the kids out.

Zed and Birch were on their way out of the country, to a place that would be safe if the unthinkable happened. Not that any place would be truly safe if Zed had to keep going to the Trials, especially without our protection. I'd wanted Blaine to go with him, to keep him safe and out of the way, but he'd insisted he could be useful, and outright refused to leave Kris and Gregor to anyone's protection but his own. Zed would have to do his traveling alone, because as much as I hated it, in truth I couldn't spare the manpower to go with him. I'd left Birch with him since the cub needed protection as much as he did.

I had a quick image of China dying, but this time it was Zed's eyes staring back at me. I clenched my fist. That wouldn't happen. It wasn't an option.

The ground of the huge courtyard rumbled below, and a hole in the concrete dilated open. Three heli-pods rose from it, their blades reverberating with a deep *thwump-twhump-thwump*. I watched them rise slowly, turn, and head away at top speed. Whatever NIX was doing, it would just be a distraction from us, something to slow down their reaction speed a little more.

I rose and took another deep breath, feeling a ball of something cold and hard in the center of my chest. All or nothing, now. "It's time," I said to the two next to me, as well as sending the words in a Window to Sam.

I adjusted the armored vest straps over my chest, pricked the back of my wrist, and fed it a few drops of blood. "Armor in place?" I asked the others, receiving positive responses.

They were all wearing the impact absorbing body armor that Blaine had been so proud of developing when we first met him. I preferred my armored vest for the top, but I'd taken the leg covers. Unless we were shot in the head, or with a high-impact round from a tank, we wouldn't die from bullets. They would still hurt like hell, though, so the plan was to not get shot.

"Let's go," I told everyone, then started to lope down the mountainside, letting gravity accelerate my descent.

Jacky and Adam moved to my right and left, slightly behind me, so we ran in an arrow-like formation.

The guards noticed us before we reached the base of the mountain and the dirt road leading to NIX's only gate: a huge, double-doored thing cut into the side of the wall. No side entrances or sneaking for us this time.

They pointed their guns at us, and someone shouted for us to stop, raise our hands in the air, and identify ourselves.

I slowed, and Jacky and Adam slowed with me, but we didn't stop. We reached the road and headed straight for the gate.

When we got closer, a guard called down with a megaphone, "Stop right there! One more step and we open fire!"

I stopped and looked up at the guns pointing down at us from the top of the wall, a couple hundred feet away in either direction. "Jacky," I said.

With only that, she crouched down and sprang up again, shooting over my head and toward the wall like she'd bounced from some epic trampoline. Combined with her Skill, gravity in the normal world was just low enough to allow her to make such a move. She screamed as she went, a screech of excitement and aggression, and tucked her arms around her head to protect it from any bullets.

She needn't have bothered, because the guards were too stunned by her inhuman jump to aim or shoot at her.

By the time they recovered, she'd already disarmed and knocked out four of them. At least I thought they were unconscious. They may also have been dead.

The others turned and started to shoot at her then, but it was too late. She used their fallen comrades as shields as she continued to take them out, moving forward unstoppably. Using the distraction she created to our advantage, Adam and I moved forward. He fiddled with a keypad beside the huge gate for only a few seconds, and it unlocked with a series of loud metal clicks. The doors rumbled open, and I stepped confidently through into the courtyard, Adam at my side. I unsheathed my claws and sank slightly lower into a fighting stance.

I was quite aware of the theatrical effect of all this to anyone watching. That was precisely the point of a show of force, after all. Cue the epic music.

From the glass walls facing the inside of the courtyard, people in different uniforms and lab coats stood and looked down open-mouthed. The panic hadn't hit yet.

Piercing alarms screeched through the compound, and the guards inside the courtyard started shooting.

The bullets were aimed for our chests, rather than our heads, but we still wove and dodged, doing our best to avoid being shot.

Adam's eyes met my own, and I gave him a nod. He shot off toward the concrete column forming a trunk topped by the huge metal sphere in the center of the courtyard. He would break through the concrete and jack into the twisting mass of wires within to gain retrograde access to NIX's computer system, and thus their whole base, along with all their top-secret information. Meanwhile, I'd protect him by putting on a display of overwhelming force, just like Jacky had taught me.

My claws sank into the closest guard's shoulder and ripped down, immobilizing the limb. I yanked them out, grabbed his gun, and smashed him in the side of the head. Lights out. I twisted and swung my leg up, slicing my toe claws across the back of another guard's neck, knocking him out, too.

I tossed the guns toward the center of the courtyard. Guns were useless to me since my DNA didn't match the guards', and I wanted the weapons as far away from my opponents' access as possible, just in case. I moved onto the next person, and the next, until blood splatters stained my whole body. Earth made me feel light after all the time spent in Estreyer, and I didn't hesitate or try to spare the guards I fought. I wasn't actively trying to kill them, but if it happened, I wasn't going to cry.

The air seemed to ripple with the force of all the alarms going off, and shouts and screams of pain filled the air, with the occasional burst of gunfire and booming crunches. A bullet barely grazed my left arm, and another hit the armor around my thigh.

Up above, Jacky was almost finished with the whole top of the wall, having disabled or killed most of the guards and disarmed the mounted anti-aircraft gun stands.

I'd almost finished with the resistance on the ground level of the courtyard. Adam was sending a few distracted lightning bolts at a group of guards who had slipped past me.

Before I could move to help him, the electronic doors all around the courtyard slid open, and soldier-types in full body armor and shields poured out.

"Damn," I said, watching them swarm into the courtyard.

They moved in formation, the front line holding shields while the center pointed guns the size of rocket launchers at us from safety. These guys were not only better equipped than the normal guards on the walls and the randoms milling around the courtyard, they were apparently prepared to fight people like us.

A soldier from the door closest to me tossed out a small metal pipe. As it arced through the air, it started to smoke, letting out billowing clouds of yellow gas.

I sidestepped and made sure not to inhale, but within seconds each little team of soldiers had thrown multiple smoke pipes, and the yellow fumes began to fill the courtyard. A whiff of it, and my head felt a little lighter, my wounds a bit less distracting. I noticed the soldiers were wearing small air filters over their mouths and lenses over one eye, no doubt to allow them to see through the sedative clouds.

"Bastards," I spat. "Don't breathe it!" I called to Adam and Jacky. I back-stepped as far away from the smoking canisters as possible and took a deep breath. Crouching low to the ground and digging in with both my hands and feet, I scrambled to pick up the canisters while holding my breath. I threw them past the soldiers, back through the open doorways through which the defenders had come.

I'd been quick enough with a few of them, but I wasn't lightning-fast like Adam, and I didn't get to the other half in time to mitigate the smoke profusion.

Still, at least some of the air was breathable. And any of the guards I'd downed before wouldn't be getting up again in a "surprise!" kind of way.

The soldiers in the front row of one group bent to a knee, and the row behind them started to shoot. I darted to the side to draw their attention and bullets.

—Almost through!—
-Adam-

It was imperative to keep him protected till he could accomplish his part in my plan. I sprinted forward, straight toward the shooting soldiers, their bullets bruising me as they punched into my body armor. I jumped over the crouching line of soldiers bearing shields and slammed feet first into the shoulders of a gun-wielding man near the edge. I knocked him out of formation and scrambled around behind him in a single movement. I couldn't use his gun past a couple bullets before it would shut down on me, so I snapped his neck and held him up, my arms wrapped around his body. My fingers moved over his, and I squeezed. Bullets sprayed through his comrades. While I was at it, I took out a few from another group not too far away.

It was a good start, but there were too many of them, and only one of me.

Already, more bullets were flying at me from all around, and other groups turned their guns toward Adam.

"Shields!" I screamed.

He ripped little scraps of paper off a pin on the side of his pants and Animated them. Three broad ink shields sprang up around him, protecting him from the sides and back. He had less than a minute before they ran out.

I slammed my back into an empty section of the wall, holding onto the soldier and using him as a meat shield from the bullets. I continued to shoot back, but I wasn't able to move from behind him without getting shot, and I knew I wouldn't be able to protect myself for long, let alone Adam. The smoke was clearing, blowing away in the breeze, but I saw more soldiers coming, lining up in the hallways leading radially out from the courtyard. Backups already arriving.

The only positive was we weren't taking fire from above, too.

Which also meant Jacky should be finished with her first assignment. "Jacky!" I said under my breath, sending it in a Window.

—On it.—
-Jacky-

A few seconds later, something plummeted from the top of the wall into the midst of a group of soldiers like a meteor fallen from space. The impact alone knocked them off their feet, and then Jacky stood up from her crouch and attacked. They didn't stand a chance.

When they were finished, she moved onto the next group. Her moves were like a crushing dance, kind of beautiful to watch, even as I thanked God she was on my side. But even she wasn't enough to shift the balance back in our favor.

My commandeered gun ran out of bullets.

Adam's shields would be running out any second.

"Damn it!"

It was time for me to step it up. As it was, I hadn't been very awe-inspiring yet. I didn't want to use my trump card this soon, but I could still make a difference. I thrust the quite dead soldier forward, hoping the bullets aimed at me would follow him. In half a second, I'd flipped around and was scrambling up the wall, finger and toe claws punching into the cement. A couple rounds punched into my back, but my armored vest repelled them with little more damage to me than a painful bruise.

Imitating Jacky, I dashed around to the other end of the wall and took a running leap off it, landing on the shoulders of a soldier. Some of the group had noticed me coming, but they were packed too tightly in their defensive formation to evade an attack from that unconventional route. The soldier crumpled under my weight, and I used my claws to slice into either side of his neck. The blood splurted out like a crimson sprinkler.

I wasn't as good as Jacky, but she didn't have claws, nor my Tumbling Feather Skill. I jumped and spun and sliced, hitting with my elbows and my knees, cutting with my hands and feet.

—Got it!—
-Adam-

Seconds after Adam sent the message, the center of the courtyard lit up. He had one hand plunged into the bare, twisting, coiling wires, and the other stretched outward as if it was trying to escape the pain of the current. Electricity jumped and branched out from him like a tree made of light.

I closed my eyes, remembering the last time he'd done something like this.

Sure enough, bright whiteness exploded, loud enough to send me rocking backward and cause me to slip in the pool of blood I'd created.

I opened my eyes after a second to be sure it was safe. My eyesight was a little dim and spotty, and my ears rang, but I made out Adam still standing in the center of the courtyard. He was the only person on his feet.

All around, charred bodies had fallen to the ground, selectively electrocuted while he avoided the rest of the team, keeping us safe.

The hair on the back of my arms lifted, though I wasn't sure if it was from the smell of cooked human or residual electricity dancing through the air.

I stood up, and saw Jacky throw a crispy soldier off her and get up, too. She rubbed at her eyes and groaned, obviously having failed to close them in time.

Adam sagged against the wires, his hand falling away from them.

I took a few steps, making sure I had my balance, and then saw the soldiers within the hallways crawling to their feet. He hadn't barbecued *them*.

—Close the doors, Adam.—
-Eve-

I could barely make out my own voice giving the command, so I knew he wouldn't be able to hear anything, seeing as he was literally in the center of that lightning boom.

He shook his head and straightened, then started to tap away at a screen embedded to his side among the wires.

Two seconds later, and the doors slid shut despite the panicked soldier's attempts to keep them open.

"How long?" I sent him in a Window.

—It won't be opening from the inside. They'll have to blast their way through. So maybe five minutes?—
-Adam-

I crawled up the side of the sphere's concrete support to the grated maintenance ledge that lay around the top.

The sphere pulsed with a faint hum of energy. Lines covered its surface, a bit like the patterning of the Seeds. All around it floated orbiting rings moving at different angles, like a way more complex version of the belts around the planet Saturn, but of different sizes, orientations, and made of strange metals unlike any I'd ever seen.

"So this is it," I said aloud. The thing that NIX used to send us to the Trials, and to track us when we went, even without the GPS trackers in our necks. I pressed the tip of my claws to its surface and walked a few steps, making tiny scratches in the metal. The sound of it rang out like a long and continuous crystal bell.

I looked out, saw people pressed up against the glass wall of the inside hallways, staring out at the scene we'd been making. I smiled at them and waved a bloody, claw-tipped hand.

The alarms stopped as Adam crackled away with electricity down below, and only in their absence did I realize that they'd been sounding the whole time.

In the silence, I took a deep breath and screamed at the top of my lungs. "Send out your leader!"

Jacky jumped up beside me, shaking the grating.

"Glad you could make it," I said, grinning.

She pursed her lips, fighting against a smile of her own. "I was busy. Didn't you notice?"

"I noticed you taking forever with those guards. And then getting buried under Adam's lightning barbecue."

She was grinning full out now. "*Me* taking forever? I remember finishing my area, and then coming down to help *someone*, no?" She gave me a pointed look. "And I may not have a flashy power like you two, but I make up for it in other ways." She flexed her bicep and wiggled her eyebrows.

I laughed. "Hmm…how about a demonstration?" I patted one of the gently moving rings that orbited the sphere.

"My pleasure." As we'd planned beforehand, she began to pound on the sphere and its rings, varying kicks and punches.

It shuddered on its stand, and some of the rings jammed up on each other when she forced them out of their proper orbit.

I added blows of my own, though they had nowhere near the impact of Jacky's. My claws were useless here, too soft to cut through the metals.

"Have you got the name yet?" I asked Adam.

"Almost…okay. I think it's Nadia Petralka," he called up to me.

"You *think*?"

"It is."

I called out again. "Commander Petralka! Come to me!"

From beside me, Jacky paused in her attacks and said, "Isn't she trapped inside along with all the others? What if she's trying, but she can't get out here?"

I shrugged. "She'll come out once they finish blasting down the doors. I'm sure they've already started. And in the meantime, we can put on a little more of the show. I still haven't gotten to bring out my party trick, remember?"

Jacky's mouth hung open for a second before she said, "Ah…are you going to do that, now?" She stepped backward.

"Yes."

She nodded and stepped back again, getting as far away from me as possible while not going so far around the circle that she got in front of me. "Should I get down?"

"You should be fine. I can control it." I raised my hands toward the sphere as if I was getting ready to push it.

She looked from my face to my hands, and then down to the ground.

I sighed. "Fine. Go down if you must."

She nodded, let out a sigh of relief, and jumped off the edge to safety.

I looked around again. People were pounding on the glass, impotent and silent behind its barrier. I turned back to the sphere, took a deep breath, and closed my eyes. In that room of serenity in my mind, I opened the chest of stillness. The box of silence was leaking black mist at the edges, which alarmed me.

As if sensing my disturbance, the misty tendrils wriggled and thickened.

I grabbed that small bit of Chaos and threw it outward, into the real world, right at the sphere. Even as the metal screamed and buckled, the sphere rocking on its stand and letting out heat as its molecules rubbed against each other, in my mind I was slamming shut the chest and locking the door, lest the rest of my power escape.

I looked at the partly damaged sphere with satisfaction, and then screamed, " Petralka!"

My voice was strong despite my spinning head and legs that threatened to buckle. A mixture of Chaos-enhanced rage and fear was keeping adrenaline in my veins and me on my feet. Using the power took a lot out of me.

Glass broke behind me, and I turned to see a group of people jumping out of the window into the courtyard, kind of like my team had done the last time we were here.

It was a group of younger people. They were dressed in a uniform quite different than the soldiers.

I smiled wide. "Players." The last time we'd done reconnaissance on the place, we'd thought maybe they were captives, or possibly test subjects. It'd been beyond us to consider someone who'd been forced into the Game would be willing to cohabitate with their oppressors. But I knew them for what they were now.

"Why, hello," I called down to them. "I don't suppose one of them is Petralka?" I directed the question toward Adam, who was standing shoulder to shoulder with Jacky, facing off against the advancing group.

"No," he said, clipped.

"Then I'm going to warn you," I called down again, leaning out over the edge of the narrow platform. "We're not here for you. Go back, and we'll allow you to live."

They didn't stop, and the hair on the back of my neck rose as both raged at being ignored and a healthy dose of wariness washed through me.

The Player at the forefront, a shorter girl with spiked pixy cut hair and a hooked nose, laughed aloud. "You were looking for the Commander? Sorry, scag. I can't make the same promise to you. None of *you* will be leaving here alive." She pointed two fingers from each hand at Adam and Jacky. "Two on one. Take them down. I'll handle the giant." She jerked her chin up to me.

I raised an eyebrow. "Now, that's a bit hurtful, don't you think? I'm just a little taller than the average—"

She shot off the ground like a rocket, slamming into me and knocking me off the platform.

Chapter 38

It was like this blackness that crept into the corners of my life until everything was grey and dirty. My insides felt burnt out, like if you cut me open, all you would find would be smoke. No heart. No bones. There was nothing left, just the anger. It followed me everywhere. It sat on my bed and watched me sleep and when I had to eat, it looked at me across the table.

— Tanya Byrne

THE PIXIE-HAIRED PLAYER slammed me into the far wall hard enough that my body armor rippled with the attempt to protect me. Something cracked. I wasn't sure if it was me or the concrete, and I didn't know which was more likely.

She stepped back, and I slid to the ground, coughing out little puffs as I tried to regain my air.

In the center of the courtyard, Jacky and Adam were fighting wildly, their backs to each other.

Before I could move, the girl stepped forward again and slammed her foot into my stomach, further winding me. She ground her flat-heeled boot into me, then brought down a fist for a quick punch in the temple.

When she pulled her fist back again, I grabbed her foot and bucked upward, slamming my bare feet into her chest while simultaneously pushing and twisting at her foot.

Her much smaller body flew backward, but she followed the force of my throw, twisted, and landed on her feet, sliding backward.

That was okay, because it gave me enough time to stand up again. I tackled her before she stopped sliding, claws out. I expected them to sink into the soft flesh of her sides, but instead they slid harmlessly forward, and I ended up in a kind of awkward body roll with her.

I used the momentum to tear myself free and jump back, staying in a limber crouch a safe distance from her, claws out and ready to slice—though I now had doubts about their ability to actually do so. I thought for a moment she might be wearing some sort of body armor beneath her uniform…then her skin turned grey and scaly, rippling out across her neck, hands, and face from underneath her clothes. Literal armored skin.

"Sorry, scag," she sneered. "Your little claws won't work here."

I grinned and lunged forward, my right hand aimed low. At the last second, I shot two fingers from my other hand at her eyeballs.

Her face twisted in alarm as my "little claws" came within millimeters of her unprotected eyes. But she threw her head backward, dipping her upper body recklessly toward the ground.

My claws missed her eyeballs and scraped across her grey-scaled forehead harmlessly.

She turned her dip into a backflip, landing it with a self-satisfied smirk that I really wanted to claw off her grey-scaled face.

To our side, Adam shot off bolts of lightning toward his and Jacky's four opponents. The arcing electricity caught two of them, and Jacky and he were on them instantly, he with his knives, and she with her fists.

I cocked my head to the side and mirrored her irritating expression. "Looks like this isn't going too well for your friends, huh?"

"Don't worry. When I'm finished with you, I'll go help them out."

"For that to happen, you'd have to still be alive at the end of this."

"Like you're going to stop me? Honey, it's obvious you don't have what it takes."

I let the smirk fall away as I straightened from my crouch. "There's a whole other side to me that you haven't seen yet, *Honey*." I stepped forward, taking a deep breath with every footfall.

Her mouth tightened, and I saw the moment when she grew wary and decided on a preemptive strike. She shot forward a millisecond later, but I was already jumping to the side.

Her eyes widened as she realized her miscalculation, but by then she was in motion, and it was too late.

I grabbed her by the arm and spun her around, throwing her into the side of one of the buildings in the courtyard.

As her face whitened in pain—I guess that armored skin didn't protect her internal organs—I walked toward her again, breathing deep and concentrating.

She made it to her feet and climbed up the side of the building, hoping to buy time or gain an advantage with the height, perhaps.

I jumped and grabbed the edge easily, and from there it only took half a second and a grip on the concrete with my toes to make it onto the roof.

But of course, me coming up after her is what she'd planned for. She was already shooting forward as soon as I'd planted my feet.

There was nowhere to go but back down off the roof, and I threw myself backward to avoid her attack, lifting my arms in a defensive stance. I was too slow.

She stopped abruptly an arm's length in front of me and slammed both of her palms forward, carrying all the energy of the full body dash she'd just aborted. Her hands smashed past my half-formed defense like it wasn't even there and crashed into my chest.

I watched as if in slow motion as my vest sank into a perfect impression of her small hands, then rippled outward like the surface of still water after a pebble is dropped into it. My body flew up and backward, bowed forward around the point where she'd hit me. My lower back slammed into the side of the grated walkway around the stalled metal sphere. I flipped backward, tilting around the axis where I'd hit, and slid along the grating, clawing desperately at the platform as I twisted before finally sliding to a stop.

I tasted blood in my mouth and gaped soundlessly in shock as the pain hit me. But I grabbed onto the sphere and pulled myself up.

She was still standing on the roof below, panting hard. Her eyes widened in surprise when she saw me rise.

This wasn't the first time I'd taken a beating or been thrown around like a rag doll, and I refused to be taken out so easily. Black spots flashed and tumbled behind my eyes, and the desire to pass out clung to me like a weighted blanket, but I tried to force my lungs to expand and take in air again. They ignored me for the moment, but I was sure they'd listen eventually. If they didn't, I *would* pass out, and if that happened it would all be over, and this would be for nothing.

So I tried harder.

My opponent jumped forward in that inhuman way that I'd only ever seen Jacky do and landed in a crouch on the platform a couple yards from me. She stood and smiled when she saw my condition, blood dripping from my mouth, a hand pressed to my chest, and barely able to stand.

Desperation raged in my chest, and I screamed at myself wordlessly. I could not be defeated here. After all that I'd been through, and how close I was to accomplishing my goal, I couldn't lose here, just because I was weak. I'd always been weak, and my enemies had always been strong, but that hadn't stopped me before. I was supposed to be stronger now.

She stepped forward and threw a punch toward my stomach.

I watched it coming, still screaming inside for my body to move, to attack, to win.

Then, everything *snapped*. The world slowed down as my whole being overloaded. Every thought slipped temporarily out of my mind except for the sight of her fist swinging forward to smash into my body, and my raging denial of my possible loss to her.

I stepped forward to meet her fist, grabbing it with my clawed palm, just so.

She was moving as if through water, her expression just beginning to change from cocky into something else as she saw into the depths of my eyes.

With one shallow breath and a sleepy blink, I unleashed Chaos.

I had very little control over my new power this time, and it roared out of me with the force of a hurricane. I slammed her into the sphere, staring into her eyes, my hand still clenched around her fist.

Visible ripples radiated through the air—her grey skin, her bones, her blood, her organs—and out into the sphere, which screeched again as the metal moved and buckled under my power like undulating water under the force of a storm.

She screamed the scream of being separated from herself, as her insides bucked and bubbled and burst. It was a horrible sound, reverberating through my bones and echoing from every surface in the courtyard.

Then her bleeding eyes rolled back in her head, and she went limp.

The overpowering storm of rage in my head hadn't calmed yet, and I wanted to continue hurting her until she died, if she hadn't already. I wanted to keep smashing her like the bug she was, until her body was nothing but an unrecognizable lump of flesh and blood and bone.

But I took my second breath, a gasp this time, and released her fist and my power.

Chapter 39

Hello, darkness, my old friend...I've come to talk to you again.
— Simon and Garfunkel

THE FIGHTING down below had stopped. Everyone still standing was staring up at me.

In the sudden silence, my knees almost buckled from the backlash of my attack. My head spun as the rage and triumph tried to take over again, and I was as tired and hurt as if I'd just fallen out of a plane with no parachute. If no one had been watching, I would have fallen to the ground and let my consciousness slip away. Using Chaos twice in such short succession should still have been impossible for me.

But this was neither the time nor place for weakness, so I straightened and put on a mask of calm confidence. "You will concede defeat," I called down to the still conscious attackers below, "or I will come down there and destroy you all."

They raised their hands, and the three that could still move backed away from Jacky and Adam. The other was unconscious and didn't look like he'd be waking up any time soon.

A muffled boom sounded from down below, and then one of the concrete doors burst open, rubble flying as an explosion ripped it apart.

A uniformed woman stumbled out, ignoring the surprised call of,

"Commander! Wait!" from behind her. Metal stripes glinted on her shoulder.

"Is it her?" I called down to Adam.

"Yes," he said.

"I am Commander Nadia Petralka," she shouted. "Please, stop now. I've come, like you requested."

"Do you know who I am?" I asked, again running my claws over the surface of the damaged sphere.

She nodded, but her eyes were drawn to the downed girl at my feet. "You're Eve Redding, one of our highest ranked Players. Stop what you're doing. There is no need for further destruction or violence."

I scowled. "You say that, but you people are the ones who started all this. And suddenly, when it turns out you may have taken on the wrong opponent, you call for peace? I warned her to leave us alone if she wanted to live."

"Is she…dead?" Commander Petralka's voice threatened to waver, and she clenched her jaw instead, keeping a calm face.

I reached down for the ruined girl's throat. Commander Petralka took half a step forward, hand lifting, before she seemed to remember herself and abruptly stopped.

I found an erratic pulse in the girl's neck. "She's alive. I'm not sure for how long, without medical attention."

"She's just a girl. She doesn't have anything to do with this. Let her go, and we can talk."

I burst out with a bitter laugh. "Why would I let her go when you so badly want her to be safe? She serves double duty for me, as a bargaining chip and a ticking clock. It couldn't be more perfect if I planned it myself." Wow, I thought, realizing how much I sounded like a comic book villain.

Commander Petralka's mouth tightened, and she snapped her ID sheath link straight, turning it into a flat screen. "You want something, and I want something, Eve. Maybe those two things don't have to be mutually exclusive." She held up the screen toward me.

On it, I saw the figures of Sam, Blaine in his mecha suit, two smaller children, and a blonde girl surrounded by people with guns. Sam and Blaine were in a protective stance, the three rescued prisoners placed between them.

—We've been caught. There must have been people waiting for us. I'm not sure if we can fight our way out or not.—
-Sam-

Sam wouldn't have waited to tell me, so Commander Petralka must have been apprised of their successful capture just moments before I was. But then again, she was probably expecting it. I suppressed any outside reaction to the news.

"It was a nice try, Eve. But did you really think we weren't keeping tabs on the Rabbit group Moderator? He was sneaky, sure, but opening that door was kind of a giveaway. It's too bad you didn't all come from that direction. We could have captured you immediately, and none of this"—she gestured around to all the bodies and general destruction in the courtyard—"would have had to happen."

I raised an eyebrow. "So you got a couple of my team. I let them attempt the rescue for their own satisfaction. A kind of reward for the work they've done. In fact, it has no bearing on my larger plan." I stood up, gazing imperiously down at her. "And do you really think you could have captured us all? Do you realize the situation you're in?" I sent a quick Window to Sam, telling them to sit tight and not do anything stupid.

I could still save them. They may be caught, but they weren't captured, and they weren't dead. "Do you know what my teammate below me was doing, besides just shooting those spectacular lightning bolts? He was gaining access to your computer system. The whole thing. Including a whole slew of data and the records of what you've been doing. In five seconds, we could have that streaming to every link in the nation." I pointed to the girl collapsed at my feet. "I've got a hostage of my own." Then I put a hand on the sphere. "And this thing that you use to send us to the Trials? A few more pushes from me, and it'll be nothing more than a crushed lump of metal. Do you think you can win against me?" I shouted.

She paused for a moment, and then smiled slowly, an expression that chilled my blood. She waved her hand in the air. "You've done spectacularly. Truly. You've got a higher score than almost any Player before entering NIX. And I'm particularly curious about that Skill you just used. But did you think we'd just allow you to run wild? You created some leverage to get what you want. I've done the same."

A familiar *thwump-thwump-thwump* sound headed our way, filling the sky. Soon after, three heli-pods came into view and sank to the ground of the courtyard behind Commander Petralka.

My heart sank.

The belly of the center heli-pod opened and three men stepped out. Two of them held my brother restrained between them, while the third held a gun to his head. Zed's mouth was covered, but when he caught sight of me, he renewed his struggled and muffled shouting, till they kicked his legs out from under him and forced him to the ground.

Birch was being held in a soldier's arms, but, when he saw me, he began his little scratchy roaring again and managed to struggle free, racing out of the heli-pod.

"Your brother," Petralka said. "From what I know of you, that's an awful big bargaining chip of my own."

How *dare* they? My tenuous control on my temper slipped, and I grabbed the grey-skinned girl by the back of the neck and jumped down from the platform.

Soldiers rushed to Petralka's side and pointed their guns at me as I strode forward, dragging the girl, but I ignored them, looking instead to the ones that still held Zed. "If he gets hurt, I'm going to disembowel you. Literally," I said to them.

I continued to move until I was close enough to smell the commander's skin and feel the warmth of her breath. I could see the beat of her heart from the pulsing in her neck. I dropped the girl unceremoniously at her feet.

Petralka's eyes followed with obvious concern, but I stepped forward those last few inches, until I could look down right into her face, almost nose-to-nose, and brought her attention back. "You have no idea the hell I've traveled through, the things I've done. If you want to deal in threats, I should let you know that I've got the bigger gun. What do you think I've been doing this whole time? That power that you want so desperately for yourself, the power of a god? I've got it. And if you cross me, I will annihilate you, and NIX, everything you've ever worked towards, and everything you've ever loved." I looked pointedly to the dying girl, who shared Nadia Petralka's hooked nose, and probably shared a father, as well. "So if you want to deal in threats, think again," I finished, snarling into her face.

She swallowed, but didn't back down. "It doesn't have to be a threat. If you cooperate, none of them need to get hurt. They're still alive as a gesture of my goodwill to you." Petralka looked down to the girl at our feet. "Take her down to medical!" she snapped at one of the guards whose gun was still pointed at me.

I smiled in my head but kept it from my face. "You want to talk? Talk." My hand darted forward and grabbed her by the neck, claws just barely piercing her skin.

To her credit, she reacted immediately, bringing one arm up in a sweeping gesture to knock my hand away and thrusting the other one forward towards my stomach. The hand she attacked with shot a dart forward from beneath the cuff of her sleeve.

I twisted, perhaps a bit unnaturally thanks to my Tumbling Feather Skill, and avoided the dart, releasing her neck for a second to grab her other arm by the shoulder. I shoved sharply forward and down, pushing her off balance, and brought a knee up into her lower back, riding her fall down to the ground. My free hand found the back of her neck and crushed her face into the dirt while I twisted her other arm up behind her in a very classic move.

No one shot me or my brother, likely because my attack happened so quickly, and their commander was in danger if they made the wrong move. A guard stepped forward, gun pointed at me, but I raised a hand and he stopped in his tracks.

"Let me return your gesture of 'goodwill,' Commander," I said. "One of my team you've got surrounded down below has a healing Skill. We'll be going down to see him, and he'll see to the girl. Of course, feel free to keep your men with guns on them," I added caustically.

She stared at me for a second, and I knew she understood my meaning. The girl's life, which she obviously cared about, would depend on my team, and therefore, on me. If Petralka tried to pull a trick, she'd pay the price. She nodded stiffly.

"Jacky, you stay here and guard Adam. Make sure none of these buffoons tries anything that'll get them painfully killed," I said. "Adam, keep an eye on things. If something…untoward is attempted, you know what to do."

Adam patted the side of the exposed wiring. "Got it." He hid his stress well, but I could see the tension in the tightened skin around his eyes.

"Zed, you're coming with us," I said.

Petralka tried to protest at that, but I spoke over her. "Lead the way," I said, clamping a clawed hand on her shoulder. "You really don't have as many options as you seem to think, nor as much authority," I murmured to her, and, with a pause as she seemed to think for a moment, she acquiesced.

ZED STRUGGLED AGAINST HIS CAPTORS, and Petralka waved a hand at them to release him. "I'm sorry," he said once he reached me. "I couldn't do anything. I know this ruins everything—"

Jacky gave him a quick blow to the back. "No worries. We can keep you safe, especially now that we're all together. Eve says the word, and we finish destroyin' the place, then bust the hell outta here."

Zed followed me and the commander, and I gave him the most reassuring smile I could. "This won't take long."

Birch mewled at me, but stayed with Adam and Jacky as I asked him to do.

Commander Petralka led the way through the concrete door they'd blasted open, looking back only once to take in the scene of destruction and carnage. "It's going to take a lot of time and money to fix all the damage you caused. The Shortcut alone…" She sighed. "Not to mention the loss of life."

I noticed a familiar face watching from the windowed halls across the courtyard.

Vaughn grinned and threw me the victory sign, forefinger and middle finger spread in a V. So that's where he disappeared to.

—I'm coming to get you, Sam. Be ready, just in case.—
-Eve-

"What's a few lives lost to you? It's nothing new," I said, turning away from the courtyard and pushing on her neck to move her forward.

She shot me a look of controlled ire and turned her face away from me, heading farther into the hallway. "Every life is my responsibility. Whether they die in the Game or defending our base, it's still on my shoulders. Whatever you think, I'm not running from that fact. But I realize there is a greater good at stake, and a reason that we are willing to sacrifice a few, in the hopes that we might save many. In the prayer that we might save us all." She was muttering by the last bit.

I stared at her back and snorted, then edged both her and I closer to Zed. Getting separated from her might not be a good idea. Any attack on us would be a possible attack on the commander, if we were close enough together. I started to mentally track our route and the necessary security passes in my head, in case I needed to leave again without a guide. The three of us continued down into the ground, and I caught glimpses of things through the occasional door window, some more interesting than others.

One small window looked into an immense room that seemed to be a mix of mechanical workshop, laboratory, and hangar. I saw what looked to be a jetpack hanging from one wall, huge glass tubes of colored liquid that looked like the cloning tubes I'd seen in movies, and what appeared to be a smaller, incomplete replica of the teleportation sphere.

I slowed and stared, just taking in the crazy.

What really caught my attention was the plane at the far side of the lab. At least I thought it was a plane. I'd never seen anything quite like it. It was a grey so dark it would look black without the bright spotlights shining at it from every direction. It looked kind of like what an airplane might look like if it was actually a stingray-shaped crustacean. Or made of a giant crustacean monster's hollowed out shell.

"Yes. Quite the oddity, isn't it?" Commander Petralka said. "We'd never seen anything like it before, either."

"This is your top-secret lab, right? Where are all the people, the scientists?"

"They evacuated, Eve, along with physical documentation of their work up to this point, and anything else they could carry. They were on their way out of here as soon as the alarms went off. Without being able to monitor you properly, we weren't exactly sure of your plan. But I believed you'd survive your little "excursion," even if no one has stayed there and lived before, so I didn't let down my guard. From where the Rabbit group Moderator was tampering around, we thought they might be at risk."

My eyes darted around, catching on Zed, who was stiff with tension, but whose attention was focused bull-doggedly on the commander. I pulled away from the window and continued on. I was struggling to keep mental focus, exhausted from my earlier display, but it wouldn't do to reveal that to the enemy. "What did you mean earlier, when you talked about my score?"

We turned a corner, and Petralka stopped at a door, which she opened by pressing her thumb to a fingerprint pad. "The Game is more than just the Trials," she said. "You know you're all being monitored?" When I didn't respond, she continued. "Of course you do. You managed to slip away from almost all our avenues of observation. You're only the thirty-fourth to ever do so. But the point is, we keep tabs on you because your actions outside of the Trials are also part of the Game. Your reactions to the situation, the danger, the artificial stimuli, the almost inevitable isolation…it's all part of a calculation. A score. A ranking, if you prefer." She stopped at the next door and swiped a card from within her jacket pocket, gave a full handprint scan, and a retinal scan.

The door beeped sharply when I stepped through behind her, but she said, "Allow guest," and continued walking till we reached an elevator.

I looked back at the door closing behind us and caught a glimpse of my reflected face. The whites of my eyes had turned blood red, every little vein and capillary burst within them. My light blue irises stood out creepily against the bloodshot sclera.

Petralka was silent while we sank downward. When the doors opened again, we stepped out of the elevator into a hallway, so deep inside the earth I could feel the weight of thousands of tons of dirt pressing down, pushing the air against my skin. It almost felt as if there was a buzzing in the air, electricity just about to snap, something just about to happen. It was strange to realize that I was walking through where NIX kept their prisoners, that people were being held, trapped, in the rooms around me.

Blaine, Sam, Chanelle, and a couple of kids who looked like Blaine were there, surrounded by a circle of people with guns pointed warily at them.

"Hold fire," she told them, and they shuffled, but didn't take their eyes or their guns off me or my team.

I stepped forward, my hand still on Commander Petralka's shoulder, and broke through the circle.

Sam let out a visible sigh of relief and relaxed his grip on Chanelle, and Blaine stood, his mecha suit unbending from its protective crouch over the children. But Commander Petralka didn't relax, and one of the guards threw a look down the hallway, the type of look you throw over your shoulder when you're alone at night and you think someone might be following you to your pod.

The hair on the back of my arms rose, and that feeling of being on the edge grew more palpable. "What's down the hall, Commander?"

"My guards are worried about more of your little surprise attacks," she said.

"She's lying," Zed interjected before I could say anything.

I turned to him in surprise, and he met my eyes with confidence. "Something important is down there, it's on all their faces, in the way they're standing."

I looked around and saw that he was right. "We like important things, don't we, Adam?" I said aloud, for the benefit of the people around me. I could have just sent him a Window, but this way they knew he was watching.

—Yes. I'll start looking.—
-Adam-

"Let's do some exploring," I said, and Commander Petralka winced subtly, as if in pain, though I hadn't dug in with my claws. That made my teeth-baring smile grow just a little larger. I pushed her forward, and my teammates and her guards followed. The tension quivering in the air grew stronger, and stronger again as we passed through one last security door.

"Commander…" one of the guards hissed, fingering the trigger of his gun.

"Stand down," she snapped as I wiggled my claws against her already slightly bleeding skin. "It's too late already."

Chapter 40

I am alpha and omega, the beginning and the end. I am the creator and destroyer of worlds.

— Eve Redding

I KNEW the details of that moment would remain forever clear in my mind. I stepped forward and looked through an observation window. On the other side, a giant was tied up alone in the middle of a large room, connected to tubes, wires, and machines, bound with enough straps and shackles to confine a large elephant. The metal slab he lay on was tilted forward so that we could see his whole body, half standing, half lying on it.

"The window is a double-sided mirror, triple paned and bulletproof. He can't see us or get to us," she said.

I felt uneasily, as if she was saying that mostly to comfort herself. A couple steps brought me close to the window, which had little wires threaded all through it.

Even bound, I could sense his terrifying strength, and a strange sense of *other*-ness that caused all the small hairs on my body to stand up in alarm. My skin was crawling with unease, but not abhorrence.

He didn't seem that different than us, if indeed quite a bit larger than the average human. In fact, he was almost beautiful, lying there with his eyes closed. Long, dark lashes fanned out on his cheeks, a contrast to the dirty, probably once-blonde hair that hung down matted and tangled, past his face and his equally unkempt golden beard. It had grown bushy and wild in whatever amount of time he'd been held there. Dark circles lay under his eyes like those of a raccoon, standing out against his pale, drawn skin.

His eyes snapped open, looking right into my own.

I jumped, and my heart tried to punch its way out of my chest. I stared back into his eyes, wondering if he could see me through the glass despite the woman's assurance to the contrary.

I *knew* him.

His skin was no longer bronze and healthy, his body no longer looked as if it held the strength of ten men. Despite it all, I knew he would rain down terror and destruction that would make my own look like a child's tantrum if he were ever freed. I had dreamed of him, living in his skin. I'd never heard his voice, and yet I knew its sound. We stared at each other for a long moment, until Petralka said, "This. This is what stands against us, coming to destroy us."

Something changed in him, then. His upper lip lifted away from his teeth in a snarl, ever so slowly. Then, like the snapping of a rubber band, he went berserk, roaring and heaving at his bindings. He strained until his face turned red, snapping his teeth at us.

An alarm started to go off, and a milky white liquid ran through a tube from one of the machines and into his neck. He weakened, a forced calm settling over him, but he still stared out from his incapacitated body with malevolence.

I stepped back from the window and turned Petralka to face me. "What are you talking about?" My fingers trembled slightly with fear, but she didn't seem to notice, too shaken herself.

"They think they're gods," she said. "And compared to us, they might as well be. Which is why we're creating gods of our own."

Blaine shook his head, his eyes slightly vacant as his mind went to work. "This is absurd…" he muttered, except his tone of voice showed how alarming he found it, so his words weren't comforting.

I opened my mouth to keep questioning her but could only shake my head.

—Adam, I'm sure you're seeing this. I need information. Everything and anything. Who is he?—

-Eve-

—Already working on it. I'll send the info to Petralka's link.—
-Adam-

IT DIDN'T TAKE him long. I had Sam strip off Commander Petralka's link and straighten it out so the screen was flat and visible to all of us, and soon after, a video expanded atop its plastine surface.

The video was blurry, shaking as something small and indistinct flew across the screen. "What's happening?" Zed asked, peering at the image.

"We weren't sure at first, either. We thought maybe it was debris in the upper atmosphere, or an unauthorized mission from another country," Petralka said, some of the tension gone from her as she stared raptly at the screen with the rest of us.

The next clip was clearer, though the image was still bad. Something grey shot through the sky far above a line of tall buildings, dipping out of the worst pockets of smog clouds every few seconds. The next was even clearer, and it showed the strange plane slicing through the air, avoiding the shots and missiles of the fighter jets racing after it. The dark grey aircraft flipped up some of the joints on its tail end, dipped one wing, and turned on a dime to shoot back at them. They fell out of the sky like fiery spitballs.

"What is this supposed to be?" I asked, having a feeling I already knew the answer. That aircraft wasn't like anything I'd seen on Earth before today. But in the last few months, I'd been introduced to a lot of things I'd never seen before. In Estreyer, the Trial world.

The commander was staring at the screen intently. "This is the first recorded and verified alien invasion of Earth. We're calling it Breach Zero."

There was a huge, silent explosion across the screen as something hit one of the ships and blew up. The blast seemed much too big and violent for the relatively small size of the ship. When the shockwave reached the recording camera, the video cut out in a short burst of static, and another clip took its place.

"The attempted air strikes, seven years ago…" I trailed off as my mind whirled.

"P.R. had to put some sort of spin on it. Something the public could understand, something they could deal with. Terrorists have always been great news. And the outcry allowed us to put more defensive measures in place against the real threat."

Next, men in hazmat suits, machine guns in hand, were walking toward the downed alien ship. The camera was obviously attached to someone's faceplate, because it dipped up and down with every step, and swung dizzyingly when its wearer looked around. The picture was grainy, and static kept rolling across the screen as if someone was waving a large magnet close to the camera.

But I could see clear enough as they pried open the side of the hatch with a large machine and inched inside, their weapons at the ready. The cameraman stepped inside after them, and the view dipped and swung as he maneuvered through the makeshift entrance. Inside, the grey walls rippled, shining like silk, but hardened instantly at the touch of one of the suited men. There wasn't much left loose, but what there had been was strewn about. A small tree with orchid-like flowers was bent in two, leaking sap onto the floor, and vases filled with colored sand had tipped and broken, spilling their contents.

They walked farther in and saw a small, dead animal on the floor. Its mouse-like body had been crushed under a piece of fallen furniture, its bushy tail sticking straight up in the rigor mortis specific to its species. There was nothing like it on Earth, but I recognized it as one of the rare semi-friendly creatures from Estreyer. A lump in my throat was making it hard to breathe, but I kept watching.

The cameraman moved past the creature as someone else bagged it in a vacuum sealed hazmat pouch. They moved into the cockpit, or command center, or whatever you wanted to call it. In the back of the room, a large metal sphere hung from the ceiling, with floating bands of different colored, different shaped metals orbiting around its axis.

"The Shortcut," Commander Petralka said. "Kind of a goofy name, but when one of our scientists figured out what it did, he started calling it that, and the name stuck."

The strangely designed controls in the front of the cockpit were abandoned, and when the cameraman stepped farther in, the body in front of the metal sphere came into view.

On the floor lay a giant, beautiful blonde man with shoulder length hair and a golden beard, trimmed neatly. He was lying on his back with one arm underneath his body and one leg twisted oddly. He had obviously been injured and fallen, and seemed to be unconscious.

I remembered the force of the explosion and amended my assessment. I would have thought he was dead if I hadn't known he was sedated in the room next to me. I felt sick.

Then the video cut, and it was the man again, this time bound and chained and locked on a huge metal slab in the center of a room. The camera was high above, at an angle, as if it was placed at a corner of the ceiling. The man had wires and patches and tubes running all over and piercing into him. His eyes were closed, but I knew he couldn't be dead, or they wouldn't have restrained him so.

A much smaller man in a white coat came in with a clipboard and poked him in the side with a metal rod. I saw the spark of electricity jumping from the end of the rod as the man in the white coat jerked it back.

The giant woke in an instant and looked around, straining against his bonds, roaring at his attacker with enough force to send the scientist staggering backward. His huge muscles bulged and strained, and the shackles around one wrist started to bend, twisting both the metal clamp and the slab it was welded to.

Before he could rip the arm free, armored men burst into the room from doors in each of the walls and started to shoot him with little darts that I supposed were tranquilizers while simultaneously ushering the scientist out.

The giant ignored the darts in his skin for a few moments, shaking his head in rage and continuing to strain against his bonds. But as soon as the men were gone from the room, the doors closed again, and thick gas started to pour from holes placed all along the outside of the walls. He was half obscured, but I could see him slump and fall back again to the metal slab, senseless.

There was another clip of him, snarling at a camera held at a lower angle. "My people…will kill…you all!" he snarled in English with a strange lilting accent.

The video clip cut off, and the screen went dark.

"I find myself completely astounded," Blaine murmured, which solicited a snort from Zed.

"The last one was taken a few months after we downed his ship and captured him. It seems his race is significantly intelligent, to learn our language so quickly. Or maybe I should say his species?" Commander Petralka, who I'd almost forgotten about, shrugged beside me. "Breach

Zero hit most major military facilities around the world. We're fairly positive it was a scouting mission. A test of our responses."

She chuckled bleakly and turned away from the link. "Unfortunately, we failed that test miserably."

I listened to her in silence, staring back through the observation window at the giant man, for once at a loss for words. This changed things. My plans had been decimated by this revelation, the same as if NIX had shot one of those ship-downing nukes at them. I was listening almost absently, scrambling to come up with a way to get what I needed out of all this.

"Almost all of their ships escaped unharmed as we scrambled to do something, anything, to counter their attacks. We destroyed a couple, but managed to take this one mostly intact, along with some of their technology, like the Shortcut. After that, every single nation of the world banded together, combining their military resources in preparation for the coming war."

"War coming, when?" I asked.

"Soon. Less than a year. Maybe less than six months. We've got a rough idea of when those that escaped will be bringing reinforcements. That is, if none of the other ships had some different form of FTL communication or transportation that we don't know about."

"FTL, meaning faster than light?" I asked, even as Blaine opened his mouth to no doubt ask the same thing.

"Yes." She opened the security door blocking off the rest of the hallway. "If it takes them as long as we've estimated to make the round trip. It all depends on how quick to mobilize military forces they are. Now, let's hurry back to the surface. Your healer has a job to do."

I motioned to Sam to keep an eye on her, took one last look at the sedated man, and followed Petralka with the rest of my team and her own visibly uncomfortable guards, who seemed reluctant to be trapped alone down there with him—or it, I still wasn't sure. In the midst of my tired delirium, it suddenly struck me as funny how these aliens looked like us, except bigger. What were the chances that two races from two different worlds in an infinite universe would look almost completely alike? I'd bet my life the odds were beyond minuscule. And if I went with the plan forming in my head, I literally *would* be placing my life on the line.

Blaine herded the three defenseless captives he and Sam had rescued, and Zed fell into step beside me, silent but watching Petralka and her guards intently.

I gave the three rescues a quick once-over. Chanelle was staring blankly ahead and following Blaine meekly, looking worrisomely catatonic, while the two smaller children were huddled together, and though also silent, showed obvious signs of tears and not a small amount of jumpiness. What had they gone through while we tried to find a way to save them?

"And you're sure reinforcements are coming?" I asked, turning back to Commander Petralka.

She stopped and stared at me for a moment, then continued walking and talking as if I hadn't asked such a stupid question. "We have permission to enforce a mandatory draft from the citizenry. Kind of like martial law except no one knows about it yet, unless they're part of it."

"Like me." I followed her onto an elevator, which started a long, dark ascent back up through the heart of the earth.

"Yes." Her lips twitched at the look on my face. "The Constitution and human rights? Is that what you're thinking about? Those don't mean as much as you might believe, especially in the face of our extinction as a species."

"Some would say the life of an individual is worth as much as the life of the masses."

Petralka snorted. "That someone would die along with the masses when these things come back. They're different than us."

"You're drafting soldiers to fight an alien invasion," I said. "How crazy does that sound?" I laughed humorlessly. "But why do it like this? It seems counterproductive to actually building and training a fighting force. You take kids, basically, with no military inclinations, and leave them to their own devices. Why not allow volunteers, or recruit from within the military, or at least cultivate them and train them from the beginning?"

"We're looking for a certain type of person," she said as the elevator doors opened and we moved back into the ground-level floor of the NIX compound. "We do recruit from within the military, if the genetics are right. We found out early on that the Seeds weren't compatible with a large majority of the population. Only people with a certain gene sequence can adapt. The survival rate is higher in younger people, which is why we aim for them. And the Game is designed to create a specific type of person, someone who will adapt, and fight, and survive against horrifying odds. The type who can make it without someone holding their hand."

"Do you need to kill half of them to do that?"

"The Trials do create strong people. But you're right; I wouldn't use them if I didn't have to. We need the Trials because the Seeds we can manufacture on our own are sub-par to what the aliens have. And the Skills are beyond our current technology entirely. But we don't create the Trials. They're entirely an invention of those creatures. The aliens are violent and horrifying in nature, and their games reflect that. They worship their 'gods' through them, and are rewarded with power."

"You send children into these 'violent and horrifying' games. What does that make you?"

"It makes me someone who's willing to pay the price. I'm not heartless. But I'm strong enough to do what needs to be done, even if I have to carry the weight of the dead on my shoulders." As if to add weight to her words, she knocked my hand away from her shoulder and walked away, back out through the blown-up security door into the courtyard, scowling.

I would have grabbed her again, but I needed some space to think where she wouldn't be analyzing my every twitch. Her justifications were bullshit, and I knew it, but it seemed like she might actually believe them. But, except for figuring out how I might use what I was learning against her, my focus was on the verbal confrontation I was about to initiate.

Zed sidled up beside me and whispered, "She was lying earlier, when she was talking about the Trials."

"What?"

He shook his head, lips pressed together. "I don't know what about, exactly. But I could tell she was lying. She's not being completely truthful, trust me on that."

And I did, but it didn't matter, except that it might make negotiations harder. "Well, that's no surprise," I muttered back.

—Guys, I know we all saw that. I'm going to take a drastic change in course. I can't leave, now, but if you want to, you still can.—

-Eve-

I got a barrage of Windows back, as if they'd all been waiting for that moment.

Sam sent me an apology for failing in the mission and getting captured, Jacky told me they were ready to come down and break me out if something had gone wrong, and Adam sent me a suspicious query about what was going on.

When I emerged through the destroyed doorway into the light of the sun, Jacky and Adam let out a simultaneous sigh of relief.

The armor-skinned pixie girl was lying on the ground, motionless, but Sam rushed over to her and touched her head. His eyes widened, but he nodded at me, communicating that she would live.

Commander Petralka's shoulder slumped a little, then straightened again so quickly I wouldn't have noticed if I wasn't watching her. "We need soldiers that can match them." She motioned to the Players still watching from the windows lining part of the courtyard.

"People like me," I said.

She stared at me for a second, surprise showing through the mask of calm she'd regained. "People like you, Eve. I'll admit, you've gone the furthest of almost any Player before entering NIX. Was that Skill before truly a Bestowal? How did you get it?"

"I took it," I said, making it clear by my tone that I was unwilling to elaborate further. I gave her a large smile. "And why don't we stop playing this game, Commander?"

"You want to escape the Game," she said heavily. "You want me to just let you go, with you knowing what you do?"

"You shouldn't make assumptions, Commander. You've misjudged me," I said, stepping closer when she frowned in confusion. "You mentioned being able to understand how the aliens work by looking at their Trials." I paused for dramatics. "I know how you work, because I've seen what the Game uses to motivate Players. Whatever fancy reasoning you want to spout for your actions, it's obvious you understand two things. Fear, and greed."

She stared up at me.

"I showed you what there is to fear from me, but it wasn't enough to sway you. It only served to fuel your greed instead. That's too bad, but it's okay." My smile was full of teeth and triumph. "Because your greed *is* enough to sway you. You want my power, and you've already proven you're willing to do whatever it takes to gain it. And I'm going to give it to you, whether you like it or not, because you're going to meet my conditions for doing so. I'll be staying here, with the other Players you deemed worthy enough to join your forces, rather than stay part of the ignorant cannon-fodder."

Her eyes widened and she blinked a couple times, obviously thrown for a mental loop. But she regained her composure quickly, and her eyes narrowed just a bit with what I thought was calculation. "You think I'd take you in, after this?" She waved her hand to encompass the courtyard and all the literal and figurative damage we'd done.

"You allowed this to happen, in part," I countered, shaking my head. "These goons weren't even shooting at our heads. Please, spare me the false incredulity."

She shook her head in self-derisive amusement. "You're sharper than I gave you credit for."

"That's okay. I aim to continuously surprise."

"But why do you want to join us? If I recall correctly, it was only a few minutes ago that you were attacking and threatening to expose our cause to the world."

"I could care less about the aliens," I said. "I'm not interested in saving the world. But I am interested in keeping all of us safe."

"Safe, by joining NIX?" Adam interjected, raising an eyebrow. He was subdued, and I thought the rebuttal was more his token role as devil's advocate than an actual argument.

I met his gaze for a moment before nodding at him subtly. Adam was smart. Maybe he'd figured out what I was doing. "Safer. If we don't want to join, we need to destroy them. But destroying them doesn't stop the Estreyans from coming. What it does is reduce the power Earth has to fight back. From what I understand, they're the only real defense the world has. But I don't work for free. There are a few other things I want that I think they might provide."

Commander Petralka's mouth twitched, and I was almost certain she was hiding a smirk. Good, let her think that she was in control.

"I want my team to be privy to the hiring negotiations. Along with everyone else watching," I said, jerking my head to the increasingly packed glass hallways.

"Let's not make a production of this," Commander Petralka said, frowning. "You said you had conditions. What are they?"

"My first stipulation is my brother," I said.

"We'll let him go. He'll not be in danger from us," she agreed, nodding vigorously.

"That's not what I mean. Of course you'll let him go. What I need is for you to remove him from the Game."

"Eve, please don't do this," Zed said. "I'll be okay. I made the mistake. You don't need to sell your soul to fix it."

"I'm not doing this just for you, Zed. Stop being so conceited." I threw him a nonchalant wink, which only made me realize how much my eyeballs were starting to hurt.

"What are you talking about?" Petralka asked.

"My brother got his hands on a Seed. He doesn't have the genetic marker needed to be compatible with them, but luckily I've got a pretty freaking amazing healer. However, because of the way the Trials work, my brother is forced into them, even though he's not a Player. I want you to fix that. I want him to have a normal life."

She seemed lost in thought for a while, then said, "Was it just the one Seed?"

"Yes."

"And he doesn't have the genetic marker? Amazing. I can't guarantee anything, but there might be a way to slowly release the particles and filter them out of his blood. I can't do that for the rest of you," she added. "It's much too late. We'll have time to get him clean. Until we can get the Shortcut fixed."

"The Shortcut isn't my concern. If I have to, I'll stop it for good."

"The future of mankind depends on us!" she snapped. "What kind of life will the boy have when Earth is destroyed by—"

I stared her down, and she stepped closer to our group so her voice wouldn't travel. Not that it would matter if one of the Players listening from up above had extremely high Perception, unless the glass was made out of something special.

"How will your brother fare in an alien invasion from the species that created the Trials, without us here to do anything to stop them?" she continued. "Especially being as weak as he is?"

"Good points, Commander. I guess it's up to you to make sure I never have to make such a difficult decision."

Her nostrils flared. "We will do everything we can to remove the Seed from your brother. Is there anything else?"

"Quite a bit, actually." I looked at Jacky, Sam, and Adam, all of whom were displaying varying degrees of uncertainty. "Those of my team who wish to join me in NIX will be allowed to."

"That shouldn't be too hard to accommodate, though they may be a bit behind the other recruits."

"If they do not choose to follow me, you will let them go, no repercussions."

She clenched her jaw but nodded sharply. "Okay."

"I assume you have leadership tiers among the others, if you're training them like soldiers?" I continued without waiting for her response. "I will keep my position as a leader, for those who will follow me. I won't accept being under the command of some random person, no matter if I'm a new recruit or not. And the same for any who follow me."

"Slightly unconventional, but doable."

"You will release Kris and Gregor"—I jerked my head toward the two children—"back to their uncle, Blaine Mendell, who I also consider part of my team. All stipulations for the team extend to him. Those conditions also extend to Bunny the Moderator. I'm sure you know who I mean, though I don't know his real name."

"I do."

"Chanelle Black," I said simply.

The girl was lying on the ground beside Sam. If the first part of the plan had gone accordingly, the antidote to the "wolf" bite should already be working in her system.

"She's yours, too," Petralka said, anticipating my demand.

"Yes."

"I think it's my turn to lay out terms for our agreement now." When I only raised an eyebrow, she continued. "You will follow orders like all the others we've taken into the fold. If you want to join us, act like one of us. You will be assigned training classes, and will be expected to attend and perform to the best of your ability. Any disruption will be punished as if you were anyone else, and you are responsible for controlling the actions of your team, if they decide to join. If they do not decide to join, they should be fully aware that your wellbeing is tied with ours. I wouldn't want anything…unfortunate to happen."

I'd expected no less, but Jacky clenched her fists threateningly. "You know what I always say, Eve. The best defense is an overwhelmingly powerful offense," she muttered.

"And one last thing," I said, raising my voice a little to draw Commander Petralka's attention back to me.

"Only one more?" she said sarcastically. "Why, please, go ahead."

"The man who killed China Black. You will give him to me, too."

Jacky guffawed and pumped her fist.

The commander's eyebrows rose. "I understand you must feel some bitterness, but I assure you he's been thoroughly reprimanded."

"Oh, really? Reprimanded?" I asked, hurling her sarcasm back at her like a weapon.

"Yes. He was demoted and put under supervision, among other things. What happened was unfortunate and unnecessary."

I held her gaze, drawing myself up to my full height as I said, "What he did is unforgivable."

"He is a valuable asset to us, and, though a bit unrestrained, he's proven his loyalty. You, however, are even more of a loose cannon"—she spread her hands to evidence the courtyard—"and you show a distinct lack of allegiance to anyone besides yourself and your little team. I won't trade his life for your gratification. If I were to execute everyone who'd ever killed anyone else, you'd be on that list, too."

"Indeed, I would," I said, deciding to let the argument go for the moment. The truth was, Petralka's permission didn't matter to me. The snake man would find himself painfully dead at my earliest convenience, no matter what she said. "Okay."

She searched my eyes for a moment, and then nodded, too. "Okay."

By the time she learned not to trust me if I acquiesced so quickly, it would be too late for her.

Commander Petralka turned her back on me, but I kept the savage grin I'd been suppressing from spreading across my face. I may have won, but I didn't know who was watching, and it wouldn't do to reveal too much.

Log of Captivity 6

Mental Log of Captivity—Estimated Day: Two thousand, six hundred forty-three.

She is a *two-leg-maggot*. When she attacked and the *screams-with-no-mouth* began to wail, the others of her kind gave me the seed of the poppy to force my tranquility so that I would not damage my body again. Though her mind was walled off, I sensed her draw near. She stood on the other side of the glass, and, fool that I was, I did not even notice her true nature. I thought only of my eyes meeting hers. Then the *most-abhorrent* and she began to hold discussion, watching me as if I was some fascinating bug. I am in *blood-covenant* with a *two-leg-maggot*. I am a halfwit. I thought my suffering complete, no pain not inflicted, no humiliation ignored, nothing pure undefiled. But the gods play a crueler game.

Chapter 41

Who shall tempt, with wandering feet,
The dark unbottomed infinite abyss?
— John Milton

I SAT atop NIX's wall, staring out at the murky evening sky. In Estreyer, the stars would just be coming out.

Birch lay on my lap, carefully grooming his paws and sharp kitten-claws.

The rest of the team was down below, considering their options. I'd left them to make their own individual decisions.

"It might be just you and me," I said to Birch, scratching behind his ears.

He grunted at me and continued grooming himself.

After the team had seen what was held below NIX, we'd talked, and I'd laid out my reasons for staying through a Window to those who could see it, with instructions not to reveal the information, which was more than just bartering for Zed's life and the team's freedom.

"So NIX continues to exist, we stay safe one way or another. And you want other people able to do the fighting, so maybe we won't have to," Adam had said aloud, skillfully holding a second conversation with me, out of notice.

—Do you really think this creature is so important?—
-Adam-

"Uh, yeah. Exactly. Plus, we'd have access to more Seeds and targeted training."

I had routed his conversation to the others, so the team members with a VR chip could see both sides of the conversation. Unfortunately, for those who didn't have one, there was nothing I could do to make them understand without revealing things to the monitoring devices NIX was no doubt smothering us with.

—I can feel it. I know that sounds strange, but the Oracle gave me the vision of Behelaino that indirectly led me here, and along with it she leveled up my non-sensory Perception. I feel like he's important, and if I leave, there won't be another chance to come back.—
-Eve-

"And in exchange for this, they keep us under their thumb and watchful eye. They control us."

"They think they control us," I'd corrected, giving them all a quick grin.

—This is an infiltration. But the negotiation I had with the commander was valid. Anyone who wants to leave can do so. I will stay, and my presence will shield you from reprisal.—
-Eve-

Zed had started out frowning down at his hands, not meeting my eyes, but as the dual conversations continued, he'd gained that strangely intense focus again, his eyes flickering from face to face. He wasn't privy to the secondary conversation, but I thought he might be aware of its existence. I'd need to find a way to talk to him, soon.

Blaine and Bunny hadn't been to the Trials before, and so had been more shocked by the day's many revelations than the rest of us. Throughout the conversation, both the scientist and the awkward-in-person Moderator seemed too overwhelmed to respond. Normally, Blaine wouldn't have been able to shut up about such a huge discovery, but I had to remind myself that now he had his surrogate kids to worry about, too.

"I know what I have to do," I had told them. "I'm worth enough to keep NIX off your backs if you decide to leave. Think about it. And… whoever is with me, meet me up on the wall. I'm kinda tired. Gonna watch the sunset."

And so there I sat, alone, thinking about distant suns and the winds of change.

"Heya!" I heard from down below.

Jacky waved up at me as she started walking across the courtyard, the others following on her heels. All of them.

I grinned and waved back, then turned to watch the red and purple streaked sky fade out as they came to join me.

Birch turned around in my lap and let out a whine.

"What's up?"

He leaned forward and started to lick my upper lip and nose, his tongue coming away dark red.

I drew back from him and brought a hand to my nose. My fingers came away bloody. "Just a nosebleed. No big deal," I said, laughing past the fear.

He nuzzled up to me and started to lick my neck, whining more insistently.

I felt the blood drip out of my ear, saw it land on his muzzle.

He whimpered again, licking more frantically.

I tilted my head back, tore a strip of my sleeve away, and used it to wipe away the blood spontaneously dripping from my nose and ear, then took a Seed out of my pocket. Commander Petralka had given them to me upon request, as a sort of signing bonus for joining NIX. "I wish I was more Resilient."

I took a deep breath, and then lifted Birch up to my head and had him lick up the rest of the dark red smears from my face and neck. "This is a secret, okay?" I said, staring seriously into his eyes. "The others can't know about the side effects of my new power. They think I've got it under control. No one can know, or we won't be safe anymore."

He let out his little scratchy growl, getting another laugh out of me, this one more genuine. "I know you'll protect us. But it's still a secret."

I turned my head to the side, where my team had just walked up the steps on the inside of the wall. I waved them over, and they settled in beside me to watch the muted sun of Earth leave us behind.

. . .

THE STORY CONTINUES in *Seeds of Chaos Book II: Gods of Rust and Ruin*. Turn the page to continue reading.

Gods of Rust and Ruin

To Jared. For I am with you.

Chapter 1

No one but Night, with tears on her dark face, watches beside me.
— Edna St. Vincent Millay

I SAT UP ABRUPTLY, choking on my own blood. I jerked out of the little cot tucked into the side of the wall and spat the liquid onto the floor in a dark splatter. The heavy iron taste in my mouth added to the terror of the nightmare I'd been yanked from. My claws slipped out and I sliced through the empty darkness, lashing out at a nonexistent enemy.

A second of flailing later, I got control of myself. I was alone. The only enemy attacking me was also the thing keeping me alive, now that I lived within NIX's compound. The Seed of Chaos made me powerful enough to be valuable, while literally eating away at me from the inside.

I gagged and coughed, trying to staunch the blood flow with one hand while fumbling for the backpack shoved underneath my mattress with the other. The only light in the room came from the small diodes on a couple of sleeping electronics, but it was enough for my augmented eyes to see. I pulled out a small pouch and fumbled for one of the large, marble-like Seeds within. "I wish I was more Resilient," I mouthed almost soundlessly, pressing it to my neck. I was long past flinching at the pinprick. I sighed in relief as the Seed injected its contents into me and took hold, stopping the bleeding.

Birch, my little monster-cat companion, woke, either from the noise I'd made or the smell of my blood dripping everywhere. He let out his scratchy little meow, the sound lilting upward at the end in an obvious question. He hadn't yet displayed the ability of his late mother to share thoughts through touch, but he was far from stupid.

"I had to take a Seed," I muttered to him, my voice low in case something was listening. "I was bleeding again, but I'm okay now."

Birch bumped me with his head and licked at the blood on my forearm with his prickly tongue.

I withdrew my arm before his tongue accidentally removed the top layer of my skin, and moved to the shower in the tiny bathroom stall. I was the only one of my teammates with private quarters. The others were sleeping in a small barracks-like room across the hall from me, stacked two bunks high. I'd glanced at their room the night before, and then promptly passed out from exhaustion onto my own private little cot.

Behind me, Birch grumbled and moved to lick up my blood from the cold hard floor. He had an excessive and disturbing penchant for raw meat and blood. Especially my blood.

I turned on the water at a temperature most kindly described as "scalding" and let it wash away the sticky red residue, along with the lingering creepy feeling from my nightmare. I'd been waking up with nightmares, *from* nightmares, for a while. But they were getting worse than ever before, and I rarely went a night without them.

Sometimes, it was the monsters of a Trial coming for me, ready to rip me apart and dance with my entrails. Sometimes, it was the last time I saw my team member China, as the light went out of her eyes and she died. And sometimes, the nightmare had no form. It was the creeping mass of decay and putrefaction devouring everything in its path. A shudder, a feeling, a smell.

When I exited the shower, Birch had finished cleaning all the blood from the floor. My sheets and pillowcase still glistened with the dark liquid, but luckily, they were black. I took them back into the shower with me and cleaned the synthetic material as best I could. No one would know what had happened.

Birch called to me from the doorway of the shower, his meow still scratchy from sleep.

"It's getting worse," I murmured.

The cub padded past the open shower door and under the spray of water, then licked my knee and peered up at me with his green human eyes. Water splashed down on him and his translucent second eyelids closed sideways for protection. He spread his downy wings to better catch the warm water.

"I'm afraid," I whispered, knowing that he couldn't reveal my secret, and the rushing water would cover any other surveillance that might have slipped through my search. "The Seeds aren't working for as long as they used to."

The Seed of Chaos grew continually stronger, as Behelaino had warned me it would. I just hadn't thought it would happen this *fast*. Every time I was forced to use it, it grew stronger, but being able to display it was the only thing keeping me—and the team—safe.

The meditation technique Adam had taught me helped control Chaos, too, but I could only do so much without more Seeds. A lot more. Without them or some other way to heal myself, the outcome was obvious. I had wanted to keep my condition a secret, but I would need to reveal it to Sam, and hope that he could help me until I could find a way to fix myself.

"I'm dying, Birch," I whispered with terrible certainty, the words no more than a breath on the air.

Chapter 2

I buried my past under a sheet of old earth, and hoped it would not rise up to follow me again.
— Ilium Troia

"I'M GOING to have to find another way to fix this," I said, voice hardening as an angry determination pushed back the fear. The words came easily enough, but I had no idea how to actually do anything about the black Seed eating away at me.

I exited the shower, turned on the lights to my room and sat on the floor, ignoring the water still beaded on my skin and slicking my hair down. Fear pounded through my bloodstream, gurgling in my stomach and weakening my muscles. When Birch crawled onto my lap, I laid my hand on his side, letting his heartbeat center me.

I breathed out and started my meditation exercises. The sun wouldn't rise for a while, so I had time. I closed my eyes and breathed in deep, until I could feel the oxygen swirling in the deepest parts of my lungs, spreading into my blood. From there, it wasn't so hard to sense the tiny particles of Chaos.

I forced them into my mental room of serenity, and put their writhing darkness in my box of silence, locked inside the chest of stillness. By its very nature, Chaos hated being confined so, and wrestled with me to escape. But if there is one thing I can be sure of in myself, it is my will of iron. I do not back down.

I stayed in my meditative state even after I was finished cleansing my body, letting my heightened Perception swirl around me. I could feel Birch's little heart beating within his body, hear the electricity thrumming through the walls, and sense the cold air blowing through the vents woven into the compound.

Desperate curiosity sparked within me again. I'd agreed to join NIX for two reasons. Partially, to gain their "protection" for myself and my team. And partially because of the alien down below. Maybe, we could have threatened NIX into compliance after breaking the Shortcut and escaped to live in peace, but when I had seen the alien, that had no longer been an option for me. Not until the urge inside me that I didn't even understand had been sated, at least.

The night before, I'd searched my quarters for monitoring devices. I found many, some of them hidden more cleverly than others. I'd destroyed them, of course. Beyond that, I'd been too exhausted to even brush my teeth before falling into bed. I hadn't had the time or the energy to learn much about NIX, or the thing it was holding far below, in the bowels of the mountain. Now I did.

I sent my awareness outward through the air, leaving my room through the vent in the ceiling. It was more difficult to force my awareness to travel through substances I wasn't in physical contact with, and as I pushed farther from my body, even moving at all got exponentially harder. So I let my mind travel through the vents and hallways and spaces where air traveled unimpeded. I sensed Players as I went, an aura of sorts thrumming around them even as they slept.

Occasionally, I passed a bright spark of power that wasn't asleep. A couple roamed the halls, or the cafeteria, and farther down a group of them had gathered in a large room along the way, but my Perception of details aside from the Seed glow was hazy at that distance, and I couldn't tell what they were doing.

I slipped past, straining to hold my concentration together. Downward, level after level, until something pinged on the edges of my alertness. I ignored it. I was used to gaining levels by that point. I'd check my stats later. I strained, but I couldn't keep hold of that strange extra-sensory Perception at such distances. It snapped, fraying like mist through a shredder, and I found myself fully back in my room, my head throbbing fiercely along with my heartbeat.

I DRESSED in the bodysuit NIX provided for its Players, wearing my blood-powered armored vest underneath it. I ignored the boots because my feet were too strangely shaped nowadays to fit into them, and the bottoms were tough enough to make footwear unnecessary. I wove my damp hair into a tight braid and checked the whites of my eyes in the bathroom mirror. I'd disabled its monitoring function the night before. The blood vessels in my sclera were still red and irritated, and patches of rusty brown showed where they'd broken and bled, which made the ice-blue of my irises stand out more. At least it looked better than the disturbing bloody color the whites of my eyes had been the day before, after I'd used too much Chaos.

Before leaving the room, I pulled up my Attributes Window to see what had happened during my mental foray into the carved-out depths of the mountain.

PLAYER NAME: EVE REDDING
TITLE: SQUAD LEADER(9)
CHARACTERISTIC SKILL: SPIRIT OF THE HUNTRESS,
TUMBLING FEATHER
LEVEL: 38 UNPLANTED SEEDS: 0
SKILLS: COMMAND, CHAOS

STRENGTH: 14
LIFE: 27
AGILITY: 21
GRACE: 18
INTELLIGENCE: 17
FOCUS: 17
BEAUTY: 10
PHYSIQUE: 12
MANUAL DEXTERITY: 9
MENTAL ACUITY: 18
RESILIENCE: 22
STAMINA: 19
PERCEPTION: 20

For some reason, my out of body awareness didn't count as a Skill.

Maybe because I hadn't gained it through a specific Skill Bestowal. I didn't advertise its existence, so anyone who didn't know and saw me using it just thought I was into meditation. The couple of Seeds Commander Petralka had given me and the others as a joining bonus weren't noted, either.

I placed my hand on the pad next to my door, and it slid open onto the slightly curving hallway. One of the barracks doors a few meters down the hall was also open. A Player leaned nonchalantly against the doorway, staring straight at the entrance to my quarters. She held my gaze long enough to make it an obvious challenge, then stepped back and waved her door closed.

Birch bared his teeth at her closed door.

I rolled my shoulders to release the tension already building there and knocked briefly on the door to my team's room before signaling it to open. I wasn't going to worry about hostility from the other Players in NIX, since there wasn't much I could do about it. Hopefully, our display the day before would keep anyone from messing with us directly. If not, maybe we would have to put on another gruesome show with the first people to try their luck.

Within the room, most of my teammates milled about in various states of undress, some still obviously waking up.

Birch shot through the open doorway, straight at Adam. He knocked Adam back onto the low bed behind him, ruffled his wings, let out a scratchy roar, and pranced off.

Kris, Blaine's young niece, let out a delighted laugh and bent down, making enticing noises at Birch.

"Be quiet," her younger brother grumbled, scrubbing at his face. Gregor's adorable bushy eyebrows drew down into a scowl like a storm cloud.

"Why does Birch hate me?" Adam said, throwing his arms out dramatically and ruffling Sam's pristinely made bed. Which he was still lying on, apparently having given up on the idea of standing back up.

Zed laughed, leaning down from his bunk above Adam. "Birch doesn't hate you. He loves you. He *loves* to torment you."

I snickered, drawing Adam's attention, and was about to add a comment of my own when a flash of blonde caught the corner of my eye. My first thought was that Blaine was combing Sam's hair. Then I realized, of course it was China, not Sam. After that, I realized it was actually Chanelle, and her hair had been cut sometime during her stay at NIX. No doubt to make it easier for her captors to care for her. She stared blankly ahead, not seeming to notice the tug of the comb on the boy-short hair of her head, or the people around her. Everything about it was wrong. China's face, even if it wasn't really her, shouldn't be so blank. And she definitely would never have chopped off her princess-hair.

Any amusement died a cold death.

Adam's eyes followed my own, and he sat up, running nimble fingers through the brown mop of curls atop his own head.

"No luck?" I said, turning to Sam, who was yanking his covers back into some semblance of neatness.

He straightened and shook his head. "I can tell something's wrong with her, or was wrong at some point, but...I can't fix it. Something's wrong with her brain, I *think*. But it seems as if it's natural, rather than an injury. Maybe, it's because whatever it was happened too long ago. I can't take away scars." He grimaced and looked away, but not before I caught a glimpse of the shiny wetness in his eyes. "If we'd gotten to her sooner…"

Jacky hopped down from her own top bunk, landing way too lightly for a normal human. She was unrealistically beautiful even with her brown eyes glazed over and her hair a tangled mess from sleeping. I would have bet money that she put more than a few handfuls into Beauty if I didn't know better. She clapped Blaine on the shoulder, causing him to drop the comb and wince from the blow. Then she patted Chanelle on the head, gently enough that she probably wouldn't have cracked an egg. "She'll get better, Sam," Jacky croaked sleepily. "We're gonna figure out a way." Then she stumbled to the bathroom, burping loudly and scratching her stomach.

"Ugh, everyone, please shut the gaping holes of loudness and stinking breath you seem to think are your mouths," Gregor said, loud and clear, just as the door opened beside me.

The room quieted for a bit, as we all turned to stare at the child in astonishment.

"Whoa," the new arrival said from the doorway. "Brush your own teeth before you start talking!" Bunny turned to me. His rumpled shirt, hair, and the slightly awkward tilt of his mouth belied the directness of his gaze. "Someone's been having bad dreams," he murmured mockingly.

I almost reacted, thinking he was talking about me, when Gregor muttered, "They're not bad dreams. I'm not an idiot!" and stalked off to the bathroom, the hems of his pajama pants covering his entire feet.

Blaine turned to Kris, a question on his face.

She shook her head and picked up the small stuffed moose propped up against her pillows. It was old and worn. "We both have bad dreams sometimes, but Mom isn't here to make them seem less real now."

Blaine stared at her through the lenses of his glasses, his hands stilling in Chanelle's hair. "Err...well...I am here now. I know I cannot compare to your mother, but—"

Kris shrugged quickly, and cut him off. "We're older now. We don't need you to help us with bad dreams," she said, carefully patting her moose on the head and settling it back against her pillow without looking at Blaine.

I felt awkward on Blaine's behalf, so I turned to Bunny and gestured to Chanelle. "Do you have any idea what's been done to her? Brain damage?"

Bunny shrugged. "That's really not my area of expertise. Besides, wasn't she all 'rabies-biter,' before?" He bared his teeth and made fake claws, swiping at the air.

I stared at him expressionlessly, letting my eyes convey how utterly humorless I found him.

He lowered his hands after a few moments, "Well, I just mean, you guys did something to her, right?" He stared hard at Blaine. "You gave her something that stopped the crazy but made her stupid instead."

Blaine stood up, clenching the comb in his hand hard enough to bend the plastine teeth. "I did *not* do this to her."

"Whoa, *calm down*. You've got to admit it. You're not a doctor, you're a scientist. Maybe you didn't consider all the side effects."

Blaine's arm jerked a couple times, his hands loosened around the comb, and he went back to untangling Chanelle's hair, not seeming to notice that some of the comb's teeth were bent. "I am a genius," he said. "I did not do this." But now, his voice was calm, almost serene in fact.

I lifted an eyebrow. Blaine, calmly accepting someone disparaging his inventions or intelligence? Maybe he really was worried that he'd done something wrong. "Well, NIX has records, right? I'm assuming they were studying Chanelle and whatever it was that infected her. We need that information. Talk to whoever you need to, and make it happen," I said to Bunny.

Bunny hesitated. "That's probably classified information. Besides... they're not very happy with me at the moment."

"I'm pretty sure everything we know about NIX is classified. At this point, does it really matter? If you don't make it happen, Bunny, I'm going to." I let my expression harden a bit.

He scratched the back of his head. "Well, if you agree to get your VR and GPS chips replaced, I could probably get that information." When Jacky, Sam, Adam, and I immediately focused on him, he rolled his eyes. "*Don't be so suspicious*, guys! NIX just wants to make sure they can keep track of you without going to ridiculous lengths, and all the other Players here have working VR chips. They run the classes with them, make announcements, all that stuff."

I felt my shoulders relax just a little. That made sense. But it still didn't mean I was going to agree to give NIX even more power over the team and me.

Jacky shrugged and returned to getting ready, while Sam relaxed with an easy smile, but Adam frowned and shook his head.

Zed hopped down from his bunk. "What about me? The boss lady said you were going to remove the Seed from me. How does that work?"

Bunny shrugged. "I have no idea. The scientists are working on something. They'll let us know when they've got it figured out."

I frowned. "How long is that going to take?"

"Not long, probably. *Don't worry,*" he said, meeting my gaze. "NIX will take care of Zed. Commander Petralka knows how valuable you are."

I wasn't that worried. But staring into Bunny's eyes, I realized that I couldn't tell what color they were. That was weird, wasn't it? I nodded, and he smiled, the skin around his eyes crinkling up in happiness.

BUNNY TOOK us first to the cafeteria for breakfast, where we garnered plenty of attention. Everyone knew who we were, apparently. Many had probably seen the pandemonium of our second invasion of NIX, and each had their own response. Some seemed afraid of me, and the power we had displayed. Perhaps unsurprisingly, that response was in the minority. Most watched and waited to see what we would do, like predators waiting for our guard to drop. To be taken in by NIX, you had to be valuable. And above all, NIX seemed to value those of us with monstrous tendencies. I was no exception.

I sighed. It was definitely going to get annoying if everyone didn't go back to minding their own business soon.

After we finished the gigantic and very uncomfortable meal, Kris and

Gregor left to go to class, which apparently was being taught by remote schooling. I was surprised, because for some reason I hadn't anticipated that NIX would ensure the kids' continued education while holding them hostage against Blaine.

Blaine left with the kids, excited to spend time with the niece and nephew he'd been separated from for so long, and then to get his lab area set up while they were learning.

Just as Bunny was about to continue our introduction to NIX, some scientist approached and requested that Zed come with him for diagnostic testing.

"He's not going anywhere with you alone," I said automatically.

Bunny sighed loudly. "*You* are the one who asked for this, Eve. *Relax*, and let the man do his job."

Zed looked uncertainly from the scientist to me, but left with him.

I watched him leave, feeling strange. Just as he was about to turn the corner, I crouched down, touching Birch on the flank. "Go after him. Make sure he's safe," I murmured.

Birch fluffed up and raced after my brother, his claws leaving little scratch marks on the floor.

Bunny shook his head, but only sighed. "Come on, guys. Let's get you signed up for classes." As we walked, he launched into a seemingly-rehearsed spiel. "NIX is very interested in helping our Players to develop and expand the utility of their Skills. With some experimentation and practice, you may find that you're more versatile than you originally imagined, or that refinement of your control significantly increases your effectiveness."

He turned to look at Sam. "NIX is particularly interested in helping you develop your Skill, you know. It's rare that we find someone with the ability to heal others, and the juxtaposition between the restorative and destructive side of the coin is fascinating. To the scientists, you know. I heard them talking."

Sam smiled, but it didn't reach his eyes, and he met my own gaze with wordless apprehension once Bunny had turned away. I knew Sam didn't want to use the destructive half of his power any more than he absolutely had to. It was too easy to kill with. "I'd love to take some of the first aid or medic classes," he said after a pause.

"Oh, definitely!" Bunny nodded. "Adam, your Skills are pretty interesting, too. Hyper Focus, Electric Sovereign, and Animus, right?"

Adam nodded silently, his fingers sparking with tiny little flashes as he rolled a coin between them.

"It's a pretty eclectic mix. We're hoping we'll be able to help you integrate them and create some really powerful synergy."

"*We*?" Adam said. "Do you still consider yourself part of NIX?"

Bunny rolled his eyes again. "You're part of NIX now, too. God, why are you all so cynical? This is going to be an ordeal. Step one, remove stick from buttocks. Step two, sigh in relief." He smiled at Adam in that infectious way.

Adam smiled back, though it was more like a smirk on him.

Jacky snorted and slapped Bunny on the back in approval. "Great advice. So, how's NIX gonna help *me* get stronger?"

I shared a look of amusement with Adam at Bunny's wince and stumble. Soon enough, Bunny would learn to brace himself when Jacky moved in his direction.

Bunny walked us around the circular, multi-leveled base, pointing out our classrooms, places we could go to spar mundanely or practice with our different types of powers, and places where we could go to review previous Player battles. "Players get a chance to contact relatives twice a month. Video chats are restricted to those with good behavior, so *you* guys won't be having those for a while. But as soon as NIX is able to find and contact your families, who seem to have 'relocated' mysteriously, we'll get you in contact with them. Wouldn't want them to think you died!" He laughed, while those of us with relatives still outside NIX shared looks of unease.

We stopped by one of the empty observation rooms. One wall was a big screen, and there were multiple smaller cubicle stations with smart-glass tabletops.

Bunny used his ID link to activate the wall display. The guards atop the wall and down below went from mostly still to kicked-anthill scrambling, in fast-forward. Then, a small figure appeared atop the wall, as if they'd leapt up, and began to attack.

"This is us," I said. "You recorded us, from yesterday."

"Of course. There are cameras everywhere, as I'm sure you know. But these rooms are mainly used for the Players to view the official mock battles. Your little rampant destruction spree was uploaded only because you haven't participated in any of the battles yet, and I'm sure the others will be eager to analyze it."

"What exactly are these mock battles?"

"Oh, you know. Just practice in military-style fights. In the Trials, you run willy-nilly for your lives, or so I hear. In the mock battles, you have objectives you have to complete, against an enemy that looks and thinks like you but is stronger than any of the normal human soldiers on Earth. We simulate protecting civilian groups or taking out enemy strongholds, that sort of thing. Based on your…'wanton destruction,' we probably won't be having any Trials for a while, so this is going to be the main way for the Players here to gain Seeds, in addition to the occasional reward for exceptional performance in class."

"So, we fight another group of Players for Seeds, and everybody else watches how we did, trying to figure out how to beat us next time?" Sam said, staring up at the screen, where I was now fighting the Player girl and getting tossed around.

"It shouldn't be that hard," a new voice said. "You're not so special. I have no idea why Commander Petralka agreed to let idiotic traitors like you join."

We turned to the Player standing in the door.

"We're the elite," he said. "You don't belong here." He stepped forward, and a group of other Players filtered into the room behind him, spreading out among the stations.

"Watch yourselves," Bunny said sharply. Without his nonchalant irreverence, his innocuous veneer slipped away.

The Player who'd spoken looked away in an obvious display of submission and stayed silent.

"Let's go," I said. "I've seen enough here."

As we left the room, I spread my awareness out just enough to keep track of anyone who might see our turned backs as a vulnerability. It irritated my head, and I was just about to reel it back in once we reached the hallway when I realized a bright spot of power was following us, and it wasn't one of my team.

I turned my head and saw Bunny exit the room.

He shook his head in exasperation. "You Players are mostly idiots, as I'm sure you're aware. Don't take it too seriously. They'll get over themselves in time, once you're all properly integrated."

I shrugged, keeping the expression from my face, and turned my head back to the front. "Where to now?"

Bunny started talking and moved to the front of the group to lead the way again, but I wasn't paying attention.

I turned and caught Adam's gaze out of the corner of my eye. I shook my head minutely.

He nodded, the motion almost undetectable.

—Bunny's a Player.—
-Eve-

—I figured. Mind control, do you think?—
-Adam-

Chapter 3

Turn your face toward the sun and the shadows will fall behind you.
— Citron Aodh

ADAM and I discussed our suspicions through Windows so that neither Bunny nor anyone watching through the cameras at NIX would notice. The need for secrecy resulted in a useful discovery. Instead of body movement or verbal cues, I could use a focused enough *thought* to direct my VR chip.

I discovered this by accidentally wishing to close the Window Adam had sent to me. With a little more experimentation, I found I could mentally dictate and send him a message back, without ever moving my body or speaking a word. Of course, I shared this discovery, and from there it was easy to communicate without fear.

—Should we tell the others?—
-Adam-

I debated the question for a bit. They knew how to keep a secret, but if NIX was watching our every move, lack of knowledge about Bunny's true nature would ensure they weren't able to accidentally give anything away.

—No.—
-Eve-

Adam's mouth twitched in a subtle grimace, but he nodded.

I watched the back of Bunny's unkempt head, my lips twitching as they attempted to pull back in a snarl. What good reason could Bunny have for hiding the fact that he was a Player? Or for manipulating our emotions? Any trust I'd ever had for him had evaporated quicker than rubbing alcohol. If I could just take him somewhere isolated… But no. If he just disappeared, NIX would notice. I couldn't remove him unless I either had a really good way to hide my own involvement in his disappearance, or I no longer needed NIX's goodwill.

We decided to keep a close eye on Bunny and his interactions with the others to make sure he wasn't doing anything too nefarious. We would tell them if it became truly necessary.

The whole situation left me feeling like I had ants crawling up my spine, and only made me more desperate to regain control of everything being swept up by the winds of circumstance. I had to fix whatever was wrong with me, first. Then, I could work on the reason I'd agreed to join NIX in the first place. The creature below. With more information about it, and NIX, I'd be able to figure out what to do about Bunny.

We had some free time after the group gathered again for lunch since we weren't yet integrated into the schedule of the rest of the Players. I left Adam to keep an eye out for the rest of the team, and grabbed Sam to come with me.

Birch stayed by Zed's side, fluffing up and growling at any of the other Players or guards that came a little too close to my brother for the creature's liking.

I led Sam out into the courtyard, where people milled around, repairing damage, examining the Shortcut, and guarding the compound and surrounding wall. We climbed up onto the top of the wall, where a guard moved as if to stop us, but stopped abruptly when he saw my face.

I listened carefully for monitoring devices and found them only on the uniforms of the guards, who kept their distance from us.

"What are we doing, Eve?" Sam asked. He looked over the side of the wall, then stepped back away from the open air.

"I need your help," I said simply. "Follow me." I walked until we were standing over the edge of the mountain, looking down on the crashing waterfall below. The sound would help disguise our voices, I hoped.

"Are you hurt, from yesterday?" he said. "I saw that you didn't look so good, but I was so preoccupied…with everything…" He pressed his lips together for a moment, as if scolding himself. "I'm sorry. Where are you hurt?"

"I'm not sure, exactly," I said. "Everywhere, I think."

He laughed, then frowned in confusion when I didn't join in. "Err… did you get really bruised up? You seem to be walking alright. Broken ribs or something? It could even be internal bleeding, with how you got tossed around." He seemed to be worrying himself more and more with every word. "Eve, you really need to stop toughing these things out and just let me know when you need to be healed. That's *what I'm here for.*" He reached forward and placed a hand on my forehead.

I watched his face carefully. What would he find?

His eyes went blank for a moment, and then he frowned. "What…" He grabbed my hand with his free one and frowned harder. "What's going on, Eve? It's like…"

"Like what? What do you…*feel*, or sense, or whatever?" Tension leaked into my voice.

"Something is hurting you, as we speak. It's…everywhere. It's almost like it's trying to dissolve you, or *eat* you. Your body is trying to heal itself, but it can't keep up. What *happened*, Eve?"

"I did something foolish," I admitted. "But it had to be done."

"What did you do?"

"I ate the Seed of a Goddess," I said simply, knowing he would understand. He'd been there when I did it, after all. "She told me my body wouldn't be enough to contain her power, but I thought I'd have more time. But…it's getting pretty bad. It's giving me nosebleeds quite often now, and when my emotions are heightened, I can feel it become agitated. It feels…almost alive, like a wild animal, or a storm that's caged inside me. I've been putting the normal Seeds into Resilience and Life, and meditating to calm it and keep it caged, but that's not enough on its own. I need you to help me stay ahead of it."

"Why didn't you tell me earlier?"

"Because this is what's keeping us safe. I didn't want everyone to feel guilty about it, because we don't have a lot of options. And I didn't want NIX to know, because if they knew I wasn't as strong or valuable as they thought, I wouldn't be such a good bargaining chip. But people might start noticing something is wrong soon, and I can't seem to get my healing factor up high enough to overcome it, so I need some help."

Sam nodded soberly, and said, "I hope you know how stupid you are, Eve," before closing his eyes and getting to work.

Seconds passed, then minutes, as his eyebrows furrowed together, and his skin grew pale. I waited to feel a difference, some feeling of relief, but nothing happened. "What's wrong?"

He shook his head silently, continuing to strain until tiny beads of sweat broke out atop his still-pale skin and his breath grew fast. Finally, he took his hands off me and stepped back. "I can't," he said. "I don't know what's wrong with me, but I can't fix it. My Skill just glances off. I can tell you're hurt, but I can't get ahold of the injury to pull it into myself." He shook his head desperately, as if denying the truth of his own words.

"Oh," I said, my voice almost swallowed by the wind. "Well, now I'm really worried."

THE NEXT COUPLE days were stressful, to say the least. I asked Sam to keep my condition a secret from the rest of the team, at least until I could come up with a solution of some sort, and he acquiesced, but made me promise I would let him help if he could be useful.

Sam volunteered his services to other Players who got injured in one way or another, which seemed to both reassure him that he could still heal, and to make him more anxious and motivated to keep doing it. I figured it must have been difficult not to be able to heal Chanelle or me.

The Player members of our team, even Zed, started attending classes. Zed had a lighter load of "Player" classes than the rest of us, since he only had the one Seed and no Skills, and spent the rest of his school day with the kiddos, working on his own normal education.

I spent most of the next few days acclimating to classes and trying to perform well enough to earn some Seeds, while any free time was spent meditating and worrying about the Seed of Chaos' effects. I spread my awareness around the base when I had the chance, but I had yet to be able to reach far enough to observe the alien, though I was aware of its location below me at all times, as if it was a beacon.

The scientists came up with a way to remove Zed's Seed, and I carefully controlled my worry around Bunny, but convinced Blaine to come observe the first removal session and make sure everything was okay.

When I arrived in the observation room, Blaine was already sitting in front of the observation window, half paying attention to the scientists below. I used my link to turn on the speakers in the room, playing some loud classical music. NIX was no doubt already frustrated by my insistence on privacy for my private conversations.

Birch pressed his ears back at the noise, his tail flicking back and forth in irritation.

Blaine didn't look up from his tablet as I took a seat beside him, but I was used to that. After a few moments, he spoke casually, as if we'd been talking for hours. "I have made some progress on the diagnosis, but none on a cure. I am not sure there *is* a cure, to be candid. This may be like amnesia, or memory loss. Something we can only hope that the body fixes on its own."

I knew he was talking about Chanelle. "What have you learned about what's wrong with her?"

"The files which Bunny," he said the name with badly hidden irritation, "got for me about what happened to her were redacted. Heavily. Apparently, my clearance level is not high enough to be privy to whatever experiments they were doing. I am going to be speaking directly to the scientists in that research department in the attempt to get more information. For the time being, most of what I know, I have discovered through my own research. Meningolycanosis affects the brain. However, I am not certain that is the entirety of what was done to her. The symptoms suggest that she was infected with something slightly different to the samples I was given to work on, or that in a human host, it interacts complexly with the body. Perhaps even both. Whatever she had seems to have affected her like an advanced, mutated cousin to the rabies virus."

"What does that mean? Are you saying the serum you made to cure her didn't work?"

Birch pressed himself against the cool floor, a small whine escaping him in response to the tone of my voice.

"No, it worked. For the most part. But the damage was already done. In the samples I studied along with your blood, the Seed organisms seemed unable to recognize the meningolycanosis, and it did not attack them and thus draw attention to itself. However, samples I got from Chanelle show an almost nonexistent number of Seed organisms. Much less than I originally estimated, based on China. It seems that somehow, they were all destroyed. It was as if they were a bacteria subject to high doses of antibiotics. Without more knowledge of the timeline of what she was given, and access to research materials, I cannot be sure. Perhaps the upgraded meningolycanosis began to attack the Seed organisms, and in doing so revealed itself for counterattack, and they wiped each other out. Perhaps the anti-meningolycanosis serum I administered allowed the last of her remaining Seeds to remove the meningolycanosis, but not in time to stop their own eradication. Both the meningolycanosis and most of her Seeds are gone. How, I do not know.

"Worrying as that may be, it is secondary to the extensive brain damage. Strangely, it has left her gross motor skills intact, and she seems to be able to understand basic instructions well enough to feed herself and carry out other rudimentary functions. It is also quite a conundrum why Sam is unable to heal her. So far, this is the only ailment I have encountered that seems to elude him, except for perhaps amputated limbs and the like."

I knew that wasn't quite true. "Blaine," I said, turning to the man whose kind features sometimes hid behind his glasses and his focus on whatever fascinating thing he was working on at the moment. "Do you remember examining samples from me, after we got back from our last stay on Estreyer?"

"Of course."

"Did you notice anything unusual about them?"

"More unusual than the two different types of Seed material mixing around within you? More unusual than the subtle ways it has been augmenting your body?"

"I'm talking about the fact that the new Seed is trying to eat me alive," I said.

Blaine hesitated, frowned, and shook his head. "I did not have much time to do an extended observation of those samples, as you know. And I did not bring any of them here. When you say, 'eat you alive,' what exactly do you mean?"

"That's what Sam said it seemed to be doing. And he can't heal *me*, either."

Zed finally entered the room below, and I turned my attention from Blaine to wave at my brother.

Zed waved back, but I could tell the joking smile on his face wasn't quite natural. A scientist motioned him onto an obviously high-tech examination table, which cocooned him in glass and began to display diagnostic diagrams and numbers all over the surface. The display was gibberish to me, but the scientists down below gathered around avidly, tapping away on the arched smartglass of the examination table and their own tablets.

Blaine watched them, explaining what they were doing and the readings the table was giving.

After a while, Zed got off the table and drank something green, gagging a few times and screwing up his face into an exaggerated grimace with each swallow.

When I used the mic in the observation room to grill them about it, the scientists assured Blaine and I the liquid was almost perfectly harmless, as long as they completed the rest of the procedure, and didn't stress Zed's liver and kidneys by having him drink it too often. Blaine seemed to believe them, and I was mollified.

Zed said something that made some of the scientists laugh, but I noticed that he didn't look up at me very often, and held himself too still. He was uncomfortable.

They pierced his arm and hooked him up to a machine that began to pull his blood out through a tube, presumably filtering it somewhere within before returning it to his body. After a while, he relaxed and sent me a thumbs up.

When I was assured enough he wasn't being harmed, I settled back again. "Maybe Sam can't heal certain things from Estreyer," I said to Blaine. "Or maybe there is some other sort of restriction on his ability that we just haven't come across until now."

"Perhaps." Blaine looked up from the simulations he'd begun running on his smartglass tablet, the worry on his face an obvious contrast to the unaffected tone of his voice and his academic language. "I do not know what to do, or how to help either of you," he said. "My specialty is science and engineering, not medicine. And I will assume that you do not want to bring the medics of NIX into this." He paused, and added in a low voice, strangely intense, "I would advise against it."

"Of course. I don't trust them. At all. But…maybe the solution is simple. If the meningolycanosis killed off Chanelle's Seeds…maybe she just needs more? You've stopped the meningolycanosis, so it can't keep destroying them, and the Seeds do a pretty good job of healing. Maybe even for things like the brain. NIX might have some research on that, if you could access it. I don't know if we'd be able to focus the Seeds into healing specifically if we're planting them in her body for her, but it'd probably do *something*, don't you think? I've been using them myself, and Sam said it is working, but just not fast enough. If we could get a significant amount, maybe it could boost my regenerative growth level above the corrosive level of the Seed. Both would keep growing stronger, but as long as my Resilience and Life stayed higher than Chaos' strength, I'd be okay."

Blaine's face brightened and his eyes unfocused from my face. "Perhaps, perhaps. Like compound interest. I would rather not duplicate the circumstances of Chanelle's situation in another living creature for testing, but…" He sobered. "But I do not have access to Seed material, despite the fact that I work here now. Access to Seeds is very restricted, and I have actually already been denied my first request. I had a small sample back at my home laboratory, but that would not be enough to make a difference, and even that is out of our reach at the moment."

"Well," I said, watching Zed down below as the cleaned blood filtered back into his body, "I will just have to find a way."

A COUPLE DAYS LATER, the team was entered into our first mock battle. The battles were announced every two or three days during breakfast, and after the announcement, teams had barely enough time to prepare and move to the arena before the battle started.

I'd been shoveling food into my mouth, because if I didn't eat enough, I knew I'd be starving well before the second meal period of the day. Adam had calculated, with his signature snark, that I ate my own weight in food about once every week. I maintained that I was just going through a growth spurt, but in truth, I worried that my body was trying to compensate somehow for the energy it expended fighting Chaos.

"Eve, you eat so much," Jacky said, smirking as she took a bite of the turkey leg held in her fist. "How often do you poop?"

Zed, Kris, and Gregor almost spit out their food with sudden laughter, while Sam stared at her in horror. The others were too busy talking at the other end of the table to pay attention.

Zed gave Jacky's turkey leg a high-five with his own, which somehow devolved into "sword" fighting, and meat flying everywhere.

Birch perked up and took a flying leap for one of the pieces, flapping his wings futilely as he snatched it from the air.

Kris looked at me under her lashes, as if worried that I'd seen her laugh and would be offended.

Gregor cleared his throat, smoothed his face, and pretended he'd never laughed in the first place.

I grinned, and Kris smiled tentatively back, then returned to making a snowman out of mashed potatoes and vegetables, while I resisted the urge to reach over and ruffle Gregor's hair. I knew he hated that, but sometimes he was so cute!

Then, the large screens cut into the walls lit up with the battle announcements.

Like creepy puppets all under the same master's fingers, almost every head in the room turned to look at the screens at the same time. The faces of my nine team members lined up beneath mine on one of the screens, number score and a ranking next to each of us. NIX tracked all its Players, both within its walls and out in the real world, giving them points for their actions. Like Commander Petralka had said, I had one of the highest scores ever for a Player *entering* NIX.

That was nothing compared to the scores of the highest ranked Players, who'd been a part of NIX for far longer.

"They're ranked twelve places above us," Sam murmured. "And it's a full squad! How are we supposed to fight a full squad?"

Now that I technically had ten people on the team, we were considered a squad. Which was a nasty bit of payback on Petralka's part. When she had agreed to my demands that Blaine, his family, Chanelle, Zed, and Bunny be under my protection, she'd done so by putting them on my team. Even though none of them were fighters, and half of them weren't even Players, my command level was still bumped up to squad leader. Which meant we'd be matched up against other full squads.

I turned my attention to the other side of the wall, where a screen showed the faces of our opponents, Squad Ridley, along with their ranking. *Shit.* Vaughn Ridley led a squad here? "The ranking isn't always indicative of real strength," I said weakly. It was no comfort. Vaughn had shown me how vicious he was in the Characteristic Trial, and I knew there was no way he'd lead a team any less driven or dangerous. Just alone, he had almost as many Skills as my entire team.

Adam shared a glance with Sam, then turned to me incredulously. "Eve." He drew a breath. "Over half of our members aren't fighters. Don't tell me you expect *them*," he gestured to the non-Players at our table, "to fight *them*." He pointed across the cafeteria, where our opponents were stamping their feet and shouting.

Zed scowled, clenching his fork so hard his knuckles turned white. "We can still help, Eve. Just because we don't have Skills and aren't superhumanly powerful doesn't mean we're *useless*. The battles apply technology, too. I can use an air-burst gun just as well as you, or fly one of the airpods, or even act as a decoy for one of you to come in and surprise attack them."

I bit the inside of my lip as I watched Squad Ridley jog off through one of the side doors of the cafeteria, moving in formation. "Let's go. We don't have much time," I said.

We moved out, our ragtag bunch not moving in anything close to formation. We had *children* on the squad, and a girl in an unresponsive stupor, so any attempts to look cool and competent were doomed from the start.

Luckily, Bunny knew exactly where our side's battle prep room was, and he led us there, explaining the rules between puffs of air as we jogged. "If we win," he said, "we'll each get twelve Seeds for defeating a squad ranked twelve higher than us, plus the normal five Seeds for winning. If we lose, but impress the Moderators, we still might get a few Seeds on an individual basis." He stopped talking to breathe for a few moments. "The prep room will have weapons or supplies that we can take, but I don't expect there to be anything really good, since they stock it depending on overall team rank."

"What?" I gritted out. "So, for our first battle, we take six non-combatants into a fight against a full squad, twelve levels higher than us, and they're going to nerf our supplies to match our average rank? Which includes the ranks of our *non-Players*?"

Bunny let out a little coughing laugh, his gasps for breath reminding me of my own first quests to exercise. Despite the situation, I felt a bit of vindictive satisfaction, since he'd been the one to give me those quests. "Don't be so surprised, Eve. Commander Petralka needs to save some face, and regain a bit of authority. Plus, she's probably," he coughed again, "angry at you. For all that…" He coughed again and apparently gave up on finishing his sentence.

Adam shared a look with me, his mouth tightened into a grimace. "This does feel very…*personal*."

Our prep room had a few grated shelves of weapons and supplies, a lot of empty space filled only with an old model airpod large enough to squeeze twenty or thirty people in a pinch, and a small screen on the wall with the battle's objective.

Bunny went straight to the screen and began to read, while the rest of us moved toward the supply racks. There were ten thin bodysuits that went over the top of our standard issue bodysuits, which were meant to evaluate when a Player had taken too much damage and was considered "dead." One for each of us, and sized perfectly for our bodies. The bodysuit would also alert medics to come save someone if they needed it. If someone wasn't critically injured, it worked the same way as the electrical immobilizers NIX had used on me when they injected me with my first Seed, and stopped you from moving.

The weapons were mostly nerfed, meant to interact with the monitoring suit to simulate damage and shut down mobility rather than actually harm. Killing the other Players in the mock battles was heavily frowned upon, and apparently resulted in a loss of all Seeds that would have been earned during the battle, but it did happen, since some Skills were more destructive than others. I bet it also happened when someone held enough of a grudge against someone else that they were willing to give up on the Seeds for the chance to kill them.

"The objective is to protect a group of civilians that have hidden about a third of the way into the arena, and evacuate them safely," Bunny yelled. "It's simulating some high priority targets mixed in with the civilian group. Scientists and politicians. It doesn't say what the other team's objective is, but based on ours, it's almost certainly to wipe out the civilian population, and probably to 'dispatch' our team as well."

"How much time left?" I shouted.

"Nine minutes."

I grabbed one of the airburst-round guns, and hooked it onto the utility belt at my waist, along with plenty of extra ammo.

Beside me, Zed did the same with competent efficiency and a tight expression.

I didn't try to stop him, though seeing him suiting up for battle made my stomach clench.

"No!" Blaine's voice rang out, sharp enough to draw my attention.

Gregor scowled up at him, holding tightly with both hands to a gun of his own. "I'm not going in there without a weapon. I don't trust you or any of these other idiots to be able to protect me!"

Kris shifted from foot to foot, looking between her brother and her uncle. "I want one, too. We don't have to be a burden to everyone else. If we're attacked, at least we'll be able to defend ourselves." She turned to me, a pleading look on her face.

Gregor stomped toward me, still holding the gun. "I can have this, right?"

I looked up at Blaine, who was staring at me wordlessly, his expression mixed between pain, anger, and resignation. "It's best if they can help defend themselves," I said to him before turning back to them. "I'm not going to send you into battle, but if one of them comes after you, don't go down without a fight."

Blaine didn't say anything, just turned away and latched a large shield onto his arm, which clamped on and then contracted down to the size of a bulky armguard.

Sam was loading up with medical supplies and a couple shields of his own, while Jacky fitted what looked like gauntlets onto herself, and Adam filled his utility belt with ink cartridges and electrical cells, which had been provided specifically for him.

"Bunny!" I called. "Come grab a gun and a shield, at least. We're running out of time."

"Oh, I was thinking I'd just..." He caught sight of my scowl. "Okay, okay. Battle gear it is."

I turned to Chanelle and helped her dress in the top layer bodysuit, then strapped a light pack onto her back and filled it with ammo and first aid supplies, just in case.

Birch yowled scratchily up at me, drawing attention to himself for the first time since the announcement had gone off. He reached up with his forepaws toward one of the smaller packs and yowled again.

With a tiny smile that left almost as quickly as it had appeared, I grabbed the pack and helped him strap it on tightly enough to fit securely, and tossed the few remaining grenade rounds in, along with some random supplies that I'd learned through experience might come in useful, and wouldn't weigh his small body down too much.

Adam tossed the rest of the guns into the airpod and started it up. We all jumped in with only seconds to spare before the hangar door on the wall opened onto a war-torn cityscape.

Chapter 4

It is easier to break than mend. For everything I learned to heal, I learned a thousand times to end.

— Sha Du

ADAM PLACED his hands flat on the dashboard and closed his eyes as little tiny sparks of electricity jumped from him into the airpod, forcefully bypassing the electrical shielding. It took about thirty seconds, but then the craft shuddered and took off, angling forward and shooting into the city.

"Stay low," I said. "If they're flying, too, I don't want them to know where we are. And Bunny, you read the objectives, so you should have the best idea where the 'civilians' are. Navigate for Adam."

I closed my eyes, letting my awareness spread out from the ship, into the life-size, three-dimensional model of the city. One whole level of NIX was devoted to the mock battles and the three-dimensional printer that created the environment anew every few days.

I didn't notice any sign of life, or the other team, which I hoped was a good thing. "Bunny," I said. "Tell me about Squad Ridley. What are their Skills, their specialties? What have people done to beat them?"

"They've never failed an objective," Bunny said. "Not completely, anyway. I know the leader has like six different Skills, or something. He pushes his team hard, and they're always training. I'm pretty sure the team is geared toward 'attack' type missions. Kinda like ours, I guess. Except, you know, they're probably way better than us. As far as *specifics* go, I don't know. I wasn't the Moderator for any of them, and I haven't really paid too much attention to that stuff."

I kept my eyes closed, since my awareness was enough to notice the fast beat of his heart through the air, contrasted with the slightly mocking smile on his face as he looked out over the front window onto the city. I wasn't sure whether he was lying, or just slightly creepy.

We arrived without incident at a large building, one of the tallest in the area. The hostages were supposedly within somewhere.

I didn't like how exposed the ship was, or how vulnerable I felt doing this type of mission. I preferred when we were the ones attacking with the element of surprise, plenty of preparation, and no one to worry about protecting. We had no experience as a team on this type of mission.

I directed Adam to fly the ship into the cover of a half-destroyed building nearby. "Okay," I said. "We've got to assume the other team also has this location and will be coming soon. How many 'civilians' are there?"

"About twenty, according to the objectives."

"Okay. Jacky, Sam, Zed, and Adam. Go get them. Highest priority on the important targets, if you can tell them apart."

They nodded and left at a run, Adam at the lead.

I hated to send so many of my competent team members away, but I had no idea if they'd encounter obstacles or difficulty of some kind, or end up needing to physically carry the 'civilians.' Their protection and rescue was the main objective of the mission, and not one we could afford to fail. I turned to the remainder of the team. "Blaine, if you needed to, could you fly this ship?"

"Not as well as Adam, but I could fly it."

"Good. I'm pretty sure there's a training program built into it. Start practicing." I paused, closed my eyes, and took a deep breath, pushing my awareness outward with a forceful swirl, like the beginnings of a tornado, quickly aborted. Still no sign of our opponents, but I could feel Jacky breaking down the door to the building, and I pushed my awareness inside on the wind, stretching to try and find the civilians. There were no signs of life, but down in the basement, I found a group of robots. Little more than mannequins capable of rudimentary movement, really. That was why I hadn't sensed any human presences, but those were undoubtedly the target. I sent a Window to Adam.

—The basement.—
-Eve-

I opened my eyes and caught Bunny staring at me curiously, his face far too near my own for comfort. "I've got a plan," I said, pushing my palm into his face and forcing him back. "Grab the extra guns."

I walked over to Birch, who was crouching near the open door of the airpod, ears pricked and teeth bared as if daring something to *try* and attack.

"Good thing you're here," I said, ruffling the fur on his little head, and reaching inside his backpack for the spool of plastine wire and duct tape.

He growled a little under his breath, not averting his attention from the self-appointed duty of watchdog.

We knocked out the windows on the ship, and fastened the guns to them, pointing outward. We disabled the weapons' safeties, and tied the wire around the triggers, strings leading inward to the center of the little airpod.

I had Bunny strap himself down in one of the seats, and tied the ends of each plastine wire to the armrests. "When they come, Blaine is going to fly this ship off. You're going to man the artillery for him."

"What!?" Bunny squawked.

"Pull the wires for the gun you want to fire. Try to be sensible about it, and don't waste too much ammo, since I doubt you're going to want to unstrap and get up to reload any of them."

"Eve, we need this ship to escape with the hostages," Bunny said, in the tone of someone trying to reason with a crazy person.

"No. We need *a* ship. This one is going to be a decoy, and I'm going to get us another one. I don't have time for you to argue," I said. "I'm taking the kids and Chanelle with me, and we'll put them out of the way where the other squad isn't going to think to come after them. You two are going to run away and fire at them as if you've got plenty of people on board that you need to protect, and I'm going to commandeer a ship to pick up the hostages and the kids."

Bunny muttered something about not being a bait-worm, and that he should have been hiding somewhere safe, too, but I'd already turned to the kids.

"Are you ready?" I asked.

They both nodded, though Kris was pale and kept wiping her sweaty hands on her suit. Gregor's face was stony, but his eyes darted about restlessly, searching for danger.

"Blaine, do you have anything to add?" I joined him at the control panel, where he was furiously fiddling with the controls with both hands.

He grunted. "Keep them safe," he said, his attention obviously on his task. "I am going to fly this ship as if I am a desperate madman. The enemy will not have a choice but to devote some of their attention to me."

I squeezed his shoulder, and with a nod to the kids, grabbed Chanelle's hand and hopped out of the airpod. Luckily, she was pretty responsive to basic physical stimuli, so she ran along with me, though I had no idea if she actually understood anything that was going on around her.

I sent another Window to Adam.

—TAKE HOSTAGES TO THE ROOF. WILL BE DOING ROOFTOP PICKUP, USING AN ENEMY SHIP.—

-EVE-

—RISKY. I'M SENDING JACKY UP FIRST TO HELP. GOT IT HANDLED HERE, NO OPPOSITION TO HOSTAGE PICKUP.—

-ADAM-

I ran along at a pace the kids could barely keep up with, though Birch seemed to manage just fine with four legs instead of two. I was just turning a corner when a glint of light up above caught my eye. I dug my clawed toes into the ground, stopping so fast that Chanelle and the kids ran into me before they could stop themselves.

I scrambled back around the edge of the building, and sent my awareness out and upward. My range was much better than it had been when this faux Skill had first developed, but I still could barely reach the edge of the roof a couple blocks over and many stories up. Even so, it was enough, and I confirmed the presence of an enemy. I hadn't even noticed them move in! Did they have airpods, or had they come in on foot? If they were all on foot, my plan was going to be ruined.

I stretched my awareness to its limits, ignoring the whispered questions from Kris and Gregor as I searched for other enemies. I found none, but that didn't reassure me. "A Player from the other squad is up on the roof over there," I said. "We have to go a different way. Gregor, I'm sorry but you're going to have to ride piggyback. Your legs aren't long enough for the speed we need."

The solemn boy nodded, his lips pressed together, and climbed up onto my back without complaint, latching on with both his arms and legs. "Run fast," he murmured into my shoulder.

And I did, Chanelle and Kris barely able to keep up with my preternatural speed.

We reached one of the other tall buildings near the hostage's hiding point, and I fed the children and Chanelle through one of the seemingly long-broken windows on the ground floor. The door to the stairwell was locked. But even though I wasn't as strong as Jacky, the lock was rusted, and a few kicks and a yank with all my might broke it open. We ran, upward, step after step. A glimpse out one of the sparse windows we passed showed an airpod arriving. It was smaller than the one we'd been issued, made for attack rather than transport.

Kris was panting, her breathing ragged. When I told her to move faster, she nodded, and kept up with me, if only barely.

Chanelle was gasping for breath as well, but in an easier way, as if she wasn't really bothered by the fatigue or muscle pain I knew she had to be feeling, without any Seeds left in her body.

Atop my back, Gregor was silent, clinging tightly so as not to unbalance me.

When we got to the door to the roof, I stopped.

Kris fell to the ground, heaving. Her face was pale and beaded with sweat, and she looked almost sick. As soon as I had the thought, she leaned over the stairwell and threw up. "Sorry," she muttered, still panting. "It's just the running. I'm okay." She wiped her sleeve across her mouth, then used her arms to pull herself up by the rails of the stairwell.

"You did well," I said, letting Gregor down. "You guys are going to stay here for now, okay? I'm going to go attack the airpod out there, and once I'm finished, I'll come to pick you up in it. Shoot anyone that comes who isn't me. And don't worry, you'll be fine."

With that, I cracked open the door onto the roof and spread my awareness once more. "Damn," I muttered aloud. Three airpods, not one. All of the attack-style variant, and closing in on the target building from three different directions.

Birch growled under his breath, hunching low at my feet.

"You should stay with the kids," I murmured to him. "Especially since you can't fly yet." On the upside, at least the enemies weren't all on foot, and there *was* a ship for me to try and commandeer, moving toward me at that very moment. I wished Blaine had a VR chip, so I could contact him and tell him it was time to go, but instead, I had to wait.

Luckily, I wasn't stuck hiding against the door of the stairwell for long.

Our ship rose from the half-demolished building, scraping against the walls a little as it did so. It fired a couple shots at the nearest enemy airpod, both from the ships' built-in guns, and from the rigged windows, and then turned at a sharp angle, racing away at top speed. Blaine handled it surprisingly well, weaving in and out among the buildings like he had a death wish.

The two airpods that had been closing in from the ten and two o'clock angle turned to follow him, already spitting shots of their own, while the one coming in from behind me, at six o'clock, seemed to actually slow for a second instead of speeding up.

Was someone inside able to sense me, maybe? I worried for a second, but the airpod sped up again, on a trajectory to pass right next to the building I was on.

I burst out of the doorway, slamming it closed behind me and running toward the edge of the roof.

The pilot must have seen me for sure, then, because the ship slowed, rotating in midair to face me.

It was too late. I jumped off the side of the roof like an animal, claws fully extended, and slammed into the side where the seam of the doorway allowed me to dig in. This close, the airpod's guns wouldn't be able to hit me.

I was digging my claws into the door, preparing to try and rip it away, when the whole door blew off and outward, with me on it. I twisted in midair, angling the door under me and looking up at the airpod, where a Player glared down at me. I had only a second to be surprised, before the door and I both hit the roof of a lower building and went tumbling.

I rolled with the momentum, tucking my arms around my head to protect it, and came to a hard stop against the lip of the roof, bruised and winded.

The Player jumped down after me, the force of her thrust making the airpod wobble for a moment before the pilot regained control. She walked toward me calmly, her eyes just a little unfocused, as if she was looking more at the area around me than directly at me.

I let my awareness wash over her, and was dismayed by how brightly she shone. I wasn't sure exactly what her Skill was, but she was strong. And obviously not afraid of me, if the slight smile on her face was any indication.

I stood up and slid into the fighting stance Jacky had shown me. Inside, Chaos swirled eagerly, and I took a shuddering breath, trying to ignore it. I attacked first, claws out in a straight thrust toward her throat.

She slid to the side as if I was moving in slow motion, gripped my wrist, and slammed her hand toward the back of my elbow.

I panicked, I'll admit it. The thought of my arm bending backward, the tendons tearing and the joint ripping apart, was enough to make me act without thinking. Chaos bubbled up in a wave from my stomach, rushing along my outstretched arm.

She released me immediately, jumping back so hard she skidded when she hit the ground and had to stretch out a hand for balance.

My attack dispersed futilely in the air, leaving only the arm of my outer bodysuit a little ripped up, as if it had been a surge of little razors that passed. The backlash hit me. I should not have used Chaos. I hadn't meant to, but now it was only more imperative that my team won, because I'd need the Seeds to mitigate the damage.

I dashed forward, but only made it a couple steps before the airpod she'd arrived in shot at me. I tried to dodge, and in an instant, she was in front of me again, her hand smashing into my face, my solar plexus, my kneecap. She swept out a leg, knocking my own out from under me, then kicked me with a forward thrust before I even hit the ground, so hard that I flew. I once again crashed into the lip of the roof.

I rolled over and pushed myself up, but my knee buckled and I barely caught myself. I let out a low keening moan and unhooked my gun.

Instead of shooting at her, I aimed for the airpod. I hadn't wanted to damage its flight capabilities, but at this point, I just needed to reduce the number of concurrent threats.

My shots didn't even come close to hitting, and I was about to turn my attention to the girl, who was now sprinting toward me, when both Kris and Gregor burst out of the nearby roof's stairwell, rounds slamming out from the muzzles of their guns.

Gregor shot down at the girl, who avoided the airburst rounds just as easily as she'd avoided my claws, while Kris doubled up on my fire at the airpod, and actually got a few hits in, which caused it to tumble away out of sight.

The girl turned her attention toward the kids, and I screamed at them. "What are you *doing*? Go back inside!" I ignored the grating sensation in my knee and pushed myself toward my opponent, hoping to distract her before she got any ideas about attacking the kids.

The airpod rose from between the two buildings, having recovered from the temporary loss of control. It shot at the ground around the kids, obviously not aiming for them directly. Whoever was inside at least had a little bit of a conscience, I guessed.

"Go back *inside*!" I screamed again, my voice breaking.

Instead, they threw a couple of the nerfed grenades from Birch's pouch at the airpod, then ducked down back behind the lip of the roof.

The force of the explosions made the airpod tumble sideways and lurch drunkenly, but it recovered, and by then the girl was attacking me again, her hands and feet lashing out even faster than Jacky's, seeming to anticipate my every move.

—Jacky, I need your help.—
-Eve-

I sent the Window with a thought, backpedaling frantically, desperately avoiding the other Player's attacks.

—I'm almost there.—
-Jacky-

She was true to her word, leaping off the side of the civilian target building, arms and legs circling as she sailed through the air. She slammed into the side of the airpod, and then jumped off again, heading toward the girl.

The girl sidestepped just as Jacky was about to smash down her, but Jacky corrected easily, touching down with absurd lightness based on how fast she'd been hurtling through the air, and spinning around to attack.

The much-abused airpod finally seemed to lose control, its side dented a little where she'd made contact.

Kris and Gregor reappeared over the edge of the roof above and threw some more grenades, which seemed to seal the deal.

I caught a glimpse of the pilot frantically manning the controls as it tumbled toward one of the nearby buildings and disappeared out of sight. I would have cheered, if not for the arrival of one of the other ships, which looked a little scuffed up, but otherwise perfectly fine. Either it had given up on chasing Blaine and Bunny, or they were downed.

The new arrival shot *directly* at the kids. It blasted them back over the edge of the roof, and they didn't stand up again. I screamed once more, and sent my awareness lashing out toward them, desperately pleading with anything out there to have mercy, and not let them be hurt over some stupid little *contest*.

Birch was crouched defensively over them, yowling at the new airpod, real snarls managing to make their way out of his tiny voice-box.

—Sam, the kids!—
-Eve-

I sent him a Window with a map of their location along with the message and immediately turned my gun toward the new airpod, shooting off air-burst rounds in an attempt to draw it away from them.

I felt Gregor stir, and together, he and Birch worked to pull Kris back toward the stairwell. Not fast enough. Gregor wasn't using one arm, and Kris lay limp.

I shot at the new airpod frantically, reloading clumsily when I ran out of ammo.

It wove in the air and avoided most of my shots, but didn't even bother to turn and shoot back at me. I sprinted toward the edge of the roof. I wasn't Jacky, but I thought I could make the jump to the airpod. I had to, because the kids were exposed still, and I had no idea how badly Kris was hurt. I could only pray that it was her top layer bodysuit keeping her limp, and not a serious injury or concussion.

That was when the side of the target building, where the others were traveling with the hostages, exploded.

I didn't have a chance to figure out what caused it, because afterimages of a man's body flickered in front of me, between me and the edge of the roof.

I skidded to a stop as Vaughn solidified in front of me, and then he broke into transitory multiples again, and something hit me, and tore at me, and I spun through the air, my outer bodysuit kicking on and enacting the electrical immobilizer.

I lay on the graveled rooftop and watched helplessly out of the corner of one eye as Jacky fell back from the other girl's attack, one arm already hanging limply at her side. Her head turned, and I saw the crushed cheekbone and eye socket, and her eyeball trailing out, connected only by a fleshy string. I wasn't sure if she was still conscious as her opponent smashed her literally down through the roof.

It was only a couple seconds later that the klaxon blared, declaring an end to the mock battle.

Chapter 5

Farewell Hope, and with Hope farewell Fear.
— John Milton

I GOT three Seeds for my performance in the mock battle. I wasn't sure I actually deserved them.

Adam got two, apparently for some impressive Skill work in his attempts to lead the other half of my team in evacuating the targets and fighting against the other squad when they came after them.

Despite not being a Player, Gregor got one.

This shocked Blaine at first, and then drove him to quiet rage.

Gregor agreed to give the Seed to Chanelle when Blaine explained to him that they might help heal her brain damage.

Blaine and the carrier airpod had been downed, and his suit had immobilized him while he was out in the middle of the city, with no way to check in or see what was going on.

Sam was already busy healing Kris and Gregor by the time Blaine learned what they'd done. Blaine berated the kids, white-faced as he watched Sam assume Gregor's broken arm and second-degree burns, and Kris' broken ribs and minor concussion. I noted idly that we had proof Sam's ability extended to brains, so that wasn't what stopped him from healing Chanelle.

After NIX's medics and Sam had done what they could for everyone, we all gathered together in the barracks. Jacky was more withdrawn than I'd seen her in a long time, and when I sat beside her, she murmured, "I'm really sorry, Eve. She just...she was *better* than me." Sam had patched her eye socket back together, but it was still fragile enough that she had to wear a bandage around her head to keep everything in place.

I shrugged. "She was better than me, too." I was just glad she was alive. I'd wondered for a moment, when I saw her injuries.

"But I'm supposed to be the fighter, no? It's my job." She hunched her shoulders. "I'm gonna train more, I promise."

I bumped her with my shoulder, ignoring the throb it caused my bruises. "We'll all train more. Don't worry about it."

She nodded, but didn't smile.

Adam was suffering from the exhaustion of Skill overuse to the point that he could barely move, and he fell asleep in his chair.

Zed drew on Adam's face with a marker while he slept, but his mischievous smile didn't ring true.

Sam flopped back on his cot and went straight to sleep, but even in repose, his face was pale and strained. I knew we relied on him too much, but his demands to heal what he could held an intensity that wouldn't be denied.

Before the end of the day, what had been wary watchfulness in some of the Players turned to open hostility in almost all of them. We'd been beaten, and whatever wariness we'd managed to instill in the other Players would be gone. I made sure the team knew to travel in groups of at least two or three, and turned my mind to making sure something like this never happened again.

The next day, Blaine and I went down together to one of the battle observation rooms and watched a replay of what had happened. His knuckles went white around the edge of the table when the kids left the cover of the stairwell, and when the airpod shot and hit them whatever he'd been containing snapped out of him. He smashed his fist into the table and the sides of the station's walls, glasses flying off and getting crushed mindlessly under one of his now-bloody fists.

I didn't try to stop him. I knew what it felt like to need a release, even if it hurt a bit. Sometimes, things built up to the point they were unbearable.

Still, every time his knuckles slammed down into something harder than they were, with another panting, desperate breath just on the edge of tears, I flinched. I had taken the kids, and I was supposed to keep them safe. I'd been the one to give them weapons. Maybe they would still have gotten hurt if I'd kept them unarmed, or left them with Blaine, but it seemed obvious that the way they had *actually* gotten hurt was almost entirely my fault.

When Blaine tired himself out, he dropped into one of the chairs and sat silently for a few moments.

Tentatively, I picked up his broken glasses and handed them to him.

He put them on, though they were lopsided on his face, and one of the lenses had been shattered and was missing. "The rest of us need VR chips," he said, almost conversationally.

I was surprised enough that I didn't respond.

"Ones that aren't," he paused, and almost whispered, "*accessible by 'outside sources,'* like the modifications I made for your team. Except we should all be able to communicate with each other freely, rather than needing to route messages through you."

I nodded slowly. "That's a good idea."

"And the kiddos need to start learning self-defense. And working out. Maybe they won't ever be able to stand up to one of you, but I want them to at least be able to fight back enough to escape." He paused again. "I am going to start doing that, too. And training with the battle technology. I cannot be useless if I am going to be an…*active* part of this…"

I reached out awkwardly and put a hand on his shoulder. He didn't push it off, but I struggled to find words. "Blaine…I'm so sorry. I'll help you in any way I can. We all will, you know." Despite my guilt, I had to force the apology out past my pride.

He nodded, and stood abruptly. "I am going to my lab. If you wish to join me, I will see if there is anything I can do to help *you*." He gave me a meaningful stare and strode off.

I followed him. Technically, the area was off limits, but Blaine ignored the alarms and the guards that responded to them, and eventually, things settled down.

Something about the irritating sirens reminded me of the klaxon blowing to signify my team's utter defeat. I'd been out-strategized, our technology had been eclipsed, and on an individual basis, we'd been outclassed by the Players of the other team.

Blaine had a small lab, adjacent to the huge one, which contained the alien spaceship. He entered it and immediately began to putter around, muttering to himself and drawing diagrams on the smartglass screen that covered one of his walls. He'd turned on some ambient water sounds, the volume high. He took samples of my blood, claws, hair, and the inside of my mouth. While he got to work, I sat in an armchair at the corner of his lab, crossed my legs, and leaned back. I was so tired. "Blaine," I murmured, "I'm just going to close my eyes for a moment."

He didn't even acknowledge my words.

I breathed in deep and exhaled my awareness. It filled the room, and then drifted out through the vent in the ceiling. NIX had huge air shafts running through the entire base, as far as I could tell. I'd thought things like that were a cliché from the films. There was always the whirling fan blade that the character had to time and jump through at just the right moment to avoid being cut in half…or flames that shot out periodically, something like that.

But any sufficiently large industrial system that needed to cool machinery or transport air deep into the ground needed an extensive ventilation system. From what I understood, NIX also had an oxygen-scrubbing fail-safe, but it was too expensive to put in place unless we were on lockdown due to a nuclear war or some sort of airborne biohazard.

I was deeper in NIX than I'd been since Commander Petralka had taken me to see what our world was up against. Maybe…I took another deep breath, trying to calm my body, and pushed out, reaching downward through the vents, farther and farther, level after level. I passed plenty of interesting things along the way, but the thing that almost distracted me was the number of Seed-imbued people as I went farther. I was pretty sure they weren't Players. Not per se, anyway. Maybe, they were Moderators, like Bunny?

I felt my attention straining, so I ignored them and continued on till I reached a sterile holding cell with enough fail-safes to contain a herd of rabid elephants. Or an alien, I guess. Since that's what it was actually containing.

I slipped in through the small vent in the ceiling, trying not to let the strange buzzing vibration that filled the room distract me and snap my concentration. Conversely, the clarity of my senses seemed to sharpen. I reached out tentatively to the angled metal slab in the middle of the room and felt the huge creature shackled to it. Power radiated from him, flowing in his veins and *brightening* him in a way that had nothing to do with sight, and everything to do with whatever non-sensory Perception the Oracle had given me. I had to consciously hold myself back from thinking of him as a man, and remind myself that though he may look like a larger version of us, he wasn't human.

I focused my attention on his face, which was half-obscured by an unkempt beard, observing him in secret as he slept. Or maybe he was drugged into sedation. He looked sick enough. I pushed forward, touching the gaunt skin over his cheekbone, mentally almost tasting the clammy sweat there.

His eyes snapped open, staring out into the empty air of his room as if he knew I was there.

We had met before, in my mind.

When I had first been injected with a Seed, I'd had glimpses of this room, and thought they were a hallucination. When I was dying after my Characteristic Trial, and after my younger brother injected himself with a Seed and I'd broken down from despair, I'd met him twice more. After I'd solved the Oracle's first puzzle, I'd had a vision of Behelaino, and then a dream. And I'd worn his body in that dream. Or maybe it was also a vision. I didn't know. I felt almost as if I was slipping into his skin, the sensation dizzying, as my paradigm of the world shifted.

I still was reeling when his rage slammed into me. He shoved my existence away with a white-hot anger, and I crashed back into my body with a searing headache.

He hated me. It wasn't just anger. He *loathed* me, and me specifically.

BLAINE DIDN'T REACT to my muffled gasp as my attention returned fully to my body.

I reeled mentally for a second, almost nauseous. I stood and moved to the doorway.

The scientists were so caught up in their work that they didn't notice me, despite the dark color of my bodysuit indicating I was a Player.

I waited at the door for a while, just watching them work and looking around at the crazy inventions. The hair on the back of my neck stood up, the skin prickling. I rubbed at it. My eyes lingered on the alien spaceship. It really was damn cool, even if it was from a species determined to wipe us humans off the face of the planet.

Something prickled at the back of my mind. Maybe it was discomfort at what I'd just experienced. But instead of dissipating as time passed, it grew as I watched the scientists, and thought back to the almost ant-like crawl of people through the underground tunnels and rooms of NIX.

I realized once again that NIX had some amazing technology and resources.

But this time, that realization scared the feeling out of my fingertips.

If NIX had been better prepared, we might not have won when we attacked. They constantly drilled us, preparing us to fight against people as strong or stronger than us. How could they have been unprepared to fight against Players, their own cultivated weapons? I didn't trust Bunny even as far as I could no doubt throw his scrawny frame, but he'd mentioned that NIX was worried I might be a Player from somewhere else. If that was true, they would have been prepared for Player-level attacks. If they'd used their technology…If they'd sent out Players to fight Players instead of weak soldiers…

I'd been cocky, sure. But I knew now we weren't the strongest, so why hadn't they sent out a group of people like Vaughn, with armored suits and some heavier weaponry, to neutralize us? I could almost feel my brain buzzing against the muffling nature of a building headache.

Had they been afraid I really *would* be able to win against them and then escape? Maybe…they wanted me to *feel* like I won. Why else send expendables out to fight me?

But if so, why? What did they gain? I looked up, and around at the chaos as scientists milled around the huge lab, working at personal stations or tables, or entering and exiting the auxiliary labs that filled this whole level of the base. There I was, standing among them, having just resolved to train harder for NIX, after getting my ass handed to me in a mock battle they orchestrated.

I stumbled back, letting the wall support me, as my legs were too weak to do so. It felt as if these questions may have been hiding in the back of my mind for a while. I had been deliberately ignoring them. And that wasn't like me. Maybe Bunny had more influence than I'd thought. That was a terrifying idea, that I resolved to explore in detail. But even so, why would they do this?

If I looked at the outcome and worked back from there to find the answer, it was easy to see that NIX got what they wanted. They now had stronger Players with special Skills under their control, and I and my whole team ended up beholden to them. When NIX was first preparing to fight off an alien invasion, they must have realized the stupid tropes in the sci-fi films weren't realistic.

No human could successfully hack an alien computer with only their ID link. The aliens wouldn't have some specific weak spot so obvious a five-year-old could point it out, which one man could exploit to bring all the invaders to their knees. An alien race that had achieved interstellar travel would probably outnumber us, would definitely outgun us in every way, and lastly, outsmart us. We couldn't just increase army enlistment and train soldiers, funnel resources and fund military research. We had to get smarter before any of that would yield quick enough results.

I'd bet my life that when NIX first discovered the possibilities inherent in the Seeds they supercharged the Intelligence of every compatible candidate they could get their hands on. Those people would be working on everything from technology, to battle tactics likely to prove successful for humans, to ways to manage Earth's population up to and during an attack.

There was no way they would have botched my recruitment. I suddenly recalled Nadia saying to me that I'd escaped *almost* all of their methods of monitoring me, praising me for my trickiness. I groaned under my breath, a low, sick sound with a hint of a whimper. How could I have missed that?

Bunny. He'd come off as a bit of an ignorant rookie, working for the bad guys but just a normal person who was a bit weak-willed. But he'd been a Player all along. Or maybe, I should say that he'd been a Moderator, all along. I knew they had psychological evaluations done on all Players before even injecting them with the initial Seed, and they probably continued to develop those evaluations afterward. It would make sense for them to pair Players with a master manipulator who monitored their every move. Someone literally built to control the weak-willed. Bunny had been chosen to be my Moderator, and even now that master manipulator was on my squad, under my "protection" from NIX's retribution.

And if Bunny had been a plant, what about Blaine? Why would a genius like him, who was supposedly being *forced* to work for them, have been allowed outside of NIX? Another valuable asset, ripe for me to acquire and turn on them. He was perfectly situated to subtly guide my choices, leading us to his masters, acting as another spy, all the time. I shook my head in denial, even as I had the thought. I didn't want that to be true.

I realized what Blaine knew, NIX might know. The side effects of the

Seed of Chaos might not be at all secret. My find filled with horror like a glass fills with water, to overflowing.

I wanted to deny it. I was jumping to conclusions, I must be. There had to be another explanation. And maybe there was. But I knew that no matter what truth came to light, things weren't how I'd thought them to be, and I couldn't trust anything around me. It would be illogical to do so.

How did I even know the others on my team came to me organically, that NIX had not been guiding my every action with an unseen hand? Chanelle, made important to me as the person to help me when I was alone and frightened, sending me to her sister, the girl who became my first ally and even a friend after that? Jacky, obviously stronger than the rest of us that first Trial, enough so that I would notice and remember her? Adam, who Bunny had me "save" from being caught in possession of a knife. Then Sam, who Bunny sent to save *me* when I was about to die, furthering my trust in the both of them.

I grew dizzy as my breath heaved in and out of my chest, too fast for comfort. I looked down at the link on my arm, pulling up the time. Zed was about to enter a cleansing session. A horrible certainty filtered down from my head, settling in my stomach like a living thing. I turned mechanically, and sat back down in the corner of Blaine's office.

Then I pushed my awareness outward again, ignoring the headache. It took me a few minutes to travel unnoticed to the vents around the lab they used during Zed's sessions, but I still arrived before he did.

Scientists and researchers bustled around the room, most wearing white coats. I could hear them clearly, chatting as they prepared the equipment. Two in the corner worked on a glass screen set into the wall, examining the display that my Perception didn't even come close to being able to render at this range.

"This subject has been amazingly successful," one noted to the other. My heart sank, and I focused my hearing on them.

"He is Redding's brother. I wonder if that has any bearing on it, or if it's solely due to the fact that he's been forcefully kept alive through the initiation by her healer. Hawes, wasn't it?"

"Samuel Hawes. Interesting Skill if I ever saw one."

Zed's entrance cut off whatever reply the second scientist had been going to give. He smiled wide and greeted all the scientists by name.

To my slight surprise, they greeted him warmly in turn. Maybe they *weren't* doing anything nefarious, but I continued to monitor them to make sure, since the true measure of their trustworthiness was what they would do when they thought no one was watching.

They did some diagnostic scans and then ran Zed through stress tests, taking samples of everything as he ran on a treadmill, caught small balls as they shot at him from machines, lifted weights while answering their rapid-fire logic questions, and so on.

My worry morphed steadily into a fatalistic dread. He was performing more like a Player than a normal human. A weak Player, true, but they hadn't had him for long, yet. I swallowed. Maybe it was just talent. He'd always been better than me at anything physical, and he was smart.

My desperate hopes died as they laid him out on a device that looked similar to the diagnostic machine they'd used the first time. But this time, as he lay on the slab like it was an operating table, they put him to sleep. Clear walls rose up from the sides of the slab, curving over and enclosing him like a stasis chamber, or a clear tomb. They gathered all around his prone form. Then, clear tubes and needles grew from the glass all around him, piercing his flesh in hundreds of places.

I clamped my hand over my mouth, holding back a whimper. I kept the majority of my focus on the room hundreds of meters away, but took a moment to reassure myself nothing was amiss near my body. Blaine didn't seem to have noticed my involuntary physical response.

Then one of the scientists with Zed pushed some buttons, and the glass lit up with electricity, though I couldn't tell what it was displaying. "Everyone knows their task for today?"

They all nodded, and he tapped on the screens. The needles injected something into my brother in a slow, continuous stream. Each of the scientists began to tap away on their section of the screen. The machine seemed to have control over the substance, sending signals to the liquid and directing it as they wished.

Some of them worked on his bones, others on his joints and muscles, others on his very organs, augmenting his lung, his heart, his kidneys. One was even doing something to his brain.

I watched them work for over an hour, biting into the skin of my palm, which I held clamped over my mouth still. I wanted to rush out like the angel of death and kill them all. I wanted to save Zed, but I held myself back, knowing that would be the worst thing I could do.

NIX mustn't know I knew, or I wouldn't be able to save us, to fix everything.

So, I stayed silent while the needles withdrew and the machine sealed all the little holes they'd left. I watched as they woke Zed up and told him they were making slow progress removing the Seed, watching with interest as he gingerly moved his aching body. I did nothing as they told him it looked like the Seed had made some permanent changes for the better, and everyone smiled.

I watched Zed leave with movements slow and stiff, and rage and helplessness burst against my insides. I memorized the feeling.

Chapter 6

Do not look for my heart anymore; the beasts have eaten it.
— Charles Baudelaire

ONCE ZED MADE it safely back to the cafeteria and sat with the team for dinner, I released my awareness, and leaned back against the wall with my eyes hooded, watching Blaine work. Chaos roiled inside me as if it could feel my distress.

Blaine seemed oblivious. He pushed his glasses up, and absently scratched at the light dusting of stubble across his cheeks. Too stressed out to shave for the last couple days, maybe.

I listened to the ambient sounds he'd turned on, and thought of his earlier assertion that we needed to keep our preparations secret from NIX. Was that a ploy to make me more trusting, or had he been loyal the whole time? I didn't know, and I needed to find out. The suspicion was like a gnawing worm in my gut. I had to find some sort of proof.

I stood up, and had to steady myself on the chair when the room spun dizzily. I was starving, I realized, and the last meal of the day was about to start. I considered joining the Player members of my team in the cafeteria, but instead grabbed a few nutrient bars off Blaine's desk, and headed back to my little room while eating them, distracted from my surroundings.

Thankfully, most of the other Players were also in the cafeteria, so I didn't run into anyone hostile enough to start a fight.

I hurried through the curving hallways back to my quarters. My face felt like a skin-mask, calm and deceiving, a barrier between me and the real world. I'd been so *stupid*.

Birch waited for me outside my room, posted beside my door like a little four-legged sentry. He mumbled angrily when he saw me, no doubt peeved at being left alone and waiting outside.

"Sorry, Birch," I said absently, striding through my door as it slid open and then closed behind us. I didn't turn the light on, and ripped the bedding off my little nook, spreading it onto the floor. I sat, and tried to focus despite myself. It took a while, but I searched my bedding and every inch of my room for monitoring devices. I'd done it all before, and destroyed everything I found, but I was newly suspicious, for good reason.

I turned the lights back on after finding nothing, then stopped. I looked up at the light. It was too high for me to reach normally, even with my size, but I took the spartan stool from the corner of the room and stood on it, then reached up to the light panel in the ceiling. It came open after I pried at the edges with my claws for a few moments. The tiny black camera and microphone attached to the edge of the light inside did not surprise me.

I'd never noticed it before, because its presence was disguised by the electric activity of the light when I searched for the buzzing of mechanics, and it turned itself off when the light did. I'd thought the little bump next to the veiled light was just part of the mechanism.

I detached the spying bug and debated whether to put it back and pretend I didn't know it was there or crush it. I crushed it. Whoever was on the other side would have seen me find it, and if I suddenly allowed it to stay, unlike what I'd done with all the other devices I found, my deviation would set off alarms.

Once I was as sure as I could possibly be that my room wasn't being monitored, I moved across the hall into the team barracks.

Zed was in the top bunk and sleeping already, though none of the others were there. Had he not been able to eat much? I watched him sleep for a bit, then reached up and put my hand on his forehead. The skin was hot, and when I spread my awareness toward him, I felt the strange substance all throughout his body.

He woke when I took my hand away, and stared blearily at me for a moment. "What are you doing?"

"Come with me," I said instead of replying.

He groaned. "Do I have to? I don't feel very well. I just wanna sleep."

I grimaced. "It can't be that bad," I said. "Get up and come over to my cell. I want to show you something." I tried to keep my tone light, while I conveyed the seriousness of the situation with my expression.

He frowned, then got up, stiffly making his way down to the floor and following me to my room.

"Just in case," I said, once I'd slid the door shut behind us. "I just found another hidden camera in the light fixture. I might have missed some of them in the team room as well."

He looked around the dark room in sudden distrust. "Oh. Is that what you wanted to talk about?"

"No. I want to talk about the cleansing session you just had." I could only hope that whatever NIX had done to him didn't allow them to monitor what went on around him, or to hurt him remotely. As I explained what I'd seen, and the epiphany I'd had, he sat weakly on the side of my bed, listening in horror.

When I got to my suspicions about our former Moderator, he interrupted me. "Wait," he said. "If that's true, I think Bunny is up to something *tonight*. He seemed nervous. I didn't think anything of it at the time, but Kris asked him if he'd help her to sew the button-eyes on her doll after dinner, and he said he couldn't because he had something to do. He ignored her when she asked what it was, and told her to calm down or something. She had been really excited, but then she just seemed to lose all interest, like he wasn't even there. You should do your astral-projection thing and find him."

I didn't need any more convincing than that. I took a couple deep breaths and pushed my awareness out along with the heat radiating from my body, ignoring the icepick spike of pain that shot through my head with every heartbeat. Skill overuse had its consequences.

I found Bunny in Commander Petralka's office, which was close enough to my own quarters that I had a mostly clear impression of it and its occupants. His presence didn't surprise me, but my hands still clenched in my lap, and my fingernails itched with my body's desire to lash out.

He was talking—*reporting*—to Commander Petralka and another man who shone with power. Another Moderator? "...shows a continued general distrust of NIX, which is mirrored by her squad. Performance-wise, she seems to be excelling, as expected," Bunny said.

"But she still believes herself to be valuable enough for us to fear?" Commander Petralka said.

"As far as I can tell, she's overconfident to the point of being cocky. Moods have been dimmed somewhat by the loss against squad Ridley, but she's the type to focus single-mindedly on overcoming the obvious obstacle. The antagonism of the other Players will provide plenty of conflict for her to focus on in the near future. Though I'd keep an eye out for serious injury. She likes to make bold statements where everyone can see. Ridley, in particular, might be a target."

"And her mental state?" This time, it was the other person, and he'd spoken before Petralka got a chance to.

She shot him a subtle glance of irritation, which he either didn't notice, or didn't care about. Interesting.

"I've noticed subtle signs of emotional turbulence. From the stresses of the situation, perhaps. Despite the slight instability, I see no reason for concern," Bunny said.

"Team relations?" Once again, it was the man. Something about him was a little strange. Almost as if he was simultaneously paying full attention and absolutely no attention at all to everything in the room.

"Control over the team is good, no signs of insubordination or insurrection. She has a way of making those valuable to her feel like they're… important, and from there they rush to fulfill her expectations. Even Mendell's young niece and nephew both have an obvious desire for her approval."

"Do you still believe she may attempt to take revenge on Kilburn for the death of her teammate Black?" Petralka asked. This time it was the man who glanced at her, though I couldn't tell anything from his expression.

Bunny nodded. "Any competent psychological evaluation would have told you she was lying when she agreed to let it go. She doesn't believe in forgiveness. She understands retribution, and her own value as the center of her universe. But I actually don't know if she's planning something, or just biding her time."

"You *don't know*?" This was the man.

"This has nothing to do with my infiltration capabilities," Bunny said with a mix of indignation and fear. "Eve—Player Redding, excuse me, likes to work with a certain measure of secrecy. She likes to be the only one to know all the pieces of her plan, and when she's ready, she reveals everything in such a way as to build the team's excitement."

"What about the locations of their families? Have you gotten any information about that?" the man asked.

"You mean you haven't found them yet?" Bunny said, clamping his lips shut as frowns deepened on both of the other two's faces. "Well, I haven't, because I didn't know you needed that. But I'll find out before the next report."

There was silence for a moment, and then the man waved his hand at Bunny. "You may go."

Bunny didn't wait to be dismissed by Petralka. As he walked down the hall away from her office, he muttered to himself, "Damn creepy Thinkers."

Back in the office, Petralka said, "Her arrogance is a good thing. It shows she doesn't suspect the truth, or our strategy to subdue her if need be. I've commissioned the cell on level sub-seventeen to be readied for a high threat level occupant."

I almost lost control of my grip on my awareness, then. But I clung desperately to the commander's office, and managed to stabilize it. I needed to hear this.

"This entire situation is precariously balanced," the man said. "It is an exceptionally delicate situation. You must do away with this volatility."

Petralka's back stiffened. "I've been doing the best I could, with the strictures on my available courses of action from *your* side. You wanted her strong? We've done what you said, applied just enough pressure to make her desperate, and now she's got a new type of Seed entirely, and it's got all the destructive capability you could hope for. You wanted her here, with room to analyze her? She's here. I can't complete two conflicting goals at once." She stood up, facing the man, though he was much taller. "Either you want the situation on lockdown, or you want her to continue to develop freely."

"There are more ways to control a situation than brute force," the man said, enunciating every word. "And more ways for you to fail than just not following our instruction. Your two sources of inside information are both unreliable. This 'Bunny,' the Rabbit group Moderator. His interest lies almost entirely in self-preservation. He may nominally be doing this for the good of our world, but his Skill is dangerous, and he grows much too free with its use. He attempted to *calm* us."

Petralka's eyes widened, and the man continued. "And Blaine Mendell's loyalty was never in question. It is to his niece and nephew, and only to them. It was clever, to use his sincere hatred of us to ingratiate himself with Redding and her team, but your petty little revenge for your niece's defeat, putting those children in the mock battle? The *reason* he follows our orders is because we keep them *safe*. If we fail to do that, he has no reason to comply."

Commander Petralka pressed her lips together. "I'll say it was a warning, and a punishment for not doing a satisfactory job of keeping us informed of Redding and her team's actions, previously. For cutting off our access to their VR chips and GPS trackers. It can be used to cement his loyalty. They didn't get seriously hurt."

"And Redding's brother? If he dies…"

"He's not going to die. As long as he keeps getting the nutrient paste for the nanites, he'll thrive. My scientists are ecstatic at how well he's responding. He may be the first working solution to the lack of sufficient Seed material. And as long as we've got him, we've also got Redding. I have this under control."

My awareness snapped back to me, then, and I slumped over to the floor. The room spun around me, and I swallowed hard to keep my stomach from heaving up the previous nutrient bars.

"WHOA, ARE YOU OKAY?" Zed asked, grabbing me by the shoulder and helping me to sit up again.

Birch mewled anxiously, butting me with his head as if to keep me from falling over again.

I groaned and waited till the room stopped spinning. There would be no more extra-sensory Perception for me that day, though I wished I could go back and listen to the remainder of the conversation between Petralka and the man Bunny had labeled a Thinker. "I'm okay," I mumbled. "Just a bit of backlash from pushing too hard."

Once my stomach had settled, and Zed had forced me to take a couple headache pills that helped with the throbbing pain, I explained what I'd heard. Then I sent Zed back to the team barracks, because we needed to act normally, and both of us were feeling so wretched that sleep was necessary before we could start to formulate a plan of attack.

A nightmare woke me after a few hours. I turned on the light to push back the darkness, and lay back down, thinking of what I'd learned, and hoping that some solution would present itself to me. I was absolutely screwed. The whole team was.

I'd been like a puppet on a string.

I sat up and reached under the mattress of my cot for my pack, withdrawing the second largest band of silver loops the Oracle had given me. With a deep breath and a roll of my neck to stretch the tense muscles, I sat cross-legged on the floor to puzzle it out.

I meditated again, forcing my brain to put all its energy into fixing what could be an answer to my problems. I strained, pushing and *pushing* for hours. And then I started to bleed, again.

My eyes caught my own desperate reflection in the surface of the first crimson drop as it fell onto the silver bands in my hands like an omen of doom. It splattered, spreading more than such a small amount of liquid had any right to. And then the next drop of blood fell, and suddenly it was a steady dribble, as the sensitive skin inside my nose succumbed to the onslaught of Chaos.

Birch mewled and tried to climb onto my lap to lick it up, but I shouldered him away, focusing my glare on the bloodied puzzle in my hands. "The Oracle got me into this mess, and the Oracle is going to get me out of it," I said. But even so, I wanted to cry.

My meditation had been helping to keep my emotions under control, but the stress of my current situation was too great. So I scrabbled with the silver bands, and tears fell from my eyes to meet the drops of blood. I couldn't help it.

I gasped, eyes widening. Pushed by the tears, my blood formed spider-web-thin lines on the bands, spreading, and converging into delicate pathways. The last puzzle, the ring, had been carved with tiny protrusions and grooves that kept it from forming up unless I matched them together exactly. This one hadn't, and I knew because I'd searched desperately for them.

What type of ridiculous prerequisite was both bleeding and crying on the puzzle before being able to solve it? I scowled at the Oracle's gift. Had she somehow known that this would happen, that I would fulfill the condition? If she really could see the future, as her name implied, maybe she had.

It took almost an hour, even after that, but I solved the puzzle, each of the bands fitting with the other perfectly, creating a woven cylinder. Nothing happened.

So, I held it with my left hand, making sure to pinch hard so none of the pieces slipped out of place, and slipped my right hand through it.

It immediately seemed to come alive, like its smaller counterpart had done, and wriggled up my forearm like a snake, clasping to the flesh. It stopped when it reached my elbow, and injected its contents into me.

My VR chip popped up with two messages a few seconds later.

YOUR NON-SENSORY PERCEPTION HAS INCREASED!
YOUR INTELLIGENCE HAS INCREASED!

Then, once again, my body was seized with pain and I spasmed uncontrollably, flailing about. I smashed my arm against the floor involuntarily, but the solved puzzle acted as a guard and stopped me from bruising it. My eyes rolled back. Flashing lights behind my lids put on a show to match the pain.

Then, I began to see, as before.

A rush of images passed, almost too fast for me to recognize them. Bright red ants swarming and stripping every ounce of flesh off a small animal, the streak of a wing passing behind a fluffy white cloud, a flash of light as a blinding sun shone fully into my eyes, and a thousand other things that passed from my memory as quick as they came.

Finally, it slowed. A moon hung over a black sea, shining silver into the depths.

A blonde man stood on the surface of the water and he pointed downward.

My sight followed the rays of moonlight into the darkness, and I saw that here and there they connected with the beams from another orb. This one was bright and almost golden, but it was crumbling. Bits and pieces fell and floated away, mixing like blood in the water. I watched them float until they were lost in the inky darkness, and when I looked back, the orb was an eye. It noticed my presence, then, and as happens sometimes in dreams, I knew that it was my great enemy, and that it knew not who I was. I lost the sense of myself in the knowledge of how little it cared for my existence, and then it devoured me, absorbing all that I was and ever could be. And I, too, rusted away into nothingness.

I woke, gasping, to Birch on my chest.

He licked my cheek with his painfully raspy tongue and yowled full force into my face.

I groaned. "Oh, shut up, please." My head throbbed so hard I felt like I could hear my brain thumping against the inside of my skull. "You're getting big enough that your voice is a weapon."

Birch quieted and scrambled off my chest, hopping around on all fours like an excited baby deer.

"What time is it?" I whispered. I pulled up the answer on a Window, then groaned again. I had no idea what the vision meant, or what I was supposed to do next. And I was late for breakfast.

Interlude 1

They had taken her off the side of the road, on her way to work. It was a simple thing, to cause the pods ahead of her to crash. Her own slowed and stopped to protect her, and he ripped the door off it.

She squinted and flinched back as his body dwarfed the breach he'd created in the tiny vehicle's side.

He bent, snapping the protective straps off her shoulders.

Her eyes widened, and then she glared at him like a rattlesnake. "*You,*" she said, fairly spitting with anger.

His eyes tracked over her face, taking in the faint wrinkles—those were new—and the challenge in her expression—that was not new. He didn't respond, simply grasping her by the shoulders and yanking her out of the pod.

She screamed for help.

No one responded, or even looked their way. His companion's *blood-borne* ability redirected the gazes of the humans around, so he didn't fear their notice or reprisal.

He forced her into their own, much larger vehicle, careful not to damage her. He remembered how fragile humans could be.

Another of his companions disposed of her vehicle, and as the pods involved in the crash pulled themselves off the main road, traffic began to move again.

She didn't bother screaming at them or begging them to let her go.

Her long polished nails went straight for the eyes, and she kicked at his genitals.

He turned sideways so her foot impacted ineffectually against his thigh, and grabbed both her wrists in one hand. "Calm yourself, woman. We mean you no harm."

She laughed, loudly and bitterly. "And yet, you are kidnapping me."

He settled back with a tiny twitch of his lips that someone might interpret as a smile. "It is for your own good."

She scoffed. "I've heard that one before. Bastard."

He ignored her.

Once they arrived at the compound, she was hustled away to stay with the other humans. He had not seen her since, but he found his thoughts drawn to her. It had been a long time.

Chapter 7

I have a meanness inside me, real as an organ. Slit me at my belly and it might slide out, meaty and dark.
— Gillian Flynn

I DIDN'T EVEN MAKE it out of my room before my VR chip malfunctioned. Screens flickered in front of my face, flashing with varying brightness, spreading, popping, and flying around. They were filled with random symbols, but nothing that resembled words or the stats that I'd become accustomed to. They came like a barrage, cutting off my vision with their numbers and movement.

I dropped to my knees, clenching my jaw so tightly I could hear my molars creaking. I held back a scream of fear. Was NIX somehow attacking me, or had the second puzzle damaged the chip? Seizures couldn't be good for the electronics attached to my visual cortex, to say nothing of their detrimental effects on my brain itself.

Birch yowled at me again, and then began to whimper under his breath as he pressed his body against my thigh.

To my relief, the Windows disappeared after another minute or so. I patted Birch on the head and made some soothing sounds until he calmed down. I was about to pull up my Attribute Window, to make sure the VR chip wasn't broken, when one last screen appeared in front of my face.

ACCESS ACCEPTED. PRINCIPAL GUIDE UPDATED. GUIDE NAME: ORACLE

I screamed, then, just a little.

FORGE AN ALLIANCE WITH ESTREYAN CAPTIVE
COMPLETION REWARD: ALLIANCE
NON-COMPLETION PENALTY: DEATH

A timer popped up, set at 24 hours. I watched, wide-eyed, as the numbers ticked down, second by second. A single day to complete the quest. I wasn't sure whether to be horrified or elated.

BIRCH FELL ASLEEP several times just during breakfast. It was quite hilarious to watch the little creature's head begin to fall as he succumbed to sleep, only to jerk awake again repeatedly.

His antics amused the whole squad, but did little to distract me from the timer in my peripheral vision. I'd tried to dismiss it, but neither actions nor words had any effect on it, and it remained like an omen of doom.

A thorough examination of my VR chip's Windows and information also showed a couple significant changes. The Skill Window was one.

CHARACTERISTIC SKILLS

TUMBLING FEATHER (KINETIC CLASS): INCREASES GRACE AND AGILITY. IMPROVES SENSE OF BALANCE AND MOTION. SKILL EFFECTS WILL EXPAND AND STRENGTHEN WITH PLAYER GROWTH.

SPIRIT OF THE HUNTRESS (SPIRIT CLASS): INCREASES GRACE, AGILITY, PERCEPTION, FOCUS, PHYSIQUE, AND STAMINA. NAILS EXTEND AND SHARPEN ON COMMAND, ALONG WITH PHYSICAL RESTRUCTURING OF HANDS AND FEET. FEET PERMANENTLY AUGMENTED FOR INCREASED PERFORMANCE. INCREASES CHANCE TO LAND ON FEET AFTER A FALL. AGGRESSIVE TENDENCIES INCREASE. SKILL

EFFECTS WILL EXPAND AND STRENGTHEN WITH PLAYER GROWTH.

SKILLS

COMMAND (MUNDANE CLASS): ALLOWS LEADER ACCESS TO THE TEAM MANAGEMENT WINDOW. LEADER CAN COMMUNICATE WITH TEAM MEMBERS THROUGH GAME WINDOWS AND ACCESS BASIC GAME INFORMATION OF TEAM MEMBERS.

WRAITH (PROJECTION CLASS): INCREASES PERCEPTION. SENSES EXTEND BEYOND THE BODY, GIVING A COMPREHENSIVE UNDERSTANDING OF SURROUNDINGS, AND MARKING AREAS OR BEINGS OF POWER ACCORDING TO DEGREE. SKILL EFFECTS WILL EXPAND AND STRENGTHEN WITH PLAYER IMPROVEMENT.

CHAOS (GODLING CLASS): LATENT ASCENSION POTENTIAL. GIVES ACCESS TO THE PRIMORDIAL POWER OF THE GODDESS OF CHAOS.

The Oracle recognized that Perception Skill I'd found so useful, and there was some actual information about Chaos.

The second change was the Attribute Window.

STRENGTH (14): ABILITY TO EXERT PHYSICAL FORCE.

LIFE (28): MEASURE OF HOW MUCH DAMAGE CAN BE ABSORBED BEFORE DYING.

AGILITY (21): PHYSICAL ABILITY TO INITIATE QUICK-TWITCH MUSCLE MOVEMENTS.

GRACE (18): ABILITY TO CONTROL THE FLOW AND CONSEQUENCE OF BODY MOVEMENTS.

INTELLIGENCE (20): ABILITY TO REMEMBER DATA AND EMPLOY REASONING.

FOCUS (17): ABILITY TO CONCENTRATE ATTENTION ON A SPECIFIC TOPIC.

BEAUTY (10): PHYSICAL APPEARANCE, CONFORMING TO THE WISHES OF THE PLAYER.

CHARISMA (12): MEASURE OF INFLUENCE OVER OTHER SENTIENT BEINGS, BASED ON ATTRACTIVENESS AND FORCE OF PRESENCE.

MANUAL DEXTERITY (9): ABILITY TO UTILIZE FINE MOTOR CONTROL.

MENTAL ACUITY (18): ABILITY TO THINK AND DRAW CONCLUSIONS QUICKLY.

RESILIENCE (23): ABILITY TO RECOVER FROM DAMAGE AND MENTAL AND PHYSICAL EXHAUSTION.

STAMINA (19): MEASURE OF HOW MUCH PHYSICAL OR MENTAL FORCE CAN BE EXERTED BEFORE BECOMING EXHAUSTED.

PERCEPTION (24): ABILITY TO SENSE THE PHYSICAL, THE INTANGIBLE, AND THE IMPLIED.

Physique seemed to have been rolled into Beauty, and there was a completely new Attribute. Charisma. I'd never put any Seeds into it, but if I calculated based off of the total number of levels it already had, it had something to do with Beauty and Physique. Not so surprising, but Charisma seemed *much* more valuable than either. Perception now also covered sensing the "intangible," which likely had something to do with the Wraith Skill's ability to sense Seed power.

There was also no indication of any "unplanted" Seeds, or even a space for it.

Zed's eyes caught mine several times during the meal, and I knew he wanted to talk with me, but we both knew it wasn't safe till we could be sure we weren't being monitored.

I watched both Bunny and Blaine surreptitiously. Our former Moderator seemed lively and carefree, joking around with Kris and Jacky easily, while Blaine had bags under his eyes, and had brought a smartglass tablet to the breakfast table with him so he could continue working on his latest project.

My claws scored lines in the back of my plastine food tray as Bunny yawned, then poked Chanelle in the side when no one else was watching. His continued presence was like a bloodsucking tick burrowing into my skin, which I couldn't even attempt to remove yet. Blaine, I could at least sympathize with. Bunny had no excuse.

When breakfast was over, Zed tried to move toward me as we left the cafeteria, but Blaine got to me first, using the noise of all the Players around us as cover for his words. "I have looked through your samples," Blaine murmured to me. "I destroyed them, and erased the data. I am sure NIX has access to my devices, and I didn't want to leave evidence of your condition for them to find."

I stared at him for just a moment too long, but he didn't seem to notice. Was his secrecy and paranoia toward NIX a ploy to get me to lower my guard, or was he truly eschewing his duties as a spy? "What did you find?" I asked.

"Not much more than Sam. The Chaos Seed material seems to be attempting to drag your body toward entropy on a cellular level. There may be a way to combat it through 'mundane' means, but I have not been able to think of any. I considered the modified meningolycanosis as a way to combat them, but there's no discernible way to target it to one specific type of Seed. And seeing what it did to Chanelle…I believe I am understandably reluctant to suggest such a thing. There may be others besides Sam who would be able to heal this with a Skill, but NIX would be made aware. The only viable solution is likely to be what you already suggested. Overwhelm its destructive capability with Seeds in the healing Attributes."

I'd suspected as much. And at this point, I'm not sure I would've trusted Blaine if he had suggested anything else. "Thanks for trying," I said simply.

"I have also started preparing the modified VR chips to implant in the kiddos, myself, and the others. Whenever the rest of the team is ready, I should be able to enable communication in their chips so that you do not need to relay messages for any of us."

"Okay," I said. "We'll set something up, maybe in a couple days. We can't be too obvious about it."

He nodded and left, ignoring the rule about traveling alone.

I spent a tense day slogging through classes and meals while worrying about completing the Oracle's quest.

Birch ended up taking several naps during my classes, which some of the Players around seemed to think was cute. One tried to pet him when I was distracted, and he woke up immediately and bit them. His human-like eyes glared at them in a manner that I imagined was somewhat disturbing, especially with his little pointy teeth glistening red.

No one tried to touch him after that.

During our shared Battle Tactics class, I sent a Window to Adam.

—NIX WIPED ALL YOUR DATA ON THEM, RIGHT? ALL THE STUFF WE TOOK OR CHANGED BOTH TIMES WE WERE ABLE TO ACCESS THE SYSTEM?—
-EVE-

—YES.—
-ADAM-

He looked at the smartglass screen in front of us with an comical load of sadness and frustration.

—YOU KNOW THE...*STUFF* DOWN IN THE BASEMENT?—
-EVE-

He looked up at me, and then back to the screen, matching my deliberately casual expression. We both knew that by, "stuff," I meant, "alien."

—YEAH?—
-ADAM-

—DO YOU REMEMBER IF THERE WAS ANYTHING ABOUT IT IN THE DATA YOU DOWNLOADED?—
-EVE-

—THE FIRST TIME, I ONLY MODIFIED SOME OF THE DATA, NEVER DOWNLOADED IT. AND THE SECOND TIME, I DIDN'T HAVE IT LONG ENOUGH TO LOOK THROUGH IT. WHEN WE AGREED TO JOIN, YOU KNOW NIX FORCE-WIPED EVERYTHING I HAD. I'D TRIED TO KEEP

SOME HIDDEN, BUT THEY DID A WONDERFUL JOB. I'M CONSIDERED A HIGH-PRIORITY RISK FOR THE INFORMATION SYSTEMS NOW. I'M NOT ALLOWED TO ACCESS THEM OUTSIDE OF CLASSWORK OR THE ALLOTTED HOURS I WORK WITH BLAINE, AND THEY MONITOR MY USAGE LOGS.—
-ADAM-

He paused a second, and then sent me a second Window.

—WHY? IS SOMETHING HAPPENING?—
-ADAM-

—YES. I'VE GOT TO FIND A WAY TO GET DOWN TO IT WITHOUT BEING CAUGHT. I'VE GOT AN IDEA HOW TO DO IT ALREADY.—
-EVE-

—THEY'VE GOT THE SURVEILLANCE SYSTEM WORKING OVERTIME. WE'VE PROVED IT FALLIBLE TWICE, BUT YOU BETTER BE CAREFUL. DO YOU NEED HELP?—
-ADAM-

—NO. MY METHOD REQUIRES MY SKILLS, SO I HAVE TO DO IT ALONE. I'M NOT PLANNING TO GET CAUGHT, SO DON'T WORRY.—
-EVE-

He looked at me doubtfully, but I was already lost in speeding thoughts.

At the end of the day, back in my room, I moved my little stool over to the vent in the corner. It was smaller than a lot of the other vents around NIX, but it was significantly bigger than it probably would have been if NIX wasn't cut into the depths of a mountain. I measured it carefully, then compared it to the width of my own shoulders.

I wouldn't be able to move my arms and legs, but if I could find a way to avoid needing to climb until I reached the larger ventilation tube that my own fed right into, I could make it. I crouched low, then sprang upward, grabbing onto the metal grate with my clawed fingers. I held myself suspended with one hand as I reached out with the claws of my other hand and unscrewed the nine rods holding the grate to the ceiling. I hid the grate and the rods in my bedding, turned off the light, then returned to the stool.

I jumped again, with my arms held close to my head and pointed straight up toward the vent. My shoulders hit the sides with enough force to bruise, but the tips of my claws caught on the edge of the main vent system. I had to let go, because I didn't have enough space to wiggle my way up.

I pulled over the small table and balanced the stool atop it, as Birch watched curiously.

My feet had changed significantly after getting the Spirit of the Huntress Skill, so much so that wearing shoes was difficult. The toes were too long, and with a little extra push, they grew claws, making it a simple thing to grip the edge of the stool for balance. The extra boost from activating the Huntress Skill also gave me the necessary power to fully reach the bend in the vent. I scrabbled with my claws and managed to drag myself up and into the larger duct.

Birch mewled pitifully and scrabbled up atop the table and then the stool, and with a motion familiar to cats everywhere, wound up for a seemingly impossible jump. His small body launched up toward me, and I caught him by the forepaws, helping him over the edge.

"Be quiet," I whispered to him. "We can't get caught."

We crawled through the metal-walled vent slowly, pausing at the grate over the team barracks. A quick foray with my extra-sensory Perception told me my brother was sleeping within. It took me longer than I'd expected to navigate through the three-dimensional maze of NIX's ventilation system, partially because of the monitoring devices I discovered hiding around some of the corners in the ducts. I cursed spectacularly in my head, glad that I'd been sensing my way ahead and had noticed them before they noticed me. I ended up having to take several detours to avoid them.

I would have been dripping with sweat if not for the cool air pumping through the shafts in a less-than-gentle breeze, and even so, I was panting from all the spread-eagled climbing and descending I had to do, taking roundabout paths to avoid the sensors on the more maneuverable shafts. If not for the days of climbing mount Behelaino, I might not have been able to do it.

As I grew nearer to the alien's cell, a buzzing sound, like a variation of white noise, filled the air and brushed insistently against my skin. It ran just beneath what I might have noticed if my Perception wasn't so heightened. As it was, I could feel the hair on my arms vibrating along with it. By the time I entered the vent that connected to his cell, it was strong enough to feel in the metal under my fingertips. I'd noticed the buzzing when I'd sent my awareness down before, but not when Commander Petralka had brought me to look at the alien the normal way. Was he causing it, or was it something NIX did?

I drew my knees up to my chest so Birch would be able to fit beside me if he wanted to, and poked my head forward to peek through a slit in the grate.

The man met my eyes, glaring up at me in complete awareness.

I jerked back without thinking, as if he'd slapped me. When my heart stopped squeezing with a combination of shock and fear, I leaned forward again and met his glare. "Don't make a scene," I whispered, almost inaudibly. "They'll come." Could he hear me? I'd heard him speaking English in the vids Commander Petralka had shown me, so I knew he could understand.

"Why should I not?" he said. His voice was hoarse, whether from disuse or from screaming I didn't know, and his mouth formed the words strangely, lilting with an accent I didn't recognize.

It must be an Estreyan accent, I realized. The realization that aliens existed hit me anew, as I realized how absolutely bizarre my current situation was.

"I doubt you are supposed to be here," he said, voice low. I hoped whatever microphones they had in the room were also affected by the white noise, and wouldn't pick up on his murmur.

"I am definitely not *supposed* to be here. But you must hate them, too. Why would you alert them?"

"You are *one* of them!" He growled up at me, lips curling back from his teeth in a feral snarl.

I shrank back. I couldn't help it. My body knew that he was a predator, and compared to him, I was prey. Great. Make an alliance with someone who hates me. No problem. "I'm not one of them. They have power over me, and they're using it to try and control me."

He scoffed, a sharp huff of air through flaring nostrils. "You wear their clothing, sleep among them, and train among them. You are just another of the..." he paused here, as if searching for a word he couldn't find, "two-legged maggots." The machines to one side began to beep more rapidly, an obvious warning. "Your kind is a horrid race, matched only in your natural weakness by your capacity for cruelty."

I opened my mouth to argue with him, and then closed it. What was I going to say? Just one look at the red, raised flesh around his cuffs, the tubes running in and out all over his body, and the sunken, bruised skin under his eyes would have made me a liar. I looked down at my own claws, which I hadn't retracted. They were evidence, too. "You're right," I said instead. "My kind is cruel. And compared to you, we are also weak, no doubt. I can feel it in the air and the way the hair on the back of my neck rises when I just look at you. But my kind also have a saying. 'The enemy of my enemy is my friend.'"

He relaxed, one deliberate muscle at a time, and the machines calmed. "Why are you here?"

"I am here *right now* on a quest given by the Oracle. I am here *within NIX*...because they manipulated me and predicted my decisions. They somehow knew that I would agree to stay, if I knew that you were being held here. But I learned that they're betraying me already, and have plans to stab me in the back in other ways. I think they might have been lying about quite a few more things, and I'm hoping you can help me."

"The Oracle?" he said, ignoring the other parts of my explanation.

"Well, that's what she said her name was. She was made of stone, and every time she moved she made music, and she used these birdbaths that played music and sent shadows of herself to fight me...ugh." I groaned. "I'm not making any sense. The Oracle is a stone...creature, from your world, who gave me three puzzles. I've just solved the second one, and it involves you."

His eyes widened, and for the first time since I'd arrived above his holding cell, I felt like I had the upper hand. That might have been nice, if I hadn't been so desperate for him to provide something other than shocked silence.

"You..." He stared at me, his eyes narrowing, but not quite with hatred. He didn't continue with whatever he'd been going to say.

"Is it true? That your kind is going to attack our world?" Why had the Oracle told me to make an alliance with him?

The alien snarled at me once again. "Yes! My warriors will come for me. We will come in force and raze your cities to the ground like the ripe grain of a field. Your putrid maggot species will be wiped from the face of this planet, no more to defile it." The machines were beeping at him again, this time more urgently, and I waited a while for him to control himself, and them to calm down.

I could take a hint. Hatred for humanity was a trigger subject. Since I was a human, I was a little worried about the likelihood of completing the quest.

Birch decided that was the moment to come forward and peek through the vent beside me. He let out a chattering sound and curled his claws around the metal of the grate.

"A…tailos?" the alien said, almost breathless.

"Yes! One of the Trials NIX sent us to was in their habitat. The retchin—you're familiar with those?" At his nod, I continued, "They were attacking, pretty much wiping out all the tailos. We fought back but we lost. The leader gave me her egg to protect, and after we got back to Earth, Birch hatched." Mentions of his world seemed to be the key to negotiating with him.

He was staring up at Birch and me with no hint of a scowl. "When you met the…Oracle, did she reveal anything to you? Did she speak with you, when she bestowed upon you the three gifts? A message, or a task?"

"Err, not really. She said I'd proven myself worthy, gave me the puzzles, and said some platitude about walking in the midst of tribulation and not wavering," I said, but he stared up at me as if waiting for more. "The first puzzle led me to a…mountain-woman named Behelaino. From her, I got a black Seed, that I'm pretty sure she called Khaos." I enunciated the "K" and "H" separately, as she had done. "She warned me that it would destroy me, but I thought maybe I was *supposed* to take it, and that it would help me do what I needed to, so that I could save…save us from NIX." I hesitated for a moment. "But it's destroying my body. So, I solved the second puzzle, and had another vision, which you were in. Then, the Oracle connected to the Virtual Reality chip that NIX implanted in my brain, and gave me a quest to come see you. I was hoping that with your background, you might have an idea about what I should do to save myself. I can't heal fast enough to keep up with Chaos' growth, even though I'm putting all the normal Seeds from the Trials into the healing Attributes."

"The 'normal' Seeds?" His voice turned into a growl. "Your kind have made a horror of the Bestowals, as you know, and yet you continue to reward yourself with the theft of my blood. You force the blood-covenant on me in pretense of a bond…" his voice grew hoarse with the strength of emotion, and guttered out.

I blinked at him. "Your blood?"

He strained against the cuffs again in sudden rage. "You pretend innocence, when I know you take my blood willingly, though I have not consented! You are despicable. I wish destruction on you and all your progeny, till the sun falls from the sky." The full force of his presence, his rage, was back again, making it hard to think beyond the instinctual need to protect myself from imminent death.

Birch growled at him, wings flaring out to make himself seem bigger.

"Your blood is what makes the Seeds," I muttered, managing to ignore his outburst. My mind was exploding like a firework. "They're not making Seeds, they're…" I looked at all the tubes puncturing his skin, running outward like a splayed mass of tentacles to the machines. "Harvesting them," I whispered, finally. I focused harder, letting my Huntress Skill sharpen my eyesight, until the faint shimmer of the substance within the tubes was clear. "Oh my god," I said aloud, inanely.

"But…how do they keep you here?" I wondered aloud. "If the Shortcut takes anyone with the Seeds in their system, wouldn't you escape back to your homeland every Trial?"

"Is that what they tell you? That my 'Shortcut' takes all who have a blood-covenant with me?"

I knew the answer without him saying it, from the look on his face. "It doesn't. That's a lie. They have complete control over who stays and who goes." I pressed my forehead against my knees, staring down at the dark fabric of my bodysuit. It meant that they didn't even *need* to cleanse Zed to keep him from the Trials. I wanted to throw up. How stupid could I have been?

He stared at me, his expression unreadable, but at least no longer radiating fury. His head jerked a few inches to the side, his eyes going distant. "They are coming. You must leave now, human. Come and talk to me again soon."

I didn't need any more prompting than that to start moving away, but paused, turning my head back to the grate I could no longer see through. "What's your name?" I asked.

"I am Torliam, son of Mardinest, of the line of Aethezriel."

"I'm Eve Redding," I said, moving away again but sure he would hear me. "No fancy titles."

He said something else, but I did not hear him past my own pounding heart and the incessant buzzing.

In the corner of my vision, the countdown timer disintegrated.

Chapter 8

Someone I loved once gave me a box of darkness. It took me years to understand that this, too, was a gift.

— Mary Oliver

THE NEXT DAY, I talked to Adam, bringing him into the loop about my recent discoveries. NIX's puppeteering, the experimentation on Zed, the second vision from the Oracle and the subsequent strange behavior of my VR chip, and the alien far beneath our feet. Technically, I had no *proof* that he wasn't also one of NIX's informants, but I knew Adam. Even if Bunny had purposely manipulated our meeting, I still trusted Adam with my life, because he'd proven through action that he could be trusted with it. There is a kind of bond that grows with another person when you narrowly avoid the cold fingers of death together.

Adam seemed to be unsure how to respond to the influx of ulcer-inducing information. His hair stood on end from a building static charge, and he took the time to give me an all-purpose, "I told you so," for all the times I'd ignored his pessimism and paranoia. "It's not paranoia if they really are out to get you," he said, lips turning up at the corners just a bit.

I raised an eyebrow. "Is that the important thing to be dwelling on right now? Yes. You were right, *some* of the times you were suspicious."

"I notice that you can no longer say, 'acted crazy,'" he said pointedly, letting the electrical build-up jump between the fingers of his hand in miniature arcs of lightning.

"We need to deal with Blaine," I said, sobering Adam handily. "He's useful, and I'm pretty sure that he really does hate NIX with a passion. It's just that our previous offer wasn't good enough to make him actually put the kiddos in danger. We need to present him with a more...*persuasive* argument."

During our free period, the entire squad moved to the courtyard to get a workout and training session in, under Jacky's leadership. The courtyard was really more like a huge, artificial caldera. It was the best place to talk unobserved by NIX because the wide-open space was free from the mics around the walls, and at such a high altitude, the wind always seemed to be blowing, even better for not being overheard.

Instead of joining in, Adam and I drew Blaine away from the main group. "A storm is coming," Blaine said. "I can smell the ozone in the air. Quite interesting, you know. A similar smell is created when..." His eyes flicked between Adam's and my own face. "What is this about?"

"Do you remember the first time we met?" I asked.

"Yes." He chuckled a bit. "You all burst in, asking who I was working for, and willing to do anything to get me to talk." He held up his hand, the crushed finger of which Sam had healed.

I turned to him more fully, looked him in the eyes, and said, as significantly as I could, "*I know.*"

He stared at me for a second, and then his eyes dilated visibly as he sucked in a ragged breath. Blaine was anything but dense. He understood exactly what I meant. He straightened. "I knew you would find me out."

That surprised me. I shared a quick look with Adam. "Then why did you do it?"

"You know why." Blaine looked to the kiddos, who were laughing with Birch as they followed Jacky's instructions. "I had no choice. I could not risk it, not when I was wagering with their lives." He paused, and then added with difficulty, "Are you going to kill me?"

I tilted my head to the side, studying him. "I would have a hard time hiding the fact that I'd killed you." I smiled kindly, for the benefit of any watching us. "But I don't think I'm going to have to worry about that. I *did* already know why you lied to me, and to all of us. I just wanted you to say what's really important to you out loud."

"You would hurt *them*?" Blaine's voice grew gravelly.

"Would that make you loyal to me?" I was doing my best to exude a sense of calm that I didn't actually feel. I noted every twitch of his facial muscles, the tone of voice, his body language and breathing, watching for any reaction that could help me navigate the conversation. "I don't think it would. It certainly hasn't made you more loyal to NIX, has it? When Petralka put Kris and Gregor into our mock battle, so that they could be hurt? Did you know she did that as a chastisement because you actually *did* turn off our VR chips and GPS trackers, instead of just saying you did while allowing them to have access?"

Blaine seemed to be trying to find something to do, or say, his body fidgeting while his eyes stayed locked to mine, the glasses making them look just a bit larger. If he were a film actor he'd play a kind kindergarten teacher. He was handsome, but unassuming. A face you could trust.

"I've learned quite a few things that might interest you, Blaine. I, too, bargained with Commander Petralka, for the safety of someone I care about. Someone defenseless. A few days ago, I watched secretly as they *experimented* on my brother with *nanites*. They're trying to overcome the limitations imposed by the fact that NIX can't create their own Seeds, and most of the population can't assimilate them without dying. As I understand, they've tried before. Subjects have died. In fact, the scientists are excited that he might be the *first* functional alternative to the Seeds."

Adam interjected then, with perfect timing. "Gregor swears those nightmares he has are real. What if something is happening to them, under NIX's protection? Even if it isn't, how long do you think that will last? How much will they try to get away with, while you continue to 'protect' the kiddos with your loyalty?"

Blaine paled even further.

"I want to keep us all safe," I said. "I'm coming up with a plan, but I know I'm going to need your help. For real, this time." And that was all it took.

ZED THREW AN ANGLED punch toward my kidney, which I avoided by twisting my body in a way that most gymnasts couldn't, and landed a glancing blow with the side of one of my clawed feet.

"Point for me." I grinned wolfishly and bounced up and down on my toes a couple times.

"This is obviously unfair," he said, though he didn't let that deter him from attacking again. "How am I supposed to compare to an alien mutant woman?"

I slipped past him and kicked the back of his knee, which made him stumble but not fall. "I don't know..." I twisted and caught his neck in the crook of my elbow, bringing his head down to thoroughly tousle his hair. "Maybe you could use some of your cyborg powers?" I said, just loud enough for him to hear.

He struggled free and took a moment to straighten his now-tangled hair. "Did you think you could give me a noogy and I wouldn't retaliate? You've taken this too far. I hope you're prepared for my retribution," he said with mock seriousness.

I slid my feet apart, settling into horse stance like a kung fu master. I beckoned him with one arm outstretched. "Bring it."

The whole team was sparring toward one side of the courtyard.

Jacky directly instructed the less experienced, while the rest of us practiced on our own, except for the occasional comment from her.

Kris and Gregor were learning to attack viciously in ways that might give them the opportunity to run away from a stronger opponent.

Blaine and Bunny were being forced to hit a punching bag in endless repetition, which Blaine took to much better than the petulant Bunny.

Blaine had kept to his word about making sure both he and the kiddos were better able to defend themselves if need be, and during the times I'd followed him with my awareness for the last day, he hadn't done anything obvious to betray us to NIX. He was exhausted from working so hard, and I believed in the fact that he was on our side fully now, though it would be a while before I could let my guard down around him, even if I did understand why he'd made the decisions he had.

Adam and Sam were sparring in a way that gave both of them practice with what they needed. Adam created Animated ink constructs, mostly animals, and set them on Sam, who could feel free to attack without fear of harming something that could actually feel pain.

Birch had volunteered himself to help Sam defeat the animals, and was also happy to rush in and attack Adam with tooth, claw, and a not-quite-fearsome roar if he saw the opportunity.

After Zed got tired enough to need a water break, I wandered over to watch the spar between Adam, Sam, and Birch. Adam had a variety of materials spread out around him, both different inks and different surfaces to draw upon. He was already panting from exertion, though except for the rare times Birch had gotten past one of his ink constructs, he hadn't had to fight physically, and in fact, had barely moved. "Have you come to distract me?" he asked, bright red paint dripping from the artist's paintbrush in his hand.

"Just curious. You can ignore me," I said, as the saber-toothed monkey he'd just created attacked Blaine while swatting Birch away with its two tails.

"I don't mind. I'm almost out of juice anyway, so this'll be over soon. I know you have questions, it's written all over your face."

"Well then. Why are you using so many different supplies? And I know you don't even need to use a paintbrush or canvas. Or...a cafeteria food tray," I said, noting what he was painting on.

"Turns out, my Animus Skill cares about stuff like this. This is mostly a fun trial run, but I've been experimenting more seriously in the Skill Handling class, and it turns out that various factors affect the quality of the constructs I can produce."

"Really? Like what?" My own Skill Handling class had been an exercise in *avoiding* using my Chaos Skill as much as possible, while working on Spirit of the Huntress and Tumbling Feather freely. I'd definitely frustrated the instructor and the scientists who'd come to "help," but they were under the impression that I just had a bad attitude, not that I was afraid of killing myself.

"It doesn't like plastic, most of the time. Either to paint with or on. Dry mediums don't work, it has to be paint or ink. It has a thing for metals, the harder or more precious the better, it seems. The constructs increase in quality when I spend a little more time on them, but that seems obvious. And a couple other things, but it's pretty inconclusive so far. There must be some sort of rule behind it, but I haven't figured out what it is yet."

"That's fascinating," I murmured. Did my own Skills have similar functions that I'd never noticed? I didn't have a chance to ask him any more questions, as a heavy *thwump-thwump-thwump* filled the air, signaling the approach of a heli-pod.

The heli-pod hovered above one side of the courtyard, waiting as a section of the concrete ground opened up to the hangar down below. People began jumping out, which would have been dangerous for a civilian. Two of them carried a cot between them, which held a body covered by a white sheet.

My eyes widened as a tall, thin man launched himself out, floating just a little too far in a way that reminded me of Jacky.

The commotion drew attention, and other Players filtered out of the various doors to the courtyard or watched curiously from the rows of glass wall and windows.

"Is that..." Adam asked, standing up slowly.

"Yes." It was the man who'd killed China. The man I'd dubbed the "snake," and a mortal enemy.

He smiled and stretched, and did not notice me among the others milling around the outside of the walls.

Jacky and Sam came over to us, dragging Chanelle, Blaine, and the kiddos with them, while Bunny watched nervously, and then sidled over to put our group between himself and the new arrivals. "Maybe we should leave, guys," he murmured, just loud enough for my augmented ears to hear him.

"He's back," Jacky whispered.

Zed moved closer to my side, Birch balanced precariously on his shoulder. "Is that the guy you told me about?"

Adam nodded. "Stay away from him. He won't hesitate to kill you if you give him an opportunity."

"Are you going to do something?" Sam asked, looking at me.

I looked around and noticed the soldiers stationed in the courtyard. There were other Players all around who already didn't like us so much, along with what I assumed were the man's teammates. They would attack with pleasure if I tried to start something in such a public space. No, we couldn't attack him now. We would never succeed, and with the amount of power in attendance, I might not even get close. The knowledge maddened me.

I carried rage under my skin like a second being. It whispered of gleeful destruction in the intervals between my heartbeats. "Yes. I am going to. But not now."

Chapter 9

Terrible things happen to good people every day.
Consequentially, I am not one of the good people.
I am one of the terrible things.
— Marianna Paige

"I'M LOOKING FOR A NEW RECRUIT!" China's killer called out. "One of my soldiers was too weak to cut it, as you saw." He gestured toward the door his other teammates had taken the body through.

The clamor grew, as people chattered excitedly to themselves. A few overheard snippets of conversation revealed that the man was called Kilburn. In fact, at least some of the other Players present had connected our history, and were looking between him and my team with greedy little eyes.

"I'll sign up for that spot," another familiar voice called out.

I turned to see Vaughn pushing through the crowd. The heli-pod sank into the hangar below, and as the cement closed back up after it, it seemed as if the whole courtyard had grown quiet with anticipation.

"My unit is elite. Are you sure you won't just end up as the next body bag?" Kilburn asked, his smile stretching too wide across his face. Did normal mouths have that many teeth?

"I have no intention of dying any time soon, if ever," Vaughn said.

"Your intentions don't mean much to me. I need someone who can prove they won't weigh me down." They were both speaking loudly, no doubt for the benefit of the crowd.

"You'd like to fight, then?" Vaughn smiled with enough charm to make me shudder.

"No. That would be silly. And you'd die. I want to see you fight *her*." He swung an arm around and pointed straight at me. Apparently, he hadn't been oblivious to me at all. "A friendly little spar should do it? You can stop if you get her to vomit blood."

Vaughn followed the line of Kilburn's finger to me. "Oh. Little Miss Spirit-type, the famous Redding. We met recently, didn't we?"

To my surprise, Blaine was the first to move forward, drawing something shiny from his pocket and pointing it at Vaughn. "Stop there. If you want to spar, you will do so under NIX's established rules."

Adam fingered the ink and electricity cartridges at his waist.

Jacky popped the knuckles in each of her fingers individually, glaring at Vaughn in obvious threat.

Vaughn looked around at the guards in the courtyard and atop the wall, who were far outnumbered by the Players. "I don't see any of the guards trying to stop us. I'm pretty sure that means they're okay with it." I was pretty sure some of them were actually Moderators, or maybe even Thinkers, but he was right. "And that gun isn't going to stop me," he said. "It's meant to be nonlethal for *normal* Players. I don't mind fighting all of you at once, but Eve, you could save your teammates if you'd just come out and fight me one-on-one. Wouldn't you like a chance to redeem yourself after the last time?" He stared at me intently, and then his expression morphed into surprise for a half second, and maybe even a little concern.

Then I felt the warm wetness on my upper lip. I slapped a hand to my face, covering my nose. "Oh, shit," I muttered. "It's no big—" my words cut off as a wave of pain cut through me. I felt dizzy and nauseous and like my blood had just begun to spontaneously boil, all at the same time. That side effect was new. I took an involuntary step back from him, half-stumbling.

Unfortunately, Adam turned around at that moment. His eyes took in the blood flowing around my cupped fingers, the expression of fear and pain on my face, and then cut back to Vaughn. "He just attacked Eve," he said urgently. A logical conclusion, I guess, if you didn't know the truth.

Jacky roared like an animal, lunging at Vaughn with a rage that I'd rarely seen in her before. She grabbed him by the arm before either of us could say anything, pushing and pivoting at the same time.

Vaughn went flying, sliding back through the doors to the cafeteria, and Jacky stomped after him, her footfalls causing noticeable tremors in the ground beneath our feet.

Players scattered to get out of the way, moving towards the outer walls of the courtyard.

I stumbled forward to stop Jacky, but the pain was still sliding through my veins, radiating through my muscles.

"Jacky, please—" Blaine called, pointing his gun down and away from Vaughn, now that she was standing in between them.

"He attacked Eve!" Jacky snarled, her face flushed and eyes wide. She kicked out at Vaughn, and he jumped back further into the cafeteria to avoid her.

It seemed fortune was not on my side at the moment, because Sam laid a hand on me, and then shook his head in desperation. "Eve, I can't do anything—"

That was all the rest of them needed to hear, I guess.

Adam's eyes flickered between my face, the blood, and my hand, braced on my knee to help support me. Within a second he'd snapped open an ink canister and surrounded me in a shield bubble.

"Wha—" I mumbled, sputtering blood away from my lips. "You guys, stop it." But they either didn't hear me within the bubble, or they were ignoring me. I tilted my head back. My nose didn't stop bleeding, but at least the blood ran down my throat instead of spilling all over the place.

I tried to relax past the pain, but couldn't, as it was different than the usual injury. I didn't feel hurt, I felt sick, and I couldn't ignore it. It faded away after a few more seconds, and I focused on the microscopic organisms of the Seed of Chaos in my blood. I calmed them perfunctorily, as quickly as I could, but it was a slow process at the best of times.

I took a portion of my awareness and pushed it outward, ignoring the fear bubbling up hotter than ever in the back of my mind. I gasped.

It hadn't been more than a minute, but the team was being decimated by Vaughn. I'd known he was strong, but they were no match for him.

Adam had stepped in to help Jacky, leaving the shield which was imprisoning me to fade away when it expired.

Sam was a few yards away, popping Blaine's shoulder back into place. The kiddos were on the edge of the crowd with Zed and Chanelle, being guarded by Birch, who was snarling at anyone who even got close to them.

As soon as Sam was finished with Blaine, he ran back toward Vaughn, who dropped forward as if about to smash his own face into the ground, then flickered out of existence in the gap of a half second, his body alternating between flashing brightly with light and disappearing in the blotchy spot of darkness that marred the vision in the light's absence.

Sam barely noticed the flicker of distortion above him in time to throw himself out of the way.

Vaughn popped back into sight, and seemingly, also back into plain old existence, just as he touched the spot where Sam had been.

Jacky jumped back toward Vaughn, bringing her hand forward like it was a hammer, while a small flock of ink birds pierced through the air, emerging from behind her and darting around in a pincer movement toward him.

Vaughn hummed under his breath, low enough I might not have noticed if I hadn't felt the vibration with my outstretched senses.

The vibration of his hum split from his throat, and a vibrating after-image pushed forward from his body.

When Jacky touched it, barely sinking into it, her skin bloomed bright red. The feeling of it in the air was like when your teeth grind together, or the way you feel when you hear nails screech across one of those antique blackboards teachers used to use. I was pretty sure her skin had just been ripped apart beneath the surface.

Jacky snatched her hand back like it'd been burned, and the ink birds disintegrated as they hit the after-image.

The after-image split in two, and then those split in two again, each of them humming a slightly different note. Vaughn had surrounded himself with a shield of sorts. One of his copies lashed out at Sam, brushing its vibrating fist against the boy as Sam yanked Jacky backward.

Adam flashed forward, two ink rods held in his hands, almost like swords. He managed to slip through the copies and clip Vaughn across the side, but Vaughn blinked out in a flash of brightness again, and Adam had to throw up a quick shield in order to escape. Adam was tired already, coming close to exhaustion, and it showed in the pale skin of his cheeks and lips, and the way he panted.

On a positive note, Vaughn's vibrating copies disappeared along with him, and didn't reappear when he flickered back into existence behind Sam. "You're good," Vaughn said. "But you're not good enough." He slammed a fist into the side of Sam's neck, dropping the boy like a sack of potatoes.

Vaughn looked down at the red crystals growing out of the side of his fist, where he'd touched Sam. "Ouch," he said, and flickered into existence behind and to the side of Jacky. He kicked her in the ribs hard enough to send her flying in my direction.

She softened her own landing, but didn't get up fast enough, and he began to hum again, bringing the copies out as he moved toward her.

Adam was running towards us, but he would arrive too late.

I let out my claws and raked them across the blackness in front of my face. I knew Adam imbued his Animations with the characteristics he desired when bringing them into the world. His shield was meant to keep things out, not trap something inside. It was already close to evaporating, and so when I attacked it from within, it ripped and disintegrated.

I ran forward, the claws on my toes scratching on the hard concrete beneath my feet with every step. I threw myself toward Jacky, who was doing her best to regain her feet before Vaughn kicked her in the ribs. Again.

I slipped around one of his after-images with a quick feint, and smashed my foot down on the front of his leg, trapping his foot on the ground without doing any real damage. "Stop!" I snarled, my voice ripping through the noise of the crowd and echoing off the walls. The sound died down as people quieted to catch every second of this new development. "This is over."

Vaughn laughed and stepped back, dragging his trapped leg away from me.

I shook my head at Adam, telling him silently to stay away. Anger had become my frequent companion, since that first time NIX had taken control of my life. It had deepened and grown along with me, and now it strengthened me with its familiar hot-and-cold chill.

"*Can* you end it?" He cocked his head to the side like a bird. "I saw what you did to little Petralka and the Shortcut. I've wondered about you since then, but I've never seen you go all-out again."

"Eve, he's strong," Jacky groaned, and I heard her spit onto the floor.

I jumped to the side, feinting, and when the copies nearest me lunged forward to block and attack, I spun back and slipped through the opening I'd created, slamming my claws toward his chest and closing my eyes. At least he wasn't clairvoyant, too.

His eyes widened, and he flickered just as I made contact, so brightly it would have been blinding if I'd seen it without the protection of my closed eyelids, and disappeared. The vibrating copies disappeared along with him, but once again didn't reappear when he flickered back into existence a few feet farther away.

I lifted the hand that had touched him, showing the blood on the very tips of my claws. There was surprised mumbling all around from our audience.

He laughed, then, and started to hum this time before flickering. His copies took a split second to reappear every time he changed location, but this time they stopped me from properly getting out of his reach or counterattacking, and where they touched me my skin fell off.

Just the first couple layers, but it seemed with every attack the damage grew. My bodysuit couldn't withstand the vibrations, but it did act as a temporary shield. My armored vest beneath it stopped his vibrations easily, simply spreading the energy along its whole surface. Unfortunately, it only covered so much of my body, and the rest of me was vulnerable to his Skill.

I let the pain sharpen my instincts. I twisted and turned around his copies like an eel swimming through the air, slashing at him when I could get close enough and using my Skill to keep track of him and his copies at the same time, even if I couldn't see them all with my physical eyes.

YOUR AGILITY HAS INCREASED!

I waved away the notification and attacked with the same movement. I knew I couldn't keep it up for more than a couple minutes at most. I was fighting against my instinct to unleash Chaos into the area around me. Despite the side effects I'd been dealing with only a minute before, I'd half convinced myself that I could release it just for a split second and end the fight.

It was to my enormous and hopefully secret relief when Commander Petralka stepped into the courtyard. "Freeze!" She roared, rage suffusing her voice. "What the hell do you homicidal imbeciles think you're doing?"

Zed lifted both hands and pointed to Kilburn and Vaughn. "They started it!"

COMMANDER PETRALKA SCREAMED a bit more and sent all the onlookers scrambling away, then berated Kilburn, Vaughn, and my team. She seemed quite suspicious that I was going to try and attack Kilburn, or vice-versa, and sent us back to the team barracks, while she kept Vaughn and Kilburn behind to chew out.

Once Sam woke up, he healed Jacky, Adam, Blaine, and me. The tension in the muscles around his eyes only grew.

Kris and Gregor wanted to know why the whole incident had happened, and I left it to Adam and Jacky to explain it to them, while Zed slipped in sporadic comments meant to distract them from their fear and uncertainty. The way Kris held her little moose to her chest made something inside me squeeze with regret, and I turned away.

Bunny sat with Chanelle in the corner of the room, trying to get her to play a card game with him, with a total lack of success. Eventually, he got up and clapped his hands together. "You guys are way too mopey. Lighten up!" he said, looking at the kiddos.

They smiled, a little, and then he turned his power on the rest of us. "'Now is the time to get stronger, so this doesn't happen again!' Eve, isn't that your line?"

I felt a new little bud of determination well up within me. I wondered if I was getting better at detecting his intrusion, or if perhaps the Oracle's second gift had made me a little more aware, with the Perception boost it granted. The foreign emotion was one-dimensional. It held none of the desperation or fear that my real determination was tinged with. "I've got a plan for that, actually," I said. My claws itched, and I relaxed my fingers so that they didn't slip out and display my feelings toward him overtly.

He smiled, oblivious to the thoughts running through my mind, or the nature of my plan. "Great. Care to share?"

"It's going to involve a lot of training. Bunny, I noticed that you didn't participate in the fight. Blaine's an unpowered adult just like you, but even he did his part." I ignored the narrow-eyed look Zed shot my way. "I want to make sure we're utilizing all of our members to the best of their ability. Maybe we could get you a gun or two, like Blaine? Or knives, if you prefer?"

"Err, that sounds…" Bunny coughed. "Eve, don't you think I'd just be a liability? You don't want to put the other members in danger if I screw up during a fight, do you?" He stared hard into my eyes.

I frowned, deliberately letting my eyes glaze over, just a bit. "Hmm…

maybe not. But…what if you put someone in danger because you can't protect yourself?"

"I'll stay out of the way, don't worry about that," he said.

When I nodded, but then frowned again as if I'd come up with a new argument, he quickly found a reason to leave the team barracks.

It took the rest of the night for me to get everything into place. Aside from the kids and Chanelle, who went to sleep early, the rest of us had a conversation about what I'd learned recently—after I'd swept the barracks for any more hidden bugs. I'd hesitated whether to reveal Blaine's duplicity to the others, but Adam took the decision out of my hands.

"They need to know, we all need to know, so that we can make sure it doesn't happen again," Adam said, not flinching from Blaine's obvious discomfort.

"He is right," Blaine said. "It is better if everyone is aware of the dangers. One or two people cannot keep watch for the entire group." He then explained his real assignment from NIX.

Jacky almost punched Blaine, but Sam stopped her. When she learned of Bunny's much more serious transgressions, her anger was directed in full force toward him.

The next day, after dinner, Sam and Zed stayed in the team barracks with Kris, Gregor, and the still-unresponsive Chanelle, while the rest of us crowded into my tiny room, where Sam had left Bunny in an artificially induced sleep.

Blaine did some relatively minor surgery on Bunny while he slept. And then, for good measure, we brought in a chair and tied Bunny to it.

Instead of Adam, who was still upset with Blaine, I assisted the scientist. I'd come up with this plan as the best option under impossible circumstances. I didn't trust Bunny, but if he died, it would undermine the team's safety. I also couldn't just leave him alone, because then he might directly sabotage our future efforts by reporting on us. Because we would definitely be doing things NIX wouldn't like. Hopefully, the Thinker was right, and Bunny was selfish enough for my plan to work.

A quick shock of electricity from Adam woke our Moderator up. He looked around frantically, but caught on to the situation quickly. "What's going on? You guys don't want to hurt me, you know. I'm on your side! And I know NIX would think it was weird if I suddenly disappeared. Eve." He turned the force of his gaze on me. "I've helped you so much. Why are you doing this? I thought you looked out for your teammates?"

I felt compassion burble up inside me, strong enough to make me choke. I ignored it. I'd done plenty of things that made me feel bad, when the stakes were high enough. Compassion wasn't going to change anything. "Do you feel that soreness on the back of your neck, Bunny? Right under the hairline?"

His eyes grew wider with desperation. "You *have* to let me *go*, Eve!"

I frowned sadly and shook my head. "I want to. I really do. I think you *know* that, Bunny."

He swallowed.

"But I can't let you go. Because you've betrayed me, and that means there are only two options."

"What are you talking about, Eve? Guys, help me out, here! She's crazy!"

Jacky pinched herself on the thigh and and kept squeezing as she spoke. "Eve is crazy. And if she's crazy enough that she thinks you have to die, I'm going to help her." She took a deep breath, then released the crushing grip on her skin. "Whoa."

Adam frowned for a bit, but otherwise didn't react, keeping to his role as the administrator of the intimidating, silent stare.

Blaine turned to me, looking down at the smartglass tablet in his hand in horror. "Eve, this *is* crazy. We just planted a bomb in his head—"

"What!?" Bunny screeched.

"I don't think I can go through with this," Blaine said.

I gestured to Jacky, who slapped Blaine lightly across the face, rocking his head to the side.

He looked shocked, then lifted a hand to the bright red imprint she'd left. His expression hardened, then, and he glared at Bunny. "On second thought, I think I can." Pain helped to break Bunny's influence.

"You're very dangerous, Bunny," I said. "Turning people's emotions against them? That must be so useful for you. I mean, you even used it on Commander Petralka and the Thinker, when you met with them the other night." I waited for that to sink in.

Bunny didn't say anything this time, but began to struggle against his bindings.

"The problem is, your power isn't invincible. It's best used subtly, and on people who have no idea that you're capable of such a thing. Once someone finds out…well, you're a threat. Insidious and self-serving." I leaned in. "I think those are the exact words the Thinker called you after you left your little meeting with him and Petralka." Kind of true, if not exactly. "If people can't trust you, the only option left is 'removal.'" I lifted my fingers up for the air-quotes.

By that time, he'd stopped struggling, and was pale and sweaty. "They…how do you know that? You could be lying. You're just making all this up to try and get me to admit to something that isn't even true!"

I raised an eyebrow. "I know that you told Petralka I, 'don't believe in forgiveness.' That I, 'understand retribution and my own value as the center of the universe.' A bit extreme, don't you think? I can be forgiving. If there's a reason."

"What—what do you want?"

"To smash your head in till I can see the white meat," Jacky muttered, which caused Adam's mouth to curl into a small smirk.

"NIX has been telling us Players some lies, Bunny. Some of them you probably know about, but I'm not sure. Like the fact that they're experimenting on my brother?" I said.

His eyes flickered away, "What? No, I didn't—"

"Lying," I said. "You're lying, so just stop there." I took a deep breath. "But that's okay. I can forgive you, because you're going to help me make sure my brother's safe. I really hope you agree to this. And I hope you can keep your word. Because I'm going to have to make sure you don't reveal this conversation before NIX kills you. That's going to be a big drain on my resources. Someone will have to monitor the devices we put in your skull all the time. Then, if you decided to talk about this conversation as a bargaining chip to convince them to keep you alive, I'd have to blow your skull apart from the inside." I grimaced.

"I'm probably going to have to do most of that work," Adam muttered. "It's a waste, if you ask me. We should just take him up to the wall and toss him off into the river below, and blow up his head on the way down, just in case."

"I can help," Bunny said quickly. "And I know how to keep my mouth shut. But whatever you're doing, you have to keep me safe. Take me with you—keep me on the list of people you're shielding—whatever. You have to promise me."

"If you're useful enough, why would I want to get rid of you? There's no chance of you influencing my decisions anymore, so you don't pose a danger in that way."

DESPITE MY EXHAUSTION after everything that had happened, I crawled down to see Torliam again that night. He was once again awake and waiting for me when I arrived. His eyes met mine, and he dipped his head in a subtle nod.

"Hello again," I said.

"You have given me much time to ponder, since our last meeting."

Perhaps being shackled there with only his mind to keep him proper company, time seemed to pass slower. "It hasn't been that long, and I've been busy."

"Tell me about the vision you received from the Oracle. The one that I was in."

"I've actually seen you in both my visions," I said hesitantly. "And when NIX first forced the Seed on me and I had the initiation sickness." And maybe a few other times, but there was a strange look on his face, and I wasn't sure it was wise to continue.

"What did you see?" His head strained forward, as if he could will himself out of his shackles and off the slab. He paused, as if hesitating, and then continued with a sneer, "I do not wish to speak of your mind touching mine, or your incredible disrespect."

Sheesh. "The first time, it felt like I was living one of your memories, or something. It happened directly after the vision that led me to Behelaino. You were in Estreyer." I paused, feeling uncomfortable. "This time, you were in the actual vision. There was a moon shining over water. An ocean, maybe. You were standing on the surface of the water. You pointed me down, and I followed the light of the moon into the water to this gold colored orb. But it was actually a giant eye, and I was like a bug in comparison to it…" I shuddered at the remembered feeling of turning to rust.

"A giant golden eye, you say? Perhaps it is symbolism for the God of Knowledge? He has been removed from mortal contact for a long time, now. Are you sure that it was *me* you saw?"

"Yes, it was you. I leaned forward eagerly myself. "Do you think this God of Knowledge might help me? With my Chaos problem?"

"The God of Knowledge is a counterpart to your Goddess of Chaos, who seems to have allowed you to ascend, if your story is to be believed. Behelaino, as you called her. The God of Knowledge has removed himself from the presence of mortals, but if there is a being in existence that knows how to save you from your own stupidity, it is he."

I ignored his continued insults, too elated by the idea that I may have found the solution to at least one of my problems. "I'll just need to find a way to get to him, then. The Shortcut is broken for now, but maybe that's where we'll be going when it's fixed…"

"No, the 'Shortcut' does not connect to his domain. It will not allow you to petition him. It is a weak tool meant to take our young to be tested when traveling far from home. The Trials connected to by my device are simple, and relatively easy, the gods lenient in accordance to their weakness. A commander works with them to shape the Trials. Usually a parent, but in this case, it is likely one of NIX's people. I am surprised, in fact, that it allowed you to connect to a manifestation of Chaos. That particular manifestation must have been much, much weaker when the destination point was originally established. You would have to travel halfway around the world to reach the God of Knowledge, or travel to Estreyer another way, and even then, it would be a long journey."

My brain wanted to be caught by the fact that someone from NIX had not only been the Examiner who explained the rules of the Trials to us, but had actively worked to shape them. Which meant that they might have been able to affect the horrific death tolls. And yet, more than half of us died within them. I blinked hard, and moved on to the currently relevant information. "Another way? Is there a way for me to get there besides the Shortcut?"

"There are other ways, but I will not be revealing them to one of your kind."

My eyes narrowed as I thought of a way around his reticence. Is this what the Oracle had intended? It was *insane*. I opened my mouth anyway. "But *you* could use them, if you were free?"

Some of the energy seemed to go out of him, and he lay more heavily against the slab. "Once, I hoped so. No more. I have found hope is only another form of torture. Until my kind return for me, there will be no escape."

"But you *could*, if you were?" I said, pressing the point.

"Yes." His eyes had caught on my expression, and seemed to be searching it for meaning.

"You have something I need…and I have something you need," I said, my mind tumbling down all the paths that could lead to an answer.

"What do you have that I need? I cannot even move."

"I need to fulfill the vision the Oracle gave me. And *you* need…to escape from this place."

I said the last part slowly, each word tripping over my lips separately. I needed a way out from under NIX's crushing thumb, too. I ignored the little voice in the back of my head that was screaming how utterly demented I was to even think of releasing a creature like Torliam.

"You make promises you cannot keep." He looked away from me, the muscles around his mouth and eyes tightening. Maybe even the inkling of hope he drew from my face and words was painful.

"You'd be surprised at the things I can accomplish, when I set my mind to it." I was still thinking, rapid-fire. I would have to take the whole team with me, as they wouldn't be safe on earth with NIX. But maybe, if we weren't constantly being subjected to a Trial, and had someone as strong as Torliam with us, Estreyer wouldn't be so bad. It might be safe there, for Zed, the kiddos, and the rest of us. At least until we could find a way to be safe back on Earth. I reminded myself of the team members' families, including my own mother. I still had to do something about that. But if I could make sure they were safe… "This might actually work," I said aloud.

"The surprise in your voice does not inspire confidence," he said wryly.

"You just made a joke!" I couldn't help my small smile of excitement. Now that I could see a possible path out of this horrible mess I'd gotten everyone into, a little bit of the metaphorical crushing weight removed itself from my shoulders.

"But… This new method of getting to Estreyer, does it scramble electronics like the Shortcut?"

His halfway-pleased expression curdled. "Why?"

"My brother is filled with nanites, which I'm worried may be affected. NIX has been experimenting on him. Without consent." That was partially a lie. If I could bring some of NIX's air-burst guns, maybe a hoverboard or two…

"The incompetence of your race causes the 'scrambling,' as you say, of electronics. Your brother will be fine."

"And a hoverboard, maybe? There will be children coming. I don't think they'll be able to keep up on their own."

"*Children*? You wish to try and escape this place while protecting children?"

"I'm not going to *leave* them, so there isn't much choice, is there?"

He grunted. "As I said, your race's simple devices will be fine."

"And you can make sure we're not dropped in the middle of a Trial? We'll go to somewhere relatively safe?"

"Relatively."

"Once we're there, how long will it take us to get to this God of Knowledge? I've got…" I stopped talking, as I realized what I was thinking. I *knew* the God of Knowledge would be strong, and if my time on Estreyer had taught me anything, it was that everything within that beautiful world wanted to kill you. The vision the Oracle had shown me didn't suggest he would be a pacifist, either. Even *she* had beaten me like a ragdoll, to prove my worth! And yet, there I was, planning to essentially repeat my first attack on NIX. I was unprepared. The *team* was unprepared, and it would get someone killed.

I swallowed down the shame. "I've had to fight pretty much everything I've ever met on Estreyer. Do you think it will be the same here? Is he the communicative type, or the 'crush you like the puny mortal you are' type?"

"Mortals who hunger for growth and power do petition the gods and attempt to prove their worth, but it is rare to succeed. Occasionally, they do succeed, and are given a Bestowal. These are your 'Skills.' The God of Knowledge is one of the few greater gods, and if he is where I suspect, a large portion of his strength will be gathered in one place. You will not find yourself winning a fight against him. I doubt you'll be able to persuade him to help at all. You can only hope that he doesn't kill you if you fail."

"That's not useful. You'll have to help me prepare." I said decisively. "This has to work, because I'm not going to die." That was the alternative, if I couldn't find a way to fix my power or myself.

A violent shudder rolled through him, as if he'd gotten cold, and when he murmured again his voice was quieter. "If you help me break the blood-covenants that have been forced upon me, I will help you fulfill the Oracle's vision, even if I must battle the gods to do it. This I swear."

"The blood-covenant, that's what you were talking about before. What exactly is that?"

"When you take my blood and mix it with your own, it forces a bond on me. I wish to be rid of your kind's defilement."

I ignored the barb, "If you do that, will the Seeds still work for us?" As a normal human, I'd probably die instantly within Estreyer.

"Breaking the bond is not pleasant, but any blood your kind have stolen from me will remain in your weak bodies."

"Okay, it's a deal. What measures have they put in place to keep you here? I need to know everything so I can make a plan to get you out."

He took a deep breath and began to speak. “I have a constant stream of paralytic pumping into me, and they are constantly draining me of my life-blood. They have found the perfect balance, where they harvest as much as possible, up to the limit of where it would begin to affect my power’s ability to replenish itself. They hold me shackled, as you can see, and if I become too active, they will stun me with electricity and spray a different mist-sedative. This room is completely reinforced, and even if I were to get out of my shackles, I could not escape if the door were not open. I am watched for signs of rage or the possibility of my escape. There are listening devices throughout the room, but I have caused the air to buzz so that they are impotent. The floor tiles are set to detect my substantial weight pressing down on them, and this table knows if my weight leaves it. And lastly, the table has clamps running along the length of my spine. It breaks my spine from the bottom up, letting me heal over the course of a few days, and then breaking directly above the previous break, till it reaches my neck and starts back at the base again. It is a never-ending cycle of pain and paralysis. They have just started back at the base of my spine. I can move my arms and upper torso, but never my legs.”

He wiggled his torso to show me, grimacing. “Many of these precautions are due to my previous escape attempts. I have tried everything I can think of. And even if you do manage to get me out of this room, we would need to retrieve my ship to make it halfway around your world before I can take us back to my homeland.”

My eyes were wide, as I imagined my spine being systematically broken, over and over, just to keep me securely imprisoned. I suppressed a shudder and vowed that I would do my best not to be placed in the cell on sub-level seventeen that was being prepared for me. “That is daunting. But you didn’t have me before. And I come as a package deal with my team. Now, please explain in *detail*, as best you can, how all of the security technology works. And hurry up, I’ve got to get to bed soon.”

Chapter 10

The devil asked me how I knew my way around the halls of hell. I told him I did not need a map for the darkness I know so well.

— T.M.T.

THE NEXT MANY days were a stressful, sleepless blur of plotting and secretive preparation. All of us had our own tasks to carry out, and after the initial burst of arguing and apprehension when I'd revealed the plan, we'd gotten to work with a vengeance.

Bunny hadn't argued quite so much as he might have, because he didn't know the real plan. He thought we were going to steal the ship and escape, but had no idea that we were also bringing NIX's alien, human-hating captive with us. I kept an eye on Bunny, or had one of the others do so, as much as possible, and attempted to make sure he believed the observation was constant. But I didn't trust him, especially because, out of the whole team, he was the only one who'd joined NIX willingly, and condoned its actions.

He'd been searching for more information on the location of my mother, and the other relatives Blaine had relocated, without any luck. "NIX doesn't know where they are. Or if they do, they're doing a really good job of lying about it. *We* don't know where they are, or at least if you guys do, I'm not aware of it. It literally seems as if they've dropped off the face of the Earth," Bunny said.

I wasn't sure if that was a good thing or not. On the upside, NIX didn't know where they were, and couldn't find them to hurt them. On the downside, we didn't know where our relatives were, and they'd disappeared. Though, if ever there was a woman who could fend for herself, it was my mother. I wasn't self-deceiving enough to pretend I cared about *other* people's families, but I hoped worrying over their own wouldn't affect my team members' work.

Blaine had finished augmenting the new VR chips and set the rest of the team up with them, then modified the settings so that every team member could communicate freely with the others.

When Bunny was out, we gathered in the now unquestionably debugged team barracks and discussed the more controversial part of my plan. I sat at the table, with the others lounging around in the few loose chairs, or on the bunk beds.

"What does it mean, that the Oracle is connecting to your VR chip now?" Adam asked. "I mean, the alien wants to kill us. What if she's on his side?"

"Then we're pretty much screwed, because as far as I can see, getting off Earth is our only option," I said. "And we can't do that without him. Not unless we want to wait till the Shortcut is finished, initiate the kids as Players, and then have it drop us all in the midst of a Trial." It didn't need to be said that that plan wouldn't fly.

"That may be, but what about surviving while we're there?" Sam said.

Blaine leaned forward. "The kids and I do not have the ability to just tear any opponents apart with our bare hands. With the release of the electronic restrictions, I have been gearing the ship up for conflict situations. The missing things will be noticed eventually—we know NIX keeps track of inventory—but if we do this right, we will be gone before they notice. By the time we leave, I hope to have enough to supply the whole team. We will be able to augment any strength deficiencies with technology."

Kris' stuffed moose was on her lap. "We've been practicing. Running, and with the guns. I know we're not like you guys, but we'll be able to take care of ourselves better."

Gregor grunted. "If they really have been experimenting on us all this time, maybe we'll be just fine protecting ourselves." He shot a dark look toward Blaine.

"I have found no evidence that they have done anything to either of you," Blaine said. His mouth tightened when Gregor rolled his eyes.

Sam looked toward Chanelle. "Well, maybe…if there are other aliens we can get in contact with…" He hesitated for a moment. "Maybe they have a Skill or some technology that can help Chanelle."

Jacky brightened. "Whoa, great! It's weird seeing China looking like that, even if it really isn't her."

Adam ran a hand over Chanelle's short hair, making it rise with static electricity. "China would have wanted us to try, at least."

"And we will. But right now, we need to finalize the preparation. We don't have time to waste." My voice wasn't loud, but it brought everyone's attention back. "This is a complicated plan, and we need to make sure that we've got redundancies in place, in case something goes wrong. The point is that our preparation will stymie NIX at every turn. I want backup plans to counter their backup-backup plans. Zed is going to need 'nanite nutrient paste,' enough to last him for a long time, just in case. How are we going to get that?"

Blaine had a few ideas about sneaking some away and stashing it in the ship ahead of time, which Zed volunteered to help with.

"You should hide weapons on your body or in your clothing," Gregor said. "In case they try to capture you or have some way to keep you from using the powers and weapons they know about."

"That's actually a really good idea," I said. "No such thing as overkill, when we're dealing with NIX. Seriously, they've been so far ahead of us this whole time. If this is going to work, we all have to step up our game. I want everyone to come up with ideas. Blaine, you may be helping to implement some of them."

"I will prepare more stimulant pills." He sighed, taking off his glasses to rub his bloodshot eyes.

"It won't be much longer now. Adam, how is the research on that cell in sub-level seventeen going?"

"You'll need our help once you're in there, but it's still the most direct route to the alien."

"Okay, good. There are a few more kinks to work out with the plan to jailbreak Torliam, but right now I want to focus on the Seeds."

I flattened my hands on the table. "How are we going to steal them?"

DAYS LATER, while I was in the vents talking to Torliam, he turned his eyes to me and said, "They are starting it."

"Starting what?"

"The Shortcut. I can feel it beginning to call out to my blood. It is being set in motion."

"Oh, shit." I turned my body to the side and moved along the ducts away from Torliam's cell. "It's too early."

We'd been preparing our breakout and spying on NIX through both Blaine and Bunny, so I knew NIX planned to use the Shortcut as soon as they had it working again. But electricity wasn't enough to get the floating rings spinning again, so they had to use some other way. I hadn't thought they'd be able to do it so quickly. We weren't ready.

As I scrambled, carelessly puncturing the walls of the duct with my claws to gain speed and maneuverability, I sent out Windows to the team.

—They're starting the Shortcut! I think we're all about to be taken to a Trial. If you're not where you're supposed to be, get there now! —
-Eve-

—I'm out of bounds, Eve. Halfway to the generator. There's no way I can make it back in time.—
-Adam-

Why was he doing that *now*? We hadn't planned for him to augment the backup generator yet. If the Boneshaker pulled him away halfway through using suction cups to crawl through the vents, he'd be caught. NIX would want to know exactly what he was doing in such a suspicious location. The plan would be blown apart. "Damn it, Adam!" I ground out. I sent a Window to the whole team.

—I'm going to stop the Boneshaker. Or at least delay it. It's probably going to cause a scene, and we may be forced to escalate our timeline.—
-Eve-

I crawled faster, my arms and legs moving like a spider as I skittered back to where I'd come down from. I ignored the team's alarmed responses. I was lucky, in multiple ways. If it had been only a little later, after curfew, I would've been in my quarters, and had no idea what was going on until the Boneshaker started.

I dropped into my room and raced out the door without even reattaching the ceiling grate, only sending a quick Window to the others, asking one of them to replace it and hide the evidence, just in case. A couple guards tried to stop me along the way, but I barreled past them as if they weren't even talking.

I slammed the cafeteria doors open onto the lit-up courtyard.

Kilburn stood on the grating around the sphere, his arms raised high as he forced the pieces of the Shortcut to move. They were gaining momentum.

I almost laughed. At least I wouldn't have to worry about holding back. "Kilburn!" I screamed. "Stop!" I knew putting the plan into motion early was dangerous, but allowing him to continue was unacceptable. Even if Adam weren't in danger, I would have been worried. The Trials were an unknown danger, one the team and I weren't prepared to deal with at the moment. It would be all too easy for NIX to have a "treat" planned for us over there, and if NIX decided to continue with the charade that anyone with Seeds was subject to the Trials, we'd also have to protect Zed and Chanelle. As it was, I didn't have a choice. At least by stopping the Shortcut's revival, I was choosing the danger I had most of a plan in place for.

Kilburn turned his head to look down at me, pausing his manipulation of the alien device. "Oh, if it isn't the little troublemaker. Am I going to have to keep you in line again?" He turned his attention back to the Shortcut.

I rolled my shoulders and cracked my neck in an imitation of Jacky. Then, I fully extended my claws and sprinted forward. I jumped and hit the side of the concrete tower that supported the sphere, clawing into its surface. By that point in my life, I had plenty of experience climbing things. A few seconds later, I tossed myself off the top of the railing, straight toward the snake.

His eyes widened in surprise, and he turned his hands from the Shortcut toward me. But before he had time to react, I unleashed Chaos in a concussive wave. Anger fueled my power, and his skin bubbled and broke as he was flung backward. The edges of my Skill clipped the Shortcut and threw off its orbiting rings. I knew I probably wasn't a match for him. I didn't have the luxury of holding back, even if there would be consequences.

The screech of bending metal was familiar, and I allowed myself a small twinge of satisfaction. It would be a few more days, at least, before it would be repaired again.

He didn't even hit the ground, instead stopping in midair like some sort of superhero, and rising back toward me as if he'd bounced off an invisible trampoline.

It was my turn to stare with wide eyes.

But I didn't wait for him to reach me, instead hurling myself at him again. I jumped feet first, my toe claws reaching for his neck.

I was on track, but before I could slice his neck open like the belly of a fish, he twitched his fingers and suddenly my legs wrenched to one side and I was hurtling toward the ground in an out of control spin. I righted myself, thanking that little boy whose name I never learned for the Tumbling Feather Skill. I landed on all fours, my joints screaming in protest. I stood, and ran a hand over the stomach area of my bodysuit, feeling the almost indiscernible bulge beneath, and undamaged. If Kilburn managed to attack my torso powerfully enough to damage what I'd hidden beneath, I'd be dead anyway from the organ damage, but I was still wary.

Kilburn cursed as he landed back on the railing above, snarling. "I'm going to play with you until they force me to stop," he said, not even breathing hard. "Just pray you're still alive by the time they get here." Sirens screeched in the air, and though the guards posted on the walls weren't intervening, I knew it wouldn't be long before reinforcements came to back him up.

I turned and ran in the opposite direction. As I scrambled atop a nearby roof, I felt a sense of deja-vu. But this wasn't my fight with Petralka's Player niece again. I wasn't trying to escape, I just needed a more advantageous position. One that didn't have my enemy looking so far down on me.

I'd done some research on Kilburn since joining NIX, and watched as much footage of him in action as I had time for. From what I understood, he had some control over kinetic energy. Basically, he could control movement. An extremely versatile Skill, and one he used ruthlessly, along with what were no doubt a half-dozen other, slightly less powerful Skills. But he had to have a range limit.

I ran farther away from him still, hoping to get out of the range of his Skill. I looked over my shoulder when I reached the far edge of the roof, and almost smiled to see him floating quickly down toward the other end.

Now that he wanted to kill me, he'd follow me. It was doubly advantageous, because he gave up his position on higher ground, and if I could drag the fight out long enough, Adam would be safe back in the team barracks.

I felt Kilburn move with my extended awareness, and a flicker out of the corner of my eye was all the warning I had. I lashed out instinctively, and that might have saved me.

He bowed forward bonelessly, moving his abdomen out of my reach.

Another swipe, with my left hand, slashing across the skin of his forehead. Blood spilled down, into his eyes, and he blinked, trying to clear it away.

I lunged sideways, claws digging into the roof beneath and leaning so far forward I felt like I might fall. Away, away, had to get away. I could feel the power gathering.

A second later the arm I'd cut him with was breaking, as he twisted and flung it away with a twitch of his fingers and a flex of power.

My arm twisted and pulled in a dozen different spots, and I tried to spin with it to alleviate some of the damage, but instead ended up sprawled on the ground. My left arm from the shoulder down was mangled, twisted several times around like an ice cream swirl, the skin split, the bones and joints shattered, and my fingers pointing outward in different unnatural directions from the lump of flesh that had been my hand.

I gasped, feeling like I couldn't breathe. Then I screamed in horror, shrieking with all the strength in my lungs, the sound grating against my throat like sandpaper. That wasn't my arm. It couldn't be. It was just so incredibly *wrong*. Not what an arm should be. Not what the arm I needed had to be.

Then the pain hit, and my screams stopped abruptly. Pain had always allowed me to focus, but I'd never felt pain like this. And to be honest, I'd never felt fear quite like this. China's blue, dead eyes flashed in my mind.

The snake turned to me, angrily trying to keep the blood running from his forehead out of his eyes. He seemed to be glowing with power, which my panicking brain thought for a second might mean I was seeing things. Then I realized it meant I was about to die, as he lifted a hand, fingers curled and trembling with anger.

I raised my own hand, the good one, and unleashed a counterattack as his power lashed through the air. There was a split second where time seemed to slow, as it so often did when I was about to die. Everything I had moved outward through the air, and things stilled for a second. Then every cell in my body contracted and burst into pain with what must have been an almost audible *thump*, and we both began to scream.

His bodysuit and skin rippled under the force of my attack, as if he stood in front of an overwhelming gust of wind. Then the fabric and flesh began to crumble away, blowing off him like he was made of dust, as my power disintegrated his existence.

He *moved* then, flinging himself backward like he was being sucked through an enormous straw.

Was he dead? Probably not, but I felt like I was on my way there. I tasted blood, my ears were ringing and half-plugged with it, and my lungs shuddered as I breathed out. This had not gone quite according to plan.

IT HAD SEEMED A LOT LONGER, but the fight had only taken a couple minutes, and before I could even think of rallying my strength, I heard Commander Petralka's faint voice snapping orders through the ringing both inside my ears and outside from the sirens. Their response time was quicker than the last time I'd made such a big scene.

A couple people wearing a different uniform than the standard Player bodysuit, but who must have been heavily Seed-augmented, jumped to the roof of the building I lay incapacitated atop. On her orders, they dragged me down, jostling the mass of pain that had once been my arm.

I almost passed out, but instead of slipping away into darkness, my mind spun dizzily, the relief of unconsciousness not to be. "I took off his face," I slurred up at Nadia Petralka, who I thought might be glaring at me. I wasn't sure, because the red tint I kept blinking away made it a bit hard to see.

"What have you *done*?" she snarled at me, and I was sure she was glaring. "One of our most *valuable* assets…if he dies—" she seemed literally too angry to speak.

The Thinker man from her meeting with Bunny appeared then, taking her by the elbow with his fishy fingers and drawing her away. They gestured to me, voices agitated, but I couldn't focus enough to hear them clearly, even though I knew it was possible with my enhanced senses. The man's voice raised, "…cell isn't even fully prepared yet! … Spinning out of control, and you…"

She responded, "…half-dead, no way she'll be putting up a fight. We have time."

While they talked, the two who had brought me down from the roof examined my injuries and shot a vial of something into my neck.

"Go 'way," I said, still slurring. But when I tried to lift my good hand to bat at them, I found that my body wouldn't move. It could have been from injuries, but I was betting they'd just paralyzed me. My face chilled in the breeze, and I realized suddenly that my face was wet for some reason. I wasn't crying, was I? I was tougher than that, surely. I let out a tiny wet cough, and promised myself I wouldn't do *that* again as pain swept through me with the movement of my chest.

They stepped back, and one lifted his hand and encapsulated me in a bubble that pulsed faintly red, which only added to the crimson tint of my world.

Oh, that didn't bode well.

Nadia returned, scowling at me through the red bubble. "I ought to have you executed," she said, little dots of spittle spraying from her mouth. "You would be, if this were a standard military operation."

I tried to raise a defiant eyebrow, but I couldn't feel my face to tell if it worked.

"You may be valuable to us, but don't think you're untouchable. It was a mistake to give you such a long leash. You've deliberately disobeyed my orders, and proven yourself a danger to our operation." She dug her nails into her own palms, fingers clenched so tightly they'd turned pale. "Damn Thinkers," she muttered, turning her head away from me. "I *would* have you killed right now if your body wasn't useful to us," she said, quieter this time. She crouched down outside the bubble and met my gaze. "But I, too, have my orders, and your body is useful. You'll wish it wasn't, soon. You'll think back to today and wish I'd had you killed immediately. Because you *will* be useful to us. But you've proven you can't be managed with anything but a stranglehold." She stepped back and nodded to the pair of differently dressed Players.

One lifted their arm, and the bubble rose, taking me with it. It buzzed unpleasantly along the skin touching it. As they walked behind Nadia, my head rested awkwardly against the side of the bubble.

Once again, I had an audience of Players, watching from the windows and a few open doorways. I wish I could say it was surprising, the number of faces which bore a look of satisfaction.

I caught a glimpse of my own reflection. Ouch. I would have winced if I could. The wetness I felt on my face was blood, as the red liquid dripped from every orifice in my skull. It dripped from my ears and nose, and my eyes were completely crimson around the blue irises, leaking blood instead of tears. I tasted it in my mouth, and every breath rattled with it. My left arm was swiftly turning purple and swollen under its own layer of leaking blood.

Apparently, I'd gone a bit too far with Chaos. I needed to get it under control. But I didn't have any more Seeds on me, and I didn't currently have the luxury of time to meditate. I wished I could pass out to escape the pain, but I wasn't sure I'd wake up again if I did.

My bubble followed Commander Petralka down into the bright white bowels of NIX, and I did my best to stay alert and memorize our path and the placement and type of security measures. I would match it up against my mental map later.

Nadia passed me off to a guard when we got down to what I was pretty sure was the seventeenth basement level. "Here," she said. The word was ominous and final, like the dust rising from a demolished skyscraper after it crumbled in on itself.

One of my captors met my eyes for a moment, and I thought I saw a spark of sympathy. Then they moved me into a small, cold white room, and the door slid shut behind me. The bubble popped, and I flopped onto the floor, eyes rolling back momentarily from the pain of being jolted. I struggled to stay conscious, noting vaguely that the air buzzed around me. What looked like thick white steam shot out of tiny holes in the wall near the ceiling. I'd seen that before, I knew, but I couldn't remember where, for some reason. I felt dizzy.

I started to separate from the pain, and with the distance came profound relief.

Then oblivion claimed me, and I knew nothing.

Chapter 11

In the midst of winter, I finally learned that there was in me an invincible summer.

—Albert Camus

THERE WAS *PAIN*, and cold, forcing me to wakefulness. I really wanted to escape from it. I couldn't, and that made me want to huddle up in the corner and sob. Instead, I opened my bleary eyes. Blood crusted together my eyelashes, and I had to blink a few times to free them. I ended up staring at a nondescript metal door. My ears buzzed, and despite lying on the floor, I felt dizzy.

My armored vest was fully extended. It had gotten enough blood to power it for a long time, I imagined.

Abruptly, my stomach rebelled, heaving bile up onto the ground so hard I felt like the convulsions were trying to turn me inside out. It hurt, but the involuntary movement that aggravated my wounds hurt even more.

The distinctive smell of stomach acid only partially masked the scent of raw, bloody meat, which I knew was coming from my own body.

My eyes traveled to the side as I instinctively avoided following that train of thought any further, and I saw a plain grey pouch lying on the concrete floor, underneath a metal flap cut into the wall. A nutrition packet.

Despite my earlier nausea, my body cried out for sustenance with a strength that overwhelmed even my pain. I forced myself to inch across the floor using my good arm and weak nudges from my legs. I tore the cap off the nutrition pouch with my teeth and squeezed some of the normally disgusting mush into my mouth with the cold-stiffened fingers of my good hand.

Yes. Yes, this was what I needed. I breathed a sigh of relief and continued to suck. After a few swallows, my agitation calmed, and I slowed to sips so as not to upset my stomach. I didn't want to be forced to expel the meager rations. And they were already making me feel better.

I closed my eyes and breathed shallowly, as the deeper breaths made me move more, and caused proportionate pain. As the nutrition mush settled, it seemed to push the pain away. It must have had some sort of pain relieving substance mixed in. I vaguely understood that might not be a good thing, but I couldn't bring myself to care past the wonderful feeling.

As my mind stopped cringing away from the sensations haranguing my physical body, I was able to clear up some of the Chaos I'd released in my earlier attack. I could only suppose that the sedative mist they'd knocked me out with had somehow also resulted in calming Chaos, either directly or through the enforced absolute calmness of my body and mind. Because I probably shouldn't have woken up again, *ever*, with that amount of power used and the damage to my body.

I didn't get very far with wrangling Chaos, because before I knew it I'd eaten the whole nutrition pouch, and then the world slipped away again.

YOUR RESILIENCE HAS INCREASED!

WHEN I WOKE up the next time, another food pouch lay on the floor next to me, and the pain had separated into distinct sections. I wasn't sure if this was a good thing or not. My head throbbed like my brain was trying to hammer its way out of my skull. My eyeballs, nose, and pretty much all the soft tissue inside of my head burned like I was grinding salt into an open wound, and my stomach simultaneously ached with hunger and threatened to force bile up my throat. My arm, however, hurt less, which I wished was a good thing. It ached deeply, throbbing with every beat of my heart, like my head, but the pain had decreased. I tried to wiggle my fingers, and found I couldn't.

Damn it. That was bad, I knew. Not that nerve damage was surprising, at this point. I might be in danger of being poisoned by my own putrefying flesh. The classes I'd taken recently in combat medicine and first aid flashed through my mind. But I had no tools, no supplies. I was trapped in a room by myself. There was nothing I could do for any of my wounds, except meditate and hope my Seeds were strong enough to heal me.

Somehow, I doubted the Seeds could do a thing for my arm.

I picked up the food pouch, bit off the cap, and slowly started to suck up the nutrient slush. It started to numb me, the sedative doing its job, so I backed off even though I was absolutely starving. I couldn't afford to keep sleeping.

"Display time," I muttered aloud, and my VR chip obligingly popped out a small Window. I mentally waved the message away, along with the level up notice. It was ten in the morning, which meant I'd been in the cell approximately ten hours.

I wondered what was happening to the rest of the team. Had Adam made it back in time? Had they been captured, like me? It had been part of the plan for me to cause trouble, be captured, and locked up down here, but not like this.

If what I knew of NIX was true, they would want to use my team in the field, not lock them up. It was a pattern with them…and wasn't it crazy that I was *hoping* to be blackmail material? If Petralka thought she could control my team without locking them up or torturing them, she would. I hoped.

With that thought, I mentally interacted with my VR chip and tried to send a message to the whole team, asking for a status update. The Window pulsed faintly, but failed to send. I grew dizzy as my brain seemed to vibrate. What the hell? Maybe my concentration was too shot to interact with the VR chip properly.

I opened my mouth and croaked, "Send Window to all team members." There. It couldn't fail to understand voice commands.

Except it did.

UNABLE TO CONTACT SUBORDINATE VIRTUAL REALITY CHIPS.

The Window popped up over the message I'd been trying to send, and the hair on the back of my neck rose as the dizziness increased. I'd slurped up the last of the nutrition mush without realizing, and my stomach decided it really would like to throw up, but I fought the urge.

I panicked for a bit, I'll admit it. Then I turned my mind to analyzing my suddenly disastrous current circumstances. I ran through the functions my VR chip was supposed to have and determined that it was functioning properly, except for anything that required outside input. Which meant that it wasn't broken, and despite my worried thoughts, whatever was in the nutrient pack probably hadn't interfered with the chip. That was both good and bad. Good because I could still eat them, and bad, because whatever was blocking my chip was beyond my immediate control.

The buzzing dizziness was coming from outside my head, as opposed to a side effect of a concussion or the like, I was pretty sure. I wouldn't take a stacked bet against NIX implementing some sort of signal scrambler, perhaps based on the vibrations around Torliam's room. Damn. I almost wondered if it could get any worse, but stopped that thought in its tracks. It didn't do to tempt the gods of irony.

I was getting tired, and that was making it hard to think. I shook my head and set aside that problem for a few minutes while I meditated to suppress Chaos again. I needed any edge I could get, and letting my body deteriorate from the inside any faster than absolutely necessary was unacceptable.

By the time I finished, my eyelids felt like they were trying to bench-press a hundred pounds every time I blinked. Damn it, I was tired.

I examined the room. My cell was similar to the one Torliam lived in. White, made of a stone or concrete-like substance, with small holes around the ceiling that had sprayed gas down on me. The solid metal door fit snugly into the wall on either side. The major difference between my room and his was that I wasn't stuck on a metal slab or attached to any machines. The room was completely bare, and my cell had a metal flap in the wall, through which someone had no doubt dropped the nutrition pack.

I scooted closer to it and tried to pry up the metal flap. It opened easily, but I couldn't get my arm into it any farther than the wrist, because opening the flap's hinge caused another flap to tilt up behind it. Instead, I tried sensing past the flap using my Perception. The square metal opening slanted slightly upward just behind the flap, and then turned sharply up, then turned again to point straight parallel to the ground, opening up into the outside hallway. It created a skewed S-shape. There was no way a human arm would bend properly to fit through that, even if the flap opening didn't guard itself.

I wasn't disappointed by this realization for too long, because I passed out again, leaning against the wall with my good shoulder.

THIS TIME, I woke up when the silvery food pouch landed in my lap. I pressed my ear up against the metal opening and heard footsteps. "Hello?"

The owners of the footsteps, two people, I thought, didn't respond. But they stopped for a moment before continuing on. I immediately dove into my senses, pushing outward through the small duct and following the duo out into the hallway.

They exchanged meaningful glances with each other, and when they were a bit farther away, one murmured to the other, "Increase the dosage of food sedative for Redding, and the strength of the inhalable for the operation. She's displayed an unusually fast adaptation to the narcotics. Waking now is…" He looked as if he was doing calculations, but continued after a few moments, "almost *twenty percent* faster than expected."

His partner glanced back at my door. "Well, at least she'll be dependent on them soon. Anything to decrease the likelihood of escape from that one is a good thing, in my book."

"Yes, but the sedatives are damaging in high doses. Her condition will deteriorate more quickly than normal."

His partner shrugged as they continued to walk away. "She's going to be 'gelded' soon anyway. Should I increase the dose in the next nutrition pouch, in prep for the surgeon? We won't have to worry so much once the VR chip is replaced with the penal conditioner model and she's locked down to a table."

"No…we want her on an empty stomach for the surgery. Just make sure the calculations for the inhalable sedative are properly adjusted."

"What about…"

The buzzing grew too strong, and my concentration too weak, for me to hear any more. I wasn't in top shape, to say the least. But I had enough to know I needed to make a move, and fast. I had no desire to meet this 'surgeon' and have him update my brain hardware.

I glanced down at the silver pouch in my lap and reluctantly away. I couldn't sleep. Judging by their conversation, by the time I would normally get the next nutrition pouch, it'd be time for surgery. Which meant I had a few hours, at most. They would knock me out with the aerosol sedative before trying to enter the room or mess with me in any way. I couldn't take advantage of them opening the door and allowing me to attack and free myself.

I needed to be gone before they arrived. How?

I had planned to be down here, and planned to have to escape. But I'd also planned more time to prepare, and hadn't expected NIX to do quite such a good job of detaining me. As counterintuitive as it might seem to be locked up in order to pull off a jailbreak, and the fact that I had vowed I'd avoid being put in this cell at all costs, it had made sense.

Torliam's room was physically and electronically reinforced to the max, as was the whole level he resided on. The security wasn't unbreachable, but any way we would have broken in by force would have alerted NIX to our plans too early. To break in and *then* break out again would have taken too much time. It was faster to get NIX to take me down to Torliam themselves, so I could work from within the prison level.

We'd had a plan. It depended on the use of our VR chips. Once I was down here, with everything else already prepared, I'd contact one of the team and give them directions through the vents to my cell. They'd bring me one of several stashes of supplies hidden among the vents system to enable me to more easily break out, before I was incapacitated any further, like Torliam.

Then, Adam would use the connection in our VR chips to lead me through forcing the door to Torliam's room open from the outside, which was the only way it opened at all.

So, without the VR chip, I didn't have a way to escape from my cell, or to open Torliam's. I'd tried to make sure redundancies were woven into the planning, but we were still working on it, and I hadn't anticipated *this*.

I let the tension flow out of my shoulders and brought the food pouch to my mouth with my good arm. I bit off the cap and took a single swallow. I didn't want the sedative to knock me out, but I needed the energy and a bit of pain relief. Plus, I was just starving. Literally. I examine my arm critically as I lowered the pouch to my lap. My body was wasting away in front of my eyes.

No doubt my Seeds were desperate for fuel and had turned to the only place they could. The almost non-existent fat deposits had been burned away first, and then they'd turned to my muscle. The bones of my wrist stood out sharply against thin, pale skin, and even small movements exhausted me.

I needed to get out of my cell, and into Torliam's. Working with what I had, how could I make that happen? I put my aching brain to the test, leaning my head against the coolness of the metal flap. It was so cold in my cell, but my head was hot, and the metal soothed some of that.

There was an extremely high chance the team hadn't been able to continue preparing after I was locked up, so I could only count on the things we'd already done. Adam had been in the middle of the critical mission. If he'd finished it, we might be able to pull this off. If he'd gone straight back to the team barracks, I was screwed.

It took me over an hour of thinking, with occasional slurps of my nutrition pouch for pain relief, to come up with a plan. It was reckless, and it was dangerous. And as far as I could tell, it was my only option.

A focused examination of my cell from where I sat revealed a few cameras, and no blind spots, per se. But if I tucked myself into the wall, they would only be able to see my back. I took another swallow of my nutrient pouch and turned toward the metal flap, blocking the view of it from the cameras.

It was a struggle to get the claws of my right hand to come out, like it hadn't been since I first gained the Skill. But after almost a minute, I had claws again, the hand morphing a little into something distinctly inhuman to go along with them. My bodysuit was in the way, so I disconnected it at my waist.

I brought my hand to my stomach, under my belly button, and sliced into the skin. It bled sluggishly, but I ignored that and slipped a clawed finger under the skin. I could feel it tugging and separating from the layer of connective tissue and muscle below with teensy little snaps. I shuddered, and felt light-headed for a second, but continued wiggling my finger below the skin of my stomach till I felt the pouch there and pulled it out.

The malleable plastic was slippery with blood, but the surface was intact, and the fluid inside undisturbed. Thank goodness. Though, I would have known if something went wrong with the tiny package, at about the same time my organs started to dissolve.

Thinking back on it, hiding a hyper-concentrated acid under my skin before getting into a fight might not have been the best idea. But Blaine had designed the pouch to be sturdy, and if Kilburn had ruptured the pouch with his power, I would have been dead anyway, from being turned into human hamburger. And Gregor and I, along with Jacky and Zed, had all agreed that hiding an undetectable secret weapon under my skin was a really cool idea. Just like a spy film. Which, I also realize, may not have been the best indicator of the soundness of the idea.

But it was going to save my ass, now. It didn't show up on scans as anything other than a fat deposit at the base of my belly.

I very carefully brought the cap of the small pouch to my mouth and twisted the lid off. I kept the cap in my mouth, in case I finished with leftover acid and needed to reseal it.

I palmed the bloody pouch gently and slid my hand under the flap. My hand hit against the rotating metal barrier, and I carefully squeezed out a thin line of liquid across the base of it. In a few seconds, the acid had eaten through, and the blocking flap toppled backward. I slid my hand farther through, being careful not to brush my arm against the acid eating a useless hole through the bottom of the small metal tunnel.

My arm started to shake, and I breathed deep, focusing on keeping it steady and strong. I only had one chance, and not a lot of time.

When I came to the first bend in the tunnel, I squeezed a line of acid out along the edge, using my awareness to guide me. I almost despaired at my own weakness. Just using my claws and the Wraith Skill at the same time was a struggle.

It took me almost an hour to turn the ninety-degree angle leading out into the hallway into a gentle slope, but the acid ate through the metal and stone of the wall valiantly. My good arm had gone past the point of burning pain into numbness at being forced to stay steady in the awkward position. Finally, I drew another thin line of acid along the metal of the outside flap opening from the hallway. It ate away the metal, but I didn't touch the flap, and it stayed precariously in place. I hoped the dissolved line wasn't noticeable from the outside.

Then, I waited.

Chapter 12

They are all gone into the world of light, and I alone sit lingering here.
— Henry Vaughan

THEY SPRAYED the aerosol sedative without warning, white mist shooting from the holes in the wall around the ceiling.

No doubt, they expected me to have completely passed out by the time they arrived, my struggle to reach out of the small vent futile. If I had not had the acid, they would have been right. I was much too weak to utilize Chaos, and they probably knew it.

I pressed my face to the vent and used careful application of my claws to slightly displace the covering on the outside wall. This was dangerous, and I could only hope they didn't notice from the outside and ruin my whole plan.

I held my breath for a while as the sedative shot down and then slumped bonelessly against the wall, my face pressed against the opening of the vent, resting on my arm. I breathed slowly, sucking in the fresh air from outside the room. I was sure I'd still get a bit of the aerosol sedative in my system, since I didn't have an airtight seal to make sure I only took in air from the vent, but hopefully, it wouldn't be much.

After a few minutes, during which I pretended to be knocked out, I heard footsteps coming down the hall toward me. Four people. They stopped outside my door and talked among themselves for a few moments while two of them entered in a code to the keypad and let it scan their eyeballs to confirm their identity.

The door slid open, and I withdrew my arm from the tunnel and flung myself at them, the claws on my good hand out and ready. Two of them carried stun batons. I knocked one of them out with a kick to the face and flung away the baton of the other before she could turn it on.

Three enemies remaining. But I was already tiring, dizzy from the sudden movement. "Freeze!" I snarled. Stupid, I know, but I hoped they'd be shocked and unsettled enough to listen to the authority in my voice without thinking about it.

They froze, and I used the opportunity to its fullest. I stood straight and tried to look imposing, despite my bedraggled state and mutilated arm. "You can't outrun me," I said calmly. "Your bodies are not fast or strong enough. Back up against the wall and raise your hands. If you run, I will kill you, immediately." I flexed my clawed hand for emphasis. "But I can be reasonable."

Two of them exchanged glances, perhaps of disbelief. The alarms began to sound, alerting the compound to my actions. I hoped my team realized what it meant, since a quick attempt to send a Window proved I still couldn't contact them. I had less than two minutes before the guards converged and forced me back into my cell.

"I need an escort," I said. "And the key to the alien's door."

The surgeon choked, took a step back and shook his head. "We will never give you access to the threat against Earth."

"Yeah, I was expecting that," I said. "I guess you'll have to help against your will." I crouched down toward the one I'd knocked out and stepped on his hand, pressing his palm flat against the ground. Then I used the last of the acid to remove his hand from his arm.

He jerked and screamed, waking from the pain.

I continued resolutely, watching as the liquid ate away at his wrist joint and corroded through the tendons. Blood pooled on the ground, but I soon had his hand detached from his body. Then I turned to face him. "Okay, that's the fingerprints. Now for the eyes."

He tried to scramble away from me, cradling his mangled stump against his chest, sobbing incoherently.

"Stop, please." One of the surgeon's other assistants whimpered, looking as if she wanted to step forward from the wall and stop me.

"I don't like doing this either." I sighed. "It's pretty disgusting. But I need a way to get through the doors down here, and you guys refused to help me." I knew I didn't have much time left before the deployed guards reached me. I wished I was strong enough to just force a couple of my captives to help, but I wasn't.

When I began to dig into the man's eye socket, I guess his screams got to the rest of them.

"That won't work!" the surgeon yelled. "You need our eyes intact, so that the pupils dilate when the scanning light shines in them. You can't just kill us."

Oh. Well, crap. I looked down at the severed hand and eyeball in my hand and let them fall to the floor. The poor medic beneath me was quivering incoherently, and the stench of his piss burned in my nostrils. I sighed. Time to bluff some more.

I stood up and grabbed the surgeon, yanking him away from the wall. "Thanks for the info. I'm pretty sure I'll be able to use my Skills to keep your head alive for a few minutes, with or without your body," I lied. I pressed my claws into the skin under his ears, hoping that panic would be enough to make him forgo his common sense.

It was. "We'll take you! I'll open the door!" He gasped, eyes squeezed closed.

"Let's go, then." I waved at the other two, who were still cowering against the wall. "Now!"

That snapped them out of it, and they ran ahead of me, moving faster at my urging.

I could hear the footsteps of guards behind us. Thank goodness the medics had snapped in time. No doubt NIX had given them training about what to do in the event of a breakout, attack, or other emergency situation. But when a situation changes from a hypothetical to the immediacy of seeing your coworker de-eyeballed while he screams…priorities change. People do things they never thought they would, given the right motivation. I should know.

Guards turned the corner in front of my little group, guns at the ready. The medics screamed and skidded to a halt, which gave me enough of a shield and distraction to get close to the guards before they attacked.

I raked my claws across one's eyes, and then grabbed his forearm with that same hand and turned. A bone in his forearm snapped and punctured through both his skin and the fabric of his uniform, but his hand stayed wrapped around the trigger, and the gun was facing his fellow guards. I used the familiar trick, squeezing my finger around his own and spraying them down with tranquilizer darts. The weapon was coded specifically to him somehow, but as long as it was technically his finger on the trigger, it would still work for me.

They dropped like puppets with their strings cut.

Well, at least I knew they were aiming to sedate, not kill me. So far.

I released the gun, then punched the screaming owner of the gun in the back of the neck. I wasn't good enough to use Jacky's signature neck chop, but he stopped screaming and joined his unconscious friends. Hopefully, I hadn't killed him. I turned back to the medics and waved impatiently at them. "Don't just stand there! We've got places to be."

One of them let out a gasping sob, but they continued running, leading the way to Torliam as I directed them.

We arrived at his section of sub-level seventeen, and they used their verification to get us through the security block.

The sound of the alarm changed then, becoming more screechingly urgent. I wasn't sure if it was because of my current location, or because my team was implementing their part of the escape plan up above.

I could feel Torliam's presence through the wall, a kind of thrumming energy that pushed against my skin like phantom waves. I itched with urgency, as I thrust one of the surgeon's assistants toward the security pad. "I know the code just as well as you do," I growled. "If you use the fake one…" I let her imagination fill in the rest. "And don't think I'm not aware that different keys have to be pushed with different fingers."

Her knees were shaking, but she gave a stiff nod and entered her code, then let the pad scan her eyeball under my intense scrutiny. The surgeon went next, and though he was more hesitant to open the door, my clawed hand resting gently on the back of his neck was all the encouragement he needed.

The huge, incredibly reinforced slab of a door slid open, revealing the back of Torliam's restraints.

The medics probably knew about the cameras that watched Torliam's room, connected to monitors far away from NIX's main base. That fail-safe may have been the only reason they agreed to open the door, even considering my threats. The fail-safes assumed that NIX's security system had been compromised, and negated the ability of those within NIX to affect the compound through any electronic method. In other words, when the second set of people watching through the cameras saw where I was and what I was doing, and how NIX had failed to stop me, they took over.

I'd barely gotten Torliam's door open when they shut down the main generator, cutting off the power source to the whole compound. The lights, sirens, and ventilation cut off, and in the sudden, absolute silence, I could hear faint yells and screams from other prisoners.

I held my breath and counted to ten. A deep, rumbling explosion sounded off below, the vibration traveling through the floor and walls around me, from deep beneath my feet. I almost lost my balance and a couple of my captives let out ear-splitting shrieks, but I ignored them, letting out a breathless, loud laugh.

I stopped laughing when I realized that I sounded a bit like an evil villain. "I'm going to have to give you a raise, Adam," I murmured aloud.

SABOTAGING the backup generator had been Adam's assignment the night before when I'd been captured, but I hadn't been sure if he'd managed to complete it or not.

"Do not enter the room," Torliam said. "I do not know what you have done, but my cell has protections of its own. It is not de-fanged." Despite the warning, his tone was tight with suppressed excitement.

"Just sit tight and wait. I'll have you out soon." I instructed my VR chip to send a Window to the team, and this time there was no backlash.

—STATUS REPORT, TEAM. —
-EVE-

It only took a few seconds for the replies to bombard me.

—KICKING ASS OVER HERE. HURRY UP AND JOIN US! —
-JACKY-

—ARE YOU OKAY? WE COULDN'T CONTACT YOU EARLIER. WE'RE IN THE LAB DEFENDING THE SHIP. —
-ZED-

—CURRENTLY HOLDING THE LAB, DEFENDING FROM ATTACK. THE PLAN IS IN PLACE. SHOULD BE ABLE TO HOLD POSITION FOR THE NEXT TEN MINS. WHERE ARE YOU? —
-ADAM-

—Are you okay?—
-Sam-

—Powering up the ship with a backup generator. We will be ready. The kiddos are already inside, safe.—
-Blaine-

—I'm okay. Down here with our friend from outer space.—
-Eve-

I thought for a quick moment, then sent a message to Zed.

—Come down and pass me the breakout supplies. Be quick, be safe.—
-Eve-

Zed would be least useful to the team in defending the lab from the rest of NIX, and in helping with any last-minute escape preparation, but he was more than competent enough to help me at the moment.

A few minutes later, Zed broke the relatively weak grate in the ceiling, making sure it didn't fall to the floor, and pushed the supplies through. They floated toward me, balancing gently on what Jacky had dubbed the "hoverboard," without touching any of the equipment, or the pressure-sensitive floor. "What's that stuff all over your face?" Zed asked, bringing out a flashlight.

"What?" I grabbed the board out of the air and stepped back further into the hall, then dug into the supply pack for the numbing spray. We'd thought Torliam might need it, along with a few other medical supplies. I shook the can and applied the contents liberally, coating my entire left arm. It helped a bit. I popped a stimulant tablet into my mouth for good measure. I could crash after we were gone. Then I straddled the hoverboard around the middle with the supply pack held in front of me and floated into the room, my good side angled toward Zed. "Don't shine that right at me. You'll kill my night vision."

"It looks kinda like…dried blood." His voice trailed off.

"Oh, yeah. I overused my Skill a bit. It's got a bit of backlash if I don't control it properly. Some of the small blood vessels in my face probably broke. It's no big deal, kinda like a dry air nosebleed. Doesn't even hurt," I lied.

"Oh." He didn't sound satisfied, but thankfully didn't pursue that line of conversation. "Who are those crying people?" Zed asked, shining a flashlight on the forms huddled outside the door.

I glanced over my shoulder. "They're the people who were going to do some surgery on me for NIX."

The two assistants were crouched by the wall next to the door, but the surgeon was pressed against the door separating Torliam's section from the rest of the level. He was banging futilely on it, calling for help.

"Do you think I should kill them? I'm not sure they're really a threat to us anymore," I said.

Zed's eyes widened, but he hesitated, and then shook his head. "Not if we don't have to." He laughed. "My life is so surreal. Here I am, breaking my sister and an alien giant-person out of a top secret base cut into a mountain. And I'm wondering whether we should kill the hostages or not."

The hoverboard brought me around to the side of Torliam's restraining slab. I maneuvered around the tubes and wires coming out from him and met his eyes. "You'll get used to it," I said absently, my concentration shot by the look on the giant's face.

Torliam's eyes were wide and feverishly bright, and his muscles tense as if he wanted to thrash against his bonds but was holding himself rigid instead. "You…are here. This is beyond my expectations," he said.

I grinned, trying to relieve some of the tension caused by the sheer force of his presence. "Don't tell me you're impressed *already*. I'm just getting started. Sing my praises when we get to Estreyer." I gripped the hoverboard tighter with my thighs, and then dug in the supply pack.

His eyes tracked my every move, unblinking.

"Shine the light over here, will you?" I waved to the side of the slab. "I've got to disable this first."

Zed swung the light, but stopped on me instead of where I'd pointed.

I frowned up at him. "Don't shine the light in my eyes. Over there!" I pointed again.

Zed ignored me. "Eve, what's wrong with your arm?"

I glanced down at the appendage that hung uselessly off my shoulder. The pain flared, just thinking about it, especially when I breathed in that raw meat smell again in full force. I squeezed the hoverboard tighter between my thighs and warded off a wave of dizziness. "Oh, yeah. I got a bit hurt while fighting Kilburn. He was reactivating the Shortcut."

"A *bit* hurt?" Zed's voice rang out, and Torliam turned to scrutinize him instead. "I…" Zed fell silent for a moment, and when he spoke again his voice was quieter, calmer. A bit of the ice I imbued my own tone with when I was angry sounded in his words. "You should have called Sam, instead of me. You are severely injured. This could endanger our escape."

I smiled up at him, squinting against the beam of light. "Logic. I like it. It's good to see you're adapting your arguments against me."

"I'm not joking, Eve! You're hurt bad." His voice rose.

"I can make it. We don't have time to heal me right now, and Sam's undoubtedly got plenty to deal with up there with the rest of them. We'll have time for healing once we're away. Otherwise, we're all as good as dead anyway. Now hurry up and shine the light where I need it. We're wasting time."

Zed complied. "Well, then you better hurry up so we can get out of here and Sam can do his job," he said through clenched teeth.

Torliam watched as I pulled a pouch of acid out of the pack. "How will you bypass the safeguards of this cell?"

I spoke as I took the cap off the pouch of acid, partially to ease the tension, and partially to distract myself from the pain and weakness sabotaging me. "I know the security measures in here aren't dependent on the rest of the base. They've got it rigged to kill, under pretty much any circumstances. Guess they thought it'd be better to eliminate you than chance your escape. But I've got a team of really smart people, too. This room may have its own backup generator for security, but in the case of a forced takeover, the base loses direct control and access to the main generator. Almost the entire rest of the base is dependent on the backup generator that just exploded below us. Which means that the other doors are all stuck closed. If the guards want to get to us, they're going to have to blow their way through every single checkpoint, or find a way to get control returned to this base. That gives us the time we need to get you out."

I squeezed a thin line of acid on the seamless metal surface supporting his slab. "This will give me access to the inner components of this table that's got you stuck here. Please don't move around too much. I'll be working with some sensitive stuff, and I don't want it thinking you're trying to escape and setting off any safety mechanisms."

The acid did its job, and I took off the sheet of metal it had eaten through and placed it gently on top of a machine that was attached to Torliam by tubes inserted into his skin in multiple places. Then I had a thought. "This is the one that filters your blood, right?"

"Correct."

"Hmm." I maneuvered the hoverboard gingerly around, examining the controls. "It's like a fancy version of those old dialysis machines, right, Zed?"

He looked at it for a second, peering down from his cramped space in the vent. "Maybe? I may have wanted to be a medic, but I really don't know a lot about those machines. And I can't tell much by looking at it from afar. Why?"

I traced the tubes coming out from Torliam to the ones going back in, and then leaned down to see a large tube full of golden shimmer. Drop by drop, more of the Seed material joined it, being filtered from his blood. "I really don't know what I'm doing," I said. "But if I do this…" I flipped a switch, then pushed a few buttons when the screen on the machine lit up. "I think it might run backward."

I leaned down again, and sure enough, the golden liquid was being slowly sucked out of the tube instead of entering it. I turned to Torliam. "Can you feel anything?"

He clenched his fist, the wrist of which had one of the many tubes entering it. "My strength is being restored. I… I thank you, Eve of the line of Redding." He looked over at another machine. "That one pumps the sedative."

I took the hint, and pinched off the tubes leading from that machine, since I didn't see an obvious "off" button. "By the time I've got you off that slab, hopefully you'll be a bit stronger." We might need his strength, because from the dizzying waves of cold that washed over my body, it seemed like my own was failing.

I took out what looked like a gun, but had a cartridge on top filled with a clear liquid instead of bullets. "This is a binding agent," I said, peering into the complicated guts inside the base of the slab supporting Torliam. "It's going to lock the pressure sensors on the slab in place, right where they are now." I reached in and began to squeeze the trigger slowly, fighting against the dangerous tremors in my hand. "So, when you get up, this thing will think all your weight is still on it, dispersed just like it is right now."

I finished that relatively quickly, warning Torliam again not to move so that the binding agent could activate and harden.

"I would not do anything to jeopardize our mission. Place your faith in that. I desire nothing more at this moment but to be free of this *thing*, and to be rid of this place," he said.

When the binding agent had dried, I twisted to look up at the clamps rooted in the slab, which dug into the flesh of his back along his spine. I could see where dried blood had run down into the tiny seams around the metal. I grabbed one and manually wiggled it with my fingers, and he grunted in pain. "Hold still. There's a catch down here, I think I can draw the clamp right out, but it's probably still going to hurt." I used a claw to pry open the catch that held that half of the clamp in place, and then grabbed the whole base and pulled.

Torliam stiffened and let out a prolonged groan as I drew on the clamp, his voice mixing with the squelching sound as the metal withdrew from his flesh.

I pulled it all the way out through the slab and brought it out of the bottom into the light. "Umm…no wonder that hurt. Are you alright?"

"I can endure whatever pain necessary. Please continue."

"That's not exactly what I meant." I pointed to the tip of the clamp, which had an angled notch cut into it. Like a fishhook, the tip of an arrowhead, or a serrated knife. It was designed to hold in place, or to mutilate the flesh if drawn out the way it had entered. "I just ripped open a chunky hole in your back."

"That's disgusting, Eve," Zed said.

Torliam glanced at the bloody half of a clamp I held in my hand, and then quickly looked away, focusing on my eyes. "Your people are indeed well versed in the art of torture, I have learned. Do not back down from what must be done."

"Well, maybe I can detach them from the slab instead of detaching them from your back. We'd still have to extract them later, but it would probably be better to have Sam do it, instead of me. He's my healer."

He nodded. "If you can."

So I used the rest of the acid to eat through the metal keeping the clamps from sliding upward through the holes in the slab. Torliam continued to watch my every move, which was slightly unnerving. "They mentioned something about implanting me with a 'penal conditioner' instead of my current brain hardware. Do you have any idea if they did something like that to you?"

"They tried. The power of my blood recognized the enemy within and destroyed it."

That was one less thing to worry about, at least. "Zed, tell me about what's happened while I was down here," I said.

"Well, when you got taken, these really strong Players grabbed all of us and brought us to individual rooms. They almost caught Adam out of bounds, but he made it back in time. We were all talking among ourselves using those awesome VR chips, even though we couldn't see each other, and we kept trying to contact you. We made sure to do it all mentally, no hand or voice signals, and Adam basically walked me through the whole interrogation."

"What did NIX want?"

"Oh, basically they threatened us that your life depended on our good behavior. We were right about that, at least…"

I nodded. When I had to start the plan so early, I wasn't sure that NIX wouldn't retaliate against the rest of the team. We hadn't put any protection in place for the others yet. I realized Zed had trailed off, and glanced up at him. He was looking off to the side, jaw clenched as he remembered.

"I would prefer to never get captured and put in an interrogation room again," he said simply.

Torliam snorted at that, with some amusement that I didn't share.

"Were you guys still being held when I set off the alarms?"

"Yeah. Kris and Gregor actually broke Adam out with one of those non-lethal guns Blaine's been having them practice with. Then Adam killed some people and busted Jacky out, and with the two of them… well, you know how she is. It was like watching a superhero film. NIX didn't even have time to react. Everything locked down, but we got to the lab before you set off the second alarms, and then the backup power blew itself up. When I left, they were killing the guards who'd already been guarding inside the lab after the scientists evacuated."

"I see." I'd have to thank the kiddos and Adam. If not for his guidance of the team and their actions, we might all be in a very different position right now. "I *really* have to give that guy a raise."

"Do you pay us?" Zed asked archly. "Isn't zero multiplied by anything still…zero?" He pretended to count on his fingers.

I shot him a mock glare. "Well, I see *someone* doesn't want their holiday bonus."

"Sis, you should know by now that you can't influence me with your grubby scheming. Bribery?" He lifted his nose in mock disdain, then grinned at me. "What type of bonus are we talking, here? 'Cause, you know, I might be convinced of the error of my ways. I could even tell the others that we're being paid with non-material coin. The coin of friendship and rainbows and all that." He rubbed his hands together in a caricature of greediness.

I had to stifle a laugh, but my amusement was quickly snuffed out when I ran out of acid. “Damn it!” I hadn't finished removing the binding on all the clamps. I looked up to Torliam, who looked faintly bemused by our antics. “Sorry to say this, but I'm out of acid. Looks like you're gonna have a few more holes in your back till we can get you to Sam.”

“Do it.” He took a deep breath and seemed to brace himself. “And hurry. We must not waste time. Only the gods know what scheme our enemies are executing as we tarry.”

I began to rip the remaining clamps from his back, wincing in sympathy. I'm far from squeamish, but even so, inflicting that amount of pain on someone not my enemy was a bit beyond my comfort level. Luckily, there were only a few left, and I finished quickly. Then I released the shackles around his limbs. “Okay. Do you have the second hoverboard, Zed?”

He quickly floated it down to me, and I caught it and held it beside the slab. “You should be able to move your arms, and anything above the level where your back was most recently broken. We need to take those tubes and monitoring patches off you, then get you onto this. You'll float out of the room with me, so we don't set off the pressure sensors in the floor. Ready?”

Torliam nodded. “I have been ready for many cycles.” He used his arms to push his torso up, suppressing any reaction to the pain it must have caused, and ripped away the myriad tubes, patches, and wires still attached to him.

“Swing your legs over first. I'm going to need to adjust the resistance. These things aren't exactly made to support people of your…considerable size.”

Zed coughed. “Sis!” He gave me a cheeky grin. “I'm shocked. I thought you were a lady!”

I sighed. “Get your mind out of the slums.” I couldn't resist, though, and added, “And whatever gave you the impression I was a lady? Surely it wasn't something I said or did?”

Torliam's lifted his legs one after the other with one arm, supporting himself with the other, and I adjusted the degree of strength variation from the hoverboard's output. “Do not reprimand your sibling. She is only stating the obvious,” Torliam said. “My enviable size is no secret. In fact, it is legend among the females of my homeland.”

My mouth fell open, and I stared at him.

Zed's voice was choked with disbelief. “Hey, Eve, I'm pretty sure our giant extraterrestrial friend here just made a dirty joke. Did you hear it, too?"

"Erm." I coughed, busying myself with the hoverboard. "It's either a shared hallucination, or you just got one-upped."

Torliam didn't respond to our commentary, too busy hoisting himself onto the hoverboard, which dipped frighteningly under his weight before righting itself.

I took a quick moment to grab the blood clotting powder from the pack and messily shake it over his back.

Then Torliam and I floated out the door to his cell, unmolested. Unfortunately, it was at that point that my body gave up on me, the stimulant pill ran its course, and I lost consciousness.

I PASSED in and out of darkness, as if my life was a strobe light, catching only brief snippets of what was going on around me.

Torliam, jamming the modified stun baton Blaine had created for this very purpose into one of the doors that blocked the hallway, forcing it open.

Blackness.

Zed, towing me behind him as he raced through the halls.

A brief lance of pain as my hoverboard idled into the wall and jostled me. Zed was shooting air-burst rounds at a group of Players, dodging their return attacks of bright light. Two of them were down on the ground. A bright blue mist drifted past me from behind, but I slipped back into darkness before I could see what it did.

Blackness.

Zooming through the larger vents, Zed riding ahead of me on my hoverboard, steering us. His forehead had been cut, and blood covered one side of his face.

The hoverboard falling out from under me, my stomach rising into my throat as Zed slammed both feet into the grate, ripping it right out of the ceiling.

Something light blue wrapping around me and steadying me on the back of the hoverboard so that I didn't fall off.

From above, the view of the huge lab, one door blown open, smoke bombs spewing into the air, burning my lungs even so far up. From the hallway, one man stepped forward and knelt on one knee, with what looked like a small rocket launcher on his shoulder. His fellows closed in around him, some kneeling and some standing, holding up their shields shoulder to shoulder to guard him.

We dropped down next to the ship, near the doorway. Adam threw up a shield of black ink, and then another one a couple feet behind that one, so that there was a double layer of protection.

The rocket smashed against the first barrier with a *boom* so forceful it half-deafened me and pushed me back with its force. Shrapnel exploded forward, peppering the wall and ceiling behind and around the team and ship. Adam's first shield was gone when I looked down again, and the second disintegrated as I watched.

He sagged, curly hair plastered to his forehead with sweat.

Jacky shouted in rage, grabbed some clunky metal thing off a table near her, and threw it like a discus, making a whole spin before she released it with frightening speed. It flew straight at the guy with the rocket launcher and smashed him backward out of their little human shell formation and into the hallway behind.

By the way his chest had caved in, I'm pretty sure he was dead.

Sam was busy trying to heal Blaine, who was standing beside Adam in a huge, skeleton-only mecha suit. Blaine's leg had a hole in it, which was leaking some blood, probably from a bullet wound. Blaine waved Sam off and moved his arms back till the elbows connected with a metal pack the rudimentary mecha carried on its back, which loaded ammo into the arms. He extended his arms forward, let out a battle cry, and the mecha shot its own little rockets at the formation of guards, blowing them backward to land amongst tons of their other downed comrades. Damn. That thing was pretty cool.

I floated down past the catwalk to land behind Jacky. "Guys, if you're finished playing around, we really should be leaving already," I groaned.

Another blank of darkness.

Zed grabbed my hoverboard to steady it against the wall as the ship lurched about, and then we were through the ceiling of the wrecked lab, rising up out of what used to be the ground of the courtyard. "Guys, I'm debating having secret aircraft hangars open up out of the ground when I get my own evil lair. What do you think?" he said, voice strained.

A blurry Window swam in front of my face, declaring my Stamina had increased. I waved it away like one might shoo a fly.

"Cliché," Jacky said with a snort of derision.

"Turret guns incoming," Blaine said. "Both air burst and armor piercing rounds. They had better not work, or…" He cut off, as a huge explosion rocked the ship's balance.

I watched as the pieces of gun, wall, and bloody chunks of the gunman flew through the air.

"They will think twice about shooting now," Blaine said.

Jacky whooped and pumped her fist in the air, jumping and floating for a little too long to be natural. "Hell yes! Keep blowing yourselves up, suckers."

Zed gave Blaine a respectful look. "You did that?"

Blaine coughed and lifted the faceplate of his mecha suit to adjust his glasses. "Merely some simple sabotage to their weapons. They test and clean them once a month, and since it was highly unlikely they would have any reason to use or inspect them outside of that timeframe, I set it up so that pulling the trigger would result in the gun backfiring. With the power and amount of ammo those guns carry, it causes quite an explosion."

Another gun turret exploded as the ship gathered speed, shooting away through the air, over the mountains and river below.

Jacky nodded wisely. "Boom." She demonstrated the explosion with a hand motion.

Birch stood on the edge of the control station next to Torliam, growling out through the front-facing window.

Bunny moved up from wherever he'd been in the back of the ship, likely making sure he was protected with the kiddos and Chanelle, surrounded by the more cushiony, protective supplies.

He saw Torliam's back, seated at the control station at the front of the ship, and paused, just staring.

"What…have you *done*?!" Bunny said, his voice rising.

There was a moment of silence, and I felt a sense of foreboding rise up, helpless to do anything about it.

"It's an alien! It wants to destroy the Earth!" Bunny screamed at me, then reached behind himself and pulled out the gun from his utility belt.

I lifted my good arm, but I was too far away to stop him.

Chapter 13

Go forth into the hollow lands, where the fears of men live.
— Ateus of the Fall

SAM, who'd been standing disregarded next to Bunny, stepped forward while everyone else was still hesitating from shock. His left hand grabbed the wrist of Bunny's gun hand, forcing it down while twisting painfully, and his right hand shot out in a straight punch that rocked Bunny's head back.

Bunny wobbled and jerked away, leaving Sam holding the gun and looking bewildered by what had just happened.

"Back down," Bunny snarled at him.

Sam went hazy-eyed and dropped the gun, stepping away with his hands raised.

Bunny lunged toward the energy cell hooked into the wall and began to pull on it. "Stay away!" he screamed.

Torliam roared and half-turned toward him, reaching an arm out.

I felt a wash of fear, partially artificial, and partially because Bunny was sabotaging our escape. If he removed the energy cell, the ship would crash, with all of us inside it.

I navigated my VR chip with a flicker of thought.

Bunny's head exploded. Brain matter splattered outward.

His body tottered for a second, then fell backward.

Blue mist sputtered and died away from Torliam's hand.

Adam wiped goop off his face and turned to me. "I told you we should have just killed him in the first place."

I grunted. "We couldn't have gotten away with that. Now it doesn't matter."

"Toss him through the waste dump," Adam said. "Good job with the gun, Sam, but your Skill is needed." He waved a hand to me, Torliam, and Blaine, who was silently using a med kit to deal with the bullet wound in his own leg.

Zed spoke up. "Eve's hurt bad. She needs to be healed ASAP. Her arm's… I don't even know what to call that. And she looks like she's been starving for weeks." He scowled at me.

Sam stared wide-eyed at the body, blinked a couple times, and then turned to my arm. He took a deep breath. "Okay." He dug out a small medical kit from one of the supply packs.

Blaine went to the back to check on the kids and keep them from coming out while Jacky disposed of the body.

Adam looked out to the rear of the ship from one of the small windows cut into the rippling walls. "No immediate pursuit, but I can only imagine they've got trackers on this thing. They'll be after us soon."

"No human ship will catch my *Lady Ladriel*," Torliam said with pride. He was still riding the hoverboard, but was using his legs to maneuver it, so Sam must have fixed his spine while I was blacked out, though it looked like all the rest of his wounds remained. Then Torliam did something, and the force of our acceleration rocked me. "*Lady Ladriel*" began to shudder at the speed. The vibration was soothing, like being inside the belly of a big purring cat, except that I knew I was actually inside the belly of a small ship that had been hit by a bomb, and then inexpertly patched up by people who didn't even understand how it worked.

"I'm hungry," I said weakly. "Could I get a nutrition bar?"

Sam waved Zed aside and out of his way, taking charge as he only did in situations like this. "Did they feed you? Your body's been eating itself, obviously."

"They fed me some. But the food was drugged."

Kris peeked around Adam's side, obviously curious about my fearsome battle wounds, and Gregor joined her. "Here," she said, handing me a nutrition bar. She took one look at my arm and drew the bar back. "Oh."

She tore open the wrapping, and then held the bar up to my mouth hesitantly.

I let her feed me, while Sam used some tiny scissors and an equally small set of clamps to cut away the sleeve of my uniform, and then peel it painfully out of the crusted blood and open wound that was now the surface of my arm. It hurt. A lot.

The kiddos gasped, and Gregor looked from my arm to his own much smaller one, obviously imagining himself sustaining a similar wound.

"Goddamit, Eve," Zed said. "What did you *do*?"

I kept eating, because somehow the pain only made me even more ravenous. "Got in a fight with Kilburn," I said, a few crumbs spewing out of my mouth.

As Sam revealed more and more of the injury, there were sporadic gasps and groans of horror from the onlookers. I resisted the urge to roll my eyes at them, but decided not to look down at my arm just yet, because I knew they weren't overreacting, and I didn't want to think about it.

"Oh, Eve…" Adam said, his face falling. "I'm…*god*. I shouldn't have…" He seemed, for once, at a loss for words. "This happened because of me."

"Damn," Jacky said succinctly.

Torliam even turned his head to see what the commotion was about, but I couldn't read his expression before he turned back to the controls.

"Not your fault. It was always the plan for me to cause a little havoc. I just went for the overkill." I grinned, but I was afraid it came out looking more like a grimace.

Gregor's little eyebrows were scowling as always, but this time with concern. "Can you even fix something like that?" he asked Sam, in a tone that was more demand than question, crossing his arms over his chest.

Sam laid his arm on the top of my shoulder and closed his eyes for a second to analyze the wound before answering. "It will be difficult," he said, instead of a true answer.

For the first time since I'd first gotten the injury, I couldn't stop the fear from slipping into my conscious mind. What if this was permanent? I hadn't known until just then how much I was counting on him to make everything better, to just…fix me.

"Hurry up, then!" Zed said.

Sam scowled at the group. "Stop pressuring me." He took a deep breath, and some of my pain just...went away, like it had evaporated through the connection of his skin on mine.

I sighed and released some tension I hadn't even known I'd been holding.

"Urgh!" Sam grunted and pushed through the others, throwing himself towards the small waste removal station at the back of the ship. He fell to his knees and threw up noisily into the basin. The smell of vomit had hardly started to spread before the ship sucked it up.

I wondered inanely where the vomit went. And where Bunny's body went. Did the ship eat it? "Are you okay, Sam?" Maybe something was wrong with the wound. Maybe something about the snake's Skill meant Sam wouldn't be able to heal me. And just like that, the tension was all back.

"I'm fine." He stood up, wiping his face, and spitting into the basin with a small amount of ration water. When he came back to my side, he was still pale and breathing hard, but he returned to normal as I watched. "It's just...the pain. I didn't even take a lot from you. How are you still conscious right now?"

A low whimper forced itself from Kris, and tears fell out of her eyes before she angrily scrubbed them away with her sleeve and turned her head away.

"I'm okay," I said, forcing my voice to sound like I meant it. "I was out of it for a few hours, under sedation. But then I needed to be awake. Don't worry about numbing me or whatever. Just work on the actual injury—that's the important part. Besides, when you fix that, the pain will follow suit."

Sam clenched his jaw and nodded. "Someone get the numbing spray from the med kit. Something is better than nothing, at least," he said. He healed my arm, bit by bit, as Adam covered my entire arm and every new piece of exposed flesh with the substance. Because of the way my arm had been twisted, Sam had to untwist it to heal it. And because he couldn't heal all of it at once, it was excruciatingly painful for parts to twist back into place while the pieces adjacent to them were still mangled. Fragments of bone slid through muscle to reattach themselves to each other. Old, clotted blood seeped out of my flesh as the skin and muscle moved, separating themselves from the marbled-swirl-cottage-cheese mess they had been part of.

I tried not to scream, I really did. But I couldn't help it.

Sam apologized over and over, white-faced and straining as his own flesh mimicked my injuries in little patches, but I gritted my teeth and told him to shut up and stop worrying about me.

Adam's hair was floating around his head in a big curly halo from all the times he'd run his fingers through it while nervous static jumped from his skin.

Kris was crying silently in the corner, while Blaine tried awkwardly to simultaneously comfort her and shield her from the sight and sound of me.

Zed knelt beside me and held my good hand, and let me squeeze his fingers so hard they would probably be in danger of breaking, if his bones weren't reinforced by those bastard nanites. But from the way he gritted his teeth, maybe the nanites weren't standing up to my Seed-enhanced strength. I figured if I did break his fingers, at least Sam could fix them later.

Torliam pushed away from the controls.

He moved the hoverboard with skillful pressure from his legs, obviously having acclimated quickly. He was scowling, and despite the fact that he still had holes along his spine in some places and the backs of metal claws poking out in others, he was imposing enough that those standing around stepped back.

Adam quickly realized what he'd done, and moved forward again, as if to insert himself between Torliam and me.

Torliam glared at him. "She will break her own teeth, grinding them like that. Move."

Adam scowled and didn't move, but Torliam shoved past him. He snapped off the strap of a nearby pack, folded the padded fabric over, and forced it past my lips, between my teeth. He settled it back between my molars. "Bite down. It will help."

I bit down, and nodded my thanks to him, panting through my nose.

Zed pushed some sweat-dampened hair back from my forehead, and then Sam started again.

I learned a new appreciation for Sam. What must it take, to willingly mutilate yourself, over and over, for someone else? Then, Sam jerked backward and stared down at where his hands had been in horror.

I didn't want to look, but I did. I don't know what I'd been expecting, but five little spots of red crystal sprouting out from my skin like a fungus, where the fingertips of one of his hands had been? I was speechless.

My eyes tracked up to meet his, and he shook his head back and forth, taking another step back. "It was an accident," he said. "My Skill... it just...*slipped.*" He was stuttering, almost, holding his hands away from himself as if afraid of them. "It's been difficult, lately. Like it's pushing back against me when I try to heal. It's been getting harder to push through, but nothing like that has ever happened before. I *didn't mean to do that.*"

"Maybe you need a break," Jacky said.

"But what about Eve?" Zed said. "You're only halfway through! And the Estreyan dude has holes in his back! Also, Blaine got shot."

"We have Seeds," Blaine said. "In the back. I could only carry two cases, but they may ensure infection does not set in, at least. I cannot use them, but my wound is relatively small. I can treat it myself. And perhaps the Seeds will give Sam the energy he needs to continue."

I looked to Torliam, and though his knuckles were white and the skin on his back had a slight sheen of sweat, he didn't say anything or turn around.

Blaine directed Adam to retrieve a metal briefcase, which clanged much more heavily on the floor than its size would indicate. Inside were row upon row of Seeds, nestled individually like eggs in a carton, and stacked atop each other. A quick calculation told me it held at least a few hundred Seeds.

I took the slobber-soaked, well-bitten strap out of my mouth and grabbed a handful of the sparkly treasures. "I wish I had more Life," I muttered, ignoring the sharp pricks as the six or so Seeds injected their contents into me. I dropped the empty spheres to the ground and grabbed another handful. "I wish I was more Resilient." I repeated the process again, then waited as the side effects swept through me, signaling that the Seeds were "planting" themselves in me.

Torliam let out a sharp puff of air that no one but me seemed to notice.

Sam took a couple handfuls himself and went to sit hunched over in the corner.

After a few more minutes, and quite a few more devoured nutrient bars, I felt a little better.

Kris looked around and frowned. "Where's Bunny?"

No one said anything for a few moments.

"He decided he was on NIX's side after all," I said.

"So he decided to stay behind?" she asked, clenching her moose.

"Yes," Blaine said, staring hard at me. "He decided to stay behind."

Gregor's eyes narrowed, and his gaze tracked from face to face, analyzing our expressions.

Sam shifted and avoided his gaze.

Gregor's eyes stopped on my own face, and he raised an eyebrow.

I raised my own in response, just a little. He was smart enough to figure it out for himself.

His expression flattened out, and he gave me a small nod. "He was weird, anyway," he said to Kris.

I grabbed a handful of the bars and moved to stand beside Torliam, still eating. It seemed like my stomach would never be sated, even with the bland chewiness I was swallowing en-masse. I ripped the wrapping off yet another bar, using my teeth and the fingers of my good hand. I waved the bar teasingly under Torliam's nose. "Aren't you hungry? I bet they starved you to keep you weak down there."

Something tightened in the skin around his eyes, his tangled beard moving as he ground his jaw under it. "They will be following. Tracking us. We have little time, and I refuse to go back."

I, too, would be afraid to return to a tiny little prison deep beneath the surface of the earth. I could understand that, and I knew what he needed to hear. "Eat," I spoke more softly, leaning down so I was closer to him. "You need to build up your strength. If you end up needing to fight…" I was confident he understood.

He reached forward and grabbed the bars from my hand, ripping one open and biting into it. The ship continued hurtling over the ocean, unconcerned. Overhead, the clouds parted sporadically, beams of sunlight shining down and making the water glow. We stood in silence, and then he spoke in a soft voice, his lilting accent making his words seem like poetry, in a way I'd never heard from a human. "It has been *cycles* since I have seen the sun. It is not my own, yet somehow, it is comforting to know that the light of a distant star shines brightly on its own world." He sniffed in a way suspiciously reminiscent of tears, and I carefully didn't look at him, in case that would embarrass him.

Sam's voice came from the back, unsure and exhausted, "I'm feeling better. Let's try again."

I looked down at Torliam's back, a few meaty holes in a row with the huge hooks still pressing into him, threatening his spine. "Come away from the controls and let my healer help you," I said. "If it comes down to it, your condition will be a lot more important than mine. Sam can heal me once we're safely away."

Torliam nodded sharply and conceded his spot, moving over to the sleeping nook in silence.

Adam moved up to take the spot at the control panel, but Blaine protested. He had emerged from the mecha suit, which was sitting crouched in the back corner beside our supplies. "I can pilot the ship," Blaine said with a smile and contrasting narrowed eyes.

Adam shook his head. "Haha! I'm the master of electronics, alien or human. This is my thing."

"I am a genius, a mechanical engineer among other things, and I know more about the alien technology than everyone else but...perhaps *one* person on this ship. And that person is not you," Blaine said firmly.

Jacky snorted. "The boys both wanna drive the cool alien plane," she said to Kris, who had thankfully stopped crying.

"Ahh..." Kris grinned, nodding wisely and crossing her arms over her chest.

"Childish," Gregor said, adding his own nod.

"Come on, Blaine." Adam pointed an accusing finger toward the powered-off suit in the back. "You've got a freaking warrior mecha suit! I think I should at least get to fly the ship."

Under the weight of that argument and all our stares, Blaine gave in.

I ate and drank till I was stuffed, sharing the pack of food bars I'd opened with Torliam, who ate stoically even while being healed. I drifted off at some point with Birch purring next to me, barely aware as Adam draped a blanket over me.

Interlude 2

Someone had hit the woman. A purpling bruise spread across her cheekbone, darkening where it surrounded her eye.

His heart thumped, and he turned to the man who held her arm in a vice grip, undoubtedly bruising her tender flesh. "What happened?" It came out an accusation.

"She attempted to escape, Eliahan. I found her climbing over the inner wall, to the east." The man rubbed a hand across his jaw, where already fading red lines marred the skin.

"And she fought back, so you hit her. A human woman who could never be your match in battle," Eliahan said, letting the words roll out as slow as mountain honey.

His compatriot flushed. "She fell, when I was forcing her back down off the wall. I did not hurt her intentionally."

The woman yanked away from him, and he let her go, shooting Eliahan a guilty glance when she rubbed gingerly at her arm.

"I will take her back," Eliahan said. "And you would do well to remember that these people are our guests, not our prisoners." He pretended not to notice when the man muttered that the "guests" weren't worth their efforts. Eliahan offered the woman his arm as they walked away.

She refused. "I know what you've done," she said abruptly. "How could you? They're only children."

Her accusatory look made him feel oddly guilty. "I have done many things wrong in my life. What exactly is it you accuse me of?"

"Kidnapping our children! The other families were talking about it. How their children started acting strange, and kept getting injured, and then just disappeared. You've been running some sort of...cult, or militant recruitment group. I didn't even..."

He frowned. "I believe you may be mistaken. It is not us who is taking your children. That is an organization called NIX. We have you here to protect both you and your children."

She seemed to deflate. "So someone *did* kidnap them? I'd hoped..."

She had hoped that he would refute her accusations? He shook his head. "They are being trained for war, in ways you cannot even imagine."

She was silent for a moment, and then surprised him. "Well, what are you going to do about it?"

When he was silent, she stopped and turned to scowl up at him, hands on her hips. "Eliahan, you damn well better be doing something to fix this."

Chapter 14

Awake, arise or be for ever fall'n.
—John Milton

TURBULENCE WOKE ME, as the ship rattled and pitched a couple times.

"Oh, what have the humans done to you, *Lady Ladriel*?" Torliam muttered, frowning down at the ship's controls. His wounds no longer oozed blood, though they were quite raw, and at least all the clamps had been removed from his back.

"How long have I been sleeping?" I asked.

"Not long," Adam said. "Twenty minutes."

"Any signs of pursuit?"

"Not yet, but there's no way they're not tracking the ship. And it won't just be our base coming after us. They could be sending pursuers from anywhere in the world. We've been gone for slightly over an hour. If this ship wasn't so fast, they probably would have caught us already," he said, fingers running along the cartridges at his waist as if reassuring himself they were still there.

"Has he revealed how we're escaping, yet?"

"The alien? No. I don't know why he won't just tell us, at this point. There's no way we're going to reveal it to NIX."

"Stonehenge," Blaine said.

"What?" I asked.

"Based on a few basic pieces of information, like our flight trajectory, size of the alien ship, and my basic knowledge of geography, I believe we are headed for Stonehenge. Our historians have never been able to unquestionably deduce its purpose. Perhaps it is some sort of portal, to those who know how to use it."

Torliam grunted, from the front. "Your historians are imbeciles. Though your race dies off so quickly, it is no surprise that you cannot properly bequeath information to your offspring."

"I will take that to mean I am correct," Blaine said, slightly smug.

"If that's true, at this speed we'll be there in about…five minutes!" Adam said.

"Do we need to prepare anything, Torliam? Pack up, etcetera? Or will you be able to send the whole ship through?" I moved up to stand beside him.

He was tapping at something on the control panel and didn't seem to hear me. He muttered something in his own language, face growing increasingly more expressionless, if that's even a thing. Then he just… sagged. "It is damaged, according to the ship's sensors. The array is completely broken. It will not work."

There was a beat of silence, and then the interior of the small ship burst into noise, everyone questioning him all at once.

I was stunned into blankness for the space of a couple breaths. Then I calmed, and my mind started to race. If we couldn't escape using Torliam's method, NIX was about to catch us.

I raised my hand and said, "Quiet."

The others complied, but turned to stare at me expectantly. As if I had an answer.

"How long do we have until NIX gets here?" I asked.

"I estimate we have about thirty minutes," Blaine said, "if they are employing their absolute fastest aircraft. And I see no reason why they would not, judging by the current situation. If they have sent word to others to cut us off, perhaps half that."

That wasn't enough time to escape, even if we had a way to do so, which we didn't. And even if we could we had nowhere safe to escape *to*. "We have no alternatives," I muttered to myself, eyes darting around in thought. "Tell me about this array. Stonehenge? What does it do? How is it broken?" I turned to face Torliam. He hesitated a moment, so I snapped, "We don't have time for this! Tell me."

"That place…the stones. They are an array that was laid down by my people when we were last on this godforsaken planet, thousands of years ago. There is a matching array in Estreyer, and this one can be used to access that one. Each can be used to transport the contents inside the circle instantly to a counterpart. But some of the stones are broken, or out of place, and some are even *missing*."

"How does it work? In a general sense, I mean. We don't have time for an alien science lesson."

"Vibration," he said simply. "I would cause the stones to vibrate, and their waves would travel across even endless space, faster than light, to pinpoint the location of the counterpart we want to access. Then…I do not know how to explain to one with such a rudimentary language and…" He stopped when my eyebrow rose in impatience. "It would *pull*, and we would be there, and NIX would not reach us."

"Okay. Stonehenge is made of what we humans call bluestone. Does it have to be bluestone? Could we fly somewhere and pick up some other rocks real quick?"

"They must be 'bluestone,' and they must have been prepared with the…'marks' by my people."

"Is there somewhere else we could go? Any other arrays like this that aren't broken?"

"There were few arrays, even before. Your world has little of worth, and we abandoned travel here long ago. The record of the array placement was not kept. When my exploratory group arrived, we did search out some arrays, but most were either also broken, or seemed to be an attempt by humans to copy something they did not understand. I did not know this one was broken."

"Most? Was there a working one, then?"

"Far from here. But it is small and rudimentary, and would not transport us all. And…I do not know if *Lady Ladriel* could make the trip. She is failing."

Well, screw that. I wasn't leaving anyone behind. I considered going to pirate the stones of that smaller array, but I realized that by the time we got there, loaded up the stones, and got back, NIX would have caught up long before.

I paced around, trying to will myself to come up with an answer. We couldn't run for much longer, and we really weren't strong enough to fight.

"Did you come here using the array?" I stopped and looked at Torliam again.

"No. They are disabled from our side. We cannot access Earth from Estreyer. My team flew here, the long way."

"And *Lady Ladriel* won't make it."

"Even if she could, we would all starve to death before even getting halfway. We do not have the preparations." He looked like a taut wire, ready to snap. No doubt I did, too.

I did *not* want to be caught by NIX. I could barely imagine the trepidation he must feel, considering the type of torment he'd endured for *years*.

"What do I need, what do I have, and how can I use what I have to get what I need?" I muttered under my breath, the words tripping on each other on the way out. My eyes passed over my teammates.

I stopped, staring at Adam for a long moment. "Could you make a passable replica of bluestone with your Animate Skill?"

His eyes widened as everyone else turned to stare at him, too.

"Your Bestowal, the 'Skill,' allows a short-lived mimicry of something, borne out of ink?" Torliam asked. "I have only seen it in action against NIX as we reclaimed *Lady Ladriel*."

"Well, yes, basically. It can bring something I've imagined and painted with ink to life, for a short while."

"I do not think that will work," Torliam said. "We might attempt it, but without the intimate knowledge of how our arrays function, I do not think it would be possible for you to replicate their effects. Or, perhaps, to hold the mimicry for long enough to complete the activation."

My faint hope evaporated. "Is there any fix for it? Or a workaround of some sort?" I asked.

Torliam didn't answer my question right away, but his face lost its expressionlessness. "I…" He tapped at the screen faster, symbols unlike anything I recognized from Earth flashing across its surface. "It would be dangerous. It will require us to calibrate the array to ourselves *specifically*."

"We will have to try," I said. "While Torliam is working on that, the rest of you, start gathering supplies. Anything you can carry, in order of importance to our survival on Estreyer."

"Food first, or supplies?" Zed asked. "Will we be able to gather food on Estreyer, wherever we're going?"

"There will be animals and vegetation where we are going. And another ship," Torliam said, meeting my eyes with understanding. "Smaller than this one, but it will carry anything we can bring to it."

"Can this ship fly on its own? If we send it out back over the ocean?"

"I hunted *Lady Ladriel* myself. She is the highest quality, and retains a small portion of her own instincts. If we tell her to go, she will go. And she can fly under the water, though a bit slower. Can your ships do the same?"

"Blaine?" I asked. He was the expert.

"Perhaps some of them. There are prototypes, but they do not compare to the speed of standard airships. If we are lucky, they will have to deploy other airships, or aquatic ones, to follow," Blaine said quickly. "But if you are planning to abandon the ship with most of the supplies inside, I must caution against it. I was already unable to fit as much as I wished into this…creature's…" he paused for a moment, seeming distracted as he looked around at the rippling walls, "…amazing cargo space. But I have already optimized based on what will be most useful for our survival. If we leave any more, I will not even have tools!"

"You'll have to make do without them, then. We're dropping off at Stonehenge, and the ship's going on without us. There isn't time for any more. And even if there was, we'd still have to be able to transport it to the other ship. We have about two minutes, Blaine. You'd better hurry."

Everyone scrambled to grab the important supplies—each team member's pack, the two cases of Seeds, some medical supplies and extra cartridges of ink and electricity, and Zed's nanite paste, which I ensured they didn't forget.

Lady Ladriel slowed as we approached Stonehenge, sliding so low to the ground it seemed like she was brushing the grass. On Torliam's order, the back of the ship opened up like a tube, and we were all sucked out by the force.

My Grace allowed me to land on my feet, thankfully, because a tumble would have been torturous to my half-healed arm. Blaine's mecha suit allowed him to do the same, with Kris and Gregor. Jacky carried Chanelle on her back, along with a huge backpack and enough side satchels that she was almost buried under them, though she didn't seem to have any problem with the weight. Blaine's doing, most likely.

Lady Ladriel shot off at an angle, the hull closing back up. Hopefully, she would draw NIX off for long enough for us to get off Earth. If we *could* get off Earth.

We ran toward the towering boulders of Stonehenge, and Torliam immediately got to work. He commandeered Jacky, and Blaine with his mecha suit, to right some of the fallen stones and move others back into position, while rearranging others.

I could almost smell the stress hormones in the air, wafting off everyone's skin.

Kris, normally quiet, snapped at Gregor. "Stop grinding your teeth!"

When Sam kept fidgeting, Adam growled at him to, "Stop looking so guilty!" Despite that, he himself couldn't keep his hands still, and his hair was floating about with a life of its own.

Sam pointed this out, which didn't help Adam calm down, but did incentivize him to stalk away from the other boy toward me.

"How's the pain?" Adam asked.

"Manageable," I said. "As long as I don't move, nothing hits the arm, and I stop breathing."

My attempt at humor didn't coax a smile out of him. "Once we get there, Sam can take some more Seeds and try again. This array thing better not cause any more injuries. Whatever's going on with Sam, I don't think we can rely on him to heal them."

"We'll make it work," I said, watching as the stones glowed with strange Estreyan symbols flashing across their surface.

Torliam was feverishly focused, hurrying around as he used the surface of the stone like a smartglass tablet. "We must calibrate the array, now. Everyone, gather with me!"

We did as he asked.

"Hold your hand over the stone," he said. "We must give our blood."

Blaine frowned at him. "Our blood… Is it taking a DNA sample?"

"We have no time for questions, human!"

I stepped forward first and held out my good hand.

Torliam waved his own hand, and a misty blue light shot out, scoring a thin line across the back. He grabbed my hand and rubbed the wound on the stone, spreading my blood in the pattern of an Estreyan symbol. The stone lit up along those lines, and when it dimmed, my blood was gone.

"Hurry," he said, eyes on the horizon. "NIX may not be fooled for long. We must not tarry."

The others followed suit, and then we gathered ourselves and the supplies in the center of the circle.

"Is this safe?" Adam muttered.

Torliam ignored him, still scanning the skies, and then he began to sound off the stones.

I shivered as the vibration traveled through me. Torliam explained that the sounds were a type of coordinate, each of them establishing a different parameter of location, far beyond simple latitude and longitude.

They felt kind of like the Boneshaker, but more powerful and less… teeth-grinding. My eyes caught rapidly growing dots on the horizon. Our pursuers.

But the waves were already thrumming through my body till I couldn't think of anything else but them, overlapping and merging and crashing. I squeezed my eyes shut and held back a tortured sob, mentally urging the array to hurry up so that the pain would relent…and then we were gone.

I KNEW we were in Estreyer first because there were no clouds to obscure the blistering sunlight. My eyes teared up at the burning sensation, and I slammed them shut till they could adjust. I wasn't nauseous like I had expected, but I was still trembling from the trauma of getting my injured pieces vibrated.

"Whoa," Kris said, looking around in wonder.

Even Gregor lacked his customary scowl.

"Is everything so *big* here?" Zed asked. "It's like some primordial paradise world."

We'd arrived within a circle similar to Stonehenge, but much better maintained. It was surrounded by tall yellowed grass. Only Torliam, myself, and Blaine were tall enough to see over the top of it, and Blaine only because the suit boosted his height by a few inches.

Torliam said something in Estreyan, and fell to his knees, his fingers digging into the dirt convulsively.

The smell of greenery and peaches hit me anew as my eyes adjusted to the alienly vibrant colors, and I realized that I, too, would be enamored of this stunning world, if my experience of it had not been tainted by terror and death. But I wasn't the only one who was more watchful than awed.

Adam, Jacky, and Sam stood facing outward warily, each of us with our back toward the others, facing into the unknown. This world killed the inattentive.

I spread my awareness out, using the Wraith Skill to sense our immediate surroundings for danger.

Birch sidled tentatively closer to the edge of the stone circle, nose twitching.

"Stay close," I said to him, though I hadn't noticed any monsters or obvious hazards, except for the slightly disconcerting realization that literally everything around me glowed almost imperceptibly with power. "It's dangerous."

His ears lowered, but he moved back toward the group, taking his disappointment out on Adam with a swipe to the leg as he passed.

"Why?" Adam sighed. "I just want to be friends."

Birch let out something that sounded surprisingly like a human snort and flicked his tail at Adam. He crouched down and jumped, landing on my good shoulder with enough force to rock me, then rising up with his hind legs on my shoulder and forepaws pushing at the side of my head, so that he could see over the top of the grass.

I rolled my eyes in commiseration with Adam.

Torliam rose from the ground, tilted his head back, and wiped his face while he breathed in deeply. "I am home," he said. He turned to me. "I thank you, Eve of the line of Redding. This will not be forgotten."

"You're welcome," I said awkwardly. "So, where's this other ship?"

"Not far. The other ship is no match for my *Lady*, but it will do. If we walk slowly, we will make it before the sun sets."

"Let's go, guys. Load up," I said.

Blaine strapped an impressive amount of supply-laden packs to his suit, challenging Jacky for the spot of most supplies carried. He seemed to be walking fine, so I figured either Sam had been able to heal the wound in his leg, or Blaine's suit was doing all of the work for him.

The rest of the team grabbed one or two packs each. I tried to grab my own, but Adam and Zed reached out to stop me almost simultaneously, and I gave up without much of a fight. My arm hurt, and I felt weak already. My skin still stretched tight over my bones, and probably would for a while. I pilfered one of the supply packs Jacky was carrying, which contained what limited food supply we hadn't abandoned, and took another handful of nutrient bars and some disgusting electrolyte-heavy water. My body needed fuel.

Birch again had his own little pack, which he seemed quite proud of, judging by the way he pranced around showing it off.

We filed out into the sea of grasses, Torliam leading the way. He walked instead of using one of the hoverboards, though I could only imagine how much muscle he must have lost in his lower body after being forcefully and continually paralyzed. We heard the sounds of a far-off monster scuffle, and then some pained yowling as one of them lost the fight, but we couldn't see it, and it was beyond the range of my Wraith Skill. After walking at a quick pace to keep up with Torliam for a couple hours, we crossed the path of a gigantic snake.

It turned to look at us when the grasses parted on it, but after a quick staring match with Torliam, it slithered off, its huge muscles rippling.

"A largely harmless creature," he said. "Though I do not doubt it would consider you humans a pleasant meal." I'm pretty sure he was smiling at that thought, though I couldn't see his face.

Shortly after that, we arrived at the edge of the field and entered a wooded area. I was relieved to see that the trees, while gigantic, weren't the same type as those twisted creations of the first Trial I'd been in. I'd had my share of dreams about those spores feeding on the still-living bodies of humans, growing into vaguely human-shaped colossals.

After another hour of walking the sun began to slant sideways through the trees, which opened up onto a clearing, within which were another ship, smaller and clunkier looking than the *Lady Ladriel*, and an Estreyan-sized log cottage.

I looked between Torliam and the cottage, and for some reason, was startled. Despite what I'd seen of Estreyer, all the technology and the abandoned cities, somehow I'd never imagined the aliens, Torliam's people, living in houses that weren't so different from a human's.

Torliam inspected the clearing for danger while we waited at the tree line, and then let us into the cottage. He was obviously familiar with the area, and I wondered if this had been his house before he came to Earth. The inside was sparsely furnished, and covered in dust and Estreyan-sized cobwebs. There were also a few Estreyan-sized spider corpses lying at the edge of the wall.

"Gross," Gregor said with a shudder, but he still leaned in close to examine their hulking appendages. He held his hand up to the body, then grinned over at Blaine. "It's bigger than my hand! Even bigger than my old pet tarantula."

Torliam waved a hand, and that blue mist burst from him again, dispersed thinly, and caused a violent gust of wind to blow through the cottage, gathering the dust and cobwebs along the way and forcing them out through an open window.

Adam and I shared a look of curiosity. Was that a Skill? Or was it just what came from being so full of Seeds that people could harvest you for them?

It didn't take long for us all to spread out in the cabin, which fit the group at least semi-comfortably because of the large scale it was built on.

"Rest," Torliam said. "We are safe for now, but you may find you need your strength later."

I didn't have any objection to that. I was exhausted. I sprayed some more numbing solution over my arm, reassuring Sam who apologized profusely when he saw me doing it. "It's okay. You need some sleep, too."

"I'll finish healing you in the morning," he said. "I promise. Whatever it takes, I'm going to fix your arm."

I fell asleep immediately, just leaning up against the wall with a couple packs for cushioning.

A bad dream jerked me to wakefulness after a few hours.

Torliam was also awake, sitting at the wooden table with his back to me. Had he slept? Or had he awakened like me? The thought that maybe he had nightmares too made me uncomfortable. He was massaging the muscles of his legs idly, and seemed to have found some clothes somewhere in the cottage that suited him better than the papery, hospital gown-like pants NIX had given him.

"Your people will have been searching for you," I murmured, "right?"

His head spun around toward me, but he didn't seem surprised that I was awake. "Of course." It was almost a whisper. While I'd slept, he had cut off the messy beard that NIX had allowed to grow untended, and trimmed his blonde hair so that it stopped just above his shoulders. Together, it went a long way to making him seem more human, and less like a crazed, killer hobo giant. "But it would have taken them a long time. The members of my crew who escaped would only have arrived back here a cycle or so ago to alert my people of my circumstances. As I said, they could not then simply enter an array to travel back to Earth. We forced our way through to here, but the other direction cannot be used by our people."

"Why not?"

"It is forbidden." His tone was final, and I took the warning not to continue that line of questioning.

"Why would it take years for them to alert people back here as to what was happening? Didn't any of the others have one of those Shortcut things in their ships? Or some other form of faster-than-light communication?"

He frowned down at the table, and then sighed and turned back to me again. "It is coincidence that my ship carried what you call 'the Shortcut.' I rue the day I decided not to discard it before the trip. Neither my crew nor myself were still at the level of needing access to such low-leveled Trials. None of the others carried something similar, especially since any transfer accomplished by such means is by its nature temporary. And… there is a…*disconnect* in space, between your world and mine. The ship's communications do not travel past it. I do not know what your people would call it. Surely you have noticed that time seems to flow differently?"

When I nodded, he turned back to the table. "I had hoped that after returning here, I would be able to contact my people, but it seems the communications system on the old ship in the clearing is broken," he said, shoulders slumping.

I sat up more fully. "Is that a problem? Can't we just fly the ship to wherever we need to go?"

"It means that no aid will be coming. We will have to make our way to the capital by ourselves, or find some other way to contact civilization. This ship does not have the fuel to make it all the way to the capital, and it will be very dangerous if we have to stop somewhere in the middle. The lands away from civilization are wild."

I groaned and knocked my head against the wall behind me. If Torliam thought an area was dangerous, the rest of the team would probably be vaporized on contact.

IN THE MORNING, Adam and Blaine joined Torliam in trying to fix the communication device in the old ship.

While they were doing that, Sam got back to work healing me. Kris came over to hold my hand, but I wouldn't wrap my fingers around her tiny ones, because I was afraid I'd squeeze too hard and break them. Instead, she handed me her moose. "I know it's just a stuffed animal. But he always makes me feel better when things hurt and there's nothing I can do about it. He'll make you feel better, too."

Gregor nodded. "Kris lets me borrow him sometimes. It's stupid, but it does kind of help."

I smiled and thanked her, then bit down on one of the pack straps, and tried not to scream. She had to go outside the cabin with the others when it got to be too much for her. Gregor stayed behind, kneeling on the ground next to Sam and me, watching the healing process in grave silence.

I'm not really sure how long it took before the pieces of my wound crying out in pain were less than the ones that had been healed, but by the time he'd finished Sam's skin was disturbingly pale, and his hands were trembling.

When he took his hands away, my arm was straight, and I could clench my fist loosely with only minor discomfort. I grabbed a nutrition bar from my little stash and offered it to him, looking at the marbled scars across my arm.

He accepted it silently.

"Are you all healed?" Gregor asked, reaching out tentatively to touch the skin.

When Sam was finished with the bar, he said, "I've done everything I can. It's not perfect. The amount of damage was…ridiculous. And something is wrong with my Skill," he added in a whisper. "But you should be okay, and you'll be able to use the arm. I recommend you take some more Seeds for Resilience and Life. I think I need some time to recover. Maybe whatever's wrong with me is just backlash from Skill overuse. This *is* the most healing I've ever done in a short period of time." He didn't sound completely convinced.

"You should rest," I agreed. "Eat something and get some more sleep."

He acquiesced, going to the corner to curl up with the supply packs and a blanket.

I found the two cases of Seeds and handed Gregor the moose so I could carry one case in each hand. My left arm ached at the effort, but it *worked.* I experimented with slipping my claws out, and though they were now a slightly darker shade than the ones on my right hand, they were as long and sharp as ever. I was going to be okay. I spared a look and a silent offering of thanks for Sam, over my shoulder. Without him, half the team would be dead several times over.

Outside, I gave Kris back her moose with a word of thanks, and the two kids accompanied me, along with Jacky, and Zed, as I moved out beside the house, in sight of the Estreyan ship where the others were working. I counted the Seeds, making sure none were missing except the ones I knew about. I held one up to the light, looking at the shimmering, swirling Seed organisms swimming within. the words MAKE A WISH rose to the surface and then sank away again.

Jacky leaned forward eagerly. “Are you going to divvy them up between us?”

“That’s the plan,” I said. I counted two hundred and sixteen spaces for Seeds, in both of the cases. I’d taken twenty-four while on the ship, and Sam had also taken a few, but that left three hundred ninety-six remaining. It was an amazing reserve of power. Enough to make a real difference. “Blaine came through for us,” I said.

Jacky knelt beside me, staring at the rows with a similar mix of awe and greed. “I guess I can forgive him for ratting on us all this time.”

“If we divide these evenly, there will be eighty-six for each of us, including Chanelle,” I said. “I’ve already had twenty-four of my share.”

Jacky looked over to Chanelle, who was sitting in the grass not far away, patting the ground like a toddler. “You think…those could make her better?”

“Maybe. We’ll definitely try,” I said. I left silent that they could also be the difference between life and death for me. That wasn’t even taking into account the power differential they represented, and how much safer the entire team would be if its Player members were stronger.

Torliam, Adam, and Blaine exited the small ship shortly after, looking crestfallen.

“We weren’t able to fix it,” Adam said, as they made their way to us.

“There is another communication array north of here,” Torliam said. “It, too, has been abandoned for a long while, but it may still be operational. Or, we may be able to use pieces from both to create a single working device.”

“Will the ship be able to make it that far?”

“We will get close, at least.” He stopped near my little huddled group, eyes dropping to the Seeds. His upper lip rose on one side, in the beginnings of a snarl. “What are you doing?”

“We’re divvying up the Seeds,” I said, standing slowly. The hairs on the back of my neck were rising. “I know they’re technically yours, but our bodies don’t just create them at the rate yours does, and we’re weak enough that they’ll make a significant difference.”

He scowled at me, a look I was becoming all too familiar with. “A blood-covenant is not something for you to throw around so lightly,” he said, snarling fully now.

I felt the muscles in my shoulders tense up in response, but I didn’t blink. "The deal we made was for you to help me. My team is also under my protection. Since we humans are weak, as you so love to remind us, you are just going to have to deal with us using the Seeds. What other way could we have the strength to fulfill the Oracle's vision?"

"Your *weakness* is not an excuse to *violate* the life blood of another. That is something that only the worst of my kind would do. When they are discovered, they are killed."

I hesitated, but pressed forward. "You are going to break the blood covenant anyway. This won't even affect you as soon as we're back in your hometown."

He stepped forward, towering over me. "I will not allow you to do this. My power is not something that can be shared among the masses like a cheap…sex-worker."

The pressure was a physical thing, brushing against my skin, pressing on my mind. My fingers trembled. I closed them into a fist to stop the movement. "These might be the difference between Chanelle regaining her mental faculties or not. You had no problem with me using them on the ship earlier. I assure you, we're not taking this lightly. We need these."

"On the ship, it was a matter of life and death."

I was gasping for breath, the sunlight burning my eyes as they dilated involuntarily. My claws slipped out. "It's a matter of life and death, still!" I snapped, pushing back against whatever force he was creating. "You know that! I need the Seeds to stay alive until we can get to the God of Knowledge." I bared my own teeth.

The pressure released with a snap. Torliam stared at me for a moment, fists clenched and breath heaving. He stomped away without another word, slamming the door to the cabin behind him.

I let out a shuddering breath of relief, rubbing my sweaty palms on my thighs.

"You're dying?" Adam asked, glaring at me along with everyone else except Zed and Blaine.

Chapter 15

There is beauty in the ending day.
— Ember Wiles

"I'M NOT QUITE sure how to say this," I said honestly. "There have been some...issues going on with me, with the Seed of Chaos that I got from Behelaino."

"'Issues?' As in, it's killing you?" Adam demanded. He looked around. "Where is Sam? Did he know about this?" he said, hair floating up.

I motioned for him to calm down. "It's not Sam's fault. Whatever's wrong with me, it's not something he can handle. I'm not sure if it's because of the problems he's been having with his Skill, or if it's something specific about whatever is wrong with me. Or maybe he's just healed me too many times already, and there's a limit. Obviously, he also can't fix Chanelle's brain damage."

"But he knew about this, and he didn't say anything?" Jacky said.

"I asked him not to, at least until I had some sort of plan to fix it. There's nothing any of you could have done. But you don't need to worry, because we have Seeds now, and with enough of them I'll be able to just heal myself. It might even turn out that loading up enough Seeds in the healing Attributes is a permanent solution."

"Do you actually *believe* that will be a permanent solution?" Zed demanded. He knew me a little too well.

"I don't know. I think the God of Knowledge might be the answer. That's the question I was asking when I solved the Oracle's puzzle, and that's the vision she gave me."

Adam shook his head. "How do you know the vision is in response to anything you asked? They could be completely unrelated."

"I don't know that. But I have to try."

Gregor spoke up, in a small voice. "But…you seem so strong all the time. And you're the one that saved us from NIX and got uncle Blaine to us. How are you dying?"

Blaine, who had kept out of the argument, patted Gregor on the head.

The boy bit his lip and looked down at the ground, scowling.

Jacky had been shaking her head slowly, but then stopped and spat on the ground. "I've been at my total worst around you. Sniveling and shaking and I didn't know what to do, and I asked you to help me. I *trusted you* to help me. But when it came time that you were down and sick and needed help, you didn't come to us. You didn't come to me."

"Ahh…" I opened my mouth, and closed it again, then reached a hand out to her.

She jerked away.

"I do trust you," I said. "I just didn't want to worry you when there was nothing you could do that wouldn't make our situation worse. What good is it, just to tell you that I might be dying and there's nothing you can do about it?"

Jacky stepped back toward me, then, jaw clenched, lips pursed, and hands fisted. "No," she said in a low, forceful voice, physically threatening despite the fact that she was significantly shorter than me. "I'm not totally useless. I coulda done something. I got Seeds, Eve! In the classes. If you woulda told me you needed them…" She jerked away from me. "What kind of friendship is that?" She left, stomping off with footsteps that crushed the grass and sunk into the ground, her power activating, perhaps unconsciously, in response to her feelings.

My arm lifted again, the hand reaching out as if to stop her, but I said nothing. I didn't have any words that could come out in response to her own.

"You're incredibly stupid sometimes, Eve," Adam said. "There's no way in hell we're going to let you die because of it, though. Take your damn Seeds."

BY THE CONSENSUS of the rest of the group, I was allotted half of Chanelle's Seeds, because if thirty-six Seeds in Resilience wasn't enough for her to show obvious improvement, any more than that would be a waste. Blaine and Sam had decided that they would give her one Seed every couple days, attempting to plant it into Resilience for her, so that a sudden influx didn't shock her system, and they would have resources remaining to change strategies halfway through if necessary.

Though Torliam scowled, he didn't say anything more about our use of the Seeds. However, he would also barely meet my eyes, and the more relaxed version of him that I'd been growing accustomed to was gone.

I stashed Chanelle's thirty-six Seeds at the bottom of my personal pack, along with the third gift from the Oracle. They would be there in case of an emergency, in case I ended up needing more Seeds in a non-healing Attribute, or if Chanelle regained her mental faculties and needed them back.

With the other Seeds, I did a mass injection into Resilience, and Life, with a moderate amount also going into Stamina, and a few others sprinkled around in the areas I thought I might find useful, and that would be harder for me to increase the old-fashioned way.

The rush of so many Seeds planting themselves at once had me shivering hot and cold, in alternating waves. I stumbled my way into the corner and huddled up under the blanket, curling up among the packs in the fetal position. Perhaps using sixty-two Seeds at once hadn't been wise. But the whole point of this was the hope that overpowering my healing aspects over a short period of time would allow them to outpace Chaos, both in healing and in growth factor.

Jacky forced Sam to examine me, but he assured her I was okay.

When the effects passed I pulled up my Attributes Window.

PLAYER NAME: EVE REDDING
TITLE: SQUAD LEADER(9)
CHARACTERISTIC SKILL: SPIRIT OF THE HUNTRESS,
TUMBLING FEATHER
LEVEL: 38

SKILLS: COMMAND, WRAITH, CHAOS

STRENGTH: 14
LIFE: 52
AGILITY: 22
GRACE: 18
INTELLIGENCE: 28
FOCUS: 23
BEAUTY: 10
CHARISMA: 15
MANUAL DEXTERITY: 9
MENTAL ACUITY: 23
RESILIENCE: 55
STAMINA: 30
PERCEPTION: 24

I felt better than I had in a while, though I was so ravenous that Adam teamed up with me to hunt some of the smaller creatures of the nearby forest, and we brought them back to the cabin and cooked them so that we didn't blow through our food supplies. I put weight back on fast enough that it was noticeable over the course of a single day or two.

A couple of nights in, while we were all gathered around a large roast, Zed turned to me. "After all this is over, and you're cured, we're going back to Earth, right? Because Mom's still there, and we don't even know where she is."

I swallowed, a bit reluctantly. "Yeah. Maybe by then we really will be strong enough to keep NIX from messing with us. I'm sure Mom is okay, so don't worry about her. She's never met a situation she can't 'manage.'" I twitched my mouth into a halfhearted smirk.

"Do you think your mom might be with my parents?" Sam said. "I'm worried that we were trying to make them disappear, and then they really did disappear."

"Probably." I nodded. "Best guess is that someone out there has a grudge against NIX. But whoever it is hasn't said anything, and there haven't been any threats. I'm hoping that's a good thing."

Adam shook his head. "It could just as likely be that your parents are being harvested for their Player-producing genes by one of NIX's enemies or counterparts."

Sam paled. "Do you think that's what's happening?"

I interjected before Adam could make us all feel even worse. "There's nothing we can do about it, if so. Whether we have to protect them against NIX or someone else, we're useless at the moment. Once we can do something about it, we will."

Sam and Zed didn't bring it up again, but they didn't look happy.

After we were all well rested and recovered, we packed up. As we filed onto the smaller, clunkier ship that sat in the clearing, Torliam's eyes followed Chanelle, who was unresponsive, but followed the group's gentle commands. "What is wrong with her?"

I stood back with him, watching her. "She's…a bit like you," I said. "NIX experimented on her, and caused some damage to her brain."

Torliam's lips curled and he spat on the ground. "*Humans*." It was a curse word, coming out of his mouth.

"I think the Seeds might be able to heal her," I said, as nonconfrontationally as I could.

He looked at Chanelle for a long while, and the anger faded away, replaced by a distant look. He entered the ship without another word. After a few minutes, Torliam lifted us off. If the ship's clunky design and worn-out body hadn't clued me into its quality compared to *Lady Ladriel*, the flight did. It was noticeably slower and shakier.

Zed stood behind Torliam, curiously watching as the giant man piloted. "How long till we arrive?"

Gregor groaned and rolled his eyes from the back. "You're *already* asking the stereotypical, 'Are we there yet?'"

Zed scrunched up his face and stuck out his tongue at Gregor, then grinned when the small boy huffed and looked away with his nose in the air.

Torliam released a small smile at their antics. "It will be many days before we arrive at the fort. This ship is little better than an old children's toy. We will not be stopping, because we are about to enter the Dark Lands. It is much too dangerous."

"Dark Lands?"

"They have been abandoned by my people, left to the monsters and… other creatures. They are hazardous even to my people, so for you…"

Zed laughed. "Yeah, yeah. I can guess what you're going to say. Us puny humans would all be slaughtered within mere moments of encountering the fresh air outside the ship."

Torliam gave a single nod. "Indeed." But I noticed that once again he failed to hide his smile.

Zed leaned over his shoulder again. "Can you teach me how to fly this thing?"

"Perhaps."

We flew for hours, and I took the spot up at the front beside Torliam, meditating under the light of the brilliant sun and rolling clouds. I turned my awareness inward, wondering if this was also a function of my Wraith Skill, and leisurely imprisoned every drop of Chaos I could find within myself. When I finally opened my eyes to the sunset, I was relaxed, almost languid.

That relaxation didn't last for long, as the first thing I saw was Torliam's tense face, looking outward toward the horizon. Dark clouds were gathering on the very edge, above a slight glint that I thought might be water. Torliam was pushing the ship fast enough that it shook uncomfortably.

"A storm?" I asked.

"Yes. But I do not think it is the type of storm you mean. Things have worsened in the time I have been gone." He pushed the ship a little harder. "I will try to outrun it."

"Can this thing fly in a storm?"

"No. But we cannot land here."

I leaned forward and looked down. I'd had my awareness focused inward instead of on my surroundings while meditating, so I gasped when I saw the forest of feathered metal spikes below us. They followed the path of the ship, swaying, and turning towards us like sunflowers toward the light. Or, more likely, like some sort of carnivorous plant following the movement of its prey.

The storm on the horizon moved faster than I thought possible, drawing near to us. I could hear the wind screaming. And I mean that literally. At first, I thought I was imagining it, but the sound was unmistakable. "What is it?" I stared at the mass of dark writhing clouds that seemed at times to have the shape of grasping hands, borne on an unnaturally fast wind.

"There is no word for it in your language. It is a storm that thirsts for blood to add to its waters."

Jacky had moved to look out the front viewport beside me, and her knuckles went white as she clenched her fists. "Gimme a monster to fight any day. *This* isn't…"

I nodded my understanding. "Same here." The ship lurched, and my insides went with it, my throat tightening in fear. I was no stranger to fear, and if I was honest with myself, it was my constant companion, but it had been a while since I'd faced the special brand of it Estreyer induced.

The ship lurched again, and I bit my lip to keep from making a sound and giving myself away. My teeth fit perfectly against the thin scar I had on the tender skin on the inside of my lip. The pain of the bite was familiar, and helped me to unclench the death grip my hands had on the sides of my seat.

"We will land there," Torliam said, pointing with his chin to a spot past the forest of spikes where boulders sat scattered about on the barren ground. The ship lurched again as a portion of the storm cloud lashed out at our tail end. "Prepare to abandon the ship. We must hide amongst the stones."

I nodded quickly and took the opportunity to occupy myself with something I could actually affect, instructing the team to put on the packs and make sure everything was tied down to them securely. We had some plastine rope, and we all worked together to tie a piece of it to ourselves. I hoped if we were heavy enough, we'd be able to withstand the force of the winds outside better, or at least someone who was could keep another from being blow away.

"Seriously?" Gregor said, his voice rising. "We're going to abandon the only thing keeping us safe from *that*?"

"The ship is meant to fly, to be carried by the wind. You may stay inside it while it does so, if you wish," Torliam snapped. He half-crashed the ship down amongst the boulders, then threw open the door. The wind flooded in, assaulting our ears with its shrieking. He let out a roar in response, but though it was defiant, I recognized the fear in it.

And that terrified me, more than the storm itself.

Chapter 16

How can I be substantial if I do not cast a shadow? I must have a dark side also if I am to be whole.

— C.G. Jung

I USHERED the team out into the gale, following right behind Torliam in a defensive formation. Strong and heavy people were positioned on the outside, with the ones who needed protection moving within the makeshift shell. I moved at the side, with Zed on my left, because I knew I wasn't strong enough to protect our back. Even with the packs weighing me down, the wind almost lifted me off my feet, so I hunched down and dug the claws of my toes into the ground for a tiny bit of extra purchase.

I knew I put on a facade of bravado for others. I needed people to believe in me, so my team would listen and follow my lead, and my enemies would fear me and hesitate to attack. I'd even hoped that if I told the lie of my own fearless power enough, it would become the truth. I had started to believe it, a little bit. But now we were back on Estreyer.

We ran, hunched over to make smaller targets, and I kept a firm grip on Zed's sleeve, just in case.

Adam threw out shields to the left and right to impede the wind, while Chanelle stumbled along next to him.

Blaine used the size and weight of the mecha suit to curl protectively around the kids.

Jacky brought up our rear, weighing herself to the ground.

I risked a glance back to make sure she was okay, and saw the cloud form a funnel and reach down to the ship, sucking it up into the roiling mass. Like it was a toy.

Jacky screamed something at me, but I couldn't hear her.

I shook my head and turned back to the front, then screamed myself when I saw the wing of dark mist swinging toward us from the side. Luckily, no one could hear me, either.

I ducked down farther as it swept over us. I opened my eyes wider instinctually as my vision was obscured. The sky had been darkening, before. Now everything was true black. My ears ached from the noise of the screams all around us. I tightened my grip on Zed to make sure we weren't separated and pushed my awareness outward.

Faces swam in the darkness, attached to formless bodies with cutting wind for hands. One swam past my vision, large and open-mouthed, as if it was moving to devour me, and along with it, a scythe-like whip of wind cut towards us from the side, formed from the dark mist.

Torliam turned toward it, with Adam mirroring him when it smashed against one of his shields and obliterated it, but the others didn't even know it was coming. At its height, it was literally positioned to cut them in half, separating torso from legs.

I attacked, slashing out with a combination of claws and a rush of Chaos that followed my movement. I wasn't holding back. I had too much to lose, and with the Seeds I'd taken and the others stashed in my pack, I'd be more than able to mitigate the side effects.

The scythe disintegrated with my attack, and the face focused on me for a moment, but looked more surprised than angry or pained. I tried again, on a nearby figure moving toward us, with the same effect. Or lack of effect, as the case may be. Maybe this storm was too similar to Chaos to be hurt by it. All I could do was return it to its amorphous state, not destroy it.

I noticed a couple of the team were starting to veer off from the course Torliam led, unable to see him or the rest of us, so I broadcast a Window to everyone, containing a constantly updating mini-map. It showed the location of the rest of the team, and the highest-priority dangers as the cloud formed attacks around us.

Zed reached into the holster at his thigh and pulled out a gun. He shot into the amorphous mass, bullets that cut through it for a while before being commandeered by the strength of the wind, and turned back on us. I sent out an alert of danger in their path, and Adam tossed up a shield to stop their progress.

—Bullets not working. It spits them right back.—
-Eve-

—How about an explosion, then?—
-Zed-

He pulled out a small cartridge from his utility belt and loaded it into the gun. The recoil knocked his hand back, but whatever he had shot detonated in the midst of the cloud in a ball of fire. The flames were quickly sucked up and disappeared, but the screams turned angrier.

—Duck! I'm zapping the area.—
-Adam-

I didn't even think, but threw myself to the ground immediately.

Torliam stayed standing, but I figured he could handle himself either way.

I closed my eyes almost too late. Despite the eclipsing mist, when Adam let loose I saw the back of my eyelids in a bright red flash.

—Dammit, Adam! My eyes!—
-Jacky-

When would she learn to close her eyes? This happened every time.

The lightning cut through the wet cloud with light and heat. Despite the fact that electricity hurting a storm-cloud seemed counterintuitive, it screeched so hard I wondered if my ears would bleed, and thinned out around us for a good distance.

Torliam used the opportunity to point to a big rock outcropping in the distance, and I read his lips scream the word, "Go!"

I scrambled to my feet, still clutching Zed's sleeve, and grabbed the blinded Jacky around the arm, hauling her up and dragging the both of them forward. The cloud was already thickening again, so I put a big beacon on the mini-map where a rock outcrop jutted from the ground and rushed toward it.

Another scythe rushed toward the more spread out group, from the other side. Too far for me to reach with Chaos, moving too fast. It was going to hit Blaine, and Kris and Gregor along with him.

But I had forgotten Blaine had a VR chip of his own now and could see the threats signaled on the Windows I'd sent, just like the rest of us. He spun, using the artificial strength of his mecha skeleton to send the two small bodies flying toward my side of the circle.

His momentum carried him around, and as the scythe of wind slashed at him, his suit let out a burst of fire from the hands. It didn't catch the entirety of the attack, and he flew backward. The split plastine rope that had been connected to him waved about in the wind like a fire hose at full pressure. He was beyond our ability to rescue by dragging him along behind us, now.

Zed and I each grabbed one of the kiddos before they could hit the ground or smash into one of the many surrounding boulders.

I wrapped my arms around Gregor, and screamed, "Hold on tight!" into his ear.

Adam was pale and his long limbs seemed to be dragging, but he closed in behind us, throwing up shields to cover our retreat.

Debris whipped through the air, striking the shields, and stabbing at us when they got by.

Some hit Gregor in the cheek, and I tugged him closer and barreled forward with him tucked to my chest, head down and arms wrapped tight around his small body to provide protection.

A piece of severed rope, only a few inches long, tore through the air almost faster than my Skill could perceive. It entered Sam's stomach from the side, slicing through it like soft cheese. He ran a couple more steps before falling.

Adam paused for a moment to grab the extra rope around his own waist, looped it under Sam's arms, and dragged Sam behind him.

They were moving too slow, Adam without the strength to drag Sam while keeping himself and Chanelle safe, and Sam too preoccupied with trying to keep his guts from spilling out of his torso to help.

Blood spread out on the ground behind them. The stones were... absorbing it. No time to worry about that, either.

Jacky lunged away from me, grabbed Sam around his knees and

shoulders, and carried him forward, faster than Adam had been able to drag him.

Behind us, Torliam turned and began to walk backward toward us, as if he would single-handedly hold off the storm. Then he began to glow. Not like radioactive glow-in-the-dark, but a shining pale blue light that wafted off him in visible ripples.

Then he swung his glowing arm, palm flat, and sliced with it toward the darkness, as if his arm extended far beyond the tips of his fingers, and was really a blade. Whatever power he was using sliced into the cloud with a faintly luminescent edge, and the storm shrieked again and drew back, giving us a few more moments of respite.

The storm gathered itself, tightening as if preparing to shoot forward in retaliation, but Torliam used the edge of his glowing palm to cut a line across the back of his opposite forearm. His blood splattered against the rocks around him, thrown about by the wind. What the hell was he doing?

The clouds sprang forward, formed like curving hawk talons that dwarfed even his Estreyan size. But before they reached him, the rocks around him tumbled together, smashing against each other with such force I could feel the shockwave, even if I couldn't hear it.

The boulders formed a humanoid shape that reminded me slightly of Behelaino's rock golems, only much bigger. The stone creature took the brunt of the storm's attack and staggered backward. But it had given Torliam time to escape, and he dashed toward us, not even looking back. As he ran, all around us the boulders began to tumble together, and the stones rose on two legs, moving to face the storm.

Torliam quickly overtook my escaping team, grabbing Blaine with one arm and dragging him along as he passed. He escorted us closely the rest of the way to the center of the stone outcrop. Once we were within, it protected us from the wind.

We all huddled together within the surrounding rocks, crouching down and covering our ears with our palms. I made sure with a tight burst of the Wraith Skill that everyone was alright, then did the same.

—Eve, are we going to be okay?—
-Gregor-

It was the first time he'd used his VR chip to talk to me.

—Yes. You're going to be alright.—
-Eve-

I didn't tell him to trust me. Instead, I smoothed my face into a mask of certainty, as if this whole situation was nothing more than an irritation to me. He was a child. I'd never let him know how completely my expression was a lie. Because even if I was afraid, I wouldn't let him be hurt. That, at least, was the truth.

Sam huddled in a corner, shaking and gasping as he pushed his insides back through the open slice, and applied pressure.

Zed and Jacky worked together to bandage him up the mundane way, and Sam kept muttering, "I'll heal, I'll heal," over and over again.

The rocks fought with the storm, releasing some sort of power that turned the mist to pebbles and forced it to the ground. Eventually, the storm retreated, and when it did, the boulders settled back to the ground, rolling apart.

Torliam let out a shuddering sigh and gave the rest of us a despairing look. "Your combat abilities are all woefully lacking. You are so weak, I cannot imagine how you managed to survive thus far."

"MY POWER HAS BOUGHT us protection, and your friend's blood has paid for time. We may stay here through the night, but no longer," Torliam said, crouching over and trailing his six fingers over a stone, as if petting an animal. The cut on his forearm was already healed. "The stones will require more blood if we do, and none of us wants to pay their price, believe me."

"Is there any safe place near here?" I asked.

"No," he said simply. "If we can pass the chasm of the North, we might stay in the guardhouse for the night, tomorrow. But it is a long journey for people with such short legs. And as we have just seen, I am too weakened to protect you all, when we encounter danger." He gestured in Sam's direction.

"I'm okay," Sam muttered weakly. "I can heal it. I just need some rest."

Jacky stared at him for a moment, then turned on Torliam. "You should train us, then, no? If we're too weak to make it, you should train us till we're stronger. You're a warrior or whatever, right?"

Torliam snorted. "I have no desire to waste my time trying to strengthen a group of humans."

Jacky protested, but he didn't relent.

Later that night, the ring from the Oracle, sealed around my left forefinger, glinted in the brightening moonlight as the second moon entered the sky. I noticed Torliam glancing at it.

"It was the first gift from the Oracle," I volunteered. "She gave them to me as little interconnected loops, like a chain. I had to figure out how they all fit together, and once I did, they shrunk onto my finger, injected their contents into me and gave me the vision of Behelaino," I hesitated, "and of you. Now they won't let go."

"It is a symbol to those who might meet you," he said. "You have solved the second one, you said. Where is it?"

"It's..." I narrowed my eyes. "You're pretty interested in this."

"I have been studying the Oracle and her sister since I was barely a man. And now, I see a gift from one of them with my own eyes, on the body of a human." For once, he didn't say the word "human" with a sneer.

"You know...I'd be happy to talk about all this stuff with you. Like the visions the Oracle gave me, the quests, the third gift that I haven't solved yet..." I waited for a beat as he turned to look at me. "But it won't come free. We'll exchange answer for answer, and only *while* you're training at least one person from my team."

Jacky's head snapped around to look at me.

Torliam's eyes widened, and for the first time I had ever seen, he laughed without malice. "You bargain like a *skirling*. I will accept your offer, though I wonder if you will regret your words once you experience my training."

Jacky didn't seem daunted by that at all, so I let him teach her first.

I sat by the sidelines, talking with Torliam while they sparred out on the boulder-strewn plain.

He was brutal, and seemed to prefer showing Jacky her mistakes by exploiting them, rather than verbal explanations. He asked me to detail the first vision I'd had, and listened intently, though it didn't seem to affect his fighting performance at all.

"Why did you come to Earth?" I asked.

"There is a Sickness, on my world." The way he said it capitalized the word in my mind. "A plague. Many of my people have given up hope for our salvation, as our world dies. But I refuse to believe we cannot be saved. There is one who can stand against the abhorrent—that which causes the Sickness. Its enemy is the Champion, a god who had disappeared some time beyond living memory." He threw an lazy punch at Jacky's stomach that sent her flying back despite the guard she put up. He waited to see if she'd get up again for more. "I have studied long and hard, and I believe he may be on your world. Most did not agree, and I was scoffed at for my theories. But, I am the younger son of a powerful family, and my mother granted my request for a small unit to quest for him, though she thought I was a fool. We flew through space for years to reach your planet, but I was not able to complete my mission before your people attacked. I did not expect your race to have advanced far enough to do more than cower in fear, but even so, I sent down my ambassador with gifts to treat for nonviolent passage."

His words were heavy. "She was killed. And then your people attacked."

I frowned. The media had told us that terrorists had caused the massive destruction of targets all over the world about seven years ago. According to NIX and Nadia Petralka, it was really caused by the skirmish between the Estreyan group and our militaries, when they sent an experimental invasion group. But in her version, we hadn't been the instigators of the hostility. "That's not what we were told…" I murmured.

His eyebrows rose, then fell again, into a deep glare. "I do not lie, *human*. Not about this, especially. Your people generated the enmity between us, altogether unprovoked."

Jacky ended their sparring session not long after.

I did my best to commit what I'd learned from watching them to memory, then stood up for my own beating.

He asked about the second and third gifts, and I rolled up my sleeve to show him the armband around my right forearm, with a promise to take the third gift out of my pack later so he could examine it.

When it was time for my question, he grimaced, so I went for something neutral that wouldn't make him angry again. "Tell me about your world. The gods, the Seeds, you know. How does it all work?"

He stared at me blankly for a moment. "That is hardly a simple matter, material for a single question or answer."

I grinned brightly in response, imitating Zed, who Torliam seemed to have taken more of a liking to than the rest of us.

Torliam caved. "Very well. But you cannot ask me to continually clarify my statements until you end up getting answers for which you have not paid."

I nodded.

"You have learned some of these things already, I do not doubt. This world, as a whole, is formed of the gods. The Champion, the one who molds, guided them to meld together and create the earth and water and the forces of nature. The gods embody principles of existence, and many of them take a physical form or two to interact with each other and us. Beyond them, there are greater forces of existence, but they are more like…" He sighed. "Laws? Absolutes. They do not interact with us. Perhaps they do not have a consciousness like our own, and do not even notice our puny existence among the vastness of…the 'everything.'" He lifted his arms and flung them wide to explain the word he was missing, gesturing out beyond ourselves, to the sky and wider.

"The universe?" I supplied, jumping toward him and attempting to slash at his neck.

He grabbed me by the arm, and showed me how he could have broken it, if he wanted. "Yes, that word suffices. In any case, I cannot tell you much about them. My knowledge is focused more on this world and its problems, its history. When you learn to read, you can read about what our scholars have theorized yourself."

I resisted the urge to point out that I already knew how to read, just not his language, and 'would he please not make everything into an insult?'

He smirked at my expression. "The mortals of this world, such as myself, traveled here along with our gods many thousands of years ago. This world sits at a junction, a place where travel is made easy. You will have to learn more about science before you can understand that.

"This planet has layers of a type, unlike your planet, on which life only dwells on the single mundane surface."

I didn't understand what he meant, but I resisted the urge to do the very thing he'd asked me not to by prying for an extended explanation. I dodged an elbow to the temple and earned a small nod of approval from him when I kicked at his knee in the same motion.

"Most of my people have retreated to the cities, where there is safety in numbers, as the world itself grows more dangerous, and our numbers decrease. To gain strength, we train and study, and if we feel we are ready and willing to risk our lives, we will petition the gods. This is what you call a Trial. We prove our worth before the gods, and if they think us worthy, they will give a Bestowal. From what I understand of NIX, the Bestowals are what you call Skills. And very rarely, a god will find among us mortals one that shines bright with promise and deign to give them a portion of their…*life-force*. They grant patronage, and give the mortal a chance to ascend. This…I wonder that the manifestation of Chaos did not do this for you," he said, searching my face for understanding, or maybe confirmation.

My eyes widened. "Um…yeah? She did. I'm pretty sure. She said something about welcoming me as a godling. Honestly, I didn't think she really *meant* it like that." My mind raced at the implications. "What does that mean for me? Obviously, it's not going so well. My body can't handle the power—it tries to kill me on a daily basis."

"My people would spend hundreds of years strengthening themselves before ever seeking to ascend. Of course your puny human body would not withstand it. Your lifespans are as short as a *light-bug*. You are like a walking corpse to my people." He stepped forward, both hands attacking in a blur of punches and jabs that sent me scrambling backward, without even attempting to block or slip past them.

"You're not being helpful," I said through clenched teeth.

He stopped and raised an eyebrow, and I realized he'd pushed me back against the side of the jutting outcrop, leaving me nowhere to run.

I jumped up, as far as I could, and pushed off the rock behind me with my legs, claws out to ward off the attack he threw to meet me in mid-air.

"If in fact you did gain her patronage, it does not mean you are a god," he said, spinning around to face me.

I raised an eyebrow of my own now that his back was to the rock wall.

He snorted, and simply stepped forward, a few quick blows forcing me to retreat again. "You have a *chance* to move beyond the mortal, if you can cultivate the power and, of course, stay alive. Unfortunately, I have no way to help you, as I do not know of anyone with your history, and I am no healer. Perhaps there will be records we can dig up in the capital that will give some hint. If not, there is no being in existence that would be more likely to know than the God of Knowledge. *If* he will concede to help us, you will have your answer. If it is possible."

"Do you think he won't help?"

"He left the mortal world long ago, his only physical manifestation settling in the wilderness. Many think he is searching for the answer to the Sickness. I have heard of the occasional person going to quest for a Bestowal from him, but I have not heard stories of any who have succeeded in recent history."

That was worrying, but the Oracle had shown me that vision, so I could only hope that my answer would come out of it. We spent a couple more minutes sparring, which mostly consisted of me either running away frantically or getting the stuffing pounded out of me.

Jacky didn't smile at me or clap me on the back when we returned to the center of the stone monolith, but she nodded, and we both nursed our bruises in semi-comfortable silence.

WE LEFT before the sun fully rose over the horizon, the kids stumbling and rubbing at their eyes. There had been nightmares during the night, and no one had gotten enough sleep. Sam was still pale, but when Zed took off the bandage, the wound had sealed over on its own.

Blaine worried about sepsis, but Sam gritted his teeth and assured him that his healing ability could handle it.

We traveled in defensive formation again, Kris, Gregor, and Sam alternately walking or riding the one remaining hoverboard until it ran out of solar charge. We were all on edge, alert for attack and aggressive toward the slightest sound.

We walked all day, ate while we walked, and took few breaks. I even ordered that anyone moving away from the group to relieve themselves take someone with them. It'd be just *wonderful* if someone walked away to pee and never came back.

Finally, we arrived at a huge chasm. Wind whipped along it, singing as it sliced along the corners of the jagged rock. It put me on edge, but this wind didn't sound like it had a mouth. The sounds it made were simple whistles and roars, created by its speed.

We walked north, then, until we arrived at a spot where the chasm narrowed. It bore the remnants of a broken bridge.

"This was once the bridge of middle North," Torliam said, "and we must cross it."

It was obvious that the bridge had once been a beautiful, arching structure that was an accolade to Estreyan architecture, made of marble or something like it. But it was broken now. Only the ends remained, and between them stretched almost a mile of yawning chasm. On the other side leaned a half-crumbled tower, made of the same stone.

Blaine frowned. "Why has the bridge not been repaired? I am no expert, but it seems this damage happened some time ago."

"The bridge was destroyed intentionally, to stop the creatures of the lands beyond from following us, when we abandoned the middle North."

"Why would you abandon an entire section of your planet? With the kind of technology you are able to field, I imagine that you could handle some aggressive wildlife."

"My people are not as numerous as they once were. Resources needed to be consolidated. The lands near population are much safer and more bountiful than where we are going. We will rest there tonight," Torliam said, pointing at the decrepit tower. "The last time I was here there was still an inner room that had not been breached. It will be safe."

"How?" Jacky asked. "Even I can't jump across something that wide. And none of us can fly, last I checked." She narrowed her eyes at Torliam. "Can you?"

"Not as such. Even at my strongest, I could not cross this with anyone else in tow. Birch might ferry us across, if he were bigger. At one point, the line of Aethezriel was known for their tailos mounts."

The creature let out a peep, making me wonder once again exactly how much English he understood.

"The hoverboard might be able to make the trip across," Blaine said. "Though it would need some modification to deal with the high winds, and without the sunlight, it would not have enough power for more than a single trip."

"I might be able to Animate a connection between the two remaining ends of the bridge," Adam said. "But I don't think I could hold something that big long enough for us all to get across.

"I can carry someone," Jacky said. "And we've got Seeds left, right? Except for Eve. A couple more into Strength and Agility, and we can just sprint across."

"We can do the rope trick again," Zed said. "Like you were telling me about when you had that Trial with the ratmen, remember, Jacky? I'm not as fast as you guys, but I'm pretty sure I'm faster than a totally normal human, and if I can't make it, you can just pull me up."

"My suit is damaged," Blaine said. "If only I had had the time to complete the protective covering before we left… I do not know that I will be able to keep up with a Player's level of supernatural speed, but I would be heavy enough to cause issues if you were to have to pull me up along with the suit."

"Just take the thrusters out of the hoverboard and use those," Gregor said. "Eve can carry me, and Adam or Jacky can carry Kris and Chanelle."

I suppressed a chuckle at the boy volunteering me to serve as his mount.

Blaine stared at him for a second. "Yes…that might work." He smiled and pushed up his glasses. "You have potential as an engineer," he said with poorly concealed pride.

Gregor rolled his eyes.

Adam got to work brainstorming bridge structures with Torliam. "You will add blood to the ink, of course," Torliam said. "How long do you estimate that you can hold the mimicry?"

"Why would I add blood to the ink?" Adam said, taken aback.

"Is yours not a significance-based Skill? I assumed…"

Adam's eyes widened.

"Do not tell me that you are unaware how your own Skill functions," Torliam said flatly.

"I've been experimenting, trying to figure out what makes a difference and what doesn't, but I hadn't been able to come up with such a broadly applicable rule yet. Tell me more. Are you familiar with other 'significance-based' Skills?"

"We do not have time for an extended lesson at the moment. However, some Skills are affected by the…importance or the…implications of *how* they are used. When you spend your time carefully designing your creations, using the highest quality materials that have the most significance to you, if I am correct, it will make a difference in the nature of the creation."

"Like when you Animated your tattoo," I said. "It was strong enough to hold back the attack of a volcanic Goddess."

"Blood is a fitting sacrifice when you do not have anything more convenient, or when the situation is dire," Torliam said.

While he and Adam continued to work on that, the rest of us set up a few meters away from the edge of the chasm and timed our running speeds.

Birch joined in, frantically flapping his wings. He failed to take off from the ground even a little bit, which made sense, because his wings hadn't even turned completely to feather yet. They were still in the awkward half-fluff stage. After quite a few attempts, he mewled pitifully and lay down, legs stretched out fully to the front and back, neck resting on the ground.

"It's okay, Birch," Kris said. "You're growing fast. Soon you'll be big enough that people can ride you while flying through the sky, just like Mr. Torliam said."

His ears perked up, and he turned to her, his human-shaped eyes projecting curiosity.

She began to weave tales of his future awesomeness and bravery to him, and it wasn't long till he was sitting straight up to listen, interjecting with little sounds every once in a while.

"I'm pretty sure he actually understands what she's saying," Zed murmured to me as I watched in bemusement. "Does that count as discovery of the *second* sentient alien race?"

"I'm not sure he'd be the second one we've met," I said. "But I think he is sentient, to some degree. His mother communicated telepathically, through touch. Maybe he'll be able to do that when he's older, too." A small explosion drew my attention.

"Nothing to worry about," Blaine said, waving away the smoke. "I know what I'm doing."

After another quarter hour of frantic preparation by some people and worried waiting by the rest of us, we tied everyone together with the same plastine rope as before. Adam had been able to re-fuse the severed pieces, and assured me it would be just as strong as the original. Those who made it across, which would likely be Torliam, Adam, Jacky, and hopefully me, would pull the rest of the team up when the bridge gave out beneath our feet.

When Adam was ready, we all got a running start, sprinting toward the edge of the bridge which ended on the open air. I carried Gregor strapped between me and the pack on my back so that my arm and legs were free to pump mostly unimpeded. Torliam had Chanelle, and Jacky had Kris.

Adam ran a little ahead of us, and when he reached the edge, he shouted, "Animus!" and threw out a spray of ink, which formed out in front of him into a narrow platform, connected to the real bridge's broken supports.

The team followed him unhesitatingly, in order of fastest to slowest. Torliam kept pace behind Adam with seemingly little effort, Chanelle's weight barely impeding him. The rest of us were straining.

Adam probably could have gone faster, but an unforeseen problem popped up. He couldn't form the ink quickly enough to keep up with his speed, and so he didn't draw too far ahead of us.

It was a problem, because it meant no one might make it across in time, and thus the slower people wouldn't have anyone to pull them up when the ink construct disintegrated.

We were about three-quarters of the way across when Adam shot a look back over his shoulder.

—The beginning's gone.—
-Adam-

He began to form the platform tilting upward, so that as the unconnected piece of ink bridge beneath our feet began to fall, we would run up it and stay at the correct level. It was a good idea, if a desperate one.

Torliam let out a familiar blue glow, then, and the mist reached around, to buoy up the ink. We still sank, but not as fast.

Adam reached the edge first, shooting forward and leaving room for Torliam to cross behind him, then Jacky. I leapt the last bit, the edge of my foot barely reaching the jagged lip of the broken bridge. My momentum carried me forward, though, and I tumbled over the edge, doing my best not to crush Gregor between the pack and my back as I rolled.

I stood immediately and lunged forward to combat the sudden tug I knew would be coming on the rope tied to Blaine, Sam, and Zed. Torliam let me slip by him, grabbing the rope behind my back and pulling on it.

The abrupt yank on the rope knocked my breath out and almost made me throw up. But my claws dug into the ground, and I kept straining forward.

It took less than a minute to pull up the rest of the team, and though they were a little banged and scraped up from smashing into the slightly jagged edge of the chasm, we were all alive. Blaine probably would have made it across with the help of his salvaged thrusters, except that he had started out behind the most of us, and there hadn't been enough room on the ink bridge for him to pass anyone. Even so, lifting him while the thrusters pushed him upward wasn't any more difficult than lifting a fat man would have been. Totally doable.

I was just about to let out a sigh of relief when Adam's eyes rolled back in his head, and he collapsed.

Chapter 17

I want to touch the fire in the sound.
— Pablo Neruda

SAM, who looked ready to sleep for about a year straight, pronounced that Adam was just extremely exhausted, suffering the backlash from Skill-overuse, and low on blood. None of which Sam could do anything about even if he wasn't using all his healing on his own wounds, since Adam wasn't actually injured. Adam would have to recover the old-fashioned way, and would be able to move with the rest of us in the morning, though he would probably be even more grumpy than usual.

YOUR AGILITY HAS INCREASED!

I waved the Window away with a vague swipe of my hand.

When I slid the pack off my back and untied Gregor, he wrapped his little arms around my waist and let out a sobbing breath into the material covering my stomach. He hadn't made a single sound as he rode on my back all the way across, not even when I'd made that final desperate leap for the edge.

But I realized now that he was shaking, his knees trembling so that he could barely support his own weight. I hesitantly patted his head, petting him a little as if he were an animal. "You're safe," I said in a soft voice. "I said you would be, didn't I?"

He nodded mutely into my stomach, then began to cry. He struggled to stop, no doubt embarrassed to lose his usual adult-like behavior, but didn't quite succeed.

I felt a bit inept, but I just petted him some more and stood still so he could hide his face in my bodysuit. He was just a kid, after all. A kid that looked like he might be seven shouldn't have to experience situations like that.

Kris noticed before Blaine did, and came over to join in our impromptu group hug, while their uncle watched them with a pained expression on his face, and took a single step towards us before shaking his head and stilling. He stood there awkwardly, but when Gregor finally let go, Blaine made a comment about how interesting Birch was, and was able to draw both kids into playful speculation about riding the creature when he got bigger, whether or not they would need a saddle, and if it would be uncomfortable. Obviously, he'd been paying attention to their interests.

I smiled at Blaine over their heads, and he smiled back, though it was strained.

We spent the night in the still-intact room of the tower and ate through a large portion of the supplies we'd brought with us. I didn't suggest rationing it, because we would surely need all the strength we could get, traveling through the Dark Lands.

Shortly after we left the bridge, sparse, prickly trees began to grow, becoming taller as we walked farther into them. They didn't affect our line of sight and were so scraggly they barely impeded the passage of the sunlight. Torliam didn't say anything, but I was watching carefully as he grew tenser and began to twitch at every sound.

Birch sensed it too, and kept growling low in his throat.

Finally, Torliam stopped us, hand raised silently in the air as he looked around. Something was up ahead, though I couldn't sense far enough to tell what it was.

He pointed to the side, and we began to circle around in a wide arc, as silently as possible. When had we stopped speaking aloud, resorting to nonverbal cues for fear of being overheard? Probably about the same time Birch stopped growling. After a certain point, you knew when it was time to run and hide rather than stand out.

Eventually, the ground sloped upward, and the trees gained some more leaves, beginning to resemble evergreens.

I reached the top of the ridge first, and caught sight of what we were avoiding.

An…amalgamation. It was settled in the center of a huge web, which stretched across the valley of scraggly trees, covering the easy path through that we had avoided. Its top half looked like a particularly lumpy-skulled monkey. The bottom was that of a spider, oval-shaped and eight-legged.

I froze unconsciously, sinking down so that I could barely see over the fallen tree trunk in front of me. The others followed suit, crawling up to look out over the edge.

The creature quivered in place, hunched down, and wrapped around on itself. The web shivered outward from the center, shaking a group of much smaller spider-monkey creatures that were huddled near the edge of the web, watching the big one.

It lifted its head slowly, as if its muscles were creaky from disuse, and turned toward the huddling group of little ones.

They flinched back, monkey faces grimacing in obvious fear.

It stood, shrieked, and waved its arms, and chased them off the web. Its stick-like, hairy legs worked in tandem to propel its body at an absurd speed. It picked up a gigantic club off the ground, obviously made out of a tree trunk big enough to match its size, and waved it at them for good measure, still screeching. Was it shooing possible competitors away from its territory?

Its shriek hurt my ears, like nails on a chalkboard mixed with a rusty grinding sound. Its body was emaciated and pale compared to the proportions of the little ones, except for the stomach of its monkey part, sitting above the junction of primate and arachnid. The stomach was grossly distended, the fur peeling off and skin stretched taut like a balloon that was one more breath away from popping.

Its legs seemed to lose control then, some of them pushing forward, and some moving back and tangling with the others. The creature crashed to the ground and flailed around with its club till the trees trembled and even more of their leaves fell off. Then, it was on its feet again and skittering back to the web, which it shot to the top of. A few seconds of calm silence passed, and then it tore into the web with the club in its monkey arms, its spider legs, and even its teeth. Foamy spit slobbered out around those fanged teeth and a lolling, blue-purple, swollen tongue.

Once the web was hanging in tatters, it stopped again. Its head swiveled towards the still-running little ones. Then it shot off after them.

It fell on a straggler first, the club smashing into the thing's head and pulping it, instantly killing it.

The big one didn't hesitate, literally falling onto the smaller corpse, and tearing at it with hands and teeth. It didn't chew, it just shoved pieces of the little one down its throat and swallowed.

The other small spider-monkeys screamed with all too human voices and expressions of terror when they noticed the fate of the straggler and ran away even faster. But it was no use, because the big one left that its first victim behind half-eaten, and did the same to another, and another.

The big one screamed out, a continuous keening wail. The sound was muffled every time it stuffed a chunk of flesh down its throat, but never cut off completely.

Torliam laid a hand on my shoulder, making me jump in surprise. "Let us go. Before it is through with them, and turns its attention toward us," he whispered.

I nodded, and we hurried away, circumventing the whole area without another peep.

Birch jumped atop my shoulders, digging his claws uncomfortably into my arm.

I gently moved Birch's paws and placed my hand on his head reassuringly.

When he judged us far enough away, Torliam stopped. His shoulders slumped a little in apparent exhaustion, and his eyes didn't quite focus on me, staring bleakly into the mid-distance. "Those were its children."

"What?"

"That was your first glimpse of the Sickness that infects my world. The creature was driven mad, till it could not recognize the difference between that which it loved and hated. Hunger overruled everything, until it devoured its children for the false hope of extending its own life. The Sickness is a traitor within you, turning you against all that you hold dear." He walked forward again, and only shook his head when questioned.

That night, while Jacky and Blaine were on lookout, I sparred with Torliam, and we exchanged answers again. "Tell me more about the Sickness," I said, perhaps slightly more imperiously than he preferred.

His eyes fell to the ground, and then rose again, locking on mine as he savagely pressed the attack. He knew defense was my weakest area. "The origin of the Sickness is unknown, even to me. If ever my people had the knowledge, it has been lost. But all know that it is the most…abhorrent thing in existence. It hits the weak and the strong with indifference, and even now, we do not know exactly how it spreads, because we cannot see it, only its effects. It seems to spread more quickly if one is in contact with an infected. Sometimes. And yet, it may also strike a lone hermit, who has not met another mortal for decades. We have found no way to guard against it, even after thousands upon thousands of years. It defies us, and takes all that we love from us, as if mocking our futile struggles to defeat it."

I made the connection. "It took someone from you," I said, my voice soft.

"My younger sister." His eyes grew distant, and the rage that had bubbled up when talking about the Sickness receded. "By the time she was born, my mother had ascended the throne."

I wanted to interrupt, because I was pretty sure he basically just told me his mom was royalty, which would make *him* royalty, but I restrained myself.

"My sister was groomed to lead from infancy, and the knowledge that the world loved her burned from her skin almost visibly. Everyone who met her doted on her."

I remembered the dream I'd had, after solving the Oracle's first gift. I had been someone else. I felt with a certainty that person had been Torliam, and I had witnessed his dream, or his memory, of a beautiful young girl, who he was describing with every reminiscent word.

Then, his expression deadened, and he began to speak in a clinically detached tone. "The Sickness affects all of life in different ways. It manifests in us as wasting disease, accompanied by a mental…dissociation. I believe that is the word. Hunger increases, a desire for living flesh, particularly that from a strong, intelligent creature. The diseased person's love and emotional connections putrefy, and everything they once loved or cared for becomes something they wish to consume. To destroy. I once saw a woman bite off the cheek of her partner, in her madness. The spark that makes a person what they are is deadened, and eventually leaves behind a creature that wishes only to destroy, desperate to prolong the life of the flesh husk wasting away around them."

He took a deep breath, and continued is a more clinical tone. "The body begins to die from the inside. Blood in the stool. Darkening veins. The limbs thin, while often the stomach bloats out grotesquely. The rate of degeneration increases more rapidly as time goes on, while in the beginning the infected may not show signs for some time. The Sickness is both the horror and the shame of our people, and our world."

He was silent for a while, and I considered what it would be like to watch Zed go through what his sister must have.

His arms dropped, and he released his fighting stance, turning away from me and walking toward the edge of camp.

I watched him as he walked away, wishing I could reach out my hand and stop him, tell him I had seen his beautiful young sister and I was sorry. But I didn't. I couldn't. I stayed silent, and he left.

WE TRAVELED for a few more days before anything else eventful happened. Sam regained his strength, the wound on his stomach leaving nothing but a scar. We had a few small skirmishes with the local flora and fauna, but nothing too exciting. We'd almost run out of food by that time, and it had been growing colder the farther north we went, so we jogged for the added benefits of faster travel, training, and the warmth it generated internally. A couple more levels in the physical Attributes could never hurt, and even the fully normal members of our group could grow stronger and fitter from the exertion.

We were constantly on guard, though, and the tension was almost as draining as the physical exertion. Our packs were light with the lack of food, and we'd been hunting the local wildlife when we could, and foraging what few plants Torliam knew to be edible.

Zed was, surprisingly, the best of us at hunting the local wildlife. He seemed preternaturally gifted with his guns, making shots at angles and distances that seemed impossible to me. "I don't think it's all my own natural talent," he said. "NIX probably did something to make me better at this. When I'm calculating a shot, something about my thoughts… changes. I do calculations on the fly that feel like instinct, but they aren't."

One afternoon, I was just about to suggest we stop and see if we could find something for a midday meal, when a whistle tore through the air, followed almost instantly by an arrow.

We scattered, some dropping to the ground and rolling, some slipping behind nearby trees. I jerked Zed and Chanelle behind a tree, and Jacky went *up* a tree, hiding in the foliage and literally dragging Kris and Gregor with her. I cursed myself for not keeping my awareness constantly extended. I'd been doing a quick scan to the limit of my reach every hour or so, which meant whoever was attacking must have come upon us quickly.

Chanelle let out a small sound of unhappiness, but I ignored her. Sam and Blaine had been slowly re-introducing Seeds into her system, and there seemed to be a response. She wasn't close to being normal, but she wasn't quite so catatonic, either. However, in situations like this, that wasn't helpful.

I pushed Wraith outward and saw that our opponents already surrounded us on three sides, and were circling around behind us. They shone with power, kind of like Torliam did, in that extra sense Wraith provided me with.

—We're surrounded. Eight of them. Stronger than us.—
-Eve-

Adam grimaced and threw up shields twice his height around us in a wide circle, roughly defending the group's location, though it also stopped us from being able to cleanly attack.

Torliam, the only one who hadn't scattered immediately at the warning shot, shouted something in his language, loud and imperious. Our attackers slowed, as if startled.

After a few seconds, someone shouted back, and Torliam lifted his arms and started to glow, that light blue luminescence wafting off him like thick smoke.

There was another shout, and Torliam turned to Adam. "Lower one of your shields. They are from a small village near here. I will talk with them, there is no need to engage in combat."

Adam looked to me for approval before complying, but Torliam waited patiently.

An Estreyan moved forward from between the trees, riding atop an ostrich-like creature. He stopped just outside the gap Adam had created in the shield line.

Torliam said something, puffing out his chest and somehow managing to look down on the man, despite his lower position on the ground.

The man scowled, but seemed unsure.

Torliam waved to us and spoke some more, seeming even more irritated.

One of the bird-rider's companions joined him, and they spoke in murmurs that I could hear clearly but couldn't understand a word of. Then the first guy nodded and said something.

"They will escort us to the village," Torliam said. "Lower the shields."

Adam shook his head. "How do I know they won't attack us when I do?"

"*My* people believe in honor," Torliam said, the inflection carrying an obvious insult.

I considered for a bit, then released Zed and Chanelle, and stepped out behind the tree to stand next to Adam. "Go ahead," I said. "They might be helpful, if they're friendly. And if they decide to attack right now, I wouldn't bet on our odds."

Adam grimaced, his hair lifting due to the tension-driven static electricity escaping his body, but he complied.

The Estreyans, probably a patrol group, closed in around us, eyeing us with some distaste. We all looked a little ragged. If they had high enough Perception, they were probably also offended by our smell. Wilderness travel doesn't mesh the best with stellar hygiene.

One of them motioned to the tree, and with a bit of rustling, Jacky and the kids fell out of it with a startled yelp.

The Estreyan who had waved his hand smirked at them, but I noticed that they all kept their mounts a safe distance away, as if worried they might get dirty from touching us.

As we began to move, I kept my awareness spread out, and noticed the looks the Estreyans shot each other when they thought we weren't looking. They were afraid.

IT TOOK about an hour to reach the village at our jogging pace, though the riders could no doubt have gone much faster on their own. I'd tried to ask Torliam what was going on, but he refused to be drawn into conversation, just shaking his head silently. The trees thinned, allowing the huge, flat-topped village wall to be visible from far away. It towered above everything, and seemed to be made of whole, huge tree trunks stacked flush against each other. Cleared land circled the village, probably for farming or livestock grazing. And for visibility from the sentinel towers spaced into the wall at intervals.

The sentinels stationed there noticed us, and by the time we passed through the guarded gate into the village, others had gathered along the edge of the street or were peeking through their windows. Visually, the place reminded me of a mix between old-timey log cabins and Asian architecture. Wood seemed to be the primary building material, but the buildings had peaked roofs that swooped down, and the aesthetics were beautiful in their simplicity.

Estreyans stopped and stared as we passed, going silent in waves that radiated outward. They dressed in thick, baggy clothing that seemed to wrap and tie around them, rather than being fitted or held up by belts. Both the people and the buildings were a bit shabby, as if they'd stopped having the resources for repairs or new materials a few years ago. Or maybe they'd just stopped caring.

One woman stared out at us, and I could feel a palpable aura of despair wafting off her. It had to be Skill-related, and judging from the way others avoided her, they could feel it too. But it wasn't just her. Despair was elsewhere among them, though less obvious.

A young woman, barely out of childhood, stared out from an alley between houses, the bags under her eyes so prominent they looked like bruises. No one would look at her, and if they accidentally did, they looked away quickly. One mother even crossed the street with her child to avoid the young woman.

My senses were still extended a few yards beyond the group, and I could tell that the villagers were powerful, compared to us. I felt vulnerable under their stares and had to resist the almost subconscious urge to slip out my claws and bare my teeth at them. My hair stood at attention, my skin prickled, and I felt like I was walking willingly into a pit of writhing snakes. There was danger here, all around us. It felt like the intro to a horror film, or maybe the aftermath of a war film.

Torliam damn well better know what he was doing, I swore silently. He was the only one who really knew what was going on, and if he screwed up or betrayed us, I was going to flay him alive with my claws.

The patrol brought us to a large, mansion-like house, and stopped outside while the leader sent someone inside. Whoever lived there was obviously important. No doubt they would decide our fate.

Many of the Estreyans we had passed on the way had followed, eyeing us curiously and murmuring amongst themselves. Perhaps they had never seen people as small as us before. Or maybe they just weren't used to outsiders.

The person who had gone inside returned with a very old woman, and a female who stood unobtrusively off to the side, perhaps a servant. The old woman was so wrinkled she looked like a half-dehydrated, human-colored raisin, but she stood straight, and I could sense the power in her. This creature, woman, whatever she was, could destroy my group, literally, within the space of a few breaths if she tried.

Obviously, the villagers respected this elder, too, because they fell silent when she appeared.

Torliam half-bowed to the elder, and when the elder nodded back, he began to speak.

At this point, I really wished I could understand the language, because the tension was high, and I was standing there like an idiot, trying to understand what was going on by voice inflection and body language. I glanced over at Zed, whose eyes were darting about, taking everything in.

The leader of the patrol group spoke then, obviously arguing against whatever Torliam had said. He waved his hand toward our group and spoke angrily, and some of the other patrol members and people in the crowd nodded at his words, murmuring softly.

Torliam's shoulders tensed, and I felt my own follow suit.

Zed grimaced, and then looked back to the elder expectantly.

—ARE YOU ACTUALLY FOLLOWING WHAT THEY'RE SAYING?—

-EVE-

Zed's eyes jumped to mine, startled.

—I'M DEFINITELY UNDERSTANDING MORE OF THIS THAN I SHOULD. I CAN'T CATCH THE WORDS, BUT I FEEL LIKE I HAVE A VAGUE CONCEPT OF WHAT SOME OF THEM MEAN.—

-ZED-

Torliam spoke again, waving his hand in the air to punctuate his words, and resting it on my shoulder, guiding me to take a step forward and stand beside him.

I met his eyes in surprise. What did he want? I couldn't speak the language, so how was I supposed to plead our case?

I copied Torliam's bow toward the elder as best I could, which for some reason caused a bit of murmuring in the crowd. When I raised my head, I saw the elder look at the sparkling multi-banded ring on my left forefinger.

Then she looked at Birch, huffing in amusement when the little creature growled at her, ruffling his little ragged, fluffy wings in a hint of threat.

The elder looked back to me, looking me up and down in a way I would have said was ogling, if she wasn't so *deadly* focused on me.

She spoke, finally, and nodded back at me, the same slight tilt she'd given to Torliam. That made the crowd murmur again, but she silenced them with her words, turning back to her doorway. She said something to her female attendant, who bowed respectfully.

Whatever it was the elder had said, the leader of the patrol didn't like it, and raised his voice in outrage.

The elder gave him a single look and a few soft words, and the younger man backed down.

He shot a glare at us when she turned away again.

"We have been granted asylum," Torliam said simply. "We will lodge in this…how do you say it? Residence?"

I raised an eyebrow. I was pretty sure there'd been a little bit more to it than that. "I need subtitles," I muttered.

The attendant waved at us to follow her inside, and the patrol leader glared at each of us as we passed by him.

I made sure to hold my head high and stare unflinchingly back at him. It wouldn't do to seem cowed or weak. Predators could sense that, like sharks smelled blood in the water. And if the creatures of Estreyer had something in common, it's that they were all predators.

"What was the argument back there?" I murmured to Torliam.

He hesitated for a bit, but finally said, "They have secluded themselves to try and avoid contact with the Sickness. The villagers were worried that we would bring it in from outside and pass it to them."

I knew I still wasn't getting the full picture, but he clamped his lips together and moved further away from me. I'd have to ambush him later and get the truth out of him. Perhaps if no one was listening in he'd be less tight-lipped.

The attendant led us to a short hallway and motioned toward the doors lining it, indicating the rooms were to be ours. I directed the weaker members of our group toward the middle doors, flanked by stronger members.

I wish I could say that being within civilization again eased my mind. But that would have been a lie.

THE ELDER'S female attendant let us rest for an hour, and then gathered us for a meal in one of the larger rooms near our hallway. When we had finished stuffing ourselves, she said something in Estreyan and motioned for Torliam and me to follow her.

He seemed unconcerned, maybe even a bit eager, so I went along with her request.

I sent him a questioning look behind her back.

"She is taking us to the bathing room," he said. "We are the ones highest in honor among the group, so we go first."

A bath sounded wonderful. "The others aren't going to have to use our dirty water or anything, right?"

"Do you bathe in each other's water on Earth?" he asked, mouth drawing down in disgust.

"No, but I hear we used to, before technology advanced."

"Rest assured, we passed that point of technological advancement *long* ago." He shook his head, as if exasperated. At the attendant's word, he split off to enter the male section. "We also separate the genders for bathing," he said with a curl of his lip that was more joke than sneer.

Birch followed me into the bath, and after we were finished scrubbing and soaking, the attendant gave me new, warmer clothes to wear over my armored vest.

A quick stretch of my Wraith Skill told me Torliam had already finished his own bath. His signature was faint, a few streets away.

Birch meowed plaintively at me, so I took him outside to relieve himself and go for a little walk, heading towards Torliam. Birch had fun sniffing about, until we passed a pair of boots airing on someone's porch. He sniffed them, growled at the scent, then crouched over them and pooped right down the mouth of one.

My jaw dropped, and I looked around to make sure no one was watching. "What are you doing?" I whispered harshly at him.

He flicked his ears back and ignored me, peeing into the other boot. When he was finished, he ruffled his feathers and pranced off with a distinctly self-satisfied hop in his step.

"Were those the patrol leader's shoes?" I asked, following him.

Birch flicked his tail.

I suppressed a snicker.

We caught up to Torliam pretty quickly, though my relaxation leached away the longer I was outside.

Torliam turned to me with some surprise, and the younger Estreyan man he'd been talking to slipped away. "You look better when you are clean," he said. He did, too. In fact, I realized this was the first time I'd ever actually seen him bathed and groomed.

"You're all…dignified," I said.

"I *am* the son of a queen," he said, but there was no malice in his voice. When Birch grunted up at him, he leaned over so that the creature could hop atop his back and scramble up to sit on one shoulder.

"What was all that about earlier? With the meeting in front of the elder's house?" I said.

"Some of them did not want us to stay, but I was able to convince the elder to grant us asylum. We are under her protection, as long as we are under her roof. Did you not comprehend this earlier?"

I bared my teeth at him. "Exactly how did you convince the elder? And exactly what do my gifts from the Oracle have to do with it?"

His stride hitched, almost imperceptibly. "It is law that should one of my line require asylum, the people must grant it. This would have been enough, ordinarily. But the fear is strong, here. It is one of the most insidious side effects of the Sickness. The uncertainty, never knowing when it might strike, or if it is already lying dormant in yourself or one you love, is difficult. There is no single way the Sickness spreads, and there are some cases where our best healers and scientists do not know how it could have done so. In some people, this uncertainty leads to them fearing anything and everything, whether there is true danger or not."

"This is fascinating. Don't think you can avoid my second question, though. You knew the elder would find the puzzle bands significant."

"Gifts from the Oracle are rumored to have been given to those with a great task or destiny to fulfill, in the stories so old almost no one remembers them anymore," he said, reaching a hand up to push the dirty blonde hair off his neck and rub the tense muscle there. "In this situation, I thought the elder would be knowledgeable enough about Estreyan history to notice them. Long ago, when my people first came to your world, it is said that some of them found the small beings on your planet pleasing, and had relations with them."

I narrowed my eyes. "Had *relations*? You mean they had sex with the humans."

"Yes. It is unfathomable, I know. Nevertheless, you may be the descendant of one of my people's lines, and I was reasonably confident she would deduce that."

As in…I'm part Estreyan?"

"Of course. How else would you survive the Seeds? They are of my world."

My eyes widened. When he put it like that… "Wait. But my brother doesn't have the gene. He wouldn't have survived the initiation if not for Sam."

"You are sure he is your brother?"

"Yes!" I said, but realized I'd never considered that question before. We had the same dark hair and tall build. I raised my hands, fingers splayed wide, looking at the scars on the edge of both pinky fingers. "I was born with an extra finger on both hands," I said. "And an extra toe. I didn't even think about it being somehow connected to your people. On Earth, it's just considered a mutation. My mother had them removed so I wouldn't be considered strange."

"She…cut off your fingers?" He said in a low voice, staring at me in shock. "Just so you could be more like the other *two-legged-maggots*?"

"It wasn't malicious. She didn't want me to be strange, to have to deal with the social stigma of being different. But my point was, Zed didn't have any extra digits. And she…was so happy about that." I muttered the last bit, a tendril of doubt wriggling into my thoughts. Why didn't Zed have the gene?

Torliam seemed to guess my thoughts, or maybe their path was just obvious. "You are most likely extremely distant descendants. It is possible, and even likely, that the human gene just dominated over the Estreyan in your brother's case."

I nodded. "So, every one of the Players is part Estreyan?" I didn't know our father, and for the first time in a long while, I wondered about his whereabouts. Was he like me? Or was it my mother who had passed on the gene?

I waited for Torliam to answer my question, but instead of talking he turned to look down the street.

I followed his gaze to the group of Estreyans gathered to one side. I'd been so focused on our conversation that I hadn't been paying attention to the mounting tension up ahead. Voices were raised within the group, and outside, people turned their faces away and scurried on.

I was reminded uncomfortably of the first Seed I'd ever taken. I'd been so sick, just left on the side of the road, and everyone around me looked away and pretended they couldn't see, if they were kind. If they weren't, they'd sneered at me and swerved away in disgust.

Bodies shifted, and I caught a glimpse of the young woman I'd noticed earlier, shoulders hunched up, head tucked down. She flinched as someone threw an egg at her dark hair.

Torliam sped up, calling out sharply in Estreyan.

I lengthened my stride to match him, preemptive adrenaline surging through my veins.

Chapter 18

The night has a thousand eyes,
And the day but one;
Yet the light of the bright world dies
With the dying sun.
—Francis William Bourdillon

WHEN WE REACHED THE GROUP, Torliam spoke again, his voice low and angry.

One of the villagers spit toward the girl and laughed, and Torliam thrummed with power, light wafting off his skin as he activated his signature Skill.

The girl said something, her voice small but defiant.

Whatever she'd said, it enraged one of the women on the inside of the circle. She raised her hand and stepped forward, swinging her arm for a powerful slap.

The girl just closed her eyes and cringed, so I stepped forward, bringing both hands above my head to catch the blow.

The older woman gaped down at me, and didn't seem to know whether to be shocked or angry.

I guided her hand down slowly, keeping my eyes locked on her face, while my awareness swirled around searching for any danger I couldn't see.

Torliam said something, and the woman's eyes moved to my glittering armband, then to him, then to my eyes.

She drew back, the angry flush draining away from her face, leaving it unnaturally pale. She bowed to me, picked up a basket, and hurried away with no more than a glance over her shoulder to the young woman. "Damn, I *really* need to learn Estreyan," I muttered.

Torliam waved his hands at the others, and the blue mist pushed them back, giving them the impetus to disperse. He turned to the girl, using more of that endlessly versatile mist to help clean the egg out of her hair.

Birch grabbed one of the girl's shoes, which I hadn't noticed was missing, and brought it back to her.

She smiled, then sniffed back tears as she slipped the shoe back onto her dirty foot.

Her murmured conversation with Torliam was interrupted by the patrol leader from yesterday, who called out angrily and stomped up.

He shoved himself between the girl and Torliam, forcing her behind him. His fists were balled up, and he glared at Torliam in challenge.

The girl laid her hand on his shoulder and said something that made him relax, pointing to Torliam, and then to me.

There was a moment of awkwardness, before he gave a small bow to Torliam, and then to me. He didn't smile, and he didn't exactly look *grateful*, but there was respect in his eyes, at least.

As he walked away with the girl, I turned to Torliam. "So, what was that about?"

"She is his sister. Her husband died of the Sickness. Some of the villagers are afraid she will spread it to them. They have been trying to drive her out, though the elder has openly stated that there is no evidence you will contract the Sickness just from proximity to one who has it, or has been exposed to it."

"I really need to learn Estreyan," I said.

He stared at me till I grew irritated. When he finally opened his mouth to speak, I prepared to snap back at him, but he surprised me. "You should learn to defend yourself," he said thoughtfully. "Both in word and in action. I am already teaching you how to fight better than a half-drowned pup. Any companion of mine should at least be *literate*."

"You're so kind," I said sarcastically.

"My benevolence is renowned." He grinned at me, the expression making him look much younger, and taking the sting off his insults.

I turned to Birch. "Why do you let him insult me like this? You'd think a good tailos would at least bite him a little."

Birch looked to me, and then to Torliam, and let out a little grunt.

AFTER THE INCIDENT, the villagers were a lot more accepting. Or respectful, at least. Zed took to spending all his time among them, and quickly charmed them with his "tiny" size, quick smile, and willingness to make a fool out of himself miming things as he learned their language.

It turned out one of the nanite chips NIX had implanted in his brain gave him an unfair advantage in that field.

Blaine speculated that they had been attempting to develop an artificial version of Skills to go with their attempt at Seeds.

Zed couldn't actively tell when the chips were working, but he was picking up the language supernaturally quickly, especially with the constant practice.

In contrast, I was quite frustrated with my own progress. My Intelligence was way higher than it had been back when I was a normal civilian, but after a couple days of intense study, I was still barely learning rudimentary vocabulary and child-level sentence structure.

Even Blaine and Gregor were better at it than me, and neither of them had Seeds at all, which was pretty depressing.

Torliam said there would be time to learn, since the village didn't have a communication device—they had purposefully isolated themselves from the rest of Estreyan society—but they did have a supply convoy that would be heading to another village that did have a comms system. It would be a while before the convoy left, but we had been invited to travel with them. In the meantime, Torliam planned to teach me and the team how to fight, and how to speak and read the language, for those who were interested. Once we had a basic understanding, he said we had been authorized to search through the village's store of knowledge for information about the God of Knowledge and the Oracle, so there was added incentive.

I was sitting at the edge of the training fields outside the main wall. It was mainly open fields for sparring or practicing with the more destructive Skills, but some of them had trees or stumps to attack, or different types of terrain.

Adam had created a bigger version of Birch out of ink, and Kris rode atop it, shrieking with laughter as she raced the original Birch across the field. Adam called out a warning, and she dismounted before the construct disintegrated, immediately begging him to, "make another one!"

Zed plopped down beside me. "Guess what I just learned?" He kept talking before I had a chance to speak. "They have a healer!" He nodded at my look of surprise. "Yeah. They were being sloppy with the new arrowheads, and Egon dropped some molten metal on his foot. They shooed him right off to the *healer*. I don't know how this person's Skill works, or if they'd be strong enough to fix what's wrong with you and Chanelle, but what if they can?"

I scrambled to my feet. "That's wonderful, Zed! Do you know where they are?"

He shrugged. "I can ask one of the villagers."

We went back to our hall of the elder's house and found Blaine and Sam both sitting with Chanelle.

Blaine was tinkering with a small ball of metal, using tiny little tools that looked more like metal toothpicks than anything, and he didn't even look up when we entered.

"She's making mental associations!" Sam said without preamble. "She can tell the difference between red and blue, and point out the correct one when I show her an example to match up with. Not every time… She gets distracted, but this is progress!"

Zed told him about the healer, and Sam grew quiet, then stood up. "I'm coming with you. Maybe…maybe this healer can help figure out what's wrong with my ability, too."

The healer turned out to be an old man with one of the nicer houses. He was a bit suspicious, but after Zed introduced us, and the man got a close look at my gifts from the Oracle, including a valiant attempt to make the ring come off my finger, he let us into his house.

He tried to work on Chanelle first, making her sit in a bare spot on his stone floor that had diagrams drawn all over it. Then he stared at her really hard. He questioned Zed, eyes widening at the response. He shook his head sadly in the universal symbol for "kids these days," and returned to staring at her. Eventually, he shook his head again and waved her away with an irritated "harrumph!"

"What does that mean?" Sam asked.

Zed talked back and forth with the man, and said, "I don't know all the vocabulary he's using, but I think he's saying that any wounds caused by the direct touch of a…higher power?" He shrugged, "They aren't something he can heal." He talked with the man a bit more, waving his hands about and miming things to convey concepts he didn't have the words for. Then he said, "So, if a god punches you in the side and breaks your ribs with its fist, you can probably be healed. If the god uses a 'power' attack—maybe like a Skill?—then a wound that breaks the skin is way harder to heal. I don't know if I'm really understanding the concept, but in any case, he can't fix Chanelle's brain."

"Maybe that's why I can't help her," Sam said, relief tinting his voice for a moment. "But it doesn't explain the backlash, and the way I can't control if I heal or hurt someone anymore."

I sat in the middle of the circle next, while Zed explained what was wrong with me.

The old man's eyes grew bright, and he peered at me even harder than he had Chanelle. He asked questions about how I'd gotten the Seed of Chaos in the first place, how I'd been using it, and what effects had come from the Oracle's gifts. By the way he suppressed an eager little smile, I had a sneaking suspicion that he wanted to know these things so he could gossip about them later, rather than because they would help him diagnose or heal me.

Finally, he sat back and shook his head, stating something final, from which I caught the word, "die."

Zed looked pained and asked him a question before he translated the answer fully into English. "He says you're going to die if Chaos does not stop attacking you. And as it is the direct power of a god causing your condition, there is nothing he can do about it. He said he knows of no healer in the world that could heal you, though there may be a couple who could keep you alive a little while longer. There is a healer in the capital who may be able to help. Ifkana of the Panacean. He recommends we go to Ifkana when we get to the capital."

Sam heaved out a sigh. "It's not my fault, thank goodness," he whispered. When we both turned to stare at him, he straightened. "Not that it makes what's happening any better! It's just—I felt like a failure. I mean, I'm supposed to be able to fix things like this, and I couldn't, and I've been so *useless* lately—"

I interrupted. "It's fine, Sam. This was never your fault." I had decided to take the Seed of Chaos on my own. Even with the warning from Behelaino. I stood up and walked out of the center of the painted diagrams. "Your turn, now."

Zed once again explained what was wrong to the healer, who sprinkled white powder on Sam's head.

When the healer's back was turned, Sam sent me a disbelieving look.

—He just dumped chalk on me. Is this old guy pranking us? —

-Sam-

I smothered a laugh and shrugged.

Finally, the old man threw up his hands, said, "Agh!" and shook his head before turning to yammer at Zed, who translated as he talked.

"He says, we come to him with unsolvable problems, do we try and mock him? The fair-haired—blonde—one is not a healer. He's not going to be fooled by us. Or maybe we're stupid—"

"Wait," Sam said. "What does he mean, I'm not a healer?" He pressed his hands to his thighs and met my eyes for a second. I knew we were both thinking of the same thing. His Harbinger Skill was of the Ruination Class.

"He says it is a balanced power. You must take what you give and give what you take." Zed shook his head. "What does that even mean?"

Sam didn't wait for him to ask the old man. "I can't heal…unless I offload that damage somewhere else?"

"Yes, basically," Zed said, after translating the question and receiving an answer back. "He says you are unbalanced, and your power will turn against you if you try to change its nature, or to leash it."

Sam didn't speak again until Zed had thanked the healer profusely, we had left his house, and were walking down the street. Then Sam stopped, and turned to me. "I don't want to kill people, Eve." His voice broke on my name.

"We'll find some other way," I said. I wasn't sure I believed it. But we'd definitely try. Even if I hadn't cared about Sam at all, the team couldn't afford to lose its healer.

IT GREW COLDER over the next couple weeks, and the green things started to wither away. I trained with Torliam and the others every day.

He thought I was sloppy and relied on my Grace too much, rather than actual skill. He also thought I was weak, slow, tactically incompetent, and remarked repeatedly how generally amazed he was that I was even alive to learn from him. And I *was* learning.

It had made me respect him in a new way, because even if your blood was *pure* Seeds and your bones were made out of steel, it would still take thousands of hours of practice to be at his level as a fighter. He knew what he was doing, and he knew what I was doing wrong. The only downside was that he liked to show me what I was doing wrong by showing me once, maybe twice, then beating it into me.

He didn't say it, but I thought I had a talent for battle, because I learned quickly, instinctually. Even Torliam couldn't fault me in that.

Sam had tried attacking Adam's Animations with the destructive side of his Skill, but the relief of "pressure" from doing that was apparently close to negligible. He didn't want to hurt animals unless he had to, so he attacked plants, taking two other people from the team with him as he ventured into the forest, making things wither, explode, crystallize, and quite a few of the other destructive effects he'd absorbed over his time as a Player. That worked better, though still *very* slowly. Still, it was a solution that didn't involve hurting anyone.

I learned enough Estreyan to inch my way through their texts. The library held everything from old books to these cool little chips that could project information right into the eye of the "reader." They were one of the surprisingly few examples of advanced Estreyan technology I'd seen in the village.

Blaine loved the library and seemed to be trying to gorge himself on the information equivalent of eating an entire blue whale. He may have been succeeding. Unlike me, he picked up the language with astonishing ease. I mean, I had already known he was a genius, but the way he worked with science seemed more like magic to me. This was something new, and I felt a healthy dose of respect and morose jealousy for his brain.

All of us who could read spent hour upon hour in the library, searching for relevant information about the God of Knowledge, and my problem. I had never been more grateful for my boost to Intelligence, because I don't think my progress would have been possible otherwise. In fact, I'd had quite a few spontaneous level-ups to my mental Attributes while learning, and even to my Stamina.

All of the electronically archived things were searchable by keyword, so finding reference to the God of Knowledge or the Oracle wasn't the problem. Finding relevant, *new* information about either of them *was.* They didn't make public appearances very often anymore, it seemed.

I found a picture of a mural with the God of Knowledge's name on it and showed it to Torliam.

Rather than being mildly interested or explaining the background behind it like I'd expected, he stared at it, frowned, and stared at it some more. "There are old paintings," he said. "From before the God of Knowledge removed himself from the presence of mortals. I have seen them, in my research into our past. He had a temple once. There is a painting of him in it, quite like this, the roof open to the sky, people supplicating before him, and golden rods shooting into the sky. Golden light stretching into the sky…everything within it…"

"What?"

"Within the range of his divination. I think those were the words. All that lies under the light is within range of his power."

"Why didn't you mention this before?"

"I—" He closed his mouth, and opened it again, with a small frown. "I had *forgotten.* It seemed insignificant." The words were fairly innocuous, but he shot me a look of silent alarm, wide-eyed and tight-lipped. His skin had paled, and his jaw was clenched so the skin stretched over it a bit too tightly.

It made me realize how weak he still must be, after what NIX had done to him. He was easily stronger than me, but I could only imagine what he must have once been. What he would be again. A creature with enough Intelligence that forgetting something was an anomaly.

"I have studied this before…" He pressed his lips together. "I have spent my life studying these things, trying to find a cure for the Sickness. They say that he secluded himself to do the same. *I have studied this before, and I have forgotten.*" His expression spoke as much as his words.

I kept my expression as neutral as possible, trying not to show my alarm. He had forgotten something important enough that it was dangerous, which meant something had *made* him forget. "How far does the light stretch?" I asked. Were we even now within the god's range?

"I do not know. But we should be wary."

That was worrying, but it didn't change the vision I'd received from the Oracle.

Torliam's head jerked to the side, staring at the blank wall with such a horrified expression that I sank into a crouch with my claws out, hair rising in alarm.

I snapped my awareness out to search for the danger, but found nothing unusual. "What's wrong?"

He didn't have to answer me, because the black cube that formed in front of my face, asking if I wished to enter the Trial, explained everything.

Chapter 19

Be like snow. Silent and cold.
— Citron Aodh

I GOT a barrage of Windows from my teammates who had seen the cube. I told them not to worry. Enough time had passed on Earth for NIX to fix the Shortcut, and they had sent their Players out on a Trial. No big deal.

Even so, the others gathered in the library with Torliam and I. Perhaps it was a subconscious thing—safety in numbers.

"How could you tell?" I asked Torliam. "You knew a Trial had started, even before the cube."

"I feel all those that I have been forced to form a bastardized blood-covenant with," he said simply. "The disconnect between your world and mine had given me some blessed relief for a while, but now they are here, spread all over the weaker lands in groups." He turned back to me, relaxing somewhat. "I hope they are all annihilated before the gods of those Trials."

Over the course of the next few hours, Torliam announced when individual Trials across the world ended, removing their still-living Players from his consciousness. It grew late, and most of the group's tension leached away in favor of fatigue, but Torliam didn't relax.

"Is something wrong?" I asked.

"One group remains. Too much time has passed. It is not likely they are still in a Trial."

"Maybe they're trying something like what my group did, escaping NIX's clutches by camping out over here. Or maybe this is a special expedition, not Players sent to petition the Trial gods. I heard they've been trying to do research about your world, pick up old technology, etcetera," I said.

Torliam was slightly pacified, but as morning came, and then evening again, and they had not left, he grew distracted and ever more on edge. That tension spread back to the rest of the team. When he revealed that the Players had begun traveling in our direction, we lost any sense of ease we'd gained since coming to the hidden village.

The other Players moved closer over the next few days, till we were all on the brittle edge of fear and anticipation, and constantly asking Torliam for updates. We speculated that they were tracing us somehow, and NIX had sent a retrieval team for the valuable assets we represented. Or an assassination team.

Then, I had an idea. I sent Windows to the team and sent Birch to retrieve Torliam, and all of us except Kris and Gregor met in the library. I spread out a large map on the floor. "Point out where we are," I said to Torliam.

He did something to a little metal tab on its corner, and the drawings on the map wavered, the contents changing, flashing through different settings like it was diving downwards through them. "It shows the main layer now, which we are on. Somewhere around here is the village." He pointed to a blank spot, with no dot or label to indicate that people actually lived there.

I eyed the map, picking out landmarks and labels. "We started… here?" There was no marking for the Estreyan Stonehenge, so I was pointing to a blank spot.

"Yes."

I drew my finger haltingly along the map. "And the God of Knowledge is somewhere around here?" I waved a big, vague circle to the northwest of the village.

"Yes."

"So…what if they're not coming for us? I think they have no idea we're even here."

Everyone was focused on me, and Adam crouched down beside me to look at the map himself, already catching onto my meaning. "They want the God of Knowledge? How would they even know where to look?"

"NIX has been piecing together information about Estreyer since the beginning," Blaine said.

"Or…" a horrible thought filled my head. "Somehow, they got the information from me, or one of us."

"I did not say anything," Blaine said.

"I didn't mean by betrayal. What if they…have mind readers, or something? I mean, would that be such a crazy Skill?"

Torliam shook his head. "Skills such as that would not be gained from the lesser gods. At *most*, their Thinkers have extrapolated information based on data."

"However, this might have indeed been incited by you, Eve," Blaine said. "You were able to gain power by going directly after a god, and then used that against them. They would obviously wish to level the playing field, or at least make up in some small way for the great loss they have incurred from our escape."

Never mind that, I couldn't allow them to ruin my chances of getting aid from the God of Knowledge. "We need to follow them," I said aloud, my eyes focused on the vague area of the map where the god resided.

"Are you crazy?" Adam said.

I FROWNED AT ADAM. "There's no way I can just let this happen without having any idea what's going."

"It could be dangerous, Eve! Why can't you just stay safely away? I know you have this burning need to be in the middle of things, but—"

"I'm dying. As far as I know, the God of Knowledge is probably the only one who can help me. I can't just let another team of Players go after something so vital, completely unsupervised! And don't worry, I'm not going to drag the whole team into it. Just me, and…" I looked around at them, judging their suitability for this mission. I'd promised myself I wouldn't put them in needless danger by rushing into an unknown, potentially dangerous situation like I had when China was killed. "And Torliam."

"What!?" Adam, Sam, Jacky, and Zed said in unison.

Chanelle whimpered, frowning at the heightened tension.

"This is a stealth mission. Recon. There's no need to bring everyone along, and it will be safer if people who don't need to be there stay behind."

"Wasn't the plan to get stronger, and maybe get Torliam to rustle up some reinforcements from his royal family *before* you went rushing off to confront another god? The last time this happened, we had to fight. Sam almost died!"

"*Exactly*. You guys don't need to do this again. You'll be safe, whether or not I complete my vision."

"I've been training, every day," Jacky said, clenching her fists. "And I still have a lot of Seeds left, if I need them. It won't be like that mock battle, or when Vaughn beat us. I can be useful, Eve." Her voice was hard, but her eyes were begging.

Adam nodded. "She's right. What if you meet the other group, and they're hostile? If they're from NIX, they're almost certainly going to be hostile. If you *do* get into trouble, you might need help. We all have different skill-sets, and that's what makes us so effective as a team."

"There's no way you'd let one of *us* do something stupid like this by ourselves," Sam said, crossing his arms over his chest like that was the end of it.

"It's dangerous," I said weakly. "This is one of the strongest gods, and I'm almost certain he isn't going to be friendly, if the vision was correct. I plan to observe from as far away as possible, but if some of the things Torliam and I found are correct, even that might not be safe."

Adam ran a hand through his hair. "You do realize why that's not a good argument?"

Zed spoke, finally. "You're the leader of this team, Eve. But you're not the boss of me. I'm coming. And you don't need to worry about me. I know you hate what NIX did to me, but at least I can protect myself now." He turned to Jacky. "You need a hand packing up?"

She relaxed a bit and nodded sharply. "Yeah." She didn't look at me as they left.

Blaine pushed his glasses up and met my gaze. "I think you are foolish to even consider going alone, but I will be staying in the village with the kiddos. And Chanelle, of course. If something were to happen, they will need someone to protect them. And my first loyalty is to my family." There was a question in his voice, like he expected me to protest.

"That's fine! I would *prefer* you stayed here."

He nodded, though the sad little look he sent me wasn't at all subtle, and left.

Sam went to follow after Zed and Jacky, but looked at me uncertainly, and then shot a questioning glance at Adam.

Adam waved a hand at him. "I'll keep an eye on her and make sure she doesn't try to escape. Go pack."

Sam nodded, then left.

"Seriously?" I groaned.

"Don't pretend you weren't thinking about escaping," he said, grabbing me by the arm. "Come on, we both need to pack, too."

Torliam grabbed Chanelle by the hand and pulled her along with Adam and me. "Your underlings are not very obedient." I could hear the grin in his voice.

"I'm not a servant," Adam snapped.

"Not a very *good* one," Torliam said, shaking his head.

THE WHOLE TEAM was ready to go in less than an hour. We already had packs ready with the supplies we needed. Add some water and food rations and we were finished.

"Do you have to go?" Kris said, picking up on the tension of our group, as we stood around outside the back of the elder's house.

"Knowledge is power," I said. "It's too dangerous *not* to go."

"That's ironic," Zed said.

Sam frowned. "Wait. If he's the God of Knowledge, does that mean he knows everything? Won't he know we're coming?"

I shrugged "If so, he *already* knows, so what difference does it make?"

Blaine frowned at me till we left, and the kids made me promise to communicate back to them with the VR chips.

Birch had grown big enough that we had to adjust the straps on his little pack. His wings were less fluffy than they had been, though I suspected it would be a long time before he could attain any significant speed or distance when traveling through the air.

The villagers gathered to watch us go, chattering amongst themselves. The news about what we were doing had gotten out, and they seemed to be excited about my "quest."

We set off at a light jog, Jacky and Zed both grinning crazily at each other as the villagers called out well wishes to us. "I can't say I'm averse to a little bit of fame," Zed said.

Adam and I rolled our eyes at him.

For the first few hours of running, we didn't communicate, except to relay what little information we had on the God of Knowledge, and to warn the others about the columns of light that seemed to be his power. I wore warmer Estreyan clothing over my vest, but the chill still slipped inside, and my breath fogged in the air.

Birch ran beside us for a while, but quickly tired from keeping up the pace and moved to a lazy spot perched on top of my backpack, claws dug in and wings furled so as not to affect my balance.

Torliam navigated for us, traveling diagonally toward the other Players on an angle that would have us catching up with them in a little over a day, if nothing changed.

The terrain morphed from the evergreen forests that had surrounded the secluded Estreyan town to rolling mountain ranges, interspersed with wide, lush valleys. Crystal clear streams and lakes speckled the valleys, and the greenery was sprinkled with tiny early-winter flowers.

I'm not sure if it was because of Torliam's presence, but the only large wildlife we saw was at a distance, and none seemed inclined to attack us. The solitude only heightened the ethereal beauty of the place.

Further out, these strange…*growths* started to appear on the plants, and in between the crevasses of the rocks. They looked like golden rods, or columns, reaching out toward the sky from every high place. They shone with a strange, harsh light, throwing shadows that were unnaturally dark. It should have been beautiful. Instead, it was creepy, like watching maggots crawl out underneath the lid of someone's wide open eye, eating live flesh instead of waste. It felt like they were watching. I could almost feel the light, sinking through my clothes, my skin, maybe even my *thoughts.*

Something was wrong.

Torliam felt the same. I could tell by the way his eyes never stayed still, drawn to the formations though they struggled to look elsewhere—anywhere else.

Birch growled, the sound low in his throat and constant.

"Sentinels? Like from the mural?" I whispered to Torliam as we ran, letting my words ghost out along with my breath.

He nodded, grim-faced.

My heart rate picked up a bit, and I had to force my claws not to come out in response. We traveled in silence again then, except for Torliam occasionally re-orienting us toward the other group of Players. The farther we went, the larger the rods grew. Some of them looked like they had been boiled, bubbles forming from the surface. Those ones were always shorter, as if they had been stunted, and everything around them was long dead. Once, a column crumbled away near the bubbles as we passed, seemingly unable to bear the vibration of our footsteps.

Menace prickled in the air. To my Wraith Skill, the columns glowed with power, similar to the way strong Players did, or the rocks and water of Behelaino's mountain.

We stopped for the night on the side of a mountain where the rocks on either side provided a modicum of shelter, not long after darkness descended. We ate a cold meal of rations. There could be no fire, of course, and though the technology for portable hand-heaters no doubt existed on this world, we hadn't brought any. With how low-tech the village seemed in general, I wondered if they even had any.

Birch crawled inside the front of my borrowed clothes, burying everything but the tip of his nose away from the biting cold. He pressed his face against the side of my neck. His cold, wet nose touched my skin periodically, and the water in his breath condensed into a clammy sheen, sucking the warmth extra quickly out of that area.

I tucked my knees up against Birch's back, and wrapped my arm around them, trying to present as little body area to the outside as possible.

Torliam took the first watch, but with the occasional sounds of monsters in the distance, and the biting cold that I was completely sure had frozen the inside of my nostrils, I couldn't sleep.

"Lean against me." Torliam's low voice came out of the moonlit darkness. "Back to back. Soldiers do it, in my world. We can share each other's warmth, and if I arise because of a threat, there will be no need to shake you awake."

I shuffled over to him, ignoring Birch's annoyed grumble, and pressed my back against his much larger one, then tucked myself back into a ball. Heat radiated off his alien frame, and I relaxed a bit in the warmth. "Thanks," I muttered, before dozing off.

He woke me after a few hours and we switched places, me facing outward into the unknown of the night. I'm not sure if Torliam slept or not, but Birch crawled out of the front of my clothes and into Torliam's for the extra warmth, so I was a bit colder until my watch was over.

We rose with the sun, stretching and preparing for another long day of traveling.

Jacky wiped a runny nose on her sleeve, then punched Zed in the arm when he said, “Eewww!”

“If you catch a cold, I can heal you,” Sam said to her. “But if it’s not serious, I’d better conserve my energy.”

“No,” Jacky grunted. “M’fine.”

Birch crawled out of Torliam’s clothes, but when his paws touched the ground, he hopped around in shock at the cold and then jumped to me, begging for me to carry him with little pitiful mewls.

I scowled at him. “What kind of pet abandons their owner to the cold half the night and then wants to be carried in the morning?” I muttered.

He blinked at me, wide, human eyes looking completely innocent. He mewled again, this time even more pitifully, and lifted his front forepaw for a few limping steps, as if it was injured. Then he stopped and looked back to me, obviously wondering if I’d bought his ‘poor-little-kitty’ act.

I sighed gustily and held out my arms to him, once again tucking him into the front of my clothes with only his head peeking out under my chin. “I guess I forgive you.”

Torliam snorted loudly, and when I shot a narrow-eyed look at him, he shook his head. “You are a slave to his every whim,” he said. But he reached out and briefly scratched the top of Birch’s head, somehow-warm fingers brushing against my chin in the process.

Adam stayed silent and glared at everything for pretty much the whole day as we traveled.

I’d been sending sporadic Windows to Blaine and the kiddos, but the farther we traveled, the higher on a mountain I had to be before they would go through. I knew there was nothing they would be able to do to help if something went wrong, but being cut off from outside communication made me antsy.

It was late afternoon when Torliam stopped us. “We are drawing close to them, and most likely also converging on *him*.” He drew two lines on the ground to represent our path and the path of the other Players, and circled our future intercept point.

We proceeded slightly slower after that, wary of being noticed by either the Players or the god. My Wraith Skill was strained to its limit, and my brain felt a bit sore, like a muscle I’d stretched too far and too long. But it was useful, because I could feel the ambient energy shining through the air as we approached something gargantuan and powerful, though still too far away for me to sense directly.

“We shouldn’t get any closer,” I said.

Torliam nodded, then pointed to the top of a nearby mountain that was taller than the rest. It would be a good vantage point.

We all climbed up the back of the mountain in tense silence, hurrying now to get high enough before the other team either reached the God of Knowledge, or the sun went down and reduced visibility.

We reached a good vantage point and moved around to the side of the mountain so that we could peek out behind a rock.

"We'll watch the rear," Adam said. "I don't trust this place." Adam and Sam stopped a few feet down from the peak and turned to face outward.

It was about thirty minutes before sundown, and the shadows of the mountains stretched long, and grew longer fast enough to track their progress.

I poked my head over the rock in front of me and looked down onto the God of Knowledge for the first time.

Chapter 20

Rage, rage against the dying of the light.
— Dylan Thomas

THE GOD'S valley was covered in gold. The shrubbery seemed to be made of it, as did the rocks and dirt, from the floor to halfway up the surrounding mountains. Golden columns shot up high, weaving and connecting together like a…shrine. Or like an open-air, majestic chapel, with one column shooting from the joining point of the others, reaching *high* into the sky.

The god himself looked like a huge, Greek statue made out gold, more *human* than the other two gods I'd seen. Or maybe, more Estreyan would be a better word. No human was quite that perfectly sculpted. Or that gargantuan.

His back was turned to us, and I had an absurd curiosity to see whether his…*bits*, were realistically proportioned, or baby-small like the statue of David.

I pushed that thought out of my mind as I saw that he faced the other team, who had come from the far side of the valley.

Torliam's arm pressed against mine. His eyes were wide and intensely focused down below. Tension fairly radiated off of him.

As I turned my attention back to the uneasy meeting down below, I noticed the valley wasn't quite as flawless as I had first thought it.

Some of the columns had crumbled away, or were affected by those strange stunting bubbles. The God of Knowledge's left arm was peeling like he'd been a victim of the worst sunburn in living history, one of his knees chipped away at the bend in the back of his leg, and his molded illusion of hair left dust trails every time he moved the slightest bit.

I frowned. It looked like he was rusting. But gold didn't rust, did it? The thought tickled a half-formed idea in the back of my mind, but I was so focused on the scene below that I didn't pay attention, and it slipped away.

The Players, moving toward the god from the far side of the valley, had brought less than a full squad. Or maybe, some had died along the way. The ones I could see looked a bit bedraggled, and some had minor injuries.

I squinted, doing my best to see more clearly against the light of the setting sun on my face.

One of the Players stepped forward, away from the rest of the group. He was probably speaking, but I was too far away to hear. He dropped to one knee in an obvious show of respect.

Was that…Vaughn? A shiver of cold wracked me as I noticed another familiar face. "It's Kilburn's team," I murmured.

"If I didn't wanna do it myself, I'd wish goldilocks here would just kill him," Jacky murmured back. It was the first unnecessary thing she'd said to me since we left the village.

"I know why you have come—cuddle." The God of Knowledge's voice resounded out and upwards from down below, loud, smooth, and nondescript in its perfection. It was like an amalgamation of so many pleasing voices blended together that the end result was unremarkable. But…"cuddle?" Was that an Estreyan word?

I looked to Torliam for confirmation, but he just shook his head with a frown and gave a one-shouldered shrug.

"You think—apple—gain power from—" That time, he just cut off, like a recording where the sound glitched out. "What arrogance! Instead, you will—hairless—my sustenance. Give thanks for this opportunity to—beefcake—a role in maintaining my strength."

I'm pretty sure the group down below wasn't expecting that any more than I was. They lost a couple precious seconds exchanging looks of wary confusion. It was more than enough time for the god to act.

They all suddenly went stiff, and wide-eyed. Vaughn was kneeling, and just low enough that his face was in the shadow of the mountains, unlike the others. He was only illuminated by the strange glow from the golden beams.

I saw his eyes flash with two pinpricks of reflected light, like a nocturnal animal.

The god strode forward smoothly, only the tiniest limp apparent from his decaying knee, and picked up two of them by the neck. They didn't react, and he tossed them bodily over his shoulders, into the area surrounded by columns that I had earlier thought of as the chapel. Two more followed them, but the fifth, he didn't throw.

He clamped down hard with one hand on her arm, right below the shoulder, then twisted right below that point, like taking the cap off a water bottle. Then he *tore* the broken arm away, and raised the bloody end to his mouth, letting the blood drip down into it.

The pain seemed to have released his victim from whatever trance she was in, because she started jerking and screaming. But she didn't reach for her shoulder or even try to escape his grip. Instead, her remaining hand tore at her own eyeballs, digging at the soft flesh till they were just bloody, pulped holes in her face, blood streaming down her cheeks like tears.

The arm stopped streaming blood, and he bit into it, bone and all. I could see the edge of his jaw from behind, chewing slowly and swallowing like he was at a formal dinner rather than holding a hysteric human in his hand and eating her raw flesh. His too-perfect voice vibrated the hairs on my skin as he moaned in pleasure.

I was frozen, my own mouth seeming to alternate between dryness and the overabundance of saliva that prefaced violent vomiting.

Jacky must have felt the same, because she ducked back down behind the rock, vomiting in the quietest way she could manage.

The girl's teammates weren't reacting, still caught in their trances, until suddenly one of the taller columns broke for no apparent reason, crumbling at the base and falling to the ground.

The Player closest to it jerked, a single sharp spasm, and then *screamed.* Voice cracking, and then breaking, then gurgling on his own bloody vocal cords.

Birch grabbed the back of my pants and kept tugging, as if trying to drag me away.

I'd heard screams like that before, in the Trials. Humans reach a certain point where the thing that separates us from animals just…breaks. We lose ourselves. And then, sometimes we scream like that.

Chapter 21

Darkness, once gazed upon, can never be lost.
— John Milton

THE GOD DROPPED his snack and moved to throw the screamer and the others who were still frozen into the chapel.

Torliam laid a hand on my arm, and the warmth of it startled me out of the trance I'd been held in, as I watched the creature down below so easily conquer the humans.

My eyes met Torliam's, and as one, we turned to go. But I looked back.

Vaughn was running frantically, apparently freed from whatever had been holding him and the other Player, who was still screaming. He saw me. A moment of confusion, then comprehension, then hope. He mouthed "help" at me, the word silent from this distance, though it must have been a scream.

No. No way was I going down there to try and save them. "Run, guys," I barked. "Run away!" I pushed off the rock in front of me, moving just a little too high above the edge.

The god stiffened, even as I turned, as if we were a spider that he had just felt running over his neck. He turned toward us with a speed that would have disabused me of any notions about his humanity, if I'd had any.

I saw his face for the first time, and it forced that last little bit of fear into me. Except for the nose and mouth, it was a smooth face. He had no eyes. No place where eyes would be. Just smooth, featureless gold. As if whoever sculpted him had forgotten the most important part.

The light hit me before I could continue my spin. Everything around me grew bright, the colors standing out even more vividly, tinged with a glowing golden hue, and the world slowed.

The brightness grew, until it overwhelmed my vision, burning into my pupils, and scorching the back of my retinas with cold instead of heat. When I was a child, I touched a piece of dry ice that was making the fog at a Halloween party. It was so cold, the skin of my fingertip fused to it instantly, and it *burned* me, just as well as touching a glowing hot coal would have. This was like that.

It burrowed past my retinas, in a scorching path straight for my brain. I had a single moment of panicked rejection, a "No," sounding in my mind, but then it was inside.

The brain doesn't have pain receptors, or so they say. Yet, I could feel the little maggots burrowing through my thoughts, like a physical sensation. They searched, and they found.

Memory exploded through my consciousness, along with a strange dreamlike *understanding*.

I was young, small, and thoughtless. I called another girl stupid when she made a silly comment in class. She clammed up and turned away from me, pointedly ignoring and avoiding me for the rest of the day. I never saw her after that year, because she moved to a lower-income district when her mother died.

I was afraid, weak, and useless. Chanelle helped me, standing beside me in my first Trial. If she'd never met me, she would not have slipped in the blood. She would not have died with her throat being ripped out by a rabid fellow Player, and would not have left her sister alone to rely on me.

I was stressed, untrusting, and protective. I told Zed to leave me alone, pushed him away, and did my best to extract him from all the new areas of my life. As the new areas, the ones where I was a Player, took over my *entire* life, I tried to push him out of that, too. He felt abandoned by the person who had been a best friend and unloved by someone he had thought cared unconditionally. He kept coming back for more abuse, desperately trying to fix whatever problem had caused it. He wondered if maybe he'd been wrong about how close he and I were. He sat in the corner of his room, slumped over, shoving fists into burning eyes in a failed attempt to hold back shameful tears. And then he got up again, and kept trying till he no longer expected a different response.

I was desperate, and selfish. I purposely took advantage of China, because I wanted her strength to protect me, just as her sister had done. I convinced her to trust me, to work with me, and even rely on me. Then, like her sister, she died. Protecting me. Her hand held out in a vain attempt to stop the oncoming threat of Kilburn's power. Her body twisting, her eyes meeting mine for the last time.

I was terrified, panicking, and selfish. I twisted the last piece of the puzzle in my hands into place, releasing myself from my cage. Across from me, the girl, who had been just as frightened as me, screamed as the black stone turned to devouring mist, sinking through her skin, and corroding her from the inside. She could feel her bones giving way first, dissolving till they could no longer support her weight, then her muscles, tendons, organs. She screamed until she could no longer scream, watched me until her eyes were gone, too, and was, in the end, thankful that even with all that, she had lost, and not allowed herself to become a monster just because of fear.

The snippets of memory and understanding hit me, one after the other, an onslaught of the times I'd made the wrong decision, hurt another person, caused pain and sorrow and death. And I was forced to not only to remember, but to understand. I saw the connections, cause and effect, and I *knew* the pain I'd created as if I'd had to endure it myself. I knew it like a lover, like the feel of my fingers, like my own reflection in the mirror, my ice blue eyes blazing back at me.

I hurt.

So bad.

And it went on and on, until suddenly, I was torn away. I could feel the cold maggots trying to keep their grip on me, but slipping away, back out through my eyes with a ripping sensation.

MY VISION DIDN'T RETURN at first. Wind whipped past my ears, a warm body pressed against me, arms wrapped around me, Birch yowled, and I tasted blood in my mouth. I'd bitten my tongue.

A loud sound passed through the air, cutting through the sound of the wind, and it took me far too long to process it. It was a roar, sounded in the melodious screams of thousands of smooth voices, too loud to be human. My body vibrated painfully at the sound, and my eardrums pretty much just gave up.

As my vision returned through dark spots like I'd been staring into the sun, I realized that Torliam had tackled me off the side of the mountain, and we were falling. It was eerily similar to the end of my first foray into NIX, and Adam's tackle that saved me from the same fate as China. That had happened because I made the wrong choices.

I had the horrible feeling that something similarly terrible had just happened, but I was too mentally overwhelmed to figure out what had gone wrong.

Each moment passed at a bovinely slow pace, but I realized finally that there was no river to break our fall, and we would no doubt soon crash into the unforgiving rocks below.

I caught a blurry glimpse of Birch, his claws digging into Torliam's back, wings flapping frantically, trying to slow us down. It was futile. He wasn't even big enough to fly.

Where were the others? Had they fallen? Were they trapped in the light, too?

Torliam began to glow. It wasn't like the glow of the golden columns, rather it was ripples of visible sky blue that looked almost liquid, a physical thing instead of ephemeral light.

Then, suddenly I was jerked sideways, and then immediately sideways again. He must have been jumping from rock to rock as we fell to slow our fall. Then, a sudden drag had my insides protesting at the change in inertia. I was flipped so I could see the ground past Torliam instead of the sky for half an instant. One of Torliam's arms released me and ripped Birch around to my side, on top of him, and then the three of us met the earth.

The impact almost knocked me out. It did knock the breath out of me, even though Torliam had cushioned the fall with his own body.

My teeth had smashed together when we hit, and my left arm had been jerked around a little bit. It ached, from shoulder to fingertip. A horrible sense of foreboding rose in me as the rippling light disappeared. I ignored my lungs' screaming for air, and peeled my body upward.

My vision had gone wonky again when we hit, but it normalized quickly when my brain settled in my skull. I looked around at the small but relatively deep crater surrounding us.

Torliam must have created the hole with his power, somehow, along with slowing our fall. And cushioning both Birch and me with his own body.

Adam, it had to be, was sliding down the mountainside inside a black ink box with a sled-like curve on the bottom. I hoped Jacky and Sam were with him, because I didn't see them anywhere else. I would have called out, but I couldn't talk, as my lungs had yet to regain the ability to breathe.

Torliam's eyes were closed, his face screwed into a grimace.

I stabilized myself on his chest with my good arm and used the left to check his pulse at the neck. It was still beating strongly, and another quick check confirmed he was still breathing. I rolled painfully off him toward Birch, who had bounced and rolled off to the side from the rebound of our impact.

Birch lay on his side, belly rising and falling shallowly as he breathed in and out with quick little pants.

I laid my hand gently on his side and stretched my Perception out, pushing the awareness of the Wraith Skill into his body, looking for what was wrong.

He had fractured bones in the wing he was laying on, and a good amount of bruising already forming. His eardrums were…ruptured? I could feel a bit of blood beginning to seep out of his large, tufted ears. I guess it wouldn't have mattered if I could speak, because he couldn't hear me anyway.

I lifted my hand and placed it gently on top of his furry head in reassurance, fighting to regain my own breath and take stock of my own injuries. My left arm hurt, deep and *aching,* though I didn't think it was actually injured. There were consequences when humans got turned into hamburger—consequences even miraculous healer Sam couldn't get rid of.

My chest and stomach ached, a sour, burning sensation. I realized inanely that it was *emotional* pain. Guilt. Regret. Uncertainty. I would have scoffed at that, but it truly, seriously hurt to the point it distracted me from my physical injuries. What had the god done to me?

More blood filled my mouth, and I spat it out, along with a large, jagged chunk of tooth. My eyes caught for a fraction of a second on the white bone amongst the bloody spatter before moving on. No time for that now.

Bruised ribs on myself as well, and one of my knees had slipped past

Torliam's side and hit the ground in our fall. Kneecap broken, but not completely shattered. I still couldn't hear anything, except for a faint, metallic ringing sound.

I felt a bit dizzy, and wondered if that was because of my ears, or if perhaps I had a concussion. I shook my head to try and clear it, which instead sent a throbbing wave of pain through it. No *time* for this! How long had it been since we hit the ground?

I scooted over to Torliam and slapped his cheek lightly. No doubt, he'd taken more impact than either Birch or I, but he was also an Estreyan. I needed him awake, and in commission, if I was going to make it out of this. And I didn't have time to wait for him. The unjustifiably beautiful monster in the valley behind us could be preparing an attack, either by physically coming after us, or using his golden growths.

Adam scrambled down into the hole, Jacky and Sam half a second slower than him. Adam threw up an ink shield over the top, drowning out what light remained. Sealing us away from the light of the sentinels.

That was why Torliam had created a hole, I knew. But in battle, if you couldn't move, you died. And we were trapped within.

I felt Torliam's groan under my hands. I sent a Window to Sam, in lieu of verbal instruction.

—Torliam is hurt. Prioritize his healing.—
-Eve-

While Sam placed his hands on Torliam's exposed skin, I reached out as far out as possible with my Wraith Skill. It hurt my brain, and I had a sudden surge of nausea, but I could feel the blindingly bright power of the god on the other side of the intervening mountain, along with many other smaller points of power where the helixes burst from the ground.

The god's power was surging, probably with anger, but he didn't seem to be physically coming after us, at least not yet. And the golden light didn't reach us where we were.

Torliam's eyes opened, and I drew back my focus, blinking to clear the blurriness.

Jacky had broken a glow stick, and its eerie light made our huddled group visible.

The distinct taste of tears washed away the blood on the tip of my tongue, and that's when I realized I was crying. I didn't even try to stop, because I knew I couldn't.

Torliam frowned when his eyes met my own, and I said, "Are you okay? Can you move?" He didn't have a VR chip, so I hoped he could understand me. It was strange to feel my voice box vibrating, and know that I was speaking, but not actually be able to hear myself.

He nodded, and then immediately winced at the movement of his head. But he rolled over anyway, then rose to his hands and knees.

I saw his lips moving, but interrupted whatever he was saying. "I can't hear you," I said. "My eardrums are probably ruptured. You weren't out long, less than a minute, I *think*. I'm not entirely sure. I may have a concussion. The God—*it's* not coming after us, yet." I realized suddenly I was almost shouting, and tried to lower my sound output, which is harder than you think. "We need to stay out of the light." I shook my head. "You know that already, sorry, I'm rambling. But we do need to move, it's not safe to stay here. And Birch is hurt," my voice broke, more tears spilling out of my eyes.

I used the gauze wrap I'd brought since Sam's healing ability was limited, and bound Birch's wings to his body. Only the one was injured, but I couldn't find a quick way to secure it while leaving the other free, and figured just the one wing wouldn't be useful for anything anyway.

Birch woke up while I was doing that, likely from the pain, and I whispered to him, "You're okay. I'm just making sure your wing doesn't get hurt anymore. We've got to move, soon. Can you walk on your own?"

He struggled to his feet, and his mouth opened, though I couldn't tell what type of sound he was making. He touched his nose to my hand, and something foreign flashed in my mind. Two human legs, blurry facial features—blue eyes, dark hair—a strong smell, and the feel of warmth.

I jerked my hand back in horror, until I realized that it had been Birch behind the images, not the god. The little creature's "first words." I regretted that I didn't have time to celebrate the momentous occasion.

Then the very ground and air around us vibrated, and my ears screamed again. All of us except Torliam winced bodily and hunched over, me with my palms to the side of my head, leaning over Birch.

When the incomprehensible sound ended, I uncurled and opened my eyes to find Torliam crouching over me, just as I was crouching over Birch. He laid his hand on my back and said something.

I shook my head silently. "My ears aren't working," I reminded him. I considered putting a couple of the Seeds I'd been saving into Resilience, but almost discarded the idea. I had so many Seeds in that Attribute, I doubted a couple more would make much difference to my eardrums in the short term. Then I remembered that those Seeds were there to offset the effects of Chaos, and were most likely busy doing that, with nothing to spare for injuries caused by outside stimuli. Maybe a couple more *would* help. Besides, I'd probably be putting them into Resilience or Life soon anyway, as Chaos grew stronger. This wasn't an injury I wanted to waste Sam's reserves on, especially not when I could use the VR chip to communicate with most of them.

So I went ahead and dug three Seeds out of their secure place in the center of my pack, and put them into Resilience. I barely noticed the side effects, except for a vague sense of physical relief.

Torliam shuddered when I injected them, and I slipped the empty Seed shells back into my pack awkwardly. He didn't react further, other than a tightening of his lips, so I tried to put it from my mind.

I was so mentally scrambled, it wasn't hard. I couldn't stop seeing the things the light had pulled from my memory and explained to me in unflinching bluntness.

Torliam laid his hand on my arm, causing me to jump and bring my focus back to my immediate situation. Damn, what was wrong with me?

He leaned forward and placed his lips behind my ear, and I stiffened despite the pain it caused me to do so, freaked out in a completely different way. Then, his lips started to move, and I felt the vibration of it in my skull. He was talking, and with a little push of Perception, I could understand him even without my eardrums.

"The god said that we might hide from his light until we grew too weak to resist him, or come out when desperation settled heavy on us, and be captured then. I believe he expects us to remain trapped here. I have remembered some of the research I did before, and from what I know of him, he is not one to move from his seat of power in a physical way. He will try and trap us in his light, but if we can escape that, perhaps we will live."

I nodded. "But how do we escape *light*?"

"In truth, I do not know. His power is made to pierce defenses. It reaches brightest into the darkness, transfixing through any shields of deceit. It speaks well to your underling's concentration that his constructs were able to shield against it."

"But we're safe here, with the earth surrounding us, right?"

"In essence. His light travels straighter than most. The…bouncing off of things? It does not happen as much. It is not like sunlight or manmade light. It is meant to travel far and straight. Does that make sense?"

I nodded again, though I wasn't quite sure. Maybe the light from the golden columns was like a laser. I sent Windows to the other three explaining this.

Sam put his hand over my knee, touching my skin through the torn fabric there. My kneecap shifted, and whatever had been broken fused back into place.

I let out a sigh of relief.

—It's only a basic join. It will break again in the same spot if you're too rough with it, too soon.—
-Sam-

Jacky inched over to me when he was finished, and found my hand in the dark.

—Are you okay? Sorry I didn't drag you away soon enough. I didn't even know what was happening.—
-Jacky-

I squeezed her hand.

—I'm okay. Can't stop crying, though. That thing did something to my head.—
-Eve-

The ink covering over our little nook evaporated, and Adam tossed out another shield with a whispered "Animus," but in the brief moment of twilight, I saw his wide-eyed look of exhaustion.

I questioned, and he answered.

—Whatever that light is, it's attacking my shield. If we weren't dug into the ground, I don't think I could keep this up.—
-Adam-

"If we had something to *reflect* the light, instead of trying to block it?" I murmured aloud. "But I didn't bring anything like that. And my Skills aren't any good for something like that."

Torliam's head lifted, then, and his eyes met my own, obviously thinking quickly. "I am of the line of Aethezriel," he said, touching me so I could interpret his vibrations.

—WHY DOESN'T HE HAVE A VR CHIP, AGAIN?—
-ADAM-

Wraith could feel the scowl on Adam's face, which I ignored along with his question, in favor of the more pressing matter.

"Okay…? You told me your last name before. What does that have to do with anything?" I frowned. "I really hope this name sharing isn't some type of before-death ritual for you guys, because I'm damn sure not giving up."

"Aethezriel is not my *name*. It is my *line*. My…ancestry. It is the line of power that has been passed down since ancient times."

"…Your Skill? Is that what you're saying? Aethezriel is the power you have?"

"Aethezriel is my ancestor, who mated with a god. But, your meaning is correct."

I tried to think about the implications of what he was saying, but I couldn't concentrate. I lifted my good arm and wiped away the line of my tears, sniffing to clear my nose. "So why is that important? Can you get us out of this?"

"My power comes from the god of the upper air. It is a greater power, like your own Chaos. It is the bloodline of a god with a wide domain. There are many aspects—interpretations—of the power, if you know how to draw them out. One of them is *light*."

I smiled then, a sudden relief coming over me. "Oh. Well, that sounds promising."

"As your incompetent scientists may have discovered, light is quite interesting. I may be able to oppose the light of his sentinels, using an opposite, ahh…*vibration*, to nullify its reach."

"You're going to cancel out—" my breath hitched as my body tried to sob and I tried to restrain it, "the wavelength, like sound." Hey, I'd learned plenty in my relatively short lifetime, and my upgraded brain was good enough to put together at least that much. "But is that even possible? You can't think faster than light."

"His light is very steady. You are correct, I may not think faster, but if I can anticipate ahead of time and set up a pattern, perchance it will not matter."

After I relayed this to the rest of them, Adam opened up a hole in the edge of the ink lid, positioned so that the light from outside wouldn't hit any of us directly. It was enough for Torliam to test his theory.

The blue light rippled out of Torliam again, and he reached a hand wreathed in it upward, through the hole up above and over the edge of the crater.

Nothing happened, other than the muscles in his face and neck straining taut. But then the area around his hand started to change. I felt like my eyes were deceiving me in the fading light, but when I reached out with my Perception, I saw the same thing. Between the light of Torliam's power and that of the sentinel was an area of darkness. Not a shadow. A place where the light just…stopped. It ceased to exist. I'd seen quite a bit in the time since I'd become a Player, but this was something else.

Something no human had ever seen before, probably. I stared for a moment, the little involuntary shudders my body was making easing as I became fully distracted from my own mind. It was beautiful, in a frightening sort of way.

Torliam pulled his hand back, and his light faded. His breath came fast, and when he moved back to me and laid his mouth against my temple, I could feel the sweat, cold and clammy on his skin.

Whatever he'd done, it wasn't easy.

"He is strong, so close to the seat of his power. And…loathe as I am to admit it, even in the height of my own power, I would have had difficulty shielding all of us." He paused, and then said, "I am far from the height of my power," with a heavy significance, shoulders drooping.

When she read my Window of explanation, Jacky squeezed my hand, hard enough that my joints protested. The sharp pain of it distracted my mind from both the images and the aching of the rest of my body.

Torliam couldn't get us out. Adam wasn't going to last much longer. Sam and Jacky didn't have any Skills relevant to the situation. And the dirt was as good a shield from the light as any. It didn't take long for me to realize what I needed to do. I kept thinking anyway, because I was hoping to come up with something else. When I didn't, I let out a drooping sigh of my own. "If we were farther away, where the sentinels were smaller and more dispersed, could you shield us all?"

"For short distances, maybe. But we would need places to hide again when my stamina ran its course."

I nodded, then closed my eyes. I didn't really need them closed to send out my Perception anymore, but psychologically, it helped. I concentrated as best I could, trying to calculate the "dimmest" areas nearby, in any direction that could lead us away from the god behind us, who I could practically feel the *crazy* radiating off of.

I found the most advantageous spot, and then with a deep breath, I gestured for everyone to move aside.

Once they'd huddled to one side of the small cavity, I pushed Chaos out with a surge, forming it into a clumsy drill of destruction, though it resisted my attempts to constrain it to any form. Still, it did what it was supposed to, and the dirt in front of me collapsed in a slide of gritty sand. Weariness washed through me. I'd put too much power into it. We didn't need sand. Pebbles would have done.

Torliam understood the plan quickly, but when I moved to start scooping away the sand with my hands, he motioned for us to move back and cover our eyes.

I did so, after making sure Birch was safely behind me just in case, and watched with my Perception as Torliam created a short, hard burst of wind that cleared the tunnel I'd made. I shook my head, letting the blown sand fall off me, and opened my eyes.

The ink lid disintegrated again, and this time, Adam couldn't reform another immediately. I slammed my eyes shut, and hunched flat to the ground, only sitting up again when complete darkness was restored.

—I THOUGHT USING CHAOS HURT YOU.—
-JACKY-

—EVE, THIS WILL ACCELERATE THE TIMELINE FOR CHAOS OVERTAKING YOUR HEALING ABILITIES.—
-SAM-

I closed my eyes, unseen by anyone except maybe Torliam in the semi-darkness. At this point, did it really matter? I'd hoped that the God of Knowledge would be the answer to my problems. Whether he agreed to help me or not, I'd hoped that I'd be able to get what I needed from him, even if I ended up having to take a piece of his Seed core, to mitigate the effects of Behelaino's. But he was crazy. Crazy like the spidermonkey. There was no way he was going to help, and anything I got from him would be tainted, anyway.

—It'll be okay. I have plenty of Seeds left.—
-Eve-

Torliam and I shared a nod, and I crouched down, shuffling the couple feet into the tunnel and repeating the drill of Chaos with a bit less force, then retreating so he could clear it again.

My knee hurt a bit every time I moved, and Torliam was so big he had to army crawl through the small tunnel, but I couldn't spare the power to make it bigger, if this was going to work. It was a lot of back and forth shuffling, to clear the volume of dirt we needed. Dirt and sand got into my clothes, my eyes, and my mouth.

I grew tired, and Torliam took over digging out the tunnel, though his power wasn't suited to it.

When he grew tired, Jacky crawled down and began to hack at the dirt and rock with her bare hands, digging like a dog. It was surprisingly effective, with her Strength and Stamina. It also peeled back her fingernails, which she ignored until I noticed and forced her to stop, so Sam could at least help her nail beds scar over.

Eventually, we got enough of the tunnel dug so that all of us could fit in it at once—though not comfortably—without being exposed to outside light from above. That allowed Adam to take much-needed breaks from shielding us against the sentinels.

Halfway to our destination we stopped and ate some of the rations we'd brought, while I took a couple more Seeds.

It took half the night to reach our destination, which was only a few hundred meters from where we'd stared. "Your turn from here," I murmured to Torliam and Adam, repeating myself with Windows to translate for those of the team who still couldn't hear as I spoke. "I don't know if you can tell, but the easiest path—with the least light—takes us in a loop around the line of rocks out there, and then a sharp turn to the right." I gestured without looking over the edge of the tunnel.

We all held hands, and Adam picked Birch up, doing his best not to press on the creature's injuries.

The blue light wafted off Torliam again and spread to cover all of us, and after a few moments, he nodded and took a step forward.

I moved in sync with him, ignoring my kneecap as it grated.

When we hit the golden light, a barrier of darkness immediately spread out where it intersected with Torliam's own. He grunted, but kept moving forward, breathing harder with each step, each exhalation visible in the freezing air. He was trembling as if he'd just completed a race when we reached the spot I'd indicated, and Adam took over, a using Animus to create a bubble-like barrier of ink around us as we hurried through the last few meters. I wasted no time unleashing my own power into the earth, creating a hiding place for us so he could release his power.

Then, we tunneled only a bit further and took a break, because Torliam would have a much harder time negating the god's light in the full light of the fluctuating sun. And because I needed the rest.

Even so, the spontaneous bleeding started again, right before we reached the end of the second tunnel, and with it came a wave of *agonizing* pain. I flopped onto the hard-packed ground below, twitching and moaning as it washed over me.

Someone put their hand on my shoulder, saying something I couldn't hear.

When the pain passed, I lifted my head from the ground, spitting out the dirt I'd bitten mindlessly into, and wiping away the stringy saliva my mouth had created from the nauseating agony. "At least I didn't bite my tongue," I muttered, forcing a small smile.

Adam said nothing back, but his hands were exceedingly gentle as he helped me back to my hands and knees, as if I were made of eggshells, or flower petals, or something.

When darkness came, we tunneled again, till morning hit.

I took another handful of Seeds, carefully not looking at Torliam as I did. My supply wouldn't last long, at this rate.

We were going to run out of water soon, and food not long after that. I hoped that we could escape far enough from the god's reach before it became an issue.

I slept deeply, aided by a touch of Sam's hand to my forehead, and whatever he'd secreted through his skin into mine.

When I woke, a Window was hanging in front of my face, from the Oracle.

Chapter 22

I have won every battle but scarred my soul.
— Laodisia

KILL THE GOD OF KNOWLEDGE
DESTROY THIS MANIFESTATION OF THE GOD OF KNOWLEDGE BEFORE THE SMALL MOON HAS DARKENED THRICE, DEALING THE FINAL BLOW BY YOUR OWN HAND.
COMPLETION REWARD: KNOWLEDGE ABOUT THE SEED OF CHAOS
NON-COMPLETION PENALTY: DEATH

WELL, shit.

I wanted to assume the Oracle was guiding me for the better. I was trying to be smart about it, and not make the same mistakes I had with NIX. It seemed like she'd been aiding me so far, cryptically showing me the path that was best for me.

But I couldn't defeat the God of Knowledge. Even with my whole team, and Torliam, we wouldn't even come close to being better than him. The Oracle had just given me a suicide mission, with the penalty for failure being death.

Perversely, the seemingly insurmountable obstacle actually helped to calm me. It gave me a problem to work on, something to solve and overcome. It was something I could actually *do* something about, and it helped give me the focus to push the memories the god had forced on me back from the front of my mind.

Working under the assumption that the Oracle wouldn't give me a quest that was literally impossible to complete, there was *something* I could do. I just needed to figure out what. As far as willingness went, I had no qualms about getting revenge on the god.

Especially if by doing so I might be able to save myself from death.

So, I bent my mind to the usual questions. My problem—I wanted to defeat the God of Knowledge. What did I have? What did I need to get where I wanted?

I had myself, probably my team, and maybe Torliam, if he could be convinced. I needed more information about the god, but a preliminary estimation put him at about ten times stronger than *all* of us.

I was forced to admit that I couldn't make the team ten times stronger before time ran out for me. Could I instead make our enemy that much weaker? It sounded nice, but I had no idea how to go about doing such a thing, or if it was even possible. Maybe I could somehow get the Oracle to work against him. She was the one who wanted him dead, after all.

I groaned and rolled over, setting aside my thoughts for the moment. My body protested against the abuse of the cold, damp ground beneath me. An aching stiffness had seeped into my bones as I slept, and I felt like an old, old woman, whose body had been forced to stay on the earth too long.

Birch lay on his stomach in the corner of our little dugout, breathing shallowly.

"Did you sleep at all?" I whispered, leaning over the cub and placing a hand gently on his forehead.

He let out a faint squeak, and I sighed. I turned to Sam, who was already awake, his back pressed against the wall of our little hole. "Is there anything you can do for him?" I said aloud, testing the sound of my own voice in my healing ears.

"I'm pretty much out of juice. And my Skill has never really worked that well on animals, anyway. I'm sorry."

I nodded. "Well, help me out, then. We're going to have to do this the old-fashioned way." I took a few deep breaths and expanded my awareness through my hand, into Birch's body. "This might hurt a bit," I whispered to him. "But try not to move."

Sam lay his hands gently on Birch's body, ready to restrain the small creature if the pain was too much.

I nodded my thanks and gave him a small smile, though my focus remained on the injuries beneath my hand. The bones in Birch's wing needed to be set. I understood vaguely what needed to be done, thanks to the mandatory training I'd received in NIX's classes, but we'd never practiced setting a *wing*.

I unwrapped the gauze, then gripped the feathered appendage in my hand and pulled, using my Perception to make sure the bones within were shifting and meeting back together as they should.

Birch stiffened and I heard the faint sound of his scream.

Sam made sure Birch couldn't move enough to hurt himself in his pain, and I splinted and re-wrapped the wing carefully, so the bones wouldn't shift around.

Birch settled down with a shuddering sigh when I was finished, but after that, he breathed easier and seemed to fall asleep.

We still had a couple hours till sundown, so we sated our hunger with a worryingly large portion of the remaining rations, and then I meditated. I should have done it the night before, but I'd been so exhausted, and distracted, that I'd forgotten. It helped, both with my physical body and with the pseudo-flashbacks.

When the sun set, we continued on, again alternating between tunneling, Torliam's strange light wave negation, and Adam's ink barriers. As we got farther away from the God of Knowledge and his sentinels grew sparser and weaker, we were able to do much more above-ground traveling. We were all hurt, tired, and scared, and my ears were still healing, so I found myself relying even more on my Perception to scan the surroundings.

It took us more than two days to get close enough for my Windows to reach Blaine again. We'd run out of food by then, and Torliam said it was okay for us to drink the water around us, but only if it was running water, and only if I used Chaos to force it to a boil first.

"I told Blaine not to come meet us," I said, my voice cracking from disuse. "Not till we're away from the sentinels." I didn't know what might happen if the god discovered them coming to meet us, but it couldn't be anything good.

"Good. There is no need to place others in danger. The Sickness has reached so far…" I thought he was finished talking, but he suddenly spoke up again. "I believe we have completed your vision quest from the Oracle, now. It is obvious, I think, that you will not be getting any aid from the God of Knowledge. I do not know the purpose of her revelation, but perhaps when I am home again, this news will bring good somehow. Or maybe, it is just a warning that the end is near."

"We have to come back!" I blurted out.

"We had a deal, human." His voice deepened ominously. "I will not put myself in danger just because you cannot accept that the Oracle did not lead you to salvation."

My stomach soured with apprehension. I needed him, or the whole quest would fall apart. I couldn't let him decide he'd fulfilled the deal and just *leave*. "You'll have to return. The Oracle sent me another quest."

Adam's head snapped around. "What? Why didn't you say something?"

"I was…in shock." I let vulnerability slip into my voice, and bit down on my bottom lip. "Because it's to kill the God of Knowledge. And I have no idea how to do that."

"That was not part of our bargain, and you know it well." Torliam loomed over me, and I'm not ashamed to say the hairs on the back of my neck rose at the sudden sense of danger.

Adam's hands twitched toward the cells of electricity at his waist, and Jacky turned her body sideways to Torliam, for better leverage to block or attack.

"The quest reward is connected to curing the Sickness!" I said.

Torliam blinked. His eyes widened and his lips parted in surprise and maybe even a bit of hope, but then they flattened down again. "You lie."

"I'm not lying. I don't know *how* it's connected, but it says one of the rewards is information on the Sickness. These type of chain quests update when you complete each stage, and the rewards keep growing. Information now, maybe a cure, later."

He just stared at me.

"I mean, why else do you think the Oracle is doing all this? I'm certainly not important enough for her attention all on my own. Maybe she's trying to fight back, through me, through *us*. I mean, she can see the future, right?" I put a few drops of innocent consternation into my voice, and I saw the disbelief break apart in his eyes. For a moment, I felt a pang of shame for my actions, but I ruthlessly squashed it, reminding myself how much I had to have his assistance, no matter how I was forced to obtain it.

However, the way he replied shocked me.

"I did…suspect, that this might be the case."

Chapter 23

Nothing gold can stay.
— Robert Frost

TORLIAM WINCED at the barrage of questions from us. "I was not certain, of course," he said, raising his hands in a calming motion. "I told you, Eve, that you were likely descended from one of the lines of my people. Matrix is the name of that line, though it seems you call yourself by the name Redding. For many generations, the line of Aethezriel had been bound to serve and protect the members of the line of Matrix, and can never be bound to another in service. Many of the line of Matrix ruled, in times past." He paused for a moment, as if thinking, and then continued, "I knew what you were when I first felt the bond with you, though the last of the line was thought to have died hundreds of years ago. You have their blood. I did not know you were a human." He clenched his fists and looked away, but couldn't quite hide his expression.

Instead of the anger he usually displayed, he was despairing. I almost felt bad, which was ridiculous because I couldn't do anything about being human, or the fact that NIX had forced me to be a Player. I would not have chosen this any more than he. But he must have thought I was one of his comrades, either come to save him, or also captured by NIX.

"Some thought…that one day a descendant of that line might bring back the one god who could fight back the Sickness. The line of Matrix is descended from a mortal who had relations with the God of…'Life.' The Champion." He frowned then, and told me the word he really meant, in Estreyan. "As we discussed previously, the word does not translate, similar to the word for the Sickness. He is the god of order, and form. Shaping. Molding? I do not know, but perhaps you can understand my meaning."

I shrugged, then nodded. "Yeah, okay. What are you getting at?"

"There are stories, maybe prophetic, about our salvation. I believe you may be the one who can find that extremely distant ancestor, and bring him back. Many believe he is the only one who can save this world. The Oracle is clearly setting you on a path."

I felt the muscles in my jaw tightening as I held back my anger. "You didn't think that maybe I might be interested in hearing about this?"

Torliam looked away like a scolded puppy, blonde hair falling in front of his face. "I did not believe in the possibility, at first. You may have some distant blood of the line, but you are…"

"Human? A two-leg-maggot?" One of my eyebrows rose high in challenge.

He didn't rise to the bait. "But with the quest you tell me of, to find knowledge of the Sickness, I am beginning to…find hope?" He forced himself to meet and hold my gaze with obvious difficulty. "I can help you. If you are indeed the one, you are on the very early stages of the path. You will need to gain acknowledgment from the goddess of Testimony and Lore. Many of my people will follow you, if we can show them the signs. Enough people, perhaps, to kill a god."

Sam spoke up. "Do you think they would agree to help us, though, if they knew that the god was infected? The villagers were so afraid of the Sickness they didn't even want to let us stay inside the walls."

Torliam looked at him and frowned. "You are right. Perhaps they would not. But we do not have time to train you humans into proper warriors. Chaos is undoing you," he said to me, his voice softening.

I grimaced. It was true.

"We *must* convince my people," he said. "It could mean the salvation of our world. My *mother-lord* may grant us the numbers we need, or at the least allow a force of volunteers to accompany us. And if necessary, we may even deceive those who would not follow us otherwise. The task is too important to fail." His words were coming faster, and he alternated between gazing far away in thought and focusing on me with excitement. "Let us tell people that we are questing for a Bestowal from the God of Knowledge, and he has said we mortals must prove ourselves in battle against him."

"I don't think it's right, lying to people like that," Sam said. "They're going to be putting their lives on the line. They should at least know the truth, so they can make a real decision."

Torliam grimaced. "You are not wrong. But this is too important. In any case…fighting to kill a god and fighting not to be killed by one while petitioning for a Bestowal are not so different. Both end in death, almost universally. At least the one will give them hope while they fight."

Sam didn't pretend to be happy about it, but he kept any more arguments to himself, having spoken up and thus cleared his conscience of the weight of the decision, I guessed.

Jacky was very quiet, and Adam was already thinking through the possible outcomes in his head, muttering about planning for the worst-case scenarios.

"So, I just have to gain a Bestowal from a couple different gods? Testimony, and Lore?" I asked.

"She is one god, with two aspects. She is called Testimony and Lore by mortals, as her true name, like that of all gods, is incomprehensible to us. But yes, in essence. Though we will have to find her, first. She, too, has been gone from mortal eyes for generations. I have some ideas, but once we are back in the village, we will be able to use their stores of knowledge to determine exactly where we might search. I have no doubt that we will find her."

Could I do this? Could I go along with this pretense that I was some kind of destined savior, meant to find and bring back the god that could forestall the death of their world? People would die for me. Others would have their spirits crushed when they inevitably learned the truth. I couldn't answer my own question.

I kept asking it of myself, even after we were safely back in the village, we were all healed up at the hand of the Estreyan healer, and the news had started to spread.

Jacky trained like mad, driving herself into the ground every day, only stopping her training to check in with the rest of us and see what progress we'd made in pinpointing the location of the Goddess of Testimony and Lore.

Chanelle's condition improved, and I hoped desperately that enough Seeds would bring back that vivacious girl I'd first met, who looked just like China and who made something inside me cringe every time I saw her looking so incredibly lifeless.

But time was passing, and I didn't have enough to spend waiting and vacillating. It wasn't like me to be so indecisive, but whatever the God of Knowledge had done to me, forcing me to relive all my bad decisions, had made me unsure. I woke up during the night, days after receiving the quest, and the answer was clear in my mind, finally. I would live. I was too afraid to do anything else. I would *live*, and others would pay for my life in blood.

I WOKE with someone's hands pressing down on my mouth, suffocating me. Pressing down, keeping the maggots *inside* me. I clawed across the arm, and they drew back with a hiss.

"Damn it, Eve!" Sam said, the curse sounding strange coming out of his mouth.

I reached those same claws up to my face, barely even feeling the pain as I sliced at my eye sockets, trying to get the squirming parasites out from behind my eyeballs.

My room's light bloomed into brightness, and I sat up. Wraith observed Adam's look of horror, since there was too much blood for my eyes to see directly.

The others piled into the room from down the hall. Blaine held the kids back from entering once he caught a glimpse of my face.

I realized then that I was screaming, and that I'd probably been doing so for a while, if the raw feeling of my throat was any indication. "They're inside me," I said desperately. "Sam, help me, help me! The maggots are inside me, burning cold in my head, behind my eyes, *burrowing* through my *brain*!" The last was a screech, as I tried to impart the desperation of my situation.

My back arched, and I slammed my head against the wall, the starburst of dizziness alleviating the sensation of infestation for a moment.

"Hold her down!" Adam snapped, reaching for my clawed hands.

Torliam was there, a hole in the wall where he'd made himself a door since my own was filled with teammates, and the blue was pressing against me, almost crushing but it hurt the maggots too and they stilled and then Sam was in front of me again, laying his hands on me *oh god thank you thank you help me.*

Then things went dark, even for Wraith, and I fell back into unconsciousness.

Chapter 24

My candle burns at both ends, it will not last the night, but ah my foes and oh my friends, it gives a lovely light.

— Edna St. Vincent Millay

"...REALLY think that's a good idea? She was trying to scratch out her own eyeballs before Sam put her to sleep," Adam's voice said, almost spitting with vehemence.

"We cannot leave her sleeping and defenseless," Torliam said.

"It's done," Sam said.

I groaned, fighting against the nausea. I didn't know where I was for a moment, but when I saw the diagram painted over the floor in front of me, I recognized the old man healer's house. Torliam, Jacky, Adam, and Sam were with me.

Someone screamed, outside.

I sat up and groaned, "What's going on?"

Adam was already at the window, looking out into the darkness of the night. "I don't...oh *shit*."

"What is it?" Sam asked.

"One of them just broke down the main gate. They're fighting back, but there are too many monsters for the villagers to kill them all. They're flooding in."

"What?" Alarm crept into my voice. I wondered if I was hallucinating, or maybe in the beginning of yet another nightmare.

"We were attacked by the God of Knowledge," Torliam said. "Mentally. I was strong enough to fight it off. You were not. Your healer forced you to sleep, and we brought you here, to fix the wounds you inflicted on yourself."

I reached up and touched my face self-consciously. The skin on my face, especially around my eyes, was a little tender, but not raw. "Is that related to whatever's going on outside?"

"Perhaps. I wonder that the god is not aware of our intentions, and has sent the attack to ensure we are not able to complete our task."

"How many are there? Monsters, I mean."

"Too many. This village will not last the night, I fear."

"We have to help them," Sam said, moving with adrenaline-rush jitteriness. "There are kids out there. And not all of the villagers are even fighters. I mean, I saw one of them with a Skill in *music*! Everyone's going to die if we don't do something."

"And what will we do, that can make a difference against *that*?" Adam said, flinging an arm out to encompass the village outside.

"We can help them escape, at least!"

The healer bustled into the room, carrying a satchel in both arms. "Supplies for the trip," he said in Estreyan. "Hurry, we must get to the stables."

I climbed to my feet, allowing Jacky to brace me when the room swayed around me. "Where are the others?"

"Back in our rooms," Adam said.

"You must escape, Eve-Redding," the healer said. "No time to pick up those who fall behind."

"No way we're leaving the kids in this shit," Jacky said, her shoulders tightening as if she expected a fight. "We're going to go get them, right, Eve?"

"Of course. No time to waste, let's go," I said, bracing myself on Jacky's arm.

She slammed open the door, and the chill in the air hit me with a sudden shock. I could see fires starting in two different places in the village, and the light of the two moons showed the dark mass of monsters boiling into the streets near the gate, flashes of light and sound flaring from the attacks of the defending villagers.

We ran as a group, the old healer keeping up easily despite the packs he carried on each arm. We passed an Estreyan mother, running terrified in our direction, her young child wailing in her arms. "Go to my home," the healer said to her. "Hide, under the floor. Tell the others."

We had passed each other before she had time to respond, but I could only hope that she obeyed and survived.

We got to the elder's house, and Adam, Sam, and Jacky burst in to grab the others and our supplies, while Torliam, the elder, and I stayed outside to keep watch for attacks on the building. In the distance, a monster with huge bat-like wings flew away, the silhouette of the man in its claws writhing against the moon behind them.

Torliam was trembling faintly, not from fear, but from clenching his muscles too tightly in rage. "The Sickness is an *abomination*. There is no place for it, in a world on which I live. One of us must be destroyed," he said in the poetic lilting of his native language.

The healer turned slightly toward him, eyes still searching outward. "Many have vowed the same. I take heart that this is the first time I have ever held hope that a mortal will be the one to survive a covenant of enmity against the Sickness."

A figure raced up the street, entering the somewhat constrained range of my awareness. The patrol leader. I still didn't know his name.

"Eve-Redding," he said, gasping, once he was close enough. He was holding one arm close to his body, obviously hurt. "Thank the gods you are safe. We must get you away safely."

"Laine?" the healer asked.

The patrol leader shook his head and closed his eyes as if in pain. "No. It was already too late when I arrived at her house."

The healer clapped him on the shoulder, head bowing. "We will repay them in death many times over."

"Their blood will pave her way to the next life." He nodded and swallowed. He turned to me. "You must stop this," he said. "The Sickness has spread through the creatures of the land. The very earth turns against us. You must find the way to cleanse this world. I beg of you. I place my faith in you."

My stomach clenched. I wasn't capable of fixing their world. "I will follow the path," I said. Not quite a promise, and not quite a lie. I couldn't force any more past the lump in my throat.

He nodded tightly, and closed his eyes once again as he swallowed hard. When he looked at me again, the faith in his eyes, the fanatical, desperate hope hit me like a blow.

I hated myself in that moment, and not for the first time.

Jacky slammed back through the door, tossing my pack at me. "We're ready."

Kris and Gregor wore their own packs. Though they were pale and obviously frightened, they held Chanelle's hands in comfort as she whimpered with childish fear. Kris climbed atop the patrol leader's back without hesitation when he leaned down to carry her, and Gregor glanced at me, but went with Blaine instead, while Torliam carried Chanelle.

Zed was checking his guns, and with a fluid motion, pulled one out of its holster and shot past my face. The gun sounded with the strange *glup* that indicated an air-burst round. I turned, and saw another of the bat-winged creatures tumble into the top of a house, just entering the edge of my range.

"Nice shot," I said. I pushed the Wraith Skill a little more, since whatever Sam had done to me was wearing off enough that it didn't make me throw up to do so.

"I'm awesome, I know. Now let's go," Zed said, his eyes asking me silently if I was okay.

I nodded, but didn't force a fake smile.

We ran, then.

The bird steeds in the stables were panicking, and one had busted through its stall and was barreling around the building, injuring itself as it ran into things in its panic. The patrol leader did something with a Skill to calm some of the birds, and we climbed atop them without even sparing the time for saddles.

We plowed back out through the doors. Jacky glanced over her shoulder, slowing her mount with a pull on the feathers of its neck so she could bring up the rear of our group. "I hate this," she said through gritted teeth, under her breath. It didn't seem like she expected anyone to hear her. "Been working so hard, but I still can't do nothing when it actually matters."

I didn't know what to say to that, or if she would have even wanted me to hear and respond, so I stayed silent. We raced through the streets toward the back of the village, and out through the back gate that led to the training fields.

There were monsters there, too, though not as many, and they hadn't been making a ruckus. When we passed through, they attacked.

Torliam brought his power together into a huge sword-like blade of blue, and slashed with his arm. They fell in a far greater circumference around him than it seemed should have been possible, sliced cleanly through from side to side.

The patrol leader did something, and another huge swath of them fell to the ground, twitching like they'd been nerve-gassed. We ran the birds straight through.

A couple monsters avoided their comrades' fate, but with the Estreyans and my own group, they weren't enough to do more than slow us down a little, and after a while, their numbers petered out. That was when Egon slowed the birds with another simple motion of his hand. "Go on from here," he said. "Do not stop until dawn breaks over the horizon."

"What about you, Egon?" Kris asked, voice pitched high. She didn't speak Estreyan very well, but had obviously picked up on his intention.

"I will go back, and fight to protect my village."

The healer dipped into a short bow from atop his own bird. "Well met, Eve-Redding of the line of Matrix, and Torliam of the line of Aethezriel," he said. "Fight with the strength of our wills behind you."

"Well met, Borogo of the line of Ambercrest," Torliam said, returning his bow.

I copied him awkwardly, and then the two Estreyans turned around, racing back toward the battle.

"No!" Kris yelled. "You're going to—" her voice broke on a sob, "—die. We have to go back!" she screamed. "We have to help them."

"They have saved us," Blaine said. "If we do not do our best to get out of here safely, we will be acting as if everything they have done for us does not matter."

Gregor's hands were fisted in the neck feathers of his own mount. "We won't forget their names, Kris. Like in the story Mom used to read us. We'll remember them."

Kris just sobbed, but she followed along without further protest as we urged the ostrich-like birds into an uncomfortable, loping run. "This world is horrible," she said, breath hitching. "Everyone dies."

Interlude 3

They had all been preparing, ever since the elder felt the rip opening up in the world, and told them that an array had been used. The training grew more desperate, the arguments among them more quick to devolve into violence.

He and some of the others had talked to the elders about making sure their guests were treated with proper courtesy, and now they were often seen moving about the place, though they still weren't permitted to leave the outer boundaries.

The woman had grown bolder, demanding answers from Eliahan and anyone else who wasn't smart or fast enough to avoid her. "What is it that has everyone so panicked? Are you going to attack NIX?"

He laughed. "You know nothing of what is coming. Perhaps that is a blessing, for you."

Chapter 25

It is not the darkness outside that invites the demons, but the darkness inside.

— Darune Imdel

AS EGON HAD INSTRUCTED, we traveled till morning without stopping. By that time, even the ostrich-like birds, which were known for their stamina, were exhausted. Riding them was…uncomfortable at best. With only two legs, they bounced with every step, and despite my lack of male genitalia, the insides of my thighs and everything between my legs was bruised and aching.

I had wanted a few more days to prepare and gather information about how best to win the Goddess of Testimony and Lore's favor, but we were pretty sure we knew her location, and there was no more village library to search through, anyway. We headed for her, a strange mood combined from sorrow, fear, and helpless determination suffusing the group at first. Over time, though, the mood lightened, growing better conversely with how exhausted we became from traveling.

It took us a couple weeks to make it almost all the way to the edge of the continent we were on, and though the bird steeds could eat almost anything they came across, including smaller animals, we didn't have extra food for them, and they grew noticeably wirier over the course of the trip.

We'd encountered a few monsters along the way, but nothing life-threatening, and since we ate some of them after killing them, we humans were fine for food, even if none of us were gourmet campfire roasters. The type of hunger that makes your hands shake is a wonderful seasoning.

The biting chill of the air froze the insides of my nostrils when I breathed it in straight, so I kept my face hidden behind the fur lip of the coat the villagers had given me. The cold made it difficult to sleep, which I appreciated, as that saved me from the nightmares. But I was so tired I found myself nodding off in the saddle, woken by flashes of screaming terror.

I checked my Attribute Window despairingly. If only I didn't have to put all my Seeds into the healing Attributes, maybe I might have *some* chance against a god.

PLAYER NAME: EVE REDDING
TITLE: SQUAD LEADER(9)
CHARACTERISTIC SKILL: SPIRIT OF THE HUNTRESS, TUMBLING FEATHER
LEVEL: 38
SKILLS: COMMAND, WRAITH, CHAOS

STRENGTH: 15
LIFE: 67
AGILITY: 23
GRACE: 19
INTELLIGENCE: 31
FOCUS: 24
BEAUTY: 10
CHARISMA: 16
MANUAL DEXTERITY: 9
MENTAL ACUITY: 25
RESILIENCE: 65
STAMINA: 33
PERCEPTION: 25

I had leveled up quite a few times naturally, from pushing myself in training physically and learning a new language, but I knew none of my Attributes were actually impressive, compared to an Estreyan warrior.

The clouds above grew thicker and more ridiculously fluffy as we approached our destination. Even the mist showing in the air from our exhalation didn't dissipate like normal, hanging in the air like a puffy trail behind us.

"We should leave our mounts here," Torliam said. "They will not survive in the sky levels."

We left the birds, loosely tied up to a small tree. If we weren't able to return, they would be able to break free.

Then we walked into the wall of fog. Ahead, it thickened, till every gasp made my lungs rattle just a little, and the loose strands of my hair started to float around my head, as if I were underwater. Between one step and the next, my foot rose and didn't touch the ground again. I flailed awkwardly as the foggy substance around me lifted me off my feet, and sent me floating gently upward.

"It is alright. The current will carry us," Torliam said, his voice slightly muffled.

I coughed, and tried to breathe calmly so my lungs weren't overwhelmed.

"Whoa!" Zed said. Instead of the half swim, half run the rest of us were doing, he stretched out in a Superman pose, then started doing flips and stretches.

Kris laughed and joined in, and though Gregor rolled his eyes at first, when Zed pulled him atop his back and pretended to swim like a dolphin, Gregor grinned and tugged on Zed's hair to make them spin different directions.

Jacky started using her Skill to pull herself around, literally zooming through the air like a superhero.

"I want to ride you, Jacky!" Kris yelled.

"That's not fair," Gregor said. "Zed's useless. We're just floating around aimlessly here. I want to ride Jacky, too. Let's take turns."

Zed stuck his tongue out at Jacky, then turned to Adam. "Think you could help me out, here? Flippers, or something?"

Adam smirked and pulled out some ink from a cartridge he'd refilled while we were in the village, and created a mermaid tail that latched around Zed's legs and hips.

My brother reared back, looking down at himself in consternation for a moment. Instead of the protest Adam had probably expected, he flicked his fin and swam through the air over to Adam with Gregor still clinging tightly to his back. "I'm going to need a trident to go with this," he said. "Could you make it spit lightning? To be authentic, you know."

Chanelle laughed, though it might have been at the sensation of floating and the light atmosphere of the group rather than comprehension of the joke. Still, it made us all smile to hear it.

Adam rolled his eyes and made a normal ink trident that did *not* spit lightning into an unknown gaseous substance. "It'd be just like you to get us all blown up," he muttered.

I hesitated for a moment. It looked like so much *fun*, and there wasn't any danger within the reach of my awareness. Even if there were, a tail would probably help me to navigate what would basically be an underwater fight even *better*. That convinced me. "Could I get a tail, too?"

Adam ended up augmenting all of us, though Jacky got octopus legs that waved through the air randomly, and Blaine got some sort of jellyfish thing that fit around his suit and propelled him in spurts. We played around for the next half hour or so, Adam renewing his Animations whenever they ran out, till the current deposited us on a layer of quartz-like crystal.

Torliam pointed the way, after consulting the map.

I frowned as we began to walk. "Isn't this the way we came? Unless I've made a mistake…but, my sense of direction is amazing. The sky was clear, this way. Wouldn't we have seen clouds? Is whatever this is going to dissipate out from under us?"

Torliam smirked. "My world is not so simple as yours. This is a new layer."

"You know, acting obtuse and mysterious doesn't make you seem cooler," Adam said.

"Trying to explain the science to you would not make a difference," Torliam said. "I doubt you could understand even the necessary vocabulary, much less the concepts."

"Try me," Blaine said. "I am a scientist, and I have been studying the knowledge of your world. Also, I am a genius."

Sam covered his mouth with his hand to hide the smile, sharing a look with Jacky, who snorted in amusement.

"He is also humble and pious," Adam drawled.

Torliam conceded, perhaps more to spite Adam than because he actually believed Blaine, but they quickly fell into a scientific discussion that I, at least, couldn't follow.

As we waded slowly through the thick air, the ground beneath our feet turned more and more crystalline, and increasingly beautiful, glittering all different colors. After a while, we noticed that the crystals were letting off light. Despite how beautiful they were, the whole thing gave me a bad feeling. Estreyer was a planet of universal viciousness, in my experience. Anything unusual was probably also dangerous.

I voiced my concerns to Adam, and he agreed that he would give us all ink mermaid tails at the first sign of danger

Despite my uneasiness, I didn't think much of the crystal beneath my bare feet growing sharper and making shallow cuts into my extremely calloused feet. It barely hurt, and I was so used to injury by that point that a few little nicks didn't register. What did manage to alarm me was the quickly growing glow of power in the fog all around us. "Stop!" I called, looking around with my useless eyes while Wraith searched for the source of the power, and found none. Yet it coalesced around us with crushing force. "Adam, tails!" I said. "Something's closing in on us."

By then it was already too late.

Chapter 26

Still she haunts me, phantomwise,
  Alice moving under skies
  Never seen by waking eyes.
  — Lewis Carroll

I LET OUT a squawk as the crystal shifted, slicing into the pads of my feet, and spilling my blood on the ground. It sucked up my blood and shot it forward, blowing mist out of the way to reveal a lump of abstruse crystal. When my blood reached it, it shifted and unfolded, uncurling upward into the form of a woman.

Jacky, Torliam, and Sam closed in on Zed and me in a protective formation, while Adam attached ink tails to Blaine, the kids, and Chanelle, giving first priority to those who had the least chance of protecting themselves.

The crystal creature was naked, but I don't think anybody was really noticing that except a little voice in the back of my inane brain. Her legs were shapely, made of jagged crystal that sharpened down to two points, with spurs, which she balanced on effortlessly. She stretched like an unfurling flower and turned to look at me.

When our eyes met, a very clear 'Oh, shit,' resounded through my brain. "Get back," I shouted to the team. "Blaine, get the kids out of here."

To his credit, he was already moving, using the tail Adam had given him first to grab a child under each arm. But he didn't get far. The mist thickened a few meters out, and after only a few seconds of trying to swim through it, he began to cough, and then his breaths began to rattle as if he was inhaling half water. He struggled, and the current brought him back, pushing him out of the thick wall of mist.

The three of them flopped gently to the crystal ground, coughing up liquid.

The creature spoke, her voice formed by shattering the crystal gills on the sides of her neck. "Welcome, mortals. Please calm yourselves, and do not try to escape. Only death lies on that path." She spoke in Estreyan.

Torliam answered her back, speaking quickly enough that I missed some of the words. "We are honored, wise…Torliam, son of Mardinest, of the line of Aethezriel…blood-covenant is Eve Redding, of the line of Matrix…by the Oracle."

Zed didn't seem to think whatever he'd said was cause for extra alarm, though to be fair, he already had a gun drawn and primed in each hand.

For the first time, I realized that obviously, alien gods and humans should have a language barrier. I wondered why I'd been able to talk with Behelaino. I wasn't sure if she'd actually been speaking English, doing some weird Seed-thing where she inserted understanding into my brain, or something equally freaky.

"She welcomes us," Torliam relayed. At my questioning look, he nodded. "This is the Goddess of Testimony and Lore, who has long been hidden."

The creature tilted her head to the side. "They are from another world?"

How did she know that?

"Yes," he said.

Crystal tentacles exploded out of the ground and pierced into each of our temples, faster than even Adam could blink.

The surprise and pain caused more than a few screams.

"Be still," Torliam said, and we obeyed. He was the one who was from this world and supposedly had experience with this sort of thing, so I hoped for the sake of my brain staying intact inside my skull that he knew what he was talking about.

The tentacles piercing Chanelle's head broke off instantly, and the crystal ground rippled violently and swept them away from the little clearing. The rest of the tentacles withdrew from our heads after only a few seconds, and pulsed light back to the goddess, as if she was drinking up something through her…"skin."

She opened her mouth, and her gills shattered and reformed repeatedly, almost faster than my eyes could track, forming sound somehow. "I…have been waiting here for *so long* without visitors," she said in perfectly clear English. "I did hide myself away, but I didn't expect it to be so…boring! No supplicants have come to quest for my Bestowals for so long, I decided to sleep so I would no longer have to count the seconds of my loneliness." Her shoulders drooped, needle-sharp fingertips trailing sadly across her thigh. "I was not made for isolation," she said. "And I am glad to finally greet you." She smiled at me. "I have received your offering of blood, and I grant your request for a Trial. You and your followers will be allowed to petition for my Bestowal."

Torliam's eyes widened, and he turned to me, eyes following my own gaze down to my feet.

"Ahh," I said stupidly. "I'm ignorant, and I did not know the ways of this land. I didn't mean to request a Trial." Oh, freaking shit on a stick.

The creature frowned at that. "Do you mean to escape me after petitioning, to abandon the covenant uncompleted after suddenly realizing your fear?" Her voice grew imperious. "You have already entered into agreement, whether by accident, as you say, or not. I will not allow you to leave me again so easily." The wall of choking fog closed in around us, and the rainbow-colored shards of crystal began to pulse with light.

I struggled to breathe, and not just from the quality of the not-quite-air, but from the power pressing down on me. The creature before me could kill us all easily, with the same nonchalance that I would kill a spider or mosquito. There was a sense of age to her, like the feel of mountains that have stood for millennia, or oceans that have lapped endlessly at the ever-changing shores. She would remain, long after we were gone, as she had done for countless others before us.

Torliam was bowing, saying something to the goddess that I couldn't hear, though I wasn't sure if it was because of the terror, or because of the air.

Chanelle had fallen to the ground and was curled up in a little ball, crying.

Gregor was also on the ground. He'd puked at some point, but he was looking at me, and I recognized the emotion in his eyes. Desperate hope. Faith.

I hated it. I couldn't bear the pressure of it. But I straightened anyway. "I will accept the Trial," I said. "But some of my team aren't warriors. They are too weak to participate in a quest for the favor of one so great as yourself." I bowed to her, moving slowly so that my trembling muscles didn't make me jerk awkwardly.

"All must participate, except the broken one," the goddess gestured to Chanelle, "and the mortal that carries none of our legacy," she said, pointing to Blaine.

"The children will die," Torliam warned in a low voice.

Immediately, everyone shifted forward to guard the children more completely, putting our bodies between them and the body of the goddess. As if that would actually protect them. It was like putting rice paper up to dam the ocean.

"I cannot accept that," I said, my voice growing colder and deeper. "Requesting a Trial was my mistake. But these are my people, and it is my duty to protect them." I settled my heart and released my claws, feeling my hands and feet shift to their more monstrous forms as my vision sharpened and bloodlust bubbled up, my stats shifting as the Spirit of the Huntress Skill prepared me for battle. Maybe if I could distract the goddess long enough, Adam could find a way to get the others out. An ink respirator to filter breathable air, maybe. He was clever like that.

The tension gathered. She stared at me till my heartbeat pounded in my ears from the force of it. Then she smiled. "I am beginning to like you. You play the role of heroine so easily. All must have a part in the story, but if you wish, you may take the burden of protector."

"What does that mean?" I narrowed my eyes suspiciously.

"You and your warrior will take the greater burden of their roles in the story, as well as your own."

Torliam stiffened beside me, but said nothing.

"My warrior?" I echoed her.

"Him, the one with which you have a…?" she turned to Torliam.

"Blood-covenant," he supplied for her.

I didn't mention that many of the others had taken the Seeds as well, fearing it would only make things worse for them.

Torliam nodded to me, and I avoided his eyes. If he, too, was filled with sacrificial hope, I didn't want to see. "I accept," I said aloud. I would die here, or I would die at the hands of Chaos. When I thought of it like that, it was calming. As always, the only way out was *through*.

THE GODDESS RAISED HER HAND. "Let us perform the story of exodus, tribulation, and the…spark-of-hope." She ran the last words together, and I realized it was once again a missing word in English.

I asked Torliam what she meant.

"It is a children's story about our history," he said, "one every Estreyan child knows in some form or another."

I didn't have a chance to ask him for a deeper explanation, because the goddess directed all those participating to stand in various places around her. Torliam and I were placed closest to her, and the non-Players and Chanelle were farthest away.

"I know you do not know the way of this dance," she said in her fractured voice, "so I will lead your movements as we perform the story together." She lifted her hands, and the crystal ground separated and broke upward en-masse, the forms of thousands upon thousands of tiny little fish swimming through the air. Though our footing was gone, we floated.

My eyes widened as I watched the coral-shaded, translucent fish swarm around me in an almost solid wave.

"Begin," she sang, her voice echoing out, seeming to bounce off and through the crystal so that it originated from everywhere, like the best surround-sound system ever invented.

The fish closed in on me, and I jerked when their fins brushed against me and sliced shallowly into my skin. They darted in and scraped up the blood that welled up from the cuts with their mouths.

I quickly learned to avoid their fins, and in doing so, realized they were guiding my movements. I sent a Window to the others before my full concentration was taken up, explaining the concept in case they hadn't realized it for themselves.

"*Before there was Estreyer,*" her voice resounded, "*our people lived in another place. All lived happily, and in harmony.*"

The crystal fish guided me in smooth, graceful movements. I felt kind of like a ballerina, or an interpretive dancer. I couldn't see the others, and the goddess' power shone so bright and pervasively in my awareness that it blotted out my teammates like the light of the sun might blot out a lightning bug.

"*Then, the unmaking came. It is known by many names. The greater-death, the end, the abhorrent. It began to destroy us all. We could not hold it off, though our warriors fought with all their strength, and many died before it, some falling to madness. So, the people petitioned the gods and the forces-of-existence, and left to create a new world.*"

I was forced to change my movements, jerking faster, in jagged motions that felt awkward and uncomfortable. The fish got some more blood out of me, and as I watched, they began to shine with it in blurry patterns.

"*We traveled far and long, hoping to escape the abhorrent by moving beyond its reach and knowledge. Our people voyaged through the breaks, and eventually came to this place.*"

I split some of my attention away from the strange dance being forced on me and saw images take shape in the light of the swarming crystal. My focus was drawn irresistibly to them, and I watched as people and creatures I'd never imagined left a planet, moving in ships the likes and size of which were almost incomprehensible. I couldn't quite comprehend what I was seeing, as I had no reference for the all-encompassing appearance of space from a wider perspective, and the anomalies which they traveled through. I was sure "break," was another concept that humans had no word for.

"*The great champion, enemy of the abhorrent, formed Estreyer of the gods, and we exist in and of the world. But then came knowledge. We would be followed by the darkness, for it was part of us, and we had brought it with us.*"

I was gazing into the crystal-bright images when a drop of blood fell into my eye. It startled me enough that I withdrew some of my attention from the story and narrative. I realized I was bleeding pretty badly. The dance had progressed, and I wasn't keeping up properly. The fish around me gulped up the thin lines of my blood with their little, puckered mouths. I tried to focus on their movements, following them so I wouldn't be sliced, but it was hard to concentrate. Something about the images and the sound of the goddess' voice resounding in my head *demanded* my attention.

I concentrated on the fish anyway, forcing myself to split my attention and follow along as their guiding movements became increasingly difficult to follow. I felt like a puppet on strings, or maybe it was the fish that were puppets, and I was the one developing the story.

"We began to search for a way to defeat it, and we built, because we knew we could not run forever. We traveled far and wide, searching for others like us and sifting through the paths of possibility. For a long time, we found nothing significant, and no force stronger than our own which would aid us. Then, there was a glimmer of hope in the paths."

I couldn't keep up, especially not without my full focus. I couldn't even *see* all the fish! The more blood the fish took into their bodies, the more all-encompassing and imperative my need to concentrate only on the narrative and mesmerizing images became. When I realized the solution, I felt like smacking myself. I pushed my awareness out again despite the blinding nature of the goddess' power, letting the Skill observe my body from every direction.

"The glimmer was small, twinkling and weak, and so far away it would be almost too late before we could meet it. Eight would accompany it, completing the Seal of Nine, one for each of the greater Trials."

My part in the dance slowed for a while, thankfully, allowing me to grow accustomed to this new method of following along, and to catch my breath. It also allowed me to faintly catch some sounds of the others, doing dances of their own.

"The Summoner, the Gale, the Gifter. The Tracker, the Struggle, the Shadow. The Black Sun, and the Veil-Piercer."

I could hear the others, faintly. Jacky cursed under her breath in between gasps for air. Someone cried out in pain and surprise. I found it hard to worry despite that, because the crystal fish were showing me things I couldn't even describe. It was like a dream, or a vision. Somehow the words and the images made sense in the moment, but I knew that when I awoke, they would slip from my grasp.

"But as such things happen, misfortune must accompany hope, and the greatest opponent of the abhorrent, our champion, disappeared."

My own movements were forced to quicken again, even faster now, after the brief respite. Even with my awareness extended, I couldn't keep up with the fish. Before, they had been opening a path for my limbs and body to move, but now they sliced into me, though I seemingly had nowhere to move. Greedy bastards. The only areas that were safe were those protected by my armored vest. As I instinctively jerked my cheek away from an almost seamless wall of extended razor-edged fins, the other side of my face pressed against the mass of fish, but pushed them out of the way without being cut. And I understood the way the game had evolved.

I needed to force my way through the correct path, as it would no longer be opened helpfully for me. I panted as the fish drove me to bend and reach and spin in ways that the human body normally never moved. I was more grateful than I thought I'd ever be for China's yoga stuff and Torliam's training. At least I had some experience with something similar, or I'd have probably fallen and sliced my throat open by that point.

"*We searched for our champion and molder of the resistance, but the Champion was not to be found. And so, time passed, and the abhorrent caught us, trickling into our midst once more. It poisoned us till flesh turned against flesh, till it seemed that the end was near. The path of deliverance was shrouded, until it seemed to have been snuffed out. Many believed that it had been.*"

My body shrank inward in sadness, curling and twirling over like a streamer in the wind, in moves I'm pretty sure no human was ever meant to perform. My legs shuddered with the fatigue of forcing my way through the syrupy mass, and my arms went numb. Still, I couldn't quite keep up, and the fish took more of my blood, and the story took more of my mind.

"*Then, the inkling of hope drew near, born in ignorance and awakened in pain. Its spark was small, and weak, and many times seemed like it would be snuffed out. And yet, it grew, and grows.*"

I jumped, stretching like a light that had been revealed in the darkness, if that even made sense. It didn't, really, but it was the image forced into my brain from the crystal fish. My body was nearing true exhaustion, that point from which willpower no longer has any effect on performance. If I didn't fear death, I would have collapsed on the floor in a quivering, bloody heap long ago.

"*Our future lies in the spark, in the hope that it will grow into a raging inferno and eat up the abhorrent. And so we nurture the glimmer, which struggles in darkness, known to us by the signs and the blood. Such is our work, and our path, to fight against the abhorrent. Only by this may we one day prevail.*"

And with that, the swarm scattered, and I was left reaching toward the sky, body stretched out and upward to my absolute limits. The others, except for Blaine and Chanelle, were gathered around me in a circle, each in their own pose. I held the pose for half a second, just long enough to be sure that the goddess was finished with me, then crumpled to the floor like a used tissue, gasping for air.

YOUR GRACE HAS INCREASED!

SAM REACHED ME FIRST, whatever wounds he'd gotten in the course of the Trial already healed. He placed his own slightly bloody hand on my slippery cheek. "Crap," he said. "I can't do much about the cuts. I've got some healing saved up, but I think this is one of those things the village healer was talking about. It's resistant. But it's okay, I'll help your blood clot." He was already doing it, making my skin itch in waves. "It won't be pleasant. Once you've scabbed over, your body can do the rest over time. Thank god none of these are that deep."

Blaine rushed over to Kris and Gregor, flailing his way through the air, all four limbs working to help him move faster. "Are you alright? All I could do was watch as you were stuck in those...*torture devices*," he spat. He picked them up gently, and moved them further to the back of the group, away from the goddess' physical manifestation.

They were alright, though a little cut up.

The horrible *itching* that spread over my skin everywhere that Sam touched distracted me. Whatever he was doing, it had to have been from the destruction half of his Skill, the itching so intense that it felt like burning, and I bucked to get away without even thinking about it.

Torliam and Zed held me down. Torliam looked like he'd been in a blood-filled squirt gun fight against three or four other people, but Zed was okay, mostly. No serious wounds, just like the others.

"You are the first creatures in a thousand years to petition me and receive the chance to experience the Lore," the goddess said. "It is unfortunate you are so weak. I honestly wondered if you might all die. What has happened, since I have been removed from the mortals? Is this really the best spark the worlds could field?"

I wasn't sure if I should be offended. We were alive, and that was deliberate on her part. Hopefully, if we could avoid offending her, we could remain alive.

Of course, Jacky decided differently, on her own. She'd fared better than Torliam or I, but had taken a fair bit of damage. Her clothes hung off her in tatters, almost completely covered in blood. Without Sam, she might end up passing out from blood loss soon. "Well, you can do something about that, right? Make us stronger, if you're so upset about how weak we are," she said loudly, fists clenched.

I'm pretty sure the entire rest of the team froze in horror.

The goddess' mouth fell open for a second, and then her crystalline brows drew down in a frown. The crystalfish that had receded swirled up again in agitation. Several shot forward from the storm with such speed I couldn't even *see* them move. Obviously, she'd been holding back on us before. One impaled the base of my throat, but the rest of the team were shot through the hand, except for Birch. At my feet, a fish slammed into Birch's forehead and knocked him off his feet with a silent puff of air.

I struggled to move, to attack, or defend, or *something,* but the rest of the swarm was on us already, holding us in place. I pushed against them, heedless of the sharp fins, but didn't get anywhere. It took me more than a few seconds to realize I wasn't in pain, and in fact wasn't being harmed at all. It was more like being constrained in a crystalfish straight jacket than an attack.

I stopped struggling, and the fish released me. "Be still, guys," I called out, my eyes still trained unblinkingly on the goddess.

"You are all quite excitable," she said with a raised eyebrow. "No harm was done to you, except perhaps a little pain. That one," she pointed at Jacky, "asked for your Bestowals. I gladly gave them."

Torliam shot a glare to Jacky, who flexed her hand and pointedly ignored him.

"A seal of nine," the goddess said, waving her hand to the teammates who'd participated in the Trial.

I reached up, touching the base of my throat where I'd been hit. My armored vest rippled away from the spot as if repelled by it magnetically. I couldn't see with my eyes, so I looked at myself with my Wraith Skill, and "saw" the dark scales of armor glinting in the light of the fish that was writhing around under my skin. That was extremely creepy, but it only got worse as the places it touched morphed into faceted sparkles that matched the substance the goddess' own body was formed from. It burned like a brand, forming one line at a time. My body buzzed like I'd mainlined caffeine into my veins.

The fish burst back out, and my armored vest formed back around the crystal so that the symbol it had created was visible.

"With a mark of Testimony," she said, placing extra power into the last word, so it seemed to thrum in the air. "The mark will draw both favor and ill-will toward you. You will be recognized by beings of power, your presence imposed on the book of existence. So I proclaim, as the physical manifestation of Testimony and Lore."

Torliam made a small sound, looking with wide eyes between the crystal in his own hand, the goddess, and me. He had a clear, faceted symbol etched all the way through his palm to the other side.

I opened my mouth, though I wasn't quite yet sure the words I wanted to speak. A question, surely.

"I am eager to end my stay in this place," Testimony and Lore announced, before I could say anything. She waved a hand. "I am not meant to exist in solitude." And with that, she left, taking all the crystal with her in a surge that swept past us like the wave of a tsunami, leaving us in foggy half-darkness.

Kris whimpered in pain, and I turned to see the mark etched into her hand. Gregor had one, too.

YOU HAVE GAINED A NEW SKILL: VOICE

I wasn't the only one to be temporarily distracted by invisible Windows in front of their face.

"She's not even a Player," I said, the words both strangely muffled and echoing. "And I'm pretty sure that just gave her a Skill." I didn't need to state the obvious. If the kids didn't have the gene, something bad was about to happen. Even if they *did*, they'd never gone through the assimilation sickness for that first Seed.

"I'm going to need to find something to hurt, and quickly," Sam said.

ADAM GAVE us fins on our arms and mermaid tails, and Blaine forced the hoverboard thrusters he'd built into his suit to work even in the damaging environment. This time, there was no playing as we raced back the way we'd come, fighting against exhaustion and worry.

It was easier to go down through the currents than it had been to rise, and we arrived back at our bird-steeds quickly. By that time, the kids' temperatures had risen to fever levels.

"I don't want to die," Gregor had said, his hands clenching Blaine's. "I don't want to die. I want to live."

Blaine turned to Sam, and by the flickering movement of their eyes, I knew they were communicating by Window.

Sam paled, then shook his head. "It won't come to that. I'll be able to offset enough through the animals. And if I need more, I'm sure the others will be able to capture some monsters and bring them for me." He untied one of the birds and led it off away from the others so they couldn't watch what he was doing to their companion.

He placed his hands on its head, and it slumped to the ground, senseless. Then he crystallized its windpipe so that it couldn't scream out, if it awoke. It didn't even twitch. From there, he moved to the feet, shuddering as pieces bubbled or melted or hardened like stone under his hands. The wings were next, and when the bird twitched, he put it more deeply to sleep. Then, he stopped to throw up before he continued torturing it to death.

I pulled my focus away from him and turned it to gathering more information. Once again, things had changed.

PLAYER NAME: EVE REDDING
TITLE: BEARER OF TESTIMONY
CHARACTERISTIC SKILL: SPIRIT OF THE HUNTRESS, TUMBLING FEATHER
SKILLS: COMMAND, WRAITH, CHAOS, VOICE

Then I pulled up my Command Window, checking the new Skills of the others.

PLAYER NAME: ADAM COYLE
TITLE: ONE OF NINE
CHARACTERISTIC SKILL: ELECTRIC SOVEREIGN
SKILLS: HYPER FOCUS, ANIMUS, BESTOW

PLAYER NAME: JACQUELINE SANTIAGO
TITLE: ONE OF NINE
CHARACTERISTIC SKILL: GRAVITATIONAL AUTONOMY
SKILLS: STRUGGLE

PLAYER NAME: SAMUEL HAWES
TITLE: ONE OF NINE
CHARACTERISTIC SKILL: HARBINGER OF DEATH

SKILLS: BLACK SUN

PLAYER NAME: ZED REDDING
TITLE: ONE OF NINE
SKILLS: VEIL-PIERCER

PLAYER NAME: KRIS MENDELL
TITLE: ONE OF NINE
SKILLS: SUMMON

PLAYER NAME: GREGOR MENDELL
TITLE: ONE OF NINE
SKILLS: SHADOW

A LITTLE BASIC deduction told me that Adam was "the Gifter" Testimony and Lore had mentioned. What others remained? The Gale and the Tracker.

One must be Birch, and the other Torliam, since they were the only ones I didn't have access to via the Command Skill.

"Hurry!" Blaine yelled, placing one hand each on Gregor and Kris' forehead to gauge their fevers.

"It's almost over," Sam called back, the words seeming to be half for his own reassurance.

"Don't worry," Zed said. "They have the gene, right? I *didn't*, and Sam still kept me alive. It's going to be okay."

"You injected yourself with a Seed from a 'mortal,' not from an *ancient alien goddess*," Blaine said sharply. "Eve was stupid enough to do that willingly, and look where she is. There's nothing Sam can do for her!" His voice rose until he was practically shouting.

Kris groaned, and tossed her head in obvious discomfort, distracting Blaine from his anger.

"I took the Seed directly," I said. "It's pretty different than getting a Bestowal, which is actually meant for a mortal."

I'd meant the words to be comforting, but Blaine stood and took a single step toward me. "You are the cause of this," he whispered scathingly. "We are here because of you. They did not want any of this. They did not do anything to deserve this fate. Why did you not send them away? Why did neither of us keep them *safe*?" His face crumpled then, and he took off his glasses, pressing thumb and forefinger hard against his eyes. "We failed," he whispered.

Jacky, who had been watching silently, stomped off and started pounding her fists against a nearby tree trunk, hard enough to splinter the bark and shake the trunk. Hard enough to break the skin of her own knuckles.

"Yes," I admitted. "But they're not going to die. I promise." I spun around, quickly spotting Torliam squatting under one of the small nearby trees. "What do the marks mean?" I snapped, moving to stand over him.

"They are symbols representing our roles in the Lore," he said.

"The Lore? You mean this whole supposed prophecy thing where I find the god who's going to save your world? The prophecy that you didn't mention pertained to anyone else but me? The prophecy that just hooked in a couple *kids*?" I found myself leaning over him, claws extended, fingers outstretched.

He hesitated for a couple seconds. "The children's story is known to us all. Most consider it a…fabrication? A story only loosely based in truth, and made to teach children, while couching the lesson in fiction. But it usually ends at a different place, before the reappearance of the light. I did not *know*." Despite the inherent contrition of his words, the barely-contained energy I could hear behind them wasn't sad, or sorry. He was excited.

My hand moved almost without my volition, slicing through the air and cracking against his cheek hard enough to rock his head to the side.

He brought up a hand to feel the furrows my claws had dug into his skin. They healed under his fingertips, as easily as that. "They will not die," he said. "They are needed for you to complete your path."

I leaned down. "You don't know that. *We could fail*," I croaked.

He stared at me for a moment, and then his eyelids flickered, and the excitement drained away. "If necessary, Samuel can use my body to shift some of the destructive side of his Bestowal. I will be able to withstand the injuries, as the rest of you will not."

I nodded without gratitude. "Good."

Chapter 27

It is easy to go down into Hell;
Night and day, the gates of dark death stand wide.
—Virgil

SAM HAD to kill all but two of the bird-steeds, but he got Kris and Gregor through the assimilation process.

We worried the whole time, Blaine the most out of all of us.

During that time, Jacky asked Torliam to keep training her, and the two of them spent hours sparring, her pushing herself desperately to keep up with him, to get better, to fight back. On the third day, she was throwing up on the ground from a punch in the gut that had literally knocked her off her feet and thrown her a few meters away.

"Rest," Torliam said. "Your human frame is weak. You cannot push yourself like a real warrior."

Not the best thing to say to someone so stubborn. Maybe he knew that and was trying to push her to break her limits.

She spat, then rushed at him in a zig-zagging manner, rapid changes of direction at high speed, aided by her ability to adjust the way gravity pulled on her body, both in direction, and in strength. As Jacky often did, she looked like a superhero out of a film, moving in ways so blatantly inhuman.

Torliam kept up with her easily, almost blurring as he met and then parried blow after blow, despite how lazy his movements seemed. He had definitely been holding back against me. And Jacky had improved enough that I wondered just how much she'd been training and practicing when I was too occupied with other things to notice. Even seventy-two Seeds wouldn't cause changes like she displayed.

Still, a lazy kick brought Torliam's shin to her chest, and she went flying back again, skidding when she hit the ground with her knees and forearms. Her back convulsed upward as she struggled to breathe, and Sam stood up, taking a few uncertain steps toward her.

But Jacky didn't stay down. She arched again and got a leg under her. She *surged* upward, rising taller than she was. Bigger than she was, as if she'd suddenly become part Estreyan.

Torliam's eyes widened, but he didn't have a chance to do more than that, as she threw herself at him again, this time moving even faster. Her steps shook the ground, and when she slammed into his guard, he slid back a few feet. He let out a short laugh of surprise, and showed us all a glimpse of how seriously we'd been underestimating him, despite knowing that every accumulated Seed of ours was only a small portion of his own strength.

He punched and slashed and kicked, all Grace and Strength and Agility. His movement whistled in the air from speed, and when he hit Jacky, it sounded like those fake blows from the old western films. Like someone pounding a slab of raw beef.

She went flying for a third time, and when she stood up, she was bigger than him.

He tried to dodge instead of block when she shot back at him, probably wisely, but she turned on a dime, in a move that should not have been possible, not just for a human, but for any object subject to the laws of physics.

They traded blows that sounded more like the cracks of close lightning, as the rest of us watched in awe. Twenty seconds, then thirty, passed.

Then Torliam blurred, disappearing for a moment.

There was a muffled bang, and then Torliam stood where she'd been, and she was flying forward, bent backward from where he'd slammed into her from behind.

The rush of displaced wind blew past me, making the loose strands of my hair flutter.

Jacky didn't get up a fourth time, and when she shrank back down to her normal size and stayed there, Sam rushed over to make sure she was okay.

"You did well," Torliam said, panting heavily.

Jacky waved Sam off and stood, limping back toward the group. She laughed aloud, gleeful and snorting. "It's my new Skill! Struggle. I've been trying to figure out how to make it work, 'cause my VR chip wouldn't give me any info."

Sam pressed a hand on her shoulder, encouraging her to sit down on one of the big logs we'd placed around the campsite. Her clothes hung half off her, torn at the seams. He very carefully looked away, and handed her a blanket to wrap around herself.

"This is going to make a difference," she said, practically glowing with joy. "I've been working so hard, and it was just like…every time something happened, I was useless." She turned to me. "I can help, Eve."

I grinned back at her, doing my best not to let any of my dismay show. I'd picked Jacky to be on my team because of her fighting prowess, it was true. And a lot of the things we'd been going up against lately had been ridiculously stronger than us, or something you couldn't fight directly. Looking at her in this moment, it was easy to see how strained Jacky had been acting lately. For a while, actually. She'd been quiet, no longer the first to crack a joke or roughhouse playfully. And I hadn't noticed.

When the kids finally broke through the assimilation sickness, they were almost as happy as Jacky to learn that they had Skills now, too, and just had to learn how to use them.

Blaine tried to convince them to let things lie, and not try and use a power that could potentially harm them, but he had no chance of convincing them.

We traveled toward the capital, then, taking turns between riding the birds and running along beside them while someone else rode. And I thought. I thought about how smoothly things seemed to be working out. How my lies were becoming truth. And I was deeply suspicious. But by that point, it was too late. I couldn't turn away from the path I'd set myself on. I felt a cold maggot wiggling in the back of my mind, and clamped down on it, doing my best to crush it with meditation, like I did when Chaos tried to overwhelm me.

OUR JOURNEY WAS...EVENTFUL. In addition to the three different types of deadly terrain we had to traverse, we were attacked by monsters over and over again. I had a feeling it was because of my Skill, which was the only one of the nine the group had gotten that started out with a description even before it was actively used and gave the VR chip data to work with.

I suspected this was because the Skill was *always* active. However, the description was nothing more than what the goddess had said when she gave it to me.

VOICE (SOVEREIGN CLASS): INCREASES CHARISMA. ACTS AS A BEACON FOR BEINGS OF POWER. ALLOWS PRESENCE AND WILL TO BE IMPOSED ON SURROUNDINGS. SKILL EFFECTS WILL EXPAND AND STRENGTHEN WITH PLAYER IMPROVEMENT.

The monsters seemed drawn to us. We had no chance of sneaking past without notice, as if I were constantly emitting some sort of dog whistle that only they could hear. I hadn't had any luck turning it off, but I also couldn't figure out how to actively make it do anything.

On the brighter side, Chanelle had started to talk and was increasingly hungry all the time, which Blaine thought might be a sign that the Seeds were healing her and intensifying her need for fuel, like me.

When Chaos gave me another bloody nose, I took the last of the Seeds I'd been trying to save for her. I didn't tell anyone. We were already traveling as fast as we could, cognizant of the literal time limit on killing the God of Knowledge, imposed by the Oracle. I could only hope we wouldn't be too late.

I wasn't the only one who was having trouble with my new Skill.

Zed couldn't figure out how his was supposed to work, at all. He was frustrated by this, because whatever the Veil-Piercer Skill was, he was absolutely certain based on the name that it would be "so cool."

Gregor felt pretty much the same way, though Blaine did his best to discourage both of the kids from even attempting to use their Skills.

Adam was banging his head against the metaphorical brick wall, trying every experiment he could think of that involved 'giving' stuff to the rest of us.

Sam hadn't had any strange phenomena occur, but I don't think he was trying very hard, due to apprehension. 'Black Sun' was a worrying Skill name, for someone like him.

Torliam, out of all of us, worked out his Skill, Tracker, with frustrating ease. "I can find anything," he said simply. "If I have a solid idea of exactly what I am looking for, over time I will be compelled toward it." He smirked at the looks he was receiving. "I am familiar with the blood-borne powers of this world. It was not so difficult a task to discern the function, *especially* when provided with a name."

Adam huffed and rolled his eyes.

One night, while we were camping in the midst of a particularly disturbing spot, where the plants whispered and gibbered unintelligibly to each other in a sinister mockery of intelligence, Kris came into her own Skill, Summon. She'd been clutching her moose tightly, eyes squeezed tight and staying as close to the fire as possible, both for the warmth it provided against the frigid night, and for the comforting light.

I'd been on watch, along with Jacky, while the rest of the camp wound down. I was monitoring the surrounding area with my Skill, and we were all very much prepared to be attacked in the middle of the night by that point, since it had happened multiple times.

A particularly loud jabbering of word-like sounds from the surrounding bushes spewed out, in a voice suspiciously similar to some of our teammates.

Kris whimpered, and her moose wiggled. She jumped, letting out a small scream and thrusting the stuffed animal away from her.

It climbed to its feet and walked over to her, circling her and facing outward in a mockery of protective aggression as she stared at it.

A couple of the others had been woken by her exclamation, and we all pretty much just goggled at the plush toy.

Gregor scowled. "What did you do?"

Kris shook her head. "I… I'm not totally sure. I was scared, and I felt something that felt…warm, like…safe, you know? So, I connected it and Moose in my mind. And then Moose started walking around."

"You made your imaginary friend come to life," he said flatly.

"No! Well, not really." She fidgeted, and Moose turned to Gregor and gave a warning toss of its plush antlers. "I think I put a ghost inside Moose."

"A *spirit*, which does not necessarily correspond to the shade of one who was once living," Torliam corrected. "That is your Skill, is it not, Summoner?" He smiled at her encouragingly.

She smiled tentatively back.

Jacky whooped and went over to give Kris a congratulatory ride around the camp on her shoulders, while Moose ran along at her feet.

Blaine woke up then. After the shock and initial rapid-fire questioning were over, he gave Jacky a good chewing out for encouraging Kris to experiment with "spirit" summoning, when none of us had any idea what dangers could be associated with it.

The rest of us very carefully didn't mention that we also might have done a teeny bit of encouraging, before he woke up.

AS WE DREW CLOSER to the capital, Torliam began to teach me how his people interacted in a formal setting, and coach me on how to navigate their politics. "The line of Aethezriel rules, now, but the decision has never been based solely on bloodlines, though often the daughter follows the mother. Who rules is a combination of favors traded and merit."

I frowned. "Wait. Daughter follows the mother? Do only women rule?"

"Not only. A few generations ago, we had a male ruler. This was before my time. But it is customary that the females lead, in the household as well as in the nation." His jaw tightened. "Over time, and as our population has dwindled, it is becoming more widely accepted that a man may be…whatever he wants. In the village, for example, a man could take any position that a female could. Of course, there is still a small percentage who feel that it is shameful for a man such as I to be an explorer and historian."

"I'm pretty sure this is the first time you've ever admitted that Estreyer might have something wrong with it, besides the Sickness," I said. "You know, Earth had the civil rights movements long ago."

"Your people die so quickly, it is no wonder change can be enacted in shorter spans of time," he said, seeming affronted. He proceeded to drill me on the different types of bows I might need to use, nitpicking every little mistake.

Zed thought this was funny, and came over to learn how to bow with me.

Unfortunately, when I collapsed to the ground, cradling my head in my hands, it meant he and Torliam both saw.

I pressed down on temples, trying to stop myself from releasing my claws, resisting the urge to smash my head against the ground. "It's the maggots." I gasped as stars floated around my eyes from the combination of pressure on my skull and the fact that I'd been holding my breath.

"Sam!" Zed screamed.

"No, no," I said, groaning. "I don't need him. There's nothing he can do."

Torliam knelt beside me, grabbing my hands, and pulling them away from my head. "It is the God of Knowledge."

The others were running toward us. I realized suddenly that the high-pitched keening sound was coming from my own throat, and stopped. This was not the way. I needed to keep it together. At first, I'd thought the flashbacks were just some PTSD. If anyone had earned some, I had. But as it continued, I became increasingly certain that something was very wrong.

"Were you singing?" Zed asked. "You have a horrible voice, Eve. Please refrain from making our ears bleed." He laughed at his own joke, absolutely no real humor in his voice.

I giggled. Once I started, it seemed I couldn't stop, till my laughs sounded more like sobs. My cheeks felt frozen and stiff, and when I reached up to touch them, I realized that behind the concealing rim of the coat around my eyes, I was crying.

I choked down the laughter, and stiffly scrubbed at my cheeks, letting the ice flake away inconspicuously.

Torliam spoke. "I, too, have been experiencing some…mental 'flashbacks.' His influence lingers. It is apparent that you have even less defense against him than I."

"How do I stop it?" I gritted out. "What do I do?"

"You will have to attack his connection directly. There is a…Trial, of sorts, in the capital. It is unpleasant. My people only use it in the most extreme of circumstances. But it will allow you to leave your body and enter your mind, to find the pieces of his power that he has left behind."

"Why didn't you mention this earlier?" I glared at him as the feeling receded and I regained some of my faculties.

"It is *very* unpleasant. Enough to drive someone mad. Only a few have completed it successfully, and there are no Bestowals. Surviving it intact is considered a gift enough on its own."

I looked at him and saw what he wasn't saying. He did not want to attempt this pseudo-Trial. "Is there no other way?"

"None that I know of. Not to remove a mental infestation directly from a god."

"Well then we'd better hurry up," I said. "Knowledge could be watching everything that we do with his little maggots."

Torliam paled.

Chapter 28

Do I fear the sleepless nights?

You have no idea how long the dark lasts when you cannot close your eyes to it.

—Tyler Knott Gregson

THE DREAMS KEPT COMING, and as I grew more tired, it grew harder for me to tell the difference between them and the surreal, cold wilderness we traveled through. I meditated, instead of sleep, but it wasn't the same.

I was trying to meditate as the sun set one evening, curled up in my Estreyan sleeping tube.

Kris tripped over my feet in the twilight, breaking me out of a mutated flashback of the Intelligence Trial, where I'd killed a girl to save myself, and then convinced Sam to do the same.

I shot upward, and she startled back from me and gasped, surprised. "Sorry!" she said. "It's kinda hard to see—"

But I wasn't listening to her words, only noticing the fear on her face, and the way it made me feel. As if I'd done something wrong. I hadn't done anything wrong.

"Do you think I'm going to hurt you?" I snapped.

"Uh…" Her eyes widened. "No, I mean—"

"Why would I do that? I said I'd protect you, didn't I?" My words weren't vicious, yet, but my tone was. "I could have hurt you *long* before now if I wanted to! I'd just slice your throat open and let you bleed out in a few seconds."

Blaine stepped between us then, scowling at me in a way I hadn't seen him do before, even when talking about NIX. "What ridiculous insanity has come over you?" he said in a low voice. "She tripped. It is dark. It was an *accident*."

Gregor stepped forward from where he'd been watching, little fists balled up tight, thick eyebrows scrunched over his nose. "You're being mean," he said, throat thick with the hint of suppressed tears. "Don't be mean to my sister."

The rage left me suddenly, like a ghost passing through and sucking the air from my body, leaving me gasping. "I—I'm sorry," I said, panting for words, or air, something to fill the hollow in the center of my chest. "I was dreaming," I lied desperately. "A nightmare. I woke up and I didn't quite realize what was habbening—" I broke off, hand shooting to my face, covering my nose.

I turned away, hiding the blood that had made me blubber, and the discordance of emotion. What was *wrong* with me? This was not normal. I could tell that. "I'm sorry," I said again. "I didn't mean what I said. Could you go get Sam for me?"

Kris nodded, wide-eyed, and ran off.

Once the bleeding had stopped, I had Sam force me into a dreamless sleep. When I woke naturally, no nightmares forcing me awake in the middle of the night, I felt better than I had in a long while. "We need to hurry," I said.

"We can be there before daybreak tomorrow, if we do not stop tonight," Torliam said.

We pushed ourselves at an exhausting pace. However, as we got closer to the capital, excitement overrode some of our weariness. Torliam, especially, seemed to brighten. "I have not seen my family or friends in so long," he said.

We arrived in the dead of night.

I had been half-dozing in my saddle, meditating to calm the effects of both Chaos and the God of Knowledge's attack.

The capital was beautiful in a way I'd never seen on Earth. Similar to some of the urban ruins we'd been sent to for Trials, the architecture was fantastical, and things seemed to have been designed strictly for beauty. A white wall of marble surrounded the city, but it didn't look particularly useful for stopping attacks—probably because little could be, against an Estreyan or the type of monsters that might attack a city filled with them.

I wondered if they had other defenses. Perhaps advanced technology of some sort was in place, leaving the wall as a symbolic decoration.

Guards called out to us when we were still far enough away that even I with my enhanced sight couldn't make out their forms. I found that surprising for a moment, before I realized that of course Estreyan guards would be picked for their Perceptive powers.

Torliam called back to them, identifying himself.

There was a pause, and then they called out to us again, ordering us to stop. They sent out a group of five to meet us on foot.

Torliam stepped forward, pulling his hood back from his face so that they could see him.

"Identify yourself!" one called, despite the fact he'd already done so.

Torliam said his full name again.

"He's telling the truth," one said.

"Torliam, son of Mardinest, has been dead for years!" another snapped back.

"I have returned," Torliam said. "I was not killed. Only...detained. Send word to my *mother-lord*. The *warrior-queen* will want to know of her son's homecoming."

With a bit more suspicious muttering amongst themselves, the group of five escorted us just inside the gates, where they set an even larger number of guards on us while someone went to wake the queen.

They took Torliam into a building to the side of the gate, where they had some sort of communication device he would use to prove his identity to his mother. He returned only a couple minutes later, a smile and an excited tension both badly suppressed.

The queen arrived about a half hour later. I knew who she was because of the golden circlet around her forehead, the honor guard of armored Estreyans following silently behind her, and the way her face changed when she saw Torliam.

She threw open her arms and strode toward him, not quite rushing.

He stepped forward, and they hugged each other. It lasted less than a minute, as they both seemed to gather themselves and return to that slightly regal bearing.

She kept a hand on his arm, though, as if afraid he might disappear if she removed her grip. "I thought you were dead, my son."

"I am alive," he said simply. "And I have much to tell you. My quest was not in vain."

Her eyes widened. "You must tell me everything. But first, food." She turned and swept an assessing gaze over the rest of us. "Your companions may stay in the south wing, near the kitchens," she said imperiously. "No doubt they are hungry, and would appreciate a warm meal," she added somewhat more kindly.

"You will be safe," Torliam said to us. "Eat, and rest." He looked at me. "I will come find you when I have spoken with my mother."

The queen didn't seem to be waiting for an answer. She waved to one of her other companions with a nod, and he stepped forward, holding out a metal staff with lines running through it somewhat like the lines that scored the outside of the Seed spheres. Little rings of metal floated around the top of it, orbiting where the crystal ball would have gone if it were a storybook magic staff. It reminded me of the Shortcut.

I realized that was probably not a coincidence when Torliam stepped forward to wrap a hand around it, below his mother's. The queen wrapped both hands around her staff and twisted. The metal slid and clicked into place, and they were gone, with a little breeze as air rushed to fill the space they'd been.

The rest of us stuck together as the guards escorted us through the sprawling city, which was filled with lights even at this time of the night, to the palace kitchens. We ate, gorging ourselves on food with actual seasoning, that hadn't been scalded over a campfire.

The palace staff gave us each a room. They were small, but the beds were suspiciously comfortable, and we were all right next to each other, close enough for me to keep tabs on everyone with my Wraith Skill.

Still, none of us quite relaxed, and Adam hadn't stopped jerking suspiciously since we'd passed the city gates. But we didn't want to cause offense in any of the myriad ways Torliam had warned of. So we accepted their hospitality, but set up a watch schedule, so that someone would always be awake to receive and read any emergency Windows.

I'd fallen asleep under this measure of security, only to jerk upright when the door opened.

Torliam slipped into my room, his body making the huge doorframe look normal. "I have spoken with the queen," he said in an odd tone.

I swung my legs over the side of the bed, placing my bare feet on the floor, and waited for him to continue.

He moved to the other side of the small room, placing his back against the wall and sliding down till he sat on the ground. "There is no force heading toward Earth," he said, head bowed.

"What?" My voice was scratchy with sleep.

"Those of my unit who escaped returned to Estreyer about one cycle ago," he said, using the Estreyan word for their equivalent to a year. "They told my mother of my fate, knowing that I might still be alive. She did not send a force back for me. Neither to enact revenge or to save me. Not even to confirm the news of my death. Political pressures have been building, she says. Other old families are maneuvering for power, and she could not spare even a scout team."

I didn't know what to say.

"I am her son. But I am not a daughter, and I am not even the oldest. She believed when she allowed me to go that I had been crazed by the death of my sister. I knew that. But I believed she would send for me when she was able. I spent years within NIX. No rescue was ever coming for me."

I cleared my throat. "You didn't need her to save you," I said. "I mean, that *sucks*. But we escaped all by ourselves. We didn't need to depend on someone else to fix everything for us." I wanted to say something comforting, but I didn't know how. Sentiment was not my strong suit.

He shook his head. "No. I could not escape. I tried. If not for *you*…" He raised his gaze to mine.

I stayed silent, awkwardly.

"My mother will try to use you to her political advantage," he said, seeming to change his train of thought instantly. "She will want you to bolster her image and strengthen the support of the populace. Fear is a powerful motivator, but it has been turning against her. Hope is even more powerful, and it is the currency you will deal in. Do not bargain cheaply."

"Tell me more," I said, leaning forward.

He smiled, but it wasn't a pleasant expression. That was okay with me.

I MET with the queen in the morning, in what she called her "war chambers." Maps and electronic diagrams, which I couldn't understand the meaning of, glowed out from the walls.

The queen stood at the head of a huge marble round table in the center of the room. She turned to me when I entered. "Welcome, Eve of the line of Redding." She gestured for me to sit across from her, and spoke in Estreyan, which I was gladder than ever I had learned.

I made sure to bow just as Torliam had instructed me. My extended awareness showed me her grimace, which had disappeared by the time I straightened and moved toward the other side of the table. My feet barely touched the ground in the chair sized for Estreyans. "I fear you may have been misinformed," I said. "I am Eve of the line of Matrix."

She raised a hand to her mouth, as if embarrassed. "Oh! I apologize. A simple mistake."

Or a power play. I smiled.

"I must thank you for bringing my son back to me," she said. "I had believed he was dead and lost to me forever. It is a horrible thing to lose a child."

"I could do no less," I said. "The blood-covenant between us allied your son to me irrevocably."

"The blood-covenant which he will be severing," she parried. "Since it was not of his will, and furthermore was spread amongst a whole *slew* of people." She waved a hand in disgust.

"Of course," I said. "That is as it should be. It is not the greatest bond between us now, in any case. Your son has been marked by the Goddess of Testimony and Lore, as I am sure he told you."

"Indeed. What a joyous revelation. He says that the Oracle has set you on the path of the spark. The God of Knowledge has told you to come back with strength and petition before him for enlightenment about the Sickness that plagues our world?" Her voice was dry, but her eyes glittered with intensity, and her fingers clenched around her staff.

"Yes." So he had lied to his mother, too.

"The spark was indeed well hidden," she said with a hint of a smile and more than a dash of irony. She stood, then, and walked over to me.

I rose to match her, and she reached forward and undid the bindings on my coat.

She pulled the coat away from me, revealing the crystal mark at the base of my neck, and the gifts of the Oracle on my arm and finger. "There should be three, should there not?"

"There are. I have not yet completed the third. I suspect I will not be able to until I have fulfilled the vision of the second."

She stared down at me. "My son says you may bring hope for my realm."

I stared back at her, feeling the ripple of her power, so close.

"He is surprisingly wise, for a young man. And a human holds no danger to my throne." She stared at me as she said it, gauging my reaction.

"I have no intention of undermining your rule, Queen," I said. What was the point in subtlety, for a statement like that? "I have a quest that may lead to some useful knowledge about how to defeat the Sickness, given to me by the Oracle." That was a lie. Or at least I hoped it was. The quest from the Oracle *could* eventually lead to knowledge about defeating the Sickness, but I had no reason to believe it would. What worried me was the acknowledgment of Testimony and Lore, in relation to a story about defeating said Sickness. But I would go along with it, because I refused to die if there was anything at all I could do to save myself. "I also have a crystal mark embedded in my flesh, given by Testimony and Lore. But the thing I really care about is that I have too much of the gods running through my veins for any mortal of my strength to survive, and I think the Oracle may be leading me to a solution. Your goals and my own meet. For now. So we should help each other."

If she was surprised, she didn't show it. Instead, she laughed. "My son told me you were bold. With you as my champion, I could give hope to the people."

I understood. She was laying out the terms of our bargain. "I would show my support publicly, and you would help me to complete my quest. I will need warriors strong enough to help me defeat a god," I said.

"Do such warriors exist?! At most, I could provide warriors that might aid you in impressing the god enough to gain a small Bestowal."

I shook my head. "It is not a small Bestowal that I need. We must prove that we can defeat the undefeatable, force the unconquerable to kneel. Nothing less will do." I hoped she couldn't hear my heartbeat, or notice it throbbing in my neck.

She drew back. "And what if you fail? It is I that will have to deal with the backlash for having sent the strongest of my forces to die at the word of a foreign girl."

I needed this. She *had* to agree. "I am a godling, progeny to Khaos," I said, enunciating clearly. And the crystal at my throat pulsed, adding an almost physical weight to my words. It was like a vibration, like the brush of wind against you from standing too close to an explosion, or like the feel of a giant foot smashing into the ground too near to you. For the first time, my Voice Skill had asserted itself actively.

Her eyes widened, and she stepped back, the movement almost a stumble.

"I will have the strongest warriors available," I said. "It doesn't have to be a command, you sending men to their deaths. Simply give me your support. Encourage volunteers. Once the hope of your people is proven to be grounded in fact, you will still reap the benefits."

Queen Mardinest raised an eyebrow. "You are not the first to claim a connection to the Oracle or Testimony and Lore. Others have created false hope, many, many times. They have all failed, in the end, and my people have grown mistrustful."

"They were not me," I said. "It is my nature to succeed where others fail."

"We will see."

THE QUEEN and I talked for a little while longer. She instructed me on the other bloodlines that might either be allies or cause trouble, sounding somewhat like Torliam did when he lectured, except that she insulted me much less than he would have. Even so, her presence radiated more intimidation than his.

I asked about sending relief to the little village on the edge of Knowledge's domain that had been attacked by monsters. Apparently, Torliam had beaten me to it the night before. A unit was already headed toward the village. I just hoped there was something left to save.

After we were done, I headed to the kitchens to sate my growling stomach. A servant caught me on the way and told me that Torliam had requested my presence after I had finished with the queen. I tried to get the servant to have Torliam just meet me in the kitchens, but she paled at the very idea of such rudeness, so I followed her with a sigh.

His quarters were on the nicer side of the castle, and *way* bigger than my own. I'm pretty sure he even had multiple rooms. He was pacing across the floor when I entered—which caused the servant to pale a second time and scurry away, presumably so she wouldn't be caught up in the backlash if he got angry.

Instead, he was awkward. "Now that we are back in my…home," he said, "I will finally be severing the blood-covenants forced upon me."

I nodded, giving him a small frown. "Okay. What exactly does that mean?"

"I know you do not fully understand the blood-covenant, but on my world, it is a way to bind people to each other. Historically, it would bind a servant to a master, or two life-partners to each other. Often, a wife and her husband will take the blood-covenant."

I raised my eyebrows. "And we have a blood-covenant."

"Yes. Well, partially. A proper bond goes both ways. My blood has been shared, but I have not received a covenant in return. I am bound to you and many, many others." He shuddered. "The covenant allows power to be shared between the two parties, to a certain extent. You and I have been able to sense each other across distances, before, and I always know where any of those with the bond are, if they are on my side of the divide between worlds. When I break the covenant, that, too, will be broken."

"What will happen to the Seeds already within people's bodies?"

"They will remain. You will not lose all your strength. But there will be a period of…acclimatization. Probably some loss of whatever strength you were drawing continuously from the bond. It can be disorienting, even painful. And as you humans," he said it without rancor, "are undoubtedly the weaker ones in the bond, in addition to not having shared your own blood, you will be affected much more than I. Do you wish to attend the ceremony? There will be healers there, bound to silence about what we do."

"Well, that seems like an obvious 'yes.' Should the others come, as well?" I asked.

"They are welcome to attend, if they wish. You should at least alert them that they will likely be feeling sick in some manner, sometime within the next hour." He turned and led the way down into the bowels of the castle in silence.

I sent a Window to the others, explaining what Torliam had told me, and sending a map of my route and location so they could follow. "How exactly does one break a blood-covenant?" I asked.

His jaw clenched. "By changing that which is shared. The method to do it is one of the old ways. It is forbidden, and highly restricted. But some still know the process, and as queen, my mother-lord has the ability to approve it. If done incorrectly, I will die."

"Whoever's doing this better know what they're doing," I muttered. "Does that also stop the other Seeds NIX took from you from being able to create new blood-bonds?" If not, the problem wouldn't be solved, since new Players could be created at will.

"It does. That is why we must do it this way."

We arrived in a big cavern, with a narrow path cutting through the stalagmites rising from the ground. It led to a large ritual circle in the center of the cavern, surrounded by orbs of colored light that lit up the ground and the tips of stalactites hanging down from far above.

People I assumed were healers stood off in a group to the side, and the queen turned at our arrival and nodded regally at us, though the tension in her body belied the serenity of her expression. Her eyes returned to the people in cheesy hooded robes who moved around the inside of the circle, setting things up.

The other Player members of the team, plus Blaine, arrived by the same path Torliam and I had taken, and though I'd heard them talking faintly before they entered the cavern, they quieted at the oppressive atmosphere of the place. They joined me, and Blaine, ever-curious, sent me a Window.

—Is this some sort of cultural...ritual magic? Not *real* magic, of course. It is just advanced science. But is it something they treat with ceremony as if it is real magic?—
-Blaine-

I shrugged and shook my head. I knew as little as he did.

The hooded people began to chant...or sing. I didn't recognize the language, and somehow the lilting, rhythmic way they spoke could have been either. The colored orbs resonated with their voices, seeming to reflect and throw them, till they seemed to come from everywhere at once, and the hair on my arms vibrated with every word as it throbbed through the air.

Torliam let out a sharp pulse of his blue misty power, and suddenly he was bleeding from the middle of his left forearm. He walked around the circle, filling the little lines that surrounded and connected the base of all the orbs with his trickling blood, in one continuous path that ended with him standing back in the middle without ever walking over the same blood-filled line twice. He looked a bit pale, and I knew that a comparatively smaller human would probably have passed out from blood-loss already.

The lilting chants grew louder and louder, the sound of it a physical thing, kind of like the way the Boneshaker moved me from the inside.

The lines of blood flared with white light, and the orbs seemed to explode. With the flash of light and sound, something *shattered.* Like a crystal chandelier breaking forever in slow motion.

When the spots cleared from my eyes I noticed that the blood was gone from the circle. Torliam knelt in the middle, sagging from exhaustion while a couple of the healers worked on him.

I looked over at Jacky, who was hunched over and looking pale and slightly green, like really old fish.

Without warning, I bent over and threw up what little was in my stomach.

Chapter 29

I have been one acquainted with the night.
— Robert Frost

THE NAUSEA PASSED QUICKLY ENOUGH. One of the healers came to make sure my team was all right, and Blaine questioned her. “I have two kids, and they were both given Skills from a goddess. I am very worried that the power is too much for them, and might backlash. Is there something you might be able to do for them? Or at least examine them to see if my worry is founded?”

The healer refused. “That is beyond my realm of ability. Beyond most healers, in fact.” She left.

“Ifkana,” I said, turning to Zed, who'd barely seemed to be affected by the bond-breaking ritual. “Isn't that the name the healer from the village recommended? He said he'd be one of the few able to extend my life.”

Zed didn't even have time to nod before Blaine jumped in. “We need to see this Ifkana, then. As soon as possible.”

I nodded. “I agree. We should take Chanelle, too, just in case. If he's able to do something for me, he might be able to help her, too.”

I passed along the plan to the others, and would have asked Torliam to accompany us, but the other healers had taken him off somewhere, presumably to rest after his ordeal and significant blood loss. I tried to ask the queen about Ifkana, but she'd disappeared, too. When we returned to the palace, I asked a servant to tell the queen I'd like to meet with her, but they said that she had left the palace, and they did not know when she'd be back.

We waited around for an hour, then grabbed another servant, and asked if they could take us to Ifkana the healer. They hesitated, but agreed, noting that no one would turn down an audience with Eve of the returned line of Matrix, even if an appointment hadn't been set up ahead of time. I was amazed by the wildfire spread of gossip, but if it would smooth the way for what I needed, I guessed I didn't mind.

We grabbed the kids and Chanelle, and followed the servant through the streets. The percentage of people walking or riding huge animals rather than vehicles surprised us.

The servant explained to Blaine that vehicles not meant for long-distance travel, goods transportation, or attack were considered lazy. "It is as if one is making a statement that they are not powerful enough to travel on their own strength," he said. "Some say our laziness of old is the cause of our fall to the Sickness, so teleportation pods and other technologies that allow us to stagnate have been abandoned." The servant brought us to a mansion almost as opulent as the palace, though significantly smaller.

We were then forced to wait in a room with very uncomfortable chairs that were too big for all of us.

Jacky leaned back in her chair, half-sliding off it. "Is this person busy healing half the population of a small country all at once, or are they just ignoring us?" she whined.

Chanelle spoke. "We are waiting to see a healer?" she asked, looking at me.

We all turned toward her, weariness instantly gone. It was rare that Chanelle could speak coherently, though increasing in frequency.

"Yes." I nodded. "He's supposed to be the best. Maybe even good enough to help you and me." It would be a wonderful thing, if Chanelle's mind could be returned to her.

She smiled, a jerky stretching of the mouth that didn't look very practiced. "That's good. I can't stay..." she paused, searching for the word, "*awake* for very long, still." She sniffed, a little like a dog. "I'm hungry. Is there any food?"

I dug out a fruit from my pack and tossed it to Chanelle.

She caught it and grinned brightly at her success, the expression looking just a little more natural this time. She stayed lucid and kept eating until the healer finally deigned to see us.

One of his servants escorted us to a larger room filled with a couple jacuzzi-like tubs of water, strange devices, and a fat woman wearing an extremely long sheet that had been wrapped around her several times in artful ways. The translucent fabric glowed, and strands of what looked like gold glittered among the rest. Obviously, she was rich, and she wanted everyone to know it. Ifkana was not a man, I realized belatedly.

She turned to us with a smile, as if she'd been distracted from something, though I saw nothing she could have been working on. "Welcome, Eve of the line of Matrix," she said. "And companions, bearing the marks of Testimony and Lore, I hear?" She tilted her head like a little bird, eyes seeking out the crystal symbols on us.

Birch coughed at her, and she cooed over him, snapping her fingers at one of her servants and instructing them to go grab a snack for the, "darling little creature. And so *rare* a species, too!"

"Thank you for meeting with us on such short notice," I said, giving one of the bows Torliam had taught me for someone who wasn't socially above me, but who I respected. "I have heard you are the best, and we are in need of your services."

She tittered, waving a sausage-fingered hand. "Oh, of course, I am the best. Queen Mardinest has been trying to retain my services since she first came into power, you know." She smirked. "I hear our *great* ruler is supporting your claim of heritage and Testimony?" The words were tinged with a hint of derision.

I raised an eyebrow. "It would be hard for her to deny it, with the abundance of proof. You are certainly well-informed, though. We only arrived in the city yesterday."

"Oh, I have my ways, you know. I am a *powerful* healer," she said, a kind of smug significance in her tone. She asked me who needed healing and of what, and then motioned me forward. She waved her hand about, and a bright purple light arced from it, almost like ribbon unfurling. It spun around me, changing colors, and making patterns which she seemed to pay only passing attention to, more interested in making conversation with me. She wanted to know about my connection to Torliam and the queen, my quest from the Oracle, and the gifts Testimony and Lore had given my team.

I felt strangely reluctant to reveal too much information, because her questions had sharp teeth, hidden behind her facade of pleasantry. I wondered if she was one of the people who wanted Queen Mardinest removed from power. They weren't allies, that was definite.

Finally, the purple ribbon returned to Ifkana, disappearing into the hand that had created it. "Your regenerative power is strong," she said. "I will boost it, but there is not much more I can do for you at the moment. When that wears off, you come back to me, and I will keep you healthy a while longer. You know that no mortal can stave off the effects of a greater god's power indefinitely, though?"

I nodded.

Kris and Gregor were next, and she told them to come forward together. Once again, she waved out the purple ribbon, and it began to swirl and dance around them, as she asked them about their Skills from the Oracle.

Gregor pouted while Kris exclaimed excitedly about summoning spirits and putting them into bodies to play with her or complete tasks she set.

When Ifkana tried to get Gregor to talk about his own Skill, he scowled down at the ground and refused to speak.

Ifkana seemed to find this more irritating than endearing, but was distracted by Jacky, who was more than happy enough to talk about her own new Skill. The purple ribbon, still focused on the kids, let out a pulse of red halfway through one of Jacky's sentences, and Ifkana's attention snapped toward it as if it had slapped her.

"What?" she said aloud, waving her arms and moving her fingers in complicated motions that seemed to control the ribbon. It turned all red. She gasped, and stepped back, hand over her heart.

"What's wrong?" Gregor asked. "Is the Skill killing us after all?"

Adam took a step forward, but froze when Ifkana screamed, "Do not move! Everyone stay still." Once her back was pressed against the wall, she spewed out another purple ribbon, this time sending it weaving among the rest of the group.

It stayed purple until it reached Chanelle, where it turned an instant bright red.

Chanelle looked down, blinking at the ribbon of light circling her. "That's…not good, is it?"

"You are infected," Ifkana said, her voice wavering. "It is not the Skills you need to worry about, but the Sickness."

Chapter 30

A star shines brightest at the edge of collapse.
— Omar Thornton

"THAT IS IMPOSSIBLE!" Blaine said. "Kris and Gregor do not have your world's disease. They are not even Estreyan!"

"It is early," Ifkana said, "but I do not err. I am the best healer on this side of the seven seas! The children have the Sickness, and the fair one," she pointed at Chanelle, "will soon succumb to it."

"We have been here a long time, now," Chanelle said, in a soft voice. "And some of us much longer than that. Maybe the weakest of us picked it up along the way." She spoke in English, and Ifkana flinched from her words, like they might somehow hurt her.

There was silence, then. My mind was reeling. Of all the things we could have learned, and all the bad news I had braced to hear from Ifkana, I had not expected this.

"What does this mean?" Gregor asked. "I'm going to die?" His breath came a little too fast.

"No," Blaine and I both said immediately.

"You should go," Ifkana said.

Blaine shook his head desperately. "Is there nothing you can do?"

"No one can heal the Sickness! It has no cure, and—" she calmed herself with a visibly shuddering breath, and looked at me. "You may find the cure for them, if you are what you say, Eve of the line of Matrix. The very marks on their hands set them on the path to save themselves." She straightened. "You should go. It is not safe for you to be here, only in part because the Sickness may spread. The *warrior-queen* may pardon those with the Sickness. Otherwise, the solution is always death. To reduce the chance of it spreading, or the affected going on a rampage and killing indiscriminately, those with the Sickness are to be killed, everything that they are and have owned obliterated from the face of the planet."

Kris whimpered, and Blaine knelt down to hug her and Gregor, glaring at Ifkana over their shoulders. "I swear I will not let that happen," he said.

"Go," she said. "Take them back to the palace."

"Don't say anything about this," I ordered Ifkana. "I don't want anyone doing something stupid."

"I will not tell anyone," she agreed, nodding rapidly enough that her second chin jiggled.

We'd waited so long for her to see us that it was night when we exited the house.

Gregor grabbed onto my hand as we hurried through the streets. "You really can fix this, right?"

"Yes. It's going to take me a bit of work, but don't worry. We won't let anything happen to you."

Sam and Blaine shared a look, and then Sam sent out a group Window, connecting everyone but the kids and Chanelle to it.

—YOUR QUEST ISN'T ACTUALLY TO STOP THE SICKNESS, THOUGH, IS IT? JUST TO GET INFORMATION ABOUT IT?—

-SAM-

I ground my teeth together. My quest had nothing at all to do with the Sickness, but everyone in the world, and now even my own team, needed my lie to be the truth.

—NO. BUT TESTIMONY AND LORE SEEMED TO THINK I HAD SOMETHING TO DO WITH THIS "SPARK" THAT THEY THINK WILL FIND THE WAY TO SAVE THEM. MAYBE THE THIRD PUZZLE WILL HAVE INFORMATION ABOUT THAT, OR I'LL GET ANOTHER QUEST.—

-EVE-

—Do we actually have time for that? How fast does the Sickness progress?—
-Adam-

—I need access to a lab. There is no way a cure is impossible without some alien god's help. Science does not work like that.—
-Blaine-

We were almost back to the palace when the blast knocked me off my feet. We'd been walking through mostly deserted streets, with what were probably shops and warehouses, since there weren't any people in their beds within.

My body and face smashed into the wall of the alley I'd been blown into, and I bounced off, dizzy and *burning*. I scrabbled blindly at my unprotected arms and neck, ripping off the smoldering remains of my clothes and pack.

"Get into the alley!" Adam screamed, throwing up a broad ink shield in the direction the attack had come from.

I rose to my feet, looking around frantically. Wraith lashed out, but found no others—wait, no—"There!" I screamed, spinning around to face the form rushing from the alley's other opening.

Zed's guns were out and shooting in half a second, but the person *dodged* the bullets as I watched, racing inevitably closer.

Adam threw out another shield, this one covering the other end of the alley.

The attacker stopped before it for a second.

Another explosion from behind made me stumble, and Adam's first shield disintegrated. He frantically created a replacement, layering multiple shields instead of just one.

"What's happening?" Sam screamed, the children and Chanelle pressed up against the wall behind him, protected by a human barrier formed from himself, Blaine, and Jacky. They'd boxed us in, attacks coming from both ends.

"We were betrayed," I said, the words coming to my mouth as soon as they formed in my mind.

The speedster took a few steps back, and jumped at the wall, bouncing off it onto the other wall, and then tossing himself over the top of the ink shield.

"I will not let you hurt them!" Blaine screamed, reaching for his own gun, and pointing it at the attacker falling straight toward us. The bullet shot out, spinning, and fragmenting outward and inward simultaneously in a way that baffled even the Perception of my Wraith Skill, and threatened to give me a headache if I focused on it too hard.

The wall of the building behind Speedster *ruptured* when the bullet hit, but he was no longer in its path. The stone statue that had replaced his form mid-fall exploded outward, chunks raining down on us.

Instead of being pulverized by Blaine's weapon, Speedster stood looking down on us from atop the building above.

Beside Speedster stood another huge form, so wide and muscular it looked like an orc.

"Agh!" Adam screamed, as his multi-leveled ink barrier against the street attacker failed. The heat grew dizzying. He was blown back when his last ink shield disintegrated under the touch of the floating female form made of magma, who must have been the one throwing fireballs.

My eyeballs burned as the water evaporated from them, and I smelled burning hair.

Blaine shot at the magma creature, and it threw a hand forward.

A blast of fire pulsed out and engulfed the bullet, the two attacks meeting above Adam. The bullet released its effects, which were enough to blow the fireball apart and tear into the magma creature, blasting her stomach apart and blowing pieces of her everywhere.

Adam *screamed* as the heat of the exploded fireball hit him, turning him pink instantly, and sizzling away the hair on his face. He scrambled backward, pushing himself along the ground with his legs, covering his face with his arms.

Blaine shot again, but the huge form up above gestured, and the slow-moving bullet was replaced by some pebbles which fell impotently onto the ground. In the air far up above, the real bullet exploded, with a similar lack of damage to anything important. Some sort of replacement-slash-teleportation Skill was at work, it seemed.

Zed shot at the two on the roof, but most of his bullets were stopped by the orcish Estreyan, and the others were dodged by Speedster, who nudged his comrade out of the way when necessary.

Jacky let out a frustrated scream, crouched down, and launched herself up and at the wall, imitating speedster's zig-zagging jumps to much greater effect.

I slipped back to take her place protecting the kids, broadcasting out a

Window to everyone. It displayed everyone's location, and any danger I thought might go unnoticed, updating as fast as I could process the same information. I didn't have any long-distance Skills, except Wraith, and maybe Voice, but neither of those was helpful, and I didn't want to leave the kids or Chanelle unprotected. If only Torliam were with us, this fight would be going very differently.

Jacky distracted Orc long enough for Blaine to get off another couple shots against Magma, but when Sam took the opportunity to try and grab Adam off the ground, it left an unprotected spot in our shield wall around the kids and Chanelle.

Blaine was distracted by the way the pieces of Magma he'd blown off her were inching their way back to the main body, globules burning snail-trails across the ground and walls.

Speedster took that opportunity, shooting himself straight down off the top of the wall toward us.

Zed clipped him in the leg with a bullet, I think, but it didn't change his trajectory.

The kids were huddled down, heads tucked into their knees and arms up for protection, but Kris looked up, and screamed. She thrust both hands out and up, as if she could stop the falling attacker in mid-air.

The crumbled statue from earlier that had taken Speedster's spot slammed itself clumsily back together, rising to fill the spot Sam had left. It thrust a fist forward to meet Speedster, but when they collided, the soft sandstone-like material of the statue crumbled and broke. Still, it seemed to do a little damage.

Speedster pushed off the statue to launch himself away from us and toward Sam instead, who was crouching over Adam. He smashed his feet into the back of Sam's head, knocking the boy out cold.

Adam launched an arc of lightning from underneath Sam, catching Speedster with enough force to throw him back down the alley.

Up above, Jacky had grown to match Orc and was using her Skill to great effect, flashing all over the place, hitting him again and again with enough force that I could feel the vibrations traveling through the walls and the ground.

Even so, Orc seemed to be withstanding the onslaught, and the occasional blow he returned hit just as hard.

Blaine ran out of the cool ammo, then, and things went to hell.

Magma floated forward, her pieces reconstituting back into the whole, ignoring the normal rounds that impacted into her body with little ripples. She raised her hands slowly, and the temperature rose with them, as if she were calling up Hell from the depths of the earth.

"Cover the Speedster," I snapped, targeting him on both Zed and Blaine's maps. I stepped around toward Magma, trading places with them as she thrust a hand forward, aiming at Adam, who was still trapped on the ground by Sam's unconscious body.

He threw up another shield, but I knew it wouldn't be enough. This had to end *now.*

I lashed out toward her with my own clawed hand, feeling Chaos scraping against my insides as it bubbled up gleefully, rushing out in a wave of dark-tendrilled destruction.

She fell apart where it touched, and launched herself backward to escape my reach, her body slagged half away in the front. That didn't stop her, though. In fact, it seemed like it just made her angry. She flew upward, dripping little pieces of liquid heat.

Up above, Orc reached for Jacky.

I realized what was about to happen, and updated her Window with the coming attack and her possible escape trajectory.

But it was too late. Orc's hands clamped down around her shoulders with unnaturally long arms.

She lifted up her feet, kicking him in the face, but though his head rocked back, he didn't let go.

And then Magma was above them, streaming fire down onto Jacky.

Jacky screamed, first in pain, then in desperate rage. Her hair crinkled and burnt from the ends.

Adam rolled Sam's unconscious form off him and sprayed out the ink from a canister with a swing of his arm.

Jacky's body shuddered, as if trying to grow even more, but the fire streamed down on her, going from dark red to orange, to bright yellow.

I screamed in denial.

Jacky sagged, and her body began to shrink.

A human-sized ink bird slammed into Magma from the side, dissolving even as it forced her over the side of the roof and slammed her into the street below.

Speedster was gone. He'd escaped out into the street while we'd all been distracted. He was out of my range, but I could follow the vague trail of his blood from where Zed and Blaine had gotten a few shots in. Not enough blood.

The sandstone statue under Kris' control, still missing an arm, grabbed Sam, and dragged him back toward us.

"Go save Jacky!" Kris screamed.

Adam, skin blistered and hands shaking, limped over to us. "I've got this!"

I leapt away, my claws sinking into the stone of the wall, puncturing it with a sound like gunshots as I crawled up the wall like a spider, muscles straining as I pushed myself faster and faster. I threw myself over the side, leaping for Orc with my claws extended. I scratched across his face futilely, and he released his grip on one of Jacky's arms, punching out at me.

I was already throwing myself back, but his punch caught my leg, and my knee buckled, hyperextending backward. I screamed. I caught myself on one foot, never so grateful for my Grace Attribute as at that moment. I leapt forward, lashing out once more.

Then I was slamming face down into the ground below, halfway down the alley.

Up above, a sandstone statue of me impacted harmlessly against Orc. The bit of Chaos I'd managed to get out before he teleported me away wasn't so harmless. It ripped into his chest.

He released Jacky in shock, and toppled backward off the roof, falling toward me.

I rolled.

He slammed into the ground next to me.

I shaped my hand like a spear, leaning over Orc, throwing my whole body into a jab toward the hollow of his throat.

Speedster slammed into me, crushing me into the alley wall at high speed. My head slammed into the stone with a crunch that I felt as well as heard.

Someone screamed. I couldn't move.

Orc got up, moving over to the group still huddled against the wall.

Zed shot at him.

"Adam, can you get them out of here?" Blaine screamed. "Just grab one kid in each arm and run for it!"

Speedster didn't give Adam a chance, jerking jaggedly around the shields Adam which threw up with shaking hands, evading before they could even fully form.

Adam must have been almost out of ink. And almost out of energy.

Blaine stepped forward to meet Speedster, but was thrown out into the street, his fingers and hand breaking around his gun grotesquely.

Adam plunged both his hands into his electricity cartridges and stepped forward away from the kids, arcs of lightning shooting off him in a pincer movement, grasping for Speedster from every angle.

Speedster went down, but Adam's knees buckled along with him.

One of the residual arcs of electricity lashed Sam, and he woke up with a dramatic gasp.

Gregor slapped him across the face, screaming at him to "get *up*!"

Orc reached Zed, unhurriedly slapping his guns aside. He smashed his forearm into Zed's neck, pinning him against the wall, and then dragging him upward against it, so they were looking eye to eye.

The sky above us filled with firelight, again.

Sam stood up, standing with arms spread in front of the kids and Chanelle.

I coughed, twitching my fingers. I had to move. I *had* to *move*.

Kris pointed, screaming. Had she ever stopped screaming? The sandstone statue obeyed, slamming into Orc, beating on his arms, kicking at his legs, destroying itself in a futile attempt to free Zed.

Zed, who was kicking and scratching, and turning purple.

Another sandstone statue dropped down close to me, its legs crumbling up to the knee when it landed. It was shaped like me, and it carried Jacky in its arms, bringing her to Sam. It dropped her on the ground in front of him and turned to aid its counterpart in attacking the Orc.

Sam dropped to his knees to heal Jacky.

Kris ran toward me.

Gregor hesitated, then followed.

They each grabbed one of my arms, trying to help me up, or to drag me.

I lifted my head, looking up to the bright body of flaming, molten heat above.

It streaked down like a falling star, landing in front of us.

Kris was blown back, landing on the ground. She scrabbled away.

Gregor had caught himself on my body and was still within reach of Magma.

I twitched my fingers, letting Chaos spear out of me. "No," I whispered. "I won't let you."

She threw herself out of the way, losing only a few pieces of her arm.

Then she reached again for Gregor.

My arm moved, pushing me upward. But not fast enough.

Gregor screamed, but there was nowhere for him to escape.

Her molten hand sizzled through his shirt, and then sank all the way forward.

I screamed.

But Gregor didn't. He didn't make a sound. The pitch-black form of darkness that lay where he had was unharmed. It stood up, moving around Magma's arm like she didn't exist. Or like *it* didn't.

Her head turned to stare in astonishment, and then snapped around, as a rip opened up in the world.

Zed fell backward into the void, and Orc slipped through it with him, my brother's hands still clawing at his wrist.

The rip in the face of the world closed up behind them, as if it had never been. One second passed, and then two.

My eyes watered futilely against the heat radiating from Magma. She turned back to me, but I couldn't tear my eyes away from the place where Zed had been.

The world ripped again, and Zed crawled out through the crack head-first, flopping onto the ground. His clothes were frosted over. His lips were blue and chattering. He was alive.

Orc didn't come with him.

Magma spared another glance for Gregor's black form, and then turned toward Chanelle.

Jacky was awake, after Sam's ministrations, but she couldn't stand.

Sam had propped her up next to Chanelle, muttering "oh god no" over and over to himself.

Magma shot herself toward them, spewing flames from an outstretched hand.

Sam stepped straight forward into it, screaming like a broken thing. Screaming defiance, and hatred, and death. He was burning, and healing himself, and burning some more. Then he changed, power pulsing from him under the sight of Wraith.

Magma stopped. Her feet touched the ground. She tried to backpedal.

Sam stepped forward, his hand grasping her forehead.

The magma turned to flesh.

He grasped her head between both hands, pressing down.

I could see her fire-bright eyes reflected in his own. But his were just black mirrors. No white, no blue. All pupil. All sucking devouring *apathy*.

She burst and crumbled and melted and was eaten away.

When he rose, he stood over half-melted stone and a pile of pieces that didn't seem as if they had ever resembled a human form. He looked at his hands, then up to me. "I don't feel…anything," he said, his voice echoing as if it had come from a deep place.

Behind him, Jacky called softly. "Sam? Are you okay?" Her voice was small with fear.

He turned to her. "Of course. I can heal you better now. But before I do that…" he turned to Speedster. "I'm going to kill him."

Chapter 31

All is not lost, the unconquerable will,
  and study of revenge, immortal hate,
  and the courage never to submit or yield.
  — John Milton

SAM DID INDEED KILL SPEEDSTER, reducing him to another small pile. Then he healed the rest of us, easier than he'd ever done it, even when I had first met him. "Should we go after the betrayer?" he asked, directing those black holes that his eyes had become toward me.

I resisted the urge to shudder. "Yes."

He nodded. "I think I'll be able to get her to talk. We need to make sure she didn't alert anyone else. And that she won't have a chance to do so again."

Gregor shifted from his Shadow state back into normal flesh and blood, then promptly passed out. Kris did the same, as soon as she gave up control over her two mostly destroyed golems.

Chanelle had a brief moment of lucidity just before we left the alley, and looked around in shocked confusion. "What happened?"

"We got in a fight," I said simply. It probably hadn't been more than ten minutes since the fight started. Fifteen at the max, still… "We need to hurry," I said. "Estreyan enforcers might be coming. People had to have heard the noise, or seen the lights."

I dug the Oracle's third gift out of the charred remains of my ruined pack, and then we gathered together any obvious evidence of what had happened that we could find.

Zed opened up another rip in the world and tossed everything through.

I stumbled back from the feeling of cold death, and he closed the rip.

I took only Sam and Jacky with me when we returned to Ifkana's house, leaving the others hidden a few streets away. A short exploration with Wraith found Ifkana in an upstairs bedroom, pacing back and forth.

Jacky jumped up with Sam, and then with me, and we entered through the balcony.

Ifkana didn't have time to let out more than a yelp before Jacky clenched her hand around the healer's throat.

Ifkana waved her hands, dark green ribbon coming out, and Jacky spasmed.

Sam pulled Jacky back to safety.

When Ifkana's eyes met his, the woman's knees buckled under her, bringing her height to just below his.

"Those three you sent after us are dead. Did you tell anyone else?" he said, staring down at her.

She shook her head slowly, face going slack. "My personal guard. I thought…they would kill you," she said. "At least the infected. The Sickness cannot be tolerated. All who bear it must be removed."

They had come close to killing us, and might have even succeeded if they hadn't been more focused on killing the kids and Chanelle than removing the rest of us from the fight.

Sam killed Ifkana. She didn't scream.

Jacky flinched, but I couldn't look away.

Zed slipped through a crack in the air next to Sam. "I got a Window. You called?" he said.

Sam pointed to the ground. "Cleanup." He turned to me. "Should we kill the servants, too? One of them might have heard something."

I hesitated, then shook my head. "It's not worth it. If even one of them escapes while we're doing it, we'll be caught. The longer we stay here, the greater the chance. And we need to get the others back to the castle where it's safe. As it is now, it would only be our word against a servant's."

He nodded, and we left. It wasn't till we'd gotten back to our rooms at the castle that the black faded from his eyes. He stumbled, and passed out, too.

Jacky tucked him into bed. Unlike the night before, we all packed into three adjacent rooms instead of all along the hallway. We'd been shown how little time there might be to react if an Estreyan attacked us. Not enough time to make it all the way down the hall.

When I opened my door, Torliam was sitting on my bed with Birch, scowling. "Where have you been?"

"We had to kill some people," Jacky said. "Hope we're not gonna get in trouble for that."

He eyed her hair, which had been burnt short, then turned to me and sighed deeply, rubbing his face. "Explain."

Chapter 32

We are born only with the loving knowledge of self-destruction.
— Kaiser Fell

I WAS hesitant to tell Torliam that Chanelle, Kris, and Gregor had the Sickness, but he didn't react like Ifkana.

He paled, but the next words out of his mouth were, "We have to save them before it is too late. The Oracle must have known this would happen. It does not mean hope is lost."

I wondered if that were true.

Torliam told me that after what had happened with his sister, his mother no longer had the authority to pardon someone from death if it was revealed that they had the Sickness. Ifkana had lied to us. It was hard to feel any remorse for her death, so I didn't try.

"Is it going to be a problem? We killed the most powerful healer this side of the seven seas, by her own words. Along with three other Estreyans. There's a good amount of property damage."

He leaned back. "Some will try to use this to their advantage. We will just have to move first, and set the tone of the situation. You were attacked by enemies of my mother when going to see Ifkana the healer to make sure the children were able to withstand their new powers. These enemies killed Ifkana before coming after you, but you were able to defeat them. Perhaps these people had the Sickness, or had been affected by it in some way."

I frowned. "Will people believe that?"

"No, not all of them. The ones who don't will notice that a powerful rival of my mother's was killed the day after we returned. They will likely see it as a statement. A power play."

"What about the servants? We didn't kill them. What if one of them heard something? Does your city have surveillance cameras? There have got to be investigative forces that will be assigned to something like this."

"Queen Mardinest is powerful. We will give her a modified version of what happened. One of her people will make sure that nothing certain ever makes it out."

I sat back, feeling somewhat mollified, but not completely satisfied. I never liked letting other people handle important things in my stead. But I didn't really have a choice here, since I had no idea how to fix the problem myself.

"Once the people believe in us," he said, "something like this will not sway them. You…*we* are going to save this world. Anyone who stands against us stands against our salvation. There is no one who would excuse that, for any reason. Once they believe."

"So how do we get them to believe?" I asked.

"Give them hope. If we can make them truly hope, they will believe as a function of that, rather than the other way around. It will be too painful for them to doubt."

Like Egon the patrol leader, and the old healer who had helped us escape from the village. I nodded, and said, "Before we can proceed, we need to enter that Fear Trial you mentioned before. It may all be for naught, if we can't remove the God of Knowledge's influence from our minds. I, for one, cannot continue to function with his maggots—" The very thought of it made them wiggle a bit. I clenched my jaw so hard my molars creaked.

Torliam didn't respond right away, and didn't meet my eyes. "I will take you there. Tomorrow. Tonight, I will speak with the queen."

WHEN TORLIAM LEFT, I took my mattress over to the next room, where Zed, Sam, and Blaine were.

Birch was pretty irritated at me, and took every opportunity to flatten his ears or look pointedly away.

"I'm sorry we left you behind," I said in a low voice, since Sam and Blaine were asleep. "You were with Torliam anyway. Didn't you have fun today?"

Birch snorted and grabbed my pillow, pulling it over to the corner and stamping on it emphatically before plopping down on top of it with his back to me.

Zed chuckled. "You didn't need a pillow anyway, right? It's not like you were planning to sleep with it."

I rolled my eyes. "Of course not. I brought my only pillow for the sole purpose of not using it."

"Well, you can't have mine." He paused. "We could probably get one of the servants to bring us another."

I sighed. "Forget it. I'm tired."

"Me, too." We lay in silence for a while, and then he spoke again. "Veil-Piercer. It's pretty much as cool as I imagined. It's like...I can see these cracks in the world. And if I concentrate hard enough, I can slip my fingers into them and peel them back. It's like our world, but...not. I've been calling it the Other Place in my mind. It's cold there. Like warmth has never existed. And I noticed it started leeching all the feelings out of me. I don't mean because it was cold. It was like it was freezing my *emotions* out." He paused. "I admit it's dangerous. I could get stuck over there."

"I wish I could tell you not to use your Skill," I said. "But I can't. And I'm not going to try. Just be careful, okay?"

"Umm, I feel like I could be saying that to *you*. How many times did you use Chaos today?"

"Three times? I'll meditate before I go to sleep. That healer Ifkana boosted my Resilience earlier. It might have been bad, if she hadn't."

"What's the plan for defeating Knowledge?" Zed asked, following the obvious train of thought.

"Gain lots of strong Estreyan supporters who are willing to risk their life against him," I said. "I'm going to do that Fear Trial Torliam talked about tomorrow. Got to get Knowledge out of my head first."

Zed snorted. "When did any knowledge ever get *in* your head?"

I knew he was worried for me, but there was nothing either of us could do about it. "You're lucky Birch stole my pillow. Otherwise, you'd be getting a face full of feathers right about now."

"*You're* lucky Sam and Blaine are sleeping it off, or being pillow-poor wouldn't save you."

With a grin, I turned over and tucked my arm under my head, meditating for a while before I fell asleep.

WHEN I WOKE in the morning, both Zed and Blaine were gone, and Sam was straightening his bedding. He noticed that I was awake, and said, "I'm okay," over his shoulder.

When I didn't respond, he continued. "I know you were probably wondering. Considering…what I did last night. I mean, it was pretty horrifying."

When he turned around, I examined his face. "Are you really okay?"

"I've decided I'm not going to feel bad about it. If I hadn't done what I did, those people would have killed Kris, and Gregor, and Chanelle. I could never live with myself if I didn't…" He sat down across from me.

If only just deciding not to feel bad about something actually worked. My own life would be much easier. "You saved us," I said.

"This time." His voice had grown hoarse, and he laughed self-consciously. "But it wasn't even *me*, you know? The Skill took over. I remember what happened, and that person wasn't *me*. If it had been me, I would have frozen, and they would have died, just like China."

I shook my head. "Sam, that's not—"

"Don't lie to me!" he said angrily. "We both know it. But the kicker is, I don't even know what it is that I did. I don't know how to turn Black Sun on, and I don't know how to turn it off. What if—if I need to be that other person again, and I can't? Or what if I can't turn it off, and I do something that I *should* regret? When that Skill is active, I don't care about anything. It's like I've got this sucking emptiness inside me. I wasn't saving the kids because I wanted to save them, I was just doing it because…I don't even know why. Because I'd wanted to before the Skill activated? Because it was interesting?"

We sat in silence, while I tried to figure out what to say. If Sam did something horrible under the influence of his Skill… "That would be bad," I said.

He snorted.

"It would be," I said. "But there is nothing outside of our control. I have to believe that. If we push hard enough, search far enough, and fight harder than we think we're capable of, we can change things. If that happened, we would just have to find a way to fix it. Maybe you'd need another Skill to balance Black Sun out. Or maybe we'd need to get the you who's under the influence of Black Sun to *agree* to act in a manner that normal Sam can live with."

He stared at the ground for minutes. When he finally raised his head, his eyes didn't glitter with agitation anymore. "That's how you do it? You just believe hard enough that you control your destiny?"

I shrugged. "Then, you have to actually *act*. Belief doesn't do much, in a vacuum. But the point is, there's no use worrying. If you need to fix something, fix it. That's all there is to do."

Sam laughed. "When you say it like that, it seems so simple."

I laughed. "I wish!"

"Anyway." He cleared his throat. "Blaine said his genius was needed elsewhere, and I think Zed went to go train with the others. Torliam stopped by while you were sleeping. He said to meet him in airship field three."

It was a testament to how exhausted I'd been the night before that I hadn't woken up while any of this was happening, despite how paranoia normally interrupted my sleep on a regular basis. I nodded and left to go find Torliam.

He had been working while I slept, if the bags under his eyes and the crustacean-shaped ship I found him in were any indication. "We leave when you are ready," he said. "I have alerted the media, and they will meet us on the mount of Phobos and Deimos. The Estreyan people will want to see this."

The idea of people spectating as I subjected myself to a Trial made me uncomfortable, but I climbed in anyway.

I'm not sure what I had expected, but Torliam set the ship on autopilot while he took a nap, and we flew silently to the top of a peaceful mountain range. Soft green grass, totally out of season, grew from the ground at the top of the tallest mountain. Black spheres, as large as a person and reminiscent of the black cubes from NIX's Trials, floated unmoving above the grass. They made my Wraith Skill hurt to look at them, and reminded me of the way Sam's eyes had looked the previous night.

"You will enter one," Torliam said, slowing the ship so that it hovered above the edge of the mountain. "It will show you the monstrous depths of your mind. If you can make it through, you will gain control, and be able to fight back. Remember, the things it shows you are not real. You have control over everything."

Behind us, the dots of other ships began to fill the sky. The Estreyan equivalent of reporters, coming to document our success or failure.

"I'm guessing it will be harder than you're making it sound?"

"Significantly. Telling yourself there is no reason to be afraid when you are terrified is not always useful."

It would be different, at least, than being forced to acknowledge that I had every right to be terrified, and having to press onward anyway. "You'll enter one of the other spheres?"

He hesitated. "Yes."

I frowned, turning to peer at him. "You don't want to do this." I said it as a statement, though I meant it as a question.

"On the God of Knowledge's mountain, when the light of his sentinels reached my eyes, he showed me…something that had happened in the past. My sister died of the Sickness, as you know. I was much younger then, and though I had known those who fell to its grasp, none of them had been so close to me. Her death spurred my search for a cure, though everyone thought I was crazed by grief, obsessed with a futile goal. The God of Knowledge showed me her death, over again. But I knew, with every day, how she felt as her mind turned against her, her body blackening and growing putrid. As we all hovered over her, and the connections she felt toward us, her family, and the people she loved…they were severed, and twisted, till she could not tell love from hate, family from…food." He shuddered. "I felt it all, knew it all, as if I *were* her."

"You're afraid to go through that again."

"Yes. I know it must be done, but…I fear I will not leave with my mind intact. I have experienced many things in my life. When I was within NIX, before they forced you into blood-covenant with me, and then again when I thought you were one of them created to torture me, I came closer than I like to think to losing my grip on the strings that connect me to myself. I am not invincible. I have almost lost myself before."

I reached out and grasped him by the elbow. "This is different," I said. "Because you have hope." I raised his hand, looking pointedly at the mark of crystal branded all the way through it. "Your suffering was not in vain. You found the descendant of the line of Matrix. And we are going to fix everything." I was lying, in a way. But I wished it were the truth.

He clenched that crystal-marked fist and stared at it. "Sentimental drivel," he sneered. But a smile followed the words, and he settled the ship down on the grass at the edge of the mountain.

The reporters swooped in, landing all around, the more eager ones hopping out of their ships before they had even settled. They carried small tubes that beamed light out toward us.

"Those devices will record everything we do and say, in three dimensions. Others will watch it, later. Be careful that you do not lie. It will be found out, under scrutiny," Torliam said, walking with me towards the black spheres.

"What?!" The word popped out of my mouth, full of alarm.

He sighed deeply and shook his head, as if continuing to talk to me would drain him of all energy. He stopped near the edge of a sphere to call out to the reporters, "Today, we conquer our minds. Tomorrow, what can hold us back?"

They burst out with questions, all talking over each other, not so different from reporters on Earth, even if their equipment was way more sophisticated.

Torliam ignored them.

With one last look towards each other, we stepped forward, into the black.

Chapter 33

It isn't the light you want to recover, it's the certainty that there is only darkness.

—Paulo Coelho

INSIDE, it was dark. I blinked compulsively, instinctively trying to get my eyes to adjust till they could see, but the light just wasn't there. I jerked when I felt the fog intruding on my mind, sifting through it.

I very likely would have panicked just from that, what with the God of Knowledge doing something so similar and all the pain it had caused me, if not for Torliam's earlier words.

I held back the instinctive shudder when the darkness started to lessen, and I felt little tiny, hairy legs—spider legs—running over my body, around my neck and down my back, in my ears and hair.

I didn't panic when that changed, and I was suddenly sitting on the ground, with my fingers resting on something that felt like finger bones.

It must have been pulling memories from my Characteristic Trial. A good place to start, I agreed, though maybe not the best.

I still didn't panic when the bones clacked to life around me, grabbing on and wrapping themselves around my body, and dragging me backward into dark water. The illumination grew, just enough that I could see things—large things—moving through the water at the edges of my vision. I'd been scared of whales and sharks as a small child and had had this nightmare before. I held my breath and willed myself to remember that this was nothing more than a dream.

My heart started to beat faster as I held my breath, the organ attempting to distribute oxygen to my burning muscles, and the beats brought with them a sour feeling, like the beginnings of real fear. Not good. The longer I could stay calm, the better. I knew things could only get worse from here. So I breathed out, and then sucked in, drawing the water into my lungs, and continuing to suck even as they cried out with the unnatural burning sensation. There was no water. I only perceived water.

And sure enough, my heart stopped pounding so hard, and as I breathed in and out, it calmed and returned to normal, the only tension in my body the discomfort of my lungs. The water slipped away, not as if it was draining from some big tub, but as if it was just deciding to be air instead.

I was on the ground, then, the area around me lit by what seemed like a spotlight, though I could see no source for the light.

Jacky walked into the spotlight with me. Without saying a word, she spat in my face and walked away.

Were they trying to make me angry? Just trying to get any emotional response out of me so that another one would be closer to the surface? I wiped off the spit and listened to her footsteps echoing away till it was silent.

There was a scrabbling beyond the sharp edge of darkness. Panting.

I grimaced, sensing a hint of what was to come.

Fingers, bent and twitching, entered the ring of light. A nose, a mouth, and a face with blue eyes and blonde hair. Chanelle, or maybe China.

She slobbered, looking crazed. Her eyes were full of hunger. Chanelle, then.

I reached out and petted her head as if she was a dog.

She rolled over onto her back, still panting and slobbering but now with a silly smile on her face as she tried to get me to rub her belly. Then she straightened and jumped up, reaching out for me, suddenly coherent and worried. "Run!" She screamed, and then her body twisted and broke, falling to the ground in slow motion as her gaze stayed locked on mine.

I took a shuddering breath and looked away. Not real. It wasn't real.

We were going to save Chanelle, just like China had wanted. And China wasn't here.

"It's your fault," she whispered from the ground, blood bubbling from her mouth.

I turned back to her, gently straightened her out a bit and crossed her arms over her chest, then pushed her back out of the light. I waited.

Zed stumbled forward, bleeding from the eyes. "Help…help," he gasped, reaching out for me desperately.

My arms lifted to stabilize him almost involuntarily, and he collapsed forward, no longer able to support his own weight. I wanted to help, but as blood bubbled from underneath his eyelids, silver-grey foam frothed up from his mouth. The nanites that NIX had invented. I'd known they needed maintenance, but we'd stolen some of their nutrient paste! He had been taking it, hadn't he? When was the last time I saw him do it? He hadn't run out, and not told me, right? That sounded like something *I* would do, I thought ironically.

"You've been eating their nutrient paste, right? Right!?" I slapped his cheek gently, trying to get him to focus as his eyes rolled back in his head. I was breathing faster, and my heart was definitely beating faster than normal. "Oh, god," I said aloud. This Trial was better than I had hoped. Or worse.

I laid him gently on the ground. "I would never let this happen to you in real life," I murmured, and walked away into the darkness. I didn't look back.

The ground fell out from under me, and I was plummeting down toward the God of Knowledge, my claws out and Chaos lashing toward him. "Ahh!" I screamed. I could see into his open mouth.

He reached out to me, hand smashing through the air, slamming into my side, fingers folding around me, crushing. He brought me down toward his mouth, which yawned open, unnaturally wide in a way that would have caused human cheeks to rip open at the crease of the lips. I could see bits of human flesh within, stuck between his teeth and rotting away.

I opened my mouth to scream again, and somehow, it, too began to open wider and wider, till it eclipsed my body, and then his. My gigantic mouth crashed down around his head, the teeth ripping and grinding till I'd severed through his neck. I chewed the crunchy metal of his head and swallowed, and his rusting golden body fell to the ground, lifeless.

My stomach roiled, first in nausea, and then in something else.

Light poured out of my eyes and mouth in laser-like beams of brightness. Chaos reacted, roiling like the sea in a storm, darkness fighting light, till my body began to break apart, the power bursting through my skin, throwing dancing light and shadows onto the world around me.

I didn't recognize this fear, but it must have come from within me, because I couldn't help the dread and overwhelming desire to reject what was happening. I wanted to scream my denial, to turn away and hide, but I couldn't.

The world around me began to crumble. The earth, the God of Knowledge's senseless body, the very air, disintegrating around me. Where it was destroyed, it revealed a…*lack*. A nothingness, behind the veil of the universe. I screamed, then, and somehow forced my eyes shut. I knew I would die if I kept looking.

I could sense it, though, even with my eyes closed. I screamed again as I began to lose my sense of self, Chaos and the power of the God of Knowledge bursting outward till my body ceased to exist.

"We have met, and we will meet again," a faint voice whispered to me.

I closed my eyes and just concentrated on my breaths, which came… increasingly slowly. And finally, I began to…*vibrate*. It started subtly, and then grew more pronounced, till I was jerking out of my own skin with every shake. I struggled to open my eyes, and when I finally did I stood, looking back at my peaceful body.

"Interesting." I turned, then, and walked out into the world of my mind, leaving my body behind.

THE ATTACKS KEPT COMING, and I kept moving, for a long time. I didn't sleep, didn't eat, and I didn't rest. Though my mind grew weary, my body did not. I tried not to stop, because I had a feeling that if I lost focus on my goal, I would forget that I had a body outside of this place that I needed to get back to.

Finally, I found what I was looking for. A huge golden gate, beyond which a great golden column reached out from somewhere in the distance, thrusting up toward the sky and piercing a hole in the…*ceiling*. It was huge, and corrupting, and it shouldn't be there. Not in my mind. It was creepy and made me feel violated.

I bared my teeth at it and ran forward. But before I could open the gate, a small golden boy stood up from where he'd been crouching in front of it.

I almost ran into him, and panicked for a second, lashing out with my claws.

He winced at my attacks, but didn't fight back.

I backpedaled and stood staring at this creature, who looked quite like another fear of mine.

The boy uncurled his body from its defensive posture and opened his golden eyelids. The eyes within glowed with a teeming mass of writhing lights. "I've been waiting, Eve. You certainly took long enough." He spoke in English, and though his voice was a conglomeration of many, it originated solely from his own mouth, unlike the God of Knowledge.

Still, I instinctively wanted to attack.

"I mean you no harm," he said in a rush, raising his hands to ward me off and flinching back a little. "And I have little strength to defend against you. Please, calm yourself."

"Who are you?" I said.

"I am a manifestation of Knowledge."

"*A* manifestation? A separate one?" Was this how the gods had babies? Even the males?

He quirked his mouth up, as if amused by my thoughts. "A *very* small one, but yes. The Knowledge that you have seen and I were once the same. Part of me—*I*—noticed an anomaly within myself. Processes being corrupted, dissociation with things that were once meaningful—I would reach for them, and find the connection within my thoughts, my memories, and my 'emotions' had been severed. Or, more insidiously, redirected. I immediately attempted to isolate the affected areas, in an attempt to amputate them, but they'd grown too much already, while I had been made *ignorant*," he spat it like a curse, "by my own power. This," he gestured to his child's body, " was all that I could do. I have enclosed what little I could safely determine was untainted, and have been trapped within myself as the rest of me fell to the abomination. When you came into my domain, I transferred a small part of myself to you, riding along with my greater counterpart's attack."

"So, you're the part of the God of Knowledge that doesn't have the Sickness?"

"Yes, in a way. The being you see before you is but a simulacrum. A tiny, tiny piece of my power. All you could bear without dying, and all I could spare without losing my fight against myself, and being re-assimilated. So much has been lost, you see. I saw you, though my diminished range of power. I have done all I could to thwart my corrupted manifestation. And I have waited for you to return, and cleanse me." He said the last with an expressionless face, but a voice that sounded heavy, tired, and resigned.

"Cleanse you…" I said, narrowing my eyes. "You mean kill you?"

He raised his eyebrows. "That is what my daughter asked of you, is it not? Death is but a metamorphosis, though admittedly quite unpleasant. You of all creatures should understand that, scion of Khaos." He stared at me with those eyes of bright power. "Oh. You have no idea." He grimaced in distaste. "No wonder your power rebels against you. My old friend did not do a good job of preparing her progeny. I'm not so surprised as I should be, unfortunately. She has no patience for such things."

"Do you know how to stop it from killing me?" I asked, trying not to let hope bloom prematurely.

"Of course. Knowledge of a thing is power over it. But that is the reward of the quest, and you have not completed it yet."

"But if I kill the big Knowledge, you'll die too, won't you? How will you tell me, then?"

He pointed beyond the gate. "The knowledge is hidden within his sentinel. Conquer and cleanse, and it will turn to follow you. When you have need of it, it will reveal itself to you."

I looked up at the golden sentinel. "What?"

He just stared blankly back at me, as if he hadn't heard my question.

"What about the Sickness?" I tried. "Do you have any information about how we can cure it? Or where I can find this other god that can fight against it?"

"Much has been lost," he said again. "You must follow the path. It has been traveled, once before. The first time."

"I'm not sure I understand. Could you be less cryptic?"

He sighed. "No, I could not. Just do what you came here to do." Then he stepped back, and sank into the gold of the gate, melding together with it till the form of the boy was gone.

I shook my head, feeling a little disoriented, woozy. It was hard to concentrate. When I tried to take a step, the ground pulled at my feet, releasing me with a suction-cup *pop* only after I threw myself forward. I realized I'd been standing still for too long.

The gate gave under my claws like butter, and where it broke apart, tiny little motes of light flew into me. I ran forward, toward the distant glare of the sentinel.

WHEN I FINALLY EXITED THE black sphere, the reporters bombarded me, shining their little pen-light recorders at me, talking over each other.

My stomach cramped from hunger, and my muscles trembled faintly, as if I was coming down off a horrible caffeine high.

YOUR MENTAL ACUITY HAS INCREASED!

"What did you see within the Trial of Deimos and Phobos?!"

"You are the first to emerge. Are you worried about Torliam of Aethezriel?"

"What is the relationship between you and Torliam of Aethezriel?"

I straightened, hoping that their cameras wouldn't catch my weakness. "Torliam of Aethezriel will be finished when he is finished," I said, not-answering as best I could. "As for what I saw…" I paused, meeting their eyes, as Torliam had instructed me would appear best for their recorders. "I saw my own fears, and my own failings, and traversed the depths of my own mind turned against me." I hesitated, wondering whether to mention that I had met with a small piece of the God of Knowledge. It was true, but if I couldn't lie…they might ask more questions than I was able to answer truthfully.

"There are rumors that the Oracle has given you three gifts, and the Goddess of Testimony and Lore has marked you! Is this true?" another reporter asked, yelling to be heard over his counterparts.

"It is true," I said.

"There are reports that Testimony and Lore has been seen traveling amongst mortals once more. Did you free her?"

I laughed. "She did not need me to free her. She was never trapped."

"What is your quest? What do they bid of you?" another yelled.

I paused for a breath, thinking of the proper answer. "I will follow the path." There, a nice cryptic answer for the media to go crazy over. I walked away, getting into the ship to wait and worry for Torliam while munching on the snacks he'd packed.

Torliam emerged after sundown, falling to his hands and knees and gasping.

I rocketed out of the ship and ran to kneel beside him.

He murmured, "Thank the gods, it is done," in Estreyan, and then collapsed.

I caught him and maneuvered him back so he didn't fall on his face. I snarled at the reporters pressing in. The press of potentially dangerous strangers, all yelling and jostling close to us while Torliam was too weak to defend himself, made the hair on the back of my neck raise. "Get back!" I growled in threat. My Voice Skill pulsed with the command, and they stumbled back, as if it had been a shockwave. I would have to learn how to use it consciously more often.

Torliam was almost delirious, but he wasn't unconscious. After a bit of water, he got to his feet, using me as an armrest to support himself. "Let us go to the edge," he said.

The reporters kept their distance, though their recording penlights stayed trained on us.

"From here," he said, sitting so his feet hung off the side of the mountain ledge, "they will not be able to hear, only to see."

"Same for the cameras?"

He nodded. "If you are willing, Eve Redding of the line of Matrix, we might give them else something to talk about."

"You're not going to try and kiss me, are you?" I narrowed my eyes at him.

He snorted. "Your beauty and power are irresistible," he scoffed. "No, idiot."

I huffed. "Well, they were all asking what our relationship was, if I was worried about you, how I felt about your mom, given our 'delicate' relationship, and stuff like that."

"This will make them chatter more than that." He hesitated, then cleared his throat. "I severed our bond. But you are more of what I originally hoped than I thought, though you are a human. As a descendant of the line of Aethezriel, it is my duty…and my honor, to offer my bond again." Less formally, he continued. "If we complete it properly, it will return some of the power you lost when the bond was broken before, and it may help to stabilize you against Chaos."

I flexed my fingers, trying not to pounce on the idea of more power, anything that might help me survive. I'd seen what the blood-covenant had meant to Torliam. "Do you really want to do that?"

"Yes."

Well, I wasn't going to *argue* about it. "Okay, then. How do we do it? I don't have any Seeds left."

"We will complete this *properly*," he said, emphasizing the word. "Do as I do." He slashed his forearm with his power, and I followed suit on my own arm with one of my claws.

"The life is in the blood. And thus, I bind mine to yours." He dipped his thumb in the blood, and wiped it on my forehead, and down over my lips, so that I tasted the tiniest hint of iron and salt on the tip of my tongue.

I repeated the process on him, having to stretch up to reach his forehead.

He grasped my forearm, so our wounds touched. "So be it."

I felt the rush, then, extremely different from before when NIX had done this to me. But I didn't have time to examine the feeling, because the reporters broke out in a roar, their voices mixing together in a jumbled wave that was no longer recognizable as speech.

I turned to look at them over my shoulder. "Should we make a statement or something?"

"No." He grinned and stood up, not bothering to offer me a hand. "People find the mysterious much more interesting. This is the time to run away!"

I laughed and ran after him.

Chapter 34

There is a dark place underneath the world.
— Sha Du

I'D SENT the others a Window to let them know I was okay while I was waiting for Torliam to emerge, but as we flew back to the palace, I got a few more.

—What the hell was that?—
-Adam-

—The news people went crazy when you guys wiped blood on each other's faces.—
-Zed-

—It itches, but Torliam says I can't wash it off. Because tradition. And publicity.—
-Eve-

The queen was waiting with Birch in the airship landing field when we arrived. Her face was pale and foreboding, and her mouth tightened when she saw the dried blood. But what she said was, "I have called a mandatory assembly of the court, for tomorrow evening. We cannot wait. After a spectacle like this, rumor spreads quickly. We want to make the announcement when it will still be a political boon to do so, and before any of my detractors have time to prepare arguments or subtle ways to undermine me. They must all be shocked and caught off guard."

We spent most of the night planning, despite how exhausted Torliam and I were.

Birch bit me on the hand for leaving him behind again, and then struggled to stay awake. He failed, and ended up curling up in Torliam's lap, snoring lightly.

First thing in the morning, Queen Mardinest summoned the rest of my team and drilled them with both questions and guidance about what might happen at the announcement, and the small part they would play in it. She included Birch in this, and didn't seem surprised by how he appeared to acknowledge her instructions.

Then she sent us off to be prepared for the assembly.

I was given a room with a bed that looked fluffy and comfortable. I wanted nothing more than to fall down into it and sleep, but the woman the queen had assigned to preparing me took one look at me and vetoed that.

"I will have to put a glamour on your face. Oh, my, those dark circles under your eyes. You look like a *pordok*!" She *tsked* her concern.

A *pordok* must be a panda or raccoon equivalent, because I was pretty sure that's what I looked like.

By that night, the girl in charge of my wardrobe and appearance had driven me crazy with her demands, but I looked amazing. My almost-black hair hung straight down my back. She'd put some paste on my face and magically removed my dark eye circles and the unhealthy hollow underneath my cheekbones, and given my skin a healthy tinge of color.

The armorer had given me a dark grey set that made my pale eyes stand out, but kept my left forearm, fingers, and my neck uncovered to display the sparkly "gifts" I'd been given from the gods.

I was pretty in love with the armor. It fit over my—now clean—vest, was light-weight and non-reflective, and still allowed me full range of motion, so it would actually be useful for battle and not just decoration. I wondered if there might be a way I could sneakily "forget" to give it back.

The servant led me toward the back entrance to the ballroom, or the throne room, or whatever it was, muttering about how she'd "tried her best."

The queen was waiting with Torliam, a little removed from the rest of my team. She waved me over and threw a long, almost-black cloak over my shoulders. It went well with my armor and covered all my sparkly gifts, no doubt so she could dramatically reveal them in front of the assembly later. She wore one of the Estreyan style dresses but had obvious knives both at her belt and strapped along her thigh. The outfit looked like something she would have no trouble fighting in.

Torliam had been properly groomed and made fancy, too, like a different person than the one I was used to. He didn't make any snarky comments or even grimace at me. He held himself proudly straight, his hair swept back and held in place by a thin circlet much less elaborate than his mother's.

With her nod of acceptance, we entered the throne room through a back door, my team following a few steps behind the three of us.

Jacky shot me a grin, pointing to her pixie haircut. The short style only served to accentuate the graceful lines of her cheekbones and jaw.

Contrary to my expectations, none of the reporters along the walls burst out with questions, and the huge crowd of high-ranked Estreyans did no more than murmur surreptitiously amongst themselves.

Queen Mardinest took the throne above Torliam and me, who stood to the side of her raised dais. She wasted no time starting her speech, thanking them for coming on such short notice. "I have summoned you here tonight for a joyous announcement," she called out in a voice that had no trouble reaching to the far ends of the room. "My son, Torliam of the line of Aethezriel, still lives."

At her motion, he joined her on the dais, bowing shallowly to the crowd.

"I sent him on a mission some time past, to search for an answer to the seemingly indomitable Sickness that plagues our land and people. Two nights past, he returned from his mission, *successful*."

There was a long beat of silence, after that. Then they broke out in sound. People exclaimed in shock, chattered to each other disbelievingly, and shouted questions, talking over each other such that my rudimentary grasp of the language failed to distinguish their words.

The queen raised her hand for silence and didn't speak again till it was quiet. "As it is said in the Lore, my son has discovered a descendant of the line of Matrix."

I joined her then, and the hair on the back of my neck raised as my subconscious reacted negatively to the weight of so many powerful stares.

The noise died down quicker that time, as people were no doubt eager to hear what she had to say.

"This is Eve-Redding, last of the line of Matrix, and my own champion."

She'd added the last part for political gain, I knew. But I was okay with it, because as far as I could tell, what was good for her at the moment was also good for me.

"Our world has been ravaged by the Abhorrent, and we waited for the spark in the darkness. Our hope waned, and we grew weary and disbelieving, and perhaps some of us even forgot that such a thing might one day come." She paused, for effect, and I did my best to project confidence and power. To look like someone they could believe in.

"Finally, we may wait no longer. Despair no longer. Stand helpless and frightened no longer." Her words thrummed with power, and for a second, it seemed like the crystal in my chest pulsed in response, a physical sensation, like the rumbling of a huge, slow heartbeat.

Eyes were drawn to the crystal, and from it to me. I wasn't quite sure whether or not to be grateful for the strange gift of Testimony and Lore, but at times like this, it was helpful to claim legitimacy.

Torliam stepped forward, then, and from the way the queen stiffened, I was pretty sure they had not agreed on this.

"I am of the line of Aethezriel," he said loudly. His voice didn't carry that same thrum of power that his mother's had, but his words caught the court's attention all the same. "For generations, my line has served the line of Matrix, bound to them in blood-covenant. Until the last died, and they were thought to be no more." His eyes traveled over them, and he waited till the last murmurer was silent, waiting for him to continue. "The line of Aethezriel stands before you, once again bound in blood-covenant to the line of Matrix." He bowed to me then, deeply and formally, dipping to a knee and baring his neck.

I did my best to act unsurprised and reached out a hand to lay gently on his shoulder.

He rose to his feet.

The queen snapped the cloak off me with a flourish, like a stage-magician, drawing attention back away from her son. "She has been given three gifts by the Oracle." She held up my hand, displaying first the ring, and then motioned for me to lift the other arm, showing off the band wrapping around my forearm, and the unsolved gift wrapped around my waist and clasped with a dark grey brooch. "And the mark of Testimony."

She touched a finger to the crystal in the hollow at the base of my throat, and it reacted on its own, thrumming a pulse of power outward that washed through those of the crowd closer to the throne. "Her companions have the Seal of Nine." She waved a hand, and my teammates lifted their hands, showing off their own crystal-embedded skin. "She is here, with a quest from the Oracle, to defeat the Sickness,"

It was a strong exaggeration, even based on what the queen believed, but I wasn't surprised.

It took even longer for the noise to die down, that time.

AFTER HER ANNOUNCEMENT, some of the higher ranked court members, judging by how rich they looked and their level of arrogance, moved up before the throne to ask official questions in front of the court.

"How do you know *she* is the one talked of in the Lore? Or even a Matrix? Has she taken the test of genealogy to prove herself?" one man asked. He kept a veneer of politeness, but his eyes were narrowed, and he looked at the queen with a kind of greasy hunger when she wasn't watching.

"There is no doubt she is a Matrix. My son has a blood-covenant with her. But we will gladly allow a test of lineage."

His cheeks twitched in what might have been a smirk if he'd allowed it to form fully. "That will alleviate some of my doubts. However, wasn't your line in *service* to the Matrixes?"

"Indeed," she said severely, as if what he was insinuating didn't bother her. But I felt an almost unnoticeable pulse of power roll off of her, and knew she'd been angered. "My *younger* son has the honor of fulfilling the historical traditions."

After him, others asked similarly leading questions, as if trying to trip the queen up, and there were many among the crowd that frowned and muttered to each other, as if suspicious. However, just as many others were staring at me with interest, or crying even as they smiled, or hugging each other with overwhelming emotion.

Finally, someone asked how we were going to defeat the Sickness.

Queen Mardinest smiled with triumph. "The God of Knowledge has met my champion, and given her a quest to gather strength, so that she may prove the worth of the mortals on this world, and gain knowledge of our path to *victory* against the Sickness!" Her voice had raised in both volume and power, and she raised a fist into the sky to punctuate the end of her sentence.

The mood washed over the assembly, and they responded with a cheer of their own, which she egged on this time rather than trying to quiet. Her Charisma levels must be off the charts. "I ask that those willing to lend their power to this quest come join us. I believe that we may eradicate the Sickness completely during my reign, and I will not rest until it is done!" She once again pumped her fist in the air, and let out a war cry laden with that almost physical intensity particularly powerful Estreyans seemed to be able to imbue into their voices. "Tonight, we celebrate!"

The whole place exploded with festivities after that, and even if anyone had wanted to ask more questions, they wouldn't have been able to over the overwhelming noise. People were crying, laughing, hugging each other and dancing.

My group stayed with the queen, talking to the people who lined up to meet me or pledge something to the cause. The Estreyans kept thanking me, reaching out to touch me or one of my sparkly gifts.

I'd reacted a bit harshly when one chubby man tried to touch the crystal at the base of my throat.

He'd been surprised and half fearful at first, but quickly laughed off my firm grip on his wrist, and the claws that pressed against his skin in warning. "We have a warrior in this one!" he called out to the people around him, which caused another irritating cheer to rise up.

I had to stay at the dais, but after a while Torliam was allowed to leave and mingle in the crowd, surrounded by a large group of people demanding his attention. He looked truly happy for the first time I'd ever seen. His shoulders were thrown back, not in arrogance, but as if the lack of burden they carried made him stand straighter. It made me uncomfortable, though I wasn't sure why.

Two weeks after that night came the day where we officially accepted applicants for the fight. The line of non-rejected applicants stretched all the way through the castle, from the huge throne room to the streets outside, and plenty of people were trying to sneak their way into the line, though they hadn't been accepted by the queen's vetting process. It was chaos.

The queen had sent out word after the Trial that we would be accepting warrior applicants to go challenge the God of Knowledge's main manifestation. Many, many people applied to follow me, but her analysts had sorted through them, only allowing the best to be accepted. "There will be limited battlegrounds in a physical sense," she said. "Even with those who can fly and do not need room on the ground. It is better to have a smaller group of those who have a real chance of defeating the God of Knowledge than clutter the place with well-meaning weaklings who will be dying like gnats all over the battlefield."

She'd also found me another healer who could boost my healing Attributes. He had seen me a few times, and warned me that I didn't have much time left before Chaos overtook me.

Even if my body could have withstood it, the time limit given by the Oracle was approaching—the smaller of the Estreyan moons had already darkened twice.

The queen stood in front of her throne, with me beside her and the rest of my team kind of milling about the room with varying levels of watchfulness. "If I were wise," the queen said, staring at the Estreyans milling about and standing in the too-long line, "I would kill you now."

My head snapped around toward her as I registered her words, and I stepped back in sudden wariness. When someone so powerful made a comment about killing me, it wasn't something I could take lightly.

She noticed my alarm and gave a slight smile that was less than reassuring. "With the number of my citizens ready and willing to throw their lives away for you, you could become the leader of a fanatical uprising. Some people place all their faith in the Lore."

She meant that I could become a religious cult leader. "That sounds like way too much work for me," I said. "I just want to finish this and retire somewhere in peace. Or something."

"Or *something*." She raised one eyebrow sardonically.

I wasn't quite sure what the joke was, but she walked away then, and I was happy to let the subject lie dormant, but not forgotten.

I stood at the front of the line of accepted warriors, listened one by one to what their strengths were—basically whatever had gotten them accepted—and formally received their pledges of alliance. It took a few hours to get through the whole line. Some of my new allies were stoic and determined, some prideful, and some looked at me like I was the messiah-figure they believed me to be.

Just when I thought it was over, the queen stood up and dramatically announced for the cameras that she was lending me two squads of her own elite fighters. You know, seeing as I was *her* champion.

Still, who turns down two squads of elite fighters? Not me. I smiled and thanked her prettily.

Chapter 35

Weep not for the shore, but become the wave.
— Sha Du

I LET OUT a scream of challenge toward the God of Knowledge, not really meant to intimidate him, but to release some of my own tension. He had really messed me up, and I'd only recently felt fully recovered from that, at a time when I already had too many problems to deal with.

In a move we'd practiced many times, my group started to move forward from the edge of the valley toward the God of Knowledge. They stayed in the shadows and kept a protective formation around me, since I had to live to make this work.

Though my eyes were closed, I watched the battlefield with my Wraith Skill.

Ahead of my group, the heavy-hitters attacked with abandon. They paused for a moment, to allow an Estreyan with two huge, beautiful blades as tall as he was to attack without taking friendly fire.

He slung the blade off his back and pointed it toward the god with one smooth motion of his arm. A point of light shot out the end of it, connecting to a spot on the other side of the god.

Half a second after that, the Estreyan had moved there, so fast even

Wraith barely registered an after-image. The sound reached me, then, like a bell ringing as something shattered.

The Estreyan's blade broke into pieces and fell to the ground.

The God of Knowledge paused, as if surprised, and started to turn to the Estreyan. There was a line scored across the back of his golden knee. The same one that was already rusting away.

The Estreyan was already pulling the second, backup blade from his back, and repeated the process before the god could even complete his pivot.

The blade broke again, after cutting across the exact same spot on the back of the knee as the first slice.

The Estreyan landed, back where he'd started, and fell down dead from the blow Knowledge had landed on him as he passed.

But my fighters didn't lose focus just because of that, instead redoubling their attacks, focused on the god's pelvis, stomach, and lower back.

At the timed command, they all stopped attacking simultaneously, and I rushed forward, surrounded by my still mostly fresh team.

I neared the target quickly, stepping over ground that was simultaneously melted, frozen, and a half dozen other residual effects. One patch glowed a comical, radioactive-green. I avoided that spot carefully.

Torliam was counteracting the light for my group, I could tell, and Adam kept his hands touching the disks his strongest shields had been painted on, in case he needed to activate them instantly.

When we neared, Adam and other forcefield and barrier-makers tossed the results of their Skills up around the god, hoping to trap him for just a moment.

The God of Knowledge tore through all the shields around him as if they were paper, raised his hand, and brought it down flat, smashing me and the rest of my group like bugs.

"Damn it!" I gritted out. A loud horn blared, and I stood up with the others, as the simulation lost some of its terrifying realism.

One of my Estreyan warriors kicked a golden tree, making it flicker and getting his foot stuck halfway inside the hard-light construct.

"Damn it," Gregor also muttered as he drew nearer.

Blaine gave me a pointed look. "Your cursing is rubbing off on an eight-year-old."

"You did well, young one," a female warrior said to Gregor. "Was it three people that you saved from death, this time?" She smiled at him with obvious affection, just one of my many warriors who'd grown fond of the kids.

Gregor scowled. "But we still lost!"

Birch coughed agreement, walking beside the boy with tail and ears drooping.

"I'm going to go review the logs," I said, walking toward the viewing room. "Maybe we can get more efficient with taking out the sentinels in the beginning."

The Estreyans I passed bowed or smiled at me, despite the fatigue and vague sense of shameful failure I knew we all felt.

Adam frowned, reflexively rubbing his eyebrows, which were mostly regrown after they'd been singed away in our fight with Ifkana's assassins.

My team and a few of the more Intelligence-focused Estreyans, or those that had large scale battle experience, followed me.

—I believe that cabin where we first arrived will be the best place to take the kids while you fight. We will be safe from the relatively weaker monsters there, and hopefully, we will not be followed.—
-Blaine-

I nodded.

—The palace has quite a few ships. You'll want to disable the comms and tracking system in one ahead of time.—
-Eve-

The Estreyans expected the kids to fight along with the rest of us because they had the Seal of Nine, but neither Blaine or I were okay with putting them in such extreme danger.

The preparations to fight the God of Knowledge took up most of my concentration, anyway. I'd been researching past supplicants and successful Bestowals, even though gaining his approval wasn't exactly the goal, I hoped to gain clues about how to win.

People all over Estreyer were doing their best to contribute even if they weren't warriors. I had become the somewhat bemused owner of several properties, air-ships, living steeds of different breeds, and tons of advanced armor and weaponry. I had someone whose *only* job was to manage the donations!

The city even had a much cooler version of NIX's simulation chamber. My team and I were the only recorded people to see the God of Knowledge in recent history. We'd helped some of the technicians make a passable model of him for us to mock battle.

The Estreyans and I had been trying to come up with a plan to defeat him. We gathered at the simulation chamber every day and pitted our strength and strategy against the modeled God of Knowledge, over and over again.

Unfortunately, we kept failing. No matter what we came up with, when we tried it out, we always lost.

Our training had made us all stronger, but without a ready supply of Seeds from an outside source, progress was slow.

PLAYER NAME: EVE REDDING
TITLE: BEARER OF TESTIMONY
CHARACTERISTIC SKILL: SPIRIT OF THE HUNTRESS, TUMBLING FEATHER
LEVEL: 38
SKILLS: COMMAND, WRAITH, CHAOS, VOICE

STRENGTH: 19
LIFE: 71(+6)
AGILITY: 25
GRACE: 23
INTELLIGENCE: 31
FOCUS: 24
BEAUTY: 11
CHARISMA: 27
MANUAL DEXTERITY: 9
MENTAL ACUITY: 26
RESILIENCE: 67(+11)
STAMINA: 34(+2)
PERCEPTION: 27

I paused the three-dimensional simulation of the battle we'd just gone through, just as the God of Knowledge batted one of my most important fighters out of the air in a move that would have killed, or at least incapacitated her in a real fight. I growled under my breath, and let the playback continue, watching the tiny three-dimensional image of her body hit the ground and turn red.

"He's too strong," I said aloud. "He can take whatever we throw at him. His inherent power makes him the worst possible opponent, because not only is he stronger than us, but he knows everything we're doing or just about to do, as long as it's within the range of his divination."

"Why don't we just make him weaker, then?" Jacky said.

I looked up at her in surprise.

She'd gone back to being too quiet, after our fight with the assassins. She trained harder than ever, but that was *all* she did.

I'd been worried about her, but when I asked her if anything was wrong, she'd told me that she was weak, and had to get stronger. "There's nothing you're gonna say or do that's gonna change that," she'd said. "I don't need mushy gushy friendship and feelings right now. I know we're friends. What I *need* is to get stronger before it's too late, so we can all *keep* being friends."

I hadn't been able to retort to that, because I understood how she felt all too well. Still, it was a surprise that she had spoken during the strategy meeting, other than to ask about things she could be doing better.

"If I knew how to do that…" I glared at the simulated god reduced to human size in front of me.

"Maybe I'm being stupid," Jacky said, her shoulders hunching in a little.

I caught something in her tone and narrowed my eyes at her. "Do you have an idea, Jacky? Tell me. I need all the ideas I can get." This hesitance wasn't like her.

"Well…why don't we poison him?" she asked simply.

Adam, and Blaine, who were working with Chanelle in the corner of the room, looked over, their attention drawn.

"He's made of Seeds, right? Or something like that."

I nodded. His body was probably a manifestation, kind of like Behelaino's, but there was probably a core of Seed material somewhere in or near it that was powering his form. In essence, the God of Knowledge *was* really just Seed material, gathered in one spot.

"That thing NIX did to Chanelle, didn't it get rid of her Seeds?" Jacky asked simply.

My eyes widened, and I'm pretty sure I gasped like a landed fish. "Jacky. You're a genius." I turned to Adam and Blaine, who were sharing similar looks with each other. "Could that work?"

Chanelle frowned, scratching her forearm. "Are you going back to NIX? I want to come."

We conferred for a few minutes, but Blaine was pretty positive it would work, and as he was the one with the most experience, I was inclined to trust his judgment.

The Estreyans were more than a little alarmed at the implications of anti-Seed weaponry, and the fact that the military force of a hostile—though primitive—planet had been developing it. Blaine's explanation of how it was almost certainly meant to allow NIX to attempt to create Players out of those humans without the necessary Estreyan gene to accept the Seeds, and not necessarily to attack Estreyans, didn't mollify *anyone.*

Still, we took the idea to the queen. She stood up and started tapping on the table, calling for some of her official underlings. "Call *door-makers* to me. I need experts in the old connections, those beyond the void. I have an immediate decree," she announced to the room. "I am re-opening the portal to Earth."

People gasped.

THE ESTREYANS who learned about the queen's plan over the next few days had the same universal reaction. Horror.

"Why is this such a big deal?" I asked. "The arrays are there for a reason, right? I mean, it worked just fine for us, and we didn't even have a *complete* one."

Torliam didn't look at me. "It is forbidden."

"*Why?*"

He hesitated. "The array technology is knowledge we brought with us, before Estreyer. We do not fully understand it any longer. There are two reasons why it is forbidden to use it, and why the doorways were blocked. The first is that we feared to spread the Sickness to others. The second... do you remember that I told you there are powers beyond that of the gods?"

I nodded.

"Some call them the eldritch. We do not understand them. Some even believe that the Abhorrent is one of them, and that is why we cannot stop the Sickness. Long, long ago, we discovered that the arrays work both ways. I do not mean between world to world. The arrays pierce through the divide. The void between worlds. When we open them, things from between may slip back through."

I vaguely remembered the glimpse of that break in existence that I had seen in the Trial for Testimony and Lore. I shuddered, suddenly absolutely sure that *something* coming from there was a really, really bad idea. "How did you know how to make the array work, if they're forbidden?"

"I am a historian and an explorer. I know many of the old things that others have forgotten."

I started to nod, then frowned. "Wait, weren't you worried that the array on Earth would let something from between through?"

He smirked. "The array opens a door to the void from the world that *initiates* the doorway. Estreyer was never in danger."

"So…we could go back to Earth only to find it's been invaded by some…eldritch Cthulhu monster?"

He nodded. "Yes."

I stared at him. "You're an asshole, you know? There are plenty of innocent people on Earth. *Children*."

His jaw tightened. "Well, it is only a possibility. And we had no other choice at the time, so do not condemn me for it now."

I conceded, though irritation simmered in my blood. "Are you coming with us?"

"I…will cross through, but I will not go back to NIX. I will stay close, and if you have need of me, I will raze the place to the stones of its foundations. But I cannot see it and restrain myself to pleasantries and subtle threats. I only restrain myself for the benefit of a greater need, and at your request. It will be nothing at all, or death."

Shortly after that, all of us making the trip piled into the two-person Estreyan ships that were small enough to fit through the array on Earth's side. I squeezed into one with Adam. Blaine and the kids were staying behind for this venture.

A group of people activated the stone circle, which glowed bright and kept glowing.

Adam flew us through, the ship flitting down from winter and up into autumn in a disorienting twist.

It didn't take long for the others to join us, and we flew toward NIX over the course of a couple hours, our tiny ships piercing through the night like crustacean-shaped bullets. When we got close enough, we exited the ships and stood around as a group, Estreyans and humans stretching our legs in tense camaraderie. We all wore full armor with no skin exposed, along with masks that covered our mouths and noses to keep from breathing in any anti-Seed warfare, which the Estreyans feared NIX might have aerosolized.

I thought they were being unnecessarily paranoid, but just shrugged and went along with it. It did make us look even more intimidating, so that was a plus.

Our goal was to both retrieve the meningolycanosis, and make sure NIX didn't have access to it any longer. Along with any other interesting or suspicious substances we happened to find. I'd convinced the queen not to order the small force of Estreyans that had agreed to come with me to wipe NIX out completely. Not that I had any sympathy for the organization, but many of the Players were just…people. People forced into this, just like I had been.

Besides, too few Estreyans wanted to risk travel through the highly stigmatized arrays, so I convinced her that if possible, we would do this through diplomacy. What a novel idea.

Atop a mountain about a mile out from NIX, our group looked down on the base.

Torliam's hands clenched so tight that his knuckles creaked, and he glared at the compound without blinking.

I turned to one of the Estreyans and nodded, huddling together with Adam, Jacky, Chanelle, and Sam.

With a loud *pop,* the five of us stood in the center of NIX's courtyard, courtesy of the Estreyan's Skill.

There was an instant of surprised silence, but only an instant. Alarms blared. People rushed into action. A group of Players sprinted inside before the doors slammed shut behind them, guards scrambled, and most surprisingly, the Shortcut fell straight down, concrete sliding over the part of the courtyard where it had stood. The gun turrets on the walls—new ones, since we'd destroyed many of the old—turned all the way around to point down at us.

Less than thirty seconds after we'd arrived, a group of people in the darker bodysuits of the special ops Player units dashed out of one of the doors, which opened only long enough for them to slip through.

I raised my hands above my head. "I'm not here to fight, guys," I called. "I just want to speak to Commander Petralka. If you find you can't resist attacking us…you *will* regret it."

They hesitated and didn't attack, though one of them spoke in a low voice, probably talking to someone on the other end of a microphone.

I realized as I looked around that NIX seemed so much smaller, so much *less* than it once did. Always before I had been afraid, within this place.

Chanelle sidled up beside me, gripping the side of my utility belt for reassurance. "It feels weird, to be back on Earth. My family is here. They probably think I'm dead, though."

I bit the inside of my lip. "After this is over, we'll come back again. We'll find them, and make sure our families are okay."

It didn't take long before another of the doors slid open, and a man in crisp military uniform exited, striding over to us. He stopped a few feet in front of me, definitely not a safe distance from someone with my abilities. He was a tall man, almost as tall as me. "Commander Petralka has been…removed," he said. "She proved herself incapable of fulfilling her duties, multiple times. You may have some idea of the instances I am referring to," he said with just a hint of a smirk, his piercing glare and the way he held himself more than a little aggressive. "I am Commander Britt. You can just call me Britt. Why are you here?"

I smiled. "I'm here to make a bargain. A trade, if you will. You have something I want…and I have something *you* really *don't* want." I looked around, noticing the faces peeking out of windows, some of them being herded away, presumably to safer places. "Why don't we go somewhere where we can talk? Your office, maybe? Don't worry, we're house-trained."

He stared at me for a little, then his eyes flicked over my small group of teammates. "You first. I think you know the way."

I led the way to Petralka's old office, escorted by a pretty large contingent of guards and special ops Players.

Britt opened the door with a complicated series of scans and identity checks, and stepped into the room, moving to sit behind a large marble desk.

A pale man with too much pudge to be considered skinny, but too bony to be considered fat, sat in the corner, his twitching hands sunk into bulky gloves. He muttered when we entered, but didn't look up at us, staring at the smartglass tablet on the walled table in front of him.

I was curious, but my Wraith Skill was really bad at deciphering how electronic displays would appear to the human eye, even at close distances like this. "Your security is much better," I said. "And you've obviously been running response drills."

Jacky, Chanelle, and I sat in the chairs in front of Britt's desk, while

Adam stood with his back to the wall, eyes darting around, though for once his hands were still. Sam stood behind me.

"Thanks for noticing," Britt said, again with the decidedly mean smirk. "What do you want?"

"I want your anti-Seed experiments. Doctor Blaine Mendell coined the term 'meningolycanosis.' I believe you're familiar."

Chanelle coughed pointedly, her big blue eyes narrowed into a glare.

The man in the corner's fingers twitched, and Britt's eyes flickered. He was receiving Window communication. Interesting.

"I am. What do you want with them?" he said.

"I believe that should be obvious," I said flatly.

He leaned back. "You're actively an enemy to NIX. My superiors have authorized me to kill you on sight, if I feel the need. If I successfully capture you, I'd get kudos for that, too. Though…I would worry that you're just allowing me to apprehend you as part of some ridiculous plan to steal even the damn Shortcut out from under our noses."

Jacky snorted.

His eyes narrowed. "Though, it would seem you don't need it. How did you get here? We found no trace of you on Earth. And we looked."

I shrugged. "Maybe you don't know all the hiding spaces."

Britt read another Window.

I had an idea, and sent Wraith out toward the man in the corner. Instead of concentrating on the screen, I read the reflection of the smart-glass tablet in the shine of his eyes. The numbers flashed across so fast I could barely read them, then settled.

"12% chance they hid on Earth."

Very interesting. I sent a Window to Adam, telling him what I'd just learned.

"You didn't hide on Earth," Britt said. "Maybe, if you'd like to share, I could get authorization to release the 'meningolycanosis.'"

"This isn't that kind of trade. Petralka got 'removed' because she couldn't handle me or my team, and she didn't realize it early and kill us while she could. Well, her Thinker didn't realize it either, as far as I could tell. But you've got a new one now." I looked at the man in the corner, who twitched. "Maybe you won't make the same mistakes. Because it's too late to just kill us."

"This is obviously a threat."

Sam stiffened behind me, then relaxed, his posture changing to something more resembling warm toffee.

I turned to look at him and had to suppress the instinctive flinch when I saw his black eyes.

His new Skill liked to kick in without his permission, especially when he felt stressed. Once it did, it didn't let him go until it had to. "This is why I should have gone to see if I could heal that group of people that had been infected by that mind-control hive bacteria. You wouldn't have to go to all the trouble of bargaining," he said.

"You're the one who vetoed that idea," I said. "When you had your morals."

"I was being stupid." He turned to Britt, staring at him with a complete lack of expression. "And yes, this is a threat."

Britt flinched back from the windows into emptiness that had taken the place of Sam's eyes.

I nodded. "I want the meningolycanosis, or I'm going to attack this base, along with help from some of my alien friends."

The Thinker's fingers twitched.

"98% chance of alien collusion."

"10% chance of attack."

I changed my mind.

The Thinker's eyes widened.

"27% chance of attack."

I changed it again.

"63% chance of attack."

Britt's eyes flickered, and he frowned.

"You see, Britt, the aliens didn't care about us Earthlings. They didn't come here to attack, at first. But we made them angry with the whole, 'imprisonment and torture of one of their own,' thing. They'll kill you and everyone here if I don't stop them."

"84% chance of truthfulness."

"If you just give me what I want…we'll go away."

"95% chance of truthfulness."

"In event of attack, 7% chance of base survival."

Britt's teeth ground together audibly.

"No one could fault your decision to comply with me, with percentages like that," I said.

He jerked.

A few minutes later, I was walking unimpeded through the lowers corridors of NIX. Estreyan guards had joined my team to make sure Britt didn't decide to betray us halfway through completing our "trade."

Chapter 36

...that which we are, we are;
One equal temper of heroic hearts,
Made weak by time and fate, but strong in will
To strive, to seek, to find, and not to yield.
— Lord Alfred Tennyson

ADAM LED us down into the bowels of the compound, moving quickly.

We turned the corner on a surprised guard at one point, and my Estreyan escorts slipped in front of me faster than he could draw his gun up.

The guard stared at my group, and then slowly lowered his gun, stepping back toward the wall for us to pass.

Sam, still under the influence of his Black Sun Skill, brushed a hand against him on the way by, and he crumpled to the ground.

I was beginning to see what the queen had meant about becoming a cult leader. It was strange, but I can't deny I liked the sense of security that came with not having to worry about dying all the time, when people were willing to literally put themselves between me and danger.

On the way to the meningolycanosis stores, we passed the Player containment area where they'd kept Chanelle. Cell doors ran along the hallway, and almost all of them had viewing windows through which we could see the condition of the Players within.

I'd known vaguely where they were, but this was my first time actually exploring the area.

Some of the Players looked sick, or depressed, or just generally unhealthy. But some were worse. Their bodies were bloated, veins turning black as the skin turned gangrenous in places. They tore at their own skin with nails and teeth, or wore restraints to keep them from doing so, straight-jackets and human muzzles. They babbled soundlessly behind the walls and twitched in seeming paranoia at things that weren't there.

Watching them made me...extremely uncomfortable. I had a feeling my mind was trying to remind me of something, a sense of vague deja-vu.

The Estreyans were even more shocked than I, and the group slowed from a jog to a walk as we all became distracted by what we were seeing.

One of them turned to me. "Your world is touched by the Sickness, too?"

I wanted to deny it on instinct, but realized that was what I'd been comparing the prisoners to. They reminded me of the infected spider-monkey I'd seen on Estreyer. "We didn't, before," I said instead, lamely, trying to ignore the horrible suspicion forming in my mind.

Sam had no compunction in blurting it out when the same thought came to him. "NIX has been experimenting with it, I bet."

There were gasps all around. Jacky shuddered, and Adam and I shared a worried look with her. Was this what had been done to Chanelle?

"What is *wrong* with your people?" one of the Estreyans asked, still staring through the windows.

"They know not with what they play," I said, slipping into the Estreyan speech pattern in my own distraction. These people were injected with meningolycanosis, if the medical charts on their doors weren't lying. The same as Chanelle. But she was different from them. Not normal, but she didn't act *insane.*

Chanelle whimpered, grabbing my hand as she looked through the observation windows. "They cultivate the abhorrent, like flowers growing in the soil. Growing in the flesh of our own kind," she whispered, eyes half-vacant, though I wasn't sure if she was losing lucidity, or if she was just in shock.

We continued on to the storage room for the meningolycanosis. We took it, and everything else in the room that wasn't bolted down, including the documentation. The Estreyans stored everything breakable extremely carefully, doubly wary of human creations now.

"I know Queen Mardinest did not order it," one of my guards said, "but it would be a kindness to these poor creatures if we razed this place to its standing stones, and killed them all. They are suffering, and the Sickness will spread."

"Nothing stops the Sickness from spreading," I said. "And maybe… maybe we will return with a cure, and these people will not need to die."

He shrugged. "If it is not soon, they will die anyway."

Chanelle squeezed my hand harder. This fate would also be hers, if I couldn't find a way to stop it.

I resisted the urge to slide down the wall and hide my head in my hands. When did saving the world become something I was seriously considering?

As we left, I carefully did not listen to the sound of the subjects' screams of pain.

AS WE WALKED out into the courtyard, which still bristled with security, I saw two faces that I never expected to see again.

I stopped in my tracks, and the others followed my gaze, up to one of the hallway windows that looked down on the circular courtyard.

Jacky *hissed.* "We don't need NIX anymore. Can we kill him now? We've gotten a lot stronger. I bet we could do it."

Kilburn looked down on us, his too thin form standing nonchalantly with his hands in his pockets.

Sam smiled, especially surprising because of his usual stoic nihilism under the influence of Black Sun. "I would like to melt his eyeballs out," he said.

Adam looked around. "It'll have to be quick. Could you guys cover for us?" he asked the Estreyans.

"No," Chanelle said.

We turned to her. She stared up at Kilburn with the kind of piercing focus so rare for her even now. "I want to kill him," she said. She turned to me. "I want to do it. But I'm not strong enough yet. Will you bring me back…later? After?" The unspoken question, whether I would bring her back after she wasn't sick anymore, hung in the air.

I grimaced, forcing my claws back into their sheaths, and nodded. "You have more right to his death than any of us," I said reluctantly.

I looked up again, but Kilburn had gone.

Near where he had been, another person who should have been dead looked out on us, pressing his hand against the glass. Vaughn glared down at me, mouthing one word very slowly. "Traitor."

I turned away, and with a signal of my hand in the air, we were gone from the courtyard, back to the mountainside with Torliam and the Estreyan teleporter.

The flight back to the array barely registered. As we passed through, I sent out a prayer that neither world had been or would be noticed by the things in between. Though I didn't know what gods might be listening.

Chapter 37

There is no chance, no destiny, no fate,
    Can circumvent or hinder or control
    The firm resolve of a determined soul.
    — Ella Wheeler Wilcox

THE NEXT COUPLE weeks were a blur of exhausted, desperate training, and sleepless nights of strategy and worry.

Blaine and the Estreyan scientists—that he grudgingly admitted were somewhat intelligent—had taken the samples we'd appropriated from NIX, and went to work testing and weaponizing them for use against the God of Knowledge. They'd also been developing visors that they thought might cancel out his light-based psychological attack. Blaine had gone without sleep for days and commandeered every useful Estreyan he could find to help him build them.

Birch discovered how to use his Skill, which with the name Gale, was unsurprisingly an aerokinesis Skill. Its first use allowed him to fly, after he displayed incredible foolishness in jumping off one of the palace balconies, only to discover that his wings were not, in fact, ready to carry him just yet.

I scolded him for his stupidity and recklessness till he crouched to the ground, whimpering with his ears flat to his head.

He poked me with his nose, sending a flashing image of a pitiful, mewling kitten into my mind. Then, walking meekly behind a figure with two long legs and a smell of strength, then a flash of my own blue eyes and the taste of dark blood.

The two-legs was me, and it seemed to be his way of saying he was sorry and he would be good in the future.

I sighed and gave him a flank of raw meat, with a short congratulation on discovering how to use his Skill.

After that, he "flew" everywhere he could, creating a constant updraft below himself to keep afloat for short bursts of gliding.

Gregor spent a lot of time training with a pair of blood-activated Estreyan daggers, which were more like swords compared to the boy's size. They'd been donated by one of my many supporters, and when Gregor spilled a few drops of blood onto their hilt, they would phase in and out of corporeality with him. They were incredibly deadly. While in Shadow form, they could pass through anything, and when they returned to reality, they retained their momentum for a short while. Gregor tested this by cutting through trees and blocks of marble, phasing back into his physical form with the blades halfway through an object.

An Estreyan puppet maker who learned of Kris' Skill came to the palace and volunteered to design and build bodies to house her summons, and they worked together creating bodies out of steel and platinum. Bodies that wouldn't crumble from the power of their own attacks and that could kill a hundred different ways.

Blaine got into quite a few arguments with Kris and Gregor, but he couldn't stop them from training. Not without alerting the Estreyans who gleefully supported said training, and fully expected the kids to have to fight against the God of Knowledge.

At that point, only Adam had yet to figure out how to use his new Skill, Bestow. He was frustrated enough about this that he considered allowing a specialist to be brought in for a consultation, but a simple request from Kris led to the answer.

Adam could gift his ink constructs. Not just creating them to attach to someone else, only to expire within the next couple minutes. With a bit of focus, his Skill allowed him to transfer ownership of his paintings to the person whose skin they were drawn on, to be Animated at will by them.

Too quickly, the last days of the countdown passed, and despite everything, I did not feel prepared. How could we be, when our goal was to defeat a god?

Still, the Estreyans looked at me with hope.

We gathered before the airships on the night before the final day, all of us nervous, checking our gear and running through the previous mock battles in our heads, over and over. Some people grew quiet, some people chattered or joked uncomfortably, and a couple people walked away to puke inconspicuously behind a tree or around a corner. Every warrior was kitted out in the most powerful weapons and armor that we could provide.

I stood a little apart from the crowd and pushed my Voice Skill to add weight to my words. "This is not a night for fear," I yelled. "This is not a night for doubt. Those nights have passed. That time when you did not know if you could ever be saved is passed. This is a night for hope, and triumph, and joy." Voice pulsed from my throat in time with my words, and I could feel the weight of the crowd's unwavering gaze on me. "Because now we know what we have to do, and it is very simple. The first step in the path has been swept clear before us. If you have fear, or doubt, throw it away. Tonight, we defeat a god. Tomorrow, the Sickness."

I wasn't any good with speeches, but Voice helped with that, and the Estreyans still cheered me, stomping their feet and clanging their weapons against their armor.

I didn't see Blaine or the kids among the crowd, and I wished them a safe escape as we filed into the ships, and our fleet lifted off, heading towards what would be the death of most of us.

When Blaine's Window appeared in front of me, dread filled my heart.

—I CANNOT FIND THE CHILDREN. THEY WERE IN THE SHIP I HAD DECOMMISSIONED. I LEFT FOR A MOMENT, AND WHEN I CAME BACK THEY WERE GONE. I FEAR THEY MAY HAVE BEEN ATTACKED, BUT PERHAPS THEY WENT WITH YOU? THEY ARE NOT ANSWERING MY WINDOWS.—
-BLAINE-

—I DIDN'T SEE THEM BEFORE WE LEFT. I WILL CHECK FOR THEM.—
-EVE-

My Wraith Skill had trouble exiting the air-tight ships and then reaching another at such high speeds, as if the passing wind were trying to blow it away. I sent a Window to Kris and Gregor instead, including Blaine in it.

—Where are you? Are you okay?—
-Eve-

—We're fine.—
-Kris-

Blaine interjected, then.

—Where are you!? I thought you may have been attacked again, or kidnapped!—
-Blaine-

—We are going to fight with the others. Don't try to stop us, it's just a waste of time. We already made up our minds.—
-Gregor-

—It's not safe. You should stay away. This isn't a game. It isn't even like when we were attacked by those assassins. A lot of people are going to die.—
-Eve-

—If we can't win, we're going to die, too, anyway.—
-Kris-

—We have the Sickness. And we have the Seal of Nine. We're part of this, and you can't do anything about that. We have more right than you do to be involved in this.—
-Gregor-

—You are children. As an adult, I cannot allow you to put your lives in danger.—
-Blaine-

—We're flying our own ship, so there's no one to make us turn around. And I was telling the truth when I said you

can't stop us. Physically, you can't stop us. We have Skills. And all we have to do is tell all the other Estreyans that you're trying to stop us from fighting the God of Knowledge, and how it might make us lose the war against the Sickness.—
-Gregor-

—We're not doing this to spite you. But we have to fight.—
-Kris-

—I'm not going to sit back and let myself die.—
-Gregor-

—We're not going to attack Knowledge directly. We'll stay on the edges of the fight, safely out of the way, and just attack the sentinels and rescue hurt people. We have the anti-light visors, and armor and a med-kit, and weapons and my marionettes.—
-Kris-

—Eve, do something about this! They will listen to you. If they won't, *make* them listen. Stop them.—
-Blaine-

I hesitated.

—I can't stop anyone from fighting for their own life, Blaine. Even if they are kids. However, if you guys are going to join this battle, you will obey me as if you are soldiers. My orders are law. You obey. You do not argue, you do not question. You won't be recklessly endangering yourselves for no reason.—
-Eve-

If I could guarantee that we could win this and keep them safe, it would have been different. But I couldn't. No child should be subjected to the horrors of battle. But no child should be subjected to a dissociative wasting disease, either.

MY ATTACK FORCE converged on the God of Knowledge from all around, the larger ships carrying ten or twenty people, while the smallest bore only individuals. We did our best to avoid the light of the Sentinels, but of course, it was impossible to do so completely. There would be no element of surprise—one of the downfalls of increased military force. The God of Knowledge had to know we were coming, but he hadn't tried to attack or given any indication that he was aware of our approach. Perhaps he was confident in his own dominance, and *wanted* us to attack. So he could kill and eat us, of course.

I ran through a last series of tests on the tracking and communication system we'd implemented, making sure everything was working properly. The anti-light visors Blaine had created allowed the Estreyan Thinkers and battlefield generals to assign tasks to individuals. It aided in extracting wounded soldiers, assigning higher priority ratings to certain objectives, and notifying people of incoming danger or attacks.

Sunrise was about an hour away, and the darkness made it easier to see the god's power. The valley of pure gold where he resided shone like a beacon in the night, the light of the sentinels cutting through the darkness with a palpable harshness. What I saw surprised me. Many of the sentinels had fallen to that strange bubbling. The god stood in the middle of the valley, his condition worsened in the time since I'd last seen him. The back of his knee was half eaten away, his skin flaked away all over, and his "hair" was lopsided, as if he was going bald starting from the side.

—HANG BACK UNTIL STAGE ONE IS OVER. THEN, STATION HERE.—
-EVE-

I sent Kris and Gregor a mapped location through a Window. It was as safe a position as I could choose without removing them from the fight altogether. From the spot half-covered by a ridge of rock on the side of the mountain, they would be able to see the battle, but still escape quickly if necessary, and there was a natural barrier against the light of some of the sentinels. Kris would be able to see to direct her summons, and Gregor wouldn't have too far to travel to reach the heavier clusters of sentinels, which he would be removing.

Stage One started. Fast-moving ships flew over the valley in a wave, dropping dark grey spheres as they went, concentrating them around the god, the bigger sentinels, and the sentinels in higher or more strategically defensible areas. When the spheres hit, they exploded spectacularly.

This had been a human idea. Estreyans preferred to do things under their own power.

Then, another wave of ships, dropping pouches that exploded into a fine dust that would float endlessly in the air, and make the path of the light even easier to see, like sunbeams through dust motes.

Stage Two. My fighters with enough immediately destructive power attacked the remaining larger sentinels, while small, darting ships and long-range attackers harried the god. Few were strong enough to do serious damage, but some were, and others worked together to chip away at the bases of the sentinels. It worked for less than a minute.

Knowledge picked up one of the broken, dimmed chunks of sentinel, and hurled it toward one of the attacking ships as it passed by overhead.

The pilot dodged, but not nearly quickly enough. The ship careened out of the sky in what was probably the worst possible way, smashing into both another ship and a free-flying warrior on the way down.

All three crashed, but the god grabbed the flyer as he plummeted toward the ground. He shoved the mortal's body headfirst into his mouth, biting down on their stomach and ripping away, so their intestines broke and spilled out.

He chewed slowly, a look of pleasure on his eyeless face. Then he twitched strangely, like a robot with a glitch, or an old tape recording with a scratch on it. "So…hungry," he murmured, swallowing, and then popping the bottom half of the body into his mouth and repeating the process. "I will not pass from existence!" he suddenly screamed shrilly. "I am—erumpent—to—widdershins—" He twitched like he had a nerve disease.

That had distracted people. There was a moment of silence, stillness, as the God of Knowledge spasmed, little flecks of his body floating away like really bad dandruff.

Then the comms blew up with commentary, as people realized. One of their gods had the Sickness.

I overrode their voices on the system and spoke calmly into everyone's ear as I watched them both in my mind's eye and out of the windshield of my ship far above. "This is the path laid out by the Oracle," I said, hoping that would give them some comfort. "We must win this battle, for the future of the world. This is our only chance. It can be done, so we must do it."

I didn't know if my words would be enough, especially as the god reached one of the downed ships and began to tear into it to get at the person within.

One team leader on the other side of the valley let out a battle cry, the sound echoing off the mountainsides, and resumed attacking his assigned sentinel frantically. His team followed suit, and then the rest of the advance attackers followed, cheered on by those watching and waiting their turns.

Once the God of Knowledge was done eating the three people he'd downed, he lifted a hand, palm facing upward, and grew a golden column out of it. He hurled it, killing the team leader who'd encouraged the others, the chunk of sentinel piercing through him and still clipping the arm right off one of his team members.

Knowledge tried the same on another group, but one of them stepped forward, throwing up a shield that ate the sentinel as soon as it touched the shimmering patch of air.

The god laughed, his strange, conglomerate voice echoing smoothly off the mountainsides all around. "You stupid, stupid mortals. You—cabal —your strength to be added to my own."

None of the Stage Two teams hesitated in their attacks.

He seemed to take that as a challenge, growing and launching the sentinels with blurring speed, despite his size, and the obvious limp from his bad knee. He spun and lunged, and we died. Sometimes, the Thinkers gave warning in time for the fighters to throw themselves out of the way, or one of the team members was able to dodge or block the attack. More often, we died.

Still, where we succeeded in cutting down some of the sentinels, their light cut out like that of a crushed lightning bug.

The god lunged toward one of the closer groups.

They retreated immediately, sprinting away at full speed.

He almost snapped up the slowest of them, but one of the extraction team waiting on the mountainside saved the trailing warrior, reaching out with a lash of power that grabbed and snapped the Estreyan forward like the tongue of a frog snatching a bug out of the air.

The God of Knowledge turned to his prey's rescuer, and with an nonchalant toss of gold, their brain was smeared across the rock behind them.

We changed tactics, then. Some teams rushed in to act as decoys and distract the god, while others continued to take out the sentinels, but this time moving in arcs that took them back to safety quickly after they entered the battlefield, and made it harder for the god to focus on any one team.

The power the Estreyans held was truly astounding. Some flew through the sky under their own energy, attacking from above or rescuing others below when escape wasn't possible on foot. Some lashed out with Skills that flashed through the air like light-shows, or created golems that pried themselves out of the ground and rushed forward into battle, or flashed walls and barriers into existence for a moment to protect their comrades.

It was sound, and light, and beautiful chaos, as we removed the god's source of control over the battlefield.

It lasted only for a couple minutes.

Knowledge pretended to be distracted by a flashy attack from above, only to suddenly turn and take out an entire team halfway across the valley. The limited attacks on the sentinels became counterproductive then, as he killed relentlessly, only pausing to eat a couple people here and there.

Time for Stage Three.

Chapter 38

In the end,
I will win.
— Eve Redding

I SENT OUT THE SIGNAL, and my ship flew to the edge of the valley, flitting low to the ground. The floor dropped out from under me, sending me plummeting toward the golden ground below.

Two other medium-sized ships did the same, my attack group falling with me. We tumbled when we hit the ground, and the ships flew away.

All around the valley, other teams did the same.

I worked best with my own team, so despite the protests of some of the Estreyans who felt they would be better able to protect me, Adam, Jacky, Sam, and Torliam crouched in the relative darkness with me, along with a few Estreyans hand-picked for their Skills.

An Attribute-boosting healer, still just a boy, laid his hands on my back, maximizing everything he could, and then pushing even harder.

When he finished with me, he moved on to the others, till his Skill was exhausted, and he collapsed to his knees. A flicker caught him, and he was gone, extracted on the orders of one of the Thinkers.

I resisted the urge to straighten and hold my head high in challenge. The rush of multiplied power made me feel as if I'd just had a shot of caffeine straight to the veins while listening to my own personal film track of epic music. However, I was aware the feeling was an illusion, as people much stronger than me were being killed like mosquitos in front of me.

I had thought the display of powers was awe-inspiring before, but now it was truly astonishing. This was the wave of heavy hitters. The attackers who could damage a god directly, and who aimed to kill or at least incapacitate him. Plus, there was me.

I stood, finally, and let out a scream of challenge toward the God of Knowledge, a familiar action from our mock battles. The Voice Skill thudded, sending out my scream in a rolling wave that shivered through the ground. Other voices joined me, first my own team, and then the others, and the valley echoed with our screams of defiance.

Patches of light and darkness flared, strange effects from esoteric Skills. They gave me a headache when Wraith tried to make sense of what was happening to the laws of space or time within them.

We moved forward as a group, traveling through sentinel-free patches whenever possible, and shielded by either Adam or Torliam when it wasn't.

In a particularly flashy move, a gigantic flower of frost-threads and blue light bloomed from the god's head, moving through the full lifecycle from bud to decay in the course of a couple seconds. The wave of cold hit me hard enough to induce a shiver, even halfway across the valley.

That was followed up by a phoenix of fire, the sudden temperature change causing hairline fractures in the god's face, the cracks sounding like cannon-fire as they formed.

It didn't even faze him, except to make him angrier.

We passed an Estreyan dragging himself across the ground, missing his legs, and Sam stopped to seal off the wounds and signal for extraction.

One of Kris' summons bounded past us, picking up the Estreyan without even slowing down. It would carry him to safety.

I noted the group forming into a wide circle around the god, each standing at equidistant points, and seemingly unnoticed by him, what with all the other attacks. Good.

Several of the fighters in this stage, including most of my own team, carried meningolycanosis samples, in the hopes that someone would get the chance to administer it to him. I fingered the cartridges of meningolycanosis around the belt at my waist, each of them with a different delivery system, at least one of which we hoped would work.

I watched as a couple warriors tried to dagger the god with it, but the injectors, though they were of various designs and materials meant specifically to pierce him, just broke against his golden skin. They died for their failed attempts. But at least we knew that there was no way we would infect him that way.

One Estreyan with some sort of flight ability had an idea, and after a particularly vicious attack by the others, launched himself right at the god's face. Once in the air, though, he couldn't move or maneuver quickly enough.

He was moving through the light, and the God of Knowledge noticed him far too soon. The flier had no chance of getting the meningolycanosis into his nose or mouth, but he threw the breakable vial anyway.

The god caught him inside one perfectly sculpted golden hand. The fingers clenched, and the Estreyan man was squeezed out between the fingers like red putty.

I shuddered. At least his death was probably instant. It wasn't a bad idea, on the Estreyan's part, but it probably wouldn't have worked. The golden body may be a manifestation of the God of Knowledge, but it was *not* the God of Knowledge. Like Jacky had said, the God of Knowledge was the gathering of Seeds that held his power and consciousness. And that's what I needed to get to.

Once my group was close enough, but still behind both the main attackers and the group who were working in a wider circle around them, we paused for a second in an area of relative shadow, crouched down almost flat to the ground.

I pushed my awareness out, trying to see past the glowing ground and sentinels, the flaring bonfires of power darting all around and expending their power, and the overwhelming brightness that was the God of Knowledge's body. I needed to see the point from which his light emanated.

I closed my eyes behind my visor, but even so, it felt like my retinas burned in the light. My eyes prickled with involuntary tears.

I vaguely saw the sun, though, hidden deep-seated within the God of Knowledge's belly, near his pelvis. I bit my bottom lip. How would we get to that? We could barely damage his skin. Despite my misgivings, I announced my findings through the communication system.

The news lent renewed energy to their attacks. A miniature sun burnt itself out against his torso from one person while tendrils of octopus-like darkness grew out of the ground around him and stabbed at his stomach from another.

Wraith saw attacks that weren't visible to the visor or my human eyes. Rents in space that ripped small pieces out of him. One person got close enough to touch his stomach with their bare hand. They were dead an instant later, squished and then eaten, but the patch they'd touched stayed frozen in midair when Knowledge stepped away, ripping off him.

Torliam fogged up with blue, building and building his power, then attacking with a lance that scored a small divot into the golden skin.

We died almost as fast as we attacked.

Finally, though, the surrounding barrier group's technique was ready. Bands of shadowy red appeared in the air, huge concentric rings that floated over the heads of the barrier makers, matching the size of their circle.

With their shout, the bands snapped inward, constricting around the god.

He jumped in surprise, but wasn't quick enough, and they tightened like a wriggling snake, then hardened, trapping one of his arms halfway bent at what looked like a painful angle. He struggled a bit against his bindings but didn't seem to be making any headway.

A surge of elation went through me, and I'm sure the rest of us mortals. But my fighters didn't lose focus just because of that, instead redoubling their efforts.

We had a minute at most to work, and the technique the barrier makers had used was not repeatable. The red bands were created somehow from the blood and will of a group of highly trained specialists, who worked in tandem to pull off a technique that was pretty much a lost art. It hadn't been performed in over a thousand years, and for good reason. Even if the barrier makers had enough blood to try again, they wouldn't have the minds to do so. Somehow, they traded their Intelligence and Mental Acuity over the course of a long period of time for the binding. They would be almost retarded, and need daily care, for the next few *years*, until the faculties which they'd traded for an instant of power finally returned to them.

The extraction team immediately removed them from the battlefield, so they wouldn't be sitting ducks.

The Skills converging on the God of Knowledge overlapped and even merged with one another. Everyone still standing was giving their all, down to the last drop of power, and the god was writhing in pain, which hopefully meant they were successfully eating away at his metallic body, opening a path for me to his Seed core.

The seconds counted down. Since we didn't know exactly long we had, we'd tried to plan within the margin for error. Like we had practiced, the attacks stopped, and the shielders used their Skills, a backup protection in case the red bands failed sooner than expected.

I saw a couple Estreyans drop to the ground in exhaustion, and just hoped the extraction team could get to them in time.

I sprinted forward, flanked by my unit. At a motion from me, one of the more powerful teleporters transported us to within a few meters of the god. The Skill residue cleared up, and I could sense that his pelvis was not fully open, or eaten through, whatever you wanted to call it.

A wave of simultaneous terror and rage at the terror ran through me, and with a snarl, I brought forth a surge of Chaos which smashed like a hungry animal into the wounds the others had created, setting gleefully to the task I'd set it. Destruction.

It seemed to be doing a surprisingly quick, effective job of it. Sometimes I felt a camaraderie with Sam, having a power so destructive I couldn't quite trust it, or trust myself with it. This was not one of those times.

The God of Knowledge twitched, tensing up as if to try and somehow move away from Chaos. But then he relaxed, somehow shrinking in on himself, and sliding his awkwardly bent arm forward, which created a bit of space within his hardened bindings.

Then, with the tiny bit of momentum that extra space earned him, his arm burst outward, striking one of the barrier rings.

It shattered, and its companions burst apart with it, even though they hadn't been touched.

The backup force fields and shields crumbled when he smashed his hands into them, even the one that had previously eaten his sentinel.

I backpedaled, my claws digging into the ruined ground as I slid, attempting to stop as if in slow motion.

The god turned to face me directly with its perfect, eyeless face, seeming to see into my own eyes despite the visor around my head. It *grinned.*

Adam had reacted as quickly as me, as had the Estreyans. He threw up a shield, and another, and another, layering them in the air only centimeters apart, two walls at an angle pointing toward the god like a giant arrow, close enough together that he couldn't step through them, and facing so the broad side would stop his huge arms if he tied to swing at us.

Torliam threw up misty blue shields of his own, reaching for me.

Time seemed to slow. My toes were still digging into the golden ground, struggling for purchase.

Torliam's hand slapped over my face, a precaution, as he pushed his Skill into creating a canceling shell of darkness around us, shielding against the light.

Others in my protective group were throwing out Skills of their own, some meant to protect, and others to attack or force the god back.

I saw one of the Estreyans in my group, whose job was extraction and rescue, reaching out for me. His Skill gathered its brightness in my mind's eye, preparing to lash out.

I had a moment of rejection, where I wanted to stop him, when I realized he could only save *me*. But it didn't even matter, because the ground *erupted*. Even with the artificial expansion of time caused by my panic, it happened so fast I could barely follow it.

Golden sentinels shot out from every direction.

One speared right through the Estreyan that had been going to save me. I was disappointed, because that meant I was going to die after all.

Things snapped back into normal speed.

The sentinels sprouted like Sam's crystal attack, bursting in every direction like a mass of coral. They killed some instantly, but trapped others within.

Adam had been close beside me, but his body was gone, as were his shields.

Torliam's hand was still wrapped over my eyes, but it made no difference. I could see everything without my eyes. He was contorted painfully, but not seriously injured. Already, his power was slicing and pushing at the sentinels, to limited effect.

A small chunk of my thigh seemed to have been ripped off, but it wasn't much deeper than the skin, and wouldn't impede me in the short term.

One of the Estreyans had been speared through the stomach. He was held suspended in the air by his wound.

Sam was trapped behind me.

Jacky was meters away, but not badly hurt, and her body was growing already.

There was no time for caution. I let out a sharp burst of Chaos, as small and precisely formed as I was able, to disintegrate the sentinels holding nearby allies in place. As before, it was effective, more so than many of the other Skills I'd seen.

But it drew the god's attention. He reached forward, the sentinels moving aside for him and releasing me and those nearest me, though they still formed a mass of impenetrable brambles everywhere else. "You want freedom?" he asked, his smooth voice making cold sweat burst out over my skin. The god leaned downward, his massive body blocking out the sky. "Knowledge is power," he said, in what would have been a soft voice if not for the sheer *volume* of it, echoing from everywhere. It was coming from the sentinels, the golden ground, and even the golden plants.

The whole valley was part of his body, I realized. How foolish we'd been, to think we could attack him like this and win. He'd been humoring us.

"When you know—fogey—thing, completely, you have complete power over it." He didn't even seem to notice the way he'd glitched out. It didn't matter. If anything, it made it even more terrifying. "And I know you, Eve Redding," he said. The grin hadn't left his face.

I was about to die. I understood that. But I couldn't quite accept it, my heart still pounding frantically, my power screaming out to be used, as if I might fight my way free, or somehow find a way out of this.

Jacky screamed and slammed into me from the side, her massive body sending me flying.

The god brought a hand down, and she activated the shields Adam had painted onto her, all at once.

His hand smashed through them, and with another scream, she lifted both arms to block, catching his blow, though the force of it made her knees buckle.

I landed, dizzy and disoriented, the golden ground beneath me seeming to turn white.

He lifted his arm back for another attack, and I screamed at her. "*Move*!"

A tear opened in the world, a couple meters above the ground, and Zed's hand came out, reaching for her.

Threads burst upward from the ground in sheets, surrounding me in the space between a blink. They formed a familiar shape around me, like a smooshed ball, with helixes, bridges, and wandering arches filling the inside haphazardly.

I howled in rage.

Chapter 39

But one by one we must all file on
    Through the narrow aisles of pain.
    — Ella Wheeler Wilcox

THE ORACLE CRAWLED out of the floor, detaching herself from the string and turning to look down at me, the sound of wind over glass bottles floating out as she moved.

"What the fuck are you doing?" I snarled. "They're getting killed out there!" I couldn't actually tell, since Wraith had been confined, just as surely as I had, but even an idiot could make basic deductions based on facts.

"Yet you are in here."

"That's my *team*!" My shriek pulsed with Voice, echoing off the walls, tearing at the threads. "Save them! Shield them inside one of your spiderweb egg sacs!"

"That would defeat my purpose." Her stone eyes were somehow still sad, though they did not weep like they had when I first met her.

"I can't do this without them." My voice broke, the enraged demands turning to a plea.

"If my goal was for you and your team to defeat the God of Knowledge, that would be true. But my father is much too strong for you."

"*He* said I was supposed to kill him, too."

She smiled at me, just a little, tilting her head to the side like I was a cute puppy or a stupid child.

"Why are you doing this?" I whispered. "What do you want?"

The Oracle ignored my question. "I am a meshing of many of the different aspects of those who begat me. The lesser aspects of Knowledge and Time allow me to see a web of existence. Possibilities. Percentages, you might call them. But the strands of the web are always shifting. My goal is to save my world," she said simply. She bowed her head in a semblance of sadness, and the sound of the movement through the lines of her body was somber, but her stone face showed no expression. "There are paths to deliverance, among the mortals. You are not the only one, Eve-Redding. I see you succeeding more often than the others. But the paths are difficult, and many things must happen for yours to pierce through. You must make the right choices, and through them, *change*."

"Get to the point."

She frowned at me. "You are naive. You have not yet learned how to *lose*. In this way, you will learn, but with my intervention, may continue living."

"What about the others?" My eyes were trained on her in an unblinking stare that was already halfway to a glare.

"That is the loss." She shrugged, the motion letting out a few notes into the air that quickly died away. "It is more likely that you find your way if they die here. But do not worry. I will still give you the promised reward. You will not die from the power of Khaos." She touched her chest, in that same spot that had once folded away to reveal the puzzle rings.

My heart pounded, and I clenched my fists, careful not to let my claws slip back out and puncture my own skin. "You want me to accept defeat, and give up. If I do, I'm more likely to save this world, and you'll consider my quest completed successfully, even though the terms have suddenly changed completely? But everyone out there is going to die, including all the others with the seal?" I touched my throat. "My brother? The kids?"

Her features twisted once again, into a mask of compassion. "This will be hard for you. But it will make you great. Besides, they will all die eventually, if you do not stop the Sickness. On this path, their loss just comes a little sooner, and the number of those you may save is so much greater."

Rage ate at my insides, eroding my control. "People will die if I don't?

Lots of people? I don't care! I'm not some savior, some martyr who's come to fix all the problems of this world just because you want me to. All people were not created equal in my eyes. I could trade a million empty numbers for one member of my team, one life I care about. Did you really think this would work? If you wanted me to work for you, you should have offered me a better deal," I snarled, panting for breath. Chaos begged to be released, to *destroy* her.

She stared at me as if bemused at the actions of a strange animal. "There is no point to your anger. You must accept defeat. It is inevitable either way. You cannot win against the God of Knowledge, and if you refuse my offer, you will only die alongside those you place such unbalanced value on." She smiled, gently amused, and too assured of herself. "I have seen your future in the web, Eve-Redding. I know you."

"You don't know me," I said hoarsely. The crystal at my throat began to thrum again. "If you did, you would know that I don't give up. I *win.* I don't care what you see in your little future webs." The crystal was thrumming along with the beat of my voice, an almost physical pulse that pushed at her angrily. "I will bend the world to my will. I swear it." I took a deep breath and straightened to my full height, which wasn't much compared to her twelve feet. "Now, you are going to send me back down there to kill your father. And when I win, you're damn well going to give me the reward we agreed on."

The Oracle's frown formed crags along her stone brow. "I cannot choose the path for you, you *foolish* mortal." She let out a sharp grunt that still sounded lovely, and with a musical shake of her head, the egg-shaped web folded and sank away as quickly as it had come, leaving me standing in the middle of a ravaged battlefield, right back in front of an enraged god.

Chapter 40

I am the master of my fate,
  I am the captain of my soul.
  — William Ernest Henley

MY CONVERSATION with the Oracle hadn't taken that long, but I hadn't really believed there would be anyone left for me to rescue. I was wrong.

I lunged to the side, claws scrabbling futilely at the golden ground for extra purchase.

The sentinels rose to block me.

I gestured forward with a clawed hand, as if drawing something from my chest, and a mass of Chaos parted the impenetrable forest like a beam, cutting a tunnel straight forward.

My awareness swirled out, and I took stock of Adam lying trapped within the sentinels, too far away to reach with Chaos. He was badly injured, one of them having punctured right through his back, from side to side. Basically, a chunk the size of his arm was just…*gone* from his lower back. His spine was definitely severed. If not for the sentinel still pressing into him, he probably would have bled to death already.

Gregor was cutting his own path through the sentinels toward Adam, in direct violation of my prior orders. Three of his sister's summons escorted him.

Sam was...*melting* a path of his own with his bare hands, moving toward me.

I could feel the effects of Black Sun on him through my Wraith Skill.

Jacky was as noticeable as the god, her Struggle Skill still in effect, though one arm hung limply, blood dripped from her head, and she looked like she could barely keep her balance in the fighting stance she'd taken. Her visor was gone, so she was fighting with her eyes closed, and that was even more impressive. She was half as big as Knowledge, far bigger than any Estreyan I'd ever seen.

Torliam's blue mist lashed out from beside her, giving her a moment to recover while he harried the god with enough force to make Knowledge take a step back.

A ship zoomed past overhead, shooting two missiles at the god as it passed. They folded inward and outward simultaneously in a familiar manner, and when they hit, Knowledge was blown completely off his feet, tumbling through the air and smashing through his sentinels, snapping them to bits in a huge swath.

I should have known Blaine would be coming, with the kids here and in danger.

The ship came around for another pass while the god was down, this time smashing straight into him in an even more spectacular explosion, while two small forms were expelled out the back.

A flying Estreyan streaked by, catching the bigger form, and carrying Blaine away from the battlefield.

The smaller form, Birch, flew down to one of the people trapped within the sentinels. His fur and feathers bristled up, and he let out a wave of wind that carried a black-tendrilled power I certainly recognized. It cut right through the sentinels, and the Estreyan fell free. How much of my blood had Birch consumed, even back before he'd even hatched? I hadn't even considered what it might be doing to him.

I formed a plan in my head, and I hoped that I had the power to pull it off.

The long-range and flying Estreyans still able to fight took the opportunity to lay down a barrage on the god, keeping him down.

I sprinted forward, creating a tunnel through the sentinels at the same rate I moved. I passed a couple Estreyans along the way who weren't dead, and I let out pulses of Chaos to help free them.

One of them still had the visor on, and seemed to realize when she was released from the sentinels, though she moved slowly, as if fighting against her own body.

The other stared into nothing, still trapped within their own mind.

I reached Sam, and he turned without hesitation, running with me. I overtook Gregor along the way, wishing I could spare a moment to glare at the boy.

At some point, Adam's blood had bubbled up around the sentinel. He took advantage of it, using his own blood as ink, which formed into bandages to staunch his wounds. He let out a shuddering gasp, the air rattling in his lungs even as he said, "Animus." His lungs had probably been punctured by his broken ribs.

Sam didn't hesitate.

I left Adam suspended, because he might bleed out too quickly even for Sam if I didn't.

Adam lifted a hand, reaching for me.

I stepped forward. "I don't have much time—"

His hand touched my forehead, the blood on his fingers spreading onto my skin. "Kill him," he whispered.

I grinned. "Okay." I ran away, requesting a pickup for Gregor on the comms system.

Jacky had shrunk, the break in the pressure of the fight while the god dealt with Blaine's attack removing the necessary conditions for Struggle to stay activated.

I ran toward her and Torliam.

She was still conscious, and had turned to make her way toward the god, good fist still clenched as if she were ready to fight.

Torliam turned to me as I neared, and when Jacky saw me, she let out a shuddering sob.

I slipped under her good arm, helping to support her. "I still need your help," I said. "So I hope you're not too tired."

"We don't get tired," she lied with an ironic grin. "What's the plan?"

"Get me into position, save a bunch of people, then get the hell out of here. Far enough that Knowledge can't reach you. I am going to kill a god. Chaos seems surprisingly effective against it. I'll just need to use more of it. A lot more. My power isn't controllable in large amounts. I don't want you anywhere near when I unleash it. Grab a long-range extractor, if you can. Maybe..." I didn't say it, because we both knew what I meant. Maybe there would be something of me left to save, afterward.

Knowledge rose to his feet, roaring. His main body was very much worse for wear, but most of it was scratches, sometimes gouges, and other than his knee, which he braced with a quick growth of sentinels in the eroded area, none of the injuries were even enough to slow him down.

I explained the plan to Jacky and Torliam as quickly and simply as possible, and then the three of us ran forward.

THE GOD OF KNOWLEDGE knew we were coming, obviously, and it was turned to face us by the time we arrived. "Your power is impressive, Eve," he said, his voice conversational, as if we were having tea instead of a fight to the death. "Quite different—amygladin—those of the others. It reminds me of…" He looked down and away for a second, as if he'd been reaching for a word, or a memory, and had just forgotten what it was. He looked back to me. "I will add that power to my own strength."

I gave him a feral grin. Perfect. "My power will never be yours," I yelled, loud enough that he, along with anyone who might be trapped but still conscious within the growth of sentinels, could hear me.

I rushed forward, a boost of Torliam's Skill behind me pushing me faster. I moved close to the god, but shot past him, with a lash of Chaos to the back of his bad knee along the way.

He swiped for me, but was just slightly too far away to reach me.

There was a puddle of blood on the other side of the clearing his tumble had created, and a couple of my fighters were trapped beyond, alive.

I pulsed a wave of Chaos their way, weakening the sentinels around them.

I turned abruptly, body tilting low to the ground as my toes dug in for purchase, and sprinted back toward the god. This time, I aimed Chaos at his pelvis on the way by.

He was prepared for it. He took one smooth, sliding step in my direction to cover the distance between us, and reached for me.

A blue, misty light slammed into me from between the god and me, and tossed me aside, to safety.

It was a bit painful, but I twisted easily in mid-air, landing half-sideways on the wall of sentinels. I let out a bit of Chaos around my lower body to stave off their attempt to grow around me, and jumped off at an angle, making it into safe range once again.

Jacky pulsed, growing larger, and then larger again. She jumped high and dropped down with a punch so forceful she cracked a sentinel with her bare hands. She spun, throwing the chunk at the god like he had been doing to others earlier.

I shot past the god again, attacking like a dog nipping at his heels, with Torliam acting as my safety net, protecting me when Knowledge got too close to catching or hitting me. When it was feasible, I aimed my trajectory so that I ended up near someone who was trapped within the sentinels. Slowly, I freed people, and if they were uninjured and still aware, they struggled their way out.

The remaining fighters converged on the god, doing their best to cover me, to distract him, to stay alive for just a little longer.

"I see through your plan, tiny one," he said, his voice seeming to come mainly from behind me, though I was facing him. "Did you—trickle—you could hide, within my light?"

The hair on the back of my neck prickled, and more cold sweat dripped down my back, under my armor. Shit.

"You cannot save them. When you are dead, I will capture them again, and they will become part of my strength as well."

I exhaled and turned to Jacky. We sprinted toward each other. When we got close enough, I jumped, she grabbed both of my hands in her one good one, and used her Skill to root herself to the surface of the planet. She turned our combined momentum into a spin, so fast that I felt like my shoulders might pop apart as I flew through the air.

She released me, mid-swing, throwing my body like a discus at the god.

In this way, my direction changed in an instant. It was almost enough to catch Knowledge off guard. But he slid his foot forward like a dancer, and lifted it, slamming the top of it into me relatively gently, like I was a ball.

The abrupt change in momentum *hurt.* My internal organs protested, and my bones creaked.

Torliam threw up a shield for me.

I jumped sideways off of it.

The god's hands were too quick, and I was caught inside gigantic bands of gold as he wrapped his fingers around me, once again almost gently.

This was the moment of reckoning. If he squeezed me, it was all over.

But I was guessing he would want me to fear, and scream. I struggled, clawing and letting out ineffectual, random bursts of Chaos that intentionally didn't do much damage, staring in my best imitation of terror at his mouth.

Sure enough, he brought me close to his mouth in slow motion, opening wide so I could see the tombstone-like teeth that would be grinding into me in a moment.

I waited till the very last second, then released the huge breath I'd been holding along with a whispered, "Animus," and relaxed my slightly angled arms and legs, using the same trick he'd demonstrated earlier to create space.

Blood wings snapped to life, a single great flap and every bit of strength I had in my legs shooting me straight forward into his mouth, with a little swirl of Chaos around my body to grease the way.

His teeth snapped together halfway down my armored feet, biting through the metal.

I scrambled forward, losing some skin and ripping the claws off my toes. But I was already inside, and I wasted no time being surprised, or disoriented, or focusing on the pain. I scuttled away from his teeth, down his throat, stopping myself with claws and spread-eagled limbs pressing against the walls of his golden esophagus, just before the opening to the stomach. The stench hit me first.

The god's internal design had abandoned all resemblance to mortal biology. A ball of light sat on a small pedestal at the bottom of the stomach chamber, with little glowing sparkles flowing in and out of it like a swarm of ever-glowing fireflies around a nest. His Seed core. It was significantly bigger than Behelaino's. My muscles clenched in a subconscious desire to retreat, as I realized once again how strong he was. I also felt a hint of greed. Power like that could do so much for me. But I wanted no part in it. Both because my body would probably just burst apart if I put any more of the gods into it, and because it was Sickness-tainted.

The assaulting stink came from the pieces of bodies scattered about. Some were well-chewed and soupy, while I recognized whole limbs in other places. The light particles swarmed over them, growing brighter before returning to the main ball. Like bees collecting honey.

I growled angrily at them, and dropped down to the bottom of the chamber, wading toward the Seed core through the putrefied human flesh sliding off the bones. I resisted the urge to throw up, once again. Breathing through my mouth didn't help. The taste of death and disease coated my tongue and throat, and I gagged, so hard I couldn't breathe past it. I reached the sphere and took the two cartridges of meningoly-canosis from their spot at my waist. I injected both of them into the sphere, hoping that it worked as we'd anticipated.

The light of the sphere pulsed strangely, as if the Seed substance was spinning in every direction at once, and had become unstable. The little particles of light swarmed out of it, dipping in and out like bees disturbed from their hive.

An overwhelming feeling bubbled up from my stomach, and I let out a gleeful laugh that echoed off the walls of the stomach chamber, making me sound crazy. I ignored the little voice in my head that was telling me it wasn't the echo that made me sound crazy.

I opened the door to the room of serenity, then lifted the lid of the box of silence, and unlocked the chest of stillness. Chaos shattered outward, tearing at me from the inside. I turned it on the core, and the god *screamed.*

That was the key, it seemed.

Chapter 41

He who fights with monsters might take care lest he thereby become a monster. And if you gaze for long into an abyss, the abyss gazes also into you.

— Friedrich Nietzsche

KNOWLEDGE WAS A TERRIBLE, beautiful thing. I could feel it flooding me, changing my brain with a physical sensation. Synapses fired, pathways of thought and knowledge forming. I found myself knowing things in a way that seemed like I'd known forever, memories and understanding from before I was born. Some of it, relevant in the moment, came to the forefront.

"Knowledge of a thing truly is power over it," I whispered in a voice so low even I could barely hear it.

Little eddies of Chaos swirled over me, around me, for the first time like a caress instead of a burning lash. I clenched my hands, then flicked those clawed fingers forward.

Dark flames, identical to those I'd seen from Behelaino, flashed to life in my palms. It burned.

I ignored the pain. My mortal body would not channel the power needed without being consumed. It was going to hurt a lot more. But that was okay. This was a pain I could find some peace in. Fear of death had kept me alive. But to live a worthwhile life, there have to be some things worth dying for.

I threw the almost solid flames at the core. They ate at it, disintegrating pieces of it in flashes of blinding light.

The chamber bucked around me as the god did, throwing me and the other contents around within his stomach cavity.

I shuddered as a half-digested eyeball slid out of my hair. I was alright, but I knew I couldn't take my time with this. I didn't have the power to draw it out, and the god would find a way to stop me if I tried.

I unleashed more of the flames, letting them spill forward from me, building upon themselves, multiplying under my direction. They were a wild, feeding mass that I would never be able to create piece by piece, or without the aid of the uncorrupted piece of Knowledge.

The god screamed, loud and animalistic, and began to rip his own stomach open to get at me.

Too late, I hoped. I lifted my arms and let the black fire wash over my skin. I threw all my power into it, watching idly as the first layer of my skin peeled away and disintegrated immediately within the grip of my power. I closed my eyes, then. Because the visual was disturbing enough to be distracting from my task. It kept hurting, as I raised the firestorm higher, feeding it with my power and unintentional pieces of my own flesh. At some point, it hurt too badly, and I was too weak to continue, but by then it didn't matter.

Chaos knew what to do.

My eyes burned away, shortly after the lids protecting them disintegrated. But I didn't need them. I watched with the last bit of my Wraith Skill as the storm consumed the God of Knowledge's corrupted manifestation.

The towering cone of black fire grew from within, as if from nothing, and then expanded, exploding outward into the valley, burning and eating away.

"Don't hurt…" *the living,* I finished silently. My lips had gone, and it hurt too much to talk with a ruined neck.

The fire ate through the gold, and the dirt and rock, deep into the mountainsides all around. An unparalleled force of destruction.

Then, Chaos turned, and moved beyond destruction. Oh, how little I had understood it, before. The fire died out, smokeless, and left behind something new wherever its devouring tongue was felt.

It pulled inward, back towards the center. Towards my meaty stump of a body, which was barely hanging on to life. I was stubborn.

Then, it was gone. And with it, the pain.

QUEST COMPLETED!

Chapter 42

I rise.
    — Maya Angelou

I ROLLED ONTO MY STOMACH, gagging and coughing up blood. Despite that, my brain was bursting with chemical euphoria. I had almost died. I had *felt* myself dying, my consciousness partially slipping away, and partially fading out of existence, while my body ignored its wounds, slipping into bliss.

I touched my face, my eyelids, my lips, whole once more. I stood up, looking around in disorientation. Something was wrong with me. Things moved too fast, and too slow. I stumbled forward, catching myself on one of the new trees.

My left arm caught my attention. "Well, that's weird." I flexed my six fingers, and then looked up slowly, interest drawn away from the strange way my body felt and moved, to the land around. I stood in a dryad wood.

It reminded me of the exact opposite of that horrible forest from my very first Trial. The angled sunlight of dawn shone sideways through the widely spaced trees. I walked up to another one, stumbling at first, seeing the wood, grown into the shape of a warrior. He had the semblance of a sword in his hand, which grew bright leaves at the end of the flat branch of wood. I looked up to his face, and vaguely recognized the features replicated in bark. Golden threads ran through the wood, veins that sparkled slightly when the sun hit them through the leaves. It was beautiful.

But I didn't want everyone to be trees.

I sobbed, once, and turned. An Estreyan was standing in the midst of the newly created wood, watching me. She looked shaken, to say the least. Pale and wide-eyed, and a bit bloody.

I laughed with relief. "You're alive!" Voice pulsed out of me, sharing my joy. Hopefully, the others would be alive, too.

When our eyes met, she dropped to the ground, pressing her face against it.

She must be exhausted, I knew. I walked on, my thoughts skipping dizzily. I passed more Estreyans as I went. Most of the non-trees were relatively unharmed, but I found a couple who were severely injured. "I'll send a healer for you, I promise," I said. My visor was long gone, and even my VR chip seemed to be malfunctioning. Or else I'd forgotten how to use it.

It didn't take me too long to find a clearing, where people were gathering. This had been where I fought the god, before being "eaten."

Adam and Sam were there, both lying on the ground and looking horrible. But they were alive, and an Estreyan healer hovered over them.

Jacky stood to the side, tears running down her beautiful, grimy face. She made almost no sound in her sadness, aside from the occasional hitching breath.

Torliam lay against a mossy rock over to one side, surrounded by some concerned Estreyans, a couple of whom I recognized as healers. He was letting out seemingly uncontrolled, and accidental, bursts of Skill-blue mist.

"Healers?" I asked. "Injured," I said, pointing back the way I'd come. My voice sounded really strange. And it felt strange. I reached up absently to touch the base of my throat, which was vibrating a little too much to be normal. Was that Voice again?

Heads turned to stare at me, eyes widened, emotions that I couldn't quite decipher crossing their faces. Were they afraid to go? Maybe they didn't understand me.

"It is okay," I added, making sure I was speaking Estreyan, and not English. "It is over. Go save them."

One of the healers bowed deeply to me, then rushed off in the direction I'd come from.

Well, at least *someone* was listening.

I swirled my awareness outward, and fell over when the world tilted, the Skill overwhelming me with the sudden rush of information. I reined it back in, but didn't bother to get off the ground. "Everyone important is okay," I said to Adam. "And a lot of the Estreyans. Make people go get them and bring them here." I waved my hand limply. "I'm too tired to do the ordering."

"Are you in shock?" Adam muttered.

I ignored him. No need to bicker, after everything.

"The god is dead?" Torliam asked.

I nodded, rolling onto my back to look up at the sky, the stars fading away into pink and blue light. "Death is but a metamorphosis," I said, sounding quite wise, in my own opinion. "But yeah. That one is gone. Maybe another one will gather here in a while, but he won't be sick."

People shifted, and I heard someone whisper, "It *is* her."

I turned to Jacky, who had fallen onto her butt, and was staring at me. "That reminds me, I have six fingers," I said, lifting my left hand to show her what I'd discovered. I frowned at it. The skin was darker and harder, segmented in geometric patterns that looked like a cross between honeycombs and scales. The fingers were clawed, and abnormally long and angular, almost like they'd tried to grow one more joint. "Weird."

"You're bigger, too," she said.

"Really? Maybe that's why it's hard to walk—Torliam, why are you flashing?" I was distracted by how irritatingly bright he was being. "Stop that."

"I cannot."

"You should probably work on your control. You desperately need it," I said.

"I think some leniency could be afforded me, as I am bound to a godling twice over, and the backlash makes control difficult." He raised an eyebrow deliberately at me as people reacted to his words.

I rolled my eyes at him and turned to Jacky. "Excuses."

As if she'd been waiting for the eye contact, she launched herself forward and slammed into me. "Idiot!" she half yelled at me. "I really thought you were dead this time."

I hugged her back, resisting the little burning tingle in my eyes. It felt good to get a hug. I was tired, really tired.

Birch arrived with Kris and Gregor, all three of them looking a bit worse for wear, but uninjured.

The injured and the Estreyans that had been separated from the main group started to join us, Blaine among them. He didn't yell at the kids, just gathered them into a crushing hug.

The clearing filled up with people, but there were so many less than there had been when we left. Still, we'd killed a god. And the people-trees made of the dead were pretty, at least.

Interlude 4

When the *scryer* finally worked out the requirements and finished preparation to open up a brief viewing window onto Estreyer, Eliahan brought the woman to watch.

The *scryer* located their target, and in the serene pool of water carved out of the stone floor, a moving image appeared.

She took a single, startled step backward, but stopped when she felt his hand on her arm.

He dropped his hand.

"What is this?"

"It is our child, grown strong. Sadly, it is also the beginning of the end."

"What are you saying?" An uncharacteristic waver entered her voice, perhaps brought on by the almost physical atmosphere of foreboding from his people.

"Words were spoken, a long time ago. A prophecy, *some* think."

"A prophecy? Like telling the future?" Her mouth twisted up on one side, but fell again when no one responded with similar amusement. "One of your…*quirks*," she said, with a resigned air of understanding. "What did this prophecy say?"

"Despair follows hope," he said simply.

"You don't believe in this prophecy?"

"They are a slippery thing. One cannot truly know the future, I believe, unless they are the God of Time, and perhaps not even then. We are no match in strength for what is coming. But the will of a mortal can be a powerful thing."

Chapter 43

I am become Death, the destroyer of worlds.
— J. Robert Oppenheimer

WE HAD MORE than enough empty ships to take the survivors back to the capital, and I slept the whole way there. I slept for the next three days, in fact.

I awoke to an opulent room with paintings on the ceiling of people using their Skills.

An Estreyan woman had been sitting beside my bed, and she squeaked when I awoke, then scrambled out of the room backward, bowing repeatedly as she went.

I got up and went straight to the bathroom, peeing for what was probably a straight minute. When I finished, I looked at myself in the mirrors on the main room's walls.

I'd grown a little bigger. Enough that I wasn't just an abnormally tall woman, but big enough to stand out as strange. My eyes had changed—upgraded to match my beyond-human levels of Perception. My facial features, too, though it was hard to say exactly how they were different. A little more angular. A little more striking. And blemish-free.

I still wore the armor from the battle, though Chaos had changed it, too, and apparently made it impossible to remove from the outside, though it had been cleaned.

The skin of my entire left arm, the one that had been turned into hamburger and was never quite the same afterward, was dark, with those honeycomb-scales, though the rest of me was still mostly normal. The arm didn't hurt anymore, at least. The Oracle's gifts were still there, sitting as comfortably as ever, despite my larger size.

My body was beautiful, in an alien, *interesting* kind of way. But not attractive in the way I often used to wish I could be. I could feel Chaos unbound within me, swirling around calmly. It didn't hurt, though it rippled at my attention, as if readying itself to be used.

I looked away from my new reflection, as the hair on the back of my neck rose up. My memories of another body, a human body, were telling me the person in the mirror wasn't me, but someone imitating me. I pulled up my Attribute Window, hoping for a distraction.

PLAYER NAME: EVE REDDING
TITLE: BEARER OF TESTIMONY
CHARACTERISTIC SKILL: SPIRIT OF THE HUNTRESS, TUMBLING FEATHER
LEVEL: 38
SKILLS: COMMAND, WRAITH, CHAOS, VOICE

STRENGTH: 23
LIFE: 76
AGILITY: 32
GRACE: 28
INTELLIGENCE: 32
FOCUS: 24
BEAUTY: 16
CHARISMA: 33
MANUAL DEXTERITY: 10
MENTAL ACUITY: 29
RESILIENCE: 70
STAMINA: 36
PERCEPTION: 33

The new body was a bit of an upgrade, if my levels were to be believed.

The door opened, and Queen Mardinest slipped into the room.

"They are calling you the godkiller," she said without preamble. There were bags under her eyes, and her skin looked thin and pale.

"It is what we set out to do," I said.

"It is not what *I* set out to do. Nor the warriors who followed and died for you."

"I know. But who would have agreed to help me kill a god?" Especially, when the reward was only to be my own salvation. It was ironic coincidence that my own power, used properly, also happened to be the thing that could cleanse the Sickness, literally burning it out.

"The world has already forgotten your treachery," she said. "They rejoice, and say the loss of life was well-spent. The celebrations spill into the streets, and your name is on every tongue. The warriors who lived exult in their good fortune, not to have lived, but to have battled with you." She stepped forward, holding up a vial. "But I will not forget," she promised.

I stepped back quickly, but she didn't move to attack, and after a couple moments of confusion, I realized what was in the vial. Meningolycanosis.

"Yes," she nodded. "I know what your people have done. I know how they prepare to kill us, steal our power, and violated my son. I know that he is likely not the only one. But most importantly, I know that they cultivate the Sickness, for use in war." She spat on the floor, turned to the door, and left.

I stood still for a moment. My stomach burned, though I wasn't sure whether it was with hunger or apprehension.

The next day, the queen called a press conference of sorts. The media had been clamoring to get at me and the team, and what had happened at the battle with the God of Knowledge was being publicized everywhere. The warriors who'd been there had been taking interviews.

News about NIX was also circulating. Estreyan scientists had talked to the media about the meningolycanosis samples they'd worked on. Uproar over that was almost as great as the hubbub over the defeat of a god.

I stayed holed up in the castle with the rest of the team. The servants bowed to us all as we passed, and the more courageous of them asked questions.

While I ate in the kitchen with some of the others, the young man who served us asked nervously, "Will you have to kill all the infected, to cleanse the world of the Sickness?"

"There may be other ways," I responded vaguely.

Chanelle smiled at me sadly, and I almost choked.

It wasn't like I'd really killed a god. I'd just dispersed it, or removed its physical manifestation, or something. The gods of Estreyer were forces of nature. Of existence. They weren't something that could be literally killed. Enough of Knowledge would form together again at some point, and he'd reform a physical manifestation. There could already be another one, somewhere else, that had been there all along and just hidden from the mortals.

The only way I knew how to stop the Sickness was to burn it away. And Chanelle wasn't like a god. She wouldn't reform over time. Neither would Kris and Gregor.

Sam watched my face, and then bowed his head, hands fisting into his hair.

"We'll find another way," I said.

Blaine's fingers clenched around his plate. "I will need to study your power, how it works. Perhaps the effective part can be duplicated, without the need for destruction," he said to me.

Adam stared at my scaled arm. "And while you're at it, maybe you could burn me some new legs?" His upper lip curled back, a mix between a sneer and a snarl.

Sam flinched. He hadn't been able to heal Adam's wound, because it was created directly with the power of a god, and had invaded Adam's body. Unlike when we'd gone through the Trial with Testimony and Lore, the wound was deep. Just clotting the blood and waiting for Adam to heal up on his own wasn't going to work. Which meant that Adam was still missing a piece of his spine, and though Sam had kept him alive, he might never walk again.

Adam shoved back from the table, an ink dog with a broad back springing into existence under him, carrying my teammate out of the room before anyone could stop him. "It's time to go to the throne room," he snapped over his shoulder.

Jacky shook her head at him. "Whadda we do about him?"

Blaine stood, pushing away from the table and following after him. "We hope that association with Eve does not cause the same level of harm to the rest of us."

I sat up straighter, face slipping into a stony expressionlessness.

Blaine was angry at me. Kris and Gregor hadn't been hurt during the fight, but they could have been. He thought I was a destructive and dangerous influence, and he wanted to keep them safe from me. If they didn't have the Sickness, and he could just run away and live somewhere peaceful and normal with them, he would have already done so.

I understood that.

But he needed me. We were in this together, now.

I shook my head at Jacky and Sam's looks of concern and stood. "Let's go. Torliam's on his way to come grab us." I could feel his location like a tickle on the back of my neck, always.

Torliam stepped through the doorway, sagging when he saw the three of us. "Where are the others? It is time to speak to the media." Fatigue dripped from his voice. He had had almost no rest since we returned from the fight. In absence of his siblings, and with his new role as media darling, it fell to him to help his mother navigate the roiling politics of the court.

"They're already on their way," I said, confirming my words with a pulse of awareness.

The information about NIX had been a blow to the queen's approval rating, despite her association with me. Her detractors were using it against her, cultivating fear. They publicized the queen's lack of involvement in the progress we'd made, how she had left her son for dead, and wasn't even aware of the forces of Earth torturing him and plotting against us.

As we paused at the back door behind the throne, Torliam visibly steeled himself, covering up the fatigue. "Are we all ready?" he asked the team.

"Let's just get this over with," Gregor said with a groan. "We love the queen, yadda, yadda, hurry up so we can get back to doing something useful. Like fixing the Sickness."

Kris nodded, but her lips were white. "Are *we* going to have to answer questions?"

Blaine put a hand on her shoulder. "That is unlikely. If they make you uncomfortable, I will step in."

She nodded, and with a last moment to brace ourselves, we entered the throne room.

I noticed the crowd first, then the big screen hung over the wall on one side, though it displayed nothing. I looked around for the queen, but her throne was empty, and I didn't see her.

The reporters didn't seem to mind, peppering us all with questions.

"How did you kill the God of Knowledge, Eve-Redding?"

"Eve-Redding! What can you tell us about what the Earthlings have been doing to the Estreyan descendants upon their planet?"

"Torliam! How do you feel that the queen left you for dead among the Earthlings?"

"How do you plan to stop the Sickness?"

"Has the Oracle given you any more tasks, Eve-Redding?"

"Eve-Redding, now that you can eliminate the Sickness, do you still plan to find the Champion?"

They didn't have time for any more questions, because the queen threw open the main doors. The sound echoed, and silence rippled through the crowd as everyone turned to look at her. She strode through the crowd up to her throne. "I have come before you today because I, too, am shocked and outraged at the actions of the Earthlings," she cried out.

Alarm bloomed in my stomach hard enough to make me nauseated. That wasn't what she had told us this was about.

—I have a feeling she's about to screw shit up.—
-Adam-

She continued talking. "We have not harmed them, and yet, they covet our power. They prepare for war, and the Abhorrent allies with them. They are creating weapons that will destroy the power and blood of our people, allowing the Sickness to eat it away, just as it eats away at our hearts and minds. This cannot be allowed." She gestured to the screen on the wall, which came to life, displaying a huge Stonehenge look-alike. Its stones were different colors, obviously newly repaired.

I moved to step forward, but Torliam grabbed me by the elbow, his eyes trained on his mother. "It is too late," he said, lips barely moving. "If you speak against her now, it will only harm you."

"Did you know about this?" I whispered severely.

"I swear I did not."

The queen raised her voice over the clamor. "Before they can destroy us, we must destroy them. We must stop them, before they strengthen and spread the Sickness even further! For the hope of our future, I hereby declare war on the Earthlings." Her hand slashed down.

On the screen, I watched as large Estreyan ships flew through the activated array, disappearing in a blink.

The crowd gasped.

I counted two ships, then five, then seven. I stopped counting. My hands started to shake.

THE STORY CONTINUES in *Seeds of Chaos Book III: Gods of Myth and Midnight.* Go here to buy Gods of Myth and Midnight on Amazon now: amazon.com/dp/B07H8FYW81

IF YOU WOULD LIKE to get:

- The chance to read the latest pre-release chapters of my upcoming book as I finish them
- Exclusive short stories/bonus chapters not available elsewhere
- Paperbacks, audiobooks, and other story-related swag, goodies, and opportunities…

Consider supporting me on Patreon: https://www.patreon.com/azaleaellis

Also by Azalea Ellis

Seeds of Chaos Series (Complete)

Book I: Gods of Blood and Bone

Book II: Gods of Rust and Ruin

Book III: Gods of Myth and Midnight

Gods of Smoke and Stars: A Seeds of Chaos Adventure—Available free to newsletter subscribers

Book IV: Gods of Ash and Amber

A Practical Guide to Sorcery Series

Book I: A Conjuring of Ravens

Book II: A Binding of Blood

Book III: A Sacrifice of Light

Book IV: A Foreboding of Woe — Coming Soon

Codename: Moonsable (Patreon Exclusive Sidestory)

The Honeymoon Suite (Patreon Exclusive Novelette)

The Catastrophe Collector: A Practical Guide to Sorcery Series

Book I: Larva — Coming Soon

More books may have been published since you purchased this copy.

Here's a Quick Link to All my Books.

About the Author

I'm the type of person that often has a wacky, shocking, or silly–but totally *true*–story to tell about my life.

(Like the time my brother and I were chased through a secluded strip of woods in the middle of the city, for over a mile, by a naked man with an erection.)

(Or the time a trucker threw an open bottle of pee out his passenger side window without looking right as I was walking by. You can guess what I got splashed with.)

I've got an active imagination that tends toward the outrageous and the macabre, which led to me being voted "most likely to borrow someone else's car to transport a dead body."

I write books about things that interest and excite me. I'm always in the middle of teaching myself something new, and if I'm not overwhelmingly busy I tend to get antsy. I believe that the impossible is only so if we believe it to be so. Therefore, nothing is impossible.

If you'd like to get updates from me, both about my books and about what I'm up to from time to time, the newsletter is the place to be, as I tend to be very scarce on other social media.

https://www.azaleaellis.com/newsletter

For more information:
www.azaleaellis.com
author@azaleaellis.com

facebook.com/AzaleaEllis

www.ingramcontent.com/pod-product-compliance
Lightning Source LLC
Chambersburg PA
CBHW030551310726
48979CB00011B/2114/J

* 9 7 8 0 9 9 9 6 7 5 0 2 1 *